1-17-14

Dialogues of the World of Nature

John G. Azzi

Order this book online at www.trafford.com
or email orders@trafford.com

Most Trafford titles are also available at major online book retailers.

Printed in Victoria, BC, Canada.

ISBN: 978-1-4269-3012-6 (sc)

ISBN: 978-1-4269-3167-3 (hc)

ISBN: 978-1-4269-3176-5 (e-book)

Library of Congress Control Number: 2010905024

Our mission is to efficiently provide the world's finest, most comprehensive book publishing service, enabling every author to experience success. To find out how to publish your book, your way, and have it available worldwide, visit us online at www.trafford.com

Trafford rev. 4/7/2010

www.trafford.com

North America & international
toll-free: 1 888 232 4444 (USA & Canada)
phone: 250 383 6864 • fax: 812 355 4082

DEDICATION

In memory of

Azzo Azzi, my Father
Lea Marabini, in Azzi, my Mother
Francesco Azzi, my Brother

and to

Eha Willemi, in Azzi, my wife
Anne Maran Azzi, daughter, her Family and grandchildren
Anthony F.Azzi, son, and his wife Kathleen
Nikolas Cameron Azzi, grandson

and, also,

to the sad remembrance
of our long departed and beloved dogs
Waggles, Cheeby, Pilly, Wootsy
and Dana

****

PREFACE

****

These writings represent a collection of stories written in a dialogue form and simple narrative, namely an account of occurrences in a journey into the intimate world of personified trees, mushrooms, birds, fishes, insects, smoke, rain, wind, clouds, books, scrolls, fairies and witches, goblins and gnomes, penguins and rabbits, and a host of other indefinable creatures, with the occasional appearance of a human being, along with some personified human qualities.

Now, long, long ago, in the far reaches of immense lands in our world, used to live some very, very old folks who, on cold winter nights, and around a warm family fire, were narrating some vague stories of goblins and gnomes, and of various other creatures living in those lands and roamimg in vast forests, and their interacting with the natural and pristine landscape and its inhabitants. Of course, these stories were never recorded or written down or preserved in any way, except in the fleeting memory of some children of those far, far away times.

One day, as I was leisurely strolling through one of those forests, in those immense lands, so exquisitely familiar to me by previous visits, being a little tired and the day yet very young, the balsamic air very comforting and only a whispering gentle breeze through the tree tops, I thought of stopping for a while, so I sat down and leaned against a large tree, feeling very comfortable and relaxed, looking up at the sky, so blue. so clear, so beautiful with not a single cloud and only a light. very pleasant breeze, but it wasn't long before a yellow and brown rabbit, suddenly, jumped in front of me, and, after welcoming me to that neck of the woods. asked me if I would be so kind and listen to his story, since no one, until then, had been at all interested in hearing it.

He was a nice and very polite rabbit, affable and pleasant, so I agreed to listen, since the day was still young and I welcomed a little chance to rest a while, and the rabbit said: "I'll tell the story which I have sent to my beloved Fortunata…."…and started the narration. While the rabbit was declaiming his story, many and various other creatures of all shapes, sizes and appearances came along, all asking me if I would like to hear their stories too and, when I agreed, they literally overwhelmed my senses with the avalanche of their narrations, to such an extent that I shook violently as if I had been suddenly shaken and aroused from a deep sleep, …!!....And, indeed, I must have fallen asleep, I thought, while the rabbit was declaiming his story, as I couldn't find any other logical explanation for the appearance of the rabbit and all other creatures and of it all…!!...As I opened my eyes and summoned some energy to get up, the rabbit was gone and so were all the other creatures as well. The power of dreams, I thought...!! Anyway, as I resumed my walking in the forest, my mind kept on thinking about the yellow and brown rabbit and all the other strange and yet cute creatures, so diligently and almost affectionately telling me in an avalanche of emphatic rhetoric their stories, I decided to jot down those stories that I had been told in earnest by all those interesting beings, be they just a dream, or a fantasy of my somniferous mind, or just a monitoring to my intellective powers, and jot it down I did, if, for nothing less, but for a memory of an unusual and curious encounter with those personalities and the stories of their natural world.

So, just as a tourist during his travels would retain in his mind an image of the world's many wonders, as he saw them, then, in the same way, this sentimental tourist of the natural world, " I, myself", I decided to assemble and compile those stories as best as I could remember them, and edit them with respect, genuine interest and with the best of care, feeling certain that I would receive a full and most enthusiastic encouragement and approval from the yellow and brown rabbit, for doing so.

****

DIALOGUE
Of
The Giant Oak Tree and The Mushroom

with the appearance and participation, also , of a Witch , a Gnome , various Birds and Insects, narrated in a personified manner for the various characters .

****

Giant Oak- Oh!...It is really cold, this morning!!....besides, there is a persistent wind ,a sort of a chilly breeze that would possibly give the shivers even to a polar bear..!!...Horrible weather the whole night through, just wind and rain...!...Foul weather , indeed ,if you'll ask me..!!......and nothing else with it to mitigate the depressing silence of our forest except for the pedantic and monotonous sound of the rain drops against my branches and my leaves...!!....without counting , of course , the usual lamenting and persistent chit-chat of the old screeching Grand Ma' Owl...!!.....just as I said,a very depressing and solitary forest ,this neck of the woods , and it might not be as bad as it is, if, at least, there would be a few houses here and there among our trees or even just a few cabins , then, this annoying and screeching Owl, would probably croak with some of her colourful companions upon the chimney-tops of those houses or cabins instead of on my branches , driving me out of my roots..!!!.....What an impudent this Owl, to go on and on the whole night, right on one of my highest branches and I cannot shake her off it...!!...and, now , the wind seems to have picked up some more strength and that makes me feel a lot colder, although this energized wind might help a little to dissipate the remaining clouds and clear the sky......I hope....an ancient great man had said something similar , some time ago, in times of severe stress and danger and seeming hopelessness, and had also expressed a similar call for hope and He had verbalized it as: " Hope springs eternal from the human bosom " , and since for my good fortune I am not human , then my hope will spring eternal from my ligneous roots.and, I guess, the difference is debatable or even superfluous ,but not for this annoying Grand Ma' Owl , telling stories of everything and everybody just when normal creatures , and I mean decent creatures, including human creatures , try to go to sleep and rest , while she sits perched on my branches and probably thinking a lot of herself....!...Personally, I think she is a phoney..........Oh ! If at least the sun could bend the rules just a little and come up sooner than usual....if he just could.......it would make me feel a lot warmer , happier , and more cheerful, and relieve me of my depression......or I shall freeze to death in complete solitude !!

Chorus of the woken Birds - The sun is rising !!.The sun is rising !! Cheer up, Brothers ,the sun is rising !! From behind the hills the first light of dawn begins to shine against the darkness of the night , causing it to slowly fade away , and now, Brothers, NOW is time to be happy ! Look...look....at the pale pink aura of morning turning gradually into a golden halo in the glow of the rising sun !.....Behold ! Behold !....the sun has risen from behind the hills and is already high on the vast horizon in front of us , flooding everything around with the warmth of its powerful rays and ever bright light !!.....So, cheer up, Brothers , and we ought to be thankful and grateful to be able to see the rising sun from behind the hills and high up in the immense sky..!!..We are free.....we are happy at the sight of the rising sun into the sky..!...Brothers...let's spread our wings and soar into the sky , so clear , so terse , so beautiful before us , behind us , above us , and below us , and everywhere ! Brothers, the sun has risen!

Giant Oak- Those blasted Birds..!!!...Every morning the same story !.....and every morning without missing a single one!! They raise Cain at the rising of the sun as if they had never seen it before, then they want to fly away, and that would be a blessing, but, instead , they linger on my branches for a while longer describing the wonderful properties of the Golden Star and how good it is to them and everybody else , and scream and yell as loud as they can for fear, I guess, of not being properly heard or understood !....and if the Birds in the morning would not be enough measure , then Grand Ma' Owl doing her thing at night and ,at dusk , the Bats..!...Damned all!!....It's crazy, just and simply crazy ! It's sheer madness, it is !!....Just plain sheer madness, I'll say..!!

Sparrow,(Mother-in-Law) - Madness !?..Madness...you said...??...But what madness are you talking about..you Big Thing..??!..My little Joseph , the poor thing, he,rather, should be the one to claim such a misfortune as he really is on the verge of breaking down with madness , the poor thing..!!...You, Big Fat Tree do not need to get mad, big as you are..!!...How impudent these Giants...!!

Giant Oak- Thank You . But, my dear Lady Sparrow , has it ever occurred to you that it might just be the other way around ? Why, then , it looks to me that" you "are more impudent than" I " ca be , small as you are and so impertinent in your attitude. Besides , what do I care about this here Joseph of yours and , furthermore , at this early hour of the morning ?

Sparrow(Mother-in-Law) -Oh ! Listen to him ! Just listen to him !!...this heartless egoist, without compassion and without fear of God.!

Giant Oak- Well!Well ! Let's go easy ,now, with insults and frivolous insinuations ! Now, what's got into you , little bird ?

Sparrow(Mother-in-Law) - Go easy, go easy, he says ,this here.......this here monster, without the fear of God and what not ! Oh ! If my little Joseph could only hear it....if he only could , my poor thing !...and this here Giant talks about insults and insinuations of I do not know what . You know what ?

Giant Oak- No: I do not know "what", dear little birdie !

Sparrow(Mother-in-Law) - Well ,I 'll tell you "what" , you big fat giant, I tell you this : I think that I have treated you far too gently , I have , you Big Monster Tree !! Big as you are, you should have taken twice as many insults and innuendoes than the ones I gave you ..You big chunk of wood and leaves !

Giant Oak- Wood and leaves..!!!...This one is really rich..!!...and , by any chance ,what else would you have expected to see in a tree if not wood and leaves, dearie ?...Your anguish must be impairing your best judgement and thinking as well as your mind altogether, dear old Lady Sparrow, and make you overlook respect for others.

Sparrow(Mother-in-Law)- Listen to him ! This big chunk of wood talks as if he were the oracle of Delphi !!..and "You," my dear and cumbersome giant, and not " I," are the one lacking respect for others and for ME..!

Giant Oak- Heavens forbid !!...My most gracious Mother-in-Law ! Not even a Giant could allow himself the liberty and the audacity to be disrespectful to a Mother-in-Law, even if only in the embodiment of a sparrow..!!

Sparrow(Mother-in-Law)- Now : that's better ! You are quick in changing your ideas, you big giant chunk of wood. : perhaps, you have as many ideas and opinions as you have leaves that come and go ,at one time or another, one by one, as they fall from your branches at the slightest change of a gentle breeze , dry ,yellow and withered.

Giant Oak- You sound as if you got out of the wrong side of the bed this morning : You seem so irritated and angry almost at any word or sentence spoken ,regardless, it seems, of its meaning or content or reference and why.....??......that's the unknown question !!

Sparrow(Mother-in-Law)- Unknown question!?!What question are you talking about ?..that ,of course , provided that you can grasp the meaning of the word " question ", hard and ligneous chunk of wood as you are, and , besides , is none of your damn business either to inquire which side of my bed I got out this morning, or to be presumptuous enough as to judge me as being irritated and angry ! Shame on you...you giant nincompoop ,and showing no sympathy at all for me when I worry so much about my poor little Joseph ! The poor thing, so unhappy , so distressed , you know...... ....

Giant Oak- I don't !!

Sparrow(M0ther-in-Law)- That figures : Big creatures and Giants never know anything about us little creatures ! Oh! Well, what's the worth of worrying ? that would not make my Joseph any happier . A real genius ,my Joseph, you know...well ..I know what you are going to say , so don't say it ...good !...and very, very unhappy...and you dare talk to me about irritation, anger and questions in moments like these !??

Giant Oak- Well, I think that you talk too much, for one thing : and, for another , apart from all those stories and tragedies, what has really happened that is so bad, to your poor Joseph ?

Sparrow(Mother-in-Law) - Terrible, terrible situations ever so much more aggravated by a conflict of emotions and personalities causing a disturbing mental status that almost incapacitates his ability to live normally and express his genius and brilliant personality !...Oh ! If you could only comprehend..!!

Giant Oak- Well, it is somewhat hard to comprehend anything if you do not know what everybody or anybody is talking about , I assure you .

Sparrow(Mother-in-Law)- You, wooden head, don't you know that geniuses are always unhappy?

Giant Oak- But, then, why do you take the situation so much at heart when you already know what the problem is , and what is "what" that is troubling him.!? If he is unhappy because you think that he is a genius , then , for the realization of his happiness as well as for your own peace of mind and spiritual tranquillity ,would it not have been better for him to have been born an idiot ?

Sparrow(Mother-in-Law) - Impertinent chunk of wood ! How dare you ?!?

Giant Oak- No harm done or said...just a thought !....Only a simple, straight forward thought !

Sparrow(Mother-in-Law)- Only a big, ugly and disparaging thought, you brute !

Giant Oak- Not quite ! Not quite so, as the way you seem to absorb it ! What I meant was that if geniuses are unhappy , then , Idiots , by pure contrast , should be happy, or, if you should disagree with my deduction, then you would contradict yourself in estimating the geniuses as unhappy when you would not agree at the idiots being happy. However , personally , I do not think that they, the Idiots I mean , are any happier in proportional measure to the unhappiness of the geniuses , so I ,and again I insist on my declaration of personal opinion only, so I , as I said , believe that the Idiots are unhappy too because of their natural inclination to lack understanding of anything , and , as a consequence of that distinctive trait , they feel very sympathetic towards the geniuses, feeling sorry for their unhappiness and since the Idiots seem to possess a natural behavioural tendency to serene goodness , they wish that all the geniuses would be idiots so that they too , the geniuses they mean , could be also happy , and in return for this charitable and highly encomiable generosity of wishful thinking , the geniuses , then , once become happy , very happy , or even just temporarily happy , none the less they could alleviate the feeling of unhappiness of the Idiots due to their worrying for the unhappiness of the geniuses as well as their own concern of being idiots, so that in the end everybody would be happy, Idiots and Geniuses, trees and sparrows , snails and snakes , tomatoes and potatoes , mushrooms and cauliflowers , lizards and frogs , and so on , and so on ,........

Sparrow(Mother-in-Law) - IDIOT !

Giant Oak- Your arrogance , my dear sparrow ,Mother-in-Law , doesn't hold much interest for me : you should know that during my long life of over a hundred years , in this old forest of ours , I have become a sort of a philosopher since I had no other choice , but to stay here , straight and solid , and see and observe all kinds of ways and forms and variations of life pass by me ,night and day , every day and every night,weeks , months and years , birds and all , and therefore, as I had just said , your unfriendly address does not bother me at all : and I happen to know quite well, and I have heard a lot of the fabled attitudes of Mothers-in-Law , as the old legend goes.

Sparrow(Mother-in-Law)- You brazen chunk of wood !Your talking is mud !

Giant Oak- I wonder ! I just wonder , my dear Mother-in-Law, but the more you get angry and throw undesirable remarks towards me and the more I begin to understand why there is and there has always been so much talk and whispering and chuckling among every day Folk about Mothers-in-Law being not always graciously inclined to be gentle , affable , agreeable , and supportive with their daughters and sons respective spouses. And that is what I always heard .

Sparrow(Mother-in-Law) -What you heard is trash !....." Mother-in-Law " you said..??..MOTHER-in-LAW......TO ME>>???!!!....Are you crazy ??!...Mother-in-Law to buggary with you !...Ah is no Mother-in-Law, you big chunk of wood ! You better watch your steps and double watch your language too.

Giant Oak- But, I called you all the time like that during our entire conversation and you never answered back or told me differently !...Why now , then??

Sparrow(Mother-in-Law)- I had thought , then , that you were joking , may be just trying to tease me a little , taking the advantage of your larger frame as well as of your imposing silhouette and having some fun at the expense of a minuscule creature like I am , very much along the usual lines of the well practiced road of the "Larger" throttling the "smaller", which representation seems to be perfectly fitting our scene and your size as a Giant Oak and mine of a tiny,fragile sparrow and that is why I had thought that you were just joking.

Giant Oak- A Giant might take advantage of a smaller creature ,but an Oak ??..Even if large and big ? Oaks are noble creatures and ,by nature, their branches always aim high, but it is of Giants who have to look down to see where they are going and often they tread on unsuspecting ground. Besides, if I were to your eyes like the image of a creature of dark shadows and shadowy tendencies, why would you,then,sit on my branches?

Sparrow(M0ther-in-Law)- Sometime desperation ,affliction or sadness make you search for an understanding hand if you were that kind of creature, but in my case, I was looking for a charitable branch. The choice, sometime, may be treacherous .

Giant Oak- But, then, little sparrow, who are you ?

Sparrow Mother-in-Law Joseph is my son , the poor boy ! And I am his Mother : NOT HIS MOTHER IN LAW !!!

Giant Oak- Oh! Now I understand ! Sorry, Really sorry about my awkward thinking ! And I am not surprised why your beloved Joseph is so unhappy ! Bless his little souls !

Sparrow Mother-in Law Bless yours too , and your stale sarcasm ,it's not even worth a penny !

Giant Oak- Well, my dear, let's call it quit with this silly bickering and now that we know who you are, who I am and who everybody else is, birds and all, why don't we try,calmly and steadily to determine the cause of your anxious worrying about your precious Joseph , if there is a plausible reason for this to sustain and justify this worrying and, if so, to see any possible avenues to mitigate it or to dissipate it altogether and relieve this dark cloud in your existencies and, to achieve this desirable goal, it would greatly help our efforts if you were coming out with it and tell me what's the matter that you may suspect drives him so unhappy and to the verge of Madness ..?

Sparrow(Mother-in-Law)- Oh! Yes! Yes!...for his sake and for his happiness ! He is so desperate, just desperate, the poor thing !

Giant Oak- Well, my dear, sweet Mother Lady Sparrow, that......

Sparrow(Mother-in-Law)- Cut out the sugar, man, and talk some sense.

Giant Oak- Oh yeah ? Well, you wretched , despicable ,old ruffled hag , you should know that if your stupid Joseph is desperate he is not alone by any means , because the feeling of desperation , and I am saying this in order to keep pace with the focal point of your worried mind , the feeling of desperation, as I was saying , is a common and almost an inalienable predisposition as well as a mandatory attribute to geniuses and non geniuses and it embraces in its frantic and destructive vice all of us , and I mean, really ,all of us in this here forest and, I heard, somewhere else too, in many other forests So, the bottom line is :what can be done about it ?

Sparrow(Mother-in-Law) - You tell me.

Giant Oak- .Very well, genius' Mother : I'll tell you. First you try to think back and make an effort to put together as many elements as you can possibly remember of various happenings, situations, events, encounters, impressions, disappointments, appointments, recurrencies ,festivities ,sickness,suspense,euphoria,sadness,headaches and stomach upsets..and so on..! Was it negligence ? Was it vane and fruitless infatuation ? Was it carelessness ? Was it madness ?

tSparrow(Mother in-Law) May be…stupidity.?

Giant Oak- Right you are ! Unfortunately, often, that is the case ,sad to say ,and it grieves me deeply to think that way, even more so because of the devious attitude of some creatures who will take the advantage of the feeble minded folks of all sorts, and that goes for all layers of earth creatures , instead of helping them out of their misery.

Sparrow(Mother-in-Law) For a brief moment, at least, we seem to have come closer together,BIG Tree ,and I feel inclined to follow your reasoning about the cause and the causes of depression, often caused by , if not straight by direct stupidity but certainly ,most often, to poor planning or some light hearted approach to problems and their solutions, or even willful neglect, but my Joseph's desperation does not reflect any of the mentioned possible patterns : his is one of insecurity, confrontation and , for the major part, lack of understanding and confused perception of situations , feelings , and belonging, the poor thing ! A typical example of what we were describing earlier , so sad , it makes me cry just to talk about it !

Giant Oak- Has he turned stupid, by any chance ?

Sparrow(Mother-in-Law) Worse than that ! The Devil has gotten into him !

Giant Oak- Then you should hire an exorcist .

Sparrow(Mother-in-Law)- But what kind of nonsense are you talking about ?!..

Giant Oak- Well, they say that they have the power and the expertise to chase bad spirits away by some special incantations.

Sparrow(Mother-in-Law) - It would take a lot more than an incantation to chase this devil away,I assure you! I am talking about a real devil and one right here on our earth and not the one and the ones that inhabit those famous regions down below where it's always dark and hot , but one right here and, to make things worse, just right on top and behind my poor Joseph ! Oh ,it's terrible, just terrible !

Giant Oak - This is extraordinary : a real hot devil , but not from down below !??... such an event has never been heard of before !...But, tell me:has he ,I mean this devil, any horns and a tail ,hair all over his body and spits flames from his mouth ?

Sparrow(Mother-in-Law)- That devil spits a lot more than flames out of her mouth, that devil !

Giant Oak Tree - But wait a a second, dear Sparrow: just wait a second .

Sparrow(Mother-in-Law)- O.K. ! I am waiting : what's up ?

Giant Oak Tree- Did you say " HER " mouth,….did you ?

Sparrow(Mother-in-Law)- But of course I did : what else..?

Giant Oak Tree- Well,well…,you hear a new one every day and I have been here over a hundred years..!!!

Sparrow(Mother-in-Law)- Oh! You haven't seen a thing yet,standing still in one place the whole of your existence and hearing only what news the wind might bring you : I told you , her tongue is like a fireball and she , wilfully and gleefully , could incinerate any decent and respectable form of address, approach ,and representation in current use among civilized creatures , wrecklessly bent, as she is, to impose her selfish wishes and absolute dominance on everybody around her ! That devil could benumb the faculties of a hundred devils , all by herself , and send railing any incantation together with the exorcist invoking it .

Giant Oak Tree- Well,well, how true that old proverb is, so popular in this here forest of ours ,that goes " You live and learn ", and I did not know that devils had a sexual configuration, in " HEs " and " SHEs", because in the common everyday usage, the distinctive and coveted appellative of devil is reserved ,selectively and preferentially , for creatures of masculine differentiation , as we say, often , look at that poor devil , he is a mad devil, a stupid devil or a louse of a devil, but to approach a devil as " you, sweety devil ", or angel of a devil, you sexy devil, or you loving devil of my heart …….

Sparrow(Mother-in-Law)- …or even ,may be, " you, impossible dream of your devil heart "….

Giant Oak Tree- Yes, yes, incredible, incredible, and ,really, I had never heard anything like this before,I assure you.

Sparrow(Mother-in-Law)- Well, you heard it now : better later than never, as the old story goes.

Giant Oak Tree- But,then, my dear Sparrow, are you talking about a "she " devil ?

Sparrow(Mother-in-Law)- …..Precisely.

Giant Oak Tree- I don't believe it ! No one has ever seen one !

Sparrow(Mother-in-Law)- Believe you me, you old Tree : they exist , I assure you , and in good numbers ! She- Devils, at the umpteenth power !

Giant Oak Tree - My,Oh, my, !.....my dear bewildered Sparrow, but has she ever appeared to you ?

Sparrow(Mother-in-Law)- But of course she has , you incredulous , naïve Big chunk of wood ! Of course she has !

Giant Oak Tree - Incredible !!....and....is this "she" devil very....hairy and very hot too and emitting smoke as a consequence of the infernal heat, with blazing red eyes and how far from down below does she come when she appears to you?

Sparrow(Mother-in-Law)- Well , she is hot and temperamental all right , aggressive too and she can flare up at any moment in a rage and ,yes , she is abundantly hairy but far from being hirsute and definitely not enveloped in a cloud of "infernal" smoke, although such a "mantle" would be quite appropriate for her personality and , her eyes....well, her eyes can be very red , at times ,when in a violent rage. Now , in regard to her tail, I do not think that she carries the one that you may have envisaged , that is one like a flexible appendage to her lower end , but one thing is very apparent : she can wag the one she has quite adequately and at the required and proper time for maximum return.

Giant Oak Tree- Really ? Amazing !

Sparrow(Mother-in-Law)- But , now , here , what importance could have the notion of :" how far from down below does she come " , when she comes to see me or I happen to see her ??

Giant Oak Tree- Well , I would not contest its importance on a basis of a needed prerequisite for her appearance but , rather , as an " importance of consequence ". I shall explain............

Sparrow(Mother-in-Law)- Please , do...!

Giant Oak Tree- Do...: " WHAT " ?

Sparrow(Mother-in-Law)- Explain , naturally.

Giant Oak Tree- Naturally.....well , I'll do my best, naturally , provided that you can follow me, my dear little Mother Sparrow , in –Law , and all that .

Sparrow(Mother-in-Law)- Hardly any problem in that , planted solid as you are !....How could anyone at all fail to.....follow you........standing there ,as you do...??!!

Giant Oak Tree- I meant mentally , intuitively and with discernment.

Sparrow(Mother-in-Law)- Try me.

Giant Oak Tree- Very well, then . So it goes , at least among "us trees " that we give a lot of weight to how far our roots reach under the ground where we were born , meaning that the deeper our roots travel , the greater will be our stability , our strength and our appearance as well as our resourcefulness to nourish and maintain ourselves even in times of stress, like in the event of prolonged droughts, shortage of nutrients in the soil , and , above ground , the ravages of the weather around us. So , I would be inclined to think that the same might apply to Devils , and how genuine and deep seated their personalities may shine…or….shall we say…..BLAZE..??!!

Sparrow(Mother-in-Law)- Oh ! I see ……well , in respect to her attitude and actions this devil couldn't have come from any far below levels than from the farthest , furthest abyssal depths of infinite profundity….the wretched devil !!...and WHY , I am asking , why should I have been endowed with such an inauspicious privilege to see… IT ! or be seen by ..IT..!!!??

Giant Oak Tree- But, my dear Sparrow , couldn't you have tried to scare this devil away from your Joseph , or is this devil so big , so frightful , so disgusting to the point of dissuading anybody from tackling…..shall we say….with her..??

Sparrow(Mother-in-Law)- More than that , and none of that .

Giant Oak Tree- That enunciation is rather strange .

Sparrow(Mother-in-Law)- Nothing is strange about devils : they represent the most realistic image, personification and mischievous intent to provoke wickedness and insure its deleterious effect : she is a viper of a devil , she is..!!

Giant Oak Tree- Ah ! That's something else !....but , really , not new. Vipers have been famous in interfering or modifying , even changing the course of events in our existences : they are known for even taking on , literally , and assume false appearances in order to allure unsuspecting creatures into the range of their fatal embrace of love and death…!!....Oh! well, sometimes facts can be gathering the dust of the legends and become , therefore, legends, so ,my dear Sparrow , why don't we go back to our pertinent conversation, and why don't you tell me….I am really curious..!....well…why don't you tell me something more about this "she " devil ? Is this " she " viper devil a beautiful she viper devil or even….shall we say:… a gorgeous devil..!??

Sparrow(Mother-in-Law)- YOU, Idiot !...what kind of "gorgeous" nonsense got into your skull!? I am talking about Ildegard, you ninny.

Giant Oak Tree- Ah! Now we come to something : Ildegard must be the name of this "she" devil, I presume ?.......an enticing name.

Sparrow(Mother-in-Law)- Despicable, I think. And she, that devil, , she is the problem and the cause of my son unhappiness , confusion , and emotional disorganization .

Giant Oak Tree- Well , well , now,my dear Sparrow , you have been very vague about this devil , except for your terrifying comment about the whole thing , and , let aside the gorgeous " stuff ", that you were so critical about , tell me : how does this " she " devil look ? As I understand and you seemed to confirm it , she has seen you and she has been seen by you ,and I further guess ,probably on several occasions.....

Sparrow(Mother-in-Law)- How painfully true..!!!

Giant Oak Tree- Well , why ,then , do you seem to have your mind preoccupied with such an obsession about IT , or HER , or HIM or what not ?

Sparrow(Mother-in-Law)- Stupid Tree, you Big tree ! Ildegard is a female sparrow , just like I am .

Giant Oak Tree- A devil sparrow ,eh ? .....That is strange : I did not know that any existed .

Sparrow(Mother-in-Law)- Devil , yes . Sparrow , yes . Strange , yes . And a female sparrow too ,a very peculiar , vicious , antagonistic , provoking , disrupting , conniving , and cantankerous devil if ever there was one and regularly supplied with all the most necessary and sophisticated attributes to drive anybody out of their wits . Does that enter your head, now ?

Giant Oak Tree- In a way , yes , it does, and, sadly too , but ,as I had somewhat suspected right from the very beginning of our conversation, this talk about devils seemed a little strange to be logically sustainable , just as it seems strange your overwhelming invective launched at a female sparrow...........the poor devil !!??

Sparrow(Mother-in-Law)- You can say that again...: just drop the " poor " .

Giant Oak Tree- Well , " and that's a deep profundity " , some garrulous creatures would probably comment, but I just say well it looks like we need to go back to the old " adage " about the perpetual obsession for the opposite sex by the masculine line of characters that boils down in a very illustrative and yet quite direct and plain form by the " saying ", which is so much more effective if chanted in the original French tongue and common in French forests among big trees , small trees , medium trees ,bees and birds , and creatures of all sizes and shapes, ..."Go,.....and search for your female companion ". as translated liberally . Of course, in the forests of any ethnic origin , that "search" goes on without much fanfare and without a need for a French translation of that encouraging refrain either , but it reflects itself in a different silhouette in the world of the human creatures who would utter with unbridled enthusiasm : " Women ! " ,"Women ", while , we trees , would merely shake our leaves. But , going back to our main subject ,your adorable Joseph........

Sparrow(Mother-in-Law)- Don't you make fun of him : he needs help , not adoration.

Giant Oak Tree- I make fun of him ? How wrong you are, my dear sparrow! As a matter of fact I am beginning to realize , even if at a rather slow pace , that what you had said earlier about your son being a genius ," a real genius ", you said, I remember it well , I believe that you couldn't have been anymore plump right about it !!A darn brilliant chap , that Joseph and…..well,a little bit of a young scoundrel too, to my way of seeing things !!....and…that Ildegard !!

Sparrow(other-in-Law)- One more mention of that name and I'll pick off all of your leaves from your branches.

Giant Oak Tree- But, my dear sparrow, you are the one that gives me the ideas that I am telling aloud, as you are precisely the embodiment of mothers reluctant to accept the taking over of their sons by another sparrow and particularly so when that sparrow carries such a …..shall we say….enigmatic name and is "classified" by you as a devil !

Sparrow(mother-in-Law)- And a devil she is . Besides, what is your business , anyway , to get involved in this family affair and even come up with some advice ?

Giant Oak Tree- But my dear upset Mother Sparrow, you had just told me ,a little while ago , that you had been flying to one of my limbs, seeking a " helping branch ". Did you not..??!

Sparrow(Mother-in-Law)- I did, but , sometime , creatures make mistakes in their lives.

Giant Oak Tree- Now, now, from anger , to spite , to recrimination to despondency : that's not the way to be.

Sparrow(Mother-in-Law)- Any suggestions ?

Giant Oak Tree- But, of course ! FORGET THE WHOLE THING !!!....In the end ,what is it to you if your son loves his newly found choice , supposed, of course that that would be the case in question , which I begin to believe that it is , if nothing else , but and in spite of your threat , that name : " ILDEGARD " !! what a romantic name that is ! And WHAT a sparrow must she be, devil or not !!....So, my dear , we must listen sometime, which means sometime and not necessarily every time, but, using some of our arboreal common sense, other creatures, particularly human creatures who attribute particular galore to the horses'common sense, whatever, common sense, I was told,means something of value, but I never grasped its value fully, anyway what I was trying to say even if a little shaky in its grammatical configuration, the reader will excuse me for that for I am only a tree and not a didactic poet , but, as I was saying or, better still, as I was TRYING to say , some time it may be worth the effort to listen and study other creatures' experiences and, as the human creatures say , women , for all it matters, female sparrows , female carrots , female rabbits, and any creature that would come under the coveted differentiation of female , will always be females , of course ,and this statistical claim, naturally , is the pure consequence of a rather simple logic easily absorbed by any creature , even by a tree, like I am , that clearly translates into an hereditary formula discovered by a famous tree in our forest , I am told , that confirms the genetic and sexual characteristics of the shape ,size , and configuration you were born with and born by , that is , if you were born a female , a female you will remain and spend your allotted time on this planet as a female , with no hope of being given a second choice , like turning into a tulip or a rose or a water melon or a frog , although several attempts were made in the past , notably by poets , to do just that, but with no significant follow-up , so , in final analysis , if you were born a female, a female you will remain , and if born a man , an idiot you will remain , and as far as women are concerned , be they sparrows females or eggplants , they have not changed a bit since the time when the fogs of our past began to clear a little and all creatures began to see each other and everything around them remained the same until….shall we say….LOVE entered " the swelling scene " and messed everything up.

Sparrow(Mother-in-Law)- Love has nothing to do with this situation.

Giant Oak Tree- But, then , why worry so much, YOU tell me , my dear !

Sparrow(Mother-in-Law)- " THAT " sparrow……That SPARROW…..she hates me !

Giant Oak Tree- Ah ! That's different !

Sparrow(Mother-in-Law)- I'll say it is..!!!

Giant Oak Tree- I agree.

Sparrow(Mother-in-Law)- Is that all you have to say ??

Giant Oak Tree- What else is there ?

Sparrow(Mother-in-Law)- My Joseph unhappiness and confusion at the hands of this manipulating female sparrow , that's " what else " !

Giant Oak Tree- Yes..my dear Mother sparrow, in a way, a restricted way though, mind you , but in that restricted way I understand you, yet, at the same time, in my long life in this forest I found out that the Merry-Go-Round of any creature's life or the "Manipulating " of their lives by whoever engages in that kind of entertainment, does not seem to have ,really , a beginning or an end , but it just keeps on going around and around and around and it has been doing so since the very beginning of time as far back as when we were able to recognize time . Now , why that is so, no one knows, yet…..well.. I probably should have said . " no one has an inkling of why that is so…", except the poets.

Sparroe(Mother-in-Law)-1 That doesn't help my Joseph .

Giant Oak Tree- Yes, my dear Mother Sparrow, I believe that you are right : No one can help your Joseph ! It is well known in the history of living creatures , at least in this forest of ours , that be they sparrows, raccoons , hedgehogs , pigeons , frogs or lizards and , for all that matters , tomatoes or cucumbers , and be they all females, in a broad sense, of course , they always seem to come in , one way or another , from below , from above , or from either side , without anyone knowing or even realizing how they manage to do it ..!!.......But they do.

Sparrow(Mother-in-Law)- And drag down to their own selfish plans and desires innocent and clean young sparrows without any consideration, respect or deference for the innocence of those unsuspecting victims and for the Parents of their targeted pray!!

Giant Oak Tree- My dear Sparrow, please, just listen to me : I want to tell you something.

Sparrow(Mother-in-Law)- I'm listening.

Giant Oak Tree- Very well, my Dear. Now , I understand your plight and your grievance and sorrow , but , may be , I have in mind a possible solution for this sad situation: would you like to hear about it ?

Sparrow(Mother-in-Law)- At this stage , I'll hear anything while, at the same time , I doubt that anything I hear will help much , unfortunately .

Giant Oak Tree- It does not hurt to listen to it..... and if you do not like it , well, you would not be any richer or any poorer , and ,instead, if you should like it , time to rejoice !!

Sparrow(Mother-in-Law)- As you say : it does not hurt to listen. Go ahead.

Giant Oak tree- Well , then : why don't you try to encourage your Joseph to turn his attention somewhere else , may be in the south-side of this Forest, quite well known for a remarkable area populated by beautiful sparrows ,some with vivacious singing and wonderful plumage and, they say, of extremely affable disposition , and there your Joseph, I am quite certain, could easily restore his emotional and mental strength and slip away from the ....shall we say.....dependance from .....my !Oh! my !!....Ildegard....... and find a sweet, adorable and gentle sparrow , marry her and bring to your nest a nice , loving , affectionate and caring Daughter-in-Law , settle down and leave that she-devil,..........Heavens forbid...!! ....of Ildegard to the winds of fortune. Now, my dear Sparrow, how does this grab you ?....I mean ,...what do you think about it ?

Sparrow(Mother-in-Law)- Fine : only one thing wrong with it....I mean , with your plan .

Giant Oak Tree- Oh ! Well.....where did I miss the boat ??

Sparrow(Mother-in-Law)- Ildegard happens to be already my Daughter-in-Law , you ninny.

Giant Oak Tree- YOUR DAUGHTER-IN-LAW......!!!!!???????

Sparrow(Mother-in-Law)- Right : MY DAUGHTER-IN-LAW .

Giant Oak Tree- Joseph's WIFE , then..??!

Sparrow(Mother-in-Law- Your mental ability in penetrating obscure matters , associated with your piercing insight into the meanings and consequences of the " logical sequences " of questions and answers , is , indeed , remarkable .

Giant Oak Tree- Thank you, dear Sparrow , for the unsolicited compliment . However I am glad that you were able to appreciate the fine tuning of my...shall we say...."insight" into "obscure matters" and bring them out clear in the sunshine . You see , with the many branches that I have , I can reach in many different directions , including those of mental endeavour as well as the more practical ones of " lending a helping branch " to a troubled bird.

Sparrow(Mother-in-Law)- TOUCHE !!....Your salty riposte balances well my belittling remarks about your mental ability! ..Now, I believe that , should we, both you and I , have hands instead of wings and branches , we should, naturally, shake hands , but ,since " that " is , obviously , not possible , I, at least on my side , will do what I can with what I have : I'll flap my wings and send three chirps .

Giant oak Tree- And I'll rustle my leaves and shake my branches !

Sparrow(Mother-in-Law)- Oh! Big Tree, you, big, big Tree, that's very fine and I'll add another three chirps to cement the conclusion of our little confrontation, and a rather silly one at that ! Is it not strange how such intellectually void confrontations of words and insignificant thoughts can come up in creatures minds and from just an original and, somewhat , presumptuous initial posture, degenerate in derogatory statements and silly, I'd rather say, stupid confrontations, as if responding to an inner, irresistible instinct to revolt and violence, regardless whether it be of words content or even physical. Is it "that " the reason why Mother Nature has made the wind available, in order to wipe out and dissipate those distorted thoughts ? Many times I have wondered about that . Have you too, Big Tree ?

Giant Oak Tree- Sometimes. But not often : you see, my dear Sparrow , that wind or breeze that you talk about, comes and takes a walk , often , through my branches and takes away those disparaging thoughts long before they can find a resting and breeding place on my leaves and branches. That is why I am blessed with my branches being long and wide apart , they do not lend themselves to obscure and mischievous thoughts .

Sparrow(Mother-in-Law)- And , yet , sometimes, you cannot help having some of those thoughts wind or no wind !

Giant Oak Tree- Oh ! No !! You are not going back to the Joseph and Ildegard duet , are you…!!???

Sparrow(Mother-in-Law)- May be I am : that situation is so deeply imbedded in my mind, my thoughts , my soul , it is not easy to just ignore it and forget all about it . You see, Big Tree , she not only is his wife , she is also his ruin .

Giant Oak Tree- Well , now : let's not precipitate things and come to conclusions in a haste and in this way reach also the wrong conclusions !!

Sparrow(Mother-in-Law)- It is a lot more than a simple "conclusion" my dear Big Tree : it is the sad truth !!....she is his ruin and she is a shameless adventuress !

Giant Oak Tree- Well , now , there is no need to precipitate things as I said ,and , even more important , not to come to hasty coclusions , dear Sparrow . I understand how you feel, but ,in this life of ours, it pays to be restrictive in the expansion of our judgements towards others , regardless of how bitterly we may feel towards them.

Sparrow(Mother-in-Law)- Wise spoken words, always good for distribution and free delivery by those who are not directly affected by an intervening problem or unpleasant situation , but of little help to those directly glued to the mess of sentiment , confusion and frustration.

Giant Oak Tree- You sound like a creature, my dear Sparrow, who is bitterly unyielding to the call of reason. You see……..

Sparrow(Mother-in-Law)- Hush ! Hush !.....there is somebody coming !

Giant Oak Tree- Who's coming ?

Sparrow(Mother-in-Law)- I think it's Ildegard . She might be looking for my poor Joseph.

Giant Oak Tree- Where did Joseph go, without Ildegard and why did he leave her alone and looking for him ?

Sparrow(Mother-in-Law)- He had left early this morning ,even before sun-rising, to get some groceries , while she, that ….so and so…..probably was still sleeping peacefully, that lazy good for nothing sparrow, by that horrible name……Hush, hush..I think she is coming…..oh! yes…I guessed right…..it is that devil !..now let's be very quiet and do not say a word and just listen : hey , You ! Did you hear me ?

Giant Oak Tree- Very well, Thank you. Let's listen , then .

17

ENTERS ILDEGARD

Ildegard - Joseph , Joseph….but where are you, my love ?

Joseph- I am here,Ildegard, my sweet love, I am here ! What is that You want, my sweetest love ?

Ildegard - Get lost with all that mawkish sentimentalism, my good man.

Joseph- Mawkish sentimentalism…!!!??? …..Ildegard !!.....What are you saying…!!???You had just called me " my love " a moment ago , my sweet soul, and now , just like out of the blue sky , for no reason that I can think of , your address has turned hostile and …..really, cruel..!! My sweet Ildegard, what have I done to deserve such a harsh treatment ?

Ildegard - Oh ! Joseph , do not take what I have said to heart : please, do not even think anymore at what I said and forget it all ! It is ,really , my anxiety and my distraught mind that causes me to be so nervous and tense and words come to my beak without any sense , just an insensate and garrulous twitting ! Don't worry, dear : I still love you very , very much ! This enormous tree where we have our love nest, could not hold all the love I have for you ,my darling !

Joseph - Oh ! My Ildegard…..the sweetness of your words overwhelms my senses and my mind !

Ildegard - You don't say !

Joseph- Oh ! yes , yes , your words float slowly and steadily to the very heart, to my very soul , and I understand you very well and I knew that something serious was grieving you !...But , do not worry , my love , I understand you and I am all yours !....for ever and ever !!

Ildegard - Oh ! Joseph , my love , your words too are to me like the honey from the hollow of a young tree in our perfumed forest ! Joseph , I am sorry if I had sounded a little upset and a little angry , a while ago, just one of those passing black clouds, that float here and there and sometime we do not even know why they were passing by : but passing by they do, from time to time, and, often, bring rain .

Joseph- I understand , my love , I understand you perfectly well and I agree with you in everything you say , in everything your precious mind , heart and soul desire ! You are the light of my eyes , the force of my will , the beacon of my very existence ! Please , my love , do not worry about what was said before and forget it all just as if it had never happened !! How about it , sweetie pie ?

Ildegard - Yes , my love , and let's forget all about what was said just a while ago in an impulsive , and I agree and consent , in quite an irresponsible and senseless manner and let our love reign supreme and guide us in the path to the highest mountain , ...well, or should I'd rather say , to the highest branch of this gigantic and majestic tree , in a voluptuous celebration and unbridled joy for our love !

Joseph - Oh!! Yes , yes ,My Love !! ...Let's do it !!

Ildegard - Joseph, Joseph ! My love ! How happy I am now, Joseph...!!!

Joseph - Me too !!

Ildegard - Joseph ?

Joseph - Yes , Ildegard .

Ildegard - Joseph , my love , now that we have reaffirmed with almost sublime dedication and commitment to each other about our pristine love , I would like to ask you for a little favour and some help , so that the glow of our love would go on shining for ever and ever !

Joseph - But , of course , Ildegard , my sweetest love , : what is it that you wish ?

Ildegard - I want you to come here and cut your Mother's throat .

Joseph - W H A T.....!!!!!?????

Ildegard - Oh ! My sweetie , adorable Joseph, do not look so stupefied at my seemingly straight forward and direct request as if your faculties had been benumbed , and do not stare at me in that stunned like look as if you had been overwhelmed with amazement ! Oh! , please, Joseph , try to understand me ..!!....You know..the neck , .the neck !! Cut your Mother's neck.....my beloved ! Is that , now , too much to ask of you in the name of our sublime and enduring love ? Tell me ,my love , tell me : is that too much to ask ?

Joseph - You have gone crazy !

Ildegard - Ah!!....have I...???...I'll be....well, is that so..,then ??....I ....gone out of my mind ??!?....Is that what you are thinking..??!!.......or....let me put it more plainly : " is that all that you are capable of thinking ?? ".......and I , an innocent victim of a cruel , almost insane tyranny on the part of your Mother, miserable failure of your so eagerly proclaimed love and its infamous demise when confronted with a simple request and the begging of a small favour by the supposedly beloved and adored wife of a coward of a sparrow....YOU....YOU....a BRUTUS.....a CASSIUS...these names, one at a time or both at the same time for completeness of intention , would be more appropriate than one stupid and insipid name like " Joseph" ,..........you...you...you are...I know, now , what you really are ......you are a big , ugly , and disgraceful coward...That; what you are ....

Joseph - I L D E G A R D !!!

Ildegard - Oh ! Quiet , you, little , insignificant sparrow , Mamma boy !! What kind of a sparrow are you , anyway ?? Is this , then , the great , immense love that you claim to profess for me ? Tell me , now , is this , then , that kind of boundless love ? Is it now..!!?? ...You , good for nothing flightless bird , son of a witch and , on top of it , a witch sparrow at that !!! ...And now , when I ask you for a simple demonstration of affection and dedication to me , there you come out your real self and shamefully reject my anxious plea and my unselfish request, just a small token to cement our great love !! YOU are a coward and a traitor and I who had believed in you and in your daring and vertiginous flights and your sweet sounding , musical chirping from the branches just above my nest, before you proposed to me !.......You...wretched bird ,you...I just hate you ! ....OH ! Oh! my head, my head....my poor head...it feels like it's bursting apart !!

Sparrow(Mother-in-Law)- addressing the Tree. What did I tell you !??...Her head...always her head ! That's what I have been telling to my poor Joseph and warning him : " Be careful , be cautious , my dear son , and be very alert , because that sparrow , that sparrow-wife of yours, has no head " , but , what I really meant was : " she hasn't got a good one " , and , now , to further dramatize the theatrical display , her head seems to burst apart ! What luck that would be if it really were to happen !!

Joseph – (upon hearing his Mother...!) Mother ! Mother, don't say things like that !!

Sparrow(Mother-in-Law)- My poor little Joseph, what a calamity has befallen you with that Ildegard !

Ildegard - Listen ,listen to that wretched witch, Joseph, my love ! ...Your Mother is an abominable wretched W I T C H !!!

Sparrow(Mother-in-Law) turning to the Tree- WHAT DID I TELL YOU ?? That despicable female is possessed by the devil, as I had always thought . She may be the devil itself ,for all I know !

Giant Oak Tree- Where is he ? Where, where ?? Where is this devil ??

Sparrow(Mother-in-Law)- Don't be stupid ! I am saying things figuratively .

Giant Oak Tree- So do I . So do I . But , where is he , this devil…figuratively ??

Sparrow(Mother-in-Law)- In your Big Head ! Of course, always figuratively , you ninny : I am always referring to that sparrow who happens to be my son's wife . Did you hear, how bitter and homicidal she is and she feels towards me ? Do you think that that is " normal " thinking ?

Giant Oak Tree- Normal thinking, certainly not, but , then , learned trees and learned turtles , all scholars of unblemished reputation in this great forest of learning , have not established ,yet , with a clear and precise formula what "normal " is , due to some difficulties in the interpretation of various and multivarious types of "normal", as , for example, if "flying " appears a perfectly "normal " attitude for a bird or certain insects and so on, the same normal, of course , could not readily apply to a tree , because if the tree could fly, used as we all are at looking at trees well and solidly planted in the soil, it would easily follow that , should we see a tree flying, we would likely think that that is "abnormal", ' although, the "flying " ,per se , is a normal feature of Nature. So ,in the uncertainty, the Great Scholars are bidding their time ,patiently waiting to see if anything at all "normal " would come down their way and everybody's way too, in order to restore a smile to our every day life. Tha is what I think .

Sparrow(Mother-in-Law)- Now, isn't that nice !

Giant Oak Tree- I think so .

Sparrow(Mother-in-Law)- But then , my dear Big Scholar of a Tree , do you think that this obsessive and disturbing impulse in my son's wife mind , to wanting to have my throat cut , is a normal or is it an abnormal thought ?

Giant Oak Tree- I couldn't tell you, my dear : I was commenting about "flying ". Well, then , in this case of yours, as you can readily justify it yourself, "flying " would be perfectly normal, since she is a sparrow and, of course, a bird. Now , for birds to be obsessed with cutting their spouses Mother's throats, that's a far more complex equation than that of why birds can fly and trees cannot.

Sparrow(Mother-in-Law)- Interesting explanation. Now I understand why you are so big.

Giant Oak Tree - Thank you.

Sparrow(Mother-in-Law)- Don't mention it.

Giant Oak Tree - I won't .

Sparrow(Mother-inpLaw)- Good .

Giant Oak Tree - So,……what's new about the two lovers ?

Sparrow(Mother-in-Law)- turning to the Tree, intimating silence. Shush !!...Be quiet and don't say a word : I seem to hear my Joseph and Ildegard arguing again !

Ildegard - Farewell, Joseph , I am going back to my mother !

Joseph - Oh! Ildegard, stop , I pray you ! Stop and reason for a moment , in the name of that love that still lingers in us ! Just do it for me, if nothing else would justify that action for your satisfaction.

Giant Oak Tree- A poet, your Joseph : he can even rhyme a common prose sentence.

Sparrow(Mother-in-Law)- Quiet, you big Ninny, quiet.

Giant Oak Tree- OK, ok, I'll be quiet, but I still think that Joseph is a poet .

Sparrow(Mother-in-Law)- Oh ! for heavens above, why there have to be so many …BIG trees in this forest ?!!!....Just be quiet and listen!

Joseph - Ildegard ! Ildegard, did you hear what I just said ?

Ildegard - I did .

Joseph - But, then , my love , are you going to think it over and not leave me , if for nothing else , at least for me and that love that still shines in our hearts !

Ildegard- Nothing shines anymore ,at least, in my heart ! And , For that " if for nothing else " , well, that is precisely so : nothing else , is right !! You'll never see me again !!!

** Ildegard exits from her nest and, perched on a branch prepares to fly away.. **

Sparrow(Mother-in-Law)- Oh!...HEAVENS be thanked '..!! Finally she's going and,,,Good riddance !!!

Joseph - Ildegard, Oh! My dearest Ildegard , I beseech you , do not leave me !

Ildegard - Joseph ,my beloved : my poor heart cannot stand this air anymore !

Joseph - Oh !! Wretched me ! Oh ! pain ! Oh! Desperation !!

Ildegard - Adieu, Joseph , my love, adieu and fare thee well , for ever !!

* (and spreads her wings , but hesitates and does not leave.....) *

Sparrow(Mother-in-Law)- Have a good trip, dearie !

Ildegard - Yes , I am leaving, but before leaving one more thing remains to be done:"Bon voyage " to you too , you horrible witch of a Mother-in-Law ! So , here I'll let you feel the fine grip of my clows at your neck, you despicable creature !

Sparrow(Mother-in-Law)- Joseph ! Joseph ! HELP !!...I am being murdered !! HELP !

Joseph - Ildegard ! Ildegard ! What on earth came over you !! STOP ! STOP ! I say ,for Heavens sake I say STOP…Ildegard ....what are you doing ! STOP ! STOP ,I say !

Ildegard - Go away, go away, Joseph and leave me alone ! I am thirsty of blood , of the blood of WITCHES MOTHERS_IN_Law .! Go away and leave me alone ! I said, GO AWAY !!

Sparrow(Mother-in-Law)- HELP, Joseph, help ! I am being murdered ! Ildegard is trying to cut my throat !

Joseph - Ildegard ! Have you gone mad ! Let my Mother go , I say , or ELSE ! ILDEGARD !

Ildegard - Go away, go away, Joseph because I want to kill this "Witch" that you call your Mother !

Joseph - Get away, Ildegard , or I will throw you down from the tree , without your WINGS ! DO YOU HEAR ME....!!!??

*(Joseph tries to grab Ildegard away from his Mother, but in the shuffle Ildegard hits her head against the tree branch and faints) *

Joseph- Now THIS !! Damn everything !

Sparrow(Mother-in-Law)- Heavens Knows !! What a collusion...!!!!...Oh, my oh ..my !!

Joseph - Mother ! Mother ! Ildegard has passed out !!

Giant Oak Tree- The poor thing !

Sparrow(Mother-in-Law)- You mind your own business .

Joseph - Ildegard ! Ildegard !

Ildegard (coming to herself)- Oh ! Joseph !....My head…my head…so much pain…!

Joseph - Do not worry my love , it does not look serious : just a small bruise, nothing serious. It will go away soon and you will be all right in no time ! Here, now , rest a little on my shoulder , like this , yes , …that's good !

Ildegard - Joseph ?

Joseph - Yes , my dear ?

Ildegard - Joseph : did you cut your Mother's throat ?

Joseph - I L D E G A R D !!!!!?????

Ildegard - Oh ! Joseph, dear , can't you understand ?? Here is either your Mother goes or I go ! That simple ! I do not want to stay here anymore , not even a moon cycle anymore , and that's final . Oh! Joseph , when will you take me away from these old branches in this thick forest and carry me far, far away in another forest where we could be by ourselves , free from the presence of …….well, I wanted to say something , but we have had already plenty of bad blood today so I will not say what I would have really wanted to say….as I was saying, how wonderful it would be if you could carry me far, far , far away from this forest, in another forest or on a high mountain or on a beautiful tree in a beautiful garden where there would be flowers and fountains and children playing and….NO MOTHERS IN LAW !.........and we could be , then , all by ourselves , free from the presence of that witch that is your Mother, to poison our love and our relationship !...When , when , Joseph, when will this happen , Joseph , my dear , my beloved Joseph? Tell me, tell me Joseph ,when,when ??

Joseph - If we are lucky , my love , at the next Lottery drawing , I promise !

Ildegard - Always the Lottery , the Lottery !!I am tired to hear it , I am sick to hear it again and again , never coming , never happening , I tell you , I am sick and tired of hearing you say that over and over every time I am asking for a little change in our lives ! Is there ,really , no other way to make it happen ??!

Joseph - I am afraid , my dear , that that's it !! No other way !...You see…….

Ildegard - I see nothing, my love , and all I can see is misery , loneliness , and the dark clouds of a forthcoming tempest driven by your Mother's venomous spirit looming over our little happiness . And , of all the odds , I am asking , what on earth has the Lottery got to do with our happiness or to the possibility of just flying away to a place as" far away" as possible from your Mother ?? That's what I am asking.....and wondering too .

Joseph- My love , my treasure,....you see.....

Ildegard - Quit with those opening salvos and try to talk some sense, instead .

Joseph - Well , my dear , I will tell you as straight as I can , if you only will let me tell it to you . in my own way .

Ildegard - You sound just like your Mother , dear .

Joseph - ILDEGARD ! ..Stop being so bitter and listen , instead.

Ildegard - I am listening.

Joseph - That's good ! So , ...you see , my beloved , in these here times we live in it's already a blessing to have a tree on which to live and make a nest on one of its branches and raise a family , if so desired .

Ildegard - Wouldn't that be nice , wouldn't it ?

Joseph - But of course it would , my dear, of course ! ...Only if everything would go along as smoothly as the moon cycles or in the perennial and regularly scheduled flights of our good representative , the Stork ! Unfortunately , things do not always glide along so happily and a few interruptions or untoward happenings could destroy even the most carefully assembled cradle of security and happiness.

Ildegard - Probably that cradle had not been "properly " secured , I guess : right ?

Joseph - Not necessarily, my dear, because , sometimes , unpredictable events seem to interfere even with the most accurate, precise and careful plans !

Ildegard - But these happenings are quite rare , I understand , and they are considered more like accidents rather than something of an organized or predetermined nature : right ?

Joseph - Theories abound on the explanation of those happenings, considered by some as purely of an accidental nature , by others as "Acts of God " , and by others still as unexplainable, or explainable only by the fact that our actions do not ,necessarily, march along in accord with Mother Nature intents and activities . Anyway , whatever the cause of those unfortunate events may be or may be caused by , the fact remains , that they do occur and , if misfortune should come to your nest , the damage from it and the consequences may be less and more tolerable and acceptable for survival ,having a stronger and more solid foundatiom......I'll give you an example: you see.....

Ildegard - Oh ! yes, please, Joseph , tell me : I am very curious to hear it !

Joseph - Well , I had a good friend , some time ago , and he lived in a forest adjoining ours, but it had been thinned out by human creatures to make way for a long line of telegraph poles , you know , the ones that send signals for long distances without anyone having to run for them or after them....

Ildegard - But, of course : the famous telegraph ! Every bird knows that !

Joseph - That's very good , then. So, anyway , to go back to my friend , he had a nest on one of those telegraph poles : a very uncomfortable dwelling , my dear , with a penetrating , disconcerting , tormenting and continuous clacking , the whole night , the whole day , with no pause ! This situation, in the long run , led to his wife finishing up in a hospital suffering from severe fatigue due to the almost impossible task of getting some rest . The first born became crazy . The second born developed a nervous condition , clicking his beak rhythmically all the time, instead of chirping . The last born , in a valiant effort to break out of that misery , married and that was the straw that broke the telegraph pole, since there were no camels around, at that time , and that was a REAL TRAGEDY .

Ildegard - What tragedy ? The marriage ??

Joseph - The telegraph , my dear , that caused the tragedy .

Ildegard - The way you said that , it sounded like the marriage was a tragedy , and not the telegraph .

Joseph - Precisely, my dear : BOTH . The telegraph , that caused the marriage , that caused the tragedy .

Ildegard - You sound like your Mother

Joseph - A tragedy, a real tragedy , the poor thing ! And he had been a good friend of mine : his name was Ulrdich , and I felt very , very sorry for him , poor Uldich!

Ildegard - Poor Uldrich ,my clows ! ...He must have been an idiot .

Joseph - O , no, Ildegard : he was not an idiot , only an unlucky sparrow. I do not think that Nature establishes well designed coordinates for its movements and activities and , for all that our experience can account for , it seems to affect the simple minded creature and the not simple minded one , the learned man and the philosopher in an indiscriminate way ,having no special safeguard built in its proceedings to save the wise and alienate the less wise or to spare the opulent tycoon and hit the pauper : " It just hits "..: and it does not seem to have any regrets either .

Ildegard - Is that the reason , then , why your Mother is so set against me ? Blame it to Nature !....right ?

Joseph - I do not know, Ildegard :I am not a Nature or a mind reader so I will have to let you work that puzzle out yourself, if you would still think it worth working on.

Ildegard - Thanks !! How magnanimous of you.

Joseph - But , my dear Ildegard , there is another episode about another friend of mine, that might shed some more light on what I am trying to prove to you ,and that is the uncertainties one can encounter in life by not digging in where he has an opportunity and ,instead , been obsessed in always looking for something else or somewhere else to go .

Ildegard - Not even after winning the Lottery ?

Joseph - I am relieved in hearing this, proof that your headache must have improved significantly. But , here is another story that happened to another friend of mine, his name was , Keeblick , and.......

Ildegard - The more you keep on talking to me about all of those friends of yours and the more it appears to me that their association with you did not bring them much luck or fortune !!....Is this , may be , a somber omen of our future , Joseph ??!

Joseph - Ildegard , look , for your own sake and well being , why don't you try to stay away from this ill-perceived tendency to fantasticate on preconceived ideas and thoughts that only further aggravate a tense situation , if one existed , instead of helping in clearing the stage .

Ildegard - To do that you should get rid of all your inner and most sacred feelings, Joseph!

Joseph - On the contrary , my dear , on the contrary ,and , please , do not think , not even for a moment , that I may be trying to contradict you , but , instead , you should accept me as purely attempting to help ease a bitter standing that carries nothing with it but only rancour , ill feelings , and distrust . You see , in the old days , when the English Language , inclusive of the inflections belonging to the birds' chirping , of course , had a slightly different manifestation of itself , now some modified like , more or less , all languages have been with the succession and erosion of time , well , as I was saying , this English Language carried and used for the purpose of the representation of these situations reflecting a repressed ill feeling , based on preconceived ideas, most of the time without even a solid or valid base for at all being thought, carried , as I said , a particular voice , a noun , " fantastication " , meaning thoughts conceived by a capricious and unrestrained imagination . This persistent and almost obsessive , shall we say , "Fantastication " of yours , Ildegard , does not help a bit our happiness ! Can't you see it ??!

Ildegard - Oh! Never mind it, Joseph ! May be , in time , if our love will continue to flourish, we, or , I should rather say , I will stop , as you said " fantasticating "!! Who knows ? We are still young , and life lies wide open in front of us , so do not worry about me and my " rancor " as you like to call it . Go on and tell me about the story of your friend Keeblick. Did he also live on a tiled roof ?

Joseph - Strange you saying that , because , as a matter of fact , he did !! Well, he....

Ildegard - I am glad that I was able to show you that I am following your stories and even more than that : I can almost anticipate their content, because they are always the same !!

Joseph- ILDEGARD ! why do you say that ! That's hurting because it tells me that you do not wish to understand the meaning of the stories and their teaching that we should have gotten from them ! But , Ildegard . those stories were not "fables ", they were real ones.

Ildegard - OH ! Joseph ,I am sorry if I gave you the wrong impression : it was, REALLY , just a little sarcasm and play to add a bit of fun to so much sobriety and seriousness to the way you told those stories ! They were rather depressing , instead of encouraging or up lifting , don't you think so ?

Joseph - If that is the impression you got from the ones I have just told you, wait and see what you will be thinking after I finish with this one !!

Ildegard - the one of your friend Keeblick ?

Joseph - Yes, Ildegard. that story. So , if you...

Ildegard - Oh , don't worry, Joseph ! I don't think that one more story would affect me that much more than the previous ones did : so , go right ahead and come out with the misadventures of your poor friend Keeblick .

Joseph - Yes, Keeblick ! The poor fellow , a nice, straight forward chap , a dedicated sparrow to the welfare of his family ,if I ever had seen one , and he lived on a roof.........o.k, yes,...you can go ahead and smile , about another of my friends living on a roof...or on a telegraph pole........saying that you could easily anticipate how my story would come out ....with almost everyone of the protagonists in the story living on a roof...but he really did , and , ...by the way.....are you going to pay attention to my story ?

Ildegard - But of course , Joseph ? why shouldn't I ? It seems to me that ,may be and after all , I am not the only one being " obsessed " by doubts and worrying thoughts, as you appear to bring forth a good example of it with your anxiety whether I listen to your stories or I do not and if I derive from that listening precious knowledge and information of practical and real life conditions . Isn't that so Joseph ,dear ?

Joseph - If I do seem .....shall I say....more " concerned " than " Obsessed " about any one listening to my stories , that is due precisely to my " CONCERN " about the only reason why I should be " CONCERNED " , that goes back to your insistent desire of wanting to ' FLY ' away , somewhere , on a mountain or on a tree in a beautiful garden, with flowers and fountains and children and leave the fairly well secure and comfortable place we have here that will afford us a peaceful existence and secluded enough not to have to worry about wanderers and strangers coming across these paths : that is not an " obsession " : that is a very sensible " REALITY CHECK " , my dear .

Ildegard - Does this " reality check " take also into consideration the presence of your Mother in this "comfortable " place ?

Joseph - It does ! And , if for some unforeseen reason, it wouldn't , then I would not give a damn whether it would or whether it wouldn't, because I am sick and tired of your bickering back and forth, at every corner or stop of the road, and , I am telling you , Baby , if this sort of thing keeps up , I am telling you , Sport, that we'll have to reconsider our respective sides of love efficiency, love making ,and love uninhibitedly luxuriant : is that CLEAR ?

Ildegard - Very . Now , what about Keeblick ?

Joseph - T'hell with Keeblick ! T'hell with stories ! T'hell with everything ! May be I'll follow your advice born out of your desire to " fly " away , and " I " , may be , will fly away instead of you and find myself a place in a nice garden with fountains, flowers , children or no children , that would not matter much , but away fron this constant , annoying , tedious needling of yours that makes me wonder whether , may be , my Mother , might have a point ,here , in being set against you : you are not trying to settle and smooth confrontations : you are doing your best to constantly create new ones!! That what you are doing ! And I am sick and tired of it.

Ildegard - Very well, Joseph : you fly away and I will kill myself .

Joseph - ILDEGARD ! That's no way to talk .

Ildegard - And that is no way , no reason , no sense for you to fly away , either ...Now, what about the story ?

Joseph - Oh ! Heavens forbid ! I give up ! There is and used to be around this forest , some time ago , an old "saying ' , a sort of a proverb like sentence that said :" if you cannot win them ",.......who ever " them " might have been or were in the imagination of those who formulated this sentence ......" join them !! ", so, since I do not seem to be able to make neither head nor tail , yes , I will tell you the story of Keeblick , and I don't care whether you will be listening to it or not! As far as I am concerned at the moment you can go to sleep, or turn your head somewhere else, or even fly away, and it will be fine with me, but , PLEASE , DO NOT SAY A WORD ANY MORE ! Did you understand ? I hope so !........Ildegard ? Did you hear what I said ? Ildegard ?....Answer me !

Ildegard - HOW ?

Joseph - By simply opening your beak and answering . That's simple.

Ildegard - You just told me not to say a word .

Joseph - Heavens !!...Thta's fine , that's fine . If only my good old friend Keeblick could be here to lend me some very needed help, the poor devil, but he ain't here to help me, unfortunately !

Ildegard - He must have been a HE devil, was he not ,Joseph ?

Joseph - He was not the type of devil you are thinking about or you would have wanted him to look like one ; he was a gentle sparrow as I had already said earlier and dedicated to his Family welfare. He had been raised in the country , had his primary education at the local Partridge School , and then ,having fallen in love with the prettiest she-sparrow in the neighbourhood , he married her and the marriage was heralded in that happy corner of the country-side as a major event, so good and congenial and friendly the gathering was that even some hawks took part in the celebration . Next , after the initial overflowing euphoria, he began looking for a suitable place where to make their house and raise a family . As I had said before , he was the type of the family man , not one of those Gigolos always in search of new adventures , no , he was looking for a suitable place where to make his and her home and raise a family. It was then, flying around over the village , that he spotted an old farm house still bearing the old type roof made out of red coloured round tiles , and ,after landing on the roof in order to inspect it , he noticed a tile that had become slightly lose........

Ildegard - That might have caused a leaky roof !

Josph - Possibly . But , I believe , the house, was not inhabited , if I remember correctly what Keeblick had told me after he had inspected the house and , the house being deserted , gave to our Keeblick a greater sense of security, the slightly raised tile gave an easier access to the place and a very good protection from the weather . So they settled down , happy in their new home which his wife had made into a very comfortable nest and it was not long before things started to move along and several eggs came along too , to the joy of the two newly weds . Every morning , early , and at dusk too, Keeblick would take a long flight out of the nest to look for food while his wife would stay home and sit on the eggs . It happened , now , that one fine day , it was a beautiful day of Spring , the air full of pollen and of sweet perfumes everywhere and the young wife, encouraged by that luxuriant display of natural wonders, felt like to take a little rest from that constant sitting on the eggs , so she got up and , making sure that she would not get too far away from the eggs, managed to get her head out from underneath the tile to get a breath of that balsamic air .

Ildegard - The poor thing , so careful and so conscientious about her "mother-to-be" duties ! She must have enjoyed that refreshing air !

Joseph - She felt great , and breathed in all that she could of that beneficial air.

Ildegard - The poor thing . So dedicated , so unselfish ! Her little offsprings should be very tahnkfull to have such a mother !

Joseph - Yes , she was a very , very ,lovely and wonderful Mother-to- be , indeed. However ,unnoticed by them , I mean by Keeblick and his wife...

Ildegard - Joseph , what was Keeblick's wife name ?

Joseph - Dagmar . Well , as I was saying , totally unnoticed by them , busy as they were tending to their nest and the eggs , some repair work had started on the other side of the roof from where they were lodged , apparently preparatory to a reappointment of the old house and , likely , getting new dwellers in it , and , now , taking the advantage of the beautiful weather , a worker had started doing some repair work on this side of the roof where the young family had their nest.

Ildegard - Stop ! Stop ! Joseph ,I don't want to hear anymore of your story : I have a feeling that it is not good and the very anticipation of it makes me nervous and sick. So , please, stop the story .

Joseph - But it is a real story, Ildegard , a true story and anything that is true, should not either upset you or frighten you but , if anything at all, rather enlarge your experience and learn about life and its vicissitudes . So , Ildegard , please, let me finish the story : it is real life !

Ildegard - Very well, then : if it is real Life !! But ,quickly , finish it up : I don't think that I could stand it much longer .

Joseph - It will not take long , now ,to reach the conclusion of this story : you know and , at the same time it is quite strange , how situations come to a quick and , sometimes , tumultuous conclusions in almost lightning speed after a preliminary build up of many and various circumstances lasting for long periods of time before coming to that "final conclusion", some of them totally unrelated yet premonitory of what is called the destiny of things and creatures . So , my dear Ildegard , poor Keeblick's wife......

Ildegard - Joseph ?

Joseph- What now ?

Ildegard - What's destiny ?

Joseph - Destiny means that which is to happen or has happened to a particular creature or thing , in other words , the predetermined and , usually , inevitable or irresistible course of events . Well , that's destiny , Ildegard , and now , to finish our story , Keeblick's wife...............

Ildegard - Joseph ?

Joseph - But , Ildegard , please stop interrupting me all the time : we'll never be able to come to the end of this story if you keep on holding me up !!

Ildegard - How did you find out what destiny is ?

Joseph - I looked in the dictionary for it .

Ildegard - Thank you , Joseph .

Joseph - Well , now , let's hurry up with this story or it will only be boring instead of being appreciated , meaningful , or pleasing . So , Keeblick's wife was totally unaware of the man , who was working , now , on her side of the roof , because he was still some distance away from where her nest was , while she was not paying attention to anything , so profoundly oblivious to anything but the unbelievable , wondrous weather and that perfumed air of early Spring , the fragrance of that magnificent day . Now , as the man kept on working , slowly but suredly , he was coming closer and closer to where keeblick's wife was , up to the point when , while moving backwards to reach for one of his tools, he inadvertently slid one of his feet which became caught in that raised curved tile where the nest was and Dagmar too , enjoying the good weather , and the tile, under that sudden and unexpected pressure , collapsed and crushed the sparrow's neck .

Ildegard - Not a word more , Joseph . I knew ,somehow , that it would have come to something like this and your story , Joseph , does not seem to be so interesting after all : rather boring , I would say , and besides ,Joseph , where is all that meaningful content and instructive guidance that you claimed it might contain ? I am disappointed and , at the same time , saddened because I had taken a liking to that poor Dagmar !

Joseph -. Two things , Ildegard : the first one , your perceived opinion . You see , the story is not completed yet , and you have already determined its effective value, a common error to the proper and logical classification of things , facts and characters . The second one , your emotionality .

Ildegard - What's wrong with my or anybody's " emotionality " ?

Joseph - It might obscure an image or an impression , which were quite limpid .

Ildegard - I don't know what you are talking about, Joseph, really !! Go on , then , and bring this story to an end . That ,in other words , means " FINISH IT " . Besides , I am hungry .

Joseph - Well , the result of that accident can be easily perceived : wife in Paradise and three eggs without a Mother . The poor father , Keeblick , upon his return from his victuals gathering flight , at that sight became shattered .! The poor thing, old Keeblick , distraught , sad and now a widower , realizes that all he could do at that time was to try to save the eggs while , at the same time., find another wife who could sit on the eggs to incubate them , as well as finding another suitable and , possibly , safer place where to build another nest . So , he sat out again looking for another suitable abode while a cat , which belonged to the new dwellers that had recently moved into the repaired house , was prowling on the roof as most times cats do , and as he passed by the collapsed round tile noticed that there was no one near the eggs to guard them ! Like a lightning pounced upon them and devoured all of them speedily . The Father , our poor Keeblick of course , upon his return from his finding mission , was stricken by this double tragedy and fell numb in utter despair !

Ildegard - Is it finished, Joseph ?

Joseph - Not quite , yet.

Ildegard - Heavens forbid ! Joseph !

Jpseph - Now, ,desolated , alone , almost deprived of his best faculties that he could use to think straight, not able or willing to stay there on that fateful roof , our poor Keeblick takes off on a flight away from all that desolation, and into the sky , distraught as he was and unaware that a hunter was crouching in the bushes : a loud shot and the little bird falls to the ground , dead .

Ildegard - Enough, enough of that : I had a feeling that it would finish up like this ! And for you , Joseph , you really have some strange ways to show your point .

Joseph - My point , Ildegard , is every body's point , mine , yours , his , hers , it , its , theirs , and all : it is just and simply life and it should carry the message that you should never complain of what YOU MAY THINK THAT YOU DO NOT HAVE when around you there are may be creatures who'd wish they had what you thought you did not have but you had it . Hard life , my dear ,and worse than those human creatures could imagine , when they naively follow our flying and smile while watching us , thinking that ours are flights of joy, of exuberant vigor , of explosion of energy . For them our shrieks are songs of joy and our soaring in the sky , exuberance of life . Oh ! how often appearances and ignorance confuse and mislead all !

Sparrow(Mother-in-Law)- turning to the Giant Tree. A genius ! A genius ! Joseph , my son , he IS a genius!What did I tell you ? What did I tell you !!! He IS a genius and had it not been for his senseless , reckless and headlong falling for that….so and so…he could have been already knighted by now . Oh ! How proud I am of my son !!

Giant Oak Tree - Astonishing .

Ildegard - Joseph , my love ?

Joseph - Yes , Ildegard ?

Ildegard - Joseph , does your story , then , indicate that we shall stay on this tree and in this forest for ever and ever ,to the end of our allotted days , in order to avoid gutters , telegraph poles , roofs with loose curved red tiles, lurking cats and vicious hunters ?

Joseph - It is a possibility ,may be even a probability, at least until we'll strike it rich at the Lottery.

Ildegard - And there you go again ! Joseph ,I am beginning to wonder……

Joseph - Wonder about what , my love ?

Ildegard - Well, I am beginning to wonder whether the sad demise of poor , lovely Dagmar might have been , in a way , her good fortune , even if saying so , might at first , seem a little strange , but, if you think a little deeper into what happened , you cannot help wondering at the very fact that ,her premature demise, actually , liberated her from a life of misery , in company and close relationship with an idiotic husband , your friend Keeblick, and a prospect of life under curved red tiles on the roof of old farm houses..

Joseph - Ildegard , if that fear is all that you have retained out of those stories ,let me tell you that “a prospect“ does not imply a definitive step in any direction and it represents something that may linger for a while in the so called “ back of your mind “ until, eventually, it goes away or modifies itself into something more positive , more pleasant and acceptable .

Ildegard - Joseph ?

Joseph - Yes , Ildegard , my dearest , what is it ?

Ildegard - Do you still love me , my dearest ,….do you still love me so much … really so much like the whole Universe ?

Joseph - Oh ! Sweet soul of love !Tender rose of my garden ! Sweet fountain of love , what are you saying ! What are you saying ! Oh! my love , I just adore you !

Ildegard - Joseph , my love , yes , Joseph, how sweet would it be to die in your arms ! Joseph !

Joseph - Ildegard , what are you saying ??! In my arms ,yes , and always , but why to die in my arms ???!!

Ildegard - Oh ! I was just trying to make it forceful , meaning, really , the dying of every day of our past , to leave it behind us , never more to think of it , only you and I tenderly entwined in the delirium of love !

Joseph - Rapturously entwined !

Ildegard - Oblivious of everything !

Joseph - Of everything !

Ildegard - For ever !

Joseph - For ever and ever !!

* the two lovers get entwined close together and travel to the land of passionate love. *

Sparrow(Mother-in-Law)- Poor Joseph ! Oh , my poor Joseph !! Bewitched ! Bewitched !.....beyond all hope !!!

* meanwhile the Birds that had taken to the sky earlier at the rising of the sun ,have returned, and , happily perched on the many branches of the Giant Oak Tree, have begun to sing the praise to their freedom and liberty and happiness. *

Chorus of the Birds- Liberty , that is so precious ,we enjoy it every single day and seeking it is not our worry because wisdom prevented us from ever losing it . Roses have thorns , seas and oceans have sharks , women darts of love and rejection , the bees honey and the sting . We have freedom and wings and we can soar in the wide blue skies any time at our pleasure .

The Representative of the bees Labour Union - Let go of the Workers !

Chorus of the worker Bees - Everybody should leave us alone : the ancient proverb says : " let the sleeping dog lie " and , if left alone , everybody remains peaceful .

A sleeping dog, now, woken up- I know of some sleeping dogs , but I did not know that the bees knew about them .....Besides ,dogs have nothing to do with bees . Bees are insects .

Chorus of the worker Bees- Watch your language ,you four-legged barking hulk !

The woken up dog - Barking is a lot better , neater and less annoying than your buzzing , tormenting flowers and getting mad and hostile towards creatures when disturbed in your activities.

The representative of the bees Labour Union - How would you like a nice sting on your tail ?

Chorus of the woken up dogs - Sleep restores strength, lets us dream , and keeps us away from trouble . Only unkind people engage in waking up folks from their beneficial sleep . We were very happy during our sleep , but , now , we are unhappy because , woken up , we realize that we are dogs and , if awake , harsh is our nature , programmed for us to run , jump , bark , bite , hunt , mount guard , pull sledges , play with children and play with folks on Fair Grounds and Circus Enclaves , guide the blind , and protect and defend the honest master as well as the dishonest one , because we were not given the privilege of the choice but only the task to obey . Mean are the people who wake the sleeping dogs from their blissful sleep.

Chorus of Mean People - When ,What , Who ...made us mean..??!......and Who , What , and When is now making slanderous remarks about us ?? Is, then , considered bad anyone who would follow his , her , or its own nature ? Oh ! World ! World so unkind and prejudiced , wavering , fluctuating from opinion to opinion , as chance would favour one or another, and, at the same time,so selfishly individual in its choices ! And , now , do the dogs , those who are still sleeping , think of us as mean creatures ?? The dogs do not know us , at least the ones who are not mistreated and who are still sleeping . Some of them might even love us : some of them !

Chorus of the betrothed Birds- Love ! Love !Oh , you sweet essence of life , sweet, indeed !!....And yet our particular love is even sweeter than sweetness itself . The love , then ,of each one of us , in particular , is exceedingly sweet.

Sweetness - And , I am asking , what kind of sense , if any , has this last sentence from the betrothed Birds ? For all I know , Love has no " particular " headings or selected areas : you either love or you don't .

Chorus of the betrothed Birds - The " particular " emphasis added to our love is only a motive intended to make us stand out in this World .

Sweetness - What Impudence !

Love - And what about me ? Everybody talks about me or the beautiful and pleasing gifts I usually bring around with me , and no one , really pays any "particular " attention to " ME " , but , sadly , only to the wonderful gifts I carry with me ! In the end, I begin to wonder:"is there,in this wide World ,anyone loving me?

Chorus of everybody - THE UNIVERSE LOVES YOU !!

Love - Oh !! My !! I am overwhelmed !!....Although its significance might be somewhat debatable...!!......But...WHO loves the Universe ....!.?

Chorus of everybody - You do ! We do ! Everybody does !! ....But , why did you say just a minute ago , a loving Universe significance may be debatable ? Wouldn't a "debatable" Universe tantamount to a question about its very existence ?

Love - Well, the way I said that is because of the way I see it .

Chorus of everybody- Tell us , then :we are very eager to hear your explanation.

Love - Well, for one reason, to begin with , the Universe, I mean this Universe is....

Chorus of everybody - Yes,by all means,Love dearest...THIS Universe , of course ! Are there any other

Universes out there ?

Love - What I really meant was the Universe we know or , I should rather say , that we think we know , and the one or its part or section that we are allowed to see with the power of our eyes if that power is good enough or powerful enough or adjusted properly to see what we see or it is just limited to see only what we can marvel at.

Chorus of everybody - And marvel it is.

Love - Granted :but the Universe that we are capable to imagine is,really,scarcely known to us and if we pose for a moment looking in a different direction , may be back centuries ago , it would be easy to recall my ancient message formulated with the help of understanding learned and far-thinking creatures of antiquity , proclaiming :" That love absolves no loved one from loving " , meaning that it should be an unswerving duty , a sort of a sentimental obligation for anyone loved to reciprocate such love , and I am mentioning this insert of old fashioned "love logic" because such a condition , when applied to the Universe , could create some sort of a difficulty , or , may be , some hesitation , even uncertainty , because of our very limited knowledge of this so called Universe , only barely visible in a barely limited view, always assuming , of course , that such Universe really exists , and , if it really does exist , who or what or when could reciprocate this love by loving an unknown lover , our unknown Universe..???

Chorus of everybody - But how could this Universe be unknown when we are looking at it every single second of our existences , the sun , the moon , the innumerable stars , the shooting stars , the Milky Way, how ,then , could this that we"see" be "unknown" ? ?

Love - Probably , by " unknown " , we , somewhat incorrectly , signify " unexplained", because , at least , as far as I know , no explanation has been rationally and positively given , yet , as to why these bodies are there , just as why are we here and what for and so on and so on, we all know that continuous conflict , and ....

Chorus of everybody - What then , dear Love ??!!

Love - Well, there is really no "WHAT" !.....but only some perpetual questions and constant guessing : for example , in our case , when you claim that the Universe loves me : well , should I reciprocate by loving ..."it" ? Or should I love "him" ? Or should I love "her" ? This would really be an arduous task . diluting the very essence of my very being , dispersed as I would become in the immensity of this unknown lover .

* HERE ENTERS THE UNIVERSE *

The Universe - "Tricky , tricky mon amour " used to be a favourite song, some time long gone by, but I am not planning any tricks or any academic dissertations on proving whether I exist or not, that 's not so important , but I could not help over hearing your long discussions over me , so I thought of putting in some wisdom of my own.

Chorus of all - Oh! We welcome you, dear ,great , immense Universe, we are honoured at being at all considered and addressed by so great and immense personality like you seem to be.

Universe - May be not as immense as you think or wish to imagine ! You know , every measure is proportional to what you have to measure it with . Anyway even if you knew me you could never find out for sure anything about me because I am moving and what you would see to-day , it may not be there to-morrow, so , relax, rest and take it easy and , as to LOVE , he does not have to worry about me , because he already has his hands full on your planet to keep him busy for a while yet . So , all the best and so long, dear all .

Chorus of all- Love! Love! Dear Love did you hear that ? Did You ? It was the Universe talking to us !!

Love - May be it was the Universe,and yet how can we be positive about it ? Could it not have been , instead , your wishful thinking making all of your hearing what you thought might have been good to hear ? As for myself , I heard nothing .

Chorus of all- Oh !

Love - Well, going back to our original conversation and explanations of Universes in Love or whatever , you should know that love is , actually , substance……

Chorus of all - . SUBSTANCE ???!!! Love , a "substance " ??!!

Love - Let me explain : well, yes , in a way , so to speak ,a substance that if not tangible at first and during the initial , preliminary and joyous introduction , it will, however, always demand , in the end , and at least in the way it has always shown its preferences , through the eons of time , a solidly structured end product , and , here , we would be confronted with another problem which would prompt a clarification as well as a definition of this yet poorly understood and visualized Universe, in order to determine its sex, per se , as well as the preferences that this Universe might choose in love making , that is if he were masculine or feminine, and , if chance would portray it as masculine, then a search should be under way to find a suitable female companion , a feminine Universe , provided of course that this newly discovered female Universe , if found , would be proper , straight and cosmic compatible , but a rather questionable situation might persist as it would be quite difficult to attract her attention, warn her , court her , entice her to a love encounter not even knowing her name or her address . Clear ?

Chorus of all- Amazing .

Chorus of the betrothed Birds - To us is of no interest to know the sex of the Universe : it is not at all important or essential to our existence . We are still very much in love !

Chorus of the Birds Elders - Brothers ! Brothers ! Come, come ,now , and listen !...What kind of senseless chirping , chirruping and chirring is this you are doing in this beautiful morning ! The sun has risen and is already high in the sky ! Your chirping , chirruping and chirring is just idle talk . The fulgent rising star is wise and never lingers to talk , chirp , or listen : may be he thinks , but we have not been able , so far , to assess , confirm or prove either one of those suspected activities. Anyway , he never pauses , never rests . Well , then , let's put aside that useless chattering and take the advantage , again , of its warmth , its bright luminescence , its immense joy and , of this last attribute , we feel perfectly sure or , if not immensely joyous , this great star would be all dark and , as we are so freely endowed with all these benefits , it should be our turn to reciprocate these wondrous gifts given us by a benevolent Mother Nature with the tacit consent of our shining and fulgent star in the sky , , therefore , if for nothing else , but , at least , to show our respect and thankfulness for such privileges , our chirping should subside .

Chorus of the Birds in love - But, respected Elders, we need to express our joy , our fervor,our happiness,and, short of flapping our wings , what else is left for us to show utter pleasure and satisfaction than singing the praise for our love with our melodious chirping? Why ,then , should our singing subside and our joy be restrained ?

Chorus of the Birds Elders - For one thing , all things considered ,for all of us in this here World , talking or chirping , are , after all , a great mystery , both of them , talking and chirping , even and still so much more mysterious for us , elderly birds of these dense forests , as we carry with us and within each of us this mystery and we partake of its strange sound as a guarded riddle to be heralded to everyone and every thing around us when we feel the urge to sing our song early in the day at the break of dawn , but not to pry in its significance , and we could not achieve that goal, anyway , even if we wanted to , or tried to attempt that daring task ,because , just as we do not get our wings any closer to the sun , while still enjoying its warmth ,so , just as well , we are far away, by infinite infinity , to the source , significance and explanation of our chirping and other creatures' talking , while still enjoying , without any prescribed restraints , the exhilarating experience .

Chorus of the Birds in love - Then , does all this long conversation mean that we may continue expressing our joyous chanting and praising of love ?

Chorus of the Birds Elders - It means precisely the opposite : since the sky is clear , open , hospitable , and the day friendly and beautiful , the sun warm and radiant , the next move is to expand your wings with joy , vigor , enthusiasm and praise your love in the open sky , while this bountiful load of natural wonders persists .

Chorus of the Birds in love - But , respected Elders ,how can love be praised while flying around in the sky ?

Chorus of the Birds Elders - Use your imagination .

Chorus of the Birds in love - Oh !

Chours of the Birds Elders - Besides , you must remember that the night that is bound to follow soon , will deny the eyes the vision of things and allow our memory to retain only a blurred vision of those things to satisfy our wishes and allay our apprehension. At first , a soft twilight , slowly deepening into a faint glimmer and then fading into total obscurity. Therefore , Brothers , spread your wings and take to the sky and enjoy its glory while there is still light.

Chorus of all- The Elders ' talk is clear and wise :their chirping , even if slightly tremulous , yet is permeated with the wisdom of experience . Let us , therefore , let aside our vane talk and let us just look around and make an effort and a commitment to understand what we see and even doing just that is a gigantic enterprise .

Chorus of the Amoretti Cupid (Little Cupids !) - We never talk , not even when we send darts of love among the birds, whether they may be perched on a tree branch or flying around : yet , how high and complex our eloquence is when reflected in our glances and in our passionate interminable silences .

Chorus of all the Birds - Come on , Brothers , let us follow the wise council of the Elders and let's fly away into the bright sky , high and higher towards the sun in this splendid morning to enjoy this gift from the heritage of our birth !

Chorus of the ignorant Birds - The "gift from the heritage of our birth" ??....And what's that supposed to be ??

Chorus 0t the Birds Elders - Flying , of course, you NINCOMPOOPS .

*** The Birds take to the air in a majestic flight, all together , smart ones and ignorant ones , hardly recognizable in that mixed , noisy departure in a flurry of chirping , chirruping and chirring . ***

* Meanwhile, the Giant Oak Tree voices a sense of relief *

Giant Oak Tree - Finally, they are gone, these damn Birds !! Just listen to the rustling sound with all those wings flapping crazily in the air ! It sounds as if a thousand winds burst through my branches , blowing all at the same time, all thousand of them ! !!.....And it is like this every morning , every day !.....The leaves, too, joining in the fun, dancing and rustling , but , at least , the leaves create some pleasant and refreshing breeze and keep me a little more bent favourably towards patience and keep me in good humour !

Chorus of the leaves - The Birds are gone , now, flown away , may be far, far away with their newly conquered lovers and we are here in this morning breeze , pleasant and refreshing , while we rock ourselves leisurely from these large and strong branches . At night ,we offer a good abode and protection to birds, cicadas , sparrows and ravens , which are also birds , naturally , and also to lizards , beetles , centipedes and, during the day , we provide some refreshing shadow to the grass around the tree and other plants closer to the ground so that everybody receives some protection from the scorching sun ,but, at the same time, we take great care not to block entirely the beneficial warmth of the sun's rays so important and essential to the well being and the prospering life of everything living. We also offer protection from the heat to the human creatures ,although not all of them will show any gratitude to us for doing that protective service.

ENTERS LADY GRATITUDE

Lady Gratitude- I believe that I heard my name being called: it sounds as if someone is calling me . That's strange !! Who in the Universe could muster so much innocent credulity and be so exquisitely gullible to at all consider addressing me , least and not last looking for me or , worse and sadder even, expect me to be real ...!!!??? Who,of all odds , who ? I wonder !!

Chorus of the leaves - It is " us ", Gratitude , ...we , the leaves of this Giant Oak Tree ..we called you . We are quite familiar with your name which frequently breezes through these branches driven by the wind and , just like the wind , comes and goes , never lingers among us so that although we are familiar with your name we do not know you in person , how you look , and your physiognomy : we wonder if you could be so kind and show yourself and allow us to treasure a glimpse of your look and learn of where you are and where you live .

Giant Oak Tree - It's quite interesting: first a flight of the fantasy with the birds and now a didactic attitude of the leaves ! They probably wanted to be greener than they are , I guess !

Chorus of the green leaves - Not really: we already know that we are green, that's not a problem . All we wanted to say to Lady Gratitude was that we would have been interested in seeing her " features " and know her abode. That' s all it was ..

Giant Oak Tree - No harm done : I was only teasing.....a little . As a matter of fact I would be also interested in making a personal acquaintance with Lady Gratitude .

Lady Gratitude- So, you are desirous to make a direct acquaintance with Gratitude and even take a good look at her , right ?......My dear leaves of the Giant Oak Tree , futile would be your endeavour to look for me because I hardly ever can be found where I should be rightfully wanted or desired and, even worse, where I would be supposed to be by natural and logical as well as honourable expectations.

Chorus of the leaves - That's disappointing. We feel that to be also very sad.

Lady Gratitude- Well, disappointing or not , sad or not, that is the very truth. Practically , I am not here or there, neither up or down , or in the epic of a triumph or in the empty memory of a good deed , and never ever in the air or in the water or in the soil , but ,most often , in the mud where people can ignore me and feel no obligation to recognize me, so , as you see, I do not exist , really , at least for the greatest majority of people eager to ignore their debt of gratitude for something fortunate occurred to them , and ,as a result of all this , I am only a word , a word that seldom if ever people feel a need to pronounce it , or use it , or write it down .

Chorus of the green leaves - Lady Gratitude , we are thankful to you for talking to us and so freely, but we are also very sorry to have to say this to you that we are not quite certain if we understood you correctly when you said that you :" do not exist " . Did you ,really , said that YOU "do not exist " ??!.......Did you ,really said THAT ??!!...or did we misunderstand you ? The wind could have moved us a little or twisted us slightly so that we could have lost the proper continuity of your saying .

Lady Gratitude- Yes , you heard me very well and quite correctly , my dear green leaves : yes , strange as it may seem at the first impression , what I had just said ,is perfectly correct : " I do not exist " .

Chorus of the green leaves - But " THAT " is incredible !

Lady Gratitude- Well , just look on the practical side of it , and......

Chorus of the green leaves - We are trying , really , we are trying , Lady Gratitude, we are really trying but green as we are to life and all of its wonders as well as all of its unpredictable and unexpected complications, occasionally we strain ourselves in our efforts to comprehend life's many mysterious facets , and.....

Lady Gratitude - Life , yes , I agree with you , is full of countless, myriad of unanswered , unanswerable and mysterious settings and complications , yet ,some of them at least , stem out of our own silly manipulations . Not to become discouraged , would be my humble advice !

Chorus of the green leaves - Of course , Lady Gratitude , we understand that , but , you see , we have only two sides of us exposed to everything and if the wind blows "this " way we hear news this way , and , if the wind blows the other way, then we hear news the other way ,leaving us no choice in what we want to, intend to ,or desire to hear like other creatures do, who can make choices of direction , perception and projection , and can move in many different ways so that "comprehension " , probably , comes easier to them .

Lady Gratitude- You'll be surprised , my dear green leaves of the Giant Oak Tree, you'll be surprised !!........because, sometimes , the ability to perceive, receive or even depict on the multi-sided reception facets of one's mind the innumerable impressions, stimulations and sensations showered on us during the everlasting span of night and day, can create confusion rather than wisdom :.......and that applies, of course , to those other creatures you have been referring to . Anyway , going back to our conversation when I was saying that " I do not exist " , well , my statement is , really , not as far-fetched as it may sound .

Chorus of the green leaves - It isn't ?

Gratitude - No : I do not think it is . Just think : have you ever seen a word in full attire , with a face , a physical silhouette , a gaze , a smile , or a frown , and breathing ? Have you ?

Chorus of the green leaves- We have not , so far . You see , we do not go around very much , except when we fall off the branches of this Giant Oak Tree and , by then , our life has completed its brightly green cycle and we are slowly preparing to help our soil rejuvenate with our help by returning to its embrace , so we , really , do not have much of a chance to meet anybody or go looking for anybody or anything, while we are alive and brightly green dangling happily from the branches of a tree or at our demise , yellow and withered , on the ground.

Lady Gratitude - I understand and , in all confidence,you have not missed anything, really , by not seeing those words because , many a time , they just ain't worth seeing .

Chorus of the green leaves - Strange case.

Lady Gratitude- May be so ,....and here is another angle to the life of the words : they do not eat , and those who use them and do not know how to use them properly ,do not eat either . Words do not drink : when they do ,on account of reckless creatures , they get all mixed up , at times , causing real trouble . Words do not breathe either : and how many secrets in the life of the World have gone unsolved because the words would die , deprived of their pronunciation by a breathless creature .

Chorus of the green leaves - The way you describe those words they seem to remind us of ourselves : they , really , do not have much of a chance either for a saying in their lives , dangling from the"breath"of a breathing creature for their existence, just like we do , dangling from a tree branch for our own existence.

Lady Gratitude- Yes , may be so : similarities abound in our lives , but , of course , the difference rests in their identification and , often , in their interpretation . Anyway , I was saying , in addition to all of the above , and in all confidence , words are not expensive items so that owning them and , of course , using them as a consequence of proud ownership , is a commodity anyone can posses ,either by pronouncing them , if they can , or by writing them , if they can, too.

Chorus of the green leaves - Lady Gratitude, you have been very , very kind , to us , explaining a great amount of almost unimaginable facts of life, and where many problems stand and where their solutions lag behind and where various creatures do not do well what they are supposed to do or do precisely the opposite of what they were supposed to do and ,all this information is very good for us and we are grateful to you for allowing us to partake of its great importance .

Lady Gratitude - It was a real pleasure chatting with you, dear little green leaves of this Giant Oak Tree , and I enjoyed talking to you and listening to you : it is not an everyday happening to find courteous creatures and pleasant ones around this World of ours..!!

Chorus of the green leaves - Thank you, Lady Gratitude : and we consider ourselves very fortunate too in being able to converse with you . Yet, something does not seem to be quite clear to us even now ,and particularly so about the words .

Lady Gratitude - Very well, then , no problem at all , and why don't you tell me what is that is not clear and we'll talk some more about it and see if we , together , can make it simpler and better understood.

Chorus of the green leaves - Thank you , Lady Gratitude.

Lady Gratitude- How refreshing ,indeed , to hear someone thanking me !!

Chorus of the green leaves - We are glad , Lady Gratitude ,that you are pleased with ......OUR WORDS !!

Lady Gratitude - Words , indeed , yours I mean , well worth keeping them in my memory because seldom, in the history of our world , creatures condescended to be grateful or thankful, and , if they ever did, it was , most often , for a motive of interest and not one of just plain joy and recognition , not much different from to-day's trend where expressing gratitude is only acknowledged by very few and, even so , " grudgingly " !!

Chorus of the green leaves - Dogs appear equipped for the better and more desirable kind of demonstration of gratitude and friendship than other creatures , particularly human creatures !

Sleeping dogs waking up - Did someone call us ? It sounded that way .

Chorus of the green leaves - Go back to sleep ; we were just praising you .

Chorus of the woken up dogs - Oh ! Thank you . Thank you , indeed !How nice to have such kind people around , particularly these days of violence and anger. Thank you ever so much and good night .

Chorus of the green leaves - Good night .

Lay Gratitude - Good dogs ! They went back to sleep ! Well, now , if I remember correctly, dear green leaves , you wanted to go over some topics about the words that did not seem to appear clear to you : right ?

Chorus of the green leaves- Yes, Lady Gratitude : that is right.

Lady Gratitude - Very well, then . In all confidence let me tell you that , sometime , they do not appear that clear to me either ! Anyway , I am ready and ,may be , together we will make a happy exit.

Chorus of the green leaves - Thank you , Lady Gratitude : you see, we have been following your descriptions attentively and as diligently as our limited supply of understanding would allow us to follow, yet we cannot help noticing that , just as we feel the soft caress of the breeze or hear the sibilant sound of a strong wind , so we can hear those words in different variations of sounds and in variable measure , when they appear to come out from the mouth of those two legged creatures called humans , and the same happens , of course not in the form of a measurable well formed sound like the humans can, yet , in a different manner ,should we say, in a sort of harmonic sound of various proportions and innumerable variations, when expressed by many other living creatures . So,.........

Chorus of the woken up dogs - Quite interesting .

Lady Gratitude - I believe that we have started something , here !!

Chorus of the font of all beginnings - Everything , and we mean really everything , has a beginning and it usually starts somewhere .

Chorus of the woken up dogs - That's the problem .

Chorus of the font of all beginnings - What problem ?.....And what dogs know about problems, anyway ? "Problem " or " problems " , is or are not a part of a dog's existence.

Chorus of the woken up dogs - That's the problem .

Chorus of the font of all beginnings - We believe that the way you carry on ,you ,really , are the problem .

Chorus of the woken up dogs - Not quite .

Chorus of the font of all beginnings - NOT QUITE......??!!

Chorus of the woken up dogs - Yes , - " not quite " - because whenever there is or has been and, most likely, and, probably, even logically, whenever there will be a new beginning so there always will be a well arranged and compensated counterpart of a new resistance to that new beginning , and that's the problem .

Chorus of the font of all beginnings- You are talking nonsense ! Well, what can anyone expect from the..........wisdom of a dog, particularly if just aroused from his sleep !

Chorus of the woken up dogs - You can expect precisely what you just said : the beginning of nonsense .

Chorus of the font of all beginnings - Are you trying to be funny or are you just scoundrel dogs taking a shot at ridiculing us and our beginnings ?

Chorus of the woken up dogs - Not at all : we are just the compensating counterpart to your beginning of questioning our wisdom . That's all.

Chorus of the font of all beginnings - This is impertinence .

Chorus of the woken up dogs - We are glad that you recognize it : didn't we tell you that any new beginning will carry a question and an answer : the latter , not necessarily always favourable . So , you got it : Impertinence . Happy , now ?

Chorus of the font of all beginnings - Disgusted .

Chorus of the woken up dogs - Well, you started it : but let us add that , apart from our questionable wisdom , you not only are the font of all beginnings but, as well , the rather naïve beginners of your business . So , we are sleepy , so we were woken up , so we are tired and so we are going back to sleep and you , as far as we care , can start it all over from the very " beginning " . Goodnight .

Gratitude - Heavens be praised, if this squabble has really terminated !

One dog not quite asleep , yet. - It has . Goodnight .

Gratitude - Thank you ! And I hope that we can have some peace now !..Well , dear green leaves , you were saying ? You had not finished your sentence yet, before being interrupted by a barrage of controversy! What were you saying ?

Chorus of the green leaves - Oh ! Yes, we were talking about sounds , words , vibrations , and harmonics , and we had come to think that the possession of an arsenal of words and their usage appears to be , and we repeat, again and again , in our limited " fluttering "kind of vay in seeing things , as we said , it appears to be a patrimony of many creatures, therefore we believe that words must have a life because if something is lifeless , that is "dead ", it could not even retain anything at all of what it had on display or private property in life , not even the vibration given to it by the very sound that accompanies it . And , then , we thought of ourselves : when young, , we rustle in the wind , talking to each other , watching all that goes on around us on the branches of the tree, the birds coming and going, the caterpillars crowling leisurely up and down, the lizards' furtive dashes here and there and then the seeming suspension of all their activities for hours and hours, the bees, the beetles and the butterflies , but gone will be our happy rustling and talking and observing when , old , dry and yellow we will lie " lifeless " on the ground .

Chorus of the old , dry and yellow leaves -

Though fallen from the branches of the trees , withered , yellow ~~and pale at the end of our existence and of our sparkling~~ green that represented our glorious youth , we still rustle when the wind picks us up and twirls us around , or , when some creatures , passing by , tread on us and we crackle , we still respond in spite of our seeming demise , but no one pays any attention to that .

Chorus of the green leaves -

We are very , very sorry if we offended you, dear old yellow Leaves , but it was not our intention to do so and not for even a split second we ever entertained in our souls the idea of lacking respect for you .

Chorus of the old , dry and yellow Leaves -

We understand .

Chorus of the green leaves -

That makes us feel good, besides , we want to let you know that in our younger years , when still at school, in the high-rated Academy of the Chlorophyll , we were always and very incisively reminded that great consideration should be due to old leaves, fallen withered from the tree branches ,because , although yellow and wrinkled, their demise was the beginning of new life mixing themselves to the soil , so that , even without any sounds , not everything was , then , dead .

Chorus of the old,dry and yellow Leaves -

These kind expressions of sympathy mean a lot to us and give us support and new courage and confidence in our destiny , so that we do not feel entirely alienated by the living world . Thank you , you dear little green leaves , and the good Old Chlorophyll be with you, till your yellow due days .

Chorus of the green leaves - And " Thank You " to "YOU " too for your kindness , dear Yellow Leaves .

Lady Gratitude - How sweet , how moving , these words of kindness and gentleness ring to my ears !....And who can say that gentleness is no more !!

Sweet Gentleness - Certainly , not I !

Lady Gratitude - Quite understandable .

Sweet Gentleness- Indeed !!

Chorus of the green leaves - Well, with all this rustling and clamour coming from the ground , it was almost impossible to continue our conversation , so frequently interrupted by overzealous creatures , I'd rather say , unrestricted creatures , desirous of notoriety ,perhaps , without anyone around at all " desirous " to note them .

Lady Gratitude - But not all of those "creatures " were desirous of notoriety or attention, dear little green leaves ! Some were well worth being noticed !

Chorus of the geen leaves - Oh ! Yes, yes, you are so right ! The old ,yellow Leaves ! You are right ! But I had no intention of including them in the ranks of the other ostentatious types . It really was only our way of justifying the interruption of our conversation by mentioning the distraction caused by the intrusion of other uninvited characters that, eventually, prompted our remarks.

Lady Gratitude - It is really not necessary to make anything out of it: I really should not have even mentioned it ! But , then , on with our conversation and to clarify all of your questions !......And.....and ...do not be discouraged by the meddling of unsolicited and uninvited creatures : it would not be our World if it were any different.

Chorus of the green leaves - Well , with renewed " courage ! " , we were saying that with all that noise we could not progress very much with our conversation and , if we remember correctly , we had intimated that words are not dead , that they are alive , and working and effective and productive .

Lady Gratutude- Well, in a way , you could say that , but , my dear green leaves dangling in the wind so graciously and carefree , it is necessary to stop at this point and take notice that the life of the words exists only as an appendage to the life of living creatures who pronounce them and as the breath brings them up to the mouth and eases them out of it , most often ,if not right always ,the wind picks them up and once outside and alone they seem to lose their courage , being without the protection of a body which kept them inside in comfort, security and care ,and seldom you ever hear them again.

Chorus of the green leaves - We understand what you are saying , dear Lady Gratitude , and we do not intend to contradict you, but ,to the best of our memory , our Ancestors had told us that it had been the sound of the words coming from the mouths of the human creatures that had been instrumental in developing and progressing ,improving the whole being of those creatures , by differentiating them from all other creatures , creatures,of course, who can also produce sounds but not so well calibrated and syllabified like the words of the human creatures.

Lady Gratitude - It can be really confusing, I agree with you .

Chorus of the green leaves - How, then, can we reconcile the lifeless existence of words with those ancient words that can still be heard now ?!

Lady Gratitude- I hear you, dear little green leaves , and I feel sympathetic towards your wondering quest . Somewhat , I have also , to some extent , experienced the same difficulty as you have , trying to blend together what seem to be two conditions so far apart and so contradictory .

Chorus of the green leaves - Tell us , please, dear Lady Gratitude , is it because of our fluttering in the breeze and wind that makes it difficult for us to comprehend things in their right proportion , depth and significance ?

Lady Gratitude - I do not think so . As a matter of fact , I know that it is not so .

Chorus of the green leaves - How can you be so sure of that , Lady Gratitude ?

Lady Gratitude - Because your "fluttering " , has nothing to do with it .

Chorus of the green leaves - It doesn't ??!

Lady Gratitude - Of course not : if it did why would Nature furnish you with the ability to flutter ?

Chorus of the green leaves - We don't Know !

Lady Gratitude - I'll tell you why : because if you flutter it means you are alive and well and you understood and followed diligently and precisely your assigned work becoming a healthy , happy and garrulous fluttering leaf , and why would then Nature deceive you in denying understanding of the significance of anything……..you became a leaf , a beautiful , happy green leaf , you accomplished your task, you followed instructions to the last letter and in the prescribed order ,so you are a smart icon of life……and that is a real big part to play.

Chorus of the green leaves - No one ever told us anything like that !! It almost sounds unreal !!!

Lady Gratitude - Reality , many a time , is what we think something is and , sometimes , we also make up wrong realities in our minds either by poor judgement , or hatred , or desperation or desolation of mind and spirit , but , as to words , it is the instructions and the continuity of the historical values that give the words that "resounding " lively configuration . I almost would dare say that they are the mummies of antiquity, providing us with tangible proof of ways civilizations progressed and perfected themselves.

Chorus of the green leaves - We are amazed , dear Lady Gratitude , at your kindness in letting us in the knowledge of so many and fascinating aspects of life , and we are very proud that you let us partake of your knowledge and your experience .

Lady Gratitude - My knowledge and experience are not much and even questionable: it is purely and simple my own thinking , and , when you pitch your thinking to the basic running of everyday life, you lose the simple link to it .

Chorus of the green leaves - But,then,dear Lady Gratitude,as civilizations progressed,improved, and heralded themselves to new vertiginous heights of nobility of intentions , chivalrous sentiments and grand endeavours , your recognition should have reached unchallenged vertices!

Lady Gratitude - It would seem that way ,but , I am afraid , it was not "that way ", at least for what regards my life .

Chorus of the green leaves - But how was it possible ??!!......in those legendary days of epic battles , mighty Gods and Goddesses and valorous champions of war and sword and romantic loves !!

Lady Gratitude - Everything is possible , when there is a possibility.

Chorus of the green leaves - You don't say !

Lady Gratitude - But I do not have an answer for it or the right answer for it.

Chorus of the green leaves - That's too bad !

Lady Gratitude - Well, I do not have the answers for what you had just said , that is the chivalrous age of make-believe , because no human creature since that foggy day when the words were invented , has ever called me or on me or by my name or even used the gracious acknowledgement of an act of good will , or of a fortunate event , or a satisfactory solution to a problem, proving themselves to be totally disinterested towards my word , that of "gratitude ", or at all inclined to even offer a favourable "glance" to any recognition of me , in fact , quite the opposite , and as the words kept on creeping up in number as in meaning , the human creatures did seem to become overtaken by a tendency to excessive self esteem and selfish attitudes , instead of feeling and being " grateful " to one another when a favourable event occurred or good fortune came by to one of their Brothers !

Chorus of the green leaves - But why didn't they teach us at school about all of those interesting facts of old history, their influence on future times still to come and present times, where we live ? Is it , perhaps , very difficult , to remember things ?

Lady Gratitude - Not difficult, I believe , but ,may be , uncomfortable and painful.

Chorus of the green leaves- It feels painful just thinking of it !!

Lady Gratitude- It is true !

Chorus of the green leaves - But , then , we guess , not all that has been written , researched and proclaimed in the history data can be taken as to be the real and uncontestable proof of the historical events of life as we know it: right?

Lady Gratitude - It depends on who is collecting , recording and writing the history of the events, I guess .

Chorus of the green leaves - But , dear Lady Gratitude , you just said : " I guess ! " !!.....How can History be " GUESSED " ???!!

Lady Gratitude - It can , by simple manipulation and complicity by the one or the ones who write it .

Chorus of the green leaves - But that kind of behaviour is just plain horrible !

Lady Gratitude - Not horrible , I would say : just human .

Chorus of the green leaves - The more you talk about all those things and the more we feel mighty glad and blessed lucky to be just , plain and fluttering green leaves and now we really can appreciate the fact that we do not even have to think about it .

Lady Gratitude - But wait : there is more !

Chorus of the green leaves - More....???!!

Lady Gratitude - But, of course : we are talking about human history and those impersonators of high stakes and low schemes ,are never contented with small , limited avenues , be they for something good or for something bad, the latter their prime exploit and pride.

Chorus of the green leaves - A rather sinister picture of human endeavours,dear Lady Gratitude , the one you are so graphically painting !

Lady Gratitude- Not sinister to them, though!! The more evil they could think of something and the more "sinister "their thinking became .

Chorus of the green leaves - How sad !

Lady Gratitude - Sad ,yes , indeed and almost incredible, I would suggest , when you consider that such creatures, able to formulate, retain and profer words, , that is beautifully articulated words and in perfect syllabic array, could , then , be satisfied with horrible thoughts and misdeeds etched out and laid down by the same beautiful words ,they themselves had created !

Chorus of the green leaves - Incredible ! Really , incredible !!

Lady Gratitude - Yes,so it was , but not only incredible , it is defying imagination as well, at least our, and as the number of the words increased and they discovered ,as the time went by , how easy it was to obtain and accumulate those words , they became reluctant in sharing them , those words I mean , and they became very selfish too of those newly acquired riches and yielded themselves with unimpassioned activity , as it is commonly the case with anything that can be easily obtained and:.......

Chorus of the green leaves - A rather unhappy development , it seems , to such a good and useful gift from Nature ,like the ability to pronounce and use words , is it not , Lady Gratitude ?

Lady Gratitude - Yes, quite unhappy , and sad , and even depressing , I would think......Anyway they , these human creatures I mean , went on using their newly acquired bonanza of word power brought to them by this almost diluvial abundance of words by managing and concocting all sorts of machinations , fomenting discord with ill-will advertising , insinuating suspicion one for the other , discovered deceit , learned to glorify illicit love and ridicule affection , to slender one another , to infuriate , to curse , to vilify , to slander and drowned themselves in an ocean of turpitudes and pointed fingers at each other in anger, frustration and infamous accusations and lost themselves in an avalanche of false prophecies , doctrines and illusions , promptly followed by disillusions ,crimes and perversities to a point where I realized that there was no more an honourable place for me to be in this newly developed World ,so I left and went into voluntary exile searching for another abode with a secret hope that , if I should find such a place , I would be welcomed there with a more sensible and favourable reception as well as acceptance for me and my beliefs.

Chorus of the green leaves - We are following you , dear Lady Gratitude , in all that you are saying, but we are stupefied and almost incredulous at this development and turn of events in the history of the human creatures and their words , that we seem to have difficulty in comprehending how all this tragic story progressed while we were fluttering happily in the breeze and the wind and knew nothing about it all ! ! Very , very strange !

Lady Gratitude - Well, yes , it may sound strange to you , dear little green leaves , but it was not to me and to the other creatures who used their words with honesty , respect , and sensible discernment .

Chorus of the green leaves- We wonder if the leaves who were in the branches closer to the ground might have had some knowledge of that going on : it is hard to tell . Anyway, dear Lady Gratitude, were you ,then , able , after leaving that corrupted , turbulent world , were you then able to find one more suitable ,charitable and pleasant than the one you had just left ? We are very , very curious to find out how it went on ,really!!

Lady Gratitude - I was able to find a new place, yes I did .

Chorus of the green leaves - That was fortunate and we are glad that you found one ,dear Gratitude.

Lady Gratitude - Yes, I had found one in a far , far away world, very ,very far from the one where I was not welcome anymore and considered an inconvenient hazard to the machinations of that deleterious society , and as to this new far away place being more pleasant , more congenial, well , it was a half way situation ,just as it happens with many things of all kinds and instances of all sorts in an average life where half of one side is good , the middle fair , the other side not so good , so the same kind of situation happened to me in my newly discovered world ,indeed a convenient and basically peaceful abode , yet life seemed rather "flat".so to speak , insipid ,I would say and with no specific spark of any interest or joy or curiosity and....

Chorus of the green leaves - We are really sorry to hear this , Lady Gratitude.

Ladt Gratitude - Well, at first ,I felt that way too, thinking that what I had stumbled in was not ,apparently , a promised type of land ,exciting and well established and balanced , and the living creatures in that particular world were going about their existences without one knowing of the other or the next to them or the farthest one away from them and seemingly without any visible interest for one another , each one taking care of his or her own affairs , in perfect apparent harmony with one another just as if each one of them was by himself or herself showing no visible or tangible interest in one another and simply living their own personal and independent lives and showed no interest or surprise or curiosity when I tried to introduce myself .

Chorus of the green leaves - Sad ,sad, sad,indeed.

Lady Gratitude - At that point, I was not even sad ,I actually was more curious than sad or disappointed , I wanted to know what kind of a world I had come in to.

Chorus of the green leaves - At least you showed a great courage in your comporting like that, Lady Gratitude.

Lady gratitude - Well, courage or no courage , I was there , so, I knew I had to do something . I then stopped in front of one of these creatures who was standing there looking at something in the distance , I could not figure out what, anyway I stopped and with the mosr gracious approach I ever used introduced myself with my name and explained my function as well as the reason why I happened to be there in their world , but much to my surprise , disappointment and frustration , I did not promote any reaction whatsoever, the creature continued to look to "something" in the distance , only to turn slowly towards me after a fleeting interval of silence and said that he she or they did not know me , and they did not know what I was talking about.

Chorus of the green leaves - That was dreadful !

Lady Gratitude - Well, I did not know what to think of that attitude ,at least no one seemed resentful of my presence ,just as well as not being at all interested in my being there , and although they had shown no disrespect or disregard and no hostility towards me , they seemed to have no reaction whatsoever of any measurable value , when hearing my name , and I found out that they had no knowledge whatsoever of Orthography ,so they were unable and , of course , incapable of identifying me , and I was left alone.

Chorus of the green leaves
Lady Gratitude, please forgive us for interrupting you , but what is : " "Orthography " ?? We know flutter , chlorophyll , wind , breeze , birds , lizards , ravens , caterpillars , spiders , and butterflies, but we have never heard of " Orthography " . Please, Lady Gratitude won't you tell us , please, what Orthography is and we'll be very grateful to you for doing so.

** Enters Lady Orthography, just passing by and aroused by her name being called out . **

Lady Orthography - Pardon me , you gentle people , for butting in so rudely in your conversation and not even invited to do so, but I could not resist the urge to address you on a subject that is very dear to me when I happened to hear my name called and a subject quite worrisome too , because much to my sorrow and disgust , I happen to be the one that helped forming those words that brought so much sadness, distrust and mischief to the human creatures .

Lady Gratitude- It was not your fault , Lady Orthography, if your expertise and refined skills were misused by a crowd of half-witted creatures .

Lady Orthography- Fortunately, a "FEW" honest creatures lent me a hand and placed me rightfully on the tip of a "needle " and wrote wonders for the World to behold .

Lady Gratitude- True , and the sensible World will always be , as it always was then , very grateful to you for your great skill and virtue.

Chorus of the green leaves - Thank you , Lady Orthography , and we are grateful too for letting us know what Orthography means , and Lady Gratitude just explained it to us in more details , being , actually, the art of proper spelling those words ,therefore ,to put it in our own jargon , like injecting the proper amount of chlorophyll into each word , just as Nature does with us to make us nice, shiny and brilliant green. Thank you, really, from the bottom of our stems .

Lady Orthography- This compliment , from Lady Gratitude and from you , dear little green leaves , particularly Lady Gratitude, the very source where thankfulness was born , is of paramount joy to me and I thank you . But , let me warn you : you will find it hard to adapt yourselves to these new shores and you will be lonely . Anyway, whatever your choice of a new abode will be , I wish all the very best for you,now and for ever.

Lady Gratitude and the green leaves - Thank you, dear Lady Orthography and the Good Spelling be with you !.

Lady Orthography- I must go now : I have so many words to write ! Adieu !

Chorus of the green leaves - No one seems to ever be longing to spend some time with us , always in a hurry , always waiting to go somewhere , busy all the time . We believe that they should learn to flutter ,instead of going around in circles !......but what happened ,then , to your newly found abode , dear Lady Gratitude ?

Lady Gratitude - Well, I found myself isolated at first , and I thought that whenever in a new place, it takes sometime for a stranger to be accepted, assimilated and introduced to the "menu " of the new land. So, I waited ,patiently, for some clearing on the horizon, enjoying in the meantime the repose from the more turbulent times in the old World.

Chorus of the green leaves - And , dear Lady Gratitude, did you have to wait for a long time before someone approached you , or said something to you, may be just a simple but encouraging : "How are You " ? ...or even just : " good morning " and a smile , or something of that nature ?

Lady Gratitude - No, no, they would not say anything at all to me, as a......

Chorus of the green leaves - Unbelievable !

Lady Gratitude - As a matter of fact , my dear little green leaves , not only they would not say anything to me but they did not even say a word to one another or address each other either , perfectly silent , each one doing their own business as if there would be no one around but each single individual. No one seemed interested in the other or , for all it matters , in anything at all .

Chorus of the green leaves - Almost incredible !

Chorus of the far, far away World - We are far away from your World, the problems of your World, and your World altogether .We do not talk much,and that is an understatement because we do not talk at all, I being the only legal Representative, the Counsel, entrusted with speaking facilities, however we can hear a whisper even if coming from a different distance from our World, so , we heard yours.

Chorus of the green leaves - Oh ! Thank you , we are glad of that .

Counsel of the far away World Legal Affairs - We are not. Besides we do not know what"Thank you"means anyway. Whatever it might mean , we trust that it is not an offensive weapon against us.

Chorus of the green leaves - Oh! no , it means well ! Only occasionally , in our World , it may be taken in a different light, but it is a rare occasion,we assure you.

Counsel of the far away World Legal Affairs - We do not expect nor we would deserve any criticism for not having adequately welcomed and recognized this new entity from your far away World . To be further noted that , even if we had known of the existence of orthography ,we could not have taken the advantage of that knowledge because our World is the World of the Universal Illiterates.

Chorus of the green leaves - We believe that you meant : " the illiterate people of the Universe", right ?

Counsel of the far away World Legal Affairs - Wrong : we are the Universal Illiterate Creatures and not the illiterate creatures of the Universe . Besides , we do not know what you are talking about when you say universe . We do not know what universe is : is it , by any chance , a relative of yours ? Even if it were , we still would not care to know how it came about that it qualified as a relative of yours , and even if you would try to explain that to us we still would not care to listen to that story.

Chorus of the green leaves - They do seem to express quite a terse rhetoric, don't they !

Lady Gratitude - Undoubtedly , quite clear.

Chorus of the green leaves - But we wonder about this seemingly unusual isolation of your World ! Was it the result of a universal accident, or an adverse sequence of unfavourable events , or was it your own creation , your own desire to live in this type of organized society, away from everybody and everything ?

Counsel of the far away World Legal Affairs - This far, far away World of ours is the only World we know , it is not our interest to know how it came about, and we do not care to know even if someone would try to explain it to us : what good would it do, anyway ? In this World of ours we do not know how to read , how to write ,and even less how to think , and we are absolutely unique, specialized and well adapted to misunderstand everything and to understand absolutely nothing and not to dwell on so many subtleties, questions and problems.

Chorus of the green leaves - We are amazed.

Counsel of the far away World Legal Affairs - We do not indulge in complicated forms of social configurations either, whatever they may represent, or anything else . As to your question about our correct address to our identity, that of being the Universal Illiterates versus what you thought we had misrepresented ourselves, like the Illiterate Folks of the Universe , well, those , are everywhere , and , having inherited the coveted privilege of harbouring and possessing the Art of Orthography , they relaxed in their own writings, declaiming and illustrating all kinds of obscenities with abundant side-dishes of highly constructive stupidity. And now , if you do not mind , we have had enough of conversation , we are tired and we want to go to sleep and we bid farewell in the hope that you would do likewise ,and leave us in peace. Goodbye.

Chorus of the green leaves - Strange ,indeed, this World, even if far , far away !

Chorus of the far away World - Not far enough , apparently , for you to find us . We do hope that you heard our saying : Goodbye .

Chorus of the green leaves - But we mean well and so does Gratitude too.

Chorus of the far away World - What importance does have the expression " meaning well " when no one asked you to come and mean anything.

Chorus of the green leaves - But had you welcomed Lady Gratitude and tried to "understand something sometime " , like for example by understanding gratitude you could have easily comprehended the meaning of " meaning well " as well as that of gratitude.

Chorus of the far away World - What for ? We are born illiterate : we do not learn , we do not acquire knowledge ,or do we dream of notoriety .

Lady Gratitude - Everything , everybody is born illiterate.

Chorus of the asparagus plants - We are not so sure about it.

Chorus of the far away World - And what have you got to do with all this ? No one asked for your opinion , who ever you are.

The asparagus plants wise man - We are liliaceous plants and we are not illiterate . We know exactly what to do, how to grow , how to look right from the very first day of birth.

Chorus of the far away World - Good on you, smart lilies ,but we do not really care ,so , if you do not mind , we wish you goodbye ,safe trip , hoping , of course that you would start one , and also that you would leave us in peace. Goodbye .

Chorus of the green leaves - well, we never.....and, dear and respectable citizens of this far,far away world , don't you have even a tiny but kinder word for Lady Gratitude ? She is really a fine example of proper living, you know , even if you are illiterate , proud of it ,and live in a far, far away World of your own !

Chorus of the far away World - We did not ask her to come. Goodbye.

Chorus of the green leaves - Well, of all the audacity...!!

Lady Gratitude - So, my dear little green leaves , here you have my story ! As you can see I am only a word which , although more or less known , does not really exist anywhere ,not even in far , far away Worlds ..!!!

Chorus of the green leaves - Yes , dear Lady Gratitude , we heard your story by leaps and bounds from the explicit narratives of total strangers but naively accurate in their simplicity as well as in their irritating ostentation . A good story in all the details and sequence of events , but a very sad one too.

Counsel of the far away World Legal Affairs - These Strangers ! All they know to do, is criticize and dramatize !

Chorus of the green leaves - Well,well, look who is here again ! We thought you had said "goodbye " and suggested we leave you in peace, and then, you are still dilly-dallying around and eaves-dropping on us .

Counsel of the far away World Legal Affairs - Dilly-dallying and eaves-dropping do not register in our regulated society : we do not know the items and we do not accept your remarks.

Chorus of the green leaves - Either do we : so, as far as we are concerned , you can all drop dead .

Chorus of the far,far away World - Same to you.

Chorus of the green leaves - And they claimed that they could not understand our ways, our attitudes and our language ! !

Counsel of the far away World Legal Affairs. - That kind of understanding is proportional to the stupidity content of the question , naturally .

The Wise Man of the asparagus plants - Beware of far, far away Worlds ! They seem to be quite " near " in their ability and resilience in picking up habits of nearer Worlds .

Chorus of the green leaves - My ,oh,my , the never ending story !!

Lady Gratitude - I wish my story would end somewhere instead of continuing its sad peregrine journey !

Chorus of the green leaves - You know, dear Lady Gratitude , at each season in our ,let us say, "near" World , and everywhere , everything comes up new , from asparagus plants, to sugar beets to birds and human creatures , so ,if we pay good attention to even subtle happenings, who knows, your "peregrine journey " might even come to an end and you could return to your natural and well deserved place among creatures and in the light of History.

Counsel of the far away World Legal Affairs - Dreamers ! Bah !

Chorus of the Asparagus Plants - Did you hear ? those far away Idiots are still around !

Chorus of the green leaves - Yes, they are still there ! But , do not pay any attention to them or they will be pestering us more and more . We are afraid that they tasted some of the sugar of our society and ,confronted with the dismal appearance of theirs, are beginning to think it over and wondering how to join us.

Counsel of the far away World Legal Affairs - Don't you know that the truth offends ?

Chorus of the green leaves - What did we tell you..!! Exactlly as predicted .

Lady Gratitude - What's the use of finding a far, far away world ....! It does not seem, really, to change the fabric of the essentials of existing .

Chorus of the green leaves - And we agree with you , Lady Gratitude , the way everything lives or, as you say , exists , does not seem to vary whether near or far away !

Wise Man of the asparagus plants - Big deal !! We , asparagus plants , knew that all the time .

Chorus of the green leaves - How strange ! Bad knowledge can spread so easily !

Chorus of the knowledgeable Wizards - Bad or good Knowledge spreads at about the same rate as the good and the bad characters among your citizens , whether in the near or in the far , far away Worlds. Are you certain , that is , positively certain, that you know what you are talking about ?

Chorus of the green leaves - We think we do. However , since your last assessment , we are wondering if we really do.

Counsel of the far away World Legal Affairs. - I knew it, and I knew it , that it would eventually come to this : the whole story, the entire encounter , the astonishingly stupid remarks and questions and answers from all sides and all interested and involved parties was ,to put it gently ,absolutely senseless , unnecessary, unimaginative, unattractive, undesirable , unimportant ~~and utterly displeasing to our exquisite sense of proportion,~~ propriety and definition.

Wise man of the asparagus plants - Applause !

Chorus of the green leaves - We believe that it is really time to go ! Lady Gratitude what are you planning to do ? Stay here a little longer or get on the road aiming at a different "far away World " ?

Chorus of the far away World - We would definitely encourage her to get on the road and find another plaçe , and , please do not misunderstand us : we mean well ! We want Lady Gratitude to find an abode suitable to her dignity and virtue and value ! That's is ,really, what we fervently wish for her .

Lady Gratitude - Thank you, Citizens of this far , far away World , but value and virtue do not seem to be viable personal introductory business items in my experience , at least in my Old World.

Chorus of the far away World - We are sorry to hear this,Lady Gratitude . But ,after thinking over to all that has been said and discussed between all of us lately , it seems to us that , after all, our principle of living by our individual ways , and minding our own business instead of the business of everybody else, may not be a bad idea.

Lady Gratitude - I really am not certain of , or , on any decision I may be entertaining in regard to moving again in search of a suitable new World : how many of these new Worlds would be there ,anyway , to be suitable and how many , not to be suitable . And THAT if there would be any available at all ! I wonder !

Chorus of the green leaves - Dear Lady Gratitude , whether you decide to get on with your journey or stay or think about it , we wonder whether you could spare us a few more minutes ,because we need or, rather , we would want to ask you something that is not yet quite clear to us , in spite of the torrential like discussions on the subject and everybody trying to get their grist to their own mill. Could you spare us a little more of your time ?

Lady Gratitude - And , if I do , would you , then ,bear me some gratitude ???!!

Chorus of the green leaves - BUT , OF COURSE !!!

Lady Gratitude- I was only kidding ! I just could not resist the impulse !!!

Chorus of the green leaves - Do not worry, Lady Gratitude, about that ! As a matter of fact your ditto made us happy because it showed that your spirit and your feelings were up and happier than ever before.

Lady Gratitude- Always kind and generous in your thinking and interpreting words, dear little green leaves , you are indeed quite something, in spite of you being little, having only two sides ,and both of them of the same green colour ,but each side just as kind, alert and thoughtful as the other side !! But , then , dear green leaves ,why still some confusion , after all the explaining that has been going on ?

Chorus of the green leaves - Well, we do understand what you are saying ,dear Lady Gratitude ,that so much has been already redundantly discussed and you are right, but our uncertainty about some icons must be probably due to our fluttering while everybody was explaining, or discussing or arguing about everything that was discussed , and we might have missed some points.

Lady Gratitude - Which ones , dear green leaves ?

Chorus of the green leaves - For example, it is not quite clear to us what everyone is talking about now, origins , civilizations , worlds of all types ,dimensions and contents , understandings , misunderstandings , attitudes , inclinations , likes and dislikes , customs and tendencies , and what our Ancestors had told us , in the Annals recorded in the stems of those Forefathers, that.....

Lady Gratitude - But, my dear little leaves, what you are saying is a little strange , because it was just a short time ago when you were actively engaged in hot conversation with various other subjects ,countering their assertions, criticizing some, rebutting others , showing almost despair at their outlandish – like statements ,and ,now , wondering if you understood all of that correctly or if you missed something in the process ! Was it, now , so dramatically different or important what was in your Forefathers Annals , that seems to be so confusing now ?

Chorus of the green leaves - Not really confusing but subtly portraying a different aspect of those Worlds we were discussing and painting them in different lines and colours than everybody else did . That is what's confusing us some .

Counsel of the far away Worlds Legal Affairs - May be it's you that are seeing different lines and colours on your fluttering constitution. We do not see any lines or any colours at all and we would be really surprised if we could see some colours and lines painted on words, phrases and sentences and paragraphs .

Lady Gratitude - That was only a "would be " representation of unwelcome appearance of expressions and ideas .

Counsel of the far away Worlds Legal Affairs - Really...!?

Lady Gratitude - But, then, go on, dear little leaves, and tell us more.

Chorus of the green leaves - Well, the Annals had recorded that long , long ago , in ancient times , there had lived human creatures who had been able to put together certain sounds and , with these , form many words that were beautiful, melodious , and with the power and influence of their harmony and near perfect proportions of common usage ,were of an immense help in the progress of the human specie and their life conditions and were , as we had already mentioned earlier , instrumental in improving and fostering civilizations: not only one ,civilization , but all civilizations. How did it happen ,then , that there seem to be some splinter ,illiterate and almost obnoxious civilizations around ?

Counsel of the far away Worlds Legal Affairs - Watch your language .

Lady Gratitude - Don't pay any attention to them , dear green leaves , they must be just trying to be noticed and accounted for .

Chorus of the far away World - That's what you think : shame on you ! We think the same.

Chorus of the green leaves - And does that make any sense ??!

Chorus of the far away World - We know that it doesn't ,but we say it just the same because we also know that it annoys you very much . It's our World and ., here, we do as we please. So, there .

Chorus of the green leaves - We are sorry , now, to have started a stampede of nonsense and a rather uncouth reception and intrusion by uninvited folks into our historical reminiscing , but we hoped that our story would explain to you what our confusion was caused by and by what sources .

Lady Gratitude - I was really glad that you brought that subject up and you are quite right in your recurring memories because ,dear little leaves , it was right at that time that I was born !!

Chorus of the green leaves - How interesting ,dear Gratitude ! Please go on and tell us more !

Chorus of the Asparagus plants - A lot of baloney !

Chorus of the far away World - We like the asparagus plants and what they say . And you ,are you all still here ? If you are still here, and it seems that you are , or we could not hear you talk, but , that alone , would not and could not be satisfactory proof that you are still here, because you could be someone else , but we can see you and , that , is a more positive proof that you are here . So, for how long more are you planning to stay and bother us with all that nonsense talk ?

Chorus of the green leaves - For as long as it will please us , you illiterate nincompoops ! Why don't you try to move a little more far , far away instead of sitting here and be grouchy ? Please,listen carefully, and we'll tell you something in our " no nonsense " way : " GET LOST "

Lady Gratitude - Please , dear gentle leaves , do not worry : I am used to disrespect and hostility : you see , to receive it is always a welcome and easy burden to wear , but an unpleasant , Herculean Labour to return thanks for it.

Chorus of the green leaves - All this saddens us .

Lady Gratitude - But don't be sad : after all that kind of attitude was invented by progressing civilizations .

Chorus of the green leaves - That's even sadder than the first one.

Lady Gratitude - I believe that THAT is just life, just existence, or whatever you chose to call it. Anyway, as I was saying , I was born in those ancient times , when civilization ~~started sprouting its first buds and people had begun~~ interacting with me and I developed in the " word" that now identifies me, but, as time went by and I reached maturity in that civilization as it progressed forward , slowly but steadily , human creatures seemed to become somewhat uncomfortable in my presence, whenever an occasion called for my rightful intervention , ...

Chorus of the green leaves - Lady Gratitude, what is a " rightful intervention " ?

Lady Gratitude - It means or, should I rather say, it should mean, giving thanks for something good obtained , and so , as I was saying , as time went by , these human creatures seemed to feel uncomfortable near me, as I just said , and began to try to move away from my presence to the point that , one day , they forgot all about me and my ways too, I having become an obsolete word in that advancing civilization and a real obstacle to the avidity developing in them to keep for themselves everything , ignoring the charitable and honourable spirit of giving thanks for the goods brought to them ,precisely , by that very civilization.......

Chorus of the green leaves - Depressing, indeed !

Lady Gratitude - Yes ,it felt the same way to me too , I remember , and even more so when these newly civilized humans became so emboldened by this very civilization that ,at that time I became totally irrelevant to them to the point that only the dogs took pity on me and adopted my word and my language and customs into their own language and customs and welcomed me among them , sharing my feelings and my beliefs and looking at me with love and sincerity .

Chorus of the green leaves - At least "someone" in that civilization showed more civility than the civilized ones themselves !

Lady Gratitude - Yes,indeed . But , as you know , dogs don't talk : they bark only, therefore since that day ,the dogs alone understood my name and they liked to share their lives with mine and adopt my ideas and my teachings..........

Chorus of the green leaves - Oh ! That was really sweet , Lady Gratitude , really sweet !

Lady Gratitude- Yes, it really was very sweet of them , while the civilized man , instead, beats the dog for being grateful and faithful to him .

Chorus of the green leaves - So,only the dogs were able to welcome your name into their own language and understanding and into their lives and customs ,since the civilized creatures had abandoned the use of gratitude, altogether .

Lady Gratitude - That is right .

Chorus of the green leaves - But ,then, Lady Gratitude ,what are names, words , at all good for ??

Lady Gratitude - I really do not know. As you have heard from my story, I have been left a solitary word , a sort of an unwelcome form of speech , creating some great difficulty for the majority of people in pronouncing it or,if confronted with the possibility that my presence would be rightfully due , they quickly turn their attention away from me as if I were a deadly missile pointed at them, for failing to be grateful .

Chorus of the green leaves - We find all this hard to believe.

Lady Gratitude - Yes, and so do I . At times I wonder whether the essence of my personality, the meaning of my word , might have actually been an error of the human creatures' conscience ,a sort of " a nice to look at " kind of thing, but not to be touched , may be a " faux pas " of the newly civilized minds .

Chorus of the far away World - You people seem to have a lot of problems in your World . We could never have any of that stuff happen in our World .

Chorus of the asparagus plants - We thought you had gone away . Why did you come back , in case you had gone away ? But , since you are here we have two possibilities: one, you never went away in the first place , and , the second , if you had gone away, then it means that you came back . WHY ??

Chorus of the far away World - We do not have to answer that to a bunch of asparagus plants. Even if we would choose to do that, we would not care to do it, anyway. You are not even good to be looked at.

Chorus of the asparagus plants - We thought that you might have changed your minds and wanted , now , to become educated ,learned and cultured , by listening to the conversation of these two strangers from another World.

Chorus of the far away World - None of that. We may be illiterate but we are not mad. We just came back to see if the two strangers from the other world had gone away and to make certain that they would do so. in the event that they would not have left yet. That is what we came back here for.

Chorus of the green leaves- Ignorance , compounded with impudence . Shame , shame , shame !

Lady Gratitude - It looks to me as if they are becoming civilized .

Chorus of the green leaves - And Heavens save us !

Lady Gratitude - At times I ask myself : why is it to be that way, but I cannot come up with an answer.

Chorus of the green leaves - But the dogs would probably have an answer.

Lady Gratitude - Yes, they probably would . Pity , really , that dogs are not the only inhabitants in our World.

Chorus of the green leaves - Yet , if there would be only dogs to whom could they ,then , show fidelity , companionship and gratefulness ?

Lady Gratitude- That situation would not come into contest at all.

Chorus of the green leaves - It wouldn't...!!??

Lady Gratitude- That's right : it wouldn't . Dogs , dear little leaves , possess two great gifts given them by a benevolent Mother Nature, that human creatures do not possess .

Chorus of the green leaves - Gifts...to dogs...??!

Lady Gratitude - Yes, dear little green leaves, exactly so : two marvelous gifts that I myself would be joyous to possess !

Chorus of the green leaves - But ,dear Lady Gratitude, do not keep us in such a suspense any longer!! Please, tell us what these magnificent gifts are , please!

Lady Gratitude- Yes , two gifts : one , the outstanding sense of smell . The other , the sense of loyalty .

Chorus of the green leaves - But , dear Lady Gratitude , are you sure that these two are those magnificent gifts that you were referring to?.....Because there are many other creatures in our World with a good sense of smell and a ....

Lady Gratitude - And a sense of loyalty too ? That is where the road takes a different turn, dear little leaves : the acute sense of smell keeps the dogs safe from approaching rotten creatures , while the loyalty rewards Mother Nature for having bestowed so much , so great , so enlightening gifts upon them .

Chorus of the green leaves - And, dear Lady Gratitude , are the dogs aware of these beneficial gifts?

Lady Gratitude - Dear little green leaves, you must understand , that dogs are not like human creatures . Dogs do not vie for riches , or honours ,or glory , or pride : they only are looking for and are happy with a handful of food and a friendly pat . Just you try to offer that kind of situation to a human creature !.....Besides, consciousness of one's gift is ,often , a regrettable motive for ostentation and overbearing behaviour .

Chorus of the green leaves - Well, of one of those " situations ", as you call them , one certainly , could benefit the human race and ameliorate its future, and that would be an improved sense of smell , we believe .

Lady Gratitude - But I doubt that it would be put to any good use !

Chorus of the green leaves- But , Lady Gratitude , why not ?

Gratitude - Because , it would be no time before the human creatures would turn it around from its original intended purpose and ……

Chorus of the Dogs - We would be very much afraid of that happening ,too !

Chorus of the green leaves - and how do you know what could happen if no one has yet said a word about it ?

Chorus of the dogs - Our good sense of smell .

Chorus of the green leaves - We do not understand !!

Chorus of the dogs - Of course not : only we can and we can tell you, right now, that ,if human creatures would be given the gift of an improved sense of smell, the stench would be unbearable .

Chorus of the green leaves - That would be disastrous !

Lady Gratitude - Yes, dear little leaves , that would be disastrous .It would create a dangerous ground to be careful when treading on it , but not as threatening as to abolish it altogether , therefore establishing a sort of a deceitful monument to the enhanced capacity of human sniffing ability, as if they did not possess enough of it yet , and a beacon of intuitive sniffing morality, embedded in this solid monument, well anchored to the ground , for fear that it could move around and preach its message.

Chorus of the messages - We do not carry messages from monuments because we do not communicate well with them , and they , these monuments , that is , do not even say a word , ever , but ,often , the other process occurs and we carry messages to them from many other creatures , who are not monuments.

Chorus of the green leaves - Lady Gratitude , what are monuments ?

Lady Gratitudes - They are reminders for creatures with short memory .

Chorus of the green leaves - Oh ! Thank you , Dear Lady Gratitude, thank you for being ever so kind, always, and taking time in explaining things to us, so slow in understanding things .

Lady Gratitude - There is nothing to be uneasy about not understanding many things . Even the most learned men of all past ages , from antiquity to present times, are often slow, sometimes ,extremely slow , in understanding "THINGS " .

Chorus of the green leaves - Really ? Even the most learned men ?

Lady Gratitude - But ,of course ! you see, the pace of knowledge , and its speed , has not been calculated quite satisfactorily and accurately yet .

Chorus of the green leaves - We are sorry : we did not know that .

Lady Gratitude - Do not worry ! No one knows the number of creatures who do not know , and , to give you a well known example of it , in ancient times there.......

Chorus of the green leaves - Oh! Yes ,yes , Lady Gratitude, tell us , please , tell us about it ..!!

Lady Gratitude - I will if you promise not to interrupt me so many times everytime I am trying to tell something to you : Promise ?

Chorus of the green leaves - Promise .

Lady Gratitude - Well, in very ancient times , there lived a famous philosopher ,a wise and learned man , who wrote ,one day , a note , a sort of a warning to the society of those days , that he forethought the amazement of future generations, centuries down the road from his present time, as they would marvel at the prevalent ignorance existing in his days about facts, discoveries and knowledge of things, that would be "common" place , to them .

Chorus of the green leaves - Thank you, Lady Gratitude ,for explaining everything so well to us. Now, we feel a lot better knowing that it is not our tendency to flutter that might have caused , at times, missing some facts, but , it seems, that the span and the speed of time did not "flutter" fast enough for news, facts and discoveries to travel to us.......... .Lady Gratitude ?

Lady Gratitude - Yes , dear little leaves, what is it ?

Chorus of the green leaves - Lady Gratitude , with so much talk, so many personages , so many "everything", we have navigated far, far away from our initial conversation , at least it seems so to us, but , we are certain , you must have notice it yourself.

Chorus of the far away personages and "everything" - We had noticed that too, and we were wondering how long, still, would your chit-chat be going on .

Lady Gratitude- Various situations had guided us on an exchange of views about facts of life and customs that took us on a slippery road where we had seen the beginning , but the end no one could have predicted on that slippery path. So, it was good that we managed to stop and take a breath.

Chorus of the green leaves - Funny : but it sounds somewhat strange , coming from you, Lady Gratitude , when you said : " time to stop and take a breath " , because, not too long ago , during our conversation, you had told us, when we were pressing you for answers about the life of words, that words do not eat and they do not "breathe" either , so , we are ,again , a little confused , when you said that it was good to stop and "take a breath "!!

Chorus of the breathless words- Why all the curiosity and the ridicule on us ? You could not be represented in this dialogue if we were not here , breathless or not. Besides ,your much praised and respected Lady Gratitude , is also one of us : She is a word too . How can she breath now when we cannot and do not ? Indeed , we believe that there has been a lot of talking for nothing to be made good or interesting ,and ,furthermore,we ....

Chorus of the green leaves - But , dear Words , all we ....

Chorus of the breatless Words - Don't interrupt .

Chorus of the green leaves - Sorry !

Chorus of the breathless Words - For all of you to know, then , that during our long , very long and fruitful life , or , if you'd rather like to have it better portrayed as a breathless life , regardless ,we were and have been and still are instrumental and influential in inspiring courage and determination , terror and despair , love and abandon , faith and dedication to breathing creatures ,so , we believe , there must be a connection if not directly in the configuration of breathing as some creatures see and use it , but as a form of response , at least , to the imagination of many creatures , even if only one of exulted imagination .

Chorus of the green leaves - Strange , but we seem to follow your narrative more clearly than that from any of the previous conversations with different sources. It is strange.

Chorus of the Breathless Words - Strangeness is in the eye of the beholder.

Chorus of the strange people - What does it mean ?

Chorus of the breathless Words- That you are stupid.

Chorus of the strange people - Is that so ?

Chorus of the breathless Words - Oh! please , leave us alone and get lost ! We are afraid that you are planning one of those endless arguing marathon, always inconclusive and , probably , inspired by your wishful thinking that you may be represented in this dialogue : right ?

Chorus of the strange people - No : we do not want that , we are not wishing for anything like that. Besides, aren't we already in , anyway ?

Chorus of the breathless Words -Fine , fine , be happy and be quiet if you can manage that , and , going back to where we were interrupted in a rather "strange "way . To continue, then , we'd like to add that we helped the breathing human creatures to build their personalities ,their Laws , their promulgations , their poems and learned treatises , their precious and informative books of historical events and the narratives of the geographic discoveries and the description of the wonders of the planet where they......lived, and we were almost tempted to say "where they breathed " and where they were building too their castles, both on the land and..in the air , and their dreams and hopes , and words of salvation , together with words of love ,affection , dedication, and pledges of faith , and cries of joy , tempests of horror and infamy, but to rescue their disturbed spirit with sublime poetry and glorious visions of exquisite forms , beauty of design , splendor of colours unbridled imagination . This all, we have done . It was done without breathing one single part of your air or anybody else's air .

Lady Gratitude - Thank you , ancient and honourable Words, for your educated and well rendered account of your interesting existence . Yes , I am one of yours, that is true , but a forgotten one at best ! Brighter were my younger years and a valiant youth , but it is undeniable that I have aged, may be the need for me has lessened in this frantic society where there does not seem to be any time to spare and smell the roses, as the human creatures enjoy describing the modern rush , but I appear to be an obsolete noun not even worth summoning when its presence and use would be not only advisable and correct but also dutiful .

Chorus of the breathless Words- We have noticed too, a decline in the use of words that may reflect an intimation of commitment , duty , responsibility , or even reason.

Lady Gratitude - At times, I am asking myself whether the meaning of my name requires such a demanding effort as to become overwhelmingly heavy to bear , an almost intolerable weight that could even crush a giant .

Chorus of the green leaves- Lady Gratitude,we understand that, in spite of our flutter, impairing to some extent our ability to sort out things speedily ,yet certain things, while arousing our curiosity, at the same time they create new problems in comprehending the real meaning of those same things. In order to be clearer ,for example, just a while ago we heard the beautiful account by the words of their remarkable achievements through the ages, in spite of those words being "breathless " !!!..Well , not long ago,you too, were explaining to us that words , and ,of course, personal names like the one you carry of Gratitude, that is also a name, so you were explaining that words have no life of their own ,meaning, we presume,that they are not living beings and ,as a consequence, we suspect, they do not breathe, and the "breathless Words" had just told us so, and they do not eat either, at least not of the foods that we partake from Mother Nature in our Big Giant Oak Tree, and then you, suddenly , seem to change course claiming or, rather ,wondering whether your name , which ,of course , is also a word , may have such a powerful effect , such a tremendous weight on the human conscience to be able to crush even a giant.

Lady Gratitude - Yes, dear leaves , I said that .

Chorus of the green leaves - But, then , do you really mean it ? Do you really mean that the weight of your name could even crush a giant ??!!!

Lady Gratitude- Not so much the name or the word , but Gratitude could .

Chorus of the green leaves - Ah! That 's what it is ! We would never have come to think of that!! Honestly !

Lady Gratitude - Oh ! Yes , many things in our lives do not come that way honestly .

Chorus of the green leaves - But , then , dear Lady Gratitude ,tell us , please:"what is your weight"?

Lady Gratitude - Mine , is a moral weight .

Chorus of the green leaves - " A moral weight " ??....Did you say " A moral weight " ???

Lady Gartitude - Yes, dear leaves , that's what I said : mine is a moral weight.

Chorus of the green leaves - Well , dear Lady Gratitude ,you must pardon us again, and , again , but we have never heard of such a thing before . In all truth we know very little about weights , as a matter of fact ,we do not know them at all ! You see, we are so light and rarely , very , very rarely we become any heavier than we usually weigh , only at times, may be just a little , when it rains or snows ,but the wind frees us of that weight pretty rapidly , so that we hardly have any notion of weights and weighing , besides the wind and the breezes always keep us up and buoyant . But, going back to what you were saying ,dear Lady Gratitude , what is a moral weight ?

Lady Gratitude - It's a formula for responsible self-discipline, invented by the human creatures.

Chorus of the Weights - We feel offended for being taken into contest with a representation of a human measure of conscientious behaviour . We consider ourselves as solid Measures and Guarantors of stability and precise definition of "Weight" . Furthermore, we strongly object to being compared to a measure of weight invented by the human creatures , a measure that we consider neither stable nor warrantable .

Lady Gratitude - (addressing the weights) - You need not take offense for just a casual representation of a comparison of your serious measure to some weighty human conscientious obligations , whether moral or otherwise . I assure you that , often , and , " often " , in human jargon , means "most often " , morality carries the least possible amount of weight that anyone is willing to carry , except for very few and rare human creatures who carry very large loads of moral weight within themselves and those rare and valiant beings , for some yet not quite limpid reason, are shunned , neglected , forgotten and , at times , even ridiculed for being conscientious with the moral weight that they carry .

Chorus of the Weights - Do those few human creatures carry those weights around wherever they go ?

Lady Gratitude - Of course .

Chorus of the Weights - And how do they carry those weights ? Do they have a cart or a horse, a mule or do they carry those weights themselves ?

Lady Gratitude - All by themselves .

Chorus of the Weights - But that's incredible ! No wonder they are ridiculed ! How could anyone in his right mind carry all those weights around by themselves and on themselves ??!

Lady Gratitude - Well, in the projected configuration of the human mind anything that is conveniently,unobtrusively and safely configurationallly configured, has ,inherently, the right weight in anybody's mind . Now , whether their minds are at all configured , that , of course , carries a different weight .

— — —

Chorus of the Weights - Ah ! We understand : it is an adjustable weight , adjustable to various circumstances as they come along and in what sort of favourable way they seem to present themselves . Ingenious set up but lacking a measurable weight of certifiable , constant and standard value.

Lady Gratitude - Human creatures do not like to be certified , experience great difficulties in being constant , and their existences are far from any form of standardization .

Chorus of the certifiable measures and standards - "Amen "!

Chorus of the Weights - Sorry to hear that . Sorry for those creatures difficulties . Anyway , we frown on measures that cannot be rigorously and systematically and definitively measured ,weighed and maintained at an unchangeable, unalterable, perennial weight. We do not look with leniency on adjustable weights , A weight is a weight and only a weight can be a weight and, if it is a weight, a weight must remain ,stay and perform as a weight because by weighing in any other way, should not, would not, could not be a weight .If a weight , that is, a weighed weight , is a weight and weighs the proper measured weight , it would not weigh its measured weight unless it were a proper weight ,as that would constitute a tampering with a measure of weight and be an act of disgracefully measured dishonesty .

Chorus of the green leaves - What would he be , then ?? We mean , that …weight ?!

Chorus of the Words - An Impostor .

Lady Gratitude - We agree . But Humans see it differently . They seem to strive in that kind of using and manipulating weights....that is ALL KIND OF WEIGHTS !!!.......But , of course , some of those creatures are also good, some very good and some extraordinarily good .

Chorus of the Words - That's understandable . How could, otherwise, the World of living creatures continue to flourish , as it apparently does ?!

Chorus of the flourishing Worlds - That really we would like to know.

Chorus of the green leaves - How true ! How true what you just said , respectable flourishing Worlds, how true ! And we too would like to know many , many more things,but our surface on each side of the leaf is limited so, we must content ourselves of whatever we can retain on that limited space. Of course , we are well known for being carefree leaves ,dangling leisurely from the branches of trees and unprepared as we are for acquiring knowledge ,we more than often miss the thread of what is being said in a discussion, its meaning and its message.

Lady Gratitude - On the contrary , my dear leaves : you are perhaps the most schooled of all things in the world ! You have in you the knowledge of Nature, of the Universe , and that possession makes you a giant in the world of knowledge and wisdom , and that is the greatest message for all, including weights .

Chorus of Wise Men - We know that .

Chorus of the Messages - Shall we carry that message ? ...And where to ?

Chorus of Wise Men - It won't be necessary : Wisdom has no forwarding address .

Chorus of the Messages - Oh ! Well , we'll just wait for the next message.

Chorus of the green leaves - It's getting late and it won't be long before the sun will disappear behind those hills in the distance far from our woods and it will be dark: time to fall asleep for a restful night. So, my dear Gratitude, Respectable Weights, Wise Men and Special Messages and, let us not forget the Flourishing Worlds.....and....theBreathless Words..!!!...Well, we thank all of you from the bottom of our stems , the greatest expanse of our leaf surfaces and with all the Chlorophyll with it, for the unprecedented symposium of almost everything , not that much progress did really accompany it , but certainly it was most pleasant, pleasurable and pleasing . Do you think, Lady Gratitude that this sentiment of our expression carries enough gratitude ?

Lady Gratitude - Just a little bit more of it and you could take my place in the history of gratefulness .

Chorus of the green leaves - Thank you , Lady Gratitude .

Lady Gratitude - Dear little leaves,you are just wonderful,so simple,so humble,so clear, it's so refreshing being with you .

Chorus of the green leaves - Thank you again , dear Lady Gratitude : you never cease to be kind ,and we are certain that what has been discussed until now has been very beautiful,interesting,captivating,and absorbing and you too , respectable Weights of such honourable measures, please, understand our deficiencies , while we admire your honesty and stability of purpose .

Chorus of the Weights - Thank you.

Chorus of the green leaves - Well, as we just said , it's getting late ,time to pause and rest . Even the wind has "calmed" down ,it always helps us stay cool and active regardless whether we show gratitude or not. Probably he has never heard of it , but we are sure that , had he heard of Lady Gratitude, he would send her a card of sympathy . The wind , anyway, always blows on its own accord, whether we are grateful or not , and we dangle and twirl in its path, enjoying it.

Lady Gratitude - How sweet !

Chorus of the green leaves - So, dear Lady Gratitude and you too , Weights of so noble heritage, thank you for your company , your interesting arguments ,your stories and your explanations on so many things, that we cannot fully understand anyway , but we are very grateful for having been allowed to listen , anyway.

Lady Gratitude - How sweet !.... And ,dear green leaves , I am the one who is grateful to you for your sweet company.

Chours of the Weights - Indeed , a beautiful thought of the right weight and a well balanced distribution .

Chorus of the green leaves - Oh! here comes a light breeze ,so gentle and moderate that makes us feel happy to be leaves .So long, dear Gratitude ,and you too, Respectable Weights of serious measure.

Chorus of the Weights - Bye , bye , little leaves ! Well ,as far as we are concerned ,all the previous chit-chat does not seem to have any weight : it did not register at all on our measuring scales . Perhaps it has a composition that does not have any weight, and we suspect that the failure to register any measurement was due to being an invention of some unregistered sources or ,may be,even humans . We are not interested ,anyway, in these kind of fleeting weights . We measure and guarantee only weights which can be weighed .

Lady Gratitude - Bye, bye ,little green leaves : may be we'll meet again ,sometime!

Chorus of the green leaves - Yes ,of course ! Come and see us again , may be in Spring time , when we are all dressed up and eager to dance . We wish you a very happy journey , wherever you may go .

Lady Gratitude - Thank you, thank you , dear little leaves , that's very kind of you .As you see , from the last remark of the Weights , before parting ,when we disconnect ourselves from any physical aspect of ourselves , and we allow ourselves to delve into non physical matters but only speculation, abstract thoughts, postulates, ideas, wishes, dreams, sentimental principles of conscience and what not, all kinds of diverging paths will start cropping up causing creatures to become proud of the intuitive prowess allowed in them and losing their touch with our more physical and terrestrial aspect and becoming entangled in endless and seldom rewarding educational ends .

Chorus of the terrestrial Aspects - Terrestrial, you said . We understand, and we believe that you referred to the aspect of life encountered on our planet , by the name of...

Chorus of the Wreights - Earth.

Chorus of the terrestrial Aspects - Should we say , then , Earthestrial ?

Chorus of the Weights - "Terrestrial" derives from the Latin word "Terra", which means Earth .

Chorus of the terrestrial Aspects - Interesting .

Chorus of the Weights - We do not think so . Utter nonsense .

Chorus of the green leaves – (Turning to the Weights) - You should not be so expressively clear in your remarks ! Shame on you !

Chorus of the Weights - Hold it an instant : that last expression you just mentioned " shame on you " , how much does it weigh ?

Lady Gratitude - No measure in the entire Universe, could ever measure it !!!

Chorus of the Weights - We do not believe that .

Chorus of the green leaves - How graceless those Weights can be.!

Lady Gratitude - They do not care and they rely on the impressive sight of their own weight and they , these weights , are in good company, I assure you !. Bye, now, and happy rustling in the breeze .

Chorus of the green leaves - Do you feel the breeze too, Lady Gratitude

Lady Gratitude - Oh! Yes , I feel it : a pleasant refreshing breeze in spite of the fact that I am without a body but only a lonely word made up of syllables and vowels ,yet ,many times ,good will ,happy attitudes and a pinch of fruitful imagination can create conditions which , at first , would be thought as totally unimaginable and totally unattainable. So, time to leave, and I hope that you will enjoy your nice breeze. See you !

Chorus of the green leaves - Bye, now! Take care ! This gentle breeze will soon put us to sleep !.

Lady Gratitude - Bye ! Bye ! Dear Leaves and good repose !

Chorus of the Weights - This particular parting expression and its sound do not seem to have any weight at all . We are unable to measure it.

Chorus of the green leaves - Fine : we are glad that you cannot measure it and ,really ,it is better that you do not, because a warm expression of sentiment at parting ,or a deeply felt adieu , if measured like any other piece of merchandise, would lose their spontaneity , their pristine meaning and so they would lose their intrinsic values as well . So,pay no attention to these Weights,dear Lady: may be they are so insensitive because they weigh too much!

Lady Gratitude - Do not worry, little leaves: as I have told you several times I am used to it . So long, dear leaves , and enjoy your gentle breeze .

Chorus of the green leaves - Bye ! Come back sometime to see us !

Lady Gratitude - I will ! Bye , now.

Chorus of the green leaves - Bye !

****

Lady Gratitude departs from the forest after exchanging warm greetings and goodbyes with the little green leaves and the little green leaves , in their turn , tired and worn out by the lengthy discussions and arguments , are lulled by a gentle breeze into a peaceful , restful sleep.

Meanwhile the forest , in the approaching crepuscular light , falls quiet : only an occasional and rhythmic clicking of some crickets breaks the eerie silence .

The Giant Oak Tree lets out a sigh of relief at the anticipation of a peaceful night refreshed by the gentle breeze after the long turmoil caused by the chatting birds and the garrulous , ostentatious, sometime senseless, overbearing oratory of various other creatures and multifarious representatives of yet many other creatures , when , much as a surprise , the Giant Oak Tree's loud voiced observations about the good prospects of some peace and quiet , apparently caught the attention of a mushroom growing close to the roots of the Giant Oak Tree , just above the ground .

****

Giant Oak Tree- Ah ! What a delightful breeze, so gentle , so soothing , just what I badly needed after the almost irreverent conversational "fracas " that went on the whole day, almost the whole day .....!! This caressing breeze will restore my faith in the worldly countenance of things and creatures. Besides, my foliage, stirred by the breeze, tickles me ! It's wonderful !!

Mushroom - Far better a good tickling ,I believe , than a hell of a noise by the Birds and everybody else that plagued you to day ,from dawn to dusk !! ...Am I right ?!

Giant Oak Tree- Ah ! Ah ! little mushroom ! Is that you down there or am I "hearing " things ??

Mushroom - Yes, Charlie, it's me , the little mushroom down here on the level ground , very close to one of your huge roots protruding through the soil and holding you firm and solid to the ground : yes, it's me and there is nothing wrong with your hearing either ! Your hearing is fine, just fine, dear Old Tree !

Giant Oak Tree - I am glad of that ! After the deafening racket that went on the whole day, I had wondered for a moment whether my sense of hearing had been impaired !!

Mushroom - I myself have been wondering about what was going on up there among your branches and leaves , and the activity as well as the agitation apparently must have been so intense and so pervasive that it was felt even by me down here, and that is quite a distance from your top branches to my hollow little place on the ground....well, Big Tree , do you hear me ?

Giant Oak Tree - But, of course I can hear you and very well ! Apparently that noisy clamor that went on the whole day, from dawn till dusk , did not damage my hearing...!!! But, tell me, little mushroom, why didn't you make yourself heard for such a long time ?? Keeping to yourself , I guess, in total silence .

Mushroom - I kept to myself...??!!...I did not make myself heard ....???!! But , my dear Big Tree , I have been trying to get your attention for the past four hours without getting any response from you !!

Giant Oak Tree - Dear little mushroom we have already talked about the noise and the fracas of this morning and of the whole day , so I probably did not hear you with all that nonsense going on right on my branches ! The noise was so great that no one, probably , could have heard the Universe fall down, if it should have been falling.

Mushroom - The Sparrows : right ? They were the culprits, right ?

Giant Oak Tree - That's right : the Sparrows and all the other friends and occasional visitors wherever from , a medley of weird characters and unvoucherable , unclassified souls , that they had encouraged around , and then the wind started to blow and the leaves ,then , felt like joining the party too !! Damn the sparrows , damn the leaves , damn the wind and damn everyone else with them !

Mushroom - Well , come on ,now, don't take it so much at heart , my dear friend ,and think instead of your health !!

Giant Oak Tree - I hear you, dear little mushroom, I hear you and you may be just right and it really would make a lot more sense for me to think of my health and my tranquillity, or "Tranquillitatis"if given a chance ,and an urge to show off some old Latin from the school days, of course !!! of course ! But, one thing seems quite clear to me :in this World there always is who is always wrong and who is always right : I mean, someone who never admits to be wrong and.....

Mushroom - That's more likely .

Giant Oak Tree- ....and someone who always has to submit ,willingly or unwillingly to someone else ,and always somebody who has to command and dictate almost everything, and someone who will always have enough to eat and someone who will always go hungry , and only a fortuitous event or an explosive collective and social violence in primitive places, void of wise and cautious laws and responsible leaders , could alter that unfair balance of fortunes ,even if only temporarily.

Mushroom- Why ?

Giant Oak Tree - Because it is a lot easier to reverse a trend with the use of force but very difficult to change instincts , interests , deep seated beliefs , convincements , in a manner that will last , as the greediness, so well established in the moulds of the creatures , all of them , human included , of course , will soon take over again from where it had ,temporarily, stopped .

Mushroom - It seems to me that you have a tendency at taking everything far too seriously, it does not matter what, whether it is the Birds , the leaves , the wind and who knows what else !

Giant Oak Tree- Well, at the same time, it seems to me that you too, my dear little mushroom, are experiencing some difficulty in believing what I am saying , but , unfortunately , it really works that way !!

Mushroom - It is not that I do not believe you ,dear Big Tree, but your approach to those historical happenings among people of the World ,appears to me excessively critical of its real meaning and value .

Giant Oak Tree - Well, value or no value , adversely critical or not , my dear mushroom , it does not make that much of a difference because , by my experience , it turns out to be a lot better to accept intelligently the facts bigger than ourselves rather than criticize them or fight against them ,just as I am doing every morning with those damn sparrows and frivolous leaves .

Mushroom - Well, that sounds something similar to what I was trying to tell you just a while ago,the only difference is that you seem to enjoy enlarging the issue as if trying to be in step with the enormous size of your form !! But , in all practical terms, you have just repeated what I had already told you ! So, in a nutshell , leave the sparrows ,the leaves and everybody else alone and calm down ! Why should you take things so much at heart, when you cannot do anything about it, to correct it to your liking and comfort , or to try to formulate a different equation of Nature's unrelenting postulate of give and take , the more logical action being to follow the road ahead ,that is "your" road ahead, the best you can, because ,it is quite clearly apparent , whether you are willing to accept it or not, that everyone and anyone has his own road to travel on .

Giant Oak Tree - Are you referring to what the human creatures call "Destiny " ?

Mushroom - I know nothing about what the human creatures call "things" , and I could not care less to know about it even if they ,graciously, would offer to explain it to me and I wonder whether their explanation would be any closer to the truth than I am to the moon , anyway .

Giant Oak Tree - I begin to suspect , dear little mushroom , that you are trying to remind me of the old French adage : " c'est la vie " !! , as it is a common refrain among French Trees : c'est la vie dans la forêt !!

Mushroom - ....Which is a mirror-like interpretation of what the French mushrooms would say : "C'est la vie , vous champignons ! " .

Giant Oak Tree - Ah ! this is really interesting ! Even the Mushroom know French ! Really, interesting !

Mushroom - But, of course, they do,dear Big Tree , of course they do !......" Mais certainement , Mon Cheri !! Certainement !

Giant Oak Tree - Voila' , c'est tres bon ! C'est tout grand !!

Mushroom - Please, quit being so stupid !

Giant Oak Tree- But you are the one encouraging others to be stupid, you should realize that !

Mushroom - But only the real stupid creatures follow through after that encouragement, O Big, Big Tree !!

Giant Oak Tree- You must think , then ,that I am stupid , right ?

Mushroom - Heavens forbid ! I would not even think of calling you that not even in my dreams !! No, no, my dear Big Tree , I am only speaking in general terms , just sticking to generalities , naturally .

Giant Oak Tree - That's better.

Mushroom - Agreed ,dear Old Tree , agreed ! But now listen to this : just going back to our French language show off , just listen what I heard being said about a young French cockerel who whispered the same enticing expression , "c'est la vie ! " , to a Portuguese hen, and it seems that they understood each other perfectly well in spite of the linguistic differences and without experiencing any problems in the translation.

Giant Oak Tree - You really are a jolly mushroom , you are !

Mushroom - But listen , listen : it is also known , in Portugal , of course , of a rumor that the hen in question did return several times to France in order to have that enticing "c'est la vie ! " , repeated to her several times over . "C'est la vie " , wins hands down !!

Giant Oak Tree - What a lucky cockerel " THAT cockerel " must have been ! These French cockerels are really great seducers !

Mushroom - Well, the way I see it , my dear Charlie , it is not necessary to use unusual ability or shrewdness in the process of seduction when , for most of the eager protagonists , is , precisely , what they are looking for .

Giant Oak Tree - You never seem to miss one single beat, dear Mushroom !

Mushroom - By the way , I hope you didn't mind me calling you Charlie , because if we should ever engage in a conversation or just in a quick encounter in the mornings , or evenings , or even , sometime , during the day ,I would have to put a lot of strain on my small frame and frail hat to address you all the time as : " Big Oak " or " Big Tree " or " Giant Tree " and so on and on , so , I hope , you would not mind me calling you "Charlie" . So , how about it , Big Fellow of the forest ?

Giant Oak Tree - But, of course, dear little mushroom, of course ! You may call me Charlie or anything you like , except bad words , naturally. As a matter of fact that kind of address will bring us two closer together and we'll be able to chit-chat with ease and tranquility . And now, by the way that we are on this subject , is there any particular way that you would like for me to call you ,dear little mushroom? I am sure that you must have a name .

Mushroom - I had a name , long, long ago, chosen by my Parents who belonged to the ancient clan of the Agaricus Campestris , but I did not like the open fields and migrated to the cool and refreshing climate of the forest : my name was Arthur, but I did not like that name either , so I changed it to Fabius, a recall from historical memories of my young school days , a name representing a highly valuable gift in the interpretation of reality in times of disruptive stress .

Giant Oak Tree - Very interesting , indeed , my dear...Fabius !... and , please, tell me now , dear

Fabius!.......and I really like your new name , really !..........so, please , tell me what was or is this precious gift ?

Mushroom - Yes , dear Charlie , this gift is really a most wondrous gift and it represents the art and skill and the knowledge of how to practice it , allowing you to keep your head steady ,and , in my particular case , to keep my large hat steady and safe on my stem , in times of difficulty , by knowing how and when to act and not to act, , or to react , or just to sit still and pause , waiting for the right and most prosperous moment before acting . That is the invaluable gift and it derives from that famous name .

Giant Oak Tree - Very , very interesting and , more than that , congratulations to you for your apparent knowledge of historical facts of so long , long ago .

Mushroom - That's why we have a large hat : the most knowledgeable among us , of course, have it.....

Giant Oak Tree - Of course .

Mushroom - .....so that pertinent information , useful notices , historical data, selected precepts, general perceptions of common knowledge, and anything of interest and importance , can be safely kept under our large hat and not be washed away by rain or dispersed by wind or forgotten by sheer neglect .

Giant Oak Tree - You were fortunate dear Fabius to have Mother Nature being so selective in bestowing upon you so much attention and refined taste : she was not so generous with me , soaked wet when it rains and beaten by the wind .

Mushroom - But wide open to the sun, its warmth and light and invigorating power.

Giant Oak Tree - You certainly can choose your words well, dear Fabius .

Mushroom - I don't think that it is the actual choice of the words that can describe a situation, or represent a visual effect ,or even express a sentiment, however deeply felt it could be , because no word , I believe , can ever match the reality of what we see or feel . Well, Charlie , thank you , anyway , for your kindness .

Giant Oak Tree- You may be right, dear Fabius, but , at the same time , with the use of words, if well chosen , we can still describe , express , and set forth the opinions, sentiments and feelings of one self and others, and that property as well as those handling qualities associated with their inherent highly efficient manoeuvrability and the skill of the individual who will write them down , should amply atone for any deficiency.

Mushroom - I believe, dear Charlie, that YOU and not " I " should receive all the praise for the choice of words !!......Well, Charlie , it's getting late ,we already talked a lot, and you had a hard day contending with all those characters that had flooded your premises ,without having been invited ! So , you need a good rest and ,I assure you , I could use some rest too , after the hectic activity that took place to-day ,down here , at our market place !

Giant Oak Tree - That must have been also something, I believe !

Mushroom - It was ,it was . I'll tell you more about it , to-morrow . Goodnight ,for now, Charlie, and I'll call you in the morning.

Giant Oak Tree - Very well, Fabius : Goodnight and I'll talk to you in the morning , and let us hope that it will be a better morning. Goodnight .

Mushroom - It will . It will . Goodnight , Charlie .

***

The Giant Oak Tree, tired and sleepy , prepares to settle down to a good night rest , while the mushroom , also worn out by the early morning hectic market activity, tries also to settle down to a restful sleep .

***

The two, then , will wake up in the morning, rested and refreshed , and ready to check the morning news.

***

Meanwhile, as the sun slowly rises in the dawn of the new day , two sparrows , early birds , and both skinny old maids, begin chatting on one of the Giant Oak Tree's branches.........

1st Spinster - Well , Andrea , good morning !

2nd Spinster - Is it good ?

1st Spinster - I hope so !

2nd Spinster - Good : keep on hoping .

1st Spinster - You must have had a bad night , Andrea !

2nd Spinster - Not at all : is the morning that worries me.

1st Spinster - But why , Andrea ? Besides , how can you know that when the day has not quite started yet !!

2nd Spinster - Presentiment .

1st Spinster - So early and so worried yet !! Presentiment of " WHAT " ??!

2nd Spinster - Of unimaginable doom .

1st Spinster - For Heavens above ,my dear Andrea , I do not see why this day should loom so devastating and threatening , particularly now that the hunting season is over .

2nd Spinster - That is not what worries me , Celeste , but this tree is !

1st Spinster - What do you find wrong with this tree, Andrea ?

2nd Spinster - I heard him talking to the mushroom below , last night, just before going to sleep, and he was saying terrible things about the birds , cursing them and :" "damn the birds " and : " damn everything " , and that's what 's worrying me .

1st Spinster - Ah ! Let him talk ! That's all he can do anyway :he can't go around or chase and threaten anybody well anchored as he is to the ground where he stands ! He has got to stay where he is and that's why , perhaps , he talks like that .

2nd Spinster - I don't know , but he seems to be buddy-buddy with the mushroom down below and you know how wishy-washy that mushroom is ! You can never tell what he thinks , his face always buried under that large hat and he makes it out also with all kinds of creatures coming to see him , as they pass by , and nobody has any inkling at all of what they may be talking about or discussing or contemplating . I do not trust any of those folks down there !

1st Spinster - But ,Andrea , be reasonable ! That kind of behaviour is perfectly normal : people come and go , and if they happen to see someone whom they know or did know and perhaps met some other time , somewhere , then they may stop for a minute to exchange greetings , inquire about the children , work and activities , their health , vacations and so on ! Nothing wrong with that ,Andrea ! and, Andrea , that's a very normal attitude among creatures of all sizes and formats , I assure you !!....Now when did you hear anything or see anything that looked suspicious to you ?

2nd Spinster - Last night .

1st Spinster - Andrea , yesterday was Market day , and hundred and hundred of creatures come to that market to get supplies, meet other creatures , exchange news and many other things , and "talking ' , at the Market , is a very predominant feature of it almost an "essential" feature of it, discussing prices , advertising and offering all kinds of goods, sometime in a loud voice and other times in just a whisper of consummate bargaining skill, manners that would probably look suspicious to the untrained eye or to the" NEW " to the mysteries of markets' wizardry but all very normal and well accepted in a market environment , and the general curiosity of finding out what the market had to offer might have enhanced the otherwise more placid and unsuspecting atmosphere of any other ordinary day.

2nd Spinster - Precisely, Celeste ,you just said it : the Market !

1st Spinster - Oh ! Andrea, I heard you !....."The Market " !!! Andrea, there is a " Market " every Wednesday and there has been one for donkeys' years !!....So , what's so strange about that ??

2nd Spinster - Not the market, Celeste , but the creatures going around in it and out of it, circulating in it and the way they seem to comport themselves, carry themselves and address others.

1st Spinster - I do not see anything strange about it , Andrea , really , and I believe that you are overreacting with an unnecessary fear or anxiety : it is a market , you know , and all kind of people come to markets and not just a selected , choicest crowd with special invitations and crowns over their heads !

2nd Spinster - I understand that , Celeste , and also I know that . What I am not too happy about is the way certain creatures go around the market.....

1st Spinster - Is it the way they walk, may be ?

2nd Spinster - No, not that , Celeste, not that !!...But I believe that, usually, people come to a market looking for goods and items to buy , but these people I am talking about , do not ever buy anything : they just seem to go in and out from the house of the mushroom ,with no packages, no satchels , no nothing : just going in and mysteriously coming out , looking around with some suspicious hesitation before taking the first step out . That , in my modest opinion, does not seem to be a "normal " market behaviour , I think .

1st Spinster - I understand very well what you are saying, Andrea , but I wonder whether the odd looking and acting people you are talking about ,could , instead and in all reality, being nothing more than simple folks going to the mushroom seeking advice , knowing of his connection with the majestic Giant Oak Tree and would only show shyness upon leaving , after being exposed to the influential magnitude of that Giant Tree and the Wisdom of the mushroom .

2nd Spinster - Shyness ?....I wonder ! May be and more likely sheer indoctrination with the majestic influence of the Giant Oak Tree and the wisdom , if any , of a tiny mushroom at the foot of a Giant ! Is now that type of wisdom worth to be sought , anyway , even by simple people ?

1st Spinster - Simple people, you say ??!!

2nd Spinster - But, of course, Celeste !! Who else would want to seek the wisdom and the advice of a mushroom and a lumbering giant in the middle of a forest ??

1st Spinster - Well, you certainly must have known from your young days at school at the history lesson that famous and valiant men and women, in ancient times and in not so ancient times either , sought advice from even less gigantic beings or even smaller ones .

2nd Spinster - Oh! Yes, history, always history ! I wonder how wisdom and advice were nurtured when history had not been invented yet .

1st Spinster - I do not know that Andrea: I was not there, then, and I am sorry that I cannot satisfy your curiosity ; but , History, Andrea, since the time it was invented as you say, has told us many , many things , some good , some not so good ~~and some downright bad and some totally incomprehensible and~~ ,then , some that would defy even the wisdom of an owl .

2nd Spinster - Yes , Celeste , you are perfectly right and some of that incomprehension appears to be right here in this market and, may be , even a premonitory glimpse or even just a stepping stone into something greater than just brewing carrots and potatoes , I am afraid !

1st Spinster - Well , Andrea , I tend to believe that you must be suffering from a doomsday type of complex so that everything you see or observe , or anything that glances back at you, always carries an image of something else that it really is because of the way that it manufactures itself in your brain through the restless vision of your eyes .

2nd Spinster - Why do you say that , Celeste ?......Of all the odd things…!!!

1st Spinster - Well, for one thing , you are so thin , almost undernourished , as if you were not eating enough oer not at all !!

2nd Spinster - But what came into your mind , now , Celeste ?! …Are , perhaps , Giant Trees and small mushrooms and the mesmerizing activities of the market affect your better judgement !!??

1st Spinster - Not at all, not at all, dear Andrea : as a matter of fact , precisely the opposite. You see ,…well what I mean is " I wont you to pay attention to what I am going to say " , if nothing else , but just to satisfy my perplexities about your preoccupations and worries about this here market and its mysterious characters mingling in it ……….

2nd Spinster - And right you are : I am worrying about that !

1st Spinster - Well, Andrea , I believe that your fears and associated suspicions about almost everything you see ,deteriorates your well being , deprives your mind of tranquil reasoning and limits your nourishment , seriously affecting your health ,your appearance and ,worst of all, your better judgement .

2nd Spinster - I am never hungry , dear Celeste . Most of my nourishment consists of dense thinking , penetrating speculation and enlightened suspicious scrutiny of events , people and , if I may say so , mysterious market going ons !!....and let me add , dear Celeste , what on Earth has my vision got to do with all that ??

1st Spinster - I had been wondering ,dear Andrea , whether you may have become so thin and so nervously worried and preoccupied about some features of a market, on account of lack of nourishment .

2nd Spinster - Lack of nourishment ??!....How can you say that, my dear Celeste ??! ...And that because of poor vision ...??!!...How do those two things pair together, Celeste ?? Please, tell me.

1st Spinster - Simple, dear Andrea : you are basically a preoccupied creature , may be with good reasons , sometime , not so good , some other times and you worry yourself sick at working out what you believe you see, convinced , of course, within yourself , that what you see is real and the contrast of your inflated perception of facts , happenings and creatures of all shapes and sizes , creates a powerful vacuum of expectations that you may have anticipated and which never eventuated ,so , you become more and more anxious , more suspicious , one image overtaking another , until you are totally unable to differentiate the whole picture in its proper light ,shape and configuration and , then , nothing anymore adds up to what it really is : That's what your vision appears to be doing to you, and that includes your food .

2nd Spinster - Celeste , I begin to believe that ,may be and after all, it is your vision that may be needing some sort of help and correction . Now I heard it all !" My vision " the cause of my being thin , undernourished , nervous , anxious, suspicious and seeing everything upside-down !!

1st Spinster - But of course, dear Andrea : you see , you seem to live in fear of everything, suspicious of almost everything you set your eyes and your attention upon, and I wonder whether in this state of fear and anxiety a minuscule worm or a larva or a flying insect might look to you like monsters and you run away from them , instead of eating them .

2nd Spinster - That's preposterous , Celeste, that's absurd ! No, no, Celeste, none of that , Celeste, none at all !!Yet , my dear Celeste, in all seriousness ,now , I would want to encourage you to take a more conservative and positive note of my vented "suspicions " : I tell you , there is something brewing there under the roof of that mushroom and this seemingly defiant piece of wood ,this enormous ,gigantic Oak Tree of ours , something like a pot on the verge of boiling over , I tell you !

1st Spinster - But what are you talking about , Andrea ? You sound so mysterious and so prophetic in a way that would have aroused the jealousy of the Oracle of Delphi !.......What on Earth are you talking about ??!

2nd Spinster - Ferment , ferment , my dear , wide spread ferment slowly intoxicating those twisted masses in the market : I tell you : ferment .

1st Spinster - You mean , all those people are drunk ?

2nd Spinster - No , Celeste , not that . I meant ferment of tempers , of feelings , of beliefs and multiform problems.

1st Spinster - Problems ? What kind of problems, Andrea , could there be on a normal, regular market day ?

2nd Spinster - The problems which are not seen but the ones that everyone worries about and is afraid to mention right under the majestic shade of this gigantic and seemingly defiant Oak tree .

1st Spinster - Are you thinking all this just because you saw some creatures go in and out of the house of the mushroom and went around the market place with hesitant gait and buying nothing ?

2nd Spinster - That and, also , the way the populace , right in the very market , seems to grow restless , the verbal exchanges between buyers and sellers seem more agitated than an ordinary purchase would normally require, the relative hurried exit from the market once the purchase is made as if fearing for something to happen, the worried look on the faces of the various sellers seeing potential selling bargains diminished for lack of potential buyers attendance and the general atmosphere of uncertainty and the way things look now , under the cover of a market day , all features that only an ultra naïve creature could pass over , but representing instead dark clouds that might threaten to blow in a revolution of some sort of all there is , inclusive of carrots , cauliflowers , beets and spinach , onions and potatoes . I tell you, my dear Celeste, "that's worries me."

1st Spinster - Andrea ?

2nd Spinster - Yes, Celeste !

1st Spinster - Andrea, may I say something to you ?

2nd Spinster - But, of course, Celeste !.......The way you ask tells me it must be something important .

1st Spinster - But I do not want you to get mad at me if I open up my heart and tell you what I think of all this ?

2nd Spinster - But, of course, no, dear Celeste ! We have always been the best friends and whatever you want to tell me, I feel certain , is meant well and in all friendship. So, go ahead , Celeste , and I am all ears and feathers.

1st Spinster - Very well, Andrea and thank you for your trust : after all that we have said, heard and discussed over , I ,really , cannot make head or tail of it all , except that we have gone a long way in figuring things out but we have no proof, evidence or any positive signs of anything impending of such dramatic proportions as you fear, so , Andrea , my simple advice is to stop for a while and we all take a pause .

2nd Spinster - You make a lot of sense, dear Celeste, you really do.

1st Spinster - Well, then , Andrea , why don't you go back to your nest and try to get some sleep. The day is young, yet , and you need some peaceful retreat and repose and let the market revolution take a rest too.

2nd Spinster - Oh, if you insist,Celeste , but mark my words : if you believe in history , how many serious tragedies in our forest could have been avoided if creatures had paid a closer attention and done some more serious scrutiny to events which may have ,at that time of first appearance , seemed just casual or coincidental.

1st Spinster - Very well, Andrea , I tell you what : you go back home and take a good rest and on the way to your nest try to grab a few worms , so as to restore your strength and , in return , I'll stay here , since I am well nourished and not perturbed at all , and ,while here, and giving no reasons at all for suspected activity , I'll try to pay attention to what may be going on with the mushroom, its suspicious visitors , and the Giant Oak Tree and see if I could work out some sense out of all that you said and suspected and prognosticated : a deal ?

2nd Spinster - Deal !

1st Spinster - Very well, then : see you at sundown , dear Andrea , and in the meantime ,pleasant dreams and good repose , shut the beak and the owl's nose .

2nd Spinster - Very , very funny ! Bye , now.

1st Spinster - Bye , Andrea .

****
****
****

Meanwhile , as the new day brightens up ,
the Giant Oak Tree and the Mushroom
become engaged in another dialogue !

****

Giant Oak Tree – (stretching his branches and yawning) Cold , cold ,damn cold and freezing , I'll say and the blowing wind to make things worse , so bad that it could give the shudders , I'll bet , even to a polar bear .

Mushroom - Really, now ?

Giant Oak Tree - Ah ! Little Mushroom , you do not seem to believe me, but it is indeed " REALLY " and it is for really " REAL " , my wise little fellow ,I am telling you .

Mushroom - It is common knowledge ,though, that usually and habitually, Winter temperatures are cold.

Giant Oak Tree - My dear little Mushroom, you talk like a philosopher , so, I'll grant it to you, no doubt about your keen observation on the Winter's temperatures ,yet, and in spite of the stringent logic about it , it is still cold, cold and damn, rotten cold ,this morning .

Mushroom - Sorry about it, dear old Tree : nothing ,really , that I can do about it .

Giant Oak tree - Oh ,well, we cannot change the weather and to complain about it, does not warm us up either, so , just to change the subject, how is the weather down there, little Mushroom and did you have a good night rest ?

Mushroom - Somewhat cold but probably not as cold as you might have experienced high up on your branches, but very,very humid down here and sticky, gluey, horrible , I would say, one of those days, a bad day , my dear Giant Tree , a sticky and horrible day.

Giant Oak Tree - Ha ! Ha ! you called me a "Giant " didn't you, ...well I know, I am tall , very tall and , may be , even too tall ,and the wind reminds me of that all the time , the wind , always the wind! The taller I grow and the more my head swings left and right . Every now and then, it is true, I get some rest , but as soon as the wind picks up again and there I go from left to right and from right to left !! If ,at all, it would blow always from the same side , as the farmer said when he was milking his cow in a windy day , but no chance ,now it blows this way ,to-morrow it will blow the other way , or it blows downward or upward or it just quits all of a sudden, without even having the common courtesy to tell you why . The wind, the wind , my dear little Mushroom, as it changes , everything changes with it.

Mushroom - Your problem with the wind is entirely your problem, and it seems to me that you are fishing for sympathy , but your wind is of no interest to me : no one feels it down here .

Giant Oak Tree - Fine charitable spirit, yours !

Mushroom - And who ever said that I was a charitable chartacter ? I certainly did not , my dear Big tree,or shall I still call you Charlie as we had agreed upon earlier yesterday when we kept on chatting for some time ?

Giant Oak Tree - But, of course, dear Fabius , your name that you assumed , unhappy with your given one, and which carries so much history with it and a stimulus to do good with it.

Mushroom - Well, then , now you know : I am not a charitable creature, yet I am not sufficiently foolish to ignore the right side of things as circumstances bring them forth, and when I said that I was not at all interested in your complaints about the cold and the wind , in particular, I only meant that there are more important problems in the life of the Forest than the wind and the cold . I, actually ,was referring myself to the time when you were still a small child ,you always had some problems, and you always complained about almost everything in spite of being fed and pampered with every possible comfort and privileges the forest could afford for you, since you belonged to an ancient and distinguished atavic clan .

Giant Oak Tree - But what do you know, actually , how can you possibly know anything about me when I was a child ??? You could not have been there because , I almost cannot believe it myself , well ,because you might have been born just yesterday ! You are telling me a lot of stories, dear Fabius !

Mushroom - May be it is true that I might have been born yesterday and , may be , even the day before yesterday , I do not remember it well , but my Forefathers who reach back in the memory of time for millennia and millennia, have left for me precisely and perfectly documented , catalogued and encoded memories proofs that they themselves received from their Forefathers who had reached back in the validated memory of millennia upon innumerable millennia and that is why I have learned to grow and live here , near you , and we....well I really meant to say :" we mushrooms and our Forefathers " , all mushrooms, of course , were there at your birth and we have known you for a very, very long time , dear Charlie .

Giant Oak Tree - Yes , Fabius , even granted that it is so as you just said , but how could you know of me and of my childhood directly and not from handed down information, when , very likely , you were born just yesterday ?

Mushroom - Well , Charlie , in two ways .

Giant Oak Tree- Go on !

Mushroom - One , we don't know which way . The other , from everyday's life happenings , gossip , news , rumors , and casual observations .

Giant Oak Tree - This last one , seems pretty ordinary and well known , my dear Fabius !

Mushroom - Everything that was not known becomes ordinary when fully known ,no mystery about that .

Giant Oak Tree - Is ,then , the other so far away from our knowledge ?

Mushroom - Well , Charlie , I do not want to sound presumptuous , but it seems to me , by pure natural common sense , that the birth and the childhood of anything and everything that comes after that , are just progress notes of an undefinable process that constitutes the birth itself because , of course , we know how it all happens , but we do not know why it happens or why it has to happen at all , so.........

Giant Oak Tree - Well , my dear Fabius , what has all that got to do with your boasting like a smart aleck about your mysteriously acquired knowledge of my birth and my childhood ??

Mushroom - Dear Charlie , you just got the words out of my mouth , so to speak , of course , since I do not have one , but you are absolutely right and it is true that I happen to be a smart aleck , that is not a stupid one and , as I was saying , the birth itself is common knowledge and it happens by countless numbers every single day of our existences , but the repetitive encoded memory of that process through the eons of time and in the perfect sequence of its beginning and progressing that defines and completes its final appearance , is the tricky component of that relatively common event, the actual birth and childhood ,the actual completed process and just the end-part of it. Now, dear Charlie, how it all started and how " YOU "' started and why it did start at all in the first place , that , dear Charlie , would require the study and the perception of a far dumber aleck than I am , if at all one could be found , that would qualify for that coveted genial representation, and that, my dear Charlie , would really be a BIG " IF " .

Giant Oak Tree - I don't know for certain " IF " I follow you entirely, my dear Fabius , as you seem to exceed the diameter of your hat , your words and enunciations falling off it at an unprecedented pace , almost in terror of remaining trapped on top of it. Would you consider , my dear Fabius , a more conventional , terrestrial and forest -like conveyance of your fulgid representation of the mechanics of my birth and early childhood ?

Mushroom - Charlie, I am sorry if I annoyed you with my inquisitive variations , I was only talking out of my hat .

Giant Oak Tree - I thought so.

Mushroom - Well , to make a long trunk short , or , as the humans would say , a " long story short " , and going back to where we started , WE , I , THEM and everybody else , have an " image glimpse " of a juvenile oak tree and his growth and his life , but , dear Old Charlie , why you were there, and why you were a child and why you grew after that , please, don't ask me because I would not know .

Giant Oak Tree - Anything else ?

Mushroom - Yes , Charlie, a lot " ELSE "and I know a lot more than you can possibly imagine , I assure you !

Giant Oak Tree - Incredible .

Mushroom - Listen ,Charlie , I can tell you " something "that you , probably , have not even thought about or suspected .....but , Charlie , if I am bothering you , I shall fall silent under my large hat and go to sleep.

Giant Oak Tree - Oh ! No , no , Fabius , I am interested : you seem to have a sensitivity about things , about life , and about vegetation and vegetation and germination, all your own style , that is quite remarkable and I shall listen with interest to that " something " you are going to tell me , and I am certain that it will be useful and informative , well , at least I hope so .

Mushroom - I hope so too, dearCharlie...and , excuse me for the interruption , but is it still in order to call you " Charlie " ?

Giant Oak Tree - But , of course , it is !

Mushroom - I was afraid that, indulging in its use , might bring in or cause some discomfort for excessive familiarity , and that would spoil the legitimacy of what I want to tell you.

Giant Oak Tree - No, my dear Fabius , on the contrary : it creates a closer understanding , even a deeper trust. So , " Charlie " , is perfectly all right with me.

Mushroom - Oh ! That's good and makes me feel at ease : thank you , Charlie .

Giant Oak Tree - Don't mention it.

Mushroom - Well , then , I really want to tell you something . Actually , I had wanted to tell you something all the time but I never happened to be in a position or in a favourable situation while talking with you that would have allowed me to enter without much fanfare into it , but , now , I feel free to communicate to you that " something " that I had wanted to tell you all the time.

Giant Oak Tree - I am glad that you feel that way , now , so that what you have to tell me might even sound more interesting.

Mushroom - You see, Charlie , there is so much talk, gossip, stories , rumors and all sorts of news , information , whispers and " low- talk " going around these days down here to fill your ears, your brain and your entire body with this avalanche of communicative endeavours , and almost impossible to escape from its entwining grip of persistent , methodical and unforgiving loquaciousness .

Giant Oak Tree - An uncomfortable feeling that must be , dear Fabius . And tell me : does that happen everyday ?

Mushroom - Oh! My dear Charlie, if that would happen only everyday , it would not really be so bad , but it is day and night , day in and day out , sundays and holidays inclusive .

Giant Oak Tree - It sounds serious .

Mushroom - And serious it is ,Charlie, not so much because of its persistent frequency but for its content .

Giant Oak Tree - Not offensive , I do hope !

Mushroom - Dear Charlie, tall and large and BIG , BIG as you are ,you must know quite well that " offensive " is a relative expression of displeasure that can be attributable to physical activities as well as to mental, brainy , that is , or emotional, affective or confrontational situations, so, Charlie , have your pick.!

Giant Oak Tree - Now you sound like a famous Attorney , defender of the Law , claiming his place in the midst of an even more famous trial of the century !

Mushroom - And something of a trial it really is ,with all sorts of people coming in and out of my house looking for explanations of things, seeking advice on anything, from the actual price of tomatoes to the real value of the beetroots these days , and how is the weather , will it rain to-morrow, or the day after to-morrow ! And no one pays for my services !

Giant Oak Tree - A sign of respect , I believe, towards your authority and wisdom and no offer to repay for your kindness in listening to their multiform requests lest they might offend your pride for not being able to offer you what you would considered adequate and what those poor people could at all afford .

Mushroom - That is , indeed , a nice escape for those so called poor people to circumvent the feeling of compensation, but what they may lack in finances , they certainly can make it up in the loquacity of their mouths and the turbid thoughts they let come out of their mouths .

Giant Oak Tree - Mushroom , you mystify me ! The more you talk and the greater the seeming confusion of statements ,facts and stories : and , as a reminder and a note of interest , my dear Fabius , you talk and talk and talk but you have not come out yet with that "something " that you seemed so keen , so eager to confide in me : well ? Where is it ??

Mushroom - You are right, Charlie, you are darn right and I took you on a tangent going around in circles and lines and triangles and forgetting to tell you what I had, really , wanted to tell you . I am glad that you reminded me of that or I might have gone on talking nonsense a lot longer : after hearing so much talk from so many creatures of all sizes, shapes and creeds, you become a robot and even act like one , that is , when totally charged , you keep on going ..!!!

Giant Oak Tree - I am glad that I was good for something ! But , now , it is up to you to keep on the main subject and tell me about thast famous and , by now , almost "stale " something , I am afraid !

Mushroom - Oh! , no , Charlie : not stale at all, but very much alive and kicking ,if I may say so.

Giant Oak Tree - Well, then , my dear Fabius , all you have to do is jump on that kicking beast, kick your spurs and tell me , please , what you wanted to tell me! I am really curious to hear it because hardly ever anything of that nature as you describe it ,ever reaches me . So, hurry up and tell me .

Mushroom - Right . You see, dear Charlie , all this talk , those stories , the endless gossip, the complaints , the questions, the thoughts , the emotions , the expressions and the worries of all of these creatures who come to see me seeking a solution, even if marginal , to their queries , do come first at my doorsteps, down here , and right on my lap, so to speak , of course , and , if I cannot absorb everything , then it might be my brother , on one side , or a cousin of mine on the right side of me, or my brother-in-Law on the left side ,let alone all the nieces and nephews, grand children and aunts , uncles and Grand Mothers , and Grand Fathers`, who will adjourn me on the recent events, stories, gossip ,and everything else ,before anything can slowly climb along your tall , tall figure and reach your head , and that is one way, but the deeper thoughts and the secret intentions or the conceited attempts at pronouncing one's most inner feelings and social and political ideas , adopt a more silent, yet very efficient way in reaching you,and that is via your roots .

Giant Oak Tree - Mushroom, I said a short time ago, that you mystify me and I feel inclined to say it again : " Mushroom ,you mystify me with your strange representation of life down there where you live in company of all those creatures that you like to describe in living colours as such a mixed-up type of living beings ! Now, my roots to carry me the story of the life and adventures of the people down there ! ...Mushroom , you need a rest, I believe.

Mushroom - I am sorry if I might have confused you a little but , you see, the roots that bring you your nourishment every day, go through our houses first before reaching you, that is they go through us , the people of the little creatures , before merging and forming one single , powerful body , giving , then , the appearance of a solid union , consistency and strength , and carrying a strong resemblance to a Nation , be it a human one or one built by ants or bees , it does not really make much difference , but as a consequence of that unity even the bees know how to run a nation and at a profitable clip too.... Yes,yes, I already know what you would be asking : " ,....and what all this has to do with the news ,stories, gossip and what not ,reaching me ..?? ", well , my answer would be : " Sir , there is a revolution in the making down here and you, apparently, have not heard even the first installment of it ".

Giant Oak Tree - Mushroom, I had just said a while ago that you kept up mystifying me with your " avant-garde " type of reasoning and reckoning , but now I begin to believe that you are raving mad .

Mushroom - Thank you . I realize that there is always room for reconsidering your own attitudes and capabilities and that feature , I understand , is not necessarily restricted to mushrooms .

Giant Oak Tree - You seem to take my remarks quite lightly, Fabius , but I do not mind it . Now , tell me , are all the mushrooms around and , in general too , always so well informed of all these news, happenings , gossips and stories as well as prognostications of impending revolutions and major disasters ?

Mushroom - Yes ,Charlie , usually all of them, save a few , late descendants of ancient wild , barbarous and ruthless tribes , who did not benefit of the wisdom handed down to them for million of years and did not adhere to those golden rules and institutions with honour and wisdom, and , on the contrary , they used that precious inheritance by becoming secret scouts to kill the naive and the careless , passing themselves as innocent specimens of delicious nature, texture and temperament so as to attract attention but then , when someone joins with them and takes them in ,they kill him in the hope to subvert , with that action, an entire nation.

Giant Oak Tree - Well, well, my dear little mushroom ,you seem to come out now dressed with new coloured clothes , like a political demagogue , in the way you can bring forth and describe the circumstances and feuding of opposite parties and their respective goals and aspirations ! Is this, then , your inheritance of the wisdom of your Forefathers ?

Mushroom - Who knows ? May be yes and may be no : the subtleties of heredity are not quite fully interpreted ,although some have been successfully deciphered . Anyway , when the time comes where heredity may have the upper hand in the decisions we make and the actions we take , no one will think of analyzing its intricacies at the time when action is needed , but the result of the action taken will determine it . Now, as to my political expertise , I have none and I crave for none. Besides , dear Charlie , mushrooms do not deal with politics. Furthermore , we mushrooms do not even comprehend its meaning .

Giant Ok Tree - Comprehension !....Yes...comprehension ! ...And this, perhaps , is the most difficult task for any creature to comprehend .

Mushroom - I do not know that, my big Tree , I really do not know that ,not even when encouraged to look at it with an exclamation mark !

Giant Oak Tree - I did not place any exclamation marks on it for you to look at .

Mushroom - But you said it in a way that sounded as an esclamation.

Giant Oak Tree - Someone else , may be , got out of line and placed the exclamation mark.

Mushroom - It must have.

Giant Oak Tree - It must.

Mushroom - Listen, Charlie, why don't we try to stay on the right track of our conversation instead of dispersing our intellectual energies while indulging in an "off the main road" speculation, dissertation and exclamation marks.?

Giant Oak Tree - Attaboy! You just hit the right key…right where the right key was…!!!

Mushroom - You see, my dear BIG, BIG tree, how easy it can be to derail our imagination and follow fantasies instead of real facts and impending concerns.

Giant Oak Tree - Well, it just occurs to me that you are going back to the "old track", mentioning, again, "facts" and, more ominous than ever, "impending concerns".

Mushroom - Unfortunately, dear Charlie, the "facts and concerns" are not on the wrong track but they are right here on "OUR" track, and, mind you, it is not that I would be afraid or hesitant in grappling with audacious postulates or frail grounds of yet uncharted intellectual avenues, but my limited capacity "to think", being "limited", I have to content myself, most of the time, in just observing what's going on around me, close enough to the ground which gave me life and, now, continues to keep me alive, and so, quietly and patiently under my "hat", I observe the coming and going of all those creatures, particularly so in a day like this which is the day of the weekly market, but, today, the atmosphere seems somewhat different, more alive, more agitated, I would venture to say, than usual.

Giant Oak Tree - I could not see anything "that" different, today, dear Fabius.

Mushroom - That's why I need to talk to you. I had tried already at the start of our conversation, but we got side-tracked by our urge to go over the limits of the intellectual power our Good Old Mother Nature had reserved for mushrooms and Oak trees, giant ones included. So, please, listen to me and let me finish what I had in mind to tell you: I believe it is important.

Giant Oak Tree - Of course, dear Fabius, go right ahead and I shall be "all ears" as the little humans would say! Besides, the way you advertise your forthcoming information, gives it I wouldn't say a sinister aspect, but, certainly, one of necessity and urgency. All right: I am listening…!!

Mushroom - So, I had started telling you about all this traffic, here, on the ground, and in and out, up and down and sideway too, right in front of my house, and in all the shops and stalls of the market, and many uneasy eyes looking up inquisitively, even contemptuously, at your large framed trunk...

which sets you out in your becomimg and beautiful ,imposing figure .

Giant Oak Tree - Thank you , for the compliment.

Mushroom - Oh ! Nothing , nothing , my dear Big tree, Charlie ! No attempt to an ingratiating compliment , just a qualifying specification of a tangible effect.

Giant Oak Tree - Thank you , just the same.

Mushroom - Well, Charlie , to-day , it was different : the atmosphere at the market was different and the people in the midst of it were also different ,usually the same crowd comes by every market day and , more or less , everybody knows everybody , they go about their business, buy stuff , exchange merchandise, pick up long discussions on the price of some of the offered goods, in other words, it is a real market, but ,to-day , it was different .

Giant Oak Tree - I am surprised at hearing what you are saying , dear Fabius , because ,as I have already told you , up here , I did not hear or notice anything different than at any other market day.

Mushroom - And that's why I am so worried , Charlie , because something was not quite as usual , particularly when you consider something that hardly ever had happened before.

Giant Oak Tree - And what was that ?

Mushroom - Usually ,no one ever bothers to come to my house to see me or talk or inquire about things , except very rarely ,if someone, an out of town tourist ,may be, inquiring where would be a good place to eat and spend the night or which would be the best way or the straightest road to the next forest . But , Charlie, to-day , it was something else .

Giant Oak Tree - Go on, go on , Fabius , what happen to-day ?

Mushroom - Well, some out of town folks did come to see me , but they looked somewhat different from the usual tourist that comes by in our neck of the woods and I did not even recognize any of them as some of the usual customers of the market , yet, they were very polite and carried themselves well and spoke well , but it was the substance of their enquiries that surprised me a little, I would say that it almost annoyed me .

Giant Oak Tree - Didn't they ask you for a good lodging or a direction for a better road or where you could get a good meal in our land ?

Mushroom - None of that ,Charlie, none at all . And that raised my suspicions as well as my anxiety : I really felt very uncomfortable and then I wanted to see you as soon as I could to tell you about it.

Giant Oak Tree - But what did they want to know , then ?

Mushroom - Well, they started , first , by praising the forest, its beautiful trees , the well stocked market ,and how well organized everything was ,and they had some packages with them , saying that they had found some good stuff at a very good price that they could not have bought in their town for the same price.

Giant Oak Tree - Well , Fabius , what's so mysterious, different or worrisome about that ?

Mushroom - Then , they changed the tune , and making the transition from one subject to another as if it had just come that way , they began asking some questions about the profitability of the market , its management , did the merchants pay their taxes, citing , as a corroborating incentive in the talking ,some problems they had had in their markets , and was the market and the City Government Offices open to the public , were the citizens satisfied with the present status of the political scene and if all citizens were equally welcome , everywhere in our town , and they also wanted to know how many ethnic groups could the City account for, were there more ants than caterpillars , or beetles than lizards , or flies than bees , or little red worms or chickens snakes and so on and on , to the point that I had to say something ,that I had some important business to attend to and would they excuse me if I could not stay with them any longer . They agreed and left after greeting me most courteously , but , had they just left then a crowd of shoppers rushed into my house telling me that those "strange Strangers " had harassed several of them while they were shopping , telling them that in their city things were run a lot better than in this one and that they should demonstrate their discontent to the local authorities, and when told that the only authority was the " BIG GIANT OAK TREE " , they told them to rebel against his poorly run Government.

Giant Oak Tree - I don't believe it.

Mushroom - I could not sleep last night because of all this and I became very anxious to see you and let you know about it . If you really want to know , I had thought that the Sparrow Mother- in Law might have warned you about it .

Giant Oak Tree - Now , what would a stupid bird know about it , I wonder !

Mushroom - You'll be surprised , dear Charlie, but they know a lot.

Giant Oak Tree - I wonder !

Mushroom - But, yes , dear Charlie , they do . You see, they come down here among us constantly making short flights down here ,particularly so during market time, and picking up precious morsels of good food left over in the hundreds of transactions, and , while here, they hear and see everything and take it with them in their nests, Charlie. You should really ask them about conditions down here and what is going on down here , that would be an invaluable font of information for you, but , from what I heard by your own statement the other day , you were very annoyed and almost furious at them, for all the noise they made.

Giant Oak Tree - You seem to know what's what, dear Fabius !

Mushroom - Neither more nor less .

Giant Oak Tree - What do you mean by that ?

Mushroom - Neither more nor less than yourself , you Spindleshanks .

Giant Oak Tree- You really make me laugh ,dear Mushroom :a while ago you proclaimed me a Giant , then , shortly afterwards , The Head of Government of a Nation of I do not know where , and , a few seconds later , you take it upon yourself to make fun of me by calling me ......a " Spindleshanks " !! You are really the living example that I was trying to classify you with : the dwarf that wants to look like a giant , by words only , of course . You really are funny, dear Fabius.

Mushroom - And may I ask : "Why not " ?

Giant Oak Tree - Because it is preposterous .

Mushroom - Everything that has not been tried, always seems preposterous . Don't you know that is a natural instinct in the creatures of this planet, and ,who knows, may be others too.....

Giant Oak Tree - Are you perhaps trying to tell me that there might be out there some other planets on which are living creatures who are dwarfs and would like to grow like giants ?

Mushroom - I do not know that and I did not say that : all I said was that you should be aware that in all the creatures that "roam " our forest there is an inborn instinct to try to raise oneself to the best possible level that their skills, their will and their strength will allow them to ,and least interests me if there are similar circumstances on some other planets and forests , good luck to them if they are there , but I am talking about us ,Charlie , and ,apparently ,that is what those strangers came to inquire with me , reflecting in their quests, possibly , the aspirations of the little people at the market ,a desire to better themselves and obtain a less demanding and constricted existence ,so it comes natural for these creatures to try to stretch their necks and look beyond the imposed boundaries of their destiny : that is what I was trying to warn you about and to let you know of this ferment and feelings of anticipation among our people, at least the ones at the market . But I heard something else too.

Giant Oak Tree - Go on , go on, Fabius , I want to hear more of this " ferment " and about what you heard more, as you just said.

Musshroom - Yes, Charlie , and I believe that it is important for you to know more, since, with your poorly guarded "attitude" towards birds, you are being portrayed among the little people as an unpleasant giant, who does not tolerate anyone else around except himself and , dear Charlie , that is not a good recommendation nor a desirable quality for a leader of a Nation, even in a forest.

Giant Oak Tree - I understand , dear Fabius, and I greatly value your genuine efforts to warn me of those unsettling news and tendencies of the little people, but ,whatever their desires , it does not stand to any logical thought or consideration for a little creature to wanting to rise so high as to become a giant , whether on this planet or on some other place or planet . There must be something else behind all this turmoil or , shall we say ," ferment ", as you like to call it.

Mushroom - They see you, majestic , tall and all encompassing and they see other trees, also tall and getting bigger, and they hear the "gospel " spread by visitors of uncertain credentials , and , having been exposed to no other comparative society , they fall easy prey of unscrupulous agents, who are just looking after their own interests or are representatives of adverse societies who may want to take over and add some other people to their revenues . It would seem to me that if our people were giants too, no one would dare pick up a fight with them. Don't you think so, Charlie ?

Giant Oak Tree - Well, in a way I follow you and I can understand their striving for better conditions and a better, less stressful existence but , dear Fabius ,there is a significant difference and a serious gap in acting like a giant and actually being a giant .

Mushroom - Whatever the difference and the gap might be in the endless search for all creatures in this Forest Nation in trying their chances for a better living and a more hopeful vision of a serene and fruitful existence , it is quite obvious, my dear Charlie , that in the type of situation of " acting " like a Giant , versus " actually " being one , the former proposition appears , definitively, to emerge as far less dangerous than the latter .

Giant Oak Tree - What do you mean by that, dear Fabius ?

Mushroom - Then listen , dear Charlie and I shall try to explain it to yoù, if you would condescend to lend your majestic attention to a humble , small mushroom , here , all wrapped up among your mighty roots.

Giant Oak Tree - I definitively will lend you all my available ears ,where ever they could be found , and I shall add that I will feel honoured to hold you as my trusted informer on the state of the Forest Nation , that is " my Privy Councilor" , and Secretary of the Department of Internal Affairs responsible for the monitoring of the delicate, unpredictable and , at times , almost incomprehensible attitudes and moods of the people at large as well as of the people within , and the Ambassador of the thin ,even occult ,connection threads of so many and various political motives and drives ,and Comptroller of the state of the Treasury , or , as the Old Oak Trees used to call it in ancient Rome - " the public money " , and .....

Mushroom - Please , dear , big , giant Tree, Charlie , do not poke fun at me : I happen to be very serious at this particular time of grave concerns about peoples shifting moods ,as you just mentioned , and uncertain attitudes and what I was planning to tell you is also a serious matter ,consisting or real history , events and facts that did really happen and not invented by the vivid imagination of some poets or writers : real happenings , free of additives of fantasy or embellishments and clearly stating the actual , terse truth of those events , so very carefully documented in the historical chronicles of those days , when these episodes occurred . So , if you will allow me , I'll explain to you the Saga of the Giants and the little people who wanted to be Giants.

Giant Oak Tree - Well , I'll listen , but it sounds somewhat monotonous and even somewhat unnecessary going through it again ,since we haven't been talking of anything else for the past several hours, but , if you wish ,then I will listen : in final analysis you and I do not have much of a choice ,stuck as we are on this ground ,real permanent and rightful residents of this land .

Mushroom - Permanent , yes ,I agree. As to the rightful , I doubt that we posses the necessary knowledge and authority, nature wise , to classify ourselves in that category of residents.

Giant Oak Tree - I do not understand, really , what you are talking about, dear Fabius, and you sound like a trial Lawyer , brilliantly pushing forward his captious caviling in the defense or the prosecution , whichever the case , of a charged party.

Mushroom - No particular prophetic statement , Charlie , other that the realization of being right here as " rightful " residents .

Giant Oak Tree - What else could we be, dear Fabius ?

Mushroom - I felt that for us to hold as an accepted Law that of being here in this Forest, asthe rightful inhabitants on this ground, might have sounded somewhat presumptuous : that' all .

Giant Oak Tree - The way I see it , my dear Fabius is different : yes , I might even agree with you if we would have the choice to move and go somewhere else, than ,yes, our claim to be in this place " rightfully " might have sounded presumptuous, but, my dear Fabius , we do not have that choice , so my interpretation of our standing stuck here on this ground without a choice to move elsewhere is that we were meant be here and , therefore , not only I thought that we were here "rightfully " but , by claiming that reality , we actually paid respect to Mother Nature by acknowledging her Will and Dispositions .

Mushroom - I have another suggestion .

Giant Oak Tree - It looks like we'll never end this criss-cross duel of explanations and interpretations of what's around us..!!!.. Well, what is now this new salvo of your imagination ?

Mushroom - You just mentioned, a while ago, that I sounded just like a famous trial Lawyer and , I feel that you are just following my steps in your flamboyant declaration of right and wrong .

Giant Oak Tree - So..?

Mushroom - So, since you argued and rightfully proved with unusual and brilliant legal skills that our rightful presence here on this ground is our rightful way to be, and I am a trial Lawyer ,well , then, why don't we open a Law University and flourish in it !

Giant Oak Tree - We don't have the time to do that ,dear Fabius ! You have not explained to me , yet , the merry-go round of the little giants and the big giants or whatever .

Mushroom - Not even funny , at its best .

Giant Oak Tree - We do what we can to help .

Mushroom - The way things are shaping up, I'll better hurry up and tell you about the giants and so on.

Giant Oak Tree - I think so too.

Mushroom - So , now , and hopefully without any more interruptions and chasing ghosts and having fun with unbridled fantasies , history , dear Charlie , teaches us in generous doses about the basic difference between " pretending " and "being ".

Giant Oak Tree - But , my dear little mushroom , it seems to me that you are singing back to me the same refrain and you have said absolutely nothing and , I repeat, ABSOLUTELY NOTHING of what you were so eager to tell me about the giants and the not-so giants . Tell me : do you feel well ?

Mushroom - Very well , indeed .Thank you. The story which has almost become proverbial in our existences , even in our Forest , dear Charlie , has shown that when times go changing and the softly pink horizons turn to darker colours, and business dies down , and some unscrupulous creatures take to unhealthy practices under the corrupted protection of condescending administrators of the Law , or by virtue of their high position in the ruling Elite , thus creating difficulties and ever increasing hardship for the little people and the less fortunate in the land , and , I tell you in all frankness, those are the most frequent causes of the little people unrest....

Giant Oak Tree - Do you blame them ?

Mushroom - Of course not , but , let me continue : so , under those circumstances , the discomfort and with it the unrest of the little people and the misfortune of many others , keep on growing ,and growing ,at first hardly noticed , then more apparent here and there, in isolated episodes of disobedience or fighting or disorderly behaviour , which, then , becomes more frequent and more widespread , more vociferous , more open and in many cases almost defiant, and , now even more agitated , louder and louder until the indignation of the little people from a subdued murmur turns into an ominous , powerful rumble : it is at this time that history tells us that many creatures who were born as giants ......

Giant Oak Tree - Are you trying to make any reference to me, by any chance ?

Mushroom - Would I ? I am not that simple to be thinking of something like that, my dear Charlie ! But , please let me finish : so as I was saying , it is at that time that we learn from the very history of times gone by but still quite close to us, that many big creatures who were Giants in their own rights, that is born and raised "ritghtfully " in Giant Families ,would try to make themselves very small in an attempt to escape the fury of that unleashed tempest , but without much success . So, going back to the heart of the matter ,it becomes quite clear and obvious that it would be far easier to become little for anyone who had never, really , been big than for someone who had never been small but born and raised as a real Giant to try in an utter helpless and vain attempt to become small . This is what I wanted to tell you in the light of the happenings at the Market , to-day .

Giant Oak Tree - Well put , dear Fabius ,but also a little far fetched your story and your prognosis . There might have been a few cases of some Giants , born as you said as real Giant, who might have wanted to conceal their true identity in order to escape more serious consequences by the fury of the little people , but I believe that if your lymph was that of a real Giant ,never will they feel ashamed or needing to hide their heritage :if a Giant , well, always a Giant

Mushroom - May be it is as you say , dear Charlie , but the experience dictated by History appears to show a different interpretation..........Ah !....You look askance at me , Big Tree ! Oh ! How thoughtless of me to mention that seeming historical contradiction while in the midst of so many Giants in this mysterious and unpredictable forest ! But , as you certainly know well , present company is always excepted .

Giant Oak Tree - My dear little mushroom, dear Fabius , please do not trouble yourself to apologize , when from the beginning of our conversation and until now you have done nothing else , practically , than bring up arguments upon arguments and theories and historical facts and doomsday prophecies about Giants and the land they live on.

Mushroom - THANKS Heaven, dear Charlie : for a moment I really felt as falling in the bottomless pit !

Giant Oak Tree- Do not worry , little Mushroom , as a matter of fact I have become more interested in your stories ,with historical backgrounds , and foreboding warning to Giants and to the unhappy people who happen to be around them and , in a way , I am grateful to you for , actually , helping me in keeping a keener look towards the little people , who , the way you just described them, are able to deliver powerful and significant accents to the political life of a nation .

Mushroom - And so it seems ,dear Charlie.

Giant Oak Tree - Well, then ,my dear Fabius ,is there anything else of interest to be heard, to-day ?

Mushroom - Nothing ,really , anymore , except to refine what has already been said .

Giant Oak Tree - And what would that be ?

Mushroom - Nothing really important, : just a refinement of the previous narrative when I was explaining how , in tempestuous times , important creatures try to make themselves small or disappear entirely , if that would be at all possible, in order to avoid the attention of the infuriated little people as well as that of the envious people, always alert at gaining from someone else's misfortunes, but the ones who were always on the small size, like little scheming dwarfs and had made themselves big ,big in time of roses and plenty , when the clouds of the hurricane appear on the horizon , all they do change their fierce and authoritative look into a sweet, innocent one and with thousands of smiles and a thousand and one sweet bowing and scraping they do not waste any time to spit venom on Giants and dwarfs indifferently ,depending on the prevailing circumstances , and in a split second they are little dwarfs again , in the expression on their faces , in their acting , and in their thoughts ,all of which they never , really , ever parted with . More than that , no one can challenge that right save the dwarfs themselves , who , for being precisely so small and without significant resources , usually have no means at all to challenge anything .

Giant Oak Tree - I'll say , dear little mushroom of the forest , you can talk . Even the sparrow Mother-in-Law ......by the way , I am sure that you have heard of her, didn't you ?

Mushroom - Yes, Charlie, I did . And how could anyone have missed the interesting dialogue you had with her some time ago ?!!

Giant Oak Tree- Yes, that's right : we did have quite some of a conversation, back then .But I was saying , even the Sparrow Mother-in Law, who always takes a nap lasting hours on my branches with a tight beak and a defiant look and her eyes always looking for something to discover or to criticize ,so , as I was saying , even the Sparrow Mother-in- Law kept very quiet and attentive just in order to hear you talk ! And THAT , my dear Fabius, 'That " is really something !

Mushroom - I really do not make much out of it , really , dear Charlie ! Talking , down here , is nothing more than an every day experience .

Giant Oak Tree - Human experience , may be yes because those creatures talk a lot and they seem to do nothing else from morning till night , but it is a remarkable achievement for any of us , plants or something similar as we are ,my dear Fabius . So , heart-felt congratulations.

Mushroom - Charlie, Thank you for saying that : you know such a remark means a lot to us , poor little creatures down here , really ! But let me say this : I believe that experience is always experience , be it human or some other type of creature in this world of ours, our forest , who ever these "others " might be.

Giant Oak Tree- But , my dear Fabius , I believe that you must be fully aware of what the "so- called " human experience has caused to our forests and I am sure that you must have heard a lot of talk about it down there where you live in the midst of all that traffic that crawls constantly in and out and up and down and , may be , even sideway , day and night , all around my roots......

Mushroom - Very true , Charlie .

Giant Oak Tree - Well , that was what you had told me and " that " was also what you had described to me in prolonged and ample details just a while ago , so , I'll say it again : you and everybody else down there do certainly know of the damage done to our forests by these "experienced " human creatures and , furthermore , I happen to hear straight from the investigative information gathered by the Sparrow Mother-in-Law , and graciously extended to my attention , that similar damage , and may be even worse , more severe and even permanent and far more extensive than the damage we suffered , has occurred in several other neighbouring Forests , and...........

Mushroom - We heard .

Giant Oak Tree - ....without taking into account the suffering inflicted to our sister Plants and to our many cohabitant creatures who roam in our pleasantly shadowed trails and to our innumerable birds (.......blessed those vociferous little creatures ...!!!) , and the beetles , the caterpillars and the ants , and the lizards, and so on and so on , without counting , of course and not least , the carrots, the beetroots , the lettuce , the tomatoes , the potatoes , and the artichokes . Now , you tell me , what kind of " experience " was that , if not the very wrong one to " experience " ?

Mushroom - In this perspective , perhaps you may have a point , dear Charlie . Strange creatures , indeed , these........." human " creatures !!

Giant Oak Tree - You call these creatures " strange " ? ! Well, you tell it right like it is and , yet , you tell hardly anything about them, dear Fabius !

Mushroom - How's that ?

Giant Oak Tree - " Strange" barely classifies them, because they are " extremely strange "in most of their doings .

Mushroom - Could it be , Charlie ,that they appear to us to be that way because we and "them " are actually quite different in form, aspect , way of living , eating, marrying and having siblings , and making love ?

Giant Oak Tree - I do not think so , dear Fabius , and my criticism of their behaviour is based on the accurate reports that our sweet Sparrow Mother-in-Law receives from creatures next of kin and associated acquaintances and the story goes that the well - trumpeted and renowned experience of these human creatures is none other than the fruit of a long existence of continuous destruction of other creatures' possessions and inclusive, in that honourable process , of the destruction and elimination of their own's and even themselves .

Mushroom - I would have suspected something of that kind . But , Charlie , are your sources of information strictly reliable ? You know , sometimes , things seen from afar or not in direct line of contact , may appear different, even distorted and ill represented to an untrained or a prejudiced eye .

Giant Oak Tree - Untrained or prejudiced eyes ?? ...Those of the owls and of the long-eared owls ? My boy , they can see through mud even on a dark , moonless night!

Mushroom - I did not know that you had a correspondence of information with those nocturnal creatures , knowing how irritable you become at being disturbed at night or woken up early in the morning by the joyous thrills of thousands of early birds !

Giant Oak Tree - Well , as you know , the old "adage " ......" if you cannot beat them , join them " , so , since I could not shake them off my branches at night when they sat there at their leisure and kept on babbling and carrying on a continuous tittle - tattle with that pedantic , yet persuasive as well as monotonous chant, and , realizing that I was running short of workable alternative options , I decided to make friends with them hoping that , in doing so , I could get their attention and their friendship and make my case , that of having some peace at night , a viable and ,possibly , an acceptable proposition by those night creatures .

Mushroom - And did you succeed ?

Giant Oak Tree - Did I succeed ?! More than that, dear Fabius , a lot more than that !

Mushroom - Really ?

Giant Oak Tree - You'll be surprised to learn what I heard from those night-creatures, something I had a hard time to digest and believe , but , nevertheless , true and real.

Mushroom - Sounds interesting !

Giant Oak Tree - Interesting is but a pale representation of what you are going to hear next .

Mushroom - Shoot, then, and let me hear it, Charlie ,you Big .Big Boy, my friend.

Giant Oak Tree - These night creatures, my dear Fabius, have told me that they had observed one day, early in the morning ,a peculiar looking nest ,very big and very large and very tall, that had grown that way over a period of several moons from a modest hole in the ground and up and up almost to touch the sky.........

Mushroom - To touch the sky ??!! How would it be possible ?! Even you, dear Charlie, big and tall as you are, cannot reach for the sky even if you wanted to ! How can, now, these human creatures do that ,and they do not even have wings!

Giant Oak Tree - Listen, listen : and these large nests have an innumerable number of holes in them ,some small and some larger and set out in a perfect alignment with the larger holes which are invariably set at the level of the ground, from where the actual construction started.

Mushroom - I wonder why.

Giant Oak Tree - It is not clear, but one senior owl seems to have noticed that these funny creatures enter and exit from the larger holes, the ones close to the ground or almost level with it, but she never saw anyone ever entering or exiting from the smaller holes above the ground.

Mushroom - That's probably because these creatures do not have wings.

Giant Oak Tree - May be. But there is something else.

Mushroom - And what's that ?

Giant Oak Tree - Not all those nests look alike.

Mushroom - Interesting.

Giant Oak Tree - Quite. Some are thin and tall : very, very tall.

Mushroom - To reach for the sky, I guess.

Giant Oak Tree - Who knows. Anyway it was noticed that the nests are not all looking the same, as I just said, some are smaller, fatter and with less holes, some others seem to have some significant variant structures somewhat more complex, more all over rounded and with some having enormously large holes at the bottom of the nest but not quite level with the ground like the seemingly simpler nests do have, and these larger holes have in front of them a long sequence of transverse lines on which these strange creatures keep on hopping while going into the nest and needing to do the hopping in order to reach the large door and the same happens when they exit , but ,then , the hopping seems to become more lively and faster than the hopping was on going in . Everything seems so strange around those nests , Fabius .

Mushroom - Strange ,indeed .

Giant Oak Tree - And another thing, that's even stranger .

Mushroom - Don't tell me .now , that they are going around on thier heads !

Giant Oak Tree - I wouldn't be surprised at all if they would, dear Fabius !! But it was something else I wanted to tell you about .

Mushroom - Yes , I am listening .

Giant Oak Tree - The screech owl and the long eared owl have been observing them while they built those large nest and , much to their surprise as well as astonishment, they saw somrthing they had a hard time to believe their eys !

Mushroom - It must have been really " something " , I believe !

Giant Oak Tree - And it was ! Can oyu imagine /! They were building those nests without even taking one mouthful or a beakful of materials to the construction site but picked up and placed together all the necessary materials by using some insects of strange form and configuration , something similar to a caterpillar but not quite as flexible as a caterpillar yet seemingly very powerful and strong , lifting considerable amounts of weight and delivering it to the construction site then returning to the collection place to pick up new materials or some different ones while other human creatures were directing other creatures , human too, to dispose of these newly delivered materials along a network of lines and sticks which grew from time to time as the nest kept on enlarging while reaching new heights . An incredible sight , I am telling you .

Mushroom - Would there be a chance , by any means , that the owl and the long eared one, might have told you a story, just for fun ? You know how crafty those two creatures are !

Giant Oak Tree - I don't think so, Fabius . You see , the Sparrow Mother-in-Law did confirm it to me ,when I had asked her about it , and I assure you that if the Sparrow Mother-in-Law confirmed it , you can be as sure as the light of the sun that the sighting was correct and real !!

Mushroom - The whole thing is very intriguing, to say the least!

G iant Oak Tree - Yes , Fabius , intriguing and perplexing , at the same time : for example , another peculiar custom among those creatures ,they seem inclined to get out of those huge nests, early in the morning and , while walking on their way to somewhere , they stop briefly by some very small nests, full of white leaves, and pick one up as they go , then seem to look in it for a short while but to either discard it or stick it into their skin and keep on going : the funny and unusual feature of that procedure is that they do not even eat a mouthful of that white leaf : they just look at it and then seem to forget all about it .Very, very strange ,I tell you .

Mushroom - Well, at least it is different from what we do, if nothing else ,: is it not ? Besides , neither you nor I do eat leaves , don't we ?

Giant Oak Tree - Right ; but we are not strange and , furthermore , we do not act strange and everybody knows that I am a tree and you are a mushroom , regardless whether we eat leaves or not . Believe it or not, even the Sparrow Mother-ion-Law knows that..!!!

Mushroom - Hurray for the Mother-in- Law, the sparrow , of course .

Giant Oak Tree - Bless her little sparrow soul !

Mushroom - Has any owls or long eared owls ever found out what those little white leaves are ?

Giant Oak Tree - The night owl that usually spends the night , unfortunately , right on one of my branches , one night , very carefully , and , as you know , owls are very careful birds particularly when hunting for something , so ,one night, this owl thought of looking into that strange thing and ,when everything was quiet and no one around, flew close to one of those white leaves that had been discarded on the ground ,as it appears that the majority of those human creatures do not seem to attribute excessive importance to the preservation of those leaves , and , coming closer to it , it seemed to contain an innumerable sequence of lines and dots and blots of all sizes and forms and how they had been produced on them it remained a mystery , since she , that owl, had never seen anything like it on a leaf, ever . Then she flew back to my branch to tell what she had seen to the long eared owl and both wondered at that finding.

Mushroom - And who wouldn't be wondering at that , dear Charlie !! I hope you are not telling me all of those things just to entertain me or add galore to the incredible stories about the whereabouts of the little human creatures !!!

Giant Oak Tree- What do you think I am ? A story- teller or a fibber ?

Mushroom - Oh! Charlie , nothing of the kind , Heavens forbid !! But you should understand that everything what has been said is very , very strange and that it is quite natural to have some difficulty in comprehending the whole thing and absorbing it too !

Giant Oak Tree - I don't blame you , dear Fabius : as a matter of fact I am wondering myself about the whole thing ,and yet , you have not heard half of it , my dear !

Mushroom - Now , this I find difficult , REALLY ! , to believe !! What else can there be any weirder than it already is, I wonder !!

Giant Oak Tree - Weird things don't come in small packages these days dear Fabius , and there is more .

Mushroom - ....If you insist..!!!

Giant Oak Tree - That is what the screeching Owl told me the other day , when I yelled at her to be quiet , but after that , she kept on " screeching " even louder ! The damn bird ! Anyway the screeching owl I just told you about , her name , she told me , is Maggie , saw several of these human creatures by focusing her eye - sight into one of the many holes in those nests which appeared full of light, and , this is even something else but we'll come to that t later on , and , as I was saying , these creatures do not let anyone come near to their nests or to them unless it is one of their own and , if by just a sheer mistake someone, be it another human or another type of creature comes closer , unexpected or uninvited, they pounce upon that creature with fury and determination , trying to chase it away and , sometimes , they seem to use some very long sticks who are very loud , at times , and ,at one end , when manipulated in a certain way , produce a lightning like flame accompanied by this very loud rumble like a clap of thunder and they level these sticks towards those poor creatures who desperately try to run away . Now , my dear Fabius , does all this I told you until now add up to solid and remarkable human experience?

Mushroom - My dear Charlie, foggy as my mind is at this moment after all the extraordinary and almost unbelievable reports on the events as reported to you by the screeching owl, sweet Maggie ,I guess, and by the long eared owl, whose name I do not know ....

Giant Oak Tree - Joshua .

Mushroom - OK ! Then , good old Joshua , as I said , I wonder if my brain under my hat and in spite of its protection so wonderfully afforded by it to my brain from violent and unsavory news and information , I really wonder if I could give a sensible answer to your question, my dear Charlie ! It is very hard to give a reliable interpretation to the behaviour of these strange creatures .

Giant Oak Tree - And I haven't told you everything yet ,dear Fabius !

Mushroom - I give up !

Giant Oak Tree - Well , the screeching owl who had already told me about some of her observations.....

Mushroom - Ah ! Yes , Maggie , I guess .

Giant Oak Tree - Right : Maggie . Well she and some of her friends ,who can see through the shadows of dusk and night , were able to set their sights into one of those holes that was full of light and ...

Mushroom - That's interesting : how do they get that light ,at night ?

Giant Oak Tree - Interesting is right ! I mention it just a while ago and, just as well , we can bring up an explanation ot that strange phenomenon as reported to me by Maggie : it appears that they have some sort of a luminescent type of beetle or spider ,quite large, which they keep in the bottom of those houses and use their luminescence at will and as needed and they seem to have some weird way of switching this illumination off when not needed by pressing their heads or their arms or hands against one of the walls of their nest and, in doing so , they can bring on or switch off that illumination .

Mushroom - Clever : you must give it to them , Charlie !

Giant Oak Tree - May be ! ...Anyway ,what the owls saw was quite interesting : these creatures, the human , I mean , do not have wings......

Mushroom - I thought that we had realized that already , had we not ,Charlie ?

Giant Oak Tree - Yes , in a way : we thought that they might not have wings , but , now , we have positive proof that they do not have wings .

Mushroom - I see .

Giant Oak Tree - Besides not having wings , they do not have antennae , they do not have feathers , and enter and exit from these nests continuously during day time, but less during evening hours and, rarely , at night time , but , during the hours when the sun is brighter, they run up and down everywhere as if suffering from an uneasy itch somewhere on their bodies and , even funnier, have their heads and body , in general , placed on only two sticks , like the birds have , but they seem to experience difficulties to hold themselves

Giant Oak Tree - (Continued) on branches , or on wires , or even on roof ,without running the risk of losing their balance and fall off those structures.

Mushroom - Ain' t I glad to be anchored solid on this ground !

Giant Oak Tree - So do I ! And ,Joshua , you know , the long eared owl , one day , while resting in a hole , high above the ground , in a steeple , saw one of these human creatures getting out of one of those holes in a tall nest and stepping on a wire which had been stretched from one hole to another hole of a nest right in front of it , and ...

Mushroom - I wonder why was that wire stretched from one hole to another when these creatures knew that they cannot walk on it well.....well, to each his own , as the good old forest saying goes..!

Giant Oak Tree - Well , whatever the reason was , that creature stepped on that wire and , one strange thing , he was holding a very long cane probably trying to get it on the other side in a direct route without going all the way down the entire length of the nest and climbing up all the way on the other opposite nest . Anyway, whatever the reason , he started ,slowly , moving along that wire , with some hesitation , at times, stopping , then going again, but always very slowly and very cautiously , it seemed , until he reached the midway mark, when, quite suddenly , there blew a strong gust of wind , the wire began to swing , the man frantically jerking his long cane , but , the gusts of wind persisting , the wire swung violently and the creature fell off and hit the ground, amid an uproar of cries and shrieks from several other creatures who ,apparently , were watching the whole thing from below.

Mushroom - What happened ,then ?

Giant Oak Tree - The long eared owl did not say : he told me that he flew away in search of food , but he had not understood the meaning of all that , if , of course , there would have been any meaning to be understood .

Mushroom - I am running out of space under my hat in cataloguing all these strange and yet extraordinary facts and information , so are there going to be any more surprises dear Charlie ? Don't you think that we have had enough excitement for one day ?

Giant Oak Tree - Surprises , not really , but something gruesome .

Mushroom - But , Charlie , for Heavens above , where are you trying to lead me , to-day, from one dramatic event to unheard of singular events and assorted weird stories of little human creatures doing strange activities ,building even stranger nests for habitation , I guess , and going around as if suffering from a predetermined compulsion about doing something regardless for the need of it or to justify that need in order to pacify their anxiety. What have you in mind , now , dear Charlie , when you bring to me some extra information of a " Gruesome " style ??!!

Giant Oak Tree - Well , my dear Fabius , it all started when a screeching owl , friend of Maggie, became witness to an observation quite dismal and revolting .

Mushroom - You don't say !

Giant Oak Tree - This young owl , a close friend of our Maggie , had the courage , one night ,....well you know , young creatures dare a lot in their young lives not quite well acquainted , yet , of the fortuities of life , anyway, this young owl dared perch very , very quietly on a branch of an oak tree that came quite close to one of those holes in a large nest building in a late evening and became a witness to a vision that she will never be able to forget.

Mushroom - Charlie , honestly , I am beginning to worry about your soundness of mind with the depiction and the memories of such grisly and blood-curdling events that you claim were brought to your attention by the unending interest of sweet, well-meaning screeching owls , who , apparently , knew very well when to screech and when it was not the right time to screech , but only to observe and report to you those revolting happenings . I am sincerely worried, Charlie !

Giant Oak Tree - Well, Fabius don't be . The story is weird , but real , therefore digestible and worth hearing it , even if " blood curdling " as you said .

Mushroom - I hope so , Charlie ! Is this new story very long ?

Giant Oak Tree - Why , Fabius ?

Mushroom - I am getting a little tired , Charlie , that's all .

Giant Oak Tree - No , Fabius ,it is not a long story but listen , and I assure you that the story is true to the last detail and , as you know , owls have a very good vision at night : what they saw cannot be anything but real.

Mushroom - Then, Charlie , go ahead and let me know about this gruesome adventure of your screeching owl and don't keep me any longer in such a suspense.

Giant Oak Tree - Listen , then : that night the moon was already high in the sky so that there was quite a lot of light all around ,when there were two young human creatures who , after securing something in front of the hole at the bottom of their nest ,through which they had entered the nest, they ,then , proceeded to to a higher level in the same nest by climbing up to the next hole above and, there , with a remarkable dexterity and a well coordinated method of movements , they began stripping off their skin and , that done , placed it carefully on the side of some platforms on which , shortly afterwards , they stretched their bodies and remained there until the next morning and , as the day light broke into their nest , they got out of those platforms , picked up the skin which they had discarded the night before and put it back on and in all earnest began to run again in all directions and with noticeable enthusiasm.

Mushroom - Almost incredible, my dear Big Tree , My dear Charlie ! Almost unbelievable, if it had not been you to tell me that !

Giant Oak Tree - I thought so too when Maggie reported it to me , but I ,then , accepted it as true because Maggie never told me anything that was not true.

Mushroom - I know and Maggie is indeed a very reliable owl, as a matter of fact , aren't they all ?

Giant Oak Tree - Nasty , but reliable : it is true.

Mushroom - Yet, I wonder , mind you , dear Charlie , I " JUST " wonder , if there would have been even a most remote possibility or probability that your sweet Maggie might have had an illicit ingestion of forbidden juices which could have caused such incredible visions ?

Giant Oak Tree - Don't be stupid . Owls do not drink " illicit " beverages , furthermore are renowned for their powerful vision acuity , and , particularly so , at night time. So , it is without any doubt that what they saw was real . The long eared owls also told me about several other activities by these strange beings, activities that seem to sequence themselves in an almost synchronous rhythm and consistent method every single day , repetitive and, some , totally void of any specific interest .

Mushroom - Would they , now , by any chance , take off their skins again , this time , in full daylight , may be ?

Giant Oak Tree - You seem bent to act a little silly , lately , my dear Fabius , but , to answer your silly question , well , YES , they seem to take off their skins every so often ,even in day light , particularly when the weather is good and warm ......

Mushroom - An interesting aspect : snakes are known to do something similar with their skins , if not on a daily basis .

Giant Oak Tree - You and your comparisons ..!! Well , yes ,they do strip off their skins even in full daylight, and,then,they jump into some holes full of water and shriek and splash around as if taken by a mad frenzy. After that performance, they put back on their skins and go about their business, again.

Mushroom - And what happened to those white leaves that they appear to scatter around?

Giant Oak Tree - Nothing. They are picked up by some huge insects as they go around the various avenues built between those tall nests. Interestingly, it appears that the more those scattered white leaves are being picked up, even more are being prepared and accumulated in large, enormous nests from where, later, are picked up by some other strange little human creatures, carried to some very small nests at some intervals along those long avenues and distributed to the passers by who, in their turn, seem to look at those white leaves for a short time, not eating them and then either throwing them away or putting them into a fold in their skins and then go about their business as usual. A very methodic type of behaviour, and, indeed, quite strange.

Mushroom - But, Charlie, I am asking myself: if they do not eat those white leaves, first I am asking, what do they feed themselves with, and second, by picking them up, looking at them and then discarding them, do they abide, may be, by an adverse and negative feature of their mental behaviour?

Giant Oak Tree - Nobody really knows, dear Fabius, about your first question and nobody knows about the second question either. As to the veracity of the observation, they are good, reliable and correct. I vouch for them myself since I trust the good, wise judgement of the owls and, in particular, of the impartial and detailed information by my sweet Maggie.

Mushroom - Charlie, I am sorry to be so persistent in my inquiries, but I do not seem able to get over the notion that they pick up those leaves, look at them and then they throw them away: it does not make any sense.

Giant Oak Tree - May be it does to them.

Mushroom - To the little human creatures?

Giant Oak Tree - But, yes. What their sense is, however, we do not know, so, for all it matters, it must make some sort of " a sense " even if we cannot fully grasp its direction.

The learned mole-cricket Creatures who throw away leaves are irresponsible creatures.

Mushroom - Even the Mole-crickets are upset, Charlie!

Giant Oak Tree - Regrettable situation, indeed, but true. Even the renowned Investigative Branch of the Ministry of the Interior of the Nation of Centipedes, did undertake a series of methodical and very serious studies of that particular situation and it confirmed the findings of the owls .

Mushroom - With all those legs they must have certainly covered a lot of ground in their investigation, I guess .

Chorus of the Centipedes - You guessed right .

Mushroom - I did not mean to be facetious , illustrious Centipedes : only a detailed remark .

Chorus of the Centipedes - You couldn't have done any better even if you had a hundred heads .

Mushroom - I am pretty sure about that : fortunately I have only a hat and that protects me from rain or snow ,and centipedes too .

Chorus of the Centipedes - You sound like one of those little, funny creatures who pick up leaves and then throw them away . They seem to talk like that to each other.

Mushroom - Charlie. Did you hear that ? The Centipedes have ears !!

Giant Oak Tree - Figuratively so , dear Fabius .

Chorus of the Centipedes - And not very large , either , like some other creatures we know and , by sheer observation , it seem to us that you have a very large......well.....let us say ....head ?

Mushroom - Centipedes !! Once a Centipede always a Centipede .

The learned mole-cricket - Regrettable . Indeed , regrettable .

Giant Oak Tree - Enough of this nonsense, all of you ! I am sorry I allowed myself to be drawn into this unbecoming squabble .

Chorus of the Squabbles - Hurrah ! For the Giant Oak ! Hurrah !....and , please , leave us out of any squabbles between all of you ! Thank you .

The learned mole-cricket - Hurrah ! And, hurrah also for the squabbles : sometime , common sense in our lives comes from unexpected sources too .

Mushroom - What about common sense ? ? Where were we ??

Giant Oak Tree - Right here where we were and always are : where else could we be ?

The learned mole-cricket - Excellent common sense , and , indeed , a rare gift and an even rarer virtue in a Giant . I am proud of you , Giant Oak .

Mushroom - Oh ! Don't tell him that or it will be impossible to live near him anymore !

The learned mole-cricket - Well , you can always try to live under him , as I most often do ,when I am foraging for myself .

Giant Oak Tree - Well put , dear Mole ; anyway I think that the mushroom was giggling under his hat when he said that !

The learned mole-cricket - Well, it's getting late, so , bye , bye Giant Oak , and it was nice knowingi you but I must leave now and join my fellow moles at the evening symposium of our Elders , " the Orthopteran Insects Guild " of the " Fasgonuroidei " Clan.

Giant Oak Tree - Bye , good old Mole-cricket : it was nice meeting you . Have fun at the Symposium .

The learned Mole-cricket - Thank you , Giant Oak . Bye , now .

Mushroom - Ta , Ta ! ...and don't forget to write , sometime.

Giant Oak Tree - You need not be so strident in return for a kind farewell from a learned insect, Dear Mushroom ! Are you , may be , jealous ?

Mushroom - Jealous of What ? Being down here , my dear Giant , you cannot afford to be jealous of anything ,not even of yourself , in order to live . With so much going on day in and day out , nights included , it is almost a privilege to be able to breathe , and , least of all , to be jealous of anything or anybody . My dear Charlie , if you only knew what's going on down here , even at night, when you are sleeping , peacefully , up there in the clear air , you probably would lose all of your leaves just for the shock of it .

Giant Oak Tree - Now that you say that , dear Fabius , I begin to think that what the owls and the long eared owls had told me the other day , makes real sense .

Mushroom - I am really glad that something begins to make some sense !What was it ?

Giant Oak Tree - I'll tell you : the long eared owls told me that they had , in turn , heard from informers , long eared owls of their own clan , who had been successful in building a comfortable and secure nest well sheltered from the weather in a niche under the roof of one of those giant nests, but , although well protected from the weather , yet they could not rest well because of the pandemonium that was going on every night .

Mushroom - Were those little humans fighting in there ? I wouldn't be surprised if they did , since it appears that they like to do that at every possible opportunity , and , if no opportunity occurs ,then they create one just for the occasion and then start a fight . Strange , though , that they would want to do it at night .

Giant Oak Tree - Well , what I heard is that those large white leaves are being prepared , actually manufactured , during the night .

Mushroom - I wonder why at night ,when everybody else goes to sleep , and those white leaves to be made at night instead in the normal daylight ,of all the odds !!

Giant Oak Tree - They are made at night because , dear Fabius , they will carry the news of the events that happened during the day .

Mushroom - Very , very strange idea . Why to give so much importance to what happened the previous day , I wonder ?

Giant Oak Tree - Well , the long eared owls tell me that they heard that these little humans seem very interested in finding out who had fallen down the ladder and who broke his head , who killed his wife or who was killed by somebody else's wife , who went bankrupt , who went to war and who did not , and who got richer and who got poorer , and who graduated from school and who remained an idiot , who married whom and who got lost along the way to a marriage and who had an affair with somebody else's wife........

Mushroom - Spicy , isn't it ?

Giant Oak Tree - That's up to anyone's fancy interpretation . Anyway it goes on and on ,and, as soon as the news are learned , these human creatures do not seem content or satisfied with what they learned and want many more news ,which are after all always the same , more or less , and so they throw away those white leaves which had the news of the previous day , anxious to get those of the next day , although the stories , to a great degree , never change much in scope and style ..

Mushroom - This is absolutely senseless . That is an inexplicable waste . I wonder whether these leaves could at least be picked up and saved for some good use , even food , may be, in case of a famine in Winter time : right ?

Giant Oak Tree -	Food for the Winter ? But not even for Autumn , Spring or Summer , my boy!! These leaves are not for eating but only to be looked at , as the Fox did when looking at the grapes set too high on the vine for her to reach them: "Oh , well , they are not ripe yet , anyway " ! ....and I hear that some of these human creatures appear to be highly specialized creatures and look into those white leaves through small pieces of ice in front of their eyes and it seems that those who wear them, command a lot of respect by wearing them, being regarded as great thinkers and highly skilled interpreters of what 's on those leaves .
Mushroom -	The more anybody talks about those leaves and the more it seems to me that those white leaves are not leaves at all .
Long eared Owl -	But they look like leaves .
Mushroom -	They may seem so , but I begin to believe that these things are manufactured things , artificially , and may be of the same category and consistency and property of the net built by spiders : instead of flies they trap and catch news. .
Giant Oak Tree -	Not quite ,dear Fabius , but the comparison you made with the spider's web fits well because many of these creatures , the little human creatures , I mean, at times can hurt you more than the bite of a spider would .
Mushroom -	How horrible .
Giant Oak Tree -	Horrible , you said ? My dear little mushroom it is well known that these little human creatures can bite too, not literally, but even more insidiously , with an "intent "to bite and,this noticeable characteristic, appears well documented by facts in our daily existences. You yourself had told me just a little while ago that some of your Ancestors , a renegade type of tribe , became aggressively angry and venomous to other creatures : didn't you tell me that?
Mushroom -	Yes , I remember telling you that but , you see , they can be easily recognized before they can do any harm .
Giant Oak Tree -	But it may be still very difficult to recognize the good ones from the bad ones, for somebody who has never seen them before .
Mushroom -	Well, they have characteristics that will be easily recognized, but the gentle little human creature can be all smiles while sweetly looking at you , and then, , when you don't look , they'll bite you .
Giant Oak Tree -	Well, let the sleeping dog lie,and let's go back to our white leaves:shall we?

Mushroom - By all means ! So , it seems to me that , in final analysis , nobody knows what these white leaves really are .

Long eared Owl - But they look like leaves .

Mushroom - Well , I understand that and I appreciate that : granted , they have on them lines , they have dots , designs and blots , but so do also many other leaves and that is the reason , perhaps , why they can be readily mistaken for a regular leaf but , perhaps , of some yet obscure order .

Long eared Owl - But they look like regular leaves .

Mushroom - White ??

Learned Owl - White , square and rectangular : some leaves inside the leaves can also be yellow , red , blue , and green . A leaf is a leaf and it always will be a leaf .

Mushroom - Square and rectangular ? I'd like to see the day when these will show up !

Chorus of the squares and the rectangulars- What would be wrong with it ? Some of the human beings are already like that .

Learned Owl - Fortunately , they are not aware of that : if they did , they would go around in circles .

Chorus of the Circles - That would be desirable : we are circles and what's in stays in and what's out stays out . We are perfect and we believe that everything should be a circle .

Earned Owl - The leaves too ?

Chorus of the Circles - But of course !....just a matter of adjustment to what they represent now .

Learned Owl - Like what ?

Chorus of the Circles - They are already in , shall we say , " circulation ", are they not ? Were they circles too they would even run faster and further . We believe that everything should be a circle : leaves , birds , bananas and asparagus , zucchini and pears, trees and mushrooms , humans and all creatures , lakes , rivers and oceans , mountains and volcanos , lizards and frogs .

Learned Owl - Oh ! For the Universe !!! The insane power of misrepresented ideas !!!

Chorus of the frogs and the lizards - Leaves , leaves , oh , you dear leaves , big , large and small and slender leaves, dear friends and indefatigable protectors of we poor little creatures ! We find refuge in you , we often rest on you , or take shelter under you . We do not know how to read you , like the human creatures do , but you are very dear to us , and we do not ever throw you away .

Chorus of the leaves- Tremulous , slender , light and graceful we are , we can be large , medium and small , also very , very small , but what importance has all this ? We are just leaves and we are very happy to be leaves . Nothing is traced on us in fancy characters , only the regular marks of distinction of our heritage , and, as the seasons go by , we carry the coveted caress of the sun , the wetness of the rain , the dust of the pollen in Spring time and the soft mantle of the snow in Winter time . Comes Autumn , our colour changes . And when we softly float down to the ground , finally to rest close to our dear friends whom we did protect from rain and the scorching sun of the Summer , we lay a soft mantle on that ground and , under that mantle , warm and safe , the little insects go busy building their little houses and are protected from the rigors of the oncoming frigid season . There is nothing ,really , to be read on us . At least , our Mother Leaf , never told us anything about it . We feel certain that , had there been something to read , we would have been told about that by our teachers at school when we were young .

Mushroom - Did you hear that , Charlie ?

Giant Oak Tree - Hear what ?

Mushroom - These chants from down here ! The frogs and the lizards praising the leaves and expressing gratitude towards the leaves for their help and friendship .

Giant Oak Tree - I have enough chants here every morning from the birds, dear Fabius , I really do not need an extra dose of chanting from frogs and lizards .

Mushroom - Their chant was touching , Charlie , nostalgic and sentimental .

Giant Oak Tree - Everything ,my dear Fabius , can be manipulated into something sentimental and touching , when you want to .

Mushroom - I don't know about that , Charlie .

Giant Oak Tree - What I meant , dear Fabius , was that there always will be other creatures different from you who will interpret things , facts , events and other creatures' feelings in a different manner , sometime even opposite to what yours were , sometime even confrontational to what yours were and , sometime again , even offensively directed towards you !

Chorus of the other creatures different from you - Oh , yeah ?

Mushroom - I hear some dissension , dear Charlie !

Giant Oak Tree - That's a normal trait in the span of our existences , dear Fabius , even in this Forest .

Chorus of the Forests - That is true ! Dissension is a necessary ingredient in the free expression and the inalienable right of trees to speak up for themselves .

Mushroom - Charlie , I am afraid that we might have just started something that we had not intended to start !!

Giant Oak Tree - Nothing to worry about ,dear Fabius ! As I said , dissensions are a normal trend in this Forest , I assure you .

Chorus of the other creatures different from you - Oh , yeah ?

Mushroom - I would suggest to leave all of them alone , before we get involved in something else , dear Charlie !

Giant Oak Tree - Disrespectful impudents these other creatures , Fabius : just ignore them and let us go back to our owls and their extraordinary investigations .

Chorus of the other creatures different from you - Oh , yeah ?

Giant Oak Tree - Yeah ! And yeah ! And yeah , again to all of you !!

Chorus of the other creatures different from you - Well, well ! What do you know ! You say that very well : congratulations !

Mushroom - Charlie , listen to me and let us go back to our owls , quickly , before we get caught into an unpleasant confrontation with these unintellectual teasers !

Chorus of the other creatures different from you - Oh , yeah ?

Mushroom - Yeah ! And go jump in the lake , if you all can find one .

Chorus of the other creatures different from you - The impertinence of those creatures different from us !

Chorus of some other creatures different from some others - Indeed !......and an unending reality ! You cannot change when you are different .

The learned mole-cricket - Wise guys .

Giant Oak Tree - Ah , dear little Mole , how come you are back ? What brought you back among us ?

The learned mole-cricket - I was getting along fine near your roots , getting something to eat , when I was interrupted in my work by a shaking of your roots . Anything wrong , dear Oak tree ?

Giant Oak Tree - Not really , dear Mole , not really . Just a few words , back and forth , with some Jokers who like to tease other creatures different from them while being total dead sacks themselves in learning how to live and behave in a changing world .

Chorus of the other creatures different from anyone else - We would not go that far in describing us : don't you know that variety and differences in style , customs , ways of representing one self , attitudes , and various and even questionable virtues , are at the basis of the interesting aspect of life , not only for us ,but for all " created " creatures and , may be, " things " too ?

The learned mole-cricket - Quite . Why don't you adopt that enlightened representation for yourselves and all other creatures different from whatever else you can think of .

Chorus of the other creatures different from anyone else - We'll try .

Mushroom - You know what, Charlie ?

Giant Oak Tree - No : I don't .

Mushroom - Not everything that's different is inherently void of some form of favourable recognition .

Giant Oak Tree- If you say so .

The learned mole-cricket - I agree .

Giant Oak Tree - Well, as the old refrain goes ,even in our Forests , " if you cannot understand them , ignore them" , so I'll go and chat with my owls and long eared owls. We seem to understand each other quite well.

Mushroom - No harm done , dear Charlie ! We are only talking ! By the way , may I join you in the conversation with the owls ?

Giant Oak Tree - Of course , dear Fabius : you are always welcome to join me in any conversation , be it with the owls , the birds or frogs and lizards ,all of whom you seem to be quite fond of .

Mushroom - Well, Charlie, if you put it that way ,I am not so sure of the actual amount of welcome I would be allowed for joining you in some conversation .

Giant Oak Tree - Don't pay any attention to it , dear Fabius , I was just talking ,and , really , you are most welcome to join me . What is your interest at this time , Fabius?

Mushroom - Yes , Charlie , when we were talking about those white leaves and all the blah, blah about unheard of circumstances and strange "visions" by investigative owls , long eared owls and centipedes , we never concluded the evidence about those small pieces of ice in front of the eyes of some notable creatures reading those white leaves .

Giant Oak Tree - It's true : we never elaborated on them . Well , Fabius , what about them ?

Mushroom - It just occurred to me that if those little pieces of ice go along efficiently in rigid weather , as I am sure they are , I just wondered , though , how would or could they survive in a warmer climate . Aren't those leaves put together also in the Summer months ? Wouldn't they melt in the Summer heat ?

Giant Oak Tree - It doesn't seem so . They appear to last Winter , Spring , Summer and Autumn . They , also , do not resemble or look exactly like ice ,at least that seemed to have been the impression of the long eared owl who had the opportunity to see a pair of those icy "things " closely , after one of those "notable " old creatures had taken those icy things out of his eyes , or so it seemed , and put them aside , while blowing his nose . The long eared owl also told me that they appeared to him even clearer than ice itself .

Mushroom - I don't know , but I have seen some ice that is perfectly clear .

Giant Oak Tree - Yes , I know , but this ice is different and , for one thing , it does not melt, ever , and , once it is worn by a creature , it never changes its configuration and its usage . In all my long existence in this Forest , dear Fabius.......

Mushroom - And that is a pretty long existence , Charlie ! A real long time !

Giant Oak Tree - Yes, Fabius , it is . Well, I was saying that in all my life in this Forest I have never seen anyone , and I mean ANYONE , using those little ice things in front of their eyes , not even our trees , believe it or not , including myself , in order to see what's going around . I tell you , dear Fabius , this is very , very and , again , very strange !

Mushroom - Do you believe that , may be , it could be a sign of some form of sickness , or an hereditary "affliction" that "affects" only these strange little creatures who often appear as totally unable to see any further than their noses . They do have a nose , I suppose ?

Giant Oak Tree - You , dear Fabius , so close to the ground as you are , should be in a privileged position to better observe these strange creatures who wander around our Forest, seemingly always looking for something : how could you have missed the opportunity to observe whether they have a nose or not?

Mushroom - I understand your point , Charlie , but , really , that is not the point .

Giant Oak Tree - What " point " would it be , then ?

Mushroom - No point , really , dear Charlie , but a question .

Giant Oak Tree - Let us hear it ,dear Fabius : you seem always to be reluctant to accept logical representations .

Mushroom - Well , let me explain why I seem unwilling to accept logical representations, for one, every time I see one of these human creatures or some of them coming around and looking here and there for something , who knows what it's still a mystery , they , most of the time , send out several dogs in front of them and these dogs run around the trees with their noses close to the ground, sniffing the soil continuously and , when they seem to have sniffed something , they stop and begin to break up the soil and dig around the roots of the trees where they sniffed something and when "something" is found , these little human creatures quickly pick up that " something " that the dogs had found and place it in their satchels and off they go again , dogs in front of them , the dogs' noses close to the ground and the merry-go-round continues .

Giant Oak Tree- Fabius , this what you just said is great , but what has it got to do with your question whether these little human creatures have a nose or not ??

Mushroom - Well , Charlie , my initial question wondering whether they had a nose or whether they did not , stemmed precisely from my observation of these creatures using dogs to do the "sniffing " for them , causing me to wonder whether they did have a nose or not , and , if they did have a real nose , this did not appear to be functioning well or giving a satisfactory performance if they needed a dog to sniff for them odours , scents , aromas and fragances.

Giant Oak Tree - But leave alone their noses , Fabius !! Forget about scents , aromas , and fragrances all of which has , at least in my opinion , very marginal importance. Sometime , not to posses a functioning nose , can be of a great help in our every day life , particularly with so many characters around .

Mushroom - Oh , well , it's fine with me . After all , this talk about strange happenings and weird human creatures , investigative centipedes and even crazy owls and crazier long eared owls does not get us anywhere in this crazy World of our Forest. What do we really care or care to wonder at these human creatures taking off their skins at night time and putting it back on as the sun comes on the horizon ? Let them do it , if they like it , and , as to the white leaves and the icy pads in front of their eyes , ...well....I just thought......it seems that only some of them wear those icy pads ,so , the mystery deepens : why not all of them ? Are , by any chance , those who wear them , members of some elite Clan ?

Giant Oak Tree - I do not know , but it is true that not all of those creatures wear the icy pads. Why it is so , don't ask me .

Mushroom - I guess , a logical explanation , possibly , could be that not all of them need those icy pads in order to see .

The learned mole-cricket - Interesting deduction .

Mushroom - Thank you .

The learned mole-cricket - Don't mention it .

Mushroom - I won't.

Giant Oak Tree - Oh, well, one thing never seems to change or even slightly deviate from a rigid and yet remarkable pattern and that is the never ever faltering resilience of youth.

Mushroom - I would readily go along with your encouraging definition of "youth " but, Charlie, what brought up, so suddenly, such a remark ?

Giant Oak Tree - You and the mole-cricket.

Mushroom - I'll be darn !!??....I and the mole-cricket the embodiment of Youth ???!!

Giant Oak Tree - but, of course, dear Fabius, and you would not expect me to be a representative of youth ,old as I am, but you, dear little mushroom, born just yesterday and the mole- cricket, likely, born the day before yesterday, fit very well in the methodical repetition of that constant Law of Nature by which you, I and the mole cricket exist, with the resilience of the young as the ice-breaker in the hard sea of our lives.

The learned mole-cricket - My Grand Mother would have loved to hear this.

Mushroom - The way you express yourself, dear Charlie, gives the impression that you descend from a Family of Universal Origins. I am very impressed.

Chorus of the Idiots - We too are very much impressed.

Giant Oak Tree - Dear Fabius, you force me, now, into the open and into the sacred meanders of my life and that of my Ancestors, but you said it well and it is true that I descend from a Family of Universal Origins of countless years when it adorned the avenues of those famous temples of learning and wisdom and the unending desire of knowledge. Yes, dear Fabius, it is true and my history should be a simple yet positive point of reference of our existences and of those bound to come, a luminous guide, if light may be invoked by simple trees, for all those trees that will follow us, to remind them that the universal knowledge is at the basis of a healthy equilibrium, physical, mental, and moral, so, my dear little mushroom, dear Fabius, I may as well represent a direct line in our universal heredity of continuity in this Forest of ours.

Mushroom - I am still very impressed.

Chorus of the Idiots- We too are still very impressed, and in praise of Continuity we will continue to be very impressed during Winter, Spring and Autumn and also during the hot Summer and we are absolutely sure that it would be absolutely stupid to do it in any different way .

Chorus of the Seasons - Continuity is fundamental essence , but not necessarily a requisite of it .

Chorus of the Idiots- We couldn't agree more ! Only stupid creatures would not understand .

Mushroom - I should be classified as a stupid creature , then , because I don't understand a thing in all this gibberish talk , with a dubious patrimony of any significance .

Chorus of the Idiots- We couldn't agree more .

Chorus of the Seasons- Nothing dubious in the significance of Continuity which reflects equally upon idiots , stupid creatures , mushrooms , trees , beetles , squirrels , leaves , rambling ivy , birds with wings , feathers and beaks as well as the other type of something like birds or , shall we say , flightless creatures in all directions, dimensions and scope , like mental acuity , who have no wings , no feathers and no beaks and who take off their skins every evening before going to bed for the night and put it back on in the morning upon waking up with the rising of the sun, except , of course , for the ones who have activities at night and who , for obvious but , yet , uncertified reasons , will take their skins off during the day and keep it on during the night . In final analysis , Continuity, encompasses every creature and everything that has been created , that is it " includes comprehensively " the entire range of what has been created and, likely , what might be created in the future , provided , of course , that the comprehension of " future " exists in the Nature's Dictionary .

Chorus of the Idiots- We are very impressed with the adamant and stringent explanation of the logic accompanying such highly flavoured enunciation of the Laws of Continuity , and we feel most emphatically and comprehensively included in whatever was proclaimed , whatever that was .

Chorus of the Seasons - As we were saying , before being so rudely interrupted by disgustedly hopeful " Discerners " of the nature of created things , declaiming sermons in the easy Temple of Hindsight , as we were saying , in our seasonal opinion we believe that Continuity has no virtual form and , as a consequence , it can be applied to whatever anyone's imagination would allow it to go . We are claiming this because we are the Seasons and we " continue " one after the other in methodical , never changing sequence of Continuity , without giving a darn to one season or another .

Mushroom - Excellent ,excellent !!........But , incidentally , who ever requested your opinion ?

Chorus of the Seasons - The Giant Oak Tree referred to us " by mentioning our name " : is it not an acknowledged form of common courtesy , to reply in earnest to the call ?

Mushroom - But of course it is , of course ! But I was not thinking about that and my thoughts were elsewhere .

Chorus of the Seasons - Where were ,then , your thoughts , dear Mushroom of the forest ?

Mushroom - Darn if I know ! It is this here big tree that talks too much .

Giant Oak Tree - I TALK TOO MUCH ???!! For all the Gods in the Universe and in our Forest , just look who's talking..!!!........You , my dear little Mushroom , have not stopped one second from talking here and then until now and , at this point , you accuse me of being a chatterbox !!......Absolutely incredible ...just incredible , I'll say !

Chorus of the garrulous Creatures- We believe that there is nothing wrong in chatting : only nervous, easily irritable creatures , plants in general and animals , always in general , of course , do not suffer our chatting . And we further consider that some simple but lively chatting , or a wholesome , prickly yackety-yak are a healthful introduction to joviality and cheerfulness , and also bring about a lifting of the spirits , promote friendship , contribute to the exchange of ideas, whatever they are or might have been ....

The learned mole-cricket - I wonder .

Chorus of the Garrulous Creatures - Well ...whatever we were saying ...

The learned mole-cricket - ...and that's about right !

Chorus of the garrulous Creatures - Right or wrong it is "whatever" and we stick by it , so , our chatting facilitates the transmission of those ideas.......

The learned mole-cricket - Whatever they may be ....

Chorus of the garrulous Creatures - Right !.....and whatever they might have been .

The learned mole-cricket - Golly !

Chorus of the garrulous Creatures- And we continue to be , unless rudely interrupted by unnecessary and intellectually tepid remarks , a vivid font of general information , news, facts , happenings , and with an added spicy accentuation of discriminating gossip . In other words , chit-chatting is good , it does not hurt , but it is a complete different story when our " Imitators " , the Supreme , Perennial , Unabashed Ladies of unbridled loquacity , those gentle Creatures who enjoy themselves in perpetual chatting , saying all and achieving nothing , whence the " blah , blah " of expression took its origin .

Chorus of the Ladies of unbridled loquacity - My ! Oh ! My !.....Just listen to these villains trying to redeem themselves for their own vices by implying that our vernacular conversations are the reason for " wasting time and accomplishing nothing " , while covering up for the distortion of their own vile , ludicrous and vulgar blabbering ,and , at the same time , trying to stick their noses into everybody's business .

Mushroom - Ah ! At last here comes someone who has a nose !!...Hurrah !!

Chorus of the Ladies of unbridled loquacity - Yes , exactly so ! They stick their noses into everything that 's none of their business, just as we were saying before being interrupted by this here microcosmic mushroom , everybody's business including ours ,these chatter boxes ..! DOWN WITH THE CHATTER-BOXES !

Chorus of the Idiots- We couldn't agree more , even if all the others did not !

Chorus of the Ladies of unbridled loquacity - And ,by the way , who are " these others " you are referring to ?

Chorus of the Idiots - The Stupid Creatures , naturally .

Chorus of the Stupid Creatures - All of you , just leave us in peace ! We do not cause anybody any harm and we do not stand in anybody's way , or interfere in the private business of other fellow creatures , so well endowed as we are of such explicit intellectual inertia that assures us of our coveted existence void of "Highs" and "Lows" in the interpretation of the basic functions of every created creature that wanders in this Forest of ours or somewhere else , if , of course, elsewhere might be found somewhere, be it a thing or a creature , the difference between the two , however , not known to us or understood by us, anyway our esteemed Directory has officially endorsed that serene literary expression of a famous essayist of antiquity who wrote : " People with dim intellects , and those are the majority ...." , the rule , of course , freely applicable to created creatures , wheresoever they may be , therefore as a consequence of that enlightened endorsement............GET LOST ALL OF YOU , and leave us in peace , you blasted IDIOTS ..!!

Chorus of the Idiots - We couldn't agree more . Very well put . Thank you .

Chorus of the garrulous Creatures- To hell with all of you , Idiots , Mushrooms , Stupid Creatures , Giant Trees, learned Moles and Others , enough is enough and more than enough of enough of all this frivolous chatting , so , with the approval of our most affectionate heart ....TO HELL WITH ALL OF YOU ! Is it , by any conceivable reason, our fault if these strange " other " creatures without wings , without feathers, without a beak and without an effectively functioning nose , as suspected by this here most illustrious Mushroom , and who take off their skins every night before they go to bed and sleep and put it back in the morning....incredible , really , incredible ,.....well , anyway , is it our fault if these strange little creatures make of our legitimate instincts and talents their own perverse vices ?

Chorus of the Vices- Vice is ,also , our business . But , by the way , who are these " strange little Creatures " you are referring to , who have no wings and no feathers and , to all current evidence , very little , if any , of anything else ? They do ,we are sure , sport a " name " , don't they ?

Chorus of the learned Elders - They go under the name of : " Humans " .

Chorus of the Vices- " Humans " ? Is that " all " ? Strange , very strange .

Chorus of the learned Elders - Why strange ? " human " is the singular voice if you are referring to only one of them , but you would correctly say " Humans " if you are indicating several of them . Now , as to your commenting expression of " strange " underlying your surprise at the simplicity of the noun used to describe these strange little creatures , that is " Humans ", which you , quite appropriately, though unconsciously were correct in its interpretation of " strange ", well, indeed , "human" is synonymous with " strange " .

Chorus of the Vices- Interesting . Now , you say that “strange “ is synonymous with “human “, right ?

Chorus of the learned Elders - Right .

Chorus of the Vices- But, HOW ???!........” strange “ is not even a headword with two meanings and does not even come close to it !!.... Besides , what does “synonymous “ mean ?

Chorus of the stupid Creatures - Oh ! My ! And we are supposed to be stupid !!!

Chorus of the Vices- Never mind and hold your mouths ! We are talking to the Elders !

Chorus of the stupid Creatures - Good . Don’t mind us and go right ahead ! We are talking to no one .

Chorus of the Vices- Sorry for the interruption ! So , please, what does “synonymous “ mean ?

Chorus of the learned Elders- “Synonymous “ signifies that a specific word has the same fundamental meaning of another and is accepted as another name for the same idea or significance .

Chorus of the Vices - So ?

Chorus of the learned Elders - So , what it means is that “strange”, because of its characteristic of descriptive unorthodox significance about the behaviour of phenomena , events , and the many and various attitudes of the creatures floating around , is also able to portray , with remarkable accuracy , the turbulent and ever changing temper of the human mind , the fluctuations of its character , the multiple spiritual tendencies from ascetic to torpid to self-indulgent and anything in-between, the infamous conceit and the serene humility , the tepid self-respect and the sublime ambitions of the human race , while , at the same time , giving rise and “some good reasons “ to reservations about human aims , purpose and deeds .

Chorus of the Vices- Very , very interesting , indeed !.....Yes , very , very interesting .

Chorus of the stupid Creatures - Not to us .

Chorus of the Vices- Well , well , here is another “interesting “ point , dear learned and wise Elders!

Chorus of the wise and learned Elders- And which one "point " might that be ?

Chorus of the Vices - Is there a synonym for "stupid " ?

Chorus of the wise and learned Elders- but of course there is a synonym for "stupid " .

Chorus of the Vices- Really , now !! We were only joking !....But are you serious about one in existence ?

Chorus of the wise and learned Elders- Positively .

Chorus of the stupid Creatures- We are not at all interested in this stupid game of " synonyms " : only dim-witted creatures would be .

Chorus of the Vices- Look who's talking..!!!.....Well , wise and learned Elders what is your "positively" assured answer ?..Please , ignore those stupid creatures .

Chorus of the wise and learned Elders- Very well , then . The synonym for " stupid " is " everything " .

Chorus of the Vices- Nice joke .

Chorus of the stupid Creatures- THERE IS WISDOM IN A JEST .

Chorus of the Vices- Very funny , but don't forget that you are included .

Chorus of the stupid Creatures- And so are you .

Chorus of the Vices- Oh, well , that synonym , anyway , does not refer to me , you stupid creatures!

Chorus of the stupid creatures- We heard that "refrain" before when we were in our infancy .

Chorus of the Vices- You heard...WHAT ...before ??

Chorus of the stupid Creatures- Yes , we did hear the story of a fox , narrated by a famous man in antiquity, and this fox , feeling hungry , was looking at some grapes wanting to eat them but , unable to reach them , being these grapes hung too high on the vine , left the vineyard saying : " Oh , well , they are not ripe ,yet , anyway!" And that's what we heard in our infancy .

Chorus of the Vices- Interesting story ,but someone, just a while ago in this Forest , had mentioned it , so , it seem to us , that it is a well " stereotyped " " type " of common usage quote to satisfy the inability of stupid creatures to speak for themselves : right?

Chorus of the Stupid Creatures- Wrong .

Chorus of the Vices- May be we " phrased " it wrongly , by using a vocabulary not compatible with the teaching at the adolescent Academy of Stupidity, in your infancy : right ?

Chorus of the stupid Creatures- Wrong , again .

Chorus of the Vices- We have to admit it that your persistent consistency in rebuking , denying , denouncing and correcting other creatures' interpretation of existencies in general , is quite astonishing , in spite of your dim qualifications .

Chorus of the stupid Creatures- Nothing is "astonishing" in stupidity .

Chorus of the Vices- We wholeheartedly agree with that !

Chorus of the stupid Creatures- Except , of course , for those who agree with it .

Chorus of the Vices- There you go again..!!!..You , little stupid and , as an extra measure ,dim-witted , spoiled brats ! Why don't you try to pay some attention to your mental health , instead of contradicting everyone at every plausible and unplausible occasion ....Now , was this senseless trend towards perpetual contradiction a basic course offered by the Academy of Stupidity in your enlightened infancy of stupidity ?

Chorus of the stupid Creatures- Wrong again and for the third time and , three times , usually , makes perfect, at least that's what they say......well , to answer your question , "contradiction" was not a basic topic of learning in our education , during our infancy and early childhood : it was entirely knowledge , study and wisdom.

Chorus of the Vices- Unheard of story !!.....And what brought up , then , the sad demise of your knowledge , study and wisdom and changed you into stupid creatures , oh , so very stupid Creatures !!

Chorus of the stupid Creatures- You did .

Chorus of the Vices- Of all the nerve and shame !!!..How dare you say such a lie ??!

Chorus of the stupid Creatures- " Lies " and " Lying " do not fit well with the fabric of stupid Creatures ! That is why we are considered stupid because we always say the truth and indicate things as they are , as they appear to be and how they appear to us, having forgotten how to say anything differently or changing its meaning or significance depending on circumstances as interpreted by creatures with enlightened intellects .

Chorus of the Vices- This is an outrage !! Worse than that : it is just rubbish ! This kind of talk can only be appropriate for impudent creatures .

Representative of impudent Creatures- We resent that unfavourable remark .

Chorus of the stupid Creatures- We too .

Chorus of the Vices- Fine , fine !!... Quiet all of you ! By the way when did you find out and realized that it was or that you thought that it might have been our supposed wrong doing to cause your knowledge , your study and your wisdom to disappear , and all of you slipping into total stupidity ?....Did you , by any chance , learn that at your famous Academy of Stupidity ? We wonder !!

Chorus of the stupid Creatures- No , we did not .

Chorus of the Vices- Where , then ? You must have come to it from some source or from some Information Agency or some School of stupid wise men or just by hearsay evidence , did you not ?

Chorus of the stupid Creatures- No we did not .

Chorus of the Vices- We begin to see quite clearly now , why stupid creatures are called stupid !!

Chorus of the intelligent Creatures- We feel really sorry for them !

Chorus of the stupid Creatures- Please , enlightened intelligent Creatures , do not feel sorry for us : we do not feel sorry for ourselves since we do not know that : only creatures who are not stupid know that we are ,or , think that , may be , they are not . As to the repeated questions by the reputable Chorus of the Vices , our answer is still the same , stupidly sad and totally and always the same , incredibly the same, exasperatingly the same , ...: " Yes , we do not ! " , because , plain and clear, there are nor there ever were any Institutions , Schools , Academies ,or Wise Stupid Men or , for all it matters , any "hearsay evidence " to tell us about the origin of our mental handicap , but we learned about it as we came of age and saw the World of our Forest and its short comings and goings , side comings and long goings , diagonal and trapezoidal comings and rectangular , circular and square-circular goings and , quite clearly in the front row view , the coming of the large cesspool of your vices .

Chorus of the Vices- YOU , STUPID CREATURES , YOU are disgusting , untrue and villainous! The appellative of stupid well fits your torpid reasoning .!

(Then , the Vices , turning to the Elders)

Well , wise and learned Elders , what do you make of all this gibberish and insolent , malicious talk ??!

Chorus of the Wise and learned Elders- You figure it out : we are not versed in passing judgements. We only care about synonyms .

Chorus of the Vices- But your answer , dear and , now , rather " evasive " Elders , your answer.....is just and simply PREPOSTEROUS !! Your "joke", we agree, was good , but , then , according to your claimed "interest"in the world of synonyms , and your apparent secure command of the reciprocal compatibility of their identities , then , according to your "synonymous" wizardry ....THE WHOLE WIDE WORLD and EVERYTHING IN IT, COULD BE , SHOULD BE , and actually IS STUPID !!! R I G H T ???

Chorus of the wise and learned Elders- You said that . We didn't . We only care about synonyms .

Chorus of the stupid Creatures- Hallelujah !!

Chorus of the Vices- What kind of creatures have we"collided " with , we wonder !!! What a depressing thought just the experience of communicating with them , if chatting with them could, at all , be considered a communication of any consequence , but , apart from that , it is a nightmare to realize that such creatures and their world actually exist ! They act like scared crows without even a puppet around to scare them !....Oh , well , we'll just repeat the same old refrain of that famous fox , apparently so popular , lately , in this here Forest , if for nothing else , just to remain respectful to the tradition of the literature of antiquity , ...that old refrain , as we were saying , that seems to apply very well to the folks we were talking to and goes something like this : " Just leave them alone , they are not ripe yet ! "

(......and the Vices prepare to leave that side of the Forest..............................)

(Meanwhile , several foxes had entered the Forest and were advancing very cautiously through the thick undergrowth and winding their way between the huge trees , when they were spotted by the Leader of the Group of the Vices as they were getting ready to leave....... ....the Leader of the Group of the Vices , then , turning to his fellow companions , said...................................)

Leader of the Vices- Hold it ! Hold it ! Dear friends ! I see some folks coming this way !

Chorus of the Vices- Some more stupid creatures , by any chance ?

Leader of the Vices- I don't think so : they do not seem stupid .

Chorus of the Vices- How can you tell that , at such a distance just at the edge of the forest and without having had a chance to converse with them ??

Leader of the Vices- They have four legs .

Chorus of the Vices- That makes sense.

Leader of the Vices- Observe : they might have spotted us because they suddenly stopped their advance and looked with some hesitation in our direction but then they seemed to regain their confidence and resumed their walk , to all indications, coming this way , towards us .

Chorus of the Vices- Why don't we try to make friends with them ? They might help us in our business as we get into town .

The Secretary of the Chorus of the Vices- May be . Let's not rush into it , and observe first .

Chorus of the Vices- But , if we wait too long , these creatures will pass us by without even stopping to throw us a furtive and inquisitive glance , may be satisfied that we are not aggressive or dangerous types and we will be missing a golden opportunity to make new friends .

The Chorus of the strait-laced Creatures - Heavens forbid !!!.....Has anyone ever heard of such shameless wickedness promising as a "golden opportunity" that of making friends with a bunch of advocates of VICE...!!!?....Heavens forbid !...what else can be new under the shies in this old Forest ??!!

Chorus of the Vices- Dear Sisters , we..............

The Chorus of the strait-laced Creatures - Don't you EVER " Sisters " us, you infamous guttersnipes of creation's lowest production line , and thieves of creatures's good faith !

Chorus of the Vices- There it goes again !!...If it isn't for the stupid Creatures , then it comes down to the Righteous Sisters of Forests and Parks and you begin to realize how difficult really is to live the life you were meant for . Oh, well , we'll go back again to the old story of ....

The learned mole-cricket - ...of the famous old fox of famous antiquity by a famous writer in the famous days of famous writers , yes ?

Chorus of the Vices- And how do you know that , wise guy ?

The learned mole-cricket - Common knowledge .

Chorus of the Vices- Never heard of such a knowledge : is it common because everybody knows about it or is it something so common , recalling it is considered too common a literary overuse ? Which one , dear Mole ?

The learned mole-cricket- I do not know which one it is or if it is anything like that . Why do you ask?

Chorus of the Vices- We ask because we do not know .

Leading Exponent of Common Knowledge- Sensible answer to an inconclusive question . Forget about it all, blockheads, and practice common sense instead of common knowledge .

The Secretary of the Chorus of the Vices- Your attention, please , your attention , please. Our Leader appears to have seen something and is preparing to pass on to us some new information about present goings . So , pay attention .

Chorus of the Vices- Welcome news . May be he is contemplating the formation of a Committee to try to establish contact with the new creatures spotted wandering in the forest towards us .

Leader of the Vices- Those four legged creatures seem to have stopped again in their advance through the Forest and appear as if looking intensely towards us .

The Secretary of the Chorus of the Vices- Yes , I can see them too, standing still in the same area as we had seen them just a while ago , probably thinking it over whether to proceed on or to retreat or , instead , to communicate with us .

Chorus of the Vices- Yes , yes ! Let's call them ! Right now !!

The Secretary of the Chorus of the Vices- Wait ! Not so fast !! Remember , rushing water rushes away but slow flowing water penetrates and goes deeply into the core of the path that carries it, the water that is , so let not lose our balance and let us temper our enthusiam .

The learned mole-cricket- Cheap wisdom of a bygone era .

Leader of the Vices- Look , they seem to be moving again .

The Secretary of the Chorus of the Vices- And so it appears . Yes , they are moving again ,ever so cautiously though!

Leader of the Vices- Very ,very slowly and guarding too !

The Secretary of the Chorus of the Vices- Yes ,they move slowly and cautiously ,and yet they seem to exhibit a lot of discerning qualities in the way they try to scout the surroundings .

Leader od the Vices- What do they look like to you ?

Secretary of the Vices- I am not quite sure at the present distance from us , but I have a pretty strong hunch that they are foxes .

Leader of the Vices- I am not sure,yet. May be what we should do would be to attempt to slowly cross their path ,at a reasonable distance making it appear as if just a casual encounter and if our presence , our looks and our countenance would stir some interest in the perceptive minds of these newly arrived creatures then, and may be only then , some sort of communication could be established, and............

Chorus of the Vices- What sort of communication , wise Leader ?

Leader of the Vices- You know , a smile , a nodding and , may be, something like : " nice weather we are having to-day ! " and see what happens......

Chorus of the Vices- All that talk while going ? We'll be far away from each other before we can even complete the first sentence !!

Leader of the Vices- We'll spread our lines thin so that what the first few of us in the front will start ,will be continued and brought to term by the last ones in the long line, giving a chance , this way , to the other party to also assess the situation and come up with a choice .

Chorus of the Vices- What if this does not work and they say nothing and let us pass by without attempting to either stop us or call to us ? What then ?

Leader of the Vices- It will mean "then " that they do not give a damn about us .

Chorus of the Vices- Sad ..!!

Leader of the Vices- But , if they should show some response , even a modest one , " THEN " some further contact could be established and an acquaintance formulated , further communication cemented and friendship , eventually , established , all excellent elements that could favour us in the further expansion of our penetration into the yet unexplored fabric of those "strange" creatures whose name , now , was revealed to us .

Chorus of the Vices- HUMANS !!

The Secretary of the Chorus of the Vices- Right !....and I believe that we would not have anything to lose and we would run no risks in trying to get acquainted with these new creatures .After all what's a vice good for if not exported ?

Chorus of the Vices- The Secretary speaks well : let us go closer and call to them in a most friendly way : may be they'll even like us !

— — —

Leader of the Vices- Easy, easy, now ! We have to be reasonable , dear fellows , because WE ,as fully fledged Representatives of a line of some of the finest vices available on the markets of the Wide Forests , as I was saying , "We" have a Reputation to protect and also we need to seriously guard our exquisitely selected vices, which we leased to our most influential Customers, so that these eminent vices would not become depreciated by allowing unknown and , may be , even undeserving potential customers , partake of our finest products .

Chorus of the Vices- Hurrah, for our Leader !

Chorus of the strait-laced Creatures - Hurrah for your DEVIL , you mean !! Your "hurrah" is just blasphemy against the nobility of creation and its glory , and your silent but alert approach to the unaware victims is like the guarded and cautious steps of a fox in search of food approaching a hen-house . You , are Infamous creatures like sleuth hounds in search of the prey . You are like slow crawling worms slithering your way into the naive and unguarded minds of so many unsuspecting creatures , presenting yourselves as the gentlest bearers of untold fountains of pleasure , oceans of joy , delectable projections and infinitely rewarding acts , but to dash those unfortunate ones into your "unyielding and firmly gripping vise" , and into perdition and death!! Shame! Shame ! Shame !

Secretary of the Vices- You know........I just got an idea !

Leader of the Vices- A good one , I hope .

Secretary of the Vices - Didn't we suspect just a while ago that those new creatures wandering in the forest were.........foxes...!!??

Leader of the Vices- Yes : we did . They looked like Foxes . They went around like Foxes .

Secretary of the Vices- Well , our Strait-laced creatures just put the right idea into our minds and the right word into our mouth !

Leader of the Vices- Are you serious ??..And what would they be these enchanted revelations?

Secretary of the Vices- Of course I am serious! FOXES ! FOXES ! The foxes "ARE" our friends!

Chorus of the Vices- Hurrah ! Hurrah ! The Foxes are our friends ! The Foxes are our friends ! Let us go to meet them and tell them who we are and , after what the Strait-laced Creatures just said , they must be very close to us in their dealings with these "strange" Creatures and their assets , whatever they might be , moral , spiritual , material or anything in-between ! So, fellows , let's go !

Chorus of the strait-laced Creatures - Oh ! Heavens above !....Listen , just , listen to these Prophets of moral doom, and their unrepenting and profane wickedness on the march ! Just listen to this ungodly , impious , immoral wickedness on the march for the final assault upon humanity's gullible second nature ! And , Heavens forbid , how many gullible creatures usually take cover in these forests , thinking they are safe , that is the forests and they themselves , when , instead , more dangers lurk all around !! Ah ! If Creatures would only know of the bottomless pit of Vice and Vices !!

****

(Meanwhile , the spinster Sparrows , the two skinny old maids , Andrea and Celeste , whom we had left behind chatting away while resting on a branch of the Giant Oak Tree and had been listening to all the latest developments that had been going on in the Forest , just close to the Giant Oak Tree and the Mushroom , looked at each other and......................)

****

1st Spinster (Celeste) - Well , my dear Andrea , did you hear all this interesting and encouraging hullabaloo of all sorts and things and wonders , an unexpected interlude of friendship , understanding and comradery. ? Did you pay any attention.........

2nd Spinster (Andrea) - Well , yes , I did . But tell me : what's " comradery " ?

?

1st Spinster (Celeste) - Close friendship...."comradeship" the folks in the next Forest probably would rather say .

2nd Spinster (Andrea) - Oh , I see . Friendliness , right ?

1st Spinster (Celeste) - More or less .

2nd Spinster(Andrea)- I see .

1st Spinster
(Celeste) - Well , Andrea , not quite satisfied about the explanation of "comradery"?

2nd Spinster
(Andrea) - Oh, yes , yes , of course !

1st Spinster
(Celeste) - So , you do remember the time when we stopped our conversation a while ago, and chose to watch for possible developments rather than talk about them and just speculate on the basis of fear , anxiety and concern ?

2nd Spinster
(Andrea) - Of course I do , Celeste ! I remember telling you how worried I was at what I suspected was going on in our Forest .

1st Spinster
(Celeste) - Yes , Andrea , I remember it quite well . How could I have forgotten it , I am asking you !

2nd Spinster
(Andrea) - Well , you did not seem quite convinced , then , of anything unusual going on down there , with mushrooms , market creatures , caterpillars , sinister looking characters and annoying birds .

1st Spinster
Celeste) - We are Birds too, Andrea ! Am I annoying you ?!

2nd Spinster
(Andrea) - Present company excepted !

1st Spinster
(Celeste) - That does not change our being birds , Andrea.

2nd Spinster
(Andrea) - What I meant was : " we are not annoying Birds " .

1st Spinster
Celeste) - I understand , Andrea , I understand : I was only teasing . Sometime , it is hard to go along even with your own kind .

2nd Spinster
(Andrea) - Yes , it is true and unfortunate too .

!st Spinster
(Celeste) - Well , it was not that I was disinterested in caterpillars , mushrooms and

sinister looking creatures , Andrea , but my nature does not allow me to become excited about something that has not happened yet or something that might or might not ever happen anyway , or about something I have no way of assessing it myself , devoid as I am of the help of secret agents , emissaries or spies, or a good instruction book to tell you how to do it .

2nd Spinster
(Andrea) - You are dramatizing the issue , my dear Celeste ! All you really need are two ears and some intuitive salt in your brain and , then , you can add one and one and figure out things for yourself .

1st Spinster
(Celeste) - I cannot count , Andrea .

2nd Spinster
(Andrea) - Too bad ! Too bad ! Anyway , my worries were in some way justified , Celeste , by just listening and observing the events which developed below our perch , in so many and varied circumstances and acted in concert with so many and various creatures and so many trends of thought and disconcerting probabilities .

1st Spinster
(Celeste) - True , Andrea .

2nd Spinster
(Andrea) - I feel dreadful , Celeste , and I fear that something unpleasant and even a dangerously tumultuous disturbance might happen .

1st Spinster
(Celeste) - Like what , Andrea ?

2nd Spinster
(Andrea) - Well , Celeste , this is what I am basing my conjectures on : just by listening to the earlier conversation of the Giant Oak Tree and the Mushroom and observing the chaotic "going on" down there , and , lately , of all the strange creatures coming into the play , the Foxes show up , ready to add themselves to "The Swelling Scene" as a Poet of times gone by had put down in verses the description of the opening scene in his poem, well , you can easily perceive that not everything is as it should be , meaning that there are quite some obvious signs of turbulence in the creatures ' minds , in their either veiled or openly professed aims and their intentions and last but not least , even the inequitable Vices seem to have joined the " swelling scene " and to be taking a lead in this apparent contest of lust , power and.......profit , and consequent subversion , of course , of our normal lives .

1st Spinster (Celeste)- Hold it for a moment , Andrea , I hear something !

2nd Spinster
(Andrea) - Something bad ?......Revolution , may be ??!

1st Spinster
(Celeste) - Worse than that , Andrea ! The Vices are approaching the Giant Oak Tree and the bright light of the sun shows up an ominous scowl on their brows.!

2nd Spinster
(Andrea) - Pay no attention: it's a typical intimidation technique of lesser caliber creatures .

1st Spinster
(Celeste) - But they look like a very large size "caliber " of creatures to me , Andrea , the way they shout themselves hoarse !

2nd Spinster
(Andrea) - Good . That way they won't be able to speak , later on .

Chorus of the Vices- That's what you think ! You want to bet , you dismal old bird ?

2nd Spinster
(Andrea) - YOU "do not scare me none " , you fetid exponent of "no good "!....Just get lost and , if you can find one , go and fly a kite too .

Chorus of the Vices- What's a " Kite " , YOU , old bag of faded feathers ?

2nd Spinster
(Andrea) - Never mind . Just get going and leave us in peace .

Chorus of the Vices- That is precisely what we are specialized for : to bring peace , joy and satisfaction , elation and reward to creatures all over this forest and Forests everywhere !

2nd Spinster
(Andrea) - The Forests are very well aware of what kind of happiness you bring in and offer to the unwise creature who will , oh ! so naively , buy it from you , and everyone knows how vicious and conniving you are at masquerading yourselves as bearers of precious and desirable gifts . Said a Roman consul, when stationed in Ancient Greece , " timeo Danaos et dona ferentes ", which means " I fear the Greeks (Danaos , in Latin) even when they bring presents", and so do" I " about you , by just substituting " Danaos " with " Vices " . So , get lost .

Chorus of the vices- You talk so tough , old bag of faded feathers , " Danaos or no Danaos" because you are perched high up on a tree limb and you can fly away at will should a sudden emergency require a prompt and precautionary retreat , resulting from an earlier unwise attitude or a "faux pas", but we wonder how brazen you would be standing down here and without wings.

2nd Spinster
(Andrea) - You forgot the " faded feathers " : how could you ?! Anyway , that is no valid comparison because , if I were to stand down there , on the ground and I had no wings , obviously I would not be a bird but , may be , even one of you or , - and here let me laugh !- , even a mushroom !

Mushroom - Hear ! Hear !Somebody's calling or , if not calling , it may even sound as if somebody was cursing ! Whichever , it is my name being uttered and not at all in a friendly way.......so it seems !

Giant Oak Tree- Ah ! Dear Mushroom , I think that all this noise came from here , from one of my branches where , for quite some time , two Old Timers , a couple of seasoned old Spinsters , you know , sparrows that is , have been perched resting and chatting and what not for a long , long time , now .! I guess that the calling or whatever that sound was , came from one of those sparrows .

Mushroom - Oh , I see ! May be someone is in a mood to-day , up there , as if there would be no more days of good moods around this Forest .

2nd Spinter
(Andrea) - Did you hear what the Mushroom said ,Celeste ?

1st Spinster
(Celeste) - Yes , of course I heard what the Mushroom said : nothing of importance it seemed to me : only complaining about creatures' moods !

2nd Spinster
(Andrea) - Exactly , Celeste ! That is what he said .

1st Spinster
(Celeste) - Wonderful ! For once we agree in full , Andrea , dear !!

2nd Spinster
(Andrea) - But can't you see how dejectedly that mushroom said that ! That meant that, in his remark , he implied the presence of a situation of uncertainty and suspense , exactly as I felt when watching what had been going on at the market , a while ago.

1st Spinter
(Celeste) - Andrea, oh, Andrea , you seem to attach too much importance to whatever you see or notice and you seem to me as going too far in your perception of

sudden doom ! Andrea , somebody's bad mood , even in a forest , does not mean "sudden Doom"...!! Bad moods , good moods are the run of the mill as an average way in our existences , Andrea .

Chorus of the vices- We can always bring good moods !

2nd Spinster
(Andrea) - YOU ???!!!....don't make me laugh !

Chorus of the Vices- We'd like to see the day when birds will be laughing ! That will be ,really, a laugh !

The learned
mole-cricket - Well, you all will be surprised but there are "laughing birds"in this forest World of ours , not exactly in our Forest , but in a far , far away Land !

Chorus of the Vices- Impossible !

The learned
mole-cricket - Not so , my dears , but very real , instead .

Chorus of the Vices- Incredible !

The learned
mole-cricket - Incredible as it may seem , yet true . Of course , with a little bit of help of the imagination .

Mushroom - And that's how it goes around , most of the time , about things and everything : IMAGINATION !!

Chorus of the Vices- And where is this far , far away Land ?

The learned
mole-cricket - It is located in a far , far away place .

The learned
Moth - Very logical explanation .

The learned
mole-cricket - But , of course !! ...Now , some special Birds in this far , far away Land....

The learned
Moth - You said that already .

The learned
mole-cricket - I just repeated it.........so.,

The learned Moth - ..." so "....so why don't you go ahead and finish your statement ?

The learned mole-cricket - I gladly would if you only stopped from interrupting me all the time !!

The learned Moth - Yes , dear Cricket , I will not interrupt you anymore and I will listen instead to your story which presents itself as going to be an interesting one , may be, an intriguing one too. We are all ears , dear Cricket !

The learned mole-cricket - Thank you , Learned Moth and All . So , as I had started saying , there live in this far away Land some special Birds who sing only in the early morning, at day break , and their singing resembles something of a varied tune , something in between the garrulous laughter of a child's gurgle and an open laugh of an adult person ,at times quite sustained , and ,when stopped , these birds do not sing anymore until the next early morning of a new day.

Chorus of the Vices- How far away is this Land with its extraordinary laughing birds ?

The learned mole-cricket - Very far away .

Chorus of the Vices- Thank you . And , by the way , would it be too "far away "for us to ask you what is the name of these Birds ?

The learned mole-cricket - not at all
Yes, I do . They are called , by the local population , " laughing jacks " .

The learned Moth - And that makes a lot of a laughing sense .

Chorus of the Vices- Your statement , dear Moth , was not very nice and hardly becoming a learned Moth , and it seemed to imply some derisive flavour , not at all called for in this case . You should be ashamed of yourself for ridiculing other creatures' expressions of treasured feelings , impressions and interpretations. We frown on frivolous types like you , clever only in bumping your heads against any luminous source you can find and that's perhaps why you cannot think straight .

2nd Spinster (Andrea) - Look, look who's talking !!!The Inequitable Vices passing terse judgements of iniquity and discredit by a questionable creature on another innocent creature !! I believe that the Strait-laced Creatures were right when they described you as being ominous creatures of moral , mental and emotional silhouette, bent to deception and depravation of anything in sight .

Chorus of the Vices- And what do these enterprising Strait-laced Creatures know about us ? Is it, perhaps , our fault if the heat from the sun, on a Summer day when it beams its radiant power on the creatures in the forest and encourages them to doze off , or is it our fault ,again , if laziness will dishearten creatures and if greed will trouble the character of the mind ? We exist and we live just as all plants do , flowers do , or insects , rocks and rivers and mountains and ducks and geese , cauliflowers and carrots do , or anything else that can be seen or even that which cannot be seen , or that which can be touched , tasted or smelled in this here Forest of ours and ,we believe , in many other Forests as well . It seems clear to us that it is certainly not our fault if creatures take the advantage of us and use us in a bad or improper way .

Mushroom - Used improperly ?.....YOU , being used IMPROPERLY..???!!......Oh! This is really a smashing novelty !....And how could it be at all possible to use a vice in a " proper way " and to a good and worthy end ???!...Of all the.......

Chorus of the Vices- To answer your question : ".....at any available point in the existence of any available creature when the creature's available thinking would stop thinking improperly " .

Mushroom - THAT WILL BE THE DAY !!!.....or , better still , " THE NIGHT " !! And keep on hoping !!......Creatures , insects , cauliflowers and carrots and.... humans , as illustrious late arrivals , to stop thinking " improperly " , and , on top of that , to even stop thinking anything bad ??!?.....Oh , that's the JOKE of the season..!!

Chorus of the Seasons - We do not think , we never think , but humans' thinking appears to shift as often as we do from one season into another . Could you , solid and somber creatures of the soil and of the dark forest , please , explain to us why it is so?

Mushroom - That would be, I suspect , a rather difficult if not impossible task for the whys to explain it to you because the " Sir Whys " hardly ever answer questions : they only ask questions .

Chorus of the Whys- Why should we be bound to answer to a question ? It is not our job . We are programmed to only ask questions and we do not even expect an answer . The asking , the inquiring or the demanding , " for or into or an " , respectively, are our trade and we adhere strictly to that code of activity . That activity is an integral part of our existence ,just as the chirping of the birds , the rustling of the leaves , the whistling of the wind , and the pelting of the rain . We are not aware of any existing Law , in effect to-day in this

Forest that would categorize " answering " as a mandatory procedure to be carried out . Apart from that , we do not even know what "answering " means . If , then , there should be anyone who would be willing to spend his, her , its or their time to "answer " anybody or anything , that procedure would be entirely his ,her , its , and their responsibility .

Chorus of the Answers - Our trade , that is basically the same as our instinct ,encourages us to answer, and we do answer any question that comes our way . Human creatures , now, , did harness us against our will and corralled us into a rigid discipline and a complex and complicated system of life that discouraged in us the pure spontaneity of a clear answering for the pure sense of the response to the answering instinct , as the simple response of a leaf to the wind , or of the water to an object thrown into it .

Mushroom - Times were hard on you !

Chorus of the hard Timers - Times were , are and always will be hard on everybody and anybody , regardless of the moon 's cycles .

Chorus of the Answers - Yes , it seems so , although we do not know much about the Moon's Cycles. How true ...anyway...!!...Yes , times were hard , indeed , and , as a consequence, the human creatures reduced us to the existence of mere slaves of their interpretation of what answers should be , leaving us no hope for a better future , and brought this state of affairs so far and to the point where the proper and correctly balanced measure of any answer in return for any measure of importance , or significance , or pure merit in answering adequately to a question , whether the question was answerable or worth of an answer or just questionable , became just a play that did not reflect an honest intention at giving an honourable and straight answer .

Mushroom - Interesting , indeed . But , what could have been a possible or probable straight answer , then ?

Chorus of the Answers - The straight answer dilemma was that a real problem existed and the problem was the loss by the human Creatures of the sense of the natural measure in formulating and giving answers .

Mushroom - Astonishing . It does not even seem really acceptable such an attitude !

Chorus of the Answers - And , yet , it was "really " true , dear Mushroom, very , very true . These little human Creatures did really lose the sense of measure .

Mushroom - But , did they ever get it back , once they might have realized that it had slipped their grip ?

Chorus of the Answers - They did not , at least then , and we mean " THEN " when everything was in the initial stages of self-reckoning , self-building , self-learning and self-orienting , something they still, particularly the self-orienting , are desperately trying to catch up with .

Mushroom - Unfortunate , isn't it ?

Representative of the " Isn't its " - Why creatures of all sizes , shapes and convictions do not use a plain , simple and clear " is it not " instead of shortening everything in such a lazy attitude?

Chorus of the Whys - Don't ask us.......Pardon us..........do not ask us : please go to the Answers : they will tell you .

Chorus of the Answers - Oh, it is not worth the effort . You'll always find some jokers who will raise criticism on everything : if something is understood , as " isn't " is , by the general environment of creatures , it means that it is viable so it will be left to a measure of preference .

Representative of the " Isn't its " - But how can that be done if what you said , just a while ago , that the sense of measure, and , in this case , the measure of preference , had been lost by the human Creatures ?

Chorus of the Answers - Simple : just forget that I said so .

Mushroom - By all the snails and butterflies in this Forest , I am bedazzled by this here latest sparkling of conversational skills and motives ! But , pardon my saying so , what does all this mean ?

Combined Choruses of Answers and Whys- Oh , pay attention ! We believe that the Giant Oak Tree is going to speak !

Giant Oak Tree - Thank you , thank you , but it is not anything much that I am planning to comment upon , but , as far as I can make it out of all that has been said , it seems that these little humans Creatures have developed some difficulty in formulating questions and producing sensible answers on account of having lost the sense of measure : am I right ?

Mushroom - Sad , isn't it ?.....Pardon me........" is it not " ?

Chorus of the Answers - You are right , dear and respectable Giant Oak Tree , you are absolutely right! And , it is true : unfortunately true , we would dare say ! Yes , these human creatures have really lost the sense of measure .

Chorus of the Whys - Now , we would like to ask , why did they lose this sense of measure ? Did they by any chance , forget where they had placed it , may be , before going out of their premises for a short shopping trip ?.....Now , you need not answer, if you do not feel like it .

Chorus of the Answers - Oh ! Dear Whys , but of course we do , we really do like to answer and we will . As a matter of fact we are going to answer that question right away , so prepare yourselves and listen carefully . It is..........

Chorus of the Whys - That's a pity , a real pity , dear Answers , but we are unable to accept your kind invitation to listen to your answer , because , as you well know , we are not meant to listen for an answer , that condition having been a long standing safety measure introduced by whoever was the first one to have started the trend of asking questions since hardly ever an answer was received , or , if received , not always of a pleasant formulation , specially when the question was an embarrassing one or a compromising one or a risque one . So , if you do not mind , we hope that you will excuse us and , while you would give an answer to the many other Creatures here waiting for a good one , we shall go somewhere else and ask some more questions . You know , we are in great demand , these days .

The learned mole-cricket - Beautifully put .

The learned Moth - Don't be ridiculous !

The learned mole-cricket - It is not " don't " , you ninny , it is " do not " , and , besides , I did not appreciate your crude address : a " please " should have been placed at the beginning of the sentence .

The learned Moth - You don't say !

Mushroom - By listening to these two learned creatures , I begin to realize how wise the Whys actually are and , also , very fortunate at not having to answer anything at all nor having to wait for an answer , but , then , I wonder and I ask myself, what's the purpose of all that ? If somebody is geared up for not wanting or not needing or not desiring an answer , why , then , to ask questions at all in the first place ?

Caretaker of the Answers' Lodgings- That same thought , interestingly enough ,occurred to me too , some time ago. As an employee at the Answers' House , I had enjoyed listening to their answers , for a long , long time , until the day when , in a sudden burst of the imagination , I felt that I needed to ask some questions as I had become infatuated by the stimulating and intriguing aspect of our Universe , you know , all those trees , shrubs , flowers , rivers running through it and mighty rocks and mysterious caves , so I went over as a gardener in the residence of the Whys , hoping that I could ask several questions about our Universe , but, just like you ,I became very disappointed after a short time by them , because they kept on asking me all the time, without any variation of subject, what was I doing there and what did I want and what kind of business was I offering , but they never listened to my answers .

Mushroom - What did you do , then ?

Caretaker of the Answers' Lodgings- I packed , left and went back to my old job at the Answers' House , but I was disappointed there too , almost immediately upon returning there , for they did not let me attend their "Answers'symposiums" anymore , telling me , when I asked of the reason why , they would invariably answer : " go and ask the Whys " .

Mushroom - I really feel sorry for you , going through all of that discomfort .

Caretaker of the Answers' Lodgings- " C'est la vie ! " the French Caretakers would say , so.....c'est la vie ,goes !!

Old Goat given to pretentious display- How true ! How true !....Indeed , there is an old saying , a proverb , actually, in the Italian language , of which I have a substantial knowledge , that goes like this : " Chi lascia la via vecchia per la nuova , sa quel che lascia ma non sa quel che trova ..." , and there is , also , another version of it , phrased slightly differently and shorter , but with identical meaning, and which I like more than the first one , and it goes : " Chi lascia la via vecchia per la nuova , mal pentito si ritrova..."....and , now , to translate it into the more understandable language in every day use by ordinary creatures in our Forest , our vernacular language.......

Chorus of all the forest Creatures - Yes , yes , we want our vernacular translation , if you know which one it is, of course .

Old Goat given to pretentious display- Of course ! ......and here it is : " Better the devil you know , than the devil you don't " . That is what it means in a loose type of translation but , if you really are after a word by word translation you could bring it about saying that if you ,for whatever reason , unhappiness , dissatisfaction , marital problems , may be , or love problems , may be too , financial problems , unsolved problems with yourself , or growing problems with someone else , or just plain " itchy feet " , feel a need or an urge to move on , the former or the latter depending on the type of the problem or situation , then , when you leave your old road, that is , your established and well known existence in order to get away from what you may think is a "rotten world " , the one you are presently in , and get on , onto the new road , you ,of course , are well aware of what you are leaving behind, but you know nothing of what really may be waiting for you in this new road, which means "uncertainty" as compared to the well known and established assured facts of what you had left behind , and , please , don't ask me to repeat it again , because I have already forgotten how I started it .

Chorus of all the forest Creatures - So , what does it mean ?

Old Goat given to pretentious display- It means , be careful and read your map carefully , before you take a turn .

Chorus of all the forest creatures - But there are no turns in our forest !

Old Goat given to pretentious display- Then go home and have a rest .

Chorus of all the forest Creatures - Which road shall we take , then ?

Old Goat given to pretentious display - The old one , please !

Representative of the NEW Roads- What nonsense ! New roads lead to new horizons , open spaces and improved communications .

Caretaker of the Answers's Lodgings- That was not " my case " , for certain , as I lost , on that supposed to be new move to the Whys' House , every communication I ever had before !

Representative of the OLD Roads- We knew that . Old roads never wear out , are strong as rocks , like the old Roman roads .

The learned mole-cricket - I begin to wonder , just as the noble Mushroom did a while ago , whether the philosophy of the Whys , to all practical purposes , is , after all , the right one, because answering to a question , even just a tiny , insignificant and innocent one , can get anyone hooked up in an endless contest of debatable and questionable value !.....Listen , listen ....it's still going on...!!!

Representative of the NEW Roads- Roman roads , my foot ! .....well , my paving bitumen , I'd rather say! ...What you just said is pure nonsense , and you know it !

Representative of the OLD Roads- I do ?

Representative of the NEW Roads- Of course you do ! Your old Roman roads had to be graded over and resurfaced in order to bring them up to the rigid and demanding standards of modern traffic , You , big , fat , obnoxious Nincompoops !

Representative of the OLD Roads- Yes , that is true , but , you see , the " direction " , never changed . It still remained the good , solid Old Road , You , small , diminutive , despicable Ninnies !

The Old Goat given to pretentious display - Well , if my saying may be worth just an acacia 's leaf , I would like to draw your attention , that is the attention of both of you , to a small , yet important detail you , perhaps inadvertently and unintentionally , overlooked , that the Old Roman Roads were , actually , NEW Roman Roads when they first were built , : right ?

Representative of the NEW Roads- ...And who's this idiot ,suddenly coming into our conversation ?

Representative of the OLD Roads- It looks like a stupid bearded Goat to us !

Representative of the NEW Roads- That figures ! It seems almost a Law of Nature that something has to be in the middle of the road of any project directed to reach new and brighter horizons of life and communication , an obstruction of some form just to aggravate the bold pursuers of that project , be it a hill, a mountain , a river or just a gentle brook or , an hyperbolic idiotic goat , as the present case seems to indicate .

Old Goat given to pretentious display- Watch it , Buster , or I'll eat your road .

Chorus of the Horizons - Did someone say that new roads lead to new horizons ?

Representative of the NEW Roads- Yes , we did !!

Chorus of the Horizons - Oh ! Yes , that's right : you did . How regretful of us to have overlooked it!! Well , we give you ten good marks for speaking well of us and , then , we take away ten marks for your incorrect interpretation of us .

Representative of the NEW Roads- How dare you be so insolent and disrespectful : I am a graduate , " Summa Cum Laude " , from the University of " Come and Get it " , which , by the way , is not associated with any kind of Food Chains or Merchandise .

Old Goat given to pretentious display- What a pity ! I could have eaten it .

Chorus of the Horizons - No insolence , no disrespect : only a more precise understanding of the meaning of " horizon " as seen from the standpoint of a new road .

Representative of the NEW Roads- And WHAT is it that "precise" understanding of yours , may we ask ?

Chorus of the Horizons - What did you say ?

Representative of the NEW Roads- WHAT IS IT that precise understanding of your horizons ?

Chorus of the Horizons - Oh ! That !.....Search us.......we do not even know it ourselves .

Representative of the OLD Roads- Wonderful , just wonderful ! We couldn't have said it better ourselves ! And it served you right ! Search for a stupid answer and you'll find plenty of them !

Chorus of the Answers - We resent that unethical remark .

Representative of the OLD Roads- It was not a remark and it was not an unethical statement : it was just an " old road " pointed in the right direction . That's all what it was .

Chorus of the Answers - That's better , whichever direction it pointed.

Representative of the NEW Roads - Incredible ! Just a while ago the Old Roads Representative was boastin that old roads never change and now , quite abruptly , are able and willing to point in another direction : the right one ! .....O tempora , O mores !!

The same Old Goat given to pretentious display - Hey ! Hey ! Go easy on that display of show-off knowledge of old history ! That's my territory !

The learned mole-cricket - It is really amazing to see where we have arrived in this exchange of words and feelings just talking nonsense and realizing that we had started form a simple old folks proverb and , on top of that , in a foreign language that no one inthis Forest can understand !

The same Old Goat given to pretentious display - True , but it was translated .

Chorus of the Translations - Oh , dear , dear All whoever you are or may be or might be , regardless , we have to serve all of you and we do our best in doing so and we try hard to remain honest , correct and impartial in the rendition of a thought or in the representation of an anecdote or the noble and all encompassing beauty of a poem ,remaining,as faithfully as we can,committed to the original sense and meaning . Sometime we come out good , sometime not so good , sometime far from the closest or more appropriate rendition of the intended thought or meaning and , sometime still , we even omit some passages or periods or sentences or words because , particularly for words , it is not always possible to find a ready available and perfectly matched substitute . However , no problem is encountered when searching for commas , full stops , semi-colons , colons , exclamation marks and so on , except when we have to translate from a particular foreign language that appears to consider every interrogative sentence upside down even before writing or listening to the question in that sentence and forcing us to become acrobats and stand on our heads in order to accommodate the question mark which ,with us in that unorthodox upside down position , naturally , will appear upside down too , without mentioning our headache for standing on our heads ..

Representative of the NEW Roads- Are the head aches severe and how do you manage them ?

Chorus of the Translations - Not really a problem . They are never so severe to need any special remedy .

The same Old Goat given to pretentious display - Do you take some simple medicines when they occur ? They may not be serious ,but , I wonder , if the case be that there would be several questions in a passage or an essay or period , the compound stress of so many standings on your head, may cause some more annoying headaches.

Chorus of the Translations - Those are rare cases , although we have incurred in some of them a few times . In those cases we just take two normal straight up question marks before going to bed and call our typographer in the morning .: you know , our printer .

The same Old Goat given to pretentious display - Sensible mode of action . However , some old shepherds claim that goat's milk and goat's cheese are the best headache remedies .

Chorus of the Translations - Really ?

The same Old Goat given to pretentious display - Well , that is what the Shepherds say . I just provide the milk and they make the cheese .

The learned mole-cricket - Cheap advertising , but right on the dot.

Chorus of the Dots - We believe that two of us taken with a glass of goat's milk before going to bed is the best way to take care of a head ache . Then , they can call anybody they like in the morning .

Chorus of the Whys - But why , we wonder , is it so necessary or important to always call somebody in the morning after taking some stupid question marks or dots with goat's milk the night before ?

The same Old Goat given to pretentious display - Well , for one thing, everybody will know that the medication worked well and that you are still alive .

Chorus of the Answers - Logical assumption .

The learned mole-cricket - Yes , I agree , and a well balanced quantitatively and qualitatively logical assumption it is .

Chorus of the Answers - Ah ! Who said that ?

The learned mole-cricket - I did .

Chorus of the Answers - And who are THOU , may we ask ?

The learned mole-cricket - " Thou " can ask questions , I see , quite a change of scenery , since I was under the impression that only the Whys could ask questions ! Well , to answer your inquisitive question , I am a mole-cricket and I am a reporter of the daily events in this here Forest of ours . Does this answer satisfy your inquisitive minds ?

Chorus of the Answers - A reporter !! WOW ! You are most welcome among us because we love the glamour and the excitement of the news , the events and frontline occurrences.....well you should tell that also to the Whys and we are quite certain that they would appreciate this kind thought , dear Reporter . ,,,By the way , if permissible , of course , what is the name of your paper or review or publication that you are working for ?

The learned mole-cricket - I am a free-lance Reporter and I sell my writings and notes and reports to the highest bidder .

Chorus of the Answers - Clever !.

The learned mole-cricket - Oh ! It's just a way to make a living .

Chorus of the Answers - Better than goat's milk and goat's cheese , for " sure " !

The learned Moth - Well , not necessarily so, if someone happens to like goat's milk and goat's cheese .

The learned mole-cricket - I do not like goat's milk and I loathe goat's cheese , so , being a Reporter, is a far better measure of compensation and satisfaction .

Chorus of the Answers - Ah 1.... We have heard that word before !!!

The same Old Goat given to pretentious display - Which word ?

Chorus of the Answers - And what have you got to do with that "which " and with that " word "?

The same Old Goat given to pretentious display - With " which " I have absolutely nothing to do , but with " word " I am interested too because ,not too long ago , I happened to be in the middle of a discussion about " that word " ,. and I say this because I have a faint idea that I may , after all , know that word . That's why I came in , when you seemed surprised by hearing that word .

Chorus of theAnswers We were-not surprised ! We were elated by the sudden reappearance of that word which represented a discussion carried on a while ago that somehow seemed to have vanished when another one appeared to have strayed into the main stream of our conversation with the Whys , the mushroom and the Vices and a couple of scholarly creatures ,and caretakers and goats too .How easy , it seems , is the shifting from one subject to another when there are so many creatures involved in a conversation , all with their own fixed agenda in their minds and totally intolerant of the other creatures's interests or preferences .

The learned Moth - And this late episode is a good representation of that phenomenon. Anyway , I remember that conversation quite well and the name of that word .

Chorus of the Whys - And why can 't anyone say that word to remind us of that conversation and pick up from where we , and everybody else , had left ,instead of going around it like a moth to a candle ?

The learned Moth - I don't see any candle !

Chorus of the Answers - Do not worry , learned Moth : you know the Whys never wait for answers ,: they only ask questions, regardless whether they are important, mediocre or just plain miserable and totally unnecessary .

The learned Moth - I understand : well , I said that just to be polite but there , really , is nothing at all to be understood .

The same Old Goat given to pretentious display - I agree : not only there is nothing to understand but nothing at all to think either , except for a lot of stray talking and just because of a stupid word that some nincompoop said in a pitifully descriptive exposition about losing the good sense of measure about something . somewhere , sometime ago !! What a nonsense !

Chorus of the Answers - Ah ! " " THE SENSE OF MEASURE " !! Yes that was the word !

The same Old Goat given to pretentious display - That's several words , not one as you claimed .

The learned Moth - Picky , picky , picky !

The learned Moth - Well ? No more comments on the famous word that had been left behind and forgotten over the advent of a stray conversation ?

Chorus of the Whys - Some time it is necessary to be persistent in asking questions , if an answer is crucial , because creatures , in general , have a tendency not to answer them at will , particularly if interpreted with ones which could embarrass them or annoy them or even incriminate them .

Chorus of the Answers - Poppy cock ! Didn't you hear what the Learned Moth just said ? It was the intrusion of a stray conversation that prevented us from giving an answer to the Whys .

The learned Moth - What about now ?

Chorus of the Answers - If you insist .

The learned Moth - I do , everyone else does too . Do you remember the story , we hope ?

Chorus of the Answers - We do : and it is well documented . We discovered it in the annals of the long living turtles and it was said that the human creatures , having distanced themselves more and more ,a little at a time , from being particular and consistent in preserving correct measures and depending on their own confidence as being always right in their doings without bothering to keep constant checks on their usage of good measures , did , eventually , become so distant from the good measure of living that , realizing their inability of catching up with the good old measures , now fading away from their sight, they thought of making up for that loss by modifying the meaning of answering so that they could always come up with a more comfortable interpretation of their misdeeds .

The learned Moth - Interesting Chronicles and seemingly persuasive in their content .

Chorus of the Answers - We too were impressed with the abundance of information , authenticity and authority of the source .

The learned Moth - What happened next ?

Chorus of the Answers - What happened next is written in the same Annals of the Long Living Turtles and it is indicated there that what the humans had achieved up until then, that is the utter disregard for the healthy habit of good measure and the unscrupulous practice of doctoring their answers to unsolicited questions, prompted them ,also , as a consequence , to take the unauspicious step in unabashedly and irresponsibly adopt and sanction those practices which set up the stage for a very poor start for the entire human race .

The learned Moth - And what was that "poor start " the Annals are referring to ?

Chorus of the Answers - For one , the alienating of the practice of good and sensible measure in their actions and their thoughts and the doctoring of their answers to unwanted , undesired or unfavourable questions about their behaviour and actions or to cover up for faults .

The learned mole-cricket - Not an unusual attitude in our Forest and , I suspect , in many other Forests.

Chorus of the Answers - May be so . May be so . Anyway , that is what they did as a consequence of that unauspicious step they had taken and , in doing so , they also lost another important sense .

The learned Moth - And which one would that be , now ?

Chorus of the Answers - The sense of values ,as it is written in the Long Living Turtles Annals .

The learned Moth - That is not a sense , dear Answers : that is a GIFT !

Chorus of the Answers - We doubt that they did realize that it was a Gift ! Had they , these humans , realized it , they would have certainly "grabbed " it and stashed it away as a favorable answer !

The learned Moth - And what a waste would that have been !!

Chorus of the Answers - Yes, indeed ! ....And a waste it was , because due to their failure to grasp its meaning they caused calamitous clashes of rivalries to take place frequently among all those creatures who had lost the sense of measure and beat each other up mercilessly , not being able to come up , ever , with a good and honest answer whenever a conflict of interests occurred .

The learned Moth - How far back in time do those Annals of the Long Living Turtles reach ?

Chorus of the Answers - Way back to the beginning of time , we believe .

The learned Moth - Nothing , then , seems to have changed much in our way of living , since those far away times .

Chorus of the Answers - Yes , it appears that way and the Annals go on describing how serious a problem that entire situation had become , a problem for the entire human race that not even poets or holy human creatures could mend and great became confused with large , but , having lost their sense of measure ,nobody could ever figure out how great or how large anything was and , as a result of having lost the sense of values on anything they knew or were aware of , they became evermore free from moral obligations and principles in their dealings and in the pursuit of their goals , forgetting modesty , humility and the virtue of grace and developed an insatiable craving for grandeur , for greatness and for largeness ,totally unable , ever , to figure out which of the three was the largest .

Mushroom - An extremely interesting story, I believe , but rather unfortunate in its development : isn't it ?

Chorus of the Answers - For the humans , yes , very unfortunate . For the rest of us , answers , quotes, question marks , commas , exclamation points , full stops ,semicolon and carrots ,cauliflowers and artichokes , apple trees and bananas and everything in between , is just the same , but the little human creatures must have been suffering , even in those early days , from a condition not identified yet in those far away days , but known to-day , called colloquially as the Saint Vitus Dance , and that's why , probably , why they could not sit still and had to frantically dance their way on to great thing , greater things and grandest things , without realizing , really , why they had to do it , but they seemed possessed with that peculiar mania of running as fast as they could to reach that far away beacon that , if reached , meant greatness or grandeur or something , and , in their anxiety to do great thing or larger ones ,whichever came first , they , actually , were running no distance at all because our forest being round as it had been found to be by the Giant Sequoia Trees' Expert Investigators that were able to observe that what they could see from the top of their great height could not be seen at the level of their roots . After a thorough scrutiny of those eventul findings they came down with a remarkable deduction , made public at the local Society of " The Forest ," as we see it ", that the horizon was not flat but must have had a curvature , resulting , then , in the inevitably logical assertion that if the Forest was round and not flat , as retained up until that significant discovery was announced ,it followed that it did not really matter how fast and hard you could run to reach a beaming beacon because ,eventually , you would finish running up , inevitably , back to the same place you had started from in the pursuit of that famous beacon of lust, power and glory and into each other's tail .

Mushroom - I did not know that our Forest was round .

The learned Moth - I have always known about the Forest being round : how could have I otherwise been able to fly in circles around a candle ?

Mushroom - Astonishing .

The same Old Goat given to pretentious display - That makes me sick .

The Representative of the sick trees - Me too .

Mushroom - But did the humans ever realize that they were running around in circles , so to speak of ?

Chorus of the Answers - According to latest observations and statistical findings , it does not seem so. They are still running and hitting their heads against some squares , others against the sides of a rectangle and some against the sides of a triangle and straight into its hypotenuse , not knowing with deductible clarity what a circle is , but ,in spite of those little drawbacks , the majority of those humans are appearing to continue to run amuck and attempt to become very great or very large, and still very awkward in distinguishing a difference between the two, but , nevertheless ,running after greatness , grandeur and largeness remains a persisting preferential tendency by many of them up to the present days .

Mushroom - Hear ! Hear ! And listen ,dear Charlie , my big and great and large, friendly tree : they are talking about you !

Giant Oak Tree - I heard and I hear ,dear Fabius ,but they are talking about humans and their inexplicable preoccupation with greatness and everything and anything connected with it : not Trees!

A Flea , just passing by - Please , excuse me for butting in ,......sorry ! I really meant to say for intruding so rudely into your conversation , but I am in transit through this forest and , having heard some souls talking ,I thought of stopping for a second because I needed to ask you a question .

Giant Oak Tree- Hey ! Little Mushroom , why don't you answer me ?

Mushroom - Please , excuse me , you Big Giant , friend , but there is here a flea just passing by who has stopped briefly to ask for some information .

Giant Oak Tree - A..........FLEA ....??!!

Mushroom - Yes : A FLEA ....Have you ever seen one ?

Giant Oak Tree- I have heard something about it .

Mushroom - Then , the whole thing is quite simple : here we have a Flea in transit through our forest who just stopped by , briefly , to ask for some information. That should be easy to comprehend .

Giant Oak Tree- You never fail to show yourself ! Well, fine , fine !....Just ask her what does she want to know , then , once you know what it is , tell it to her ,if you happen to know it , of course , and let her go on her way , wherever that will take her . This , also , should not be too difficult to comprehend .

Mushroom - Oh ! Dear Charlie , don't be so grouchy for just any little thing that does not quite please you ! You should be well in your knowledge as a Great figure as you are , that it always becomes the Greatest to understand , and be condescendent towards the small , the simple and the humble .

Giant Oak Tree- Oh ! Go on !! Get away with you ! Those are old stories and stop drawing things out . But , tell me , is she travelling alone or in company with someone else ?

Mushroom - And what difference does that make whether she is travelling alone or in company with someone else just to ask for some information ?

Giant Oak Tree - An enormous difference : it all depends whom she is the travelling with ,how her companion or companions look like , if decent folks or rough types...... ......or they could be secret agents in disguise ..

Mushroom - What on earth are you thinking of , to-day ? ! May be it is the wind that blows harder than usual , today , up there in your head .!

Giant Oak Tree- You can never be too careful these days , my dear Fabius !

Mushroom - This is your problem, dear Charlie : you are too big , too high and so stuck on the ground , you cannot move , you cannot bend or turn and you have to rely on everyone around you to be able to see , to hear , because , by yourself , you could not do it , and the result is that you become nervous , annoyed and irritated about even the silliest thing around .

Giant Oak Tree - You are exaggerating . What to you appears as irritability and uneasiness on my part , is nothing more than my concern about safety and the awareness of the dangers surrounding us : that' all .

Mushroom - Dangers surrounding us ?!......From a flea , causing you unimaginable and concealed turmoil and worry ? I can tell you one thing , my dear Giant of a tree , and my friend too , that I believe that I am a lot happier as a small mushroom than you are , so big and with so many headaches .

Giant Oak Tree- Oh ! quit being always so critical of everything ! Just ask the Flea what does she want to know and then let us continue our conversation .

Mushroom - Would you like to ask the Flea yourself ? That would , probably , allay all of your fears .

Giant Oak Tree- There you go ! No one can tell you anything and you come in sulking right away !

Mushroom - I am not pouting .dear Charlie , but you expect too much from souls around you .

Giant Oak Tree- Not really, dear Fabius :all I want is to be able to continue our conversation. That's all I want and this interruption causes us to lose time and , on top of that , of all odds , because of a passing Flea seeking some information !!!

Mushroom - Flea or Elephant , when they would ask for something , would that perspective call for a preferential treatment , depending on their size ?

Giant Oak Tree- Ah ! Think what you want and I don't really care ! Just get through with it and cut it out .

Mushroom - O.K ! Charlie !....(then , to himself ....).......It must be one of those days ,I am afraid !! ....(Then , turning to the Flea.......) ....Flea ? Are you still there ?

Flea , - Yes , I am still here , of course !

Mushroom - Sorry to keep you waiting !

Flea - No problem : I am fine . As a matter of fact this little pause while waiting gives me a chance to rest a little : so , please , do not worry . I am fine .

Mushroom - This giant tree to whom I was talking , he wants to know if you are travelling alone or in company with someone else .

Flea - Why would he ask that from you ? Can't he ask me himself or is it that he cannot see me ? Is he blind , by any chance ?

Mushroom - No , he is not blind but he is so large , big and tall and you are so minute and almost infinitesimal and far away from his top , you know , those branches high, high up there almost touching the sky , that he has difficulty in seeing and hearing you .

Flea - That situation is inconvenient ,indeed . In the country where I come from life goes on by leaps and bounds , so distances in all directions cause no concerns , regardless of how high , or how big or how small anyone is .

Mushroom - Well , that must be quite something , but , tell me now , how would all that jumping in leaps and bounds help the present situation between you and this Giant Tree , a situation you described as inconvenient ? I cannot see that!!

Flea - It would help , I believe , because there would be no problems in reaching out or communicating or dealing or asking questions with anybody , everyone being well within range of each other, regardless of how high, large , small, or long they would be , to be considered also the advantages due to our jumping , like the ability to acquire and posses things of interest or of curiosity or of necessity without having to wait or to beg for someone else to grant those entities to you.

Mushroom - Is it difficult to learn how to jump in leaps and bounds ?

Flea - Learning how to do it would spoil its inherent ability to be useful : you see, we are born that way !

Mushroom - Why wasn't I born a flea...!!!

Giant Oak Tree - Hey ! Fabius , dear little Mushroom ,did I hear you yelling something down there ? Are you all right ?

Flea - He is fine , Your Highness ! Our Mushroom , here , Just got a little excited by trying to jump too high .

Giant Oak Tree- Jumping too high?!.A Mushroom jumping...too high.?! Never heard of it !!!

uMushroom - Don't worry , Charlie , everything's fine : I am still talking to this young Flea and it won't be long now .

Giant Oak Tree - I hope so . May be you might want to suggest to her to come and see me up here and ask for the information she wanted .

Mushroom - Let me see ,may be a minute or two more , and I'll be with you as soon as the Flea will leave : Just be patient for a second .

Giant Oak Tree - Patience ! Patience ! Always Patience with little creatures ! Bah ! What kind of stupid and annoying Forest am I ruling, these days ! !

Lady Composure
a Lady-in waiting
of Princess Patience- Sir, Your Excellency, Your reference to Princess Patience has been noted, but , unfortunately ,the Princess is on vacation and has left instructions not to be disturbed .

Giant Oak Tree - Oh! How fortunate and I am very proud that the Princess has considered my Forest to be the place that could offer her Ladyship some adequate rest.

Lady Composure
a Lady-in-waiting
of Princess Patience- I am quite certain that the Princess will feel sympathetic about Your referral and understanding , at the same time , of Your need for that referral , yet , the Princess needs some rest due to her recent use of all of her energies in trying to alleviate and dissipate the horrors of the tog of war that has ravaged , lately , with almost irresponsible violence ,several fields of potatoes and tomato plants and it took all of the Princess's patience and fortitude to prevent and defuse a premature catastrophic salad of the entire situation .

Giant Oak Tree - I understand : You know , as the King of this Forest , I am well aware of the problems among so many different vegetables and plants , to which you can add Birds , Bees , caterpillars , mosquitoes , lizards and frogs , not to mention mushrooms and fleas .

Lady Composure
a Lady-in-waiting
of Princess Patience - I will refer our encounter to the Princess as soon as she recovers from her stress and regains her strength . The Princess just needed some rest exhausted as she was .

Giant Oak Tree - My deferent homage to the Princess .
Lady Composure- Your obedient servant , Your Majesty .

Giant Oak Tree - What a refreshing interlude !I really needed something like that, today !

Mushroom = Hey ! Charlie : the Flea is leaving ..

Giant Oak Tree - Oh ! That's good news .

Mushroom - Yes , she told me that she wanted to get on her way and she wished you all the best and also her deep respect .

Giant Oak Tree - . Jolly good ! Jolly good ! Thank you ! But , what was it that she wanted to know ? Didn't she stop here because she was supposed to have wanted some information about something ?

Mushroom - Yes , that had been the general idea , but , after all the talking back and forth between you and me , she had lost track of what she had wanted to ask . Then , she hesitated a little and went on saying something more , but in a quiet type of talking , just like a whisper , but I still heard......

Giant Oak Tree - You heard what ?

Mushroom - I am not quite certain , but it sounded like a subdued talking , all to herself , and I do not know if I understood all of it or only some words of what she was saying . So , I am not really sure .

Giant Oak Tree- But , then , come on ! What were those words that you could understand? That might have been just the important part and it could have given us an insight into the whole situation of why she was passing by and asking for some information and allay my apprehension of possible spies infiltrating this Forest of mine ! Come on , Come on , Fabius : You must certainly remember at least some of those words that you said you could hear, right?

Mushroom - Well , I feel a little uneasy myself wondering if what I heard was really what I heard , or if I heard something that I was not supposed to hear , or if it was something not to be heard "real" loud , but only whispered in a subdued and concealed tone of voice .

Giant Oak Tree - For Heavens above , my dear Mushroom , how long do we have to wait to hear what you heard , like a famous Roman Orator by the name of Cicero, in ancient Rome, said to Lucius Sergius Catilina , a noble and aristocratic Roman patrician as well as a conspirator against the State of Rome , his conspiracy unveiled by Cicero who ,then , in the presence of the full Roman Senate ,said to Catiline :" usque tandem , Catiline , abuteris patientiae nostrae ? " which , roughly translated , would go something like this :"how long would you, Catiline , take advantage of our patience ? " So , speak up , man.......pardon me.........Mushroom !

Mushroom - Well , if what I heard is true to what she said , that is what the Flea said, of course,and if I heard correctly what she might have whispered, and that's always what the Flea had whispered, of course , then it might have sounded something like this : " If you grow for so long and if you grow so tall, stretched out of sight towards the sky ,so that you cannot see or hear what's going on at your feet ,that is , of course , for creatures who have feet , otherwise it would be " roots " , then your brain may finish up very thin and wrinkled at the top of you " , and , after taking a couple of giant leaps , disappeared in the depth of the wood .

Giant Oak Tree- Ah ! That's nothing ! That's pure nonsense ! Probably she did not know what else to say or to justify her presence among us and , in some way , it is possible that she might have been an intellectual Flea out of work , having lost her job for being insolent ,disruptive and over critical of her Peers and her surroundings , and incapable to refrain from her attitude even among strangers !! Anyway , this clears my mind about this flea being a spy :, and I know , now , that she is . definitely , not one of them .

Mushroom - But how do you know that ??!!

Giant Oak Tree - "Elementary , dear Watson " , would have said *Shelock* Holmes , because Real Spies do not take giant leaps and then fade away into the woods. Real Spies just leap frog their way in and stay very well put into the woods .

Mushroom - Charlie ! You should have been a *Sherlock* Yourself , and you would have been a really clever sherlock , a real fine detective , that is, instead of a ....

Giant Oak Tree - Very well : say it and I will not be mad at you

Mushroom - .....great , tolerant and a very patient King .

Princess Patience - Did someone address me , I wonder ?

Mushroom - Oh ! No , not really . I was just praising the good qualities of our beloved King . and , excuse me for being audacious enough for asking , but whom may I have the honour to speak to in this beautiful Forest of ours ?

Princess Patience - No Audacity at all, dear little subject of this luxuriant wooded Kingdom of Bonavia and to answer your"audacious" question , I am Princess Patience and I happen to be here ,taking a vacation in this beautiful Forest .

Mushroom - I am overwhelmed by your sight and humbled by your presence , Princess!

Princess Patience- Oh ! Dear little mushroom,you need not be so bashful in my presence. : You see, I am only a very patient type of a Princess and I do not expect or desire to be adulated , but only request some gentle patience when someone , anyone .wishes to converse with me . So , just be Yourself and tell me all about your beautiful Country .

Mushroom - My dear Princess , Your Ladyship , I am not much of a narrator and I am just a mushroom and, fortunately, not a poisonous one , although my respected and beloved King , you know ,the Giant oak Tree , sometimes , during our conversations , feels differently about it , believing that ,if not poisonous altogether yet I do seem to have an “inclination” to come close to it .

Princess Patience - Oh! Yes ! your King ! Now I remember what my Lady-in-waiting told me just before I started out for a little walk after my very beneficial and much needed rest , that His Majesty the Oak , had made some reference to me and probably was desirous to exchange a few words with me , is it so ?

Mushroom - That might be so , Princess , would you like for me to ask him ? He is so tall ,his head high up there ,he hardly ever knows what’s going on down here so , usually , I pass on to him all the information and necessary news when they occur .

Princess Patience - That would be very gracious of you , dear little mushroom . It would be nice to find out if His Majesty is still interested in talking to me , before I resume my refreshing walk in your beautiful forest .

Mushroom - Very well : I’ll call him....pardon me ....I’ll call His Majesty , promptly . Hey ! Charlie ! There is here a Princess who wants to talk to you ! Are you there ?

Giant Oak Tree- Of course I am here ! Where else do you suspect that I could be ? Did you say a.... Princess ?

Mushroom - Yes I did . She told me that her Lady-in-waiting , Lady Composure , had just told her , upon rising from her rest , that you had made a referral to her a little earlier and she wanted to know if you still wanted to talk to her before she would resume her walk through the forest .

Giant Oak Tree - Oh! Yes , and you were the cause of that referral !

Mushroom - “ I “ !!!!!?????

Giant Oak Tree - Yes , you ! Don’t you remember when you told me to be “ PATIENT “ when I was urging you to expedite things with that itinerant Flea and I , then , disdainfully regretted being the Ruler of such a Kingdom ? At that time I advocated the word Patience a few times , and that must have been the time that alerted the Princess Patience’s entourage to my calling .

That ,I believe , must have been it . But ,of course , Fabius , I will not only be delighted to converse with the Princess , if she would be graceful enough to accept my humble company , but also honoured by her presence in my Kingdom . So , please , dear Fabius , go tell the sweet Princess that I am at her disposal .

Mushroom - Your highness , Princess Patience , The Giant Oak Tree , out beloved King , has expressed to me his anxiety and desire in anticipation of your meeting whenever Your Ladyship would be comfortable to proceed into it.

Princess Patience - My dear Mushroom, you can tell your King that , although I am pleased with the respect and kindness and deference afforded me , yet there should not be an excessive wall of formalities because , if so , then there could not be a clear , open and sincere exchange of views , feelings and ideas in addition to the fact that by prolonging that excess of protocol you would create a condition of impatience : and I am a proven expert at it.

Mushroom - Your Majesty , Princess Patience .

Giant Oak Tree- Welcome to my Kingdom , my dear Princess , it is a pleasure and an honour to see you here in our country .

Princess Patience - I am honoured too to be able to meet so great a King in this Forest and I am also eager to learn what was the essence of your referral to me , a while ago , as reported to me by my Lady-in-waiting , Lady Composure .

Giant Oak Tree - Yes , I had summoned your name Patience, my dear Princess , as I was being harassed by various occurrences and aggravated by a confounded erratic itinerant Flea , to the point of causing me to lose my….patience !

Princess Patience - Oh ! I understand perfectly well what you might have been going through , not an unusual occurrence in the existence of all creatures , an occurrence that, if not kept under control and sensible scrutiny of cause and effect , could generate discomfort , hostility and be even dangerous .

The learned mole-cricket - The Princess has a good insight and excellent experience about all that .

Princess Patience - "Patience" , which can be an inherited character in some creatures , can also be learned by conscientious practice . It is a great virtue possessing it but a greater treasure is to know how to use it .

The same Old Goat given to pretentious display Ah ! Very good expressions ,indeed for every day use which add luster to a good school book or on the lips of an amateur philosopher but I wonder if they would hold good for the ordinary creature who has to deal every day , day in and day out , with the frivolous and , many a time , just plainly annoying trifles of so many frivolous and plainly annoying creatures in this Forest .

Mushroom - Careful , Old Goat ! You are talking to a Princess !

The same Old Goat given to pretentious display - I know she is a Princess , by definition at least and etiquette of protocol all of which is history of times gone by long ago. This does not make me less respectful towards the Princess whom I respect more for what she is and for what she represents than for a title that anyone can print .or brag about it .

Mushroom - But , regardless of what you are saying , the fact remains that she IS a Princess .

The same Old Goat given to Pretentious display And so " it remains " ,also , that I AM a Goat .

Mushroom- No mistake about that !

The same Old Goat given to pretentious display Mistake or no mistake , I remember my old Folks ,when I was very young and growing , telling me about a famous old philosopher of ancient times by the name of Plato and his famous saying about lineage of ancient peoples and his all encompassing definition of that myth , as quoted by a more recent and just as famous a philosopher of ancient times , by the name of Seneca , a Roman , born two years BC, who , when addressing one of his disciples , by the name of Lucilio , told him in answer to his pupil's inquiry re lineage of personalities , as we said , quoting Plato's maxim : " ......and remember , Lucilio , that there is no king who would not claim among his ancestors a slave , and there is no slave who could not claim among his ancestors a king...."

Mushroom - And what's the meaning of all this display of history , Old Goat ?

The same Old Goat given to pretentious display Simple : one of the Princess 's Ancestors could have been a Goat .

The learned Moth Interesting development .Yet ,slightly perplexing as to its pertinent relationship to the present conversation .

Mushroom - I think so too .

The learned mole-cricket - Me too.!

Giant Oak Tree - You see , my dear Princess , what I do have to put up with every day of my existence , contending the path of an uncertain equilibrium between stupidity and daily squabbles about absolutely "nothing" of significant value " or of any constructive consequence ! Some days it is almost impossible to hold your temper , to keep your temper , or , not to have a temper at all and lose all of your patience , even if you try as hard as you can to remain calm and positive . I am telling you , my dear Princess , it is almost impossible , at times ,to remain patient under those provoking circumstances : believe me !

Princess Patience - I hear you , my dear King , but I'd much prefer to call you more affectionately as I heard your little mushroom calling you a short while ago........I believe it was ......" CHARLIE " !.....

Giant Oak Tree- But , of course , Princess , and how really sweet of you to think so graciously towards me ,and , addresses of this nature fill my lymph with undescribable joy . But , then , could I dare venture to call you too with a more loving name than the one so restrictive of Princess ?

Princess Patience - Yes .....CHARLIE ! ...By all means ! ......call me Butterfly !

Giant Oak Tree - What an enchanting name , that is, my dear Butterfly ! .....and you remind me of something that happened ....

Princess Patience - Yes , her name was immortalized in a musical drama , by a famous Composer....and I chose that as my nickname because she ....

Giant Oak Tree - Yes , Yes , you are right , and I remember now , some time ago , a nightingale was singing some of those "arias" while visiting some friends on one of my branches ! Oh ! and how beautiful it was ! ....But , I interrupted you , I am sorry ! You were saying that you chose that name as your nickname because ......

Princess Patience- yes , Charlie , I chose her name as my nickname because she on account of her precipitous and emotional impetuosity disregarded the wise disposition of patience , that is , to be patient and ponder before reacting incoherently to misfortune or disenchantment ,or despair.

Giant Oak Tree- Butterfly, my dear Butterfly, I never thought that a conversation with a princess could be so interesting and enticing , with common sense and mixed with love and sympathetic understanding . .

Princess Patience And I am grateful for your kind show of appreciation of my company and conversation , and your comment will be a good corollary to my vacation in your beautiful land .

Giant Oak Tree - I envy you , my dear Butterfly, and I wish I could be as relaxed as you are and ,in a way , so contemplative about our existences , while , instead I have to show signs of irritability and impatience at every corner of my existence !

Princess Patience - I fully understand what you are complaining about , Charlie , and I appreciate the difficulties you are confronted with every day , but ,then , that should be one more good reason to practice patience and treasure it

Giant Oak Tree- I think so too , many times , but , unfortunately , only after the storm has passed and the damage has already been done !

Princess Patience- Well , Charlie , think of it this way : there is ,also , another significant and quite Big advantage in using and practicing patience , and that is the extra span of precious time afforded you between thought and action , which represents an excellent and golden opportunity for all sides of the situation to reach some favourable and satisfactory balance whichever that situation might be , whether a contest of principles , or a dispute of propriety or the ownership of something important, between great and not so great creatures , or only between great creatures or just small creatures or a mixture of great and small creatures , and that golden opportunity is that it gives to one side extra precious time to review the core and the meaning of the problem and to the other side extra bonus time to ventilate its own fury to exhaustion ,without causing any extra added fuel to the fire by responding to the problem with ill advised impetuosity and ......IMPATIENCE .

Giant Oak Tree - The Golden Rule of sensible living , I'd call it !

Princess Patience - And an important and extremely useful and supporting disposition as well as a wise attitude for any creature whose responsibility is the safeguard of the interests of a nation, be it a forest , a mountain or an ant hill and for the Ruler who has the reins of Government in his power.

Mushroom - Excuse me , Charlie , Your Ladyship, but there is someone here that would like to ask for some information : what shall I tell them ?

Giant Oak Tree - Oh ! Just tell them not to bother me , that I am busy and have no time to talk to anyone and , most likely , about a lot of nonsense !

Princes Patience - Well, Charlie , what happened to the ...." Sensible Golden Rule of sensible living " You were praising just a minute ago ???!!

/Giant Oak Tree - Yes , of course , I remember that quite well and I still fully subscribe to that statement of mine , but we must not overlook what you , my sweet Butterfly, had mentioned earlier , that the virtue of patience and its practice richly become the Ruler of a Nation as well as the Authority who has the reins of government in order to protect and defend the integrity and the welfare of that Nation , and this rule is , indeed , wonderful as long , though , that it is managed without loss of credibility and without appeasement to unfair opponents or enemies of that Nation ....

Mushroom - Hurrah ! For our King !

Giant Oak Tree - ...And I am saying this , my dear Butterfly , to justify the attitudes of Rulers and Kings when , at times , patience would indeed be a noble expression in contrast to what it might be necessary , some other times , to have a firm hand and a resolute stand that would not and could not tolerate either patience or hesitation , but accept only a swift and solid rebuke of any attempt to a Nation's Sovereignty .

The learned mole-cricket - BRAVO !!

Giant Oak Tree - And yet , I can prove that patience is no stranger to me !

The learned Moth - I'd like to hear that !

Princess Patience - Dear Charlie , I am sorry if I caused you to get into such an emotional reaction to my question , I had only meant to tease you about your previous statement about the " Golden Rule "! It was just an impromptu response and, at that time , it seemed to fit the occasion ! But I fully understand and appreciate what you just explained to all of us and I fully agree with you . You know , there is ,also , a common saying about patience in general ....and it says : " Patience isn't limitless " and it covers just what you just said . So , I believe that , after all , you and I are in perfect agreement .

Mushroom - Oh! What wonderful news ! I am so happy about the King and the Princess being in full agreement .

Chorus of all the Creatures of the Forest - Does that mean that we can celebrate the happy event , to night ?

Mushroom - Of course ! It does !

The learned Moth - Good idea . A noble salute to the wisdom of Power and Fortitude .

The learned mole-cricket - Well put ! Count me in .

the Syndicate of the aggregate Vegetables - We'd love to be part of it !

Chorus of the Birds - We'd love to fly in !

Chorus of the Frogs - We'll leap frog into the party .

Chorus of all the creatures of the Forest - Hurrah ! For our King ! Long live the Princess !

Mushroom - Quite a massive and enthusiastic response to Your visit Your Highness , Princess Patience ! Every creature in this Forest seems to have fallen in love with you !

Princess Patience- Thank you , dear Mushroom , but it is more representative of a crowning reward for your King ,and well deserved too !

Chorus of all the creatures of the Forest - And for YOU too , Princess !

Princess Patience - Oh ! Thank you , dear all , you really have shown a lot of patience in listening quitley and calmly to our long conversation and that does you honour .

Chorus of all the creatures of the Forest - Thank you , Your Highness , Princess Patience ! Thank You !.

Giant Oak Tree - Patience ! That word has some magic in it , the embodiment of tolerance , stability , and self possession , the expression of fortitude and courage in adverse circumstances , Yes ! Patience !......And I agree : it is a good virtue for the human creatures to learn about it , practice it and cultivate it, but , for us , creatures of the soil , trees , plants , grass and roots , it does not play in the same way because we do not practice it , we do not live by it.......we are BORN right into it and , since that birth , we patiently stand firm in the same spot , endlessly ,until our departure for other Forests in the Heavens , just as I have grown and still growing steady as a rock in the same place for the past two hundred years and still waiting for my forest in the Heavens , patiently , oh! so very patiently , to reach this greatness of mine !

Mushroom - Charlie ! Your Highness , Princess !

Giant Oak Tree - Yes , Fabius , what's up ?

Mushroom - Well , that someone I had just talked to you about , a short while ago , well , that someone is still here and keeps on asking if …well..if " he " or " she " , I really do not know which is which , but , apart from that , keeps on asking if some information could be obtained about "something" : what shall I tell them or him or her , whatever ?

Giant Oak Tree - Did you say " Tell THEM " ? How many are there , Fabius ?

Mushroom - Oh! Nothing to it , Charlie : that was just a way of saying it : all I see , really , is only one and it looks like…..

Giant Oak Tree - Like…..WHAT ?

Mushroom - Well , I hate to have to say this , but , unless my eye sight is failing me , it has all the appearance of a fully fledged flea .

Giant Oak Tree - Oh ! No !! Not another flea !

Princess Patience - Why , Charlie ? This would be an excellent experience for using patience so that you could remember me by practicing it , while thinking of me .Why don't you try ,Charlie ? Yes , Charlie , just for me ?

Giant Oak Tree - Dear Princess , my dear Butterfly , not even a King , not even the solid wood of an Oak Tree King , could remain refractory to your sweet invitation and encouragement !! So , I will try , and I will try my best , I promise you , my sweet Butterfly , my sweet Princess .: …

Princess Patience - Atta Boy .!

Mushroom –
(turning to the Flea)- Our King has granted you an audience : His Majesty would appreciate the courtesy of your kindness if you could pronounce the kind of information that you may be seeking of His Majesty .

The little Flea - What does it mean ? What do I have to do ? Please, be so kind , gentle mushroom, Your Excellency , and help me in answering the right sentence, if you will !

Mushroom - Don't be so anxious , my dear flea, nothing's so dramatic : all His Majesty would like to know in advance is , pure and simple , the nature of your inquiry. That's all ! Nothing terrible about it , isn't it ?

The little Flea- I understand , only that I seem a little awkward `and hane some difficulty in expressing myself effectively and clearly, but I'll come to it in a jiffy .

The learned Moth - An old proverb says : " slowly but surely " .

Mushroom - Yes , go on , please !

Little Flea - You see , I am a peaceful flea and I do not even jump as high as most of my Sisters do , I do not bite or tickle dogs , on the contrary I make friends with them and , in return , the dogs , because of my disposition for a favourable coexistence,let me stay with them , nicely tucked in among their fur so that I am very warm during the rigid Winter days , when it is terribly cold outside !

Mushroom - I understand , little Flea , but could you come to the point a little faster, without ,of course , jeopardizing the " sure " path of " surely " ?

Little Flea- Yes, yes , I'll do my best , Your Excellency , I'll come to the point , presently.

Mushroom- That's reassuring .

Little Flea - You see , when I was in my Country and growing up , I always dreamed to travel to other Lands and I became fascinated by some travel brochures depicting your Land as the Land of Wisdom , where Mushrooms were the actual Archives of the Laws and of the Rules and of the Registry of the Kingdom , The Birds were the heralding Ambassadors of good will and the Frogs and Lizards made up the pacific and contented population of this Land ,further described as " enchanted " !! So , I wanted to see it and ask many questions about enchanted things and about the enormous , great trees , their greatness reaching the sky ! This is what I am anxious to inquire about and learn about the life here , in your Forest . Sorry it took me so long to come to this point .

Mushroom - Don't worry ! The wise Moth just said , " slowly " , and , certainly , your coming to it WAS rather slow , but , at the same time , it got us home without a hitch .

Giant Oak Tree - Well, Fabius , have you found out what this newly arrived flea wants to know ?

Mushroom - Charlie , this Flea seems different from the previous one and it just seems to occur to me , now , that she might be a "she " because she is so gentle , almost fragile in her speech and expressions , humble and serene in her attitude and gracious in her asking for attention , and she seems more desirous to learn rather than teach everybody

Giant Oak Tree- I am proud to hear all that , dear Fabius , but you haven't told me yet what she is after ! Are you , by any chance, falling in love with her ??.

Mushroom.- Who..? I ??....Falling in love with a flea ??....Charlie !!

Giant Oak Tree - Well , the way you described her sounded like you had been mesmerized by her ! Do you think that , may be , and I just say , may be , she could be a witch in disguise ??

Mushroom - Positively not !

Giant Oak Tree - How can you be so sure ?

Mushroom - She was not carrying a broom .

Giant Oak Tree - That's refreshing , in a way . Well, now , and again , what did she say that she wanted?

Mushroom - Back in her Country she had become fascinated about some advertisements ,found in a travel brochure , representing our Land as an "enchanted Land " or even touted as the Land of " wisdom " and so on , and she became so enthralled by it ,that she decided to leave her home and travel to this Forest of ours to find out things for herself .

Giant Oak Tree - Poor thing ! ..And I cannot imagine who might have been that idiot who would write such rubbish and , on top of it , advertise it too !! He must have been trying to add a few more bank notes of the Acacia tree for his underground nest for the Winter season , I guess , and this gullible flea fell for it .! The poor thing ! But , what else did she become fascinated about ?

Mushroom - One thing , in particular , fascinated her fantasy to the point that the initial hesitation , whether to leave her house and get on the road and travel to our land , was easily overcome and she left the safety of her house to come to us .

Giant Oak Tree - That's fine, but did you ask her ,then, what it was "that particular thing"that fascinated her more than everything else she had seen in the travel brochure ?

Mushroom - Yes , I did .

Giant Oak Tree - But , then , Fabius , say something !!! What was it ??

Mushroom - The almost incredible greatness of our trees .

Giant Oak Tree - Oh !! Dear Me !

The learned Moth - May be the little young Flea does not really understand what "greatness" is in a tree .

Lady Greatness - May be I can help .

The learned Moth- Ah ! Someone else is here ! Welcome to our Forest , gentle Sranger ! And may I ask who are thou , wandering alone through these thick woods and so sure , so willing , so concerned ?

Lady Greatness - That's my trait . I am Greatness .

Little Flea - Oh ! Thank you , dear Lady , for answering my quest and I am very , very happy to hear someone wanting ,trying ,to answer my questions and I hope that your needed attention will not cause you any undue discomfort as a consequence of my simple questions .

Lady Greatness - No question is simple if asked with a sincere heart , provided , of course , that the one who asks has one .

Little Flea - Lady Greatness , in my Country , the so called and far away Land of Jumpcadilly , I happened to come across a travel brochure which was advertising the almost unimaginable greatness of the trees in the Forest of their Land , the Land of Forests as the brochure advertised it , if I remember it correctly , and I think I do , and I became so impressed with it that I left my home to come here and see the greatness of these trees .

Lady Greatness - I understand what you are saying , child , but what is your question that you need to have answered ?

Little Flea - Lady Greatness , do you think that I did wrong by leaving my home just to come here to see this greatness ?

Giant Oak Tree - What's going on ,Fabius ? What happened to the little ,gentle Flea who wanted some information ?......FOR ALL THE HEAVENS IN THE UNIVERSE , WILL SOMEBODY TELL ME SOMETHING , SOMETIME , in this supposed Kingdom of mine..???!

Princess Patience - Now , now , Charlie , this is as good as any time to practice patience and wait and listen .Why don't we just stay quiet ,here , and try to follow what these two creatures will say. They seem to be getting along quite comfortably , I see !

Giant Oak Tree - Dear sweet Butterfly ,you never fail to be yourself , and I give in and you take the centre stage !

Princess Patience - And I'll take it gladly , Charlie ! So , let us be quiet and listen .

Giant Oak Tree- As you wish , my Princess !

Lady Gratitude - Now,about your question ,dear little Flea, let us see :You want to know something about greatness : right ?

Little Flea - Yes , that's right ! The greatness of these trees .

Lady Greatness - Well , to begin with , and that is at the beginnin of your question , greatness is greatness wherever it is found to be ,and not necessarily an exclusive prerogative of trees .Sometimes it shows itself on something that is not as great as a great tree but it can still be great , and , sometimes , it does not fall on anything at all and things ,then , do not look so great.

Little Flea - Oh ! Gentle , Great Lady of Greatness , you can certainly talk , but I do not understand very well what you are talking about , not that I blame you for it , but , you see , back in my Country I was thought of being a little slow in my ability to comprehend things and all .

Lady Greatness - Do not feel badly about that , little Flea , and I assure you that you are not alone suffering from that condition because very many other creatures, and not necessarily fleas , suffer from the same problem, some of them more acutely so , some less affected , but , as an average , they are distributed in great numbers all over many forests , because "great" is inherently a form of measure , be it in height ,width , volume , or weight, just to say a few and , about weights , they are of many different grades and levels of greatness , heavy weights , like boxers , or heavier weights , like Geniuses ,or lesser weights ,like feathers , but , in the practical analysis , always a sort of measure , a mathematical equation which may assume several different aspects , forms and sizes , but , perhaps , most important is the perception of greatness by the one or the ones who look at it and reflect its real appearance in their own minds , that perception greatly variable depending on the available receptive sites in their brains .

Little Flea - WOW !

Mushroom - I'll be....

The learned Moth - I would not have expected or anticipated that myself in a thousand Moons!

Chorus of the Frogs and Lizards - We too .

Little Flea - I am confused .

Lady Greatness - Don't be : confusion too can be great or minimal , but that's not what we are talking about and , as I was saying , to me greatness is greatness wherever anything great is found , and whether on the way up , like these giant trees, or , all the way down ,like this miserable mushroom or a potato under ground .

Mushroom - On behalf of the Department of the Potatoes and myself, I resent that remark which I consider inappropriate.

Giant Oak Tree - I concur with that statement.

Princess Patience - There you go again, all of you! What's the use of preaching something good and see the "good"disappearing as fast as fog at the rising of the sun,and the teachings greatly ignored!

Giant Oak Tree - But Your teachings, my sweet Princess, dear Butterfly, did not imply for any of us, in accepting them, to become practice punching bags for insults and vilification ....or ...did you imply that? I am beginning to wonder!

Princess Patience - Is that what you are thinking?

Giant Oak Tree - It's not a question of thinking or not thinking : that is an activity for creatures with brains. We ,trees, do not have brains, so we cannot think, but, at the same time, we can become as hard as wood, if annoyed or confronted or attacked.

The learned mole-cricket - And they have very solid roots! I can vouch for that!

Princess Patience - Those solid roots should represent an asset in the process of thinking, contrarily to your......beloved King's statement about brainless trees.

The learned mole-cricket - How's that?

Princess Patience - An old proverb of a once antique and ancient Country ,yet, very much alive today, in these modern times, goes like this in its own native language : " Scarpe grosse, cervello fino ", which, possibly, roughly translated in the prevailing lingo of this Forest, would read : " rough shoes, but keen intellect. "

The learned mole-cricket - But trees do not have shoes!

Princess Patience- Elementary, my dear and learned mole, just substitute roots for shoes and there you have it!

The learned mole-cricket - I had not thought of that.

Princess Patience - Evidently you do not wear rough shoes or you would have easily thought of it.

The learned Moth - A veritable assertion .

Lady Greatness - There you are , just a matter of measure for everything , big , large , great , small, medium , extra large and impossible .

The learned Moth - That last one , impossible , probably is the most appropriate of them all .

Chorus of the Lizards and the Frogs - We think so too . The whole thing is simply preposterous .

Giant Oak Tree - RIGHT ! Some order is necessary before we turn everything into a pandemonium out of nothing!!!..... MUSHROOM !

Mushroom - Yes , Sire !

Giant Oak Tree - Call out the Guard !

Mushroom - The….What ??!

Giant Oak Tree - The Guard , you idiot ! The Guard !

Princess Patience - Patence ,patience , Charlie !......Charlie ? Why do you act like that , all of a sudden, just out of the blue ?

Giant Oak Tree- At the moment , my dear Princess , I feel just " suddenly out of the blue , the green yellow , orange , pink , and sepia " if you want to know the truth!

Princess Patience - This saddens me greatly , Charlie !

Lady Greatness - Do not worry ,Princess , and do not be sad either : all you need to do is , first , to measure your sadness and see how great it is , then , when that measure is known , beat the daylights out of everybody around in the appropriate measure that you had calculated .

Princess Patience - Oh! I cannot believe what I hear !! I , Princess Patience , to beat the daylights out of everybody because of my sadness about Charlie's lack of self-control and a little flea's fanciful and capricious images of extra large and extra tall trees and the greatness of trees ,....this is totally unacceptable !!

Lady Greatness - It was just a suggestion .You should really figure out yourself the best way you would like to go about it . To me it is nothing more tan a matter and a manner of measure and that is ,everything .

The learned Moth - And where to ,now , from here ?

Lady Greatness -	I , personally , would like to continue my conversation with the little Flea, left alone there , possibly wondering what's going on !
Little Flea -	Oh ! Dear Lady Greatness, I was all ears listening to all that tit for tat going on between those illustrious personages . but , really ,I too would rather continue our conversation , rather than remain here inactive among these upset creatures .
The learned Moth-	Nobody is upset here : they are only irritated .
Lady Greatness -	You see,dear little Flea : what was I telling you ?
Little Flea -	Yes , I remember : something about .....wait....what was it ....wait ..was it perception ? Am I right ?
Lady Greatness -	RIGHT !! Very right ! and you are learning fast, my dear . You see , the good old Moth had her own view , that is , her own...perception of the emotional atmosphere among all those creatures . Another Moth, for example,might have had an entirely different impression of the whole thing !
Little Flea -	Everything seems to come together a lot easier when you explain it, Lady Greatness!
Lady Greatness -	And you tell me that back in your Country , Folks say that you are slow ? Shame on them ! I wonder if in your Country there are enough mirrors for them to look at themselves : they might change their minds as to who , really , may be the slowest .
Little Flea -	Oh! Lady Greatness , thank you for talking to me so gracefully and even encouraging me to think more positively about myself and my ability to understand things .
Lady Greatness-	My dear child , well , my dear Flea , that was not much what I did, really !
Little Flea -	To me it was !You see , back in my Country, I am not looked upon as a smart flea but rather,as a dum one.You ,probably , would say ,a stupid flea! ....
Lady Greatness -	No , not I , dear Flea , not I would call anyone like that , not even a stupid one . I happen to be too great not to be stupid myself .
Little Flea -	Well, anyway , at home , I am considered a very stupid flea,interested only in big trees , instead of thinking seriously of marrying and having many little fleas
Lady Greatness-	But that is simply dreadful, poor little Flea ! How can they be so crude !.

Little Flea- It really hurts .

Lady Greatness - And it upsets me too , and .thinking back at one of your earlier questions , "did you do wrong leaving home " , I cannot really blame you for doing it!

Little Flea - I know , but what can you do when you are labeled as a stupid creature ? Everybody believes that you are stupid , then . They smile ,and keep on going and you remain stupid for the rest of your natural life .

The learned Moth - Veritable words .

Little Flea - Lady Greatness, tell me ,please , if you could , how does a stupid flea look like ?

The learned Moth- Ask a stupid question and , most likely , you;ll get a stupid answer .

Lady Greatness - I do not think that you can tell right away if a flea is stupid or not by just looking at it : you see , generally , fleas are quite a sort of smart cookies , they jump so fast, so high and so far that it is difficult for anyone to have enough time to look at them long enough to pick up some positive signs to pass a sensible or accurate judgement .

The learned Moth- Veritable words , indeed .

Little Flea - Oh! I see ! So it seems to me that the higher and farther you can jump, the smarter you are , right ?

The learned Moth - Veritable words, but will the fleas ,back in her Country , believe it ?

Lady Greatness - Not really so , dear little Flea ,not in a true sense but you'll be surprised of how many creatures there are in this Forest who would like to jump that high and that far , and cannot do it .

Little Flea - Are those the stupid ones , then ?

Lady Greatness - They do not think so .

The Secretary of the stupid Creatures - Lady Greatness ,Your Highness , the significant verbal contribution by You to the existence of all of us has aroused our curiosity and that's why we have decided to make an act of presence and introduce ourselves .

Lady Greatness- You are most welcome, Sir , and our anticipation to hear you is great .

The Secretary of the Association of the stupid Creatures - We heard the plight of our little unfortunate Flea and felt sorry for her !

lThe learned Moth - Yes , a real sad story .

The Chorus of the stupid Creatures - Every story is sad , unless it is not a sad story .

The learned Moth - Why would you want to say something so absurd and so stupid ?

The Chorus of the stupid Creatures - We said that , in that way , because that is our business . Had we said it in a logical way , we couldn't have remained stupid any longer and we would have had to turn intelligent , and that would have been terrible! Simple , is it not ?

The learned Moth- Same as "not" . I am turning stupid too.

The Chorus of the stupid Creatures - Welcome to the Club !

The learned Moth- Thank you for the invitation , but I am afraid I can't get in .

The Secretary of the stupid Creatures- Why not ?

The learned Moth- It's too crowded ,already .

The Secretary of the stupid Creatures - We always have plenty of room set aside and available to new comers . What's more refreshing , more simplifying , and more dispensing from any form of behaviour , obligation , or comprehension than that of being stupid ?

The learned Moth - Something to think about , but I doubt that it needs any advertising because its appeal is already and always well patronized .

The Secretary of the stupid Creatures - But of course : that's natural . Creatures enjoy stupid things ,they look for them , they laugh at them , they feel relaxed when confronted with them and why ? Because doing so carries no weight of responsibility , no implications and no partnership with their doings . After all ,what can a stupid thing do if nothing else but laugh and look stupid even if inside that thing might cry because she does not understand what stupid means and the intelligent creature is not yet smart enough to have mastered the language of the stupid people . It all boils down to a measure of an unequal divider between the two intellectual expressions .

The learned Moth- But the way you express yourself sounds something of an intellectual nature . Are you sure that you are stupid ?

The Secretary of the stupid Creatures - Well, it's a long story . Yes , dear learned Moth , I used to be intelligent but, then , considering the significant advantages of being on the low side of the intellectual spectrum , I joined the swelling crowd of those happy and fortunate creatures of low intellectual range and became their Secretary by a unanimous vote of confidence , due to the recognition of my utter and unenviable stupidity for selecting this latter for the former intelligence .

The learned Moth- The grandest of the grander of greatness of utter intellectual chaos .

The Chorus of the stupid Creatures - "Greatness ,you said ?....Didd you say.......GREATNESS ??....Well , for your information , greatness has no meaning for us : none whatsoever, except in the case when a regular stupid thing gains notoriety by attaining a taller stature which , in our simple lingo , means height .In other words, to us , greatness occurs when a regular stupid sister or brother of ours displays a remarkable increase in its stupidity status . In this case , then , it is considered a great stupid thing . Reversely , if reduced to a very small size , it is referred to as an insignificant stupid thing , to be further considered that in between all of these extreme cases , there exist several variations of stupid greatness, the smallest of them , usually , looking up to the one on the higher level , of stupidity ,of course , and , the one on the higher level , looking down on the smallest of them on the lowest possible level .

Little Flea - For the blessing of all the trees in this Forest , these creatures can certainly jump as high , if not higher , than I can , with their imagination !! Oh , Lady Greatness , did you hear all this verbal pandemonium of such confusion and illiterate contradictions that would make raise the hair on anybody's head , at least for those creatures who happen to have both of them , that is a head and hair on top of it ?

Lady Greatness - I did , I did, and may be you are right and it is appropriate for me, at this time, to get in the middle of the whole mess and try to make some sense of it , if for nothing else but to prevent anybody's hair to go straight up on their heads ! That really would be a serious handicap and an extremely difficult and precarious situation as well as a contingency for those who , as a rule , do not have any hair on their heads .

The learned Moth - An interesting development , but I am somewhat uneasy about its probable follow -up .

Lady Greatness - Respectacle parties , I am Lady Greatness ,and I'd like to come in into your present discussions and add a little further information about the variations of greatness as described and , subsequently , explained by the respectable ensemble of the stupid Creatures and that is that there are several harmonic variations of the level of anyone's stupidity , a significantly common phenomenon of mathematical proportions between the great stupid things and the smaller stupid things , an harmonic variation of a level that becomes noticeable ,at times , in any of those categories , but , stealthy as a ghost , it makes itself noticeable a little at a time ,gaining a silent and discreet access to that selected someone's fabric , and that keeps creeping on and on ,slowly, subtly , but inexorably forward , until it reaches the limit of tolerance of any acceptable variation of the harmonics of the great stupid creatures and of the small stupid creatures ,and , once reached that point , the variations seem to disperse themselves and fade away into ,let's say , " thin air " , and precisely at that point , everybody loses its head . This is considered a very stupid thing to do , because , when so many creatures and so many things lose their bearings , these creatures and things are no longer called great stupid creatures or things or small stupid creatures and things ,but only crazy creatures and things .

The learned Moth- Scary , isn't it ?!

Chorus of the stupid Creatures- We heard you , Lady Greatness , but we are not capable of such "refined" explanations of our behaviour and we are not even sure that we could learn about them , or ,even use their wisdom ,all of those ingredients being refractory to our comprehension . Basically we are and remain extremely stupid entities out of an extremely clear stock of stupidity and of extremely pure racial descent of stupidity , and we have no way to comprehend , feel or memorize any "harmonics" of our existence . Stupidity is our character , and our intelligence as well . It is our heredity and our pride too .

Chorus of the intelligent Creatures- We are the mediators between the great stupid things and the great intelligent things. We , usually , do not care much for the small things of either identity. Now , whether we or they are at all necessary in this Forest of ours , that is something we do not know , in spite of numerous efforts to find that out by even more numerous eager explorers of our existences ,but , we reasoned , what would be the use of knowing that anyway , when , should the possession of that knowledge indicate that the time had come to leave this Forest-Planet, we could not leave it anyway , not knowing how . In final analysis , final for us , that is , but still on-going for what is around us and we may not even be aware of it , so , in final analysis we just observe our Forest, our World ,the one we can see and, so to speak , touch , and , then , work with it while he is working for himself totally unaware that we are here watching him ,night and day ,and then we criticize it , investigate it and utilize it the best we can .

The learned Moth - What is there left that has not been said yet and can still be said ?

Little Flea - Dear little Moth , don't you think that enough has been said already , even too much ? My head is swirling with so much commotion caused by so many verbose creatures ! I feel dizzy ,really ,and to think that all I wanted to know when we started was some information about the remarkable greatness of the trees and an assessment of my personal mental acuity , if any , and a favourable one ,if possible , on that score . Instead we were corralled into a most peculiar match of words , sentences and personal opinions , rather than pay any attention to my quest or ,at least , to offer the simple courtesy of an acknowledgement and I feel very saddened about it . All the way from my far away Country and I am experiencing a funny sensation of having wasted my time , diluted my enthusiasm about the greatness of the trees , worn out my curiosity about the Forest , and having achieved nothing but only given a lot of stimulation to completely strange elements , unfamiliar creatures and feuding parties to foster their own vested interests and objectives . Is this ,then , the greatness of the trees ?

The learned Moth- Little Flea , Lady Greatness is here and wants to talk to you.

Little Flea - Oh ! Yes , yes , I want to see her !

Lady Greatness - Dear little Flea , although I have met you only a short time ago , yet , during our conversations I had the opportunity to formulate quite a few well measured opinions , ideas and impressions that gave me the necessary tools to gauge your personality and your potentials , and this is my conclusion : " YOU ARE GREAT ! " .

Little Flea - Oh! Dear Lady Greatness, how nice , how sweet of you to say that , but , you see , your words , even if deeply felt , are just words and they probably could not fly high enough and far enough to reach my Country and spread the good word ! I shall still remain a big tree dreamer , over there , and nothing else .

Lady Greatness- You are wrong , my dear Flea ! You see , one good thing to remember is to have confidence in yourself ! Confidence , I say , because you are not alone in this World,.....well, I should have said ,in this Forest , but what's the difference anyway , so , as I was saying , you are not alone in this Forest , dreaming , or wishing , or longing to be something you either believe in or are fond of , or wish for , therefore you should not be discouraged because , and you just think of it for a second ,because if time means anything anyway in any creatures'desires , so you just think for a second why could you not be just as big or great or even greater than a big tree ?

Little Flea - But dear Lady Greatness ,could that be at all possible ? Lady Greatness I cannot believe it !

Lady Greatness - Well, do believe it !

Little Flea - But , Lady Greatness , how can that be ??! I can go that far in understanding why , may be , a big tree would be wishing to be as big as the one next to him or even bigger , but ,dear little me !....I am so small , Lady Greatness , how could I possibly compete with a tree , least of all a big one ???!

Lady Greatness - Simple , my dear little Flea, quite simple : CONFIDENCE ! . You see , the reason is that you could be as great as a big tree and even greater , bigger and larger ,because the big tree cannot do what you can .

Little Flea - I do not understand . Could it really be so ?

Lady Greatness - Yes , not only it " could be so " ,but , actually " is " so .

Little Flea - But....how ??

Lady Greatness - Because you can jump and he cannot .

The learned Moth - The big tree could not fly either , like I do .

The little lit candle- Am I glad of that ! I really would not like to have a big tree flying around me !

Little Flea - Lady Greatness , I believe that YOU are great !

Lady Greatness - If I were great , really great , that very , very great , you could not see me , dear child , because that classification has not come into use ,yet .

The learned Moth - Veritable words ! Noble words ! A little presumptuous , may be , but nevertheless words .

Lady Greatness - And now , dear little Flea , you have seen the big trees and found out about their greatness and ,in the process , you have discovered your own. You must now go back to your home because , remember , regardless of how bright , how inviting , how pleasant any other abode may look , it will never be as sweet as your own home ,and , above all , never , never , never ever lose your confidence . Goodbye , now , gentle little Flea, and good will speed to your home .

Little Flea - It's hard to say goodbye to such nice creatures as I have found here and particularly so to dear Lady Greatness , but I understand that this is the right thing to do: what would be the use ,then , of learning something and , then , not putting it into practice? So , goodbye Trees , goodbye creatures and things of all "harmonics" of intellect , goodbye pretentious Billy Goat, goodbye mole cricket , goodbye little Moth and ,please , do not fly too close to your candle ! That bright light may be deceiving with the allure of its brilliant appearance,so , beware , because that enticing light might draw you closer and closer to her and then….it burns you ! Oh ! I'd hate to see that happen to you , dear little Moth , so , please , be very , very careful , always .

The learned Moth- Do not worry about that , dear little Flea , it is all perfectly normal : don't we all fly eagerly , at first , towards that alluring flickering candle of our individual lives ? Sometimes the flickering persists to the end of the wick, and , sometimes , it doesn't , and , when it doesn't …..well ,why to bring in sad thoughts at this moment of parting ! Let us be happy that we were given the opportunity to meet , that we learned about each other and that the candle has not gone out yet !!

The little lit candle- The way you go about saying these things ,it makes me cry and that's bad because ,if I start crying , then the wick will get wet and the light will go out !

The learned Moth- You need not cry , little bright candle , this is not the time for that : it's time for saying goodbye to the wonderful time we all had and go forth , now , with renewed energy , in our flying around our destiny and don't you dare knock off your flickering flame but keep it up for me with confidence .

The little lit candle- I will, I will , and I am very confident that my flickering little flame will not go out ! You know , I am made of ancestral quality wax of century old heritage , just in case you did not know or had overlooked to notice .

The learned Moth- Give them an inch and they'll take a mile ! Pretty normal behaviour , isn't it , dear little Flea ?...Well, then ,back to our adieus ! So , little Flea , "good will" speed to you ,back to your home and , please , do not ever forget and always keep alive in your mind and in your little heart what Lady Greatness told you : do you remember it ?

Little Flea - Yes , dear Moth , I do remember it : " CONFIDENCE " !!

The learned Moth - Wonderful! and good luck to you ,dear little Flea !

The Old Goat - Bye , little Flea , and don't forget to write , sometime . We all want to hear from you .

Little Flea - Thank you , you all wonderful Creatures I was very fortunate to find you, meet you and learn your ways and I love all of you .Goodbye , now .

All the Creatures of the Forest - Bye, little Flea ! We love you !

.............and now the little Flea , full of Confidence ,
takes a spectacular leap in the air and disappears from view ....

****

Giant Oak Tree - Fabius ,....little Mushroom down there...Fabius !

Mushroom - Yes , Charlie ,what's up ?

Giant Oak tree - Fabius , I can feel some more quiet down there now : have ,may be , some of those creatures left by any chance ?

Mushroom - Yes , Charlie , they have left , most of them ,and the little Flea has left too but I am not sure if some might still be milling around .

Chorus of the Others milling around - We are leaving too,and some have already left . You know , we can always take a hint .

Mushroom - Oh! Do not take it that way : our King did not phrase his question in a way of expressing inpatience at your being here : he just was anxious to see if everything was in order : that's all .

Chorus of the Others milling around - Yes , your Excellency , Chief of the King's Privy Council , please , kindly report to the King that everything , at least up to this point , is in perfect order. After this point , we could not possibly vouch for anything .

Mushroom - Does your sibylline , cryptic answer imply a mysterious content of impending prognostication of doom or something of that nature ?

Chorus of the Others milling around - Not that we know of : nothing enigmatic in our saying , just a common way of everyday use that we know what has happened and what is happening now but what 's going to happen next is anybody's guess . That's what we meant.

Mushroom - I understand ,but there was a lot of talking going on when the little Flea was there chatting and chatting with all of you before eventually leaving and you all must have had something interesting to talk about !

Chorus of the Others milling around - Nothing really of any major significance . All we have heard being talked and discussed and learnt was that the little , gentle Flea got a lot of courage built in her after talking with Lady Greatness who had inspired in her the all important notion of confidence and , after that , the little Flea , happy and full of confidence , with a giant leap which she could never have achieved before, rose into the air and disappeared ,anxious to get back to her home and spread the good word .

Mushroom - Do you mean the word of....confidence ?

Chorus of the Others milling around - But , of Course ! What else ? And with that confidence she will wake up the dormant spirit of those tribes in her Country and changes will occur for the better .

Mushroom - Revolution , you mean ?

Chorus of the Others milling around - Well, we wouldn't be so radical ! Shall we say , some wise changes for the better ?

Mushroom - It sounds just the same to me ! Anyway that ,then , was all the talking about, all that chit-chat and agitation : priming each other to do great things ! Well, if I remember correctly , hadn't that little Flea come to our Forest precisely to find out about the greatness of our trees ,and ,I wonder , could it have been just a cover up for wanting to know the secret of that growth and ,once known its mechanism , devise ways of destroying it ?

Chorus of the Others milling around - Yes , of course ,she had come to find out the reason and the cause for that unbelievable growth but purely in a peaceful way and on an information seeking visit , out of sheer and honest curiosity. Nothing mysterious about her visit, no revolution planning , no subversive attitudes , no hostile feeling towards our Forest , our King , our.....mushrooms ,lizards or frogs , just a simple visit to fulfill her curiosity about our Giant Trees.

Mushroom - Thank you , thank you , but details are not necessary : we just were interested to know what all that chit-chat was about ! I'll refer the report to the King .

Chorus of the Others milling around - Our King and our Minister , His Excellency the Mushroom, seem to have a lot of worries and fears , and visions of rebellions and revolutions on their minds ! We would not like to live like that ,under that constant anxiety of something turning upside down , but , thinking of that Flea , the way she had changed by the time she left , well , we wonder , she could really stir something up !

............meanwhile.......................................

........meanwhile , the two old maids sparrows.
Andrea and Celeste , whom we had left
perched on a branch of the Giant Oak
Tree, silently but attentively observing
the unfolding events below on the ground...............

1st Spinster
(Celeste) - Well , Andrea , you see, a lot of talking but no foul play as you had been afraid of .

2nd Spinster
(Andrea) - The day's not over yet , dear Celeste ,and I am still uneasy and fear for the worse .

1st Spinster- But, Andrea, did you notice how nice ,how sweet and friendly everyone was among all those creatures down below ,near the Mushroom , and right there, close to the market place ,everybody talking about something ,freely and openly and not a hint of any observable impending doom !!

2nd Spinster - What you just described ,dear Celeste , is precisely what happens when "doom" strikes ! No one ever pays attention to the subtle signs which precede it , either ignoring some seeming superficial changes or considering them as just slight and insufficient variations of creatures' individual perceptions, sometimes unable to absorb and represent to one's self the reality of a impending situation and its deeply hidden meaning .

1st Spinster - But that kind of mental preparedness ,Andrea , is tantamount to almost a mental complex , like a perennial suspicion about everything that happens around us !! You cannot live like that , Andrea , or you'll finish up in a mental home ! That's , plain and simple , Paranoia !

2nd Spinster - I do not know what you are talking about , dear Celeste , but Patagonia or not, or whatever you said , has nothing to do with what I am talking about . I still feel very uneasy about the whole situation and this seeming peace and quiet is just something like the calm before the tempest , I am telling you !

1st Spinster - But , Andrea , all I was able to observe were the same folks that were there before , no one else " infiltrating " among them or anyone with a suspicious look and....a Flea !....and all these creatures ,inclusive of a Flea , I wonder how they could have represented such a momentous and foretelling aspect of impending doom !....Come , Andrea , I believe that you are building up anxiety unnecessarily, and if you think that a little Flea had in her mind revolutionary instincts , well , she leaped eagerly into the air to dispense them to her own house, far away from us .

2nd Spinster - Yes, she leaped away , but the message remained there , Celeste !

1st Spinster - The message ??!.....What Message !??

2nd Spinster - " CONFIDENCE " , Celeste , " confidence "!!

1st Spinster - But that is not a "message " , Andrea !

2nd Spinster - What is it , then ?

1st Spinster - It's an "Inspiration" , Andrea !!

2nd Spinster - Dear Celeste, I really do not know what you are aiming at , but , inspirations or aspirations or inhalations , whichever you 'd like to choose, make no big selective difference to me , as they all, in one way or another, always point in the same direction : Revolution !

1st Spinster - But , Andrea ...!

2nd Spinster - Let me finish , Celeste , please.! That is the message , Celeste , for all those little creatures to feel confident in themselves and ,as a result of that exhilarating feeling , feel as great as anybody else ,inclusive of the Giant Trees .

1st Spinster - But this is fantasy , Andrea !!

2nd Spinster - Not quite . You see , Celeste , the subtle underwriting to that apparent superficial veneer of sentimental encouragement to that aspiration, inhalation or inspiration , as you like to describe it , nevertheless an incitement at competing , even if not surpassing , the greatness of great things or that of great creatures , that , to me , my dear Celeste , is not a benevolent nod to enlighten Creatures's moods and minds , but it is a clear call to subversion , rebellion and revolution and the wresting of power from those who feel so big , so great and so tall that no one would ever dare to challenge them .

1st Spinster - I do not feel that way, Andrea .

2nd Spinster - Well, Celeste , I cannot make you believe in what I believe , but you just give time to this boiling pot and it will be boiling over , and don't tell me then , that I did not warn you ! I am leaving , now , Celeste , and see you later , may be ,should things , unexpectedly , calm down.......may be ! .

1st Spinster - And where are you going , Andrea ?

2nd Spinster - To warn my Family , Celeste , and alert them that a revolution may be approaching and to take refuge and seek shelter wherever possible !

1st Spinster - Very well, Andrea , if that is the way you feel !

2nd Spinster - Are you staying here , Celeste ?

1st Spinster - Yes , Andrea : I have nowhere else to go , besides Revolutions don't happen in Forests but in big Cities first , and , slowly , begin spreading to forests too and by that time , then , that they will reach me I might have found another forest and another giant Oak Tree to live in with some more peace and common sense .

2nd Spinster - Goodbye , Celeste , and good luck !

1st Spinster - Bye , Andrea , and take care !

****

Andrea , the old maid , the one indicated as the 2nd Spinster , takes to the air in earnest , to go and warn her Family of the possible approaching peril of a revolution of some sort, while Celeste , the one indicated as the 1st Spinster , has decided to remain on the branch of the Giant Oak Tree and closely follow developments and listen carefully to the discussions and talk of the Giant Oak Tree and his faithful Minister , Fabius , the Mushroom .

****

Giant Oak Tree - Some peace , again , for a change : rather unusual , yet a very welcome change !

Mushroom - Yes , Charlie , even the two Old Maids have quieten down , and one has already left !

Giant Oak tree - Praise the Lord ! I wish the other one would leave too !

Mushroom - Well, this one does not seem to be the trouble-maker type: she just sits there ,perched quietly on your branch and she just seems to listen to our conversations !

Giant Oak Tree- So , it seems to me , then , that everybody is gone , by now and you and I have remained alone .

Mushroom - Yes , Charlie , we have been left alone in this deep and shady Forest of ours .

Giant Oak Tree- Fabius , do I seem to pick up an inkling of sadness and a touch of a somewhat disconsolate feeling in you , now that all of that excitement of voices and talk and clamour has gone away and left the place empty and desolate , right , little Mushroom ?

Mushroom - I am neither sad nor disconsolate , but, instead , I wonder if you might be on account of everybody leaving instead of lingering around and give praise to you and hail you as their most beloved King , as you , probably ,had been wishing for .

Giant Oak Tree - Amusing, dear little Mushroom , amusing ! You really make me laugh, dear Fabius , mind you , just a modest laugh, of course , but, dear fellow , have you ever aspired to become a giant mushroom ? Or didn't you ? Come , now , Fabius , I wasn't born yesterday !

Mushroom - What need do I have to aspire to such a status , such a height above the ground , when among my Forefathers there lived ,in ancient times , mushroom so big , so large and so tall that were called Giant Mushrooms and their size was so enormous that they were able to provide a comfortable dwelling for Gnomes and Witches !

Giant Oak Tree - Did your Forefathers tell you that ? The way you look to me ,now, you could hardly hold a speck of dust on your head !....without collapsing !

Mushroom - Of course , Charlie, my Ancestors told me that several times and , besides , it is common knowledge that , in the Middle Ages , Mushrooms , Gnomes and Witches , were regular and common dwellers of deep , thick forests like ours .

Giant Oak Tree - Do you know, Fabius , the language spoken by Gnomes and Witches ? I was wondering if you might had received some knowledge of it from your Forefathers .

Mushroom - Only some words , some sentences and some cheap vernacular of everyday usage in the deep forests , but I know my own language , the language of the mushrooms ,and if only people could listen to our simple lingo of Tatterville, and particularly so the human creatures, they could learn a lot of sensible knowledge . Instead , and strange as it may seem , these human creatures pick us up , they examine us attentively and diligently as if trying to extract from us all the wisdom that we are supposed to contain within our heads , they value us and ,after all that systematic and devoted attention , they eat us, they digest us rigorously and satisfactorily , and assimilate us within their own internal mechanisms but , at the same time , they seem totally incapable or ill equipped , to absorb anything good of the sentiment and wise thinking derived from our natural World . These creatures , the human creatures I mean , are so scrupulously and presumptuously withdrawn into themselves, that ,sometime , I feel almost glad when some among us , the ones more aggressive and bent to violence than the majority of us , literally poison their lives .And they deserve it !

Giant Oak Tree - Now, now , dear Mushroom , Dear Fabius , do not demean yourself to such a low feeling of intransigence to the point of wishing somebody harm !! You should consider the more prevailing thought that , even if arrogant and presumptuous , not all of them are like that , to begin with, given wide and large latitudes like in anything in our lives, and there must be some good ones too among the bad ones . Well, didn't you just mention that about your own ?

Mushroom - May be you are right,Charlie , and I gave in to my inner resentment towards the human characters , and I forgot my better judgement .

Giant Oak Tree - Do not lose heart, dear Fabius , we are all like that, in one way or another , and all the hesitations that constantly seem to plague our thoughts and cause confusion in our sentiments and feelings , keep on alternating in our daily lives' thinking and pondering , and , for all it matters ,really , in the existences of everybody and anybody , be they humans or members of the animal and vegetable worlds ,or the far away stars ,nebulae ,galaxies or the closer companions of our atmosphere , the rain . the clouds and the wind , just to mention a few , and ALL these entities , from Humans and all the way to Galaxies , and everything in between , seem to change , at times , their behaviour and activities in an unpredictable way as if so commanded to do by an invisible and undetectable directive, causing significant disruptions in many ways , ranging from just simple misunderstandings or emotional outbursts of various nature as well as suspicions and dejections among humans , and progressing to acts of cataclysmic proportions and unforeseen events of unbelievable consequences in and from the yet mysterious world of stars ,planets and Galaxies inclusive of the involuntary but temperamental inner soul of our own planet , and , dear Fabius, involving, in these various and exhilarating proceedings , equally bad and good creatures,without any distinction or consideration and yet , most of the time , all of these entities look inherently beautiful , harmless and , in a sense , incapable of such astonishing changes .

Mushroom - Frightening, isn't it ?!

Giant Oak Tree- I don't know , Fabius , but it does not appear so ,since no one in this Forest of ours seems to be more concerned now than they might have been millions of years ago .

Mushroom - How can you tell, Charlie ?!

Giant Oak Tree- Just pure deductive imagination , dear Fabius , since hesitation and confusion are still common ingredients of human life , and cataclysms and disasters of all sorts and dimensions for humans as well as for the worlds of plants and animals , still plague the daily existences of us all .

Mushroom - Still frightening !

Giant Oak Tree - May be so , Dear Fabius , may be so, frightening perhaps as a collective sensation of fright ,but even that diminutive amount of fright and anxiety, so well divided among the innumerable entities of creatures and things existing in this Forest ,will be further diluted in the immense crowd of all of us to such an extent that its ever present impendence seems almost inherently accepted and even expected , strange as it may seem .

Mushroom - Strange ,indeed ,dear Charlie !! You see , Charlie , we ,the little people down here feel the same about you !!

Giant Oak Tree - About me ??!! That's something new to me , by all the birds in this Forest, I'll say !!.......and WHY , I wonder !!

Mushroom - Well, Charlie , the other day a centipede just passing by , a real gentleman by his look , was complaining of poor visibility down here where your huge size and large frame and enormous trunk cast a very dark shadow and obscure visibility .

Giant Oak Tree- What was he doing down there that so called gentleman and why didn't he choose a better lighted place in the open where he could see on what ground his numerous feet would tread ?

Mushroom - I asked him that !

Giant Oak Tree - What did he say , then ?

Mushroom - He answered that he worked better at his doings while in a shade but he had not anticipated your shade to be that dense .

Giant Oak Tree - Oh!! That's really interesting !

Mushroom - Is it ?....And why , Charlie ?

Giant Oak Tree - Because it reminds me of something else , something of immense importance for the history of mankind , you know , the fellows that go roaming in our Forest on two legs,a large body and a small head without antennae, an event for those creatures that occurred centuries and centuries ago !

Mushroom- Really, Charlie ? This is really interesting !....What did it remind you of, Charlie ?

Giant Oak Tree - Leonidas .

Mushroom - Who ?

Giant Oak Tree - Leonidas. You know , of course , who Leonidas was , right ?

Mushroom - I don't . Sorry , Charlie : not the slightest notion .

Giant Oak Tree - For all the Gods of Mount Olympus , my dear little Mushroom , you do not know who Leonidas was !!!???

Mushroom - Yes , I do not know who Leonidas was .

Giant Oak Tree - Your lack of knowledge constitutes an unpardonable gap in academic glory .

Mushroom - Same goes for your Leonidas . May be he did not know me either .

Giant Oak Tree- Dear Fabius ,your personal cheap wits will not absolve you or anybody for dispensation from knowledge , as it is commonly taken for granted that ignorance of the Law , for example , among civilized creatures , is no excuse , so ignorance of something important in the events in the life of mankind should not go ignored .

Mushroom - Charlie , I am sorry to keep on retorting , but has it occurred to you that you have had well over a hundred years of existence to accumulate your knowledge as against my only a couple of days ? Even your Leonidas, was older than I , I am sure !

Giant Oak Tree - Yes, dear Fabius , he certainly was and do not worry about me chastising you for your lack of academic knowledge , I get carried away about history , sometime , particularly this ancient history, that made a substantial difference to the way the existing world of those days shaped up .

Mushroom - I understand, Charlie , and do not pay attention to my silly talk : after all what can you expect from a small mushroom ??!....So, Charlie, please , tell me more about Leonida : after all this rhetoric of academic knowledge and what not,I have become really curious to hear something more about your Leonidas

Giant Oak Tree - When things are placed in this type of contest I seem to lose my vein for describing historical events : they do not seem so important any more , represented with such a superficial aspect , and void of genuine interest . So , should you still be taken by a "genuine interest" of hearing some more about Leonidas, I would suggest that you travel to the Thermopylae and look at the inscription placed there , where Leonidas spoke his famous words .

Mushroom- Charlie , who were these Thermopylae ?

Giant Oak Tree - It was the name of a narrow passage in a mountain in Thessaly, Greece , where the famous event occurred .

Mushroom - Was this Leonida's of yours habit to talk to the mountains , Charlie?

Giant Oak Tree - Dear Fabius , your naïve countenance overpowers me to the point that I am not quite certain whether to continue this conversation with you or quit altogether !

Mushroom - But ,Charlie , what did I do wrong ,now ??

Giant Oak Tree - Nothing ,really. May be it's me that I am over-reacting to your simple but genuine questions : really , at a second thought, there was nothing wrong about your question if Leonidas talked to the mountains as a usual " habit of his "......since you knew nothing about Leonidas or his deeds and that famous event that crystallized his memory and that of his 300 Spartans in the history of the World .

Mushroom - Sorry , Charlie, to annoy you with my ignorance , but I understand and you have no fear : I am not laughing at your story and ,now , I want to hear it all and , please , kindly explain to me , in simple words, what this " talking " at the Thermopylae , was all about.

Giant Oak Tree - Fabius , what Leonidas said at the Thermopylae meant that he was at that famous narrow Pass in that Mountain when he pronounced those famous words and not that he was talking to the Mountains , of all the odds !!

Mushroom - Sorry , Charlie , really sorry ! I won't say a word any more , but , please , finish the story.

Giant Oak Tree- Very well, Fabius , if you insist .

Mushroom - I do .

Giant Oak Tree - Fine . Then , Fabius , just listen to this "little" episode that after almost three thousand years has grown in its military and , even more so incisively , in its moral stature to a magnitude of universal proportions, so simple , so nitid and yet so magnificent that its happening may have absolved human turpitude a million folds over .

Mushroom - But , Charlie , when is the story coming ?

Giant Oak Tree- Patience , my dear Fabius , patience , a Princess told us so , not too long ago , and , remember : Rome was not built in one day , you know !

Mushroom - But , Charlie , we are not in Rome , now , or in Thessaly , but here , in this Forest of ours and , as far as I can tell , this Forest was not built in one day either , let alone Rome and Thessaly . But , Charlie , what has all that "temporizing" got to do with you telling me the story of Leonidas talking at the Thermopylae ?

Giant Oak Tree - Because , Fabius , it was the poised , self assured , calm and immovable posture of that Greek King who , with his three hundred soldiers , kept at bay a Persian Army of two million men led by the Persian King Xerxes , long enough to give time to the other Greek towns to get together and prepare to defend themselves , a fatidic struggle in a glorious and destiny filled historical event which they were able to achieve for themselves and for the sake of human history because of the heroic and stand fast Spartans's resistance , its magnitude , magnificence and far reaching historical significance still echoing back to our bewildered imagination , even to-day , Fabius .

Mushroom - Charlie ! Charlie !....But WHEN is the story coming ????!!!!....I understand all about the magnitude , the magnificence , the echo , the bewilderment and the historical destiny and consequences and everything else but , Charlie , HOW LONG DOES IT TAKE TO KNOW WHAT LEONIDAS SAID AT THE THERMOPYLAE !!!???? ...For Heavens above , Charlie , come out with it !!!

Giant Oak Tree - I would have told you the story already a hundred times over if you, stupid little mushroom , wouldn't have interrupted me a hundred times over because your inherent ignorance of history and your candid simplicity , prevent the proper functioning of the brain !.....but here is what Leonidas said.....

Mushroom - Did he say to the Thermopylae that all the Mushrooms are very ignorant of History and are also very stupid ?

Giant Oak Tree- Don't be so silly , little Mushroom ! This, the story we are about to tell , is a serious happening in the history of mankind and , certainly , not fit for a joke ! So, dear Fabius, as the enormous army of Xerxes was approaching the narrow pass of the Thermopylae, Xerxes, the King of the Persian Host, sent out several scouts to inform the Spartan King, Leonidas, to "Lay down" his arms, and Leonidas replied " Tell your King to come here to get them !" and to that answer, Xerxes, the Persian King replied...

Mushroom - Charlie, you have repeated those names a hundred times ! Do you think that I am deaf ?

Giant Oak Tree- May be I am repetitive : just look at how many branches I have ,and all the same !

Mushroom - I rest my case.

Giant Oak Tree- So the Persian King sent new words to Leonidas.

Mushroom - Charlie, you left out „" the Spartan King ", when mentioning Leonidas.

Giant Oak Tree- I know. I did that on purpose to see if you were paying attention.

Mushroom - Bingo ! So, I WAS !!

Giant Oak Tree - And the new message said : " our arrows will be so many, their multitude so large ,so thick that their swarm will obscure the sun !!

Mushroom - And what did Leonidas answer to that new threat ?

Giant Oak Tree - " Better so, we shall fight in the shade ".

Mushroom - Charlie, the way you describe things and events it makes you feel as if you were there ! Extraordinary !

Giant Oak Tree - Yes, for that great King the shade was not an invitation to rest and sleep but, instead, to emerge even more glorious in his historical niche, and, back tracking on our earlier conversation about the centipede's comment about my shadow, this should not be bothering anybody, on the contrary, it should be quite instrumental in refreshing creatures' strength and alleviate the heat of the Summer days.

Mushroom - Charlie, the shadow you are casting is not interpreted down here, at least until now, as an obstacle against anything : sometimes, things are said just for the sake of saying them ,without any particular reference to anybody or anything. It is just an harmless expression of what one sees and says as it appears to him, or to her or to it. Besides, Charlie, you should not be astonished in hearing that so few creatures know about your Leonida and his three hundred soldiers,when the little creatures down here are trying to scratch a living in this damp and miserable environment , day in and day out , every single day of their existences ! Besides ,Charlie , your Leonidas was a human creature and I am just a little mushroom together with all the other small fellows down here and I never had to confront the Persian arrows , but only Persian stomachs and I assure you that , under those circumstances , we have killed a great number of them ,a little everywhere and not at the Thermopylae only .

Giant Oak Tree - Differences , dear Fabius , seem to fade and , some time , even dissipate , when certain basic aspects of our very existences come into play .

Mushroom - Like what , Charlie ?

Giant Oak Tree - Like the right to live , to breathe , to be free . You see , Leonidas was Great not only because he and three hundred of his soldiers kept in check the immense Persian Army long enough to give their Greek Allies time to regroup and prepare for a counter offensive , but also for his unshakable faith in the principles of Liberty against Tyranny , an he and his three hundred died fighting only because of the treason of a renegade Greek creature , and , yet , notwithstanding that treacherous act , Leonida and his braves kept the entire Persian Army blocked at the Pass of the Thermopylae for a long enough time so that the highly envisioned expedition of Xerxes into Greece became a total failure .

Mushroom - As usual , dear Charlie , you speak like a well written book ! You see , and we too , precisely for that venom that flaws in the blood of our more aggressive and valiant among us , since the day that Mother Nature thought of placing us down here in the damp obscurity at the feet of trees and others , we defended ourselves , and we defend ourselves ,and we shall defend ourselves from Tyranny and from the abuse of the larger and more abusive creatures around , with our venom , not really as glorious a method as the one used by Leonidas , but a method nevertheless and quite effective .

Giant Oak Tree - You are just as poisonous with your words, dear mushroom !

Mushroom- Our words alone , dear Charlie , without the poison , wouldn't have done any good against the Persian men of Xerxes.

Gant Oak Tree - is it not strange , dear Fabius , that after so many centuries of known history , living creatures have not found yet a satisfactory way to live in peace ?

Mushroom - The way things are going on these days , even in our Forest , it looks more like that the living creatures have found a satisfactory way to live AT WAR !!

Giant Oak Tree - Unfortunately so , dear Fabius , and the ever perplexing question in my many branches , Fabius , is that there have been , throughout the known History of Creatures and things , innumerable attempts to envision , organize and bring about a peaceful way for all living Creatures to flourish in progress, quiet and brotherhood , and none of those plans ever succeeded in spite of the remarkable physical , intellectual and spiritual capabilities of the ones who were so naïve as to try to implement it .

Mushroom - Depressing realization , isn't it ?

Giant Oak Tree- Well , I am not quite sure , Fabius !

Mushroom - But , Charlie , how could that thought of yours make itself known to you , if you , Yourself , were not quite certain about it ??...Strange , isn't it ?

Giant Oak Tree - "Strange" , dear Fabius , is not in the Dictionary of Nature .

Mushroom - It isn't ? But , then , where is it ?

Giant Oak Tree - In the heads of those creatures with two legs , a large body and a small head on top of it and no antennae .

Mushroom - Always the two legged ones with a small head !! Why don't you try to examine your own head , for a change , Charlie ?

Giant Oak Tree - That's the problem , Fabius . My head is smothered with frustration and , I should really say , FrustratiONS , so what's the use of examining my own head when millions and millions upon millions and even more heads run around without any control or intellective discipline but only screaming and yelling at anything that seems to have the appearance of order , logic and intelligence ?

Mushroom - Have you ever tried their intelligence , Charlie ?

Giant Oak Tree - Again , Fabius , what's the use ? For eons mankind and our own world as well in this Forest of ours , have tried to organize , educate and enlighten all concerned without any positive results , except the constant crying refrain of " Tyrant , Oppressor , Dictator " and a multitude of other not so encouraging appellatives , many a times ,without even knowing for certain what they are yelling and screaming about , but they scream their discontent anyway because everybody does and the finger of culpability always points in the direction of the one who dared propose a better way of existence for everybody , regardless of the idea behind it .

Mushroom - Depressing , isn't it ?

Giant Oak Tree- I would rather say " unreasonable ", dear Fabius .

Mushroom - What does "unreasonable " mean , Charlie ?

Giant Oak Tree- Unreasonable , Fabius , is the opposite of reasonable .

Mushroom - Is that so ?

Giant Oak Tree - What is unreasonable is not favourably looked upon by what is reasonable.

Mushroom - Interesting . .

Giant Oak Tree - Unreasonable and reasonable derive from the noun reason who sired the two .

Mushroom - And , Charlie , who was the Bride ?

Giant Oak Tree - Bride ??!...What are you talking about , Fabius..??!

Mushroom - Well , if Reason fathered Unreasonable and Reasonable , must have had a BRIDE , or , if not a bride , if the whole thing happened in licentious times, at least a girl-friend or a lover , right ?

Giant Oak Tree - I see what you mean ,Fabius , but in that kind of world there is no sexual distinction : you either reason or you don't .

Mushroom - Rather dictatorial , isn't it ?

Giant Oak Tree - Sometimes , there is no other way to induce creatures to understand reason.

Mushroom - But , Charlie , to encourage creatures to follow certain ideas by just telling them to do it or else , does not seem to me a pleasant manner to smooth things into anybody's mind and a very questionable way of creating happiness , satisfaction and smiles for everybody , right ?

Giant Oak Tree - But , it's being done and it has been done for centuries and centuries and millennia , dear Fabius !

Mushroom - But a repetitive error should not earn a mark of approval , in my opinion, Charlie , simply because it has happened before .

Giant Oak Tree - That's when unreasonable comes in , Fabius .

Mushroom - You don't say ! Well , now , I guess , is my turn to say : " What's the use to try to be reasonable ? " , Charlie ?

Giant Oak Tree- It is still worth trying ,if nothing else , just to absolve your own spirit of that burden , but , I was saying , Dear Fabius ,all you need to do to see that so called error being repeated and approved is to observe what average creatures do every day with their own siblings when they do something wrong and they want to teach them how to do it right .

Mushroom - That's different ,Charlie. That's not imposing a system but only simple and correct education .

Giant Oak Tree - The difference , Fabius , appears to me just as the face of a coin .

Mushroom - Do you mean , Charlie , that the error appears as an economical factor ?

Giant Oak Tree- No , Fabius , not that , but , you know , a coin has two sides ,one different from the other and , yet , part of the same coin .

Mushroom - Interesting deduction , Charlie .

Giant Oak Tree - Don't be silly , little mushroom .

Mushroom - I am trying my best , Charlie .

Giant Oak Tree - Good and try to stay that way ! …So , as I was saying , dear Fabius , like a coin ,everything can be perceived with two sides,one pleasing someone , the other side pleasing someone else ,but to make the two agree on the value of the coin as a whole, purely based on their preference for their side of the coin , would be a task that would bankrupt even Job's famous patience !

Mushroom - Really ?

Giant Oak Tree - Oh ! Dear Fabius , you know better than just your silly "really "!! With so many ,or I'd rather say , with the innumerable little heads milling around in our Forest , Your "really" would come in more appropriately in describing the patience it takes to deal with all the turbulence whirling in so many heads !

Mushroom- But , Charlie , REALLY, I had just thought that you,instead of worrying and criticising the "turbulence", as you identify it , in the little heads of creatures milling around our Forest , should, just for a change, examine your own big head ! You might be surprised what you may find out !

Giant Oak Tree- Ah! You speak wisely , dear little Mushroom , and many a time the thought has occurred to me to change my identity as well as my appearance and cease to be a giant tree and become , instead ,a small creature and live in peace in a hollow of a tree or a burrow and away from everything and all responsibilities and just look after my health and well being !

Mushroom - From a Giant to a dwarf ?! Charlie , what kind of thinking is this ? Have you lost your marbles or , rather , your acorns ?

Giant Oak Tree - No , my dear little Mushroom , I have not lost my marbles or my acorns , so do not worry about my saying !But I have been wondering all along what kind of an advantage or profit being great and large and tall brings us when it is well known how little the small creatures value the larger ones, and that is not all , but they fear them as much as they despise them and ,at the same time , they nurture envy, to such a degree that this latter ,then , fuels the fear and the contempt , senselessly overlooking to comprehend what great stands for and why great is a respectable icon .

The Great Icon - I had always believed that greatness was the ability to recognize the limitations of one's reach .

The Small Icon - I had always believed that what the Great Icon had said , was not so .

The Great Icon - That figures .

The Small Icon- FIGURES WHAT ?

The Great Icon - It just figures .

The Small Icon - I do not know about that , but it might figure just the same .

Mushroom - Those Icons had no business to butt into our conversation, particularly offering such stupid remarks . They really need a long study of their limitations .

Giant Oak Tree- Fabius , I tell you something ....

Mushroom - Yes ,Charlie , what is it that you are trying to tell me ?

Giant Oak Tree - Oh! I do not know : I just forgot what it was that I wanted to tell you ! You'll have to excuse me, Fabius, but at my advanced age , such little memory lapses are quite common occurrences.

Mushroom - Yes , Charlie , I understand and , please , do not worry about that, but going back to what you were wishing to become, from a giant to a dwarf , it means,then , that you feel that greatness is not everything in a creature's life , right ? Or ,may be , even a burden to carry on for your entire natural existence , depriving you of the essential little pleasures of life. Is it so , Charlie , or are we , may be , making a mountain out of an ant-hill ?

Giant Oak Tree - Oh ! I do not really know, besides it is not so important anymore to even talk or discuss about it : that discussion has been going on for centuries and it does not seem any "greater" now , than it was small then , or vice-versa . Sometime , I complain about my little problems, more out of boredom than real need , and short comings are an every day menu of our daily existences , regardless whether you are great or small . But , you , Fabius , don't you have anything to complain about ?

Mushroom - Yes , Charlie , I do , just as you said , and it's a natural instinct to complain about something and , about that , I could fill up an entire library with my written complaints ! Take for example the rain : it rains or it doesn't rain , and that's pretty natural . However ,when it comes to just plain spatter , every so often , a drop here and a drop there ,tic,tac and tic, tac and ,then , a larger drop here and another there ,that sort of thing is not conducive to a pleasant existence . Since I was born , I have not been able to close my umbrella yet.

Giant Oak Tree - Notwithstanding your grumbling , dear Fabius , about your existence, there must be still a great peace and tranquility down there in your world , if you are able to hear the sound of single raindrops falling !

Mushroom - The wind , Charlie , is not so strong down here as it is up there around your big head with all those branches and leaves and ponderous thoughts of government and politics , but , since the greatest part of your subjects are small ,live down here and have small heads just as small as their thoughts are , and with restrained and limited desires , the wind is hardly ever felt and on that account we , the little creatures of the world of the little creatures ,are able to hear a lot more and clearer of news , events , problems ,accidents and incidents and serious as well as frivolous gossip than you can , up there . But don't be mistaken : great peace and tranquillity have no reservation seats for anybody .

Giant Oak Tree- I doubt they would have enough tickets to accommodate the requests ! As to the wind , dear Fabius , barring an occasional headache when it blows somewhat more impetuously,yet it brings me news,stories and information from other giant trees in far away Forests and, in spite of the importance of the secret messages that I receive from there, transported to me by the pollen , information of the highest priority of classified information apt at securing and promoting our continuity and stability of government for the future of the young generations , many a time I cannot help myself at envying your little world where ,probably , there is less solitude than the one I experience up here , all alone , by myself .

Mushroom- Truly, we little creatures do not have that problem, a problem that afflicts Giants and which goes under the name of "solitude". Down here ,in the World of the little creatures ,being little means being able to accommodate more creatures in a restricted space and that creates more company and less solitude .

Giant Oak Tree - Yes , dear Fabius , and I agree that you have more company if not necessarily a better one that could be available elsewhere , yet a company and a good refuge from solitude : I , myself , tall and big as I am ,have hardly any companions of my stature and , even those that could be available , are few and scattered around , solitary giants whipped by the wind and drenched by the rain , and have become centered in themselves .

Mushroom - The wind , is well known , changes directions, frequently , but it is not its fault if the creatures and things he encounters are unable to contain it or absorb it successfully or understand its purpose and mission , and here the rumors that go around appear to indicate that everything in the changes of the weather ,inclusive the wind , is due to the shifting variations of the Atmosphere .

Giant Oak Tree - As I expected , well worn as I am in the old adage that there is a reason for everything , now we have changes in something new , the Atmosphere, and its changes and all the mess that we have to endure .

Mushroom - But ,Charlie , it was you , really you , just a minute ago, telling me that the wind , although a little uncomfortable at times, yet it was very important in bringing you the coded secret pollen of far away giant trees for government reasons and the necessary means for the continuation of the powers of the State of the Forest and the stability of the Kingdom as well as the welfare of the next generations ,so, possibly , the changes in the Atmosphere are just as important in the overall equilibrium of the forces of Nature , don't you think ?

Giant Oak Tree - Yes , of course, I understand all that, although it is a little difficult for me to fully grasp its significance , only I would like to see a less aggressive type of Atmosphere where the changes would not be so frequent and so violent as they are, sometime .

The Atmosphere - Dear big and little Creatures , I heard you talking about me ,so I thought of spending a little time with you and put in some of my aethereal wisdom in order to be congenial and in an effort to dispel untrue notions about me and my habits and I do hope that you would not mind my intrusion into your conversation ! May I butt in , dear folks ?

Giant Oak Tree - Welcome , welcome , aethereal Atmosphere , we were "just"talking , as you probably know , a time-revered pastime of creatures in this Forest, but we did not mean anything of an unfriendly nature ..."just talking "......

The Atmosphere- You do not have to apologise , dear Giant Tree , and I assure you that you are not alone complaining about my habits !!

Chorus of the Syndicate of Complaints - We are constantly being taken the advantage of by all kinds of Creatures but , to a greater measure , by the two legged ones , the ones with a large body, a small head on top of it and no antennae, who use us indiscriminately when things do not seem to go well for them .

Mushroom - The Syndicate is right: it is so much easier to complain than to praise , particularly so when the praise is directed to someone else other than one's self .

The Atmosphere - I was just going to add : " the world will be world , it does not matter which way it turns ", as a follow up to your description of praise , but, then , I thought , I would be complaining and I did not want to join that crowd .

The Secretary of the Syndicate of the Complaints - Madam , we are not a "crowd" : we are a Syndicate .

Giant Oak Tree - For your information , distinguished Secretary of the Syndicate of the Complaints , in my Kingdom free speech is the norm , is the Law and its practice is respected , implemented and defended . The Atmosphere meant, in all reality , very likely "group".

The Secretary of the Syndicate of the Complaints - Why didn't she say so , then?

Giant Oak Tree - Are you trying to joke or are you serious ?

The Secretary of the Syndicate of the Complaints - We are very serious .

Giant Oak Tree - If YOU ARE , then stop COMPLAINING

The Secretary of the Syndicate of the Complaints - I'll be.......

Mushroom - Watch it ! Cursing is prohibited in this Kingdom .

The Atmosphere- Thank you, little mushroom , for your timely intervention in that semantic digression , it was very kind and friendly of you , but , at the same time , let me remind you that ,just a while ago , it was you complaining about the rain, the raindrops' monotonous , irritating , persisting , pedantic tic-tac ,as well as the dampness and the gloom of the rainy stage and the weather instability .

Mushroom - Ah ! Dear Atmosphere ,we just talk , and , our talk , although specifically directed to a certain entity , does not carry a great deal of weight , if any at all , because , anyway , there is nothing much that can be done about the weather , changing or modifying it !

The Atmosphere - Yes , that is also what I was told when I was born and was growing up and I understand that one of your two legged creatures , with a large body and a ....well , this one , for a change , had a larger head on top of his body , well , this one , with the larger head and , may be , with hidden antennae, because he was rather smart´, this one had said : " everybody talks about the weather ,but no one does anything about it "....,so , as I had already said to the Giant Oak , you need not apologize : I understand .

Giant Oak Tree- Are you just passing by , dear Atmosphere or planning to spend a little time in our Forest ?

The Atmosphere - Ah ! My dear Giant , you just asked the question that I have been asking for time immemorial , for eons and eons , actually , since the Universe ,as we call it , came into being .

Giant Oaqk Tree- Did you ever get an answer ?

The Atmosphere - Not ever .

Mushroom - But , dear Atmosphere , how long ago was the coming into being of the Universe ?

Giant Oak Tree - Fabius , please , don't ask silly questions !

Mushroom - But , Charlie , what's so silly about that ?

Giant Oak Tree - Because that is an elementary question : everybody knows that .

Mushroom - I don't .

The Atmosphere - Either do I , and , still , I do not know it now .

Giant Oak Tree - Have you then , dear Atmosphere , been around this Forest for ever ?

The Atmosphere - Longer than that .

Mushroom - Gee ..!!!

The Atmosphere - Yes ,that is what I said too, when it all started : " Gee , Universe , what now ? ", and I began to realize that I had been assigned to be the envelope of several of the created things ,without knowing what or why , because no one ever told me that , but the fact remains that I am all wrapped up like a loose undergarment in this planet ,floating here and floating there , on its surface and why it has to be so , I do not know, but , in spite of all my efforts I cannot get rid of this little ball of yours that keeps me so jealously attached to itself.

Mushroom - Is it then , dear Atmosphere , at that time , when you tray to run away from us , away from our Forest , or planet as you call it , that things go topsy-turvy and everything gets tossed around without mercy or grace ?

Giant Oak Tree - Fabuys , you should not ask embarrassing questions like that !

The Atmosphere - Ah ! Do not worry , Giant Oak Tree , I have heard worse sentences than that !....And , yet , the Mushroom may have something in it ! You see , if I pull myself on one side , it shrinks on the other side , and if I try to break loose form one side , then the opposite side gets all stirred up and it starts pulling ,pushing , and tousling and twisting me all up to such an extent that I have to keep on changing course and direction many times,over and over, up, down , side way , upside down , trying to escape that kind of unfriendly approach to my usual more benevolent character . Since I came into existence, and that was a long time ago, I have tried to break free from this trap that has glued me like a glove to this little ball of yours , but all of my efforts have been , so far , in vain . The more I try to get away and the more confusion and turmoil seem to follow my attempt at freedom that ,in return, only rewards me with insults , anger and resentment from all creatures around, as you just were doing , before we introduced ourselves .

Mushroom - But we did not really mean it ! Scout's honour !

Giant Oak Tree - I didn't mean it ,either ! Oak Tree honour !

The Atmosphere - Don't worry ! I am not upset or mad . But my existence here , on your little ball , is rather unpleasant , because I am constantly bothered by all kinds of weird machines going through me all the time , without anyone worrying whether I like it or not ,and anyone even having the courtesy to ask : " may we go through ? " ....and if I do not show my best side ,everybody gets mad , they shout at me , they curse , they scream ,they almost seem to go beserk , but no one does anything about telling the Universe to change its directive . They just curse ME and scream at ME !

Mushroom- We feel very sorry about all this , dear Atmosphere,and we understand your problem and we partake of your anguish . But ,tell us now ,when did you first became aware that you had been, more or less, imprisoned in our Forest ,I mean in our place , on this ball of ours, as you call it ?

. The Atmosphere - I didn't ,at first , thinking it was just a temporary mission in one of the planets floating around ,just to give it a good start and make it breathe on its own , then , as time went on and nothing changed , the illusion suddenly dropped in front of me and I realized that I had been trapped on your planet….

Mushroom - Planet ??!

The Atmosphere- Well, OK, trapped on your Forest , and that I had lost my freedom in the immense wide space of the Universe ! It was a terrible shock and it made me mad to the point that since then I engaged in all possible and almost impossible , unbelievable and frantic efforts in trying to free myself from this ball !

Giant Oak Tree - Ah ! That is why , then , sometime we experience so much fury in our weather !

The Atmosphere - May be ,and may be not . I am not in control of the weather ,but I have a saying in it ,now and then. Oh! I hope, I do hope , I so much, so very , very much do hope that a day will come ,a far away day , may be , when I shall be free again from the bondage that has chained me to this ball and I will be able to fly away , free , totally free , and into the immense wide void of the Universe , that coveted unending space that constantly calls me!

The Space - "We",the Space,we do not call anybody and we don't particularly like anyone calling us . The Atmosphere is wrong, she does not understand anything about the wide space ,spaces or what not in the Universe ,besides we do not even know where he is , the Universe that it ,and we do not even know if there is one anywhere available for residency . Now, we use this appellative of "we" and not " I " as the space ,singular , because we are not quite sure of how to identify ourselves or just a single self ,the fact being that we have never seen ourselves ,we do not know how we look,or if we have a look at all or if there is only one space or many spaces or no spaces at all , and in all this uncertainty and confusion ,we do not even care or intend to get into any discussion about the whole darn thing,or the sentimental problem of the Atmosphere ,that just makes us sick because too mushy, or any other problems this sentimental Atmosphere may have.

he Atmosphere- So good for those representatives of the spaces and it is quite interesting to realize how,in any Organization ,there always seem to be some hidden areas of intellectual anorexia , and "space"must be one of them. So, in final analysis,what that "space"was saying will carry any significance only if any significance is given to what they were saying ,and , that not being the case , what they said has no significance ,at all, as far as I am concerned .

The Space - After this bombastic, high flown delirious outburst of poorly repressed and deficiently managed sentimentalism , possibly due to the influence of her volatile constitution , and not quite a pretentious assertion of herself, doubtably capable of one, if at all , in her effort to qualify her reply , this now gives us further proof and a well descriptive representation of Atmosphere's intellectual twisting, which reflects very well in her physical performances of irrational, highly emotionally charged actions and meaningless,vicious,destructive and disrupting acts of vandalism. So, there .

Mushroom - But why are these here "spaces" so much bent against you ,their behaviour even more puzzling since they , themselves , do not even know who they are or if they "are", AT ALL !!!

The Atmosphere- That's something that has been going on since the whole rigamarole of the Universe started and ,please, dear Mushroom , pay no attention to it or to them or to nobody , whichever comes first. Their outrageous attitude stems from the depressing realization that they do not seem to have any "definition" of themselves and , although they do not quite understand it, they very uncomfortably feel the lack of any identity ,and they have become bitter ,irritable and have developed a tendency to pick on anybody or anything that comes within their vicinity and range and ,then, they beat on it so that ,many times , those entities that have the misfortune to become close to them , cannot stand it or bear it anymore and blow themselves up , just to get away from them.

Giant Oak Tree - Ah ! That explains ,may be , those strange lights , those obscure changes, those peculiar sightings in the sky which we observe from time to time but we never understand what they mean or meant.

The Atmosphere- May be : I cannot really tell you what those sightings of yours are since I have never seen them, but I am not denying that you might have seen them. So many things go on in this Universe that it is hard to keep a reasonable track on all of them. Anyway , going back to those silly "spaces" , I do not pay any attention to them and , to me , space, whatever that is or may be or shall or should be, or should not be , does not amount to a heap of beans, as it is commonly said in your language, and space to me means liberty from the tyranny of this here little ball floating around in a monotonous ,constant trajectory, and which keeps me tightly close to herself , so jealously , so possessively ,so forcefully ,that does not think of anything else except herself and those little crazy creatures with two legs,a large body and a small head on top of it with no antennae who run up and down her skin , doing nothing but crazy things .

The Elite Chorus of crazy Creatures- We do not run, we never ran and we will never run on anybody's skin, that being a difficult act to perform. Madness , instead ,runs on our skin, inside the skin and under the skin. We have nothing to do with the Atmosphere or with the space or spaces , and our business is strictly reserved for crazy Creatures and of these we have our hands full.

The Atmosphere - As usual, as soon as I move or say something , everybody becomes aroused,alarmed,excited and, irresponsibly illogical, in their assertions,and everything is my fault ,without even pausing for a moment of reflection, and realize that, without me around ,this little ball that keeps on floating and running and twirling on itself as a "Prima Ballerina",would be nothing else but a little stone ,dry as a bone ,no water, no life , no nothing .

Chorus of the Stones- We are very proud of being stones: we are strong, solid and useful as well.

Chorus of the Pebbles - We are healthfully conscious of our rightful place on this twirling and floating ball and we are very proud to be the fragmented descendants of the big stones, in spite of being constantly trampled on by everybody . We represent the solid and safe foundation of everything that can be trodden upon without running the risk of getting bogged down in mud when it rains . We always offer a clear , clean and smooth surface ,pleasant to look at and to sit upon. The Lizards know that well.

The Joyful Lizard- I love the stones ! I sit on them and worm up in the sun.

Chorus of the Pebbles - And what about us ?

The Joyful Lizard- I love you too! So little as you are and yet vivacious and plentiful,you give out a sound all your own when pelted by the heavy rain or when you are carried along ,one on top of the other, by rushing water or when trodden upon by something or somebody , and , you have an extraordinary flare in organizing yourself when you display your excellent ability to achieve a solid and firm compactedness under the stress of turbulent weather or in the worst calamitous circumstances in spite of being so small and loose .

Chorus of the Pebbles - You are a very kind and gentle Lizard and we thank you from the bottom of our mineral composition for the gratifying compliments that we feel should be fully extendable to our relatives , the stones .

The Joyful Lizard- But , of course !

Chorus of the Stones- Really and surely ,dear Lizard , we solidly thank you !

The Choir of the Joyful Lizards -

Little Pebbles and Big Stones
to our hearts they closely feel
and the Ones who break the stones
have their hearts made out of steel.

The combined Ensemble of the Big Stones and the Pebbles - Goodbye , little Joyful Lizards , and come back to see us , sometime!

Giant Oak Tree - Little Mushroom , Fabius , what happened to the Atmosphere ? I heard her talking to someone or some ones ,quite excitedly , but then I lost contact. Is she still there or gone gallivanting somewhere?

Mushroom - She is still around . She got into a sort of a side-talk ,triggering a more substantial talk with stones, pebbles and lizards and this conversation has now ended and ,I believe ,our dear Atmosphere is getting ready to move on ……..as a matter of fact, here she comes , probably to say goddbye.

Giant Oak Tree- Are you dreaming, Fabius ? Did you say " stones, pebbles and lizards " ??

Mushroom- Yes, I said it and I am not dreaming either .

Giant Oak Tree - Well, if that is as it appears to be , no wonder everybody is up against the Atmosphere, if she is so diversified to even entertain stones ,pebbles and lizards ,obviously confused and getting here and there and banging herself into anyone that is stupid enough to get in front of her !....And what is she doing now ?

Mushroom- Nothing much : just fetching some weather .

Giant Oak Tree - Naturally.

Mushroom - Bah ! It looks like that whether we like it or not , that's the way it has to be in this Forest of ours or, to please the way the Atmosphere said it , on this planet of ours .

The Joyful Lizard ,just on her way out, on hearing the Mushroom's remark, stopped briefly and said :

The Joyful Lizard- Planet ??

Mushroom - Planet.

The Joyful Lizard- What ...PLANET ??!

Mushroom - The planet Earth .

The Joyful Lizard- I did not know that the Earth ,as you call it , had a surname .

Mushroom- She doesn't have one .

The Joyful Lizard- But you just said so !

Mushroom - I didn't .

The Joyful Lizard- But I insist and you just said it : you said Planet Earth..

Mushroom - That ,I did say.

The Joyful Lizard- But then ?

Mushroom - But "then" WHAT ?

The Joyful Lizard- But Then What, but then What !! What does it mean ?! You said distinctly Planet Earth .

Mushroom - And I said ,also : "that, I did say " !

The Joyfull Lizard - But then what you said means a full name,with name and family name, right ?

Mushroom - Is that what a full name means ?

The Joyful Lizard- But,certainly:it's supposed to mean just that,at least in my vocabulary,of the Lizards,of course, but I do not know if it would carry the same meaning in your Dictionary,that of the Mushrooms, of course!

Mushroom - Lizard , what are you getting to ?

The Joyful Lizard- My dear Mushroom, you had said "Planet Earth",right ?

Mushroom- Right.

The Joyful Lizard- So ,"planet Earth", Earth name and ,planet , surname . Or ,is it Earth surname and Planet name ? So , please, dear Mushroom ,tell me which is which,if you do not mind .

Mushroom - I do not know it. I do not think that they represent two names either . They are together because one explains the identity of the other but they are not to be considered as part of a Family set up .

The Joyful Lizard- But,then, dear Mushroom, in what way does one of those names identifies the other and why, to start with , is it necessary to identify the Earth, I guess, when we seem to live on it already as if we had to have some visual instructions in order to find her ??!!

Mushroom - Yes, it may seem a little confusing,that is ,confusing if you try to find out whys and whats and what for and what for not and so forth ,but , not confusing at all, if you just accept things as they are or appear to you and carry on ,without fancy deviations, on your road and pay no attention to enticing road signs advertising the very best of everything in their place . So, anyway , to shorten this story , dear little Lizard , Earth is the "name" of this Planet, and our planet is one of many floating around , at least that is what people who have been in famous Schools of Learning tell us, hoping that their Schools were kept up-to-date on inter-planetary information .

The Joyful Lizard - What does "planet" mean, Mushroom ? Does it mean something plane , smooth and flat like a pebble found in a river or a flat rock or stone ?

Mushroom- That was what most creatures thought ,at first , and that was not too long ago either. Then ,after a lot of controversy and shameful regressive thinking by some people with dim intellects ,as a famous literary Essayist later said , it was found out that the Earth was not flat but round, actually ......

The Joyful Lizard- Like an apple ?

Mushroom- Not quite, somehow more like a pear, may be a little bit more flattened at its poles, but , basically round.......

The Joyful Lizard - Ah! That's why the Atmosphere called it a ball !

Mushroom- May be so and ,also, because the Atmosphere wraps herself all around it, sliding and twisting all around without ever finding something to hook up to and use that as a spring board to get away from this ball that the Atmosphere claims it has imprisoned her against her will!

The Joyful Lizard - So, in conclusion, and apart all the sentimentalism, we live on a ball, right?

Mushroom- So it seems .

The Joyful Lizard- I wonder why it took so long to find out that the Earth was like a ball .

Mushroom- I do not know. To fathom that question,it would be better to leave it to the professionals who delve in the mysteries of those arduous questions. For us , little creatures of this Forest of ours....planet, if you will, the best is to keep on going on our road, hoping it is the right one , and work , grow, produce and ,above all, be honest in your thinking and actions,and, if you can master that, that will be the best knowledge ever ,regardless whether the Earth is flat or round or the Atmosphere is angry or not.

The Joyful Lizard- That is just wonderful, dear Mushroom, but instead of waiting so long to find out about the shape of the Earth by Scholars trying to find it out by themselves , why couldn't have they, instead , asked directly the Earth about it , something like " dear Earth , we are here ,living on you, could you or would you mind telling us how you look, so that we could appreciate more the kindness afforded us by letting us use your wonderful abode ? " ,that would have been a kind approach and the Earth ,more likely , might have appreciated it .

Mushroom - It is not possible to talk to the Earth, dear Lizard.

The Joyful Lizard- And why not ? Is she deaf ? Or talking to her is not possible because she is analphabetic and does not know how to express herself or is it because the famous Scholars did not know the language of the Earth ?

Mushroom - Who knows ! May be a little of everything . You see, everything acquires importance when somebody finds some interest in something, otherwise everything slowly gets through , ages and then disappears ,and that applies to everything , the objects of our love , our desires , our aspirations and even our necessities , not one remains intact for ever and , we ourselves , one day shall not be here anymore and ,at the same time , I cannot tell you also for what reason we are here now.

The Joyful Lizard- I know why I am here !

Mushroom- YOU ??!!...You know why you are here ??!!

The Joyful Lizard- Yes : I do know it . Does that surprise you ?

Mushroom- Yes, it does, and profoundly !

The Joyful Lizard- But why ?

Mushroom- Because the question of our existence has always been one of the most tantalizing postulates that has preoccupied , occupied and disturbed the creatures of this Forest, well let us say , of this planet ,from time immemorial .

The Joyful Lizard- It has never bothered me .

Mushroom - I am referring to the human creatures that you have certainly been able to observe in our Forest as they stroll through it ,from time to time, on their errands and business or pleasure tracking .

The Joyful Lizard- The ones with two legs ,a large body and a small head without antennae and who move by first pushing one leg forward and ,then , following with the other and repeating the same procedure in the same order and with the same rhythm, sometime slow, some time faster and , some times still, even faster: are these the ones you are referring to ?

Mushroom - Yes : those are the ones .

The Joyful Lizard - If these two legged creatures have some problems that disturb them , I feel sorry for them , but the problem is all theirs. They have my sympathy , but that is the best I can come up with to alleviate their sorrows . As I have already told you , I have no such problem . Do you have that problem ?

Mushroom- Not really . All I have is only some curiosity of those yet unexplained conditions. You see,Mother Nature has created me in a sort of a pensive mood , with a large head and an umbrella to protect it,and you could not even imagine ,in your wildest imagination, how many thoughts and worries and anxious moments are constantly going through this large head of mine !

The Joyful Lizard- I am sorry . But ,then, why dom't you close your umbrella , from time to time ? That might give some fresh air to your brain and restore your strength .

Mushroom - I cannot do it , because is permanently open like that .

The Joyful Lizard- For security reasons, I guess , and to safeguard your many ,important and valuable thoughts . Couldn't you even just trim your umbrella , a little ?

Mushroom - I doubt it : and trimming it, would not help much.:more likely it is a faulty design ! Besides you too could not cut off your head if it gave you trouble, ,right ?

The Joyful Lizard- Not the head but I have a choice to cut my tail ,that is just about the same.

Mushroom- The human Creatures....

The Joyful Lizard- The ones with two...

Mushroom- Oh! cut that out ! We have gone through that already enough and we should be able by now to know whom we are talking about without having to go through all that rigamarole of explicit lettering ! So , as I was saying, the humans do not think so: according to them the head is more important than the tail .

The Joyful Lizard- They sound rather presumptuous thinking that way . May be , one day ,they will grow up and change their minds, well, I should have said , their tails .

Mushroom - May be, but I seriously doubt it . They are like the Atmosphere that envelopes the Earth and they follow steps and are enveloped in themselves so tightly that rescuing them from that illusion is almost impossible. But, there again , sometimes is better to be in a state of illusion than knowing facts as they are or the real truth, because , either of them , could be disastrous to anybody's mental balance and ,not knowing it , makes it a lot easier.

The Joyful Lizard- Makes what easier ?

Mushroom- Makes living a lot easier .

The Joyful Lizard- I have no difficulty at all to be able to live : I know why I live ,that's why .

Mushroom- That's right ,you told me that already ! And it really surprised me ! And, I wonder , how can you know that ,when no one else has found it out yet !!

The Joyful Lizard- I had never suspected that no one else knew about it. Of course ,it's not my problem , if no one knows about it , but ,at the same time , it is puzzling to think that I ,a little lizard , know it and those creatures with two...

Mushroom- I am warning you, dear Lizard, not that again....

The Joyful Lizard- OK ! OK, anyway, as I said, it is very strange that I know why I live and why I am here and nobody else knows it . Very, very strange .

Mushroom - OK, then, tell me why do you live and why are you here , if you are so sure of yourself .

The Joyful Lizard - Simple and elementary , dear Mushroom: I live to warm myself on the stones . What's so difficult or mysterious about it ?

Mushroom- Blessed be naiveness !!

Chorus of the naïve Creatures - We are the sons of Ingenuousness ,our revered Mother, and that is our name : we are called the Ingenuous ones . In all truth our Mother was always happy ,it was natural for her to be that way,satisfied always and always contented and we are contented and happy too because our Mother was always happy and contented. Being self-assured ,as we are and our Mother was , in our belief in the character of simplicity and naiveness, this condition of our make-up gives us comfort in what's around us and simple but genuine hope for our existences . We are always satisfied in what we see and in what we hear and in what we are able to touch , look at , consume and treasure,without the need to carry on interminable discussions on the value or usefulness of each of those entities and ,that saved time , gives us extra time to smile and be happy with what we have got. Our reputation among the average creatures going around in this Forest of ours is that we are rather insipid and ,basically , rather stuipid creatures but ,even in this rapport , no one has yet been able to establish a clear distinction between the two aspects of our portrayed character,and so we consider this kind of reputation a compliment rather than a deficiency.

The Joyful Lizard- Well, dear Mushroom ,what do you think of that spontaneous expression of sympathy towards my understanding of my own being and where my own being is ,and what my own being is meant for ?

Mushroom - To each his own , dear Lizard !....To each his,her or its, own !

The Joyful Lizard- Well, enough has been said and argued and epitomised ,time to rest a little! Don't you think so , dear Mushroom ?...I see you nodding your large hat so I'll take it as a sign of approval , and I myself, really , need to get on a nice ,smooth stone and warm up in the sun and , this time, it will be an exhilarating experience ,one never ,never felt before !

Mushroom- And why do you say that,dear Lizard ?

The Joyful Lizard- Because ,now , when I warm up in the sun , I will know that I am on a planet .

Mushroom- Fine,fine! But, what's that got to do with your warming up in the sun ?

The Joyful Lizard- Because ,before ,I thought I was warming up on a stone.

Mushroom- Same difference ! Just a matter of personal interpretation , if you ask me.

The Joyful Lizard- But I am not going to ask you, because I do not want to spoil that wonderful , newly discovered and acquired exhilarating feeling ,and have it dashed down by your negative interpretation. I have "interpreted "mine and I'll stick with it ! And ,now , my dear Mushroom,is time for me to really go and find myself a nice smooth……planet and sit on it and warm up. I hope to see you again, sometime , and, please, my kindest regards to all when you see them. Bye , now.

Mushroom- Bye, bye, dear Lizard , and thank you for your company and have a good trip, wherever you may go and leisurely sun baths,and come back to see us, sometime: we'd love to see you again..

******

The Giant Oak Tree ,now directs his attention back to the Mushroom after the Atmosphere had departed from the Forest on a mission to the Himalaya Mountains and so terminated her conversation with the Giant Oak Tree .

****

Giant Oak Tree- Ehi ! There, little Mushroom ! What's up "down" there ? Atmosphere had to leave in a hurry called on a far away range of mountains ,so I heard you chatting with someone and wanted to know what you were up to .

Mushroom- Nothing much ,really. I was just thinking aloud , may be , about how fortunate beings the lizards are .

Giant Oak Tree - The...Lizards...??!

Mushroom - Yes ,Charlie : the lizards .

Giant Oak Tree - Fabius, we were engaged in a conversation with the Atmosphere,just a few minutes ago,when you picked up some sort of a side conversation with somebody else and left Atmosphere and me to ourselves , and , now , you come up with a remarkable statement about Lizards ? What on Earth have lizards in common with the Atmospheric Pressure ,I wonder ??!!

Mushroom - I don't know, Charlie ! Could it be , may be , something in common with the stones ?

Giant Oak Tree - In common with the...STONES ??!!

Mushroom- Yes, Charlie , the stones . You know : those hard substances , rocks , boulders, pebbles . Mountains and rivers are full of them .

Giant Oak Tree - Have you gone mad ?

Mushroom - Even if I were , what difference would that make to the Atmospheric Pressure ?

Giant Oak Tree - Probably none to the Atmospheric pressure ,but a significant difference to YOURS .

Mushroom - Ah! All that has not so much importance, Charlie, as there are other problem, far more important than that ! The Great Creatures ,as we already talked about , suffer from solitude and we, the little creatures of the everyday life, down here , in the boon-docks of this Forest , suffering from a problem that afflicts us more than your solitude saddens you and which goes under the name of poverty ,indigence ,that is , dear Charlie !

Giant Oak Tree- I find it difficult to understand what you are saying, dear Fabius : just a while ago you were all peppered up qnd alert, vivacious and full of ….well, yes full of witty remarks and all sorts of things and now , really, all down hearted and almost turned upside down ,from riches to rags ,so to speak , and for what reason , I really cannot understand !

Mushroom - Charlie, it is not customary to go around constantly complaining of adverse situations , and we , in this Forest , are no exception to that custom , always trying to keep up a smiling face even in the circumstances of adversity or misery, but indigence is here , Charlie , is here with us ,behind the doors of many creatures of your Kingdom , on the roads , in the markets ,like the subdued but meaningful murmuring of the little creatures in our big market , on market day , and certainly not an encouraging sign of approval, and it is in the chimneys , in the beds , in the shoes and on the tables , in the pockets and in the underpants , socks and stockings and so on and so on, Charlie , if you only could be down here for a little while !

Giant Oak Tree - But , Fabius , if the indigence ,the poverty ,is such and so great and wide-spread as you describe it , why then is it you alone complaining about it when no one else says a word ?

Mushroom- I am your friend , Charlie, and your faithful Minister so I am in a privileged position of reciprocal respect and I feel that I can talk to you openly ,not only ,but that ,in a way I am even expected to be open with you as it becomes my duty to keep you informed of what's going on in your Kingdom , to the best of my ability, Charlie ,but " the Others", the little, little creatures that go about scratching a meager living day in and day out , they are afraid to say anything and they feel that some poverty is still far preferable to prison or the guillotine .

Giant Oak Tree- I greatly appreciate your candor, Fabius , my trusted Minister,and your concern in alerting me to the possibility of developing breeding conditions of discontent due to economic stagnation . That was very wise for you to do so and it was an encomiable act as well , and , we hope , may be a good omen too for a peaceful and ordered solution of this problem .

Mushroom - Yes , Charlie , if we act now and wisely , may be the whole situation will correct itself without too much discomfort or danger for everybody .

Giant Oak Tree- We'll do everything in our power to forestall any worsening of this case at the next Council Meeting ,which is due to-morrow,I'll promise you .

Mushroom- Thank you , Charlie , ...Sire ....and the sooner you'll take action on this situation, the better it will be for the entire Kingdom : your Subjects will be grateful to you for your interest , care and wisdom on their behalf .

Giant Oak Tree - That's all well said ,Dear Fabius ,and consider it just as good as done and that goes for that problem ,but, I have to confess that , at times , I feel some curiosity for this world of yours, the one you describe so vividly with faded colours of misery, hopelessness and dejection, to the point that I find myself thinking at inspecting this ,let us say , this lower world in our Forest , that is to say ,for me to become little for an instant and see and watch this strange and miserable world , as you seem to describe it, for myself and directly , face to face ! A rather drastic event but likely very interesting.

Mushroom - Interesting , perhaps ,yes ,just for "an instant", but sad and depressing for those who have no other choice but to live in its middle!

Giant Oak Tree- Do you believe ,then, by chance ,that my solitude ,the variable and ,at times , the fierce winds and the grave ,ponderous and ,at times again, the dramatic situations of Government and its constant concerns of the conditions of the entire kingdom ,without even throwing in the important and laborious thoughts of State for the management of its Laws, the promulgation of new ones, and the correct guiding of the fiscal responsibility , are more palatable and appealing than your restricted and so distraught world of the little creatures ?

Mushroom - A hundred times better:Your world !

Giant Oak Tree- Oh ! You big fool! You are easily deceived by sheer appearances !

Mushroom - No, my dear Charlie I am not deceived and I do not intend of being deceived either any sooner ,and I repeat ,clearly and openly , that solitude, violent wind and "grave" thoughts , as you describe them , are a hundred times better than the misery down here . How exciting they must be those "grave" thoughts driven by the wind and tormented by solitude and the whole stage full of mystery and wild, unforeseen expectations !

Giant Oak Tree- Fool ! Fool ! A hundred times a big fool ! How can you be so gullible !

Mushroom- And why is that so ,Charlie ?

Giant Oak Tree- Because , dear Fabius , you act contrary to reason . You opt and wish for the wind today , to turn around and curse the rain tomorrow, and that attitude just for"a superficial and vain spirit of variety"as the wife rebuked her husband when she caught him hiding in a bush of their garden in the company of another woman !

Mushroom - Not bad , isn't it ?

Giant Oak Tree - Don't misunderstand me ,little mushroóm ....just as the husband explained to his perturbed wife ,when he said :" my dearest , please, do not misconstrue my actions : this woman here ,is my cousin .", naively ignoring the obvious implications , by thinking that the less said , the better and passing over the dubious need of hiding in the bushes in order to foster family ties . So , my warning to you too, dear little mushroom, dear Fabius , do not believe everything you hear or you suspect or you desire at first sight , because even if the wind would feel exciting it is quite variable too and ,at times , even injurious and , if the sight and appearance of fatuous changes in creatures and situations may appear as a relieving means to a heavy mind , it represents only a vague and never lasting relief to the heart and soul , and the wide ocean of solitude and loneliness increases at each change of settings ,rather than decreasing .

Mushroom- My compliments ,Sire , for the excellent explanation of the responsible and difficult tasks of Government and the appendages belonging to the Kingdom with the subtle interpretations of all those variations that so often influence and modify the moods of crowds, but , deeply sorry as I feel to contradict you , Sire , I still feel that the wind ,the rain,the bushes and the cousins and the solitude too are a hundred times better and preferable . When you are rich and powerful a little solitude is not that onerous ,the wind more tolerable , the bushes do not bother at all , and cousins of the gentle sex are always welcome.

Giant Oak Tree - I believe ,Fabius , that sheer envy lets you talk like that ! You do not seem to have a good grasp on the responsibilities and problems that confront, day in and day out , the officers and the subordinate trees in our Kingdom, and throughout all the "branches" of Government , and the Giant Trees .

Mushroom - And You,Sire,although so Big and so Great ,You do not seem to comprehend the little creatures , working and trying ,as I have already told you before , to scratch a living out of this land of our, this Forest, and paying taxes and , and then denying them much of the fruits of their labour, something similar as to let the child lick the marmalade and then take it away from him, with the result that , even at the cost of getting into trouble or even hurting himself , the child will frantically try to find that marmalade and , if found , eventually , he will eat so much more of it, because of the long experienced passion in finding it , than he would have probably eaten had it been available to him all the time . You see, Charlie , this is always the great error committed by the big Trees ,that they often forget that they were small themselves in earlier times .

Giant Oak Tree- I cannot understand what's come over you, so suddenly ,my dear little mushroom, and I wonder whether the mixture of Lizards , stones and pebbles might have had anything to do with it , but ,to all practical signs , at the moment you seem to talk with the intellect and the brain of a flea !

Mushroom - Ah! Charlie,what 's in the name .....calling out to the fleas , again ??!!

Chorus of the Fleas- Ha ! Ha ! What fools , what darn fools are mushrooms and giants. We are small, we are ,really , very ,very small but we can leap very high ,then we can come down too, very fast , from great heights ,then we can fly even higher ,at any given instant and we eagerly and indiscriminately suck the blood of great creatures and small creature alike and , if so desired or useful or profitable, we can even suck the essence of the Atoms .

Chorus of the Atoms - From a whole one to a half , from half to quarters ,from quartes in octaves, from octaves in sixteens and so on to infinite we can divide ourselves, at least that is what we were told , and we do not carry within our system any essence that could be good or useful or palatable to some very stupid fleas.

Chorus of the Fleas- Watch your language ,you bullies of the Universe ! We can still jump on top of you even if you do not have any "palatable" essence.

Chorus of the Atoms - For your information we usually choose to say whatever it pleases us usually to say and there is nothing anybody can do inclusive the fleas , and from the centre of created things....

Mushroom - If there is a center......

Chorus of the Atoms - We do not particularly excuse interruptions....so, as we were saying ,from the Center of Created things to the Center of things not created yet ,we are everything : fleas , scorpions , giraffes , elephants , yesterdays , tomorrows, mushrooms , giant trees, idiots and geniuses , musicians and philosophers , donkeys and horses, frogs and toads , flowers and tomatoes, cucumbers and melons......

The yellow Beetles- We love melons .

Chorus of the Atoms - Do not interrupt us ! As we were saying , we are everything and everyone, whether you like it or not . And that goes for the Fleas too .

Mushroom- Lord have mercy ! And we were amazed a while ago, at the noise that the wind and the birds were making ! Heavens knows , it looks like the Atoms and the Fleas could stand a cmpetition with a favourable edge of success against the Atoms !!

Giant Oak Tree For your surroundings down there , dear Fabius , the sound must or seems to be very loud but , for me , up here , I barely can hear anything or notice anything unusual as far as the noise that you are complaining about ,but , of course , I would be saying a different story when the Birds start their morning rituals , early in the morning , just before sunrise , and right on top of my head !!

Mushroom - But , dear Giant Tree.....dear Charlie...those little Birds, so gentle , so delicate , how could they possibly be so annoying , so disturbing to your peaceful majestic being ?

Giant Oak Tree - But they are annoying , Fabius , they certainly are and how !! And they are annoying and disturbing in spite of your sentimentally sick portrayal of their delicate innocence about the disturbing noise .

Mushroom - But , Charlie , just think ,instead , how dreary and depressing everything is down here , and , that alone would not be so bad or so difficult to tolerate and get by it , but , under that coat of uncertain feelings , it seems to hide a fleeting murmur of discontent of undefinable meaning and not a pleasant one either , but anxiously foreboding of worse to come !

GIANT Oak Tree - But what a cantankerous type of mushroom are you !! Constantly complaining,constantly on the look out for dramas , tragedies and unfortunate events ! What should I say , then , with all those sparrows, young ,old , middle aged ,spinsters ,oh ! ,yes ,particularly the spinsters sparrows , and so on that do nothing but “scream” the whole day long just as the Devil said about Proserpine , you know , also known as Persephone, the daughter of Zeus , abducted by Pluto, the Devil , and made his wife .

Mushroom - I do not know what you are talking about and , even if the Devil took a bride for himself , that is not an extraordinary event , but a rather common occasion even for a Devil, as there are thousands of poor devils in our Forest , who get married , anyway , every day , and you should remember the old “adage“ , :” When man and wife squabble ,’tis wise not to meddle” so , leave the Devil and his wife alone !.....By the way , how could anyone have found out that the Devil, Pluto that is , had abducted Proserpine , made her his wife and then complained about her when she started protesting ,may be ,or wanting more and better clothes or to get out of it altogether ?

Giant Oak Tree- It’s an allegory : an expression of dissatisfied husbands in the choice of their wives !

Mushroom- Well , as they say , let the sleeping dog lie ,so let us leave our good Devil take care of his own problems and , instead , let us go back to our problems, well, I should rather say "your" problem and it seems difficult to even imagine how those dainty, almost sweet little creatures , tender and soft as a wad of cotton, or wool ,or velvet ,with feathers of various colours and the sweet song of their chant and the splendid ,fast and wondrous flight ,could possibly annoy you !

Chorus of the Fleas- The Mushroom appears to be in a state of an overpowering emotion as he utters in ecstatic delight the almost poetic description of the sweet beauty of the little Birds , his blood must be hot, our stomachs empty , so ,what are we waiting for ? Forward , we say , to the Mushroom's blood ! Of great and small creatures we are the arbiters ! What's better than to seem small ,as we are , and then be the greatest of them all !

Chorus of the unemployed Atoms- Amidst the grand void of no creation, we roam incessantly in the hope to find new friends , who more fortunate than we are , did find employment in the immense void of the Universe , and then , may be , we shall also be given a chance at being interviewed , examined , calibrated and ,if all the examinations would prove satisfactory , we could also find a suitable employment and make a decent living , all very busy and in constant motion carrying on great businesses in this infinite variety of creation. We, and not the Fleas , are the smallest entities available and We are the arbiters of great and small creatures and things . We were also told ,at orientation classes , that ,in the future, whenever that will be , some smaller units of us may also play a significant part of the grand void , but their time table was not yet available . WE BELIEVE that the Fleas must be suffering from a serious sick disposition towards mental ostentation . Perhaps they tend to pose as unsurpassed wonder jumpers because they can leap very high , without realizing that they would not be able to remain at that height which they achieve with their extraordinary leaps , whereas WE are constantly at the highest of all the heights ,continuously.

Chorus of the Fleas- How pitifully envious , these Atoms !

Chorus of the envious Creatures - After all , what for , why then , is our name and custom of living so inappropriately used ? Why wouldn't you say ,instead : "how pitiful ...." and then followed by the name of those or who had made you the object of envy ,instead of using our name and ,in doing so , place us who know nothing of your strife , in an antagonistic attitude towards the Atoms, of whom we know nothing of their style of existence ,their descent, or if they at all qualify as respectable entities or if they have a clean police record, as far as we care .Besides we seriously doubt that they can read or write , so small as they are . World, world ,how true it is that it is made of trouble-makers !

horus of the unemployed Atoms- NONSENSE !! The Fleas are crazy ! They are crazy as a crazy creature can be , and that is to say the least ! All they can do is suck blood , jump high in the air and chase dogs ! Is that , now , something to be so excited about ??!

Chorus of the Fleas- Nothing , really , to be so excited about , you dumbbell Atoms nincompoops! But , have you ever tried to do it like we do it ? ......You silly megalomaniac particles of nothing !

Mushroom - Ah ! Did you hear them ? Did you hear them ?!! ...Heigh ! Charlie , did you hear them ? ?! They scream so loud and throw names at each other in such a way that I feel almost certain that even the Universe would get sick of them !

Giant Oak Tree - And why do you pay any attention to them ?

Mushroom - What other choice do I have , Charlie , stuck as I am on the ground and endowed by the complacency of our good Mother Nature of front row seating in the Grand Opera House of our existences ? ...Heigh , Charlie ? ..Did you hear what I said ? It explains my seeming sick tendency to anxiety, as you claim .

Giant Oak Tree - Yes , Fabius ,I heard you . Please , excuse me just for a couple of minutes, because I am right in the middle of receiving some coded messages from some distant trees about some problems in their Forest , some sort of turbulence , I am told , but the actual nature of it has not been clearly established yet . They warn me , though , to be on the lookout for some stragglers who seem to be up to no good !..I'll be with you as soon as I shall clear up this urgent communication , and thank you , Fabius for your patience!

Mushroom - Fine , Charlie : I understand . No problem and take your time: may be we'll get some important information .

****

Meanwhile, the two Spinster Sparrows , Andrea and Celeste , the two old maids , are together again , following closely the situation perched comfortably on a branch of the Oak Tree and Andrea , who just not too long before had left to rush to her Family and warn them of possible problems in their far away Forest , has now returned to the Giant Oak Tree bearing news of the potentially explosive situation back in her far away Forest , a situation that she had construed as a preamble to a fully fledged revolution , based on the aroused and inflamed attitudes of some of the inhabitants locally and fearing for the worse and for the possibility of an infiltration and spreading of the same situation even to this Forest.....................................

****

" The two Spinster Sparrows , now , exchanging their views on the present situation and recent events.... ..."

***

Celeste - Welcome back , Andrea ! Did you have a nice trip back home, and how's your Family ?

Andrea - Safe , Celeste ,quite safe , thank you . As soon as I got home , I gathered all of them and took them to a safe place not too far away from their home but far enough to be out of the way of possible turbulence and, may be , an unlikely place to become involved in any rioting or other dangerous activities , mainly because that place is only of minor importance as a centre and very sparsely populated . But tell me ,now , Celeste : when I was away , in my Forest , I had heard through the grapevine that some discontent seemed to have surfaced here and there in your Forest too and that some worrisome signs of unrest seemed to have been brewing as well , and a few already quite noticeable , so tell me now , Celeste , is that true ? And ,also , how is the Mushroom ?

Celeste - Well, Andrea , I am not quite certain , but I know that the Mushroom appears gravely preoccupied about some activities going on in the Kingdom and he keeps on worrying the King , you know ,the Giant Oak Tree , thinking that his concern in keeping His Majesty informed as accurately as possible of any development that could forecast an impending doom , befalls his duty as the King's Minister of the Privy Council , His Privy Seal, particularly so when he hears reports from his scouts of growing expressions of discontent accompanied by subdued murmurs of disapproval of present conditions of squalor in which some of his subjects are forced to live .

Andrea - Well , Celeste , what did I tell you ? Do you believe me now or are you still floating on a pink cloud , with a lolli-pop in your beak and a peacock feather in your head and still thinking that all of that is just pure fantasy ?

Celeste - Oh ! Believing is not so difficult , Andrea : anybody can believe easily in anything anybody wants to believe in , but , to match facts with belief , takes a different form of thinking .

Andrea - And what kind of thinking are you talking about , Celeste ?....in moments like these , when anything and everything can explode , all of a sudden , with a big , a very , very Big Boom , thinking does not help much and you need positive action instead of thinking , and .....FAST !!!

Celeste - Well , what do you intend to do , Andrea ? Nothing has happened yet,to warrant our need for increased alertness and intensified readiness, and I haven't heard any BIG BOOMS, either .

Andrea - But , Celeste , my dear and seriously naive girl , you can be certain that you will hear that Big BOOM and , unfortunately , may be even sooner than you think !......Oh ! Look , look , Celeste , the Mushroom and the Giant Oak Tree have started talking to each other again !

Celeste - Yes, they had to cut short their conversation just a few minutes ago due to an urgent coded message sent to the King from another Forest .

Andrea - I wonder if that coded message could have come from my Forest !! But I doubt it ,so far away as my Forest is and also because all available communications had been cut off just as I was getting ready to leave and there was a lot of talking about getting an advance squad of armed beetles making a foray and spreading disorder among the beech-trees , the birch-trees and the oaks in another Forest about one day away on a straight flight, as a diversion to the revolution there .

Celeste - It was very fortunate for you, then , Andrea ,that you could at all be able to leave that turbulent area, without incurring in grave danger !

Andrea - Yes , Celeste , I believe that I was really lucky , considering the grave situation developing there . I left ,very early in the morning , from that isolated place where I had taken my Family and ,at that early hour, nobody was around . I flew as high as I could and encountered only a large flock of Duck-Hawks flying in formation and the Leader had told me that they were flying directly to what I undersood was the Forest that I had just left , and they were flying to that Forest to reinforce the besieged garrison there . After that first encounter I met no one else on the way and I landed here on the Giant Oak .

Celeste - I'll say it again : you were really fortunate , Andrea , and I am very glad for you . I see that the Mushroom and the Giant Oak are talking , Andrea , so let us listen quietly and try to pick up as much of their conversation as we can : that will , may be , allay some of your fears and , at the same time , give us some extra information as well as the latest news . So , let's listen carefully , Andrea !

............as the two Spinster Sparrows remain quiet and attentive hoping to hear some news on recent developments in this Forest as well as, hopefully, in other ones , the Giant Oak Tree and the little Mushroom resume their interrupted conversation which had become interrupted , as we had noted , when the Oak Tree had to divert his attention from the Mushroom and concentrate instead in the hard and tedious work of deciphering the secret coded message from another Forest .

Giant Oak Tree - Sorry , dear Fabius , for keeping you waiting so long , but the message was a long one , complex and it required some extra time in deciphering it because the code was the combined type used by the Birch-Trees and the Copper-Beech Trees Forests adopting a system compatible with their method of transmission under the coded name of *Fagus Sylvatica Atropunicea* and our Technicians had to double translate it so that it would *enter* our system of the *Quercus Genus* and be , finally , interpreted and understood . But , I am here , now , and we can pick up from where we had left .

Mushroom - Very interesting ,Sire, and I feel sorry that you had so much trouble with that code , but Charlie….Sire ..Do you think that we'll have time to resume our leisurely conversation , if something should happen ? Sire , how were the news you received in the coded message ? Good or…. Bad ..??

Giant Oak Tree - Bad , Fabius , very bad !

Mushroom - I was afraid of that .

Giant Oak Tree- Well , the coded message warned me of the existence of a band of Stragglers , undisciplined and irregular , but well armed , who are roaming in a Forest not too far away from ours and , by the way that they seem able to foment disorder and dissent among the populace they encounter in their violent forays it was noticed that large crowds of ordinary citizens are joining them and some more vociferous exponents among them are inciting the entire mob to go further and create disorder everywhere , so the legitimate Authorities of that Forest and Government representatives wanted to warn me so that I could take appropriate and timely measures to protect our Kingdom .

Mushroom - I was afraid of that !

Andrea - Did you hear that , Celeste ? Hadn't I told you something similar already several days ago , even before I had left ? But you were very hesitant in believing me and did not think that revolutions are possible . Well, Celeste , it looks like that revolution might just be around the corner right here in this Forest !

Celeste - In a while I'll be looking around the corner to see if something is coming . Who knows ? It might just be the milk man .

Andrea - Celeste !....You are incorrigible !!

Mushroom - Sire , do you have any orders to be carried out in order to cover this developing situation and come up with some plans in case things would take a turn for the worst ? Because , now that we know that trouble has erupted somewhere and not too far away from us , if we do not take some action now, we may finish ill prepared to face the problems that might come .

Giant Oak Tree - I really do not have anything in mind at the present time , Fabius , except to wait a little bit longer to see if we can pick up any positive signs of trouble and , then , we will be in a better position of knowing what would be the best way to act . Don't you think so , Fabius ?

Mushroom - May be you are right, Sire.....Charlie !.....Yet I feel very uneasy about the whole thing .

Giant Oak Tree - May be it isn't as bad as it is being presented and it might just fade away after a while , on its own accord , if no further interferences occur .

Mushroom - Charlie...?!

Giant Oak Tree - Yes , Fabius , what is it ?

Mushroom - Charlie , I thought for a moment that I was hearing something .

Giant Oak Tree - I did not hear anything , Fabius . As you know , up here , it must be really something BIG before I can hear it .

Mushroom - Well , Charlie , I am afraid that we might just be hearing soon something really BIG , because I can hear that sound more clearly now , and also some cries and shouts mixed in it .

Giant Oak Tree - Now , Fabius , I seem to hear something too : that sound, whatever it is , must have edged a lot closer to our Forest ,but it is still faint : were you able to find out what that noise was ?

Mushroom - Yes , Charlie , and what I see does not surprise me now as much as it did worry me earlier when I had not seen the nature it was made of .

Giant Oak Tree- Well , at least it does not seem so dramatic and upsetting as we had originally suspected that it might have been .

Mushroom - Yes , in a way , we might look at it that way , but , knowing now who the protagonists of this fracas are , I would not be so hasty in dismissing the potential danger that might still be lurking in their bombastic shouting and aggressive attitude .

Giant Oak Tree- But ,then , did you or did you not identify these troublemakers ?

Mushroom - Yes , Charlie , unfortunately , I did !

Giant Oak Tree - Who are they , then ?

Mushroom - They are those little creatures ,with two legs ,a large body and a small head on top of it and no antennae , who appeared , suddenly , from nowhere , screaming and shouting at each other and , when some more of them arrived from a different direction , they all got into a fight and really let go of their civic restraints , if ever they had any in the first place , and caused this horrendous fracas , the reason for its cause , as usual , unaccounted for and , very likely , bearing no serious reason at all !

Giant Oak Tree - Strange creatures , indeed .

Mushroom- And dangerous , Charlie , as well as destructive , without regard to damage or disruption they may cause with their activities and the wanton greed of everything and anything they can lay their hands on , because , in addition of having a head ,they also have hands .

Giant Oak Tree - Yes , Fabius , we know that , and the terrible damage as well as destruction caused by their inconsiderate actions to our pristine Forests , not too far away from our own . I wonder ...I just wonder ....

Mushroom - Yes , Charlie......Sire...what is it , now , this sudden expression of amazement or doubt ? Do you feel or perceive the presence of an immediate danger ? Charlie...?

Giant Oak Tree - No , Fabius ,not that , yet , but I , quite suddenly , began wondering whether all this confusion , restlessness and agitation in our Forest and in the neighbouring Forests , as we have been witnessing during these last hours, might be due , precisely , to the almost irresponsible behaviour and greediness driven turbulence displayed by these creatures with two legs and all the rest . I just wonder !

Mushroom - You may have somethimg there , Charlie , and we know quite well how destructive they can be to our Forests and totally indifferent to the consequences that these destructions may cause .

Giant Oak Tree - Yes , Fabius , and this just brings back to my memory the sadness and the hopelessness of what happened , long , long ago , to my old Family , my Mother and Father , my Grand Parents and my Great Grand Parents along with thousands of other similar Family Clusters , uprooted from their native soil and destroyed just for their insatiable greediness of these same two legged creatures , with no religion and no respect for anybody else's life , if their lives happened to be in the way of their wanton fury in squandering indiscriminately Nature's precious heritage , like ours .

Mushroom - Sire , far from causing so much distress to you was my illustration for the fracas made by these poor representatives of Mother Nature , or , at least , appearing to be some sort of production of Mother Nature, but that is not for me or for us to comment upon or worry about , since our impression of them and any judgement we may feel likely to pass on their behaviour may be influenced either by our ignorance of them or by our fear of them. But ,if this visible attitude of their behaviour , so openly and violently displayed , is any indication of their intentions , these intentions ,then , bear no good omen ..."for sure " !

..........the two little Spinster Sparrows , perched on a branch of the Giant Oak , had been listening very attentively to the conversation of the Oak and the Mushroom and Andrea , the more worrisome of the two spinsters , turning to Celeste................

Andrea - Dooms-Day 's coming , Celeste and it's right here , now !! Fearful and desolated as I am ,yet I can feel it and it won't be long before you and I will have no more a home where to rest and talk and gossip or just sing our happiness to the rising sun , because the Executioners of the trees are here... NOW...!!

Celeste - Not yet : they might come , of course , but they have not attempted to destroy our Forest yet .

Andrea - Keep on hoping and keep on dreaming on your little pink cloud, if you so wish ! After all ,denial of reality is a known aspect of inner fear .

Celeste - I am not afraid ,Andrea . I feel sorry , instead , for the Giant Oak and the little Mushroom who will lose his best companion in this Forest , once it is destroyed .

Andrea - Sentimentalism will not protect this Forest , Celeste . Soldiers are needed , and brave soldiers , well equipped and courageous who would fight for the preservation of the independence of this Forest .

Celeste - And where are these soldiers ,Andrea , so courageous and so brave , ready to defend our Forest ? You know , there are no Spartan Trees around "no more" with their King , Leonidas , to keep in check the hordes of the invading enemy !

Andrea - I am no Prophet and I am no Wizard and do not put down cards or read the messages in the stars , but "something" tells me that there will be soldiers and that this Forest will be saved .

Celeste - What made you change your mind , Andrea ? Just a minute ago ,you were criticizing me for not believing in a DOOMS_DAY approaching as a sure thing and , now , throwing a rainbow over the dark clouds as if a sudden inspiration had come down to you from the stars !

Andrea - May be it came from the stars : after all , in any situation of utter hopelessness , hope is still a viable option . Let us watch the unfolding scene , Celeste and ponder .

............and the giant Oak and the Mushroom continue the assessment of the situation..........

Giant Oak Tree- Fabius , anything new down there ? I can hear that noise , now , a lot louder than I did before but still not at all disturbing . Are those creatures still fighting among themselves ?

Mushroom - Yes, Charlie , they are, but what they seem to be fighting about is something that worries me .

Giant Oak Tree - Oh ! Something serious or bad or threatening ?

Mushroom - Well , Charlie , something that I believe seems to be more ominous than that !

Giant Oak Tree - What could be more ominous than the possibility of impending death ?

Mushroom - You just said it , Sire : death !

Giant Oak Tree - Fabius..!!..You frighten me and perplex me, at the same time !! Why are you saying such a mournful prediction ?

Mushroom - Because , Charlie, that is what they are talking about and the fighting is about which of these opposing groups will have the privilege to go into the Forest and do the slaughter .

Giant Oak Tree - Are they arguing and fighting on whose right it is to own and dispose of our Forest and its worth ? Is that what it is all about , Fabius ?

Mushroom - Yes , Charlie ! That is exactly what it is all about !

Giant Oak Tree - Well, Fabius , we all have to go ,one day or another and , if it isn't the malice of the two legged creatures to dispatch any of us , it may be , then , the fury of the hurricane or the Lightning Rod of Zeus , but , sooner or later , for whatever reason or cause ,the day of our departure from this Forest , was declared , long ago , at our birth .

Mushroom - Yes , Charlie,and I understand ,but I grieve over this adversity .

Giant Oak Tree - Fabius...hold it a moment...!......because ....well...I am not sure ...but something.......something there ...Fabius ...in the middle of the deep Forest,......I am not sure....but , yes , I can see something and this something is catching my attention ,Fabius..........

Mushroom - Yes , Charlie , I can hear you ! Charlie , is what you seem to see something bad , threatening or worse ?

Giant Oask Tree- I am not quite certain yet , but , from here , tall as I am , I can see a lot better than I can hear and I seem to be able to make out some shimmering in that midst of bushes and thick branches . I wonder what that could be .

Mushroom - Could it be the sun rays , may be , filtering down through the branches of the trees and through the bushes and giving out that appearance ?

Giant Oak Tree - I am not sure , but it looks something that moves and it is not standing in one place but it seems to appear here and there in different places and all at the same time and the shimmering , now and then , appears more intense , more apparent and more visible . Very , very strange sighting .

Mushroom - Could it be due to some more two legged creatures coming into the Forest to join the excited crowd already here ?

Giant Oak Tree - As I told you ,I am not sure yet, but that shimmering has not gone away , as a matter of fact it seems to have somehow increased in intensity.....very strange sight.....I have never seen anything like this before.....FABIUS !!! .....FABIUS !!.....I can't believe it...!!!!

Mushroom - Sire, are you all right ? What happened , Sire ??!

Giant Oak Tree- That shimmering , Fabius........that shimmering.........

Mushroom - Sire ! Are you all right ??!

Giant Oak Tree - Fabius ! That shimmering is.......Oh ! I can't believe it ....that shimmering .Fabius......are....Oh! I can't believe it , that shimmering Fabius , are SWORDS and ARMOR and SHIELDS ......THERE ARE KNIGHTS IN ARMOR THERE ....Fabius !!

Mushroom- Sire , I still cannot see it , but I believe that what you are seeing is a true sight and not just the work of your distressed imagination .

Giant Oak Tree - Fabius , What I see it is real ! Very , very real !....And a large host of those knights advancing rapidly from many directions and in battle formation ! Who could they be ?

Mushroom - Sire, I do not know but I can venture a wild guess : they may represent an advance host of a relief armoured unit sent by a friendly neighbouring Forest Government to your aid !......Now , whether they are Knights, the real ones in shiny armor , or something else , this I cannot vouch for , ...yet .

..........the two Spinster Sparrows , aroused by the excited and exclamatory enthusiasm of the Giant Oak , appear to become better motivated, particularly Andrea , the more pessimistic of the two , for a brighter outlook on the perilous situation...

Andrea - Celeste ! Celeste ! Did you hear what the Giant Oak said and what the Mushroom answered ? Did you ?!......Celeste !....We might be on the verge of being rescued from this terrible impending doom by fabulous Knights in shining armor !!.....Celeste ! The Knights are here !!!

Celeste - I am really glad about that and feel very excited about their armor being so shining . It would have been , really , very disappointing had their armor been reddish and rusty .

Andrea - Celeste ! How can you be so"terse"in your "expansive" feelings and register no unbridled excitement about it all ??!! Doesn't the very name of "KNIGHT" raise the mercurial column of response in your tenuous brain and fill you with unbounded joy ?!

Celeste - Of course it does , but , Andrea , I really like my excitements in small doses .

Andrea - Oh ! I am so different !

Celeste - That's no secret !

Andrea - If I had arms instead of wings , I'll join that host of shining knights and make certain that my armor would not be either reddish , brown and rusty!

Celeste - Yes , Andrea , all that sounds very exciting but do not overlook the fact that , sometime , just "looks" do not always convey the whole story of an apparel , not even , and , "even" more particularly so , that of a coat of shiny armor !

Andrea - Celeste , I believe that you were born with the enviable prerogative to extinguish any fire of genuine interest , enthusiasm and desire in any living creature .

Celeste - Andrea , you may be right : I couldn't have extinguished anything in a dying or dead creature , of course .

Andrea - Oh! Well , that's small talk , anyway , Celeste ,and we have allowed ourselves to be drawn into it instead of looking forward to the deep meaning of this day when the dark clouds of that terrible impending doom that was coming at us with its ugly and ferocious look and full of vicious intent and unrestrained greed , were removed from our doors , our thoughts and our Forest .

Celeste - Yes , we certainly allowed ourselves to slip into a silly, empty dialogue : but , you know , Andrea , that kind of diminutive talk that we were doing, following the period that we were under severe , dramatic and persistent stress , is not considered a mental aberration or a silly expression of light-hearted thinking but , instead , it is suspected of representing some form of an emotional "discharge" from an over tensed , over charged , over stressed defense mechanism in all creatures , when , suddenly , the primary stimulus to have caused the initial start of that distress.......

Andrea - Like the fear of civic turbulence or even a revolution , as we were so apprehensive about such a possibility ...isn't that so , Celeste ?

Celeste - Yes , precisely so , Andrea ,and , as I was saying , that seemingly light, almost insensate type of discourse following dramatic , prolonged , severe and persistent stress may come to the surface of those exposed creatures 's speech once the primary stimulus that caused the initial start of that stress and its unusual prolonged persistence far longer and in excess of the usual and, commonly , quickly resolving shock, rapidly dissolves and disappears, relieving the entire scene .

Andrea - That kind of "emotional mechanism" , Celeste , would apply , of course , to the weak-minded and the over-excitable types of creatures ,but surely not applicable to sparrows and , least of all , to old maids like us !!

Celeste - You certainly have a way to express untoward situations, Andrea !

Andrea - No, Celeste, is not that . I have enough self confidence in me and enough courage to permit myself to be taken down by despair or loneliness or fear. May be I run the risk of being looked upon as a self conceited sparrow but that is the way I am and no enticing circumstances would ever change me.

Celeste - And you are right to feel that way if that is the way you feel . You must be yourself ,always or, really, you would fail the program that Mother Nature manufactured in you .

Andrea - Thank you , Celeste . You are a good friend .

Celeste- Andrea ?

Andrea - Yes ,Celeste .

Celeste - Andrea , can you see , by any chance , if the milk-man came along with "them" Knights too ?

Andrea - Stupidity , generally, in a normal life's setting is hardly ever well accepted or even tolerated , but, I'll have to admit that in cases like this it is a real comfort to the soul of beleaguered creatures !...I'll give up…!!!!!....How was your night , Celeste ?

Celeste - Very good ,thank you , Andrea : and yours ?

Andrea - It couldn't have been any better than yours , I am sure , Celeste !

Celeste- I am glad of that , Andrea , and now let us pay more attention to the recent extraordinary development and the sudden insertion , in the midst of this riotous mess , of the imposing and fanciful sight of shining armors and shining Knights !

Andrea - I just started wondering , Celeste , whether they are real Knights .

Celeste - If you think they are ,they are Knights .

Andrea - But , Celeste , I do not see any white horses . Aren't Knights in shining armor supposed to come charging on white horses ?

Celeste - Usually , yes , but , sometime white horses may not be readily available when needed so any other colour will have to do, and ,if even other colours are not available, the shining Knights will have to go on foot or hire a cab .

Andrea - Or hire a,,,what ??!

Celeste - Never mind : it was just a silly joke that, really , belongs to the Societies of Creatures that will live down the road several centuries from our present century , so pay no attention to it .

Andrea - Incredible !!!.......But…but …Celeste, how could you know about it ???!!

Celeste - Some time ago, while I was on vacation in a foreign Forest, I met, just by chance , an old Witch who had just returned from a trip in some of the Forests of those several centuries scheduled for the future,visiting a Wizard , an old friend , and she had liked that joke and told it to me.

Andrea- Did you ask her , I hope , what did the joke mean ?! I hope you did !!!

Celeste - Yes , Andrea , I did ask and the Old Witch told me that the joke was referring to a means of transportation and , when I asked again what did that name mean , you know……..

Andrea - Yes : the "cab" , right ?

Celeste - Yes , right : the "cab", she said not to pay any attention to the word because it indicated only a type of locomotion and nothing more and , she added , certainly not as important a locomotion as my way of moving around with my wings, flying high and swiftly in the sky , or as useful and practical as her broom .

Andrea - What a story , Celeste !!....But ….what does it all lead to ?

Celeste - Nothing more than just you'll have to do with what's available at the moment you need something and do the best you can with it .

Andrea - So , then , those warriors may still be real Knights , even without horses, white or any other colour ,and even without ….what was that other thing…?

Celeste- " cab " .

Andrea - Yes ,yes ,"cab" , and ,so, they could still be real ,fanciful, romantic and fascinating Knights ,even without a cab . Amazing !

Celeste - Well, dear Andrea , if they, those warriors I mean , do have an armor , if they are armour-clad , if they carry offensive weapons like drawn swords and defensive shields ,they must be Knights , may be horseless Knights but, nevertheless , Knights , and do not ever "wash" your imagination clean of all its subtle and inventive intuition by removing a "shining" cover from a questionable truth .

The learned sweet Gopher - I agree , whatever that means .

………………..the Mushroom , who had remained watching the progress , if any , of THE SHINING KNIGHTS in armor-clad suits , turning to the King…………

Mushroom - Sire !..Those shining armour-clad Knights are advancing ,and fast ! I can now see distinctly their swords , their shields and the flowing feathers on their helmets !

Giant Oak Tree - Fabius , I am dumbfounded :.....I can't believe it ! But what could be the intentions of those warriors ?

Mushroom - Sire , I believe that they are coming to disband and even destroy this mob of unruly and pretentious outlaws .

Gianr Oak Tree - "Thanks be to the Heavens" , Fabius , my Great Grand-Father would have said !

Mushroom - Yes , Charlie , if this will prove to be the case , then , "thanks to the Heavens" will be in good order , provided that the intentions, as you are wondering , of these iron-clad Warriors are as highly intentioned and honest minded as their mission , if their mission , of course , is the one we hope it is , to destroy this mob , but , should it not be so , than their mission would turn out to be getting rid of the screaming mob and take over for themselves what the very mob had wanted first !....Indeed , not a very favourable prospect, Sire .

The learned smart Gopher - An old proverb says :" The devil you know, is better than the devil you don't know " .

......and Andrea butts in.........

Andrea - And you , stupid Gopher , what are you trying to say with such totally inadequate , unrealistic , inappropriate and out of focus sentence ?

The learned smart Gopher - Nothing , really .I was just curious to hear what your reaction to it would be . That was all .

Andrea - And did my answer satisfy your curiosity , confounded Gopher ?

The learned smart Gopher - Yes , Your Excellence , it did : now I know that you are very stupid .

Celeste - Do not waste your time like that , Andrea , by letting yourself be dragged into a silly verbal confrontation with a total stranger . Let's pay attention, instead , to the swords , the shields and the would- be Knights who hold high the shiny swords !

Andrea - And let us hope that they'll hold high our hopes too !

.......and the King resumes his conversation with the Mushroom.....

Giant Oak Tree - What did you mean, Fabius , by saying provided that their intentions, that is the intentions of those Warriors , would be honest and unselfish and purely meant to bring us help. Isn't their arrival , Fabius , a sign of hope and one of encouragement for the safety of our Forest ?

Mushroom - Yes , Sire , provided ,again , that our first impression would not have deceived us at first and deceive us completely later if , by chance , their arrival would mean ,then , let us say , "just" a "change of the guard" and they ,these shiny Warriors , taking the place or the entire thing over for themselves , rather than coming to save us !!

Giant Oak Tree - They would have shown some hostility towards us already by now, Fabius, and, besides , I believe ...I just remember now and I had forgotten to mention it to you when I had received the secret code , stressed and preoccupied as I was ,that it slipped my mind , but , the Government Representatives had informed me that they were trying to send some relief columns of armoured troops to our Forest ,trying to relieve our beleaguered status . So , I believe that these Knights are the ones promised by the friendly neighbouring Forest and that they are here to help us rather than harm us.

Mushroom - Charlie , I did not know that and I did not know it because you had not told me that .

The learned smart Gopher - That makes a lot of gopher's sense and it makes me very , very happy .

The wise and quick Squirrel - Obviously .

Mushroom - And , Charlie , let us hope , though , that all these latest developments may entice a lasting peace for our Forest !.....This kind of two legged creatures , whether they are armored shining Knights or plain shining mobs without armor , are not to be trusted , Sire . They are known to change their minds, their loyalties and their intentions just like the wind does . And that is saying the least !

Giant Oak Tree- I understand your concern, Fabius, and I trust your judgement as my friend and my trusted Minister , but , at this moment I really do not see any subterfuge or any signs of the possibility or probability of a secretely planned attempt to our authority and sovereignty, so what I have in my mind presently is a loud "WELCOME" for our saviours in shining armor and "thanks to Heaven" for their help and intervention ....look, look, Fabius , how shining those shields are and the swords in their hands , and the helmets with flowing plumage on their heads and the bright cuirasses on their chests,so imposing on the frightened looks of those screaming and shouting mobsters who , now , try desperately to run away and disperse in the thick of the Forest and in all directions to avoid annihilation !

Mushroom - Yes , Charlie ,that's what they are doing and the image never changes, never fails and it is always the same .

Giant Oak Tree - What's now , Fabius ? Aren't you glad that , this time , we might have escaped a miserable end and I might have been sent to rejoin my long departed Family in that Greater Forest above all of us ? So , what seems to be your complaint ,now, Fabius , or your uneasiness ?

Mushroom - No complaints , no uneasiness , Charlie , really , but only the realization of how persistent and well ingrained certain attitudes are in living creatures of all kinds , including and ,particularly so , in the two legged ones .

Giant Oak Tree - And what kind of attitudes are you talking about now , Fabius ?

Chorus of several learned Gophers - That's what we would like to know too !

Mushroom - Smart Alecks , you Gophers , aren't you !

Chorus of several learned Gophers - May be smart but not Alecks , our name is Gopher and Gophers for several of us ,if in a group . But that is not what we want to talk you about and we believe that you shouldn't have used that archaic noun of "ingrained" ,so high-touted and ostentatious , instead you should have used the simpler, clearer and up-to-date , modern term of "deep seated" .

Mushroom - I know who is really "deep seated " and I leave it to your imagination , you goofing Gophers .

Giant Oak Tree - Leave the Gophers alone , Fabius , and pay attention to me , instead : tell me , what's worrying you now ?

Mushroom - Not really a worry , Charlie , but more of a subtle sadness in realizing how the essence or the inherent beauty of things is most often overlooked to give room instead for admiration of the rougher or the less polished or even the violent aspect of things like this show of shining armor , the brandishing of the swords , the carved and blazoned shields and all the show of force and violence that those artifacts represent , instead of admiring and praising and greatly partaking of the beauty of the steel itself and per se ,the steel of which those weapons are made , or the elegant style and configuration of the same and the splendid artistry of their veritable aspect , considering further that it seems rather dubious the need for all that exquisite art to be displayed so ostentatiously and openly on artifacts built for war and with which those Warriors strike and bash each others with crushing blows and with such fury that it makes you think that they have lost their head and their brain, provided ,of course , that a brain was in it to start with, and that would be a difficult chore to clarify .

Chorus of the learned Gophers- Heigh ! Mushroom ! Did it ever occur to you that it would be appropriate to ask the swords and the shields and the cuirasses as well as the helmets with the flowing plumage what they think about it ?

Mushroom- Such dim-witted "occurrencies " are not in our arsenal of stupidity ,but we encounter no problems ever in referring them to the most appropriate sources .

Chorus of the Swords - We ,the Swords , are very proud of our heritage and of the fine steel we are made of. The Mushroom is right and there seems to be some subtle contradiction in the beautiful shape we were forged and engraved and the assignment given us to perform , but , then what about the beauty of the human figure and its remarkable power of reasoning and the side view of his existence with turpitude , violence , murder and meanness ? It is said that the Truth rests on the tip of our blades , of course , that statement is truthful to the extent of who, actually , is brandishing us .

Chorus of the Sheaths - And we , with our body of solid steel and felt-padded ,inside , we are the ones to hold Truth and Honour wrapped in us with a will made out of steel.

Chorus of the Halberds - "WE" ,the haughty Halberds , we hold high on our blades Truth and Honour to shine in the fulgent light of the sun ,when the sky is not overcast or when it doesn't rain , because when the weather is bad , no one likes very much to fight anyway , and our blades are flashing in war and hearts and steel are all and one thing in the fury of the battle : now , before or to morrow . "WE" do not make any use of sheaths because the Truth and the Honour that we bear on our blades are chaste even naked .

Chorus of the Sheaths - The ordinary ,every day creature , is content with even a veneer Truth , but to the Knight belongs the supreme Truth .

Chorus of the Shields - And "WE", the protectors on an equal measure of ordinary creatures and Knights ,we protect whatever it is possible to be protected and , in our

	long and defensive experience , the real Truth is only one : the one that best pleases the victor .
Shanghai , an itinerant Flea -	The Shields are right !
Sibyl , also an itinerant Flea -	Oh ! What a pleasant and unexpected surprise , dear Traveler , and what good news do you bring with you ?
Shanghai -	Oh ! Nothing much ,you know , the usual going from place to place , meeting a few dogs and from dog to dog , trying to make a living without breaking my neck .
Sibyl -	I do the same, dear...... and how shall I call you , dear ? My name is Sibyl: what's yours ?
Shanghai -	My name is Shanghai ,but I am usually called Shag , for short , by most of my fellow travelers whom I meet on the road . My Family was originally from China : and Yours ?
Sibyl -	My Family ?......Well, I'll be open with you : I never had a Family. . Incidentally , they all call me Sib ,for short .
Shanghai -	I am sorry to hear that , Sib , and I can well understand your feelings about that , but how did it happened such a sad and tragic situation ?
Sibyl -	War . My Family was destroyed by war when I was barely a few months old and I was raised by some Gipsy Fleas who had found me in the rubble of my destroyed house , as they were passing by , I the only survivor .
Shanghai -	Then you must have heard all the talking and comments of those eminent exponents of elite weaponry and the shining Knights and all the rest !!!
Sibyl -	Yes , I did , and it did not fill my mind with admiration either : because , for me , war and swords and cuirasses and Knights are just and only sad memories , their actions left me an orphan , lost in the World of Forests without a Family .
Shangai -	Yes , Sib , and I feel very , very sorry for you , and you must have suffered a lot and missed the affection of a Family around you ! Life , as my Grand Father used to say , is not a Garden full of Roses but only full of dogs .
Sibyl -	Yes , I heard the talking and the boasting of all those Warriors and their shields, swords, helmets with flowing feathers and Knights with shining cuirasses and , in a way and to a certain extent , they may be right , yet in

the climax of a war , at its highest point , and when the last furious battles rage violent and cruel.......to me those actions denote the result and the consequence of the loss of mental reasoning , and I am not blaming those who get into a war to straighten things up but I am very rigorous in my judgement for those who started hostilities just for hatred ,ambition or fanatic belief in their own selfish interests at the expense of other righteous nations and cultures and Creatures of the other Forests !.......But , what's the use to talk about it ,anyway , as we all know but too well that not only the weather can be unstable but creatures' minds too !

Shanghai - So , you poor thing , you had no one of your own to confide in or be loved by, and is that why you became a traveling Flea ?

Sibyl - In a way , yes . Somehow , I couldn't stay in one place for any length of time without becoming agitated , nervous and feeling uncomfortable , constantly assailed by the realization of being practically alone , having no one to whom I could refer my thoughts, my feelings and my life's experiences , so sedentary life became intolerable but also incompatible with the other Fleas around me who had and had had a normal Family life .

Shanghai - I understand : travelling ,sometime , can distract you enough to put a damper on your troubled and unhappy thoughts .

Sibyl - Oh ! Well , that was a time that belongs to a long , long time ago , so why don't we leave alone those unhappy thoughts and delegate , instead , the shields , the swords and all of their worthy companions to continue to praise themselves and we take then another road so that I can tell you something that happened to me lately during one of my travels : Would you like to hear my story , Shag ?

Shanghai - But of course , Sib , and not only I would enjoy hearing your story but I would be most interested to see how you did come through your adventure : I am really very curious to hear it !

Sibyl - Well , it all happened precisely during one of those battles of mighty Knights in shining armors, flashing swords and flowing feathers on the Knights Helmets, and the clash of arms was deafening and the roar of the infuriated Warriors was like the roar of lions , and I happened to find myself in the middle of it all !

Shanghai - Oh ! Please , go on , go on , Sib , I can't wait to hear the story ! It's almost incredible : you in the middle of one of those battles !!!......No Wonder you do not like wars and battles !!!

Sibyl - Very well !......So , you must know that during one of those battles I found myself trapped inside the cuirass of one of those fighting Knights ,and.......

Shanghai - Lor'have Mercy !! Trapped into a Knight's cuirass…!!! What a strange situation that must have been !!

Sibyl - Strange…??!......Embarrassing , my dear , rather embarrassing , I tell you !!

Shanghai - But , if the situation was so distressing ,couldn't you , Sib , have jumped out of the cuirass or from the entire armor, somehow , or was the armor so tightly conjoined that even you , small as you are , couldn't have gotten out of it ?

Sibyl - Yes , Shag , you are right thinking that way , but inside that steel frame everything was extremely dark : of course , I could see a couple of holes in that steel cage , but , as I am a creature of good manners , my natural reserve compelled me to look frantically somewhere else , side ways , up and down and everywhere , for a crack or a chink in that armor where I could see a ray of light , even if very faint , but coming from a reasonable and respectable site of that tightly jointed steel cage .

Shanghai - What an ordeal that must have been..!!!

Sibyl - Yes , it was an ordeal : a real one, my dear !!....But , then , as I was jumping around desperately, trying to get out from that cage of steel , when , suddenly, , there was a great roar and a crushing sound of armor hitting the steel cage where I was in , and a larger chink opens up in that steel armor , just above me , where I was standing , horrified and terrified and , Heavens be merciful…!!.....What did I see …!!!!!

Shanghai - But what ,what , what did you see ??! Tell me , what did you see !!??

Sibyl - Heavens above !.....I shudder at the very thought of what I saw !!

Shanghai - Then ,tell me what you saw and don't keep me in such tantalizing suspense ! What on earth did you see ???!!

Sibyl - That inside that steel cage there was a human creature .

Shanghai - For all the Stars in the Heavens and all the Fleas in the Universe , what was , now , so strange to see a human creature inside that steel frame ? Are you trying to tell me that you never made a personal acquaintance with one of them in your past ??!

Sibyl - Nothing of that or of anything else , Shag , but I had never seen in my entire existence ,until now , anything like what I saw then inside that steel cage .

Shanghai - But you already told me ,"Sib", that it was a man, right ? A human creature : right ?

Sibyl - Yes, of course : and right you are , it was a man .

Shanghai - So what , then ?

Sibyl - So, what , Shag : that man was a "complete" one, all meat and bones !

Shanghai - What else did you expect to find , Sib ?? Some silver florins , diamonds ,or , may be , a royal crown or an antique Roman stole ??!

Sibyl - Shag : that Knight was just as he was ,with his armor and his weapons .

Shasnghai - Very good I guess: I would have been very surprised if he hadn't had his weapons on him, Sib !!

Sibyl - And nothing else .

Shanghai - Nothing else ... what ?

Sibyl - Exactly so ,Shag : nothing else ! Not even a shirt !

Shanghai - I can't believe you !

Sibyl - But it is the truth !....Very , very embarrassing , Shag , very !

Shanghai - Do you mean to say,Sib , that the shining Knight was not wearing ......well , any undergarments ..??

Sibyl - Exactly .

Shanghai - O Tempora ! O mores !! , What times are we living in and what happened to the quality of being decent in these Forests of ours , I wonder...???!!!

Sibyl - Well , dear Shag , at that time , desperate as I was trying to get out of that trap, I wasn't giving much of a thought to decency and customs of our times, but in my natural capacity of an educated Flea , I was trying my best, jumping continuously with giant leaps , without rest or pause, here and there, up and down and everywhere ,looking for a crack somewhere, that could have given me the possibility to get out of there in a dignified manner even for a Flea, but to no avail..!!!...The more I was jumping and the more that shining Knight was bouncing and vaulting and wielding his sword in a vertiginous sequence of violent blows, thrusting his armored chest into the thick of the battle ,and giving out shouts and ferocious-like roars and performing unbelievable high jumps never seen before in a Knight so heavily armored and with his sword flashing blows after blows, right and left without remission , pity or respite, so that anyone that would come close to him in the middle of the fray would fall down, cut in a thousand pieces , while, at the same time , this maddened Knight in his rage,would erupt livid abusive language of obscene vituperations .

Shanghai - That's a serious charge for a Knight, dear Sib, that he would allow himself to a disastrous downfall from the pinnacle of ancient Chivalry by professing such injurious verbal expressions !......How did you know or how were you able to fully understand the meaning of his saying, particularly considering the conditions that must have existed in that pandemonium of clashing arms , the tumult , the deafening noise of armor against armor and the cries of the injured warriors . What kind of abusive language and even obscene language did he speak ?

Sibyl - I am not quite sure and I do not know exactly how it was , but, after the battle , I , intrigued by the stressful experience , asked the opinion of the Learned Scholars of the Academy of Fleas and they told me that the shining Knight , while fighting furiously , was uttering all kinds of horrible insults to all the insects in this Forest and , with particular fury , cursing the Fleas .

Shanghai - Those learned Scholars must be quite proficient in the languages of the Creatures of the Forests !!

Sibyl - I , of course , was not proficient in the human language ,but those sage and wise Scholars understood the language of the human creatures ,due to personal experiences , and they thought that the Shining and Valorous Knight became furious ,violent beyond control and ferociously aggressive , because he was trying to get rid of me driving him crazy ,while I was jumping up an down inside his armor .

Shanghai - Highly valuable Scholars , those learned wise and wary Fleas , and I wonder how the Shining Knight would have behaved himself if , instead of you , some of those learned Scholars had been inside his armor .

Chorus of the learned Scholars- No "wonders" would have happened, dear curious Shanghai, because we would not have been in that Knight's armor , to begin with . We only take refuge, sometimes , in the warm coat of dogs , and dogs , as far as we can ascertain , do not wear armor .

Shanghai - But , then ,"Sib", how did everything finish up ?

Sibyl - The Knight won the battle !

Chorus of the Itinerant Fleas - Of the great and the humble we are the task-masters . Of their destinies , we are the shapers .

Shanghai - It looks like a new contest shaping up, and it won't be the Knights',this time!!

Meanwhile, the Giant Oak Tree , greatly relieved of the impending trouble in the Forest that could have spelled disaster for himself and his Kingdom , glad and grateful for the timely and successful intervention of the Mighty Shining Knights in scattering the turbulent revolutionary mobs and destroying those who could not or would not scatter voluntarily , now tries to take a tally of the situation following those harrowing events , by calling his trusted Minister , the Mushroom, but , unable to receive an answer, becomes impatient and calls repeatedly……………………..

Giant Oak Tree - Fabius !.....Fabius , little Mushroom , do you hear me ? I guess you must be there just as I am here, having no other choice , but that's beyond the point , but why don't you answer me ? Fabius ….Fabius, please , try to answer me , or is something wrong down there that you cannot answer me ?....Fabius , for Heavens sake , please , answer me!

Mushroom - Yes ? Someone calling ? I cannot hear a thing ! Yet some sound came down from the tree ! I wonder if it could be Charlie ! I am not sure : the noise here is almost unbearable !

Giant Oak Tree - FABIUS ! ….For all the Gods on Mount Olympus , will you answer me ?! Or Are you fast asleep ?

Mushroom - I seem to hear something , still coming from the tree, it seems . Could it be Charlie ? I thought that he was busy with the State representatives of the neighbouring Forest thanking them for their help with their choice and elite troops contingent that saved the kingdom from total ruin and destruction , but he might be over with that ceremony and he may want to consult with me. I'll try to call myself from here to see if I can reach Him…..C H A R L I E !!!!!!!

Giant Oak Tree - Thunder and Lightning ,…if it isn't old Fabius…!!!...Yes , Fabius , what's going on , why did you not ever answer my calling ? I have been calling and calling and calling , but …dead silence !! What does this kind of negative behaviour mean , Fabius ? Is by any chance the shock of the recent experiences left you completely worn out that you cannot even answer when somebody calls ??!

Mushroom - I still can hardly hear anything down in this place: who's calling? The noise is such that I can't hear anything !

Giant Oak Tree - I am the one calling , Fabius ! I am Charlie , the Oak Tree , in case….

Giant Oak Tree - ...... the stressful events of the day did weaken and confuse your memory a little . I am Charlie , the King of this saved Kingdom , Fabius , and you are my trusted Minister , don't you remember ? And why can't you answer me or are we facing a serious aftermath to the harrowing shock of the day's tumult?.....I surely hope not ,because that would be a very sad outcome to a very fortunate and happy end of a serious trouble , but , Fabius , why can't you still answer me , even if it were so that you are deopressed , tired or displeased with the harrowing experience ? I have been calling you for hours and received no answer !.....What's going on down there , Fabius ? I thought that the worst was over and things were getting back into shape and normal settings !.I just dismissed the Foreign Dignitaries Delegation from our neighbouring Forest Government ,after extending to them , their Government and their People ,our deepest appreciation and thankful sentiments for the help so timely offered and acted in our support by sending in their elite Warriors , the Shining Knights, that saved us from total disaster and death as well as the complete destruction of our Forest !...So, why can't you answer me ?

Mushroom - Oh ! Charlie , ...Sire , is it you ? I am so glad and so relieved to hear your voice again , although I can hear it with great difficulty and just, just barely hear it!!.....If you only could be down here and listen to the pandemonium around me and around your roots , Charlie , you ,probably , would better appreciate why I seemed to have had some difficulty in hearing your calls , Charlie !!

Giant Oak Tree - That's strange , Fabius , because ,up here , I cannot notice or hear anything unusual or different from the average noises of every day .

Mushroom - It is difficult for you , Charlie , isolated as you are up there in the fresh air and the sunshine and the blue skies , when it does not rain , of course , to comprehend that overwhelming stir and uproar and for no one to be able to escape from the confusion of thousand of voices , all talking at the same time and trying to force each other voice on top of all the others ,making it almost impossible to hear anything , particularly sounds that come from high above these damp and obscure grounds .

Giant Oak Tree - But why now , Fabius , this confusion and this wild "chatting", now that the worst danger has past and peace and normality have been reestablished ?

Mushroom - Now , Charlie , if I understood correctly your question in spite of this deafening hub-bub, I hear whispered by many of these creatures that all this excitement is , at least , partially due to their figuring of the possibility that a new dawn may be at the horizon for them , after the latest events that , they believe , might have shaken the highest Authority , and that's YOU, Charlie ! .....so that they believe that this Authority might have been woken up from its benevolent torpor of governing and these same events stimulated this austere and complacent form of Government to look deeper and with renewed seriousness at the needs of its subjects : after all ,Charlie ,the revolution , although now quashed , still it had been triggered by some motive of unhappiness for their miserable existences and a need to improve conditions and basic life's standards .

Giant Oak Tree- But why was I not informed of all this by you , Fabius , my most trusted Minister ,and kept abreast of such developments so that timely and accurate attention could be paid to that situation ??....What triggered the whole mess ?

Mushroom - I believe that it could be a cognizable reaction to the trepidation suffered following the fright and the alarm of the past events , a reaction that equals if not surpass the frenetic attitudes of those frenzied and raving maniacs during the recent civic disturbances , and that makes it almost impossible to clearly hear anything while one screams on this side and the other roars on the other side , and one steps on somebody's toes and gets clobbered on the head , the other spits in somebody's face to seal and confirm his own opinions and gets beaten up by other bystanders ,while in another place some excited creatures sing and dance as if intoxicated with the glorious victory they stole from those who had obtained it for them, others arguing on the preparedness of the Armed Forces of our Forest and its ability to withstand another Insurgency, so , one thing and another , it is simply a pandemonium down here and, I tell you the truth, dear Charlie , I have had enough of it all !!

Giant Oak Tree - Now , now ,little Mushroom, Fabius ! Take it easy ! Steady does it , you know , and ,besides , I am wondering whether your world down there is, after all, really as bad and unpleasant as you make it if so many creatures are apparently so violently competing for it !!....As you can see , no one vies for a visit or a staying up here .

Mushroom - You, dear Charlie, although you are the king of this Kingdom , you do not seem to understand very well your subjects and their thinking, aims, desires and dreams , and what interest would these creatures have to come and see you up there ,when , in a moment of wanton madness , they could cut you down and see you comfortably at their level!You just don't know these folks, Charlie !

Giant Oak Tree - That's a big , big talk for such small creatures .

Mushroom - And there you go again , Charlie , and you really do not seem to understand these little Creatures ! Yes , you are right , they are small and ,yes , they brag a lot , but when they become excited and infuriated about something ,be it for something good or for something bad , they become as one person , a solid ,compact mass of creatures ,an impenetrable mass and a formidable one like the tumultuous ,rushing waters of a flooding mighty river .

Giant Oak Tree - Fabius , fortunately we do not have any rivers around here, mighty or not mighty ,so ,may be , things will be quiet , at least for a while, I hope . So, what did you have in mind to tell me with that comparison of impenetrability of my subjects , if they were to turn mad , and turning like a violent torrent if they were to get even madder ?

Mushroom - Just a sobering reminder , Charlie ,of how fragile are our existences ,happy, flourishing and grand one day , down in the dumps the next . So you should be happy with your status ,Charlie and you are the King and Nature gave you that privilege associated , of course , with a little clause .

Giant Oak Tree- And what would that clause be , Fabius , the one you are hinting at ?

Mushroom - The ponderous responsibility of a Monarch towards the welfare and the safety of his subjects , a privilege that shines outside like a golden apple but it carries a hard core inside !

giant Oak Tree - I am proud of that responsibility , Fabius , even with the potential dangers and difficulties associated with it !

Mushroom - Dangers ,Charlie , yes , and sensible responsibility, yes , but difficulties, that commodity is to be clarified .

Chorus of the little creatures - Go ahead, Mushroom , and tell the king about us and our problems !

Mushroom - Charlie , the difficulties are not up there with your chirping birds , the sun shining, when shining , the gentle wind when not so violent ,and the fresh air, but the real difficulties and the hardships are down here , Charlie , where the little people are trying to scratch a living ,day in and day out , without any sun shining, or any gentle breeze caressing their daily hard work and no praising whispers of encouragement either,or a"uniform"of respectable dignity made out of the finest cloth with medals and ribbons and gold buttons across the chest . There is so much distress down here Charlie, at times desperation too , that all the tears in your lymph would not be enough to wash them away ! !

Giant Oak Tree - Come now , little Mushroom , don't let these retrograde thoughts get you down and make you feel miserable : after all we should be glad ,rather than sad , for having been rescued from a possible horrible end of our very lives ! These are times to be glad to be alive and we should not be taken down by a melancholic sense of sadness .

Mushroom - Who said anything about sadness ? Sadness ,my foot, but since I do not have a foot, sadness can go to bugaboo ! As I had mentioned before , you still do not seem to be able to understand a thing about what life is like down here, with your head in the fog and low clouds ,shaken by the wind and deafened by the joyous singing of hundred of cheerful birds ! So, let me finish.........

The Giant Oak Tree , somewhat perturbed at the mushroom's sudden change of attitude , is becoming puzzled and worried and begins to reflect on this disturbing sign....................

Giant Oak Tree- (to himself } - Our little Mushroom appears very upset ! What could have caused this sudden change in him and such a display of irritability and almost rebellious attitude ? Did I , may be , affect his sensitivity when I encouraged him to be happy rather than sad ? Well , we better listen to whatever more he has to say: that , probably , might clear this mystery .

Mushroom - So , Charlie , let me finish : as I had already told you , you do not know anything of what's going on down here ! I would certainly want to come over there one day , up there at the very top , even if only for one time , and enjoy that pure and fresh air ,far away from this hell down here in the midst of all of these disturbed , perturbed and obnoxious creatures that all they have in mind is an eager desire to crave for fomenting disorder , discord and confusion along with perplexing and unclassified instincts to create discontent, resentment ,hopelessness and even hatred among themselves , while claiming to vie for precisely the opposite of all of above and in the middle of some time off to take a breath , they engage in the sporting activity of steeling from each other precious food from the ground of this Forest , beat down the weak and the defenseless among themselves , promoting in this way the uncensored attitudes and behaviours that promote and even sanction violent inclinations without an inkling of respect for civic dignity and safety , order , personal rights and beliefs . ....Oh !...If I only could climb up there ,to the very top , and even if only for one day , may be even just half a day or even just for one hour.....Oh !....if I could only,,,,,,,

The learned sweet Gopher - How about just for a few minutes , you stupid mushroom of the Agaricus Campestris genus ?

Mushroom - Go and get lost ,you nincompoop of a Gopher, you , diminutive brain gopher of the well known "pocket gopher"size type as well as the also known"snake gopher"denomination ,so well descriptive of your malicious inference in the "none of your business"reminder,YOU,miserable "Glomys Bursarius" of the infamous "Citellus Genus" ! Get lost !

Giant Oak Tree- But , Fabius ,to whom are you screaming with so violent and furious voice down there ? Are the revolutionary crowds at it again ??!!

Mushroom - No, Charlie . Just a Gopher .

Giant Oak Tree
(to himself) - Now the mystery really deepens : from raving mad mobs and threatening surges of revolution just witnessed and , fortunately , relegated now to history , all the way to conversational exchanges with gophers and not of the most pleasant ones either , these exchanges ,I mean , it just makes me wonder if I am dreaming or am I still alert and in control of my normal functions .

Mushroom - Oh ! Yes , !Yes ! Oh ,YES !...if I only could climb up to that very top branch , to that imposing vertex symbolizing power, dominion and possession of that power , yes ,yes , even if only for a day , alone and above everybody's else in this Forest , I would really feel King for a day, and what a feeling that would be ,what a sensation of well being , of a grand moment of being something ,being somebody whom everybody looks to as their Protector, their Defender , their righteous Ruler ,in the elite company of the other big trees , the other Giant Trees and rest in that splendid peace and serenity !

The learned
sweet Gopher - The Mushroom has gone nuts !

Giant Oak Tree –
(to himself) For a million Birch trees , I am becoming really worried about the behaviour of our Mushroom ! Lately , and particularly during the last couple of hours , he has talked with an apparent lack of coordination of meaning and intent, almost a complete reversal of all of his previous proclaimed philosophy , and contradicting all his stated principles !!...What's happening to him ???!!...Is this a post-traumatic shock from the dreadful experience of the revolution , or could it be an impairment of his physical health , or just a severe depressive trend countersigned by a manic impulse , or , even worse , a counter productive recrimination of his limited , down-sized and diminutive importance in the line of gifts and values distributed to him by Mother Nature as She usually does to all her creatures ? This is really a worrisome thought !

The learned
sweet Gopher - I would not worry so much about him : he is just a stupid, senseless , ignorant Mushroom , likely suffering from all the ailments just mentioned by you , except one : brightness .

Giant Oak Tree - Gopher , I know that there is freedom of speech and expression in my Kingdom but , at the same time and as your King , I would want to remind you that nothing good ever comes by adding fire to fire .

The learned
sweet Gopher - Sire , Your Wisdom is well known in this Forest of Yours and Ours , but for

the necessary means for survival in this competitive natural world, well…the crippled creature or the athlete, the rich or the poor, the honest frog like the dishonest frog, the thief or the policeman, the learned man or the analphabet guy, and , as it usually always follows in the existence of the combined riff-raff of all classes of living creatures, every single one of them is going about its needs for survival not in any much different way than anyone else in this Forest! And what's at the head of that glorious carousel? There goes quite prominently the inexhaustible host of the ……IDIOTS…!!

Chorus of the Idiots- We are rightfully proud of being a host, even if inexhaustible.

Mushroom - Night and day, day by day, night by night, hour by hour ,someone this way, another the other way, somebody up, somebody down, looking, sweating ,running around and troubling one self to death without rest to find anything that can be found and finding nothing or little or not enough! What kind of existence is this, I am asking myself!! ...But, up there, Oh !... up there how different will be my world, my Forest...! !...Blue skies with a shining sun and the...sweet song of the birds at sunrise and the stars at night!

The learned sweet Gopher -The Mushroom is irrational! He has gone mad, I begin to fear!!!

****

While the Mushroom continues his tirade with unabated furor, the Giant Oak Tree is in a state of utter desperation, fear, confusion. and incapacity to absorb in its entirety the present development of the seeming and alarming alienation of the better faculties of the Mushroom and, associated with it, the loss of the help for consultation, advice, opinion and counsel from his Prime Minister, the Mushroom who, apparently, has gone berserk, likely overwhelmed by the magnitude of the undergoing events, and totally unable to respond in any sensible way to the needs of the Giant Oak Tree...his King!! !

The situation is becoming increasingly serious.

The GiantOak Tree has no one around him whom he could trust and, apart from that, there actually would not be anyone around that he could even attempt to address….and time is running short…….

The Giant Oak Tree, then, invokes the Gods! .

Giant Oak Tree - Oh ! Mighty Gods on Mount Olympus , majestic , sacred , ancient Mountain, would your far reaching Wisdom ever be able to decipher for me this terrible and frightful and bizarre sudden subversion of thought , attitude , loyalty and convictions in a mushroom ? I fear the worst for my trusted Minister !

The Gods , from Mount Olympus- Mortal , We heard your plea ....Life will guide him back to himself .

Giant Oak Tree- Oh ! Mighty Gods , it might be too late , by then !

The Gods , from Mount Olympus - Nothing is late in the Universe .

****

Perched comfortably on a branch of the Oak Tree, our well known Spinster Sparrows , the two old maids , Andrea and Celeste , have been resting ,a much needed rest after the consuming stress of fear and horror at the possibility of a severe civic disorder,even the risk of a fully fledged revolution, yet alert ,monitoring any changes below............

****

Andrea - Celeste ! Did you hear the lamentations of the Mushroom ? Even the Oak Tree seems perplexed at the Mushroom's sudden change of spirit and thought !!

Celeste - Yes , Andrea , I heard it .

Andrea - And what do you make of it ? The Mushroom appears to exhibit a mixed attitude of anger , sentimentalism , despair and frustration , along with some anxiety and criticism of the conditions and living standards down there : an almost incomprehensible turn around from his usual self !!!

Celeste - Mushrooms , Andrea , here in the Forest , are known for being prone to pessimism ,anger , despair , anxiety and insecurity , because they are constantly either picked up from their houses by the human creatures , or used by Gnomes as a stool for resting and observing the world around them ,or by Goblins , you know, those mischievous Sprites of the Forests , whose intents are ,most often , on the trouble-making side ,or eaten up by worms in times of insufficient availability of victuals in the Forest, so their assessment of situations , any situation , should always be taken with a grain of salt ....I know, we Birds do not use salt , but it makes good sense , anyway .

Andrea - I understand that , Celeste , yet , even "taking" the Mushroom's findings with a grain of salt , even with several grains of salt, we can observe also something by ourselves and , rightly or wrongly , he is literally blasting everything and everybody in this Forest ,this Kingdom , if you want it , since he is the Minister , and, for the Minister of the Government of a Kingdom to go on such a melodramatic rampage at a time when , instead , a firm ,steady, sober mind and attitude are needed for the restoration of the confidence in the Government and the encouragement due to its subjects , seems to me a rather poor way of restoring confidence in anything . He just is blaming everything and everybody for what has taken place, including the King !!!

Celeste - Yes , it is a sort of a very sad and distressing situation, also made worse because there does not seem to be a solid explanation for the Mushroom's sudden change, whether he just talks loud and excitedly secondary to the shock and the distress suffered during the past harrowing experiences or his nerves are so badly frayed that he has lost ,at least , some partial control over them and his ability to distinguish propriety of communication .

Andrea - May be a little of everything , and it's a mess !.......Listen , listen , Celeste !!.... He has started yelling again !!

Celeste - Oh !....My…!!

Mushroom - Damn all these creatures ! Damn , damn , damn all of them ! Every day , every night , the same thing !.....The sun rises and there they start roaming here and there , endlessly !!...Damn these creatures !....Night comes ,and another bunch of desperado-like clowns takes to the woods , running into anything and everything , and that includes me ! Damn , damn , damn , these fetid creatures !....as if the humidity , the dismal aspect of these surroundings, the cold ,the misery would not be enough to let me age prematurely , but "NO"….there,our unenviable neighbours must come in to add even more weight to our grievous and heavy woes than Nature had intended in the first place…..this scum of Neighbours…..and these repulsive insects do not even have a brain ,at least it appears that way by their actions and doings ,good for nothing but to pry on other creatures' assets . Down with the Insects !

Andrea - Incredible !......and a Minister of the King !....Incredible !!

Giant Oak Tree - Lord have mercy ! This poor Mushroom is raving with fever ! He doesn't know what 's he is saying !!!...The Insects have their place in the existence of all of us , in one way or another , just as anyone of us and all the other creatures have their place to be and live in this Forest !...What has come upon this poor Mushroom and what so disturbing has seized him ??!

Mushroom - What a rotten world! What kind of life is this ??!...I am asking !.......and I am asking the question myself because it is I who suffers and not the Giant Trees, always standing there high and proud and indifferent to the problems and the hardships facing us ,little, humble creatures, every single day of our meager existence!!.. Is this at all a way to live ? Nothing but mud, filth ,trash and despair , and , in the end , what comes to us from all that ? .....There comes someone , picks us up and enjoys the taste of our flesh and no one will ever shed a tear at our demise because no one ever knew of our existence ! Oh ! If only I could grow as tall, taller may be , even grow to be the tallest of them all, and dominate all of these giant trees, including you, my dear enormous sweet and conniving Despot.......Oh!...yes , then , that I would put everything and everybody in their proper places ...!!

Giant Oak Tree- Oh ! Numina ! Divine Spirits !....The Greed that destroys Reason !

Andrea - Celeste, the Mushroom is bent to cause irreparable damage to this Kingdom and his King !

Celeste - Andrea , it has been known for centuries and centuries that a little worm can turn a beautiful fruit into a rotten pulp.

Chorus of the Worms - Why do you blame us for something that Nature programmed us to do ? Blame Nature, instead , if you feel that Nature was wrong in doing so .

Andrea - Dear Worms , Celeste , who is my best friend , did not mean any hostile thought against you, she just commented on something that everybody can openly observe and observing , per se , is in no way offensive or denigrating .

The learned sweet Gopher - We concur with that explanation ,we feel that it was well expressed , even if its explanation was totally unnecessary .

Mushroom - Damn the Gophers ! Damn, damn them all , those useless creatures ! After the Gophers I would cut all these haughty tall trees in half and settle several mushrooms on top of those halves ....ah! .....idea , idea ...... so that when those halves would start sprouting again , which process is widely acknowledged as usually forthcoming , as it is a probable occurrence for all the great things that were destroyed by inadvertent or ignorant or malicious creatures purely for their lack of imagination or genius to produce some new and even better ones , so ,as I was saying , if those halves of trees would start sprouting again , as they probably would , they would start growing , becoming taller and taller and I ,with my compatriots , would also rise to the sky and become a Giant !! Oh ! then , I really would fix everything and place everybody in its proper place , right there below me , in that humid, dark and putrid ground .

Andrea - Celeste , I have no doubt now : the Mushroom has gone mad !

Giant Oak Tree - Heavens above !...This confused little mushroom seems to appear even more rigid in his posture now, probably due to his frantic attempt to tower over his surroundings and assuming a threatening stand !.I am at a loss !!!.I couldn't believe my eyes , if I had them !

Andrea - Celeste ! I am worried !

Celeste - So am I , Andrea .

Mushroom - I always said that , preached that , believed in that : this world down here is very strange , obscure ,forgotten , down trodden and neglected because some creatures who carry responsibility and could inspire changes favourable to the improvement of this society ,feel themselves too big and too tall to go to the discomfort of lowering themselves to our humble level ,and yet these proud and empty creatures have their feet , their paws and ,likely , their feelings and thoughts too, down here in this mud even if , at the upper level , their necks stretch like Giraffes above the humble grounds . That has to change ! I swear !

Giant Oak Tree- He's turning green with livid thoughts and then changes to a dark red colour in his front and a grim , sinister look in his appearance and he is foaming under his large umbrella ! He is turning into a hideous creature !! Could it be that he has been poisoned by some secret revolutionary cells of the Worms and the Centipedes ??.....Strange things can happen these days !

Mushroom- When I shall be at the top , my first act of Government will be " First thing , First ! " , so , the Worms will have to be annihilated . Out with the Worms !

Andrea - Did you hear , Celeste , did you hear ??!

Celeste - What , Andrea ? What was I supposed to have heard ?

Andrea - The Mushroom is on a rampage , at the present moment only a verbal attack against the Worms and he threatens to exterminate them !....What's going on down there , Celeste ? I had thought that everything had been cleared up among the creatures of the Forest, and harmony reestablished in the Kingdom, as the Shining Knights came in , but , now , I am not so sure , anymore .... Listen ..listen , Celeste ..! Now the Worms are picking on the Mushroom ! How long , I am wondering , will this dangerous jousting last , prodromal to worse times to come ??!

The learned sweet Gopher - If you have a round object , like a ball, and an incline , like the sides of a valley , and you let the ball run down the incline , the ball will keep on rolling down the incline ,until the incline will ease up in a plain, or in a lake,or in the sea,or the ball will stop sooner if confronted by an obstacle of whatever form or size,that might have surfaced in the ball's trajectory . Quite simple, really .

Andrea - The ball might be in your head , you silly Gopher , or you might be the one rolling down the "incline" in some far away "valley" ! What has your remark got to do with my worry about the possible far reaching implications and dangers of this prolonged jousting among the creatures of this Forest ? You tell me that , smart rodent .

The learned sweet Gopher - I will tell you that , young Lady , and as I had said before: "quite simple " .

Andrea - Simple and make it snappy , old buddy .

The learned sweet Gopher - Very well : instead of a ball think of a square . A square , a cube , does not roll and it would not roll easily down an incline because it has too many sharp corners or the incline would have to be very steep for the cube to roll down ; RIGHT ? Right . Now , then , think of jousting , the situation that seems to worry you greatly , as a ball and when the two armor clad Antagonists , the "armor" not a mandatory one of steel but, and more often ,an armor of spite, hatred and intolerance , start rolling along on each side of the stretched carousel with spears aimed at each other and the horses at full gallop , nothing can stop them unless they themselves or one of them decides to stop or someone else intervenes to stop the jousting , then , as you see , the "ball" will stop. Happy now ?

Andrea - I have never heard a more stupid , idiotic , senseless , preposterous , inadequate , confused , pathetic , pedantic and incomprehensible story in my life !

The learned sweet Gopher - It is also said that ,in anybody's life , there always comes a time when somebody learns something new : you should consider yourself lucky because you just learned one .

Andrea - You are an impertinent , unpleasant creature and ,apart from that , what does your story try to explain about my worry about the consequences of the verbal jousting going on in our Forest now, with the Mushroom in a frenzy and angry with everyone ?

the learned sweet Gopher - I should not even answer you ,after that sophisticated introduction, but , sweet as I am , I'll tell you : I DO NOT KNOW !!

Andrea - Thanks , so much : that was really sweet of You , rotten clown .

The learned sweet Gopher - Don't mention it .

Mushroom - Damn the Worms ! Out with the Worms ! Death to the Worms !

Worm #1 - That mushroom is crazy . Did you hear what he just said ?

Worm #2 - Yes , I heard it . Don't pay any attention to it and to him : since his birth he has always found something to complain about ! So , ignore him and continue to suck his roots which must be very nourishing considering his extraordinary loquacity .

Mushroom - Quiet , you shapeless Worms : your noise displeases me . Prepare to die .

Chorus of the Worms - Oh yeah ? He talks big and he can't even move , the darned idiot !

The Leader of the Worms - Fellow Citizens, I have grave news !

Chorus of the Worms - Hear ! Hear !

The Leader of the Worms - I have heard several notices circulated among the Internal Affairs Ministries of the Centipedes and the Beetles that mention the highly probable breaking out of a revolution in the Forest , spear headed by the soldiers Ants , the Hymenopterous Citizens of the Nation of Farmicidea . However we have not been able to obtain any official confirmation of its impendence .

Chorus of the Warrior Worms - To War ! To War ! Death to the Mushrooms !

The Leader of the Worms - Order ! Order ! Not one move until the Diet of the Wise Worms will verify the news and confirm the correctness of the notices . Self restraint and honour are the marks of distinction of the Combined Nations of the Platyhelminths , the Nemahelminths and the Annelids : We pride ourselves of being Worms .

Andrea - Celeste ! Celeste , we better make ourselves scarce : the Worms are preparing themselves for war, or so it seems , and if they would hear us , see us and realize that we consider them as our most honourable menu ,they probably would not take to us with unbridled sympathy .

Celeste - Yes ,in a way , Andrea , you may be right, but , anybody in this Forest of ours, and , I am pretty sure , also in many other Forests , knows but too well that old refrain that goes : " dog-eat-dog" , in the natural selection set by our congenial Mother Nature in this fierce competitive Forest of ours , as well as everywhere else creatures live , of all sizes , shapes and classifications .

The learned sweet Gopher - The situation appears serious .

Giant Oak Tree - Immortal Gods !.Oh ! Mighty Zeus !What do I hear ? Revolution ?! Again ?! We jus got out of one and are these "Jockers" playing a"domino effect"type of game with such a light hearted attitude that reflects utter and irresponsible civic respectability short of being intrinsically irrational and murderous . This is serious.......

The learned sweet Gopher - I just said so .

the Diet of the Wise Worms - We feel likewise .

Andrea - Just take a second to look down below at the Mushroom : he appears raving mad , shaking his umbrella as if it were a flying disk from outer space ,most likely where his brain is at this time, anyway, and creating a fracas down there., and more confusion among those already highly confused creatures !

Giant Oak Tree - Revolution !.... And what else is new , these days , I wonder ? Creatures do not have anything else in their minds than a sense of commotion , disruption and dissent as a means to bring justice to all !....And here , up here , I mean , at my elevation , not a soul to give me some help , some friendly advice, not counter balanced by the courtesan type of second thought behind it hoping for a return in benefits , but genuine , straight from the heart counsel , if a heart is still a standard instrument in the make up of some creatures we know .

Chorus of the Standard Hearts - As far as we are concerned we keep on carrying on the programmed activities endorsed to our responsibility in the functioning of certain created structures, but we do not know which ones they are and we do not know how well instructed they may be in the maintenance of our mechanisms .

The learned sweet Gopher - Did you ever consider adding an Instruction Leaflet in your packaged matter?

Chorus of the Standard Hearts- Leaflets....??.All we know is that we have a few leaves in our mechanism. We were told that,but we have never seen them, and if the creatures provided with our system ,read them or not , that's not our business .

Chorus of the future Mechanisms- Ignorance is no solution for problems,or disinterested creatures,or green frogs. A day looms in the horizon when creatures of wisdom will be able to read these leaflets .

Chorus of the Standard Hearts- What's the use of praising something that's to come and is not here yet !

Chorus of the future Mechanisms - What a stupid question !

Chorus of the Standard Hearts - We do not think that our question is stupid .We believe, instead, that you are .

Chorus of the future Mechanisms - Really ?

Chorus of the Standard Hearts - Yes , Really !...By divulging , now , what's to come down the road in the unknown time ,you forfeit the Created Creatures' Right and Privilege to become excited and proud and encouraged and invigorated in the pursuit of a better existence , when a new discovery is brought forward in their horizons . By divulging the future you take away from the created Creatures their coveted and appetizing desire for discovery .

Chorus of the future Mechanisms - Poppy Cock .

Chorus of the Standard Hearts - Same to you !

The learned sweet Gopher - Shall we proceed with the main course ?

Chorus of the Standard Hearts - By all means !!....And let us hope that these pedantic Mechanism of Timbactu will leave us in peace !

The learned sweet Gopher - They will : as a matter of fact they are already far , far away froim us investigating many new discoveries.

Chorus of the Standard Hearts - Good ! So we may continue our interrupted conversation in peace , while we pray for them that when they'll "discover" their own destiny , it wont be too hard on them .

Chorus of the Destinies - We do not think that we are a representation of hardship on anyone created or on the way of being created:our purpose in their existences is just like a dinner: you start eating it and,when the dinner's over,so is the life of the creature , and it is a rather simple process called Demise .

Chorus of the Standard Hearts - We wish that everyone around us would call a general dinner's end and proclaimed a successful demise of everybody so that we may continue our so much interrupted conversation ! So, may we continue ?

The learned sweet Gopher - Go ahead and proceed with a wide open horizon in front of you: the Destinies have left in hot pursuit of the Future Mechanisms to tell them a thing or two, so you may resume your conversation , at leisure .

Chorus of the Standard Hearts - If we remember correctly , we were deviated from our main discourse by the remark of the Learned Gopher, about the feasibility of attaching an Instruction leaflet to our mechanism so that it could be understood and well taken care of by detailing steps for its proper use and maintenance, so, picking up from there without going into details again, already so profusely exposed , we keep on our tasks and nothing , really , short of the premature end of a dinner or the missing of some entrees, keeps us from performing our assigned duties.

Chorus of the dutiful Icons - We appreciate your adherence to our principles . It is well known about how many illustrious creatures were made famous , rich and respected in their lives because of their unflinching perseverance and exact delivery of performance of their assigned duties .

Chorus of the Standard Hearts - Thank you . Needless to say that in Ancient Times We occupied a position of great respect and consideration because we were considered the depositories of everything ,including love, affection, thoughts , imagination ,feelings and an innumerable other forms of functions until ,lately ,a great part of those functions were ascribed to another mechanism called Brain .

The learned sweet Gopher - Did that reassignment of properties and duties irk you or displease you to some extent ?

Chorus of the Standard Hearts - Not really . As a matter of fact it felt as a relief, not having to follow the strange peregrinations of Lovers'Fantasies, the sensuous lamentations of Poets and the angry impulses of murders or of fanatic Warriors or the mystic recriminations of Men of Charity and Compassion .

The learned sweet Gopher - I wonder why it had not been thought to be that way from the very beginning , instead of waiting so long ,centuries and centuries , I am told by the Wise Lunar Moth , before finding out that , may be , it was the Brain that controlled all those functions , originally conferred upon the Hearts !! Strange, is it not ?

Chorus of the Standard Hearts - May be not so strange , after all . You see , by sheer comparison with us , so plump and deep crimson red as we appear and sensuously configured in a shape all of its own, the Brain , by sheer contrast , did not offer an attractive sight , by exhibiting a rather shabby appearance with a sickly colour, all wrinkled up and kept under constant guard as if........

The learned sweet Gopher - Are there any Guards around it ???!...It just sounds incredible !

Chorus of the Standard Hearts- No, not Guards proper but something like being kept as if under house arrest in a hard enclosure, some of those enclosures harder than some ,having no way to expand , and not pulsating at all like we do, so it is a rather monotonous piece of furniture and , to the best of our knowledge , no arrows have yet been shot into it, like they have been shot into us for ages because of our softness and probably not in the Brain because of the very hard composition of the walls of its housing , but , instead , we have been told that the Brain itself is capable of shooting arrows of its own that can do a lot of damage . Now, and in spite of that mechanism having been assigned the overall direction of whatever form it may have been inserted into , We , the.......

The learned sweet Gopher - Really sorry to interrupt you ,dear Hearts , but ,then , is the placement of this mechanism that you call Brain a random procedure ?

Chorus of the Standard Hearts- More or less .

The learned sweet Gopher - Then it is possible that some creatures may not get a brain at all : right ?

Chorus of the Standard Hearts - How very right you are and to think that you are only a Gopher !

The learned sweet Gopher - No big deal , really : we are used to dig deep, naturally. .....But , then , I am sorry that I interrupted you !

Chorus of the StandardHearts - Yes, no problem dear Gopher and I'll be through in a jiffy, and, as I was saying,We, the Hearts , continue to do our job because we love the thumping of our body ,we enjoy the sound produced by our thumping and we like the distinctive and soft cadence of our rhythmic beat and , in some way and in spite of all the new directives and discoveries , if we would stop thumping , the Brain , we are told , would stop thinking and we were just wondering if , in certain instances , that could be a blessing .

The learned sweet Gopher - It might : why not trying in order to find out !

Chorus of the Standard Hearts - That would be against our programmed activity and it is not possible on our own initiative , but we know of several instances where the Brain stopped in its function while we were still pumping everything we had through it . We were told that , in one case , it was a matter of the creature getting crazy , and in another case , it had been an accident ,the hard head that contains the Brain being hit ,very hard , and yet in another instance ,it was due to a strange condition that the two legged Creatures , the human ones, call Jealousy . So , in one way or another , this new piece of equipment does not seem to be as strong as we are, a rather shifty type of matter, hard to regulate, to feed, to control .

The learned sweet Gopher- I just heard His Majesty the King , expressing satisfaction at what he was able to listen and learn from your explanation of the vicissitudes of Hearts and Brains in your long history of adjustments and diversities and he is grateful to you for giving him at least some much needed moral support .

Chorus of the Standard Hearts - Please , tell His Majesty , that We are proud to be in this Forest as his devoted subjects and that we were flattered by his appreciation and praise of our stories.

Giant Oak Tree- And to think that so much ruin can be caused, in a sudden revolt, by the deliberate incompetence of just a few ill advised creatures and ill disposed elements who always seem to benefit from the general confusion and the uncertainties , the gullibility and irresponsibility of so many naïve creatures as well as a common a patrimony for those who have nothing to lose in any state of confusion and disorder, while prone to happily ignore that the ruin of everything that was before , even if not perfect , yet functioning in some form of serenity and peace , that ruin would hit them too while they will revolt against it , as if the fury of their actions, in destroying it would in return create a new one ,may be., even worse than the one they had and wanted destroyed .

The captain of the King's Guards - Sire , Your Minister , His Excellence the Mushroom , has just now unfurled the Flag of the revolutionaries and is addressing them with inflammatory speeches!

Giant Oak Tree - Oh! Mighty Zeus , I see the approaching storm drawing closer, and I see the creatures taking leave of their own senses , wisdom languishing and violence and opportunism galloping ahead of the Apocalypse itself !...

The Captain of the King's Guards - Sire ,You should take refuge. in our midst to prevent this rousing mob from storming Your Majesty's Enclave .

Giant Oak Tree - What usefulness is my greatness, then , to the little creatures when they do not even know that it exists?....Oh ! You , Merciful Zeus, our destiny is now into your hands ,there, up on that lofty Mountain where You with a lenient glance observe the good deeds of your Creatures just as You loathe, I am sure, their wickedness and , if the revulsion of those vile acts offends your magnanimous Spirit ,You fling your bolt of lightning which ,at times ,in the fury of your offended perception at their iniquitous deeds, strikes the righteous creatures while sparing the guilty ones !

The Captain of the King's Guards - Sire , the Guards are standing at the perimeter of the enclave , armed and ready to repulse any attempt to storm our grounds. In here,among the Guards , Sire , You are safe .

Giant Oak Tree - Oh! Great and Powerful Zeus , why on this Forest is that so that Great and Small creatures do not seem to ever understand each other and stop in time from the perilous edge of an abyss ?....And how even stranger it seems that wisdom and madness, both at the same time , become crushed in the storm of passions and discomtents ! Woe to all of us , Oh , Mighty Zeus , woe to the Mushroom , poor, naive ,credulous and ill advised creature !

Mushroom - Thunder and Lightning !....Oppressed creatures !!....Time has come to revolt against the tyranny of the Giant Trees who force everything and everybody to pine and suffer in their dark shadows while they indulge in the breathing of pure and refreshing air at their vertiginous heights, caring nothing for the little creatures who are drowning in this infamous life of mud and despair, without any hope and without an even faint glimpse of a better future in this gloomy quagmire under these haughty Giant Trees ! To arms ! To arms !......and rebel against the dictatorial stance of these oppressive Giant Trees !........To arms, my valorous host of braves ,and death to the Worms , death to the Giant Trees and extermination too of all the Centipedes ! To arms ! To arms ! My Braves ! and a "Hurray" !...for the Great Revolution of the oppressed little Creatures of the Forest !!

1st Centipede - What did I tell you , the other day ?....That mushroom is a real problem , a fully fledged paranoic , raised to the nth power ! Just let me shout something in his face to shut him up !

2nd Centipede - Don't be foolish , Alambert ! The Secret Police are everywhere !...Just lie quiet and let the ones who have nothing , who own nothing , who care nothing , do the yelling and the screaming and have the privilege to hurl outrageous invectives to the governing Authorities : these creatures , usually , have nothing at stake or to lose , but , may be , something to gain , instead , in this turmoil !

1st Centipede - But somebody will have to rebuke such ostentatious boldness from a pathetic and mischievous mushroom or " I ", Alambert Piedileone of the Piedileoni will not let go unpunished this miserable and paranoic saprophytic plant !

2nd Centipede - Fine , fine , Alambert ,dear , but calm and steady nerves are needed now . Heigh ! ..Come a little closer: I want to say something quietly, so, listen : in these times it is very risky to speak in a loud voice and you'd better keep your big mouth shut and , even if…………

Some sparse voices in the distance - Down with the mushrooms ! Death to the mushrooms !

1stCentipede - Ah ! At last ! Somebody has seen the light ! By Jove, I am with you, whoever you are ! Death to the mushrooms !

2nd Centipede - Be quiet!For Heaven's sake ,Alambert , shut your mouth ! You are endangering our very lives with your boisterous and insensate attitude !

1st Centiped - Quiet , my one hundred feet ! Here , we triumph or we die !

2nd Centipede - Let us hope for the best : I opt for the triumph .

1st Centipede - Zantavius , you are a coward !

2nd Centipede - Alambert , I am not a coward .

1st Centipede - Zantavius , you are a coward .

2nd Centipede - Alambert, you are irresponsible .

1st Centipede - Irresponsible ?..".I "….Irresponsible ??!..Watch your language , Zantavius ! I, Alambert Piedileone of the Piedileoni of Valcoccola , I do not fear anybody , not even myself , and this shows what sort of a Centipede I am !.....And now is the time to let every creature in this Forest know of my free, pure and noble feelings and let my fierce indignation , my utter disdain for this vile , vulgar mushroom be brought forward, or I am not the Alambert Piedileone of the Piedileoni of Valcoccola !

2nd Centipede - By all means ,Alambert , by all means and we shall let all the creatures of the Forest be informed of that message by special delivery from our mailing,

mailing resources ,unless our delivery page will stall ,fearing of a possible attack on his person by the opposing parties , but we will certainly try , I promise you . In the meantime, common and prudent sense , so pervasive , anyway, among the Gens of Centipedes , should prevail, until the situation either clears out or becomes better delineated and represented . So what I wanted to tell you was that when I was at school , in my younger days ,of course , I ....

1st Centipede - Come on ! What happened when you were at school? Besides, what have your school memories to do with our situation at hand ??!

2nd Centipede - Not much, really, just a diversion from the tension of this dreadful instance of an impending revolt , or rebellion or revolution ,whatever you prefer , but, regardless of what you may call it , always an unpleasant show of life's futility and its difficult to comprehend meaning .

1st Centipede - Is that what you learned at school ?

2nd Centipede - No, Alambert : that is what I am learning now .

1st Centipede - Fine ! We have been at school . We have learned our lesson . The teachers are happy. The school Master is delirious with our academic progress, so what are we waiting for ? Let's get the hell out of here and rush to fight the mushrooms, attack them from all sides , cut off their heads and destroy their lairs ,so victory will be ours !

2nd Centipede - Alambert, you never fail to amaze me ! Where the hell do you intend to go to fight the mushrooms? There are none around here:just one under the Giant Oak Tree , and he is crazy. Now, does an Alambert Piedileone of the Piedileoni of Valcoccola wishes to go and fight and cut off the head of one only mushroom, crazy on top of it, or, may be ,the valiant Alambert of the Piedileoni of Valcoccola had paid too much attention to the adventures of "Don Quixote", the chivalrous personage who charged the windmills on the presumption that they were hostile Giants with their spread arms to get him?

1st Centipede - One less , crazy or not , will always be better than one plus .

2nd Centipede - That's second hand reasoning , Alambert . Why don't we , instead,pay more attention to our situation and try to avoid unpleasant surprises. So I intend to move to that portico that is at the corner with that narrow and dark alley so that we can be protected from any sudden surging of a mob or repaired from the rain in the event that it would rain, of course , always a possibility, particularly so in time of bad weather, either natural or social, either one of little importance to Mother Nature, anyway it will afford us some protection from a multitude of possibilities while still allowing us an excellent view of the main thoroughfares so that we can easily observe the movements of the various demonstrators and be aware of any other developing contingencies , while still having at our back the little dark alley that would afford us a quick and practical escape,in the event.........well, don't be alarmed now, ...Alambert .....

1st Centipede - Escape ?...Did you say ESCAPE ???!!...The Piedeleoni never "escape"!! They only and ever go forward , never retreat .

2nd Centipede - That is a very fine attitude of courage and determination, but , in case they would change their minds , or you would change yours , you know.....one never knows what can happen in life......well, as I was saying, just in case and if really needed , we would have an easy way out of a possible unpleasant or even dangerous situation.

1st Centipede - Unpleasant and dangerous would only apply to our enemies and the mushrooms : the Piedileone Knights never act unpleasantly and danger is their coveted guiding star .

2nd Centipede - Do not misunderstand me , dear Alambert : I am not denying or belittling your valorous and valiant abilities of war, but , I had thought, that easy accessible lane could be extremely useful, in the event that one of us would become sick : so , no need to fret over simple and commonplace things .

1st Centipede - All right ! All right ! ..As you wish, but you cannot see anything from here! Darn it !!

2nd Centipede - Patience , patience , my dear Alambert!! In life, "patience" is a mandatory commodity !! Besides, our theater, I mean this riotous atmosphere around us, that just looks to me like a live performance of vaudeville, appears to have just now taken some impetus ,so let us see how things will develop.

1st Centipede - Delaying the showdown with the mushrooms will only give them more time to fortify their positions , ask for reinforcements and be better prepared for resisting our impetuous charge .

2nd Centipede - Well, listen , anyway , to what my teacher used to say when I was at school in my younger days: he always said to be careful with mushrooms because, although they all look funny and cute , yet many of them are poisonous and told us too how to distinguish the poisonous ones from the ones who are not .

1st Centipede - ....When you were...at school ??......Great Scott ! There you go again...!!!

2nd Centipede - Yes , Alambert, when I was at school . And what's wrong with that ?
1st Centipede - By George ,Zantavius ,to talk about your school days in times like these ??!

2nd Centipede - Alambert , you might think that I am a little too insisting and pedantic in my conversations and explanations of facts and events, but,honestly,when I was in school our teacher used to caution us young ignorant kids of being aware of mushrooms,because some of them, although looking nice and plump, actually were ,not only bad but even dangerous for your life, if ingested, because they were poisonous and cautioned us about those mushrooms , in particular the ones which had a large umbrella thickly pleated on the inside, these being particularly poisonous ,among the many others ....

1st Centipede - Poisonous ??....Rotten...I'd say !

An Itinerant Centipede - Rotten ,You say ?? Rotten is not enough : putrefied , would be more appropriate ,for "them" mushroom , in my view, the damned things . .

1st Centipede - The Stranger talks sense : welcome ,stranger , and I shall add : " putrefied and with worms "..!!....These fetid mushrooms !

The Secretary of the Worms' Syndicate - Gentlemen , you are bearing an hideous insult towards the United Nations of the Flatworms , the Roundworms , the Acanthocephalans , the Nemerteans , the Gordiaceans and the Annelids . An apology would be in order .

2nd Centipede _ You see, now , Alambert, what kind of a mess you are getting yourself into and, on that account , me too, by your unpredictable and inconsiderate style of expressions and definitions . Fortunately we have our little lane right behind us : quick, now , let's get out of here before we get into some more serious trouble. Come on , Alambert : quick , this way : come!!

1st Centipede - Come..??..Alambert...?..this Way...??......Quick!.......Come this way ??!....to me ???!!...I am Alambert Piedileone !! NEVER EVER , my chicken-livered unworthy centipede by the name of cowardly Zantavius , NEVER EVER will an Alambert Piedileone of the Piedileoni of Valcoccola , ever , ever retreat by the way of a dark little lane !! This here Alambert of the Piedileoni of Valcoccola will, instead, utter as loud as possible his disdain , revulsion, repugnance for the Worms ,the Mushrooms and anybody else represented with them ,Nations , Empires , Lizards and Frogs , and Associates .

2nd Centipede - Be reasonable , Alambert , please, please , be reasonable !!

1st Centipede - Reasonable ?....BAH !! HUMBUG !!

2nd Centipede - Quiet, Alambert, please, be quiet ! Instead of boasting your fierce intentions why don't you listen and observe, instead, something right in front of us? Can you see what I can see ?

1st Centipede - Can I see WHAT ??....I cannot see anything !

2nd Centipede

But yes, Alambert , look down there, towards the edge of the square: can't you see two somewhat vague figures with only two legs below their large _bodies and two more, probably something like legs but not quite ,on the upper part of the body, a little indistinct now because of the prevailing fog and the dim light that pervades the square at this hour ,tell me, can you see that?

1 st Centipede

I can barely see what seem to be two shadows, in the fog, and in a dimly lit square. Now, I am asking myself: what's so important, what's so exciting, what's so captivating about two stupid shadows in an even more stupid square, in an even more idiotic brain like the one of my companion Zantavius?

2nd Centipede

Alambert ,those two shadows, as you choose to identify them, they cause me to be perplexed about them ,that's why I am interested in finding out who may they be .

1 st Centipede

May be just "shadows" and they'll be gone once the sun rises and clears everything out .

2nd Centipede

May be . May be! Yet, I became intrigued because, at first , I had thought something siniilar to what you just told me now, but, then , I seemed to have. observed some movements in them, well, I thought, they may be trees, with only a few branches left and slightly stirred by the wind, but, then, I saw them move from where they were originally standing when I saw them the first time, and they moved again , so I started thinking: " trees do not move from where they are",although, I am thinking, they would like to do that, sometime, if they could!. In final analysis I concluded that they were not trees. What could they be? But, Alambert, can't you see them?

1 st Centipede

Now, listen here, my dear Zantavilis, I just don't give a damn to look at your shadows, very likely some forlorn Centipedes who have only four limbs left after losing the other 96, may be , in a fight among themselves or with the Worms and the Mushrooms!! But you better heed my advice, my dear friend, and look around instead of looking somewhere else, mesmerized by visions of shadows and ghosts with only four legs! Look here, instead, just close to you, to us , that there is a phalanx, a legion, a formidable host of Warrior Worms heading our way to solicit our kind attention. Fortunately, the armored advance units of our Armed Forces have taken up defensive positions and they are under the command of our highly experienced and brave General Vetralius .

The Commander of the Warrior Worms -

To Your Highness, General Vetralius, Commander the CentipedesArmored Division ! "Greetings" from the Commander of the 5th. Armored Corps, the Warrior Worms, General Annalius .

General Vetralius — To the Commander of the 5th Armored Corps of the Warrior Worms} His Excellency General Annalius : Greetings accepted and reciprocated With our sincere sympathy, by order of General Vetralius.

General Annalius — General Vetralius ,Sir}! am proud to be able to see you personally and I hope to be able to bring to a peaceful solution what seems to have caused some problems between our two Great Nations.

General Vetralius — General Annalius ,dear Sir , ! was told about the occurrence ,lately, of some disparaging comments by unidentified citizens of our Nation of Centipedes, remarks that, according to witnesses, amounted to denigrating assertions about the aspect of mushrooms and referring the known Worms' activities on dead matter as a comparison of the mushrooms' character identity :we are sorry for that unfortunate comparison, while, at the same time , we appreciate the resentment of your noble Nation for that totally unnecessary altercation.

*** Meanwhile, the Giant Oak tree. on hearing that... ***
....

Giant Oak Tree — I feel some subtle murmurs coming up here and there from the midst of the Forest, a mournful whispering that does not promise good news. If ,at least, some sense would have gotten into the brain of that damned Mushroom, we could, at least, have talked to each other and come up with a better assessment of the situation, but "harebrained" as he has turned out to behave, no communication with him is at all possible! Lord, have pity on us !

*** The Oak Tree, sad and depressed ,continues to listen***

Genaral Annalius — General Vetralius, Sir , I agree with you about your report which seems to be quite comparable to the one I received. Yes, there seems to have been some unfortunate exchanges of "rather hard and offensive words and r would suggest, if you also would agree to it ,to let the parties involved in the affair to confront each other and explain their deeds, so that they would likely know better what really happened than we ,informed only by second hand reports. Would You, Dear general, agree to this arrangement?

General Vetralius — Excellent Idea, Sir , General Annalius ,and I am in full agreement: let us in the two parties and let them come up with the best solution ,supported by our best wishes.

General Annalius — Then it is agreed. I'll give orders to my guards to let the two parties meet andafford them protection. Genera.Vetralius, my deferent homage...!

General Vetralius — Agreed. Our party will also be there and I believe that your Guard will be sufficient to guarantee the peaceful conclusion to this unpleasant episode. My best wishes and regards, General Annalius , and from our Nation too. .

** The two Parties ,Worms and Centipedes , are invited to sit together under the protection of the Guards of General Annalius,and begin deliberations...**

Chorus of the offended Worms- (addressing the Centipedes) – Sirs , we have asked repeatedly of you for an overdue apology on account of the injurious vocabulary used in reference to us, our nature and our respectability, verbal injuries which greatly offend our dignity.

Chorus of the Centipedes - Regretfully we acknowledge the unpleasant episode that occurred between some irresponsible individual , quicker with their mouth than with their wits .

Chorus of the offended Worms- We understand that and we appreciate your recognition of that fact. Matter is that during the heated exchanges of unmentionable vocabulary, a referral was advanced portraying us as "putrid", a designation of appearance that was totally unacceptable to our pride and dignity .

Chorus of the Centipedes - We fully appreciate that raised point in the matter at hand and we understand the mechanism that accelerated the deterioration of that verbal confrontation. Therefore we offer our apology : we did not mean to offend you .

Chorus of the Offended Worms- However these two Centipedes Esquires, here now present among us , who appear also as being two gentleman more by the look of their attire than by their own looks, called us, liberally and openly ,that we were not only just worms but "putrid " worms .

Chorus of the Centipedes - Dear Sirs, we feel confident that the two gentlemen Centipedes here present that they did ,indeed, act in a reprehensible manner towards the exponents of the party of Worms, but we wish also to acknowledge that the particular vocabulary used was in keeping strictly with the Natural Laws of Putrefaction and for academic adherence to the terminology of Science.

***

The two Centipedes , No.1 and No.2 , on hearing that highly encouraging explanation , do not waste their time and , belatedly , merge themselves into the ongoing conversation.......................................

***

** By now , our well known No. 1 and No. 2 Centipedes , No.1, the blow-hard type of braggart and No.2, the more thoughtful and coordinated type of brain ,are eagerly approving the trend being taken by the parties in their explanatory discussions , hoping to get out of it with their "skins" still on them , and interject with passionate ardour in the Centipedes Delegation 's explanatory sequence of the choice of the offensive language by attributing it to strict adherence and respect for academic correctness...**

2nd Centipede - Precisely so, Sirs , without the minimal hesitation in affirming it,with no intention of a protective veil of mistaken choice of voice and with pure and only and absolute respect for the Scientific Terminology , if so pleases this Eminent Commission.

1st Centipede - But what kind of a masquerade is this ??!!.....and"precisely so" ..can have my full one hundred feet !!That kind of answer is an"eye wash !

2nd Centipede (turning to the 1st one, pleading...and in a soft voice, just as if commenting on the actual proceedings....) - Alambert !! Please be so good and sensible to listen to reason, at least once in your life and don't jeopardize our safety , our lives , our future ,with your negative, absurd and obstinate attitude towards the proper handling of creatures public relations........

(then, turning ,again , to the Eminent Commission of the examining body)......

Sirs , Respected Members of this Eminent Commission, please be as kind and well understanding of our position , due to my companion's birth defect in his compromised ability in discerning and choosing the correct vocabulary when engaged in any conversation and his "genetic directed " deficiency that limits his vocabulary strictly to nouns of profanity and vulgarity .

Chorus of the Centipedes - That lucid presentation of the cause and the unfolding of the unhappy circumstances that brought us here together , clearly and without aim at subterfuge, amply clarifies how the problem originated and developed in a major civic confrontation , simply and purely , out of the control of any of us, Worms , Centipedes and fully conglomerated matter, that "matter", of course, belonging to one of our citizens ,the No.1 Centipede , here present , in our Assembly now , whose genetic configuration was not a compatible match for normal civic and civil relationships.We offered our apologies : we feel free of any offense .

Chorus of ALL - Hurrah! Hurrah! For the Centipedes ,the Commission and all !!!

Chorus of the Worms

We are grateful for the offered apologies and we are certam that this will have pleased our Eminent Commission too . We further understand and appreciate that,if the term of abuse was pronounced in the exclusive interest of high Terminology and in the strict adherence to the academic code of scientific doctrine, then we feel very proud of being pointed out as"Putrid Worms", and. in a gesture of deeply felt thankful sentiment we are contorting our segmented rings in devoted deference.

Chorus of the Centipedes

With deference and renewed friendship we are tapping with enthusiasm our one hundred feet. Hurrah! for the 5th Armored division of the Warrior Worms I Hurrah I for General Annalius I I

Chorus of the Worms

Hurrah! for the Centipedes Armored Division! Hurrah! for General Vetralius !

General Vetralius

General Annalius, Sir , I would like to address the combined Armored Units of our two Nations elite soldiers, on account of this memorable occasion and as a follow up .t9 the brilliantly resolved dispute in confrontof the Glorious Nation of Worms and that not less but equally fulgent ofthe Nation of the Centipedes, and bear open an Idea that just flourished in my mind as the proceedings of the Investigating Commission came to a very satisfactory and happy conclusion. General Annalius ,Sir, would you be willing to concur with me in this impromptu address?

General Annalius

The wish and the opinion of General Vetralius is mine too and my soldiers will feel very proud to be addressed along with your brave Warriors, by a soldier like you whose reputation goes beyond the boundaries of any Nation. General Vetralius , I will listen with interest and anticipation to your address.

General Vetralius

Thank you ,General Annalius .

..The Address ..

Soldiers! Citizens! of our two Great Nations, The glorious Nations of the Worms and of the Centipedes, I salute the happy occasion with proud enthusiasm and I express my deeply felt best wishes for a glorious and propitious triumph over all the Giants, whether trees, mushrooms, gophers and
what else, Heavens only knows!...... In all... ....

Chorus of the combined armored Corps -

Hurrah for our combined Forces I Hurrah for our Generals!
We will march to Victory! To Arms I To Arms!

The interrupted address of the General by the majestic roar of approval and enthusiasm by the soldiers of the combined armoted Corps is now continuing with General Vetralius.......

" ....in all truth, I should have phrased my address not in the first person, as I did, but, more appropriately, as "WE", since We are all here united and bound together in the joy of the favourable outcome of our discussion ,a solid proof that we are able to understand each other, to talk problems over with each other, solve problems with each other and ,above all, to have the desire to cooperate with each other for the good and benefit of all of us . "

Chorus of the combined armored Corps	Hail! Vetralius ! The Warriors salute you!
General Vetralius continues.........	"Thank you ,my Braves, but I'd rather say and with my deepest respect for General Annalius, "OUR" Braves!! "
Chorus of the combined. armored Corps	Hurrah! Hurrah!for our Generals and our two Great Nations!
General Vetralius continues.....	" .... So ,realizing that under this almost overwhelming show of comeradeship and unity we appear to be a united Group of valorous creatures with similar tendencies and goals and in the light of this incredible occasion that let the sun of justice shine on our souls ,I have a proposal to make to all of you and to all the honourable Citizens of our two Nations. "
Chorus of the combined armored Corps	HEAR! HEAR!
General Vetralius continues	" I propose to create right now a " Solidarity League " that would comprise a combination of aspects, that is friendship,

cultural and gastronomic, progressIve, sensallonal and with air conditioning, this League ofWonns and Centipedes to go under the "banner name of" The invincible WORPEDS " , so avoiding the full use of the word "Worm" and that ofl the word Centipede with so many feet, a curse on our body by the wicked minds of the mushrooms. "

Gen~ral Amuillus

My whole hearted praise, General Vetralius, for your incisive and generous speech and I will fully support to the .best of my aoIlity and Power Your erillghtened proposal for the creation of the Solidarity League between our two Great Nations and I will undertake personally myselffue taSk with my Governm~nt to assure a prompt and speedy ratification of the League and the fonnation of a powerful annored Unit ITom the combined Forces of oUr two Great Nations, under the .banner of" The Invmclble WORPEDS " . General, our troops salute you!

Chorus of the combined Armored Corps

Hurrah! for the new League of "The Invincible WORPEDS" Hurrah! for our Great Nations! And our glorious Generals! Death to all the mushrooms!

Giant Oak Tree -

What a commotIon down there,ill my Forest! I never ever dreamt smce I became of age and inherited the throne of this Kingdom, that I would be one day confronted with such a tuibUlent time "! I also never thought it possible for a trusted Minister to desert not only his King but *also* and ,far worse, to desert Jus own pledges and lJeliefs ! Poor little MuShroom, naive and inebriated with the dream of P9wer , unable and impotent to foresee the dark clouds menacingly gathering on .his large .head.! What, on an the stars in the sky , went on in his head, dreaming of revolutions, of fights against a
multitude of famelic creatures, angry and obsessed by the very existence of mushrooms and he . so small and unable to move while his enemies are frantically seeking his destrucnon and that of all the other mushrooms! Poor little Mushroom. how could you be so simple, so naive not tQ 1Ulderstand the subtle connedion .between the use of Power and the simple, childish instinct to take away from someone and keep it for yourself, just as a child would with a toy in the .hands of another child! Nature, I'm afraid , and Destiny have reserved a sad awakening for you!

Chorus of the Watrior Mushrooms

Destiny is ours ,0 Giant Oak Tree !Why don't you pay more attention to your own Destiny instead of won-ying for the one of others?

Giant Oak Tree

It is the privilege of Kings to worry abouHhe Destiny of their subjects.

* Meanwhile, the newly organized Corps. of the combined armored Divisions of the two Nations of Worms and Centipedes, are fast assembling and getting ready in all earnest for battle, among patriotic chants of power and glory **

** The two now allied Generals, Vetralius for the Centipedes and , Annalius for the Worms, issue their orders by the way of a subordinate Officer to the combined armored Division.................... **

Subordimi.te Officer — Friends ,Allied troops, Soldiers! By the proclaimed orders of your Generals instructions have been handed down to me for the activation of the anticipatedoperational activities for the battle plan and thrust into enemy lines and the" well planned assault to the defensive fortifications of the Mushrooms, who are our final object selected for total destruction.

Chorus of the combined Armored Corps – Hail for the Battle Plan! Hail for the Generals!

Subordinate Officer — Soldiers! Marshal your forces and draw the lines for battle: the heavier armored units in the front advancing edge, the light armored units to follow closely and the rapid engagement Companies to protect the wings of the advancing Main Armored Corp. The hour is upon us ,so, FORWARD MARCH! .

Choms of the Soldiers — Forward March! To Battle! Death to all the wicked Mushrooms and the tyrannical Giant trees!

Giant Oak Tree — Poor little Mushroom! If I only could warn him ofihis impending disaster! It appears that the host of the combined forces of the Worms and the Centipedes are advancing in battle formation ready to attack with a ftontal thrust the weak defences hastily arranged by the Mushrooms !

Chorus of the Warrior Mushrooms — Do not worry, Giant Tree ,about us . We can take care of ourselves and we have friends in this Forest who will join us in the defence of our territory and our lives and livelyhood : rather think safely about your own safety in these turbulent times where old grudges and dormant hatreds seem to suddenly surface as if born then and there! You stand straight and tall and you cannot hear .the soft murmurs just below you, down on the dim and misty ground where the real life goes on without any real joy or the hope for any "rewards and where *tbe* sun never shines. There seems to be a breeze down here that is not the one that induces peaceful sleep and happy dreams. So, keep alert, Old Chap, together with your Giant Companions . We are now out to war !

Giant Oak Tree .: . It is quite incredible how in times of stonny weather of all types and categories, tumults, natural and political and social changes, the -entire picture, rather confused ,as a rule , in its begimring, yet ,suddenly, seems to become overcrowded with a profusion of ready-made wisdom from Philosophers- and. Clairvoyants of all sorts ,sizes and songs. I wonder!!

Chorus of the Warrior Mushrooms No, 0 Giant Oak ! Not so : this is not an aura for Philosophers and Soothsayers, but a simple and clear reality. Listen and iisten carefully again: the sounds of the open rebellion of the little people of the Forest will reach high up to your highest branches!

1st Centipede

** Meanwhile, our wen known ,by now, Centipede No.1, the boisterous One (!), bursts into the swelling scene of the aroused soon-to-be combatants with unrestrained zeal and ebullient exuberance of words as well as of body contortions .(please, do not forget that he is a centipede, therefore ,well used to body contortions) ..**

Choms of the assembled soldiers Hurrah! Long live the Worpeds ! Long live Liberty! Hail to the fteedom of the oppressed little creatures! Death to the Mushrooms! Death, to the Giant Trees, the haughty Protectors of the despicable Mushrooms! Long live the Great Nations of the Worms and of the Centipedes! Victory shall be ours! To the Palace! To the Palace!

Tbe learned sweet Gopher... (just sticking his nose out of a hole in the Giant Oak Tree roots, he had just bored in) ......" PALACE ?? What palace ??...There are no palaces around here! I am afraid that all these excited soldiers have lost their sense of reality as well as of direction and vision if they see or expect to see PALACES down here in these surroundings! The Poor things !!!

The official Historian attached to the soldiers It is customary to have a "palace"in the forefront of any attack by revolutionary forces: it gives their cause the aura and auspices of past enterprises with similar backgrounds and a larger mark of reality as well as enhancing and justifying the intention of the assault. Without the existence of a"Palace"to be assaulted , no revolution would amount to anything worth mentioning.

The learned sweet Gopher But "THAT" is absolutely absurd!!

The official Historian You said it!

1st Centipede - To the Palace ! To the Palace ! My Braves ! My Soldiers ! To the Palace !

2nd Centipede - Alambert ! I plead with you! Be REASONABLE ! You are unwittingly and naively getting the wrong hand of the stick , my poor Alambert, and you do not even really understand what all these creatures really have in mind. If you ask me, I believe that they do not even know that themselves, and that includes their Generals too . Alambert, let's get out of here: the whole thing does not look good .

1st Centipede - Zantavius, it is not "these Creatures" that I do not understand ,but it is "YOU" that I do not understand ! You seem to be completely oblivious to the highly exciting and momentous happenings, the omen of a brilliant future , a new life , new ideals and of a never before experienced well being, even if not altogether deserved . Zantavius ! Wake up !!

Chorus of the Worms - And what do you mean by that : "even if not altogether deserved"? Aren't You by chance ,with us or have you already changed sides...???!

1st Centipede - That remark was intended for the Nation of the Centipedes and directly for me too,as one of the Leaders of that Nation and a representative of that Chivalrous Elite . The remark was meant to emphasize the Centipedes' slow in coming yearning for liberty and for the destruction of the tyranny of the Mushrooms and the tyrannical Giant Trees . That was what my remark was directed to.

Chorus of the Worpeds - In that contest , we believe that the Chivalrous Centipede of the Elite Nobility of the Nation of the Centipedes , has expressed a genuine thought of high density and which we consider genuinely very patriotic .

Chorus of the real Ancient Patriots - Everybody and everything is considered patriotic when it is convenient or safer to labeled that way.

2nd Centipede - Fortunately ,in the middle of so much confusion , even creatures'reasoning remains confused and the answers to questions and their interpretations remain as confused as ever!Praise be the Heavens for that, as the little human creatures are used to say! My dear impulsive , irrational, incorrigible Alambert , even this time you got out of it with your skin still on your back !!!

1st Centipede - Zantavius , you don't ever understand anything ! This , this fulgid moment of glory is a great moment, Zantavius and these are the words of a Piedileone ! Far better to day , better dead than slaves , better Centipedes than Worms . To Arms , my Braves ! To Victory !

2nd Centipede - But ,Alambert, have you lost your better sense???!! Have you gone really mad?

If the Worms would have heard what you just declaimed with almost delirious emphasis " better Centipedes than Worms " ,what use would have served all that hullabaloo of just a little while ago with all those "Hurrah" and cheers and chants of glory and victory in celebration of the formation of the League of the " Worpeds" , Worms and Cetipedes, together , in total solidarity and aim of purpose when you, suddenly and, I am pretty sure, with some hidden and lingering well hidden but poorly repressed feeling about the Worms ,come out with such incriminating and devastating assertions that could have really been a disaster for us if not something far worse than just a disaster : may be even our demise !!

1st Centipede - Our demise ? Our danger ? What danger ,Zantavius ? For us ? We are among friends , Zantavius, and we are their friends : Danger for us ? None whatsoever!

2nd Centipede - I doubt that, Alambert. Your reference to the fact that it is better to be a Centipede than a Worm would not have been taken lightly by the Worpeds and I seriously doubt that they would have abstained from challenging it, with possible very serious consequences for you and , unfortunately , for me too.!

1st Centipede - Ah ! Do nor worry about it ,Zantavius ! It is really nothing ! Just a "lapsus linguae", a slip of the tongue !

2nd Centipede - Alambert : we do not have a tongue .

1st Centipede - Better ,even ! So we will be exonerated from any responsibility .

Chorus of the Worms - Notwithstanding the fact that our Counselors were able, by pure chance of international correspondence , to intercept the somewhat equivocal expressions of Sir Alambert, it was unanimously decided not to attribute great weight to them , there being a revolution going on and we needing our allies , as we have here , our good friends ,the honourable Centipedes under the combined Forces at the Banner of the Worpeds , so it was decided not to pay undue attention to this, shall we say,"soft"episode, or ,rather ,unhappy case of misplaced vocabulary expertise and our Great Wizard has assured us , after exacting scrutiny of the Books of theTwelve Wise Worms , has assured us that the gentleman bearing the heraldic noble name of Sir Alambert Piedileone of the Piedileoni of Valcoccola, at the time when his turn will come to leave this abode for the vague,misty and ethereal one on the Immense Forests above all of us,so as to regularly or in an irregular way passing to another type of life ,like we all are expected to do , sooner or later, depending now whether he will pass away of normal ,regular and happy old age or die, irregularly, a violent yet glorious end in battle but, regardless of that slight percetage difference,he will be confronted with three possibilities : Paradise ,Purgatory ,or Hell . Not all of them are necessarily open and ready for his personal choice but to a greater degree there is a chance , and a more likely possibility as described in the complex and intricate calculations as they appear iri the Books of the Twelve Wise Worms, of a possible unspecified time in Hell, the reason being not one of prefabricated. judgement but because of the existence of an"extremely"long waiting line in front of the first TWO. This assessment did please us sigirlficantly .

1 st Centipede

Did you hear, Zantavius ? The Counselors of the Wonns have deliberated in a very positive way towards me,showing high regard for my status and my valuable participation to the COIl1IIlon cause of Worms and Centipedes and formulating the best and most prosperous wishes for my future . They are really great friends, a really Great Nation.

2nd Centipede

Are you sure?

15t Centipede

But, of course ,r am sure! These Worms are legitimate creatures in their thinking and they always try to absorb and normalize various situations even if some of them may be unpleasant, with cautious intuition and solid wisdom ,so, time now for you to prop up your courage and follow me in this epic day!

2nd Centipede

"Day", yes. As to the "epic" part ofit, I am not so sure .

15t Centipede

But are you still doubtful about the intrinsic idealistic image of the impending triumph of Liberty for all, the downfall of the tyranny of the Mushrooms,always in the protective shade of the Giant Trees? [tell you, Zantavius ,down and death to the mushrooms! Death to the Giant Trees! ... Will you follow me, Zantavius ??

2nd Centipede

Just a moment, Alambert, just a moment. While you were practicing your large collection of dramatic expressions and stimulating slogans for war and glory, for our friends the Worms, I happened to catch a glimpse of something that looked to me rather strange.

15t Centipede

Something strange? Oh, this is a good one ! Wh~t could there be ,now, more strange than this fatidic day, harbinger of epic glory and the resurgence of Liberty and Justice for all the little creatures with honour and the destruction of Tyranny ?

2nd Centipede

That is fine, Alambert: that is all very, very fine, and it has been made very plain and clear by the bountiful demonstrations of explosive enthusiasm ,particularly by those who were not in the first advanced lines of the frontal attack positions ,and everything is in perfect harmony and everybody seems very happy, at least on this side of the"celebrations' theatre", but, you see, I just happened to notice only a couple of minutes ago, against the dark background of that edifice at the comer ofthe square, the silhouettes of two forms who were standing straight on only two legs, those being the lower ones of their body, and the other two legs, or whatever they may be, hanging on the top of the body, were, instead, moving in all directions as if blown by a twisting wind, the way they were flapping!!

1 st Centipede

Couldn't that wind, Zantavius, have blown, instead, your wild imagination to a a far away land where "strange "things may happen frequently and just of a sudden out of the blue ?

2nd Centipede - Well. Alambert, have you ever observed any one of us Centipedes standing on two legs , flipping two more on a higher level in all directions and forgetting all of the remaining 96, as if disappeared by magic ? And have you ever seen any of us climbing up a large tree and, once reached the top, remain attached to the tree with the two lower legs and bring one of the upper legs or whatever they are, to the forehead, because these creatures have a head, and then ,as if repairing their sight from something in the air with that raised upper leg , they slowly comb the ground and the trees looking for something and then they climb down and do a lot of talking among themselves . Did you happen to spot any of us doing just that , Alambert ? To me, the whole thing looks very , very strange.

1st Centipede - Ah ! Confound all your "strange findings and encounters " ! I have had enough of them! And , frankly, as far as I am concerned , they can all go to the Devil !

2nd Centipede - But , Alambert, the Centipedes do not have a Devil . It is only the Human kind who has found one .

1st Centipede - My dear Zantavius , you are so richly endowed with your tasteful naivety!! You should, instead, observe how in times of turbulence and confusion even Devils are looking for some company and camaraderie, whenever and wherever they can find some.

2nd Centipede - But ,I am telling you, Alambert , Devils or no Devils , those two "things " just ain't Centipedes .

1st Centipede - Calm down , Zantavius : may be they are two Centipedes acrobats .

2nd Centipede - No , no , Alambert : those two "things" do not seem two Centipeds at all !

1st Centipede - May be they had some touching up done with plastic surgery, that's why they may be looking a little different !

2nd Centipede - But that is preposterous, Alambert ! Centipedes do not have surgeons , period !! Let alone plastic surgeons ,of all odds !!! Alambert . are you OK ? Did you hear me ?....Alambert ,Centipedes do not have surgeons !!!

1st Centipede - We don't ? Well, may be some unhappy old maids hired some skilled plastic surgeons from a nearby Forest more advanced than ours ,like in this case, where TWO unhappy old maids Centipedes probably did , in an attempt to a renewed entry into the vortex of mundane life.

2nd Centipede - But what kind of plastic surgery...and I feel ridiculous even just mentioning it....

so, Alambert , I am saying it again , what kind of plastic surgery could benefit at all any of us, that is, any Centipede that may still be preserving some old fashioned common sense?You just talk nonsense , Alambert , you just talk through your hat, but , since you do not wear one , I forfeit that vocabulary expression, which ,although pleasing to me , does not seem appropriate to our way of being and dressing , leaving it to the judgement of posterity : and how did you like that , Alambert ?

1st Centipede - What a mixture, Zantavius, of one thing into another , beginning with one and finishing with another and totally disconnected one from the other!Be a good pal and tell me which one do you want me to answer first ?

2nd Centipede - Oh ! come ,now, dear Alambert ! You know very well what I mean ! Just a little fun , a little variation from this cloud hanging on our , well, shall we say , skin standing on one hundred of our feet and wondering where these many feet will take us in the next few minutes ! But my main curiosity is still about the kind of benefits that plastic surgery could offer to a Centipede : do you know that, Al ?

1st Centipede - Well, not that I do know for certain , but , I guess it could give to a Centipede the chance of, for one , to add another one hundred feet to the existing one hundred, bringing the total to two hundred feet : with two hundred feet it would be possible to chase the prey a lot faster , to be feared and to command more respect from our neighbours and , for those two gracious old maids that we were talking about , renewed hope for a faded past .

2nd Centipede - To talk with you , Alambert , it requires the patience of Patience herself and it almost forces any one out of his,her or its wits:why can't you stop talking in such a stupid fashion ,instead to pay a more sensible attention to what's going on around you, actually and unfortunately , around us..!! I am telling you again and , I repeat , I am telling you again for the nth time : those two "THINGS" just ain't Centipedes !

1st Centipede - How can you tell so surely ? That's what I'd like to know !

2nd Centipede - Because they "talk" to each other : that's how .

1st Centipede - We talk to each other too and have been doing so for quite some time !!

2nd Centipede - We can talk to each other because our writer puts the words in our mouths !

1st Centipede - But , then , couldn't it be the same for those two "strange" figures you seem so preoccupied with ?

2nd Centipede- I do not know : I overlooked to ask that from our writer.

1st Centipede - Dear Zantavius , then , listen and it is about time that I talk to you clearly : little by little you seem to have deteriorated in your ability to see , observe and recognize things to the point that I am becoming worried about you . What kind of a sense that makes , that you bring forth , about "our" talking , the "talking" of the writer on our behalf ,of all the odds!!!.....and your wondering about the benefits of plastic surgery or whatever ,for the Centipedes !! ....You , Zantavious , appear to me as being on the verge of becoming mentally ill , if not already so ,right now !!

2nd Centipede - Alambert !...The nerve of you !...And , more than that , your inexplicable failure to see what's really going on around you ,is simply appalling ! You , I am afraid , and not I , are on the brink of becoming crazy and , furthermore , as you choose to say , you may already have fallen off that brink !

1st Centipede - Ah ! Quit those philosophizing techniques good for ordinary Centipedes but not for an Alambert Piedileone of the Piedileoni of Valcoccola !...Besides , what difference does all of this make to what's going on now , the momentous hours of this day , the unimaginable portent of the realization of the mighty alliance of the Worms and the Centipedes,and, on top of it the dismal vociferous interference of a stupid writer wasting his time to put words in our mouth as if he had nothing better to do for himself, a stunt certainly not of the "portentous" type !

2nd Centipede - The difference is rather simple ,"Sir Alambert" of Valcoccola , and it is represented in the fact that we have one hundred legs and no brain ,while our writer has a brain and only two legs : that's the difference, whether you like it or not .

1st Centipede - And if that Sport who writes words and sentences for us to say is so primitive to have only two legs , I am afraid that ,contrarily to your suggestion , he may not have a brain at all or , if he had had a hundred in the past......lucky he.....he might have lost all of them by now !

2nd Centipede - That's fine ,Alambert . It is easy to poke fun at things that lend themselves to it but another thing is to face reality when it becomes splashed right into your eyes ! Alambert, I have no longer any doubts : those two"THINGS"are definitely no Centipedes and definitely moving , acting , looking and glancing in a way I have never ever seen a Centipede do likewise , in addition to peering into the surroundings with a suspicious attitude .

1st Centipede - Everybody seems to be suspicious in times of revolution and civic confusion when everything is upside down and in a mess .

2nd Centipede - Revolution or no revolution, there are still creatures with some good"brakes" in their heads to control unnecessary wild and inconsiderate sudden jerks and violent skiddings and still"logical"enough not to become overwhelmed by unusual events and those two creatures seem to be totally unconcerned about our revolution, or our fraternization with the Worms and even totally unconcerned about a possible break out of hostilities and open war with the Mushrooms . They seem to be looking for something "else"and"that"something else is what worries me as they keep on shifting their sight ,back and forth, from the trees in the Forest, then to us and the Worms and any other little creature that they can spot on the ground .This Pair of infiltrators appears to me more like a pair of predators ready to swoop on the prey than just interested by-standers . I really wonder who could they be !

1st Centipede - Perhaps they are vagabonds !

2nd Centipede - Centipedes vagabonds? Like many who wander around our Forest trying to get away as much as possible from those two legged "monsters" always anxious to do something or may be they are scouts for the two legged monsters to bring them advance information on the conditions around and ahead : may be , but who knows ?

1st Centipedes - Zantavius, please stay here and do not move until I'll come back: I just saw a signal, a military signal , that means it's time to muster up for readiness for battle. As soon as the review of the troops is over I'll come right back here and, then , we'll see what next . Please, do not move from here , understood ?

2nd Centipede - Yes, Alambert , do not worry: I'll be here until you will be back and I hope that that will be soon.

1st Centipede - It shouldn't take long . See you soon. Bye , now .

2nd Centipede - Bye !

** the Giant Oak Tree ,quite isolated and without a way to receive any reliable information on the developing scene, becomes agitated and despondent.................................... **

Giant Oak Tree - If I only could have a glimpse of what's going on down there ! From time to time I can hear a confused sound of voices , some louder than other , and there seems to be some indication of confusion and disorder as well and no message from the Mushroom ! I still hope that everything is in order with him and that nothing bad has befallen him . I have also noticed the tops of some other tall trees , in the other end of the Forest , swaying , as if suddenly caught with malaise and some of them slump to the ground as if unable to stand straight anymore . This seems very starnge to me because I have not noticed any wind , mild or strong , no rain to make the soil soft and shifty ,no hurrucane type of weather , no hail and no lightning able to possibly cause such indisposition in those trees and such malaise. I only hear some strident sounds coming from the far away end of this vast Forest in my Kingdom , sounds as like metal stricking metal but I do not know what that could be . If only I could get some sort of communication with that Mushroom.!....

Chorus of the Warrior Mushrooms - Your "little Mushroom" , o Giant Oak ,is over burdened with the preparations and the tasks of war and cannot spare any time to converse with you at this difficult and perilous time . But far more ominous and threatening is the act of aggression being conducted in some of the remote areas of this Forest by a number of strange creatures with two legs below their bodies and two hanging in the upper part of it, who are carrying with them some horrifying offensive weapons that appear to destroy everything that comes in their path !

Giant Oak Tree - Ah ! Now I begin to see more clearly into the whole thing and now I begin to understand what it was that peculiar screeching-like sound I was hearing from one of the far edges of the Forest and I was observing some of my tree-friends fall to the ground and I had thought, then, that they were being taken ill with malaise! They were being killed ,instead !! Oh! Immortal Gods of Mount Olympus !.What other horrible and ghastly sights will I have to witness before my own end is readied for me ??!..........

** Meanwhile , our two Centipedes ,Alambert and Zantavius , reunited since the return of Alambert from the muster drill, are picking up their conversation from where they had left it , amid increasing anxiety , particularly on the part of our more cautious, more sensible Zantavius, the No.2 Centipede . **

1st Centipede - Here I am, Zantavius , back from the drill and everything seems to be in the best of order in the preparation for the forthcoming attack to the fortified positions of the Mushrooms : it was a magnificent display of efficiency , discipline and ability on the part of all the assembled armored units and it was amazing to see how well each of the Units fitted into the ranks of the combined Division as if they had been training together for ever ! I felt so proud, that I almost forgot to come back to see you! So,tell me ,Zantavius, did anything unusual happen while I was away?

2nd Centipede - Nothing more than what we had already seen before you left .

1st Centipede - You see,Zantavius, what did I tell you ? You are worrying too much, too soon about everything that happens around our lives or anywhere else ! You ,yourself have just said that nothing new, apparently, did happened since I left, so what about those two "GHOSTS" that you have been following with the long range sight of an eagle ?

2nd Centipede - They are still there, Alambert, and more active than ever. They go here and there,they seem to go close to the trees and go around them ,even seem to be "patting"them , looking at them and then moving to the next tree and repeating the same theatrical-like routine, then they get together and do a lot of talking.They are dangerous types ,believe me , Alambert ,and they are up to no good .

1st Centipede - Come, come,Zantavius , do not get over-concerned with those two"THINGS" or whatever they are , because far more important "THINGS" are at stake to-day for us to watch, absorb and digest : days of glory are these days, Zantavius ,and days that will shine for ever in the History Annals of the Nation of the Centipedes when the brave soldiers of the combined armored Divisions of the Worpeds will throw their mighty power against those infamous, despicable and spongy Mushrooms....Charge! My Braves! Hurrah for Liberty!Down with Tyrants !Death to the Giant Trees ! Death to the Mushrooms ! To the Palace ! To the Palace !.......

2nd Centipede - But, Alambert , if you keep on "screaming" like this , you run a serious risk of exposing yourself to grave danger !!

1st Centipede - Expose myself to danger ???!!.....I , Alambert Piedileone of the Piedileoni of Valcoccola , am supposed to become fearful of impending danger ??!!..I know of no danger anywhere : I wish I could individualize some and charge with all my ebullient spirit into it ! ....And , Zantavious, of what "danger" are you worrying about ? Are you, perhaps , "pointing" to those two confounded "ghosts" that have ruined your existence right up to this moment by suggesting in you a perpetually surging anxiety ?.....For your information ,Zantavius , I am not agitated or over-excited or out of my best wits and restraints but purely expressing my genuine enthusiasm for this extraordinary day so bright and crowded with portentous signs of glory and victories to come !

2nd Centipede - My dear "Sir Alambert", I don't believe that so much rhetoric as yours has ever been recorded in the History Annals of the Nation of the Centipedes ! But that is beyond the point of what I want to say :I have studied those two shadows, now , for a "sufficient long time", and I trust that you will agree with this statement of mine......

1st Centipede - Lor'have Mercy !! don't I !!!!

2nd Centipede - Well, then , I have come to the conclusion that these two "intruders" are the ones who always chase us around and if we didn't use to our advantage the exit speed inherent to our 100 legs that Nature granted us purely for compassion as well as for repentance for failing to come up with a better functioning make up of us, we could never get away in time before being "squashed" and finish up our"glorious days", as you claim, as a nice and flat omelette .

1st Centipede - To-day, my dear Zantavius , we skall be the ones to squash them and let them finish their "inglorious days" flat as pancakes !

2nd Centipede - You are wrong, my dear Alambert and it seems to me that you didn't ever pay much attention to them ,but these intruders ,and I am pretty certain to have clearly examined them and recognized them for what they really are, can see you a lot better than you can see them and they are unbelievably deft in quickly spotting us as well as any other of our cousins similar in looks and ways of life as we are and, then , they happily go on a rampage and ....I feel mournful just to think and talk about it.....and ,then......they "squash" us !!!....And I know but too well how horrible and cruel these"monsters"can be because I lost several members of my close Family to these monsters' irrational cruelty ! For this reason ,Alambert, please, I beg of you , trust your best judgement and press your most selective reasoning to the forefront of everything else and come away , right now ,before it is too late....if it isn't too late already !!

1st Centipede - Reasoning ?...and about what, Zantavius ? Here we are in the middle of a mighty revolution and even the Mushrooms, the ones we are going to fight shortly , well, even they have rebelled against the oppression and the tyranny of the Giant Trees, even the Lizards , in these fatidic days, have assumed an erect posture as a sign of opposition and rebellion , even the stones and rocks have started rolling down the sides of mountains in support of this turning point in the history of the little creatures and the Snails seem to have come possessed of an incredible capacity for speed , unequalled in any previous generation of the same , and ,now , in the middle of all this you would expect me , Alambert Piedileone of the Piedileoni of Valcoccola , to stand here with my mouth wide open , goggle-eyed ,in an utterly stupid posture of amazement , frozen solid in admiration of the swelling scene and lose my "preferred seat" in this revolutionary historical and wondrous day ??!

2nd Centipede - As it is well known , reasoning with unreasonable creatures is not recommended and it is just wasted time, so, my dear Alambert , I have done all I could to warn you of the impending danger,of the possible traps around us and of the sadlly and terribly misguided creatures who seem to have lost any sense of reality, trying to fight Giants with blades of.....grass !! I only hope that your uncontrollable audacity would not lead you to an unhappy end, finishing your "glorious" days as a pancake , compliments of the two legged Monsters !

1st Centipede - And so be it, if that is what's written in my destiny and programmed in my birthday electronic chips , but , as for myself , I shall sally forward to battle ,to glory and Hail Liberty ! Down with Tyrants !, regardless how many of them, whether they may have one hundred , two hundred and even three hundred legs or just TWO ! To Battle , my braves , to victory !

Chorus of the Electronic Chips - Isn't it a little too early or even inappropriate for a Centipede ,at this time , to talk about electronic "programming", "chips", and make it sound like an everyday type of thing well accepted in the daily life's routine and kmowledge ,when even in the days where the Electronic function will come into an everyday being , many creatures still will not understand a thing about it , so how can a Centipede know of electronics at this time when nobody knows anything about them YET....????

The learned Moth - Knowledge , original , posthumous or future, has no time settings , I believe , but then , I am only a moth .

2nd Centipede - Someone , I guess , must have come in and into our conversation, somehow , but I couldn't figure out the villain ! Did you find it out , Alambert ?

1st Centipede - I did : the usual smart Alecs who know everything and believe that everybody else "don't" (!) know a thing ".

2nd Centipede - Did they, at least, introduce themselves ,just out of pure and expected courtesy ?

1st Centipede - They did and said that they were Electronics , but from which Forest they did not say . Probably their Forest was so crowded ,twisted , overgrown and all tangled up, that they had to find a way out in order to survive and ,as they emerged from that situation they happened to bump into some credulous creatures who took care of them purely out of pity for their plight and misery .

2nd Centipede - Credulous , may be , and ain't we all !!...But kind and charitable , I see .

1st Centipede- And they took them into their homes, their caves , their lairs doing everything they could to alleviate the stress and the anguish of these poor Electric Trones who had to leave their native land, but, after the initial support outdid itself extremely well, no one was ever capable afterwards , to ever get them out of anywhere while these fiendish Electric Trones were teasing their hospitable hosts out of their wits, day in ,day out , night and day and having a great fun in watching the hospitable hosts running in circles,squares, octagons, rectangulars, trapezoids, rhomboids, angles and semi-circles , and in all directions , trying to catch them and make them behave in a more civilized manner .

2nd Centipede - So, good for the Electric Trones ! As for you ,Dear Alambert, I do not know anymore what to say and I have exhausted all my resources . I want you to know that I liked you and that I loved you very much and I would have wanted to be near you but ,at this crossing of our roads, a bifurcation has appeared in front of us and we stand each at the entrance of each branch , poised to enter the road to our destiny : goodbye, Alambert, and the good Electric Trones be with you !

1st Centipede - Goodbye , Zantavius ! You have still time to change your mind and follow me into battle and the glory of this fateful day !

2nd Centipede - No, Alambert, I am not the glorious type of Centipede who is looking for fame to be handed down to Posterity! Posterity, and I am certain of it , will be perfectly and satisfactorily served even without a single word about me,so , I am going to stay here a little longer as I am still extremely curious about those two strange "THINGS" and who might they be and their names !...I wonder , mind you , I just wonder, if they could be, by any long shot chance, real live representations of those creatures whom the Witch Queen used to refer to as "human creatures "and I myself had already a pretty strong suspicion that they might have been two of those two legged Monsters ,as I had already warned you about them, just a while ago : remember ? I just keep on wondering, Alambert !

1st Centipede - And who has ever heard of them , anyway ?

2nd Centipede - Lucky you , if you have never heard of them , and even "luckier" and "very , very lucky" if you never met face to face with them,or, rather , foot to foot ,with them !

1st Centipede - Zantavius , you never fail to amaze me with your almost inexhaustible ability in the way you dramatize and work up tragic consequences about almost anything around you or anybody else !

2nd Centipede - Alambert , apparently you do not seem to know much about these two legged and weird creatures who enjoy the destruction of anything they can place their hands on, because you should know that they have hands, two hands, one at the end of each upper leg , a mechanisms by which they can easily and dexterously pick up and manipulate what they had picked up , and ,once done that , either keep it in their hands or throw it out , or throwing it far away or putting it inside a fold of their skins ,or , at least, so it seems , for keeping purposes .

1st Centipede - Do you think, then, that those two "THINGS" with four legs, two on the lower body and two on the upper part of the body, could be the "THINGS" that the Witch Queen talks about ?

2nd Centipede - Yes, I do, Alambert , and they carry the detailed aspect the Witch Queen was telling me as well as the content of their thinking, because the Witch Queen can read creatures'minds , provided that they do have one, of course , and she ,the Witch Queen I mean , was also telling me that these creatures are known as "human creatures", a type of roaming beings who think of nothing else but themselves or, if they ever think or pay attention, favourably, towards something or somebody else, human or not , it is only if they can see in that thing something good in return . Now, ain't it weird ! ?

1st Centipede - Well, I had thought that the only weird creatures were the mushrooms and their protectors , the Giant Trees , but , as they say , you live and learn !

2nd Centipede - It would be interesting if we could pick up some of their conversation , but the question of the language may be an obstacle unless we.........

1st Centipede - What do you have in mind,Zantavius ? Another of your visions , may be ?

2nd Centipede - No, none of that, Alambert, : I was just wondering about the language, if we could in some way find a means that we could match their words with ours, but how ?

1st Centipede - I have an idea , Zantavius ! It just popped up in my head and I am talking about those smart Alecs, who so rudely pushed themselves through our conversation just a while ago, do you remember..?

2nd Centipede - You mean.....the Trones ?

1st Centipede - Yes , Zantavius , the Electric Trones, who had interfered in our conversation just a while ago and you were wondering who those fellows, so sadly lacking in manners, could have been : remember ?

2nd Centipede - Oh , yes , Alambert , I remember it well : as a matter of fact some famous Movie Star , will say that expression in the future , in one of his moving pictures ,so we were told by our Clairvoyant .

1st Centipede - Movie..??!....Moving pictures...?? Zantavius ,are you feeling well ?

2nd Centipede - Very well,Alambert : Thank you : and you ? What seems to be the problem ?

1st Centipede - Somehow I have a feeling that there must be something suspicious floating in the air to-day totally disconnected and dissociated from the festivities and scene galore of trepidation for the forthcoming patriotic events, and in an awe-inspiring type of atmosphere that adversely challenges my most fervid imagination.

2nd Cetipede - May be a touch of what's called Clairvoyant's "fever" ?

1st Centipede - I do not know about the fever but I know about the Fantasy World of Clairvoyants!

2nd Centipede- No, Alambert , it was not a World of Fantasy, but it was during an impromptu and highly interesting lecture given us by our Royal Clairvoyant regarding the advance historical "pictures"of the coming-to-be "PICTURES"of the future that will be called " moving pictures ", so..........

1st Centipede - You will excuse my invasive and petulant and persisting negative approach to your story , but , in all seriousness, where are those "pictures" going , if they keep on moving ??

2nd Centipede - They'll go, we are told, from one Centipede, holding one end of a long thread, to another Centipede, holding the other end of the thread , so , it is true ,they do move but , at the same time, they remain in the same place .

1st Centipede - It is somehow hard to believe it !

2nd Centipede - Amazing ,I would say.

1st Centipede - But , then , you are likely to get a phenomenal headache while your eyes , for those creatures,of course, who have them, or while your antennae, like in our case........by the way do we have antennae or some other way of seeing movies ? That would be interesting as well as helpful to know, anyway,antennae or not, it's going to be very trying to go back and forth from one Centipede to the other and back again and again and again for the entire length or duration of the thread , until you drop dead .

2nd Centipede - That would be hardly the case ,Alambert, because , to begin with , when you look or, and let us be more correct and say when you shall see these movies in the future, like our Claivoyant said , you'll be seated comfortably in an adequate seat so it would be difficult to fall from a seat unless , as you just said , you dropped dead .

1st Centipede - Granted that you would not fall from your seat, yet it might still be rather cumbersome and difficult to see these movies if they keep on "moving" without "moving", a rather weird mechanism that smells to me like sorcery , I would want to say, like high caliber wizardry . I wonder if our old venerable Merlin had anything to say about all this new magic ?

A passer-by, a Knight of King Arthur round table - As a matter of fact, Old Chaps, our Merlin has just watched one of those "magics", the one he had readied for history keeping and as a documentary of the chivalrous times of those days of foggy memories and veiled visions of acts of consequence for our Forests, and He enjoyed it immensely and predicted ,after seeing it , that it will have a very good future for generations and generations to come .

Chorus of the listening Centipedes- And what was the story about , Sir Knight, just passing-by in our Forest , and the title of the movie ?

A passer-by, a Knight of King Arthur round table - The Round Table of King Arthur .

Chorus of the listening Centipedes- OoooooooHHH.......!!

2nd Centipede - Satisfied, Alambert ? You see , even the past is accepting the future, or viceversa, and , personally , I think that it does not make any difference to me one way or another ,as we Centipedes were not created to be either Wizards , Historians or Philosophers and so on , but they seem to be running after each other in endless circles .

1st Centipede - It looks to me , the way you put it , that it goes something like the magic in your "moving pictures to come " . You see them , you don't see them , they run and they don't , you sit and watch and you finish up looking like an idiot .

2nd Centipede Now you are talking...!!!

1st Centipede - That I look like an idiot ?!

2nd Centipede - Not that ,you ninny ! What you just commented about the "moving pictures to come", is precisely the actual beauty about them, Alambert , and here is the gimmick : while moving , they go nowhere , yet they move in such a way that one picture representing something ,follows another picture representing either a continuation or a sequence or a completion of the first picture, or it moves to another picture representing something else, once the first picture has been thoroughly and satisfactorily portrayed .

1st Centipede - And these pictures do not move at all while showing all these different scenes ? That's incredible !

2nd Centipede - Well, that's what I thought also when I heard of it the first time, but it didn't look that forbidding to my imagination once our good Royal Clairvoyant explained the mechanism in full : actually you may be transported to far away places , places you have never seen, some magnificent , some dismal, some full of life ,some other showing acts of was like the one we are trying to get under way here and now.........

1st Centipede - Oh ! That "moving picture " I'd really like to see !

2nd Centipede - Pehaps.But our Clairvoyant discouraged us from looking at any of those war pictures because there are scenes of destruction so frightful , so violent caused by unbelievable types of weapons that can wipe out an entire Forest with one single blow !

1st Centipede - Why ? That is precisely what we would need now to wipe out Mushrooms and Giant Trees, all at the same time and "ONE SINGLE BLOW" , by George !

2nd Centipede - Shame on you , Sir "Lancelot" ,without a lance ! Shame on you for such terrible thoughts ! I was doubtful, then , when our Royal Clairvoyant was warning us that in the future of the future ,there will be even more destructive weapons made available capable of destroying not one Forest in one blow but a hundred Forests in one blow !

1st Centipede - I would certainly opt for the second generation of those weapons !

2nd Centipede - I was terrified .

1st Centipede - Cheer up, Zantavius : your Royal Clairvoyant talks about the "future of the future" and ,possibly , even further down the road than that, so I do not see any immediate danger of being confronted with one of those refined offensive instruments and I am certain that there will be several "moving pictures" of those weapons as they will become available,so let them be where they may be now, and ,instead, let us keep our minds to the facts of this day,here, around us : and how about that, Zantavius ?

2nd Centipede - Fine with me , Alambert , but I had not quite finished the full illustration of those movies : you see , in order to facilitate the watching of the various pictures, and here comes another beauty about those "moving pictures to be", there is a flash....

1st Centipede - Ah! Now we come to something ! I knew it all the time that there was something missing in all this rigamarole !.Now we have a flash, and this flash makes some light that lights up the whole thing ! Right ? Well, now , are ,by any chance, a squadron of Fireflies being employed for the purpose ? You know , our friends and cousins , the Glow-Worms ? They really shine , the poor thing getting stuck in that funny business ! I didn't know that they were in the movies !

2nd Centipede - Stop joking and listen instead and I believe that it wouldn't hurt you a bit learning something more about,,,,shall we say....the future ? You see, you and I need "that"future badly, not knowing at the present moment which way our existences are going to ....go ! These new movies to-be ,Alambert , do represent the embodiment of the civilized communications of the future .

1st Centipede - For me the future consists in the destruction of the mushrooms and of the Giant Trees . You do not need any"moving pictures"or any"civilized communications" for your glorious or infamous deeds, regardless, or the deeds of anybody else, to be handed down to Posterity ! Why , did Rome Greatness have "moving pictures" to immortalize the majesty and the grandeur of its achievements ? Did Moses have "moving pictures" made of the delivery of the Commandments ? Did Noah's Ark have pictures of its floating in the diluvial waters ?

2nd Centipede - Of course not, but it would have been interesting if they had them .

Chorus of the future Movies - Do not temper with what is not yet , or will be later . The future should not be called in to justify your deeds of to-day and ,besides , whether we would be here already or not at all, it would not make any difference to your present status . Why don't you behave like some good kids and go to sleep instead of bothering us with your fervid imagination and live your day as it is and not as it could or you would or somebody else might make it look . So, goodbye and all the best to all of you.

2nd Centipede - Now, Alambert , you have done it again with your impulsiveness and your immature attitude, always swayed by your emotional and, at times, almost irrational impulses. You just scared those good civilized Communicators of the future away !

1st Centipede - About time ,too !

2nd Centipede - And miss all the pleasure and comfort of watching history made, being made and catching the one not made yet? And in all comfort because you would be able to see the movies move while you'll be sitting at that time without having to run after them in order to see the next scene at the risk of breaking your neck and avoiding , this way , the overcrowding of hospitals and expensive treatments. Of course, I have to admit that everybody at that impromptu lecture of our Royal Clairvoyant, the one I talked to you about just as we briefly were interrupting our conversation on another subject ,when I made that remark about your question and I said , intentionally:"Yes, I remember it well " and added that a famous movie Star of the future would say that identical sentence in one of his best known movies and you asked me if I were feeling well after hearing my talking about "movies" and "future" "Stars" ! Do you remenber ,Alambert ?

1st Centipede - "Yes , Dearie !.....I remember it well...!! "

2nd Centipede - You made my day with this one, Alambert ! I assure you!....Wow! You can certainly pick up from where someone else left ! Well, anyway, let me finish what I had started to tell you and that I have to admit that at that lecture ,everybody felt somewhat leery of that advanced projection of divination about the "movies-to-be" of the "future" , yet , it was a unanimous consensus that also Clairvoyants have a right to make a reasonable living , somehow .

1st Centipede - That's fine ,Zantavius , and quite interesting too , and you did not have to explain in such anxious details how you came to this unravelling magic splendor-like vision of the future . As a matter of fact I had heard some similar stories when I was a cadet at the Military Academy of "Catchthemup"in the Capital City of the Empire of the Centipedes and I was quite impressed with it , but , now , we were talking about something else , Zantavius and what I had in mind was to try to get the attention of our good old Trones and see if they might have any suggestions of how to help us find a way to match "human" words with our "centipedian" ones, therefore establishing a line of communication never thought at all possible between two so different types of species : don't you think so too, Zantavius?....and it was YOU, not I , to think at such a possibility and to wonder how it could be achieved .

2nd Centipede - Alambert, please,do not give me merit for something I did not do : it was you who thought right away of the Trones as the ones most likely capable of making our plan a reality .

1st Centipede - I did so because YOU, by your keen intuition,"pushed the accelerator"of my thought engine and the "motor" started !

2nd Centipede - ALAMBERT !!! YOU FRIGHTEN ME !!!

1st Centipede - I do ?

2nd Centipede - You mentioned something that is not here yet !!

1st Centipede - Oh ! Don't be alarmed , my dear : those things are here all right ! They are already here and not in the future either !

2nd Centipede - How can you possibly know that ?!

1st Centipede - Some time ago,during a safari in a very busy town, my best friend and travel pal was killed by one of those machines with a rumbling motor, by being run over by its tires : the poor thing !

2nd Centipede - You never told me that !

1st Centipede - I didn't want to alarm you , that's all .

2nd Centipede - Sad, a very sad story .

1st Centipede - Yes, it it was and it still is a very sad story, at least for me . But , now , how to get in contact with those Electric Trones !

Chorus of the Electric Chips - Don't worry, we are here and we have heard all that you just said , and we are prepared to help you if you will help us !

1st Centipede - We'll do our best , but how ?

Chorus of the Electronic Chips - Simple : you stay in contact with us while we decipher those two beings' vocabulary, we will "format"it, then, once it has been "formatted"into your language it will remain into the minds of those two beings for as long as you want to hear what they are saying, without them ever knowing that you are there listening : satisfied ? We do hope so, but you must promise us that you will not withdraw from your promise to stay there and let us control the flow of the outgoing messages or the "magic"will dissolve and disappear .

1st Centipede - It sounds great ! We will not withdraw and we will stay there !

Chorus of the Electronic Chips - Very good, then ! ..and here we go: are you ready ?

2nd Centipede - Dear Trones, excuse me for being curious as well as worried, but how can we hear anything among this terrible hubbub mixed with the marching of soldiers of all sizes, ,shapes and uniforms , with the Frogs and the Toads in their fatigue uniforms getting busy junping here and there, the snails going around with their backs loaded with the much needed supplies of food and ammunitions and for securing the flow of the logistic build up, the lizards on patrol duty for their extraordinary agility and their ability to a lightning strike and the most visible of all the uniformed soldiers , the Beetles, so well cuirassed and in their bright uniforms and powerful aspect,ready for the decisive thrust through even the most formidable fortifications, so , in the middle of all that , how is it possible to hear any sound at all !

Chorus of the Electronic Chips - That "hubbub",as you call it, will not interfere with our communication because you will be able to see it in your minds and read it translated into your own language and any external sounds, regardless of how loud or intense, will have no bearing on it.

2nd Centipede - But...Trones, Alambert.... WE cannot read or write !

1st Centipede - Extraordinary !!

Chorus of the Electronic Chips - No matter : we'll read those messages for you and then we'll tell you verbally about their content .

1st Centipede - Extraordinary !

Chorus of the Electronic Chips - So , when do we start ? Are you ready now ?

2nd Centipede - I am ready now .

1st Centipede - So am I .

Chorus of the Electronic Chips - Good . Now you just wait a few minutes until we can "hack" into their minds and pick up their vacabulary, then do some detailed "formatting"of it, adaptable to your language and, when that's done, you will be able to understand what those two figures are saying . So , in the meantime , and until we are ready , just occupy yourself with your daily chores or, in the particular aura of this seeming momentous day, attend to your military or civic duties and, when ready, we'll call you !....Until then ,tank you for choosing the Trones for your electronic needs .

2nd Centipede - Thank You .

1st Centipede - At a second thought , Zantavius, I do not really know for certain, but I feel that the whole thing is going to be just a big ,long drawn loss of time !

2nd Centipede - Quiet , quiet , Alambert.! It seems to me that they are talking to each other now, and it looks something important by the way they throw those upper legs around and in all directions, and it is hard to know which ones are the two legs with shoes.

1st Centipede - SHOES ???!!...Did you say.... shoes ..?

2nd Centipede - Yes , Alambert , I did , and it is difficult to figure out if all of the four legs have shoes or only the lower ones wear shoes .

1st Centipede - Are you sure of what you are talking about ,Zantavius ?

2nd Centipede - Absolutely ! You see, dear Alambert, they must be wearing some shoes on some of those legs because the Witch Queen used to tell me that those peculiar Creatures, the little human ones , of course , these little Creatures, then , whenever they would be challenged on some of their actions or their activities or enterprises or even over the interpretation of any problem or event or new Rules and Laws, if they were then to give a wise and, at times , even a spectacular answer to their Challehgers' question, they would get in return a lot of deferent respect and almost an aura of awe by the bedazzled challengers and the little human Creatures would then give back a quick glimpse of a sly wink and mutter in their own language an old proverb of theirs that goes this way:" scarpe grosse , cervello fino" that could be roughly translated into something like:"someone may be wearing simple, rough worker's boots , but the brain is far from rough..." , on the contrary ,they imply, "rough boots but a sharp brain", so,more or less, that's what the proverb basically means : you may be doing a simple job or considered an uneducated nobody but the brain ,surprisingly, may still be brighter than an educated "show-off ". I surmised that this translation-interpretation to be fairly representative of the original proverb .

1st Centipede - Zantavius, this is a marvelous story , exteremely interesting about boots, shoes and brains right in the middle of a revolution and I have to give it to you but your calm, self control and composure are remarkable, but , in all honesty,where are you trying to take me with this strange story ?

2nd Centipede - Nothing to worry about ,Alambert, just a confirmation that these two suspicious characters are definitely not Centipedes for the simple reason, quite self explanatory, that they wear shoes as indicated by their own proverb : simple .

1st Centopede - Obviously such a proverb would not apply or exist in our own language !!

2nd Centopede - In our Centipedian language couldn't it be like: "many legs and no brain" ?

The University Dean of the Centipedes - We are wary of that sentence which we just heard , definitely one without brain.

2nd Centipede - Sirs ! My deepest apologies ! It was not my intention to poke fun or to be insulting, only my simple effort in trying a plausible translation of that proverb in our Centipedian Language ! Apparently not very successful, I am afraid !!

The University Dean of the Centipedes - We accept your apologies and , at the same time, we praise your valorous attempt at an adequate translation of such interesting, astonishingly intellectual proverb and a great representative of universal wisdom to be found wherever Wisdom is and that is a very big question in itself . But , as to your sentence and the astonishing translation of that famous proverb, it will be codified, "cum laude", in the official Archives of this eminent University of " Centipedius ad Astra " , and preserved for Posterity .

1st Centipede - Now, YOU , Zantavius, got yourself out of trouble and embarrassment the easy way and you should pay more attention at what YOU ARE SAYING...rather than about what " I " am saying and......hold on to your Laurels !!!

2nd Centipede - Perhaps I made a mistake the way I said it ,I mean , the way I worked around that proverb: I should have said ,instead:" many feet ,without shoes": better this way , right ?

1st Centipede - I think you are mad !

2nd Centipede - I mad ? May be! Yet, Alambert , I believe that madness is a matter of perception, don't you think ?

1st Centipede - I don't think of anything at the moment and I am not particularly interested in the study and explanation of what madness is. My thoughts are on the battlefields with my soldiers, triumphantly advancing towards the nefarious enemy !

2nd Centipede - That's a good thinking for a soldier, but I am not a soldier, so , I was thinking , that madness is a matter of perception , and I am talking about subtle madness, the one that seeps unseen and unsuspected through the tenuous fabrics of creatures'ill prepared minds and when creatures with similar signs look at each other ,they do not think at all of madness possessing them, but they are perceived to be mad, even if just "subtly", by another bunch of Creatures , generally considered wise and mentally and emotionally solid, even if that gratifying classification is most often a self-appointed one, and who think that they are not or could not possibly, Heavens forbid, be at all mad themselves, not even an inkling of that terrible malady , but , sadly, the dividing line separating the two aspects of the behaviour of all these creatures is a rather sinuous one, irregularly defined , sometimes even difficult to discern its borders .

1st Centipede - That's an old story, Zantavius , and my teacher when I was a young boy at school was making a joke of that description of madness ! So , Zantavius, nothing new, as they say , under the sun !

2nd Centipede - Did it ever occur to you that your teacher might have been mad ?

1st Centipede - Oh !...You..!!!!

2nd Centipede - Quiet...Alambert !...It seems....I believe that they are talking to each other again....

1st Centipede - They...who ?....The Trones ?

2nd Centipede - No , Alambert : I am looking at those two"THINGS" in the square .

1st Centipede - Ah ! They are still there ! Do they look agitated ?

2nd Centipede - Who ? The two Things ?

1st Centipede - But of course !!...Who else is there ??!!

2nd Centipede - Not easy to see from this distance : there could be hundreds of them behind these two,may be , a thousand...!!

1st Centipede - Well , while you are there counting ,why not come up with a million of them !

2nd Centipede - If you don't believe me, why don't you have a glimpse yourself and see what the situation may look to you ?

1st Centipede - Well, of course I could, but at the moment I am keeping an alert eye on the many developing movements on the parade field where the troops are assembling with all their armored equipments and I cannot look in two directions at the same time, Zantavius !!

2nd Centipede - And why not ?

1st Centipede - Zantavius , you make me sick !

2nd Centipede - Oh ! I wish those Trones would hurry up with their promised communication link-up with those two threatening "THINGS ".......

1st Centipede - They will, and don't you worry, now : they were quite impressed with your sharp intuition into their technical and electronic capabilities and I am certain that they are following us, monitoring our chatting, and are fully aware of our anxiety ! So, just wait patiently, Zantavius , and they'll be calling us , I am sure , and soon !

Chorus of the Electronic Chips - Not only Zantavius but WE are following you too, o mighty Alambert Piedileone of the Piedileoni of Valcoccola !!

1st Centipede - I'll be.....!!...Well..., I'd better not say it : that might be interpreted in an adverse contest by the Electronic Trones so proficient in future as well as past and present ways of expression and communication but, may be ,not altogether well versed in the exotic and quite colourful ,volatile, and highly impressive exclamatory vocabulary of surprise or even contempt, so pertinent to our Century's impressive comradeship and familial lingo.........but how on this Forest....!!!.....did they know my name???!!.........Well, what a silly question am I raising in the middle of those Electronic Wizards who seem to know everything there is to know...???!!

Chorus of the Electronic Chips - Dear Sir Alambert! WE HEARD your exclamatory vocabulary which is well known to us : you see, its print was ready eons and eons ago of innumerable eras, but mankind , the ones belonging to that specie, were slow in bringing it to life by, finally, being able to print it, bur we knew of it because.......well, this may be a little difficult for you to grasp, but that expression was floating with us aimlessly, before the little human creatures became aware that we were there too, going around with them !

1st Centipede - With all that knowledge suddenly thrown at us I feel confused if not altogether and completely stunned, dear Wizards of knowledge : you seem to know all !!

Chorus of the Electronic Chips - Well, WE would not go that far by saying that we know everything, but, may be , a thing or two and , by the way , here again we want to congratulate your worthy companion's unusual display of refined intuition at guessing if our help could have been instrumental in building a phonetic liaison between the spoken words of the human specie and the purely and , most likely , and possibly , and probably, but not certainly, the magnetic ones, the words that is, of the Centipedes, so that THEY, Humans and Centipedes, could understand each other and, if that will be possible, it will be an event of historical magnitude, as it is well known to us how poorly the human specie scores on that "understand each other"type of sentiment . But we will , and you will ,soon , find out if the experiment will work as soon as the "formatted" electronic translation sequences will be completed .

2nd Centipede - Will that "soon" be really soon, dear Wizards ?

Chorus of the Electronic Chips - It will be....soon !

1st Centipede - Zantavius, you should not prod the Trones into rushing their offered help !..It is already an almost incredible privilege for us to have received their willingness to help us ! So , be patient and wait !

2nd Centipede - Oh ! I still wish that those Trones would hurry up with their forming a viable link of communication or "formatting " one as they say it and I do not know why they have to say it that way, but , anyway they say it regardless whether I like it or not, so , let us hope that something will be "formatted " pretty soon, as not to miss too much of the conversation of those two NO GOOD THINGS at the corner of the square !

1st Centipede - I guess they are still there , right, Zantavius ?

2nd Centipede - Yes they are ,and now , as I feared ,they have been joined by two others and they are all talking together quite excitedly too . Oh ! I wish those blessed Trones would hurry up..!!

Chorus of the Electronic Chips- We heard your plea , we measured your level of anxiety and we found it to be in the high level response, therefore genuine and real and we have good news for all of you........WE have successfully "hacked"into their minds ,the minds, of course, of those two creatures at the corner of the square ,and we have been blocking first and then sorting and assembling their vocabulary and translating it into your own way of communication ,adapting "meanings " of words and sentences to the form of perception compatible with the mechanisms of your way of living , and it will not be too long before we are ready, and while performing the final steps for the completion of the project, we want to extend to you, eminent Centipedes, our warmest electronic kicks..... pardon us !.....we mean electronic CLICKS for your kindness in allowing us to penetrate the minds of those "THINGS" that are worrying you so much, and we have obtained now an excellent overall coverage of their systems and our renewed thanks for helping us to achieve this end .

2nd Centipede - Oh! Thank you , and thank you a million, dear Trones ! Now we will be able to listen to the talking of those threatening looking creatures, probably trying their best to intervene in the making of our revolution either for their own self-interests or for any advantages that might surface at the successful completion of the event or just simply for the mean intention to cause confusion in our assembled Armies, possibly as infiltrators sent from the opposite Camp!....but we will be watchful for all that and , in the meantime, our renewed Thanks and You have the high esteem of the Glorious Nation of the Centipedes and the CLICKS be with you, for ever !

Chorus of the Electronic Chips - But, dear Centipedes, " WE ain't going no where " !...You let us in and here we stay . It's a wonderful place to have our headquarter and send messages from here to anywhere we want to, much to our advantage and purpose, while undetected and perfectly safe from any outside or inside interference !......WE ARE THE ONES THANKING YOU ....!!!!!!!!

1st Centipede - What nice chaps those Trones ! They are not the touch and go types of creatures: they remain faithful to their acquisitions and work !

2nd Centipede - Yes, that's true and their attitude of performance indeed commendable and that's wonderful , but what is not so commendable and wonderful are those two guys at the corner of the square, now, as I have already told you, four of them, and I have kept my eyes on them all the time! Alambert , revolution or not , and the mighty assembly of the combined Armies of Worms and Centipedes fully appreciated, should not put wool over our eyes and underestimate the potential danger from those THINGS! Now, that we can hear their talking, let us pay very close attention to what they say and let us open our ears , large and wide ,and try to figure out what they do have in mind .

1st Centipede - Zantavius , We do not have ears .

2nd Centipede - But we have "them" , in this episode .

1st Centipede - Are you crazy ? ...HOW ??!

2nd Centipede - Our Writer does not know it : so, keep it quiet.

1st Centipede - Oh ! Mon Dieu ! Une révélation stupéfiante !

2nd Centipede- But, Alambert ! What ! I didn't know that you spoke French !!

1st Centipede - Oh ! No, my dear Zantavius, I do not speak French and I have never been in France, although some friends of mine have .

2nd Centipede - But, then , how did you come out with such perfect French exclamation ??

1st Centipede - It happened one day, long, long ago, when I was travelling on a boat and I heard it cried out by a French sailor when, as we reached the port , I was trying to get out of the boat .

2nd Centipede - You must have a very good memory to remember that after such a long time !

1st Centipede - Not really, but that expression has remained firmly impressed in my mind since that day when that French sailor literally cried out that sentence right at the very moment that he was attempting to strike me with his foot while I was desperately trying to hurry out of that boat .

2nd Centipede - What an experience..!!!...No wonder you remember it so vividly , even in FRENCH !!

The Scholarly Centipede - The existence of all Creatures is always in danger wherever and whenever any of those Creatures may be or might be near danger , regardless of their size : Big, or Medium ,or Small, even when the sun shines brightly and the sky is cloudless and blue .

Chorus of the University Centipedes - Wise words, soberizing conjecture even if not of established and confirmed data , yet a remarkable assessment of the Theory of Probability , with a sentimental and philosophical value associated with a significant proof of high knowledge of the Laws of atmospheric conditions with the choice referral to the sun's shining image and the vivid representation of a cloudless blue sky . These "remarkable remarks" will be catalogued "cum Laude" in the Archives of the University of the Centipedes, "Centipedius ad Astra", to be preserved for Posterity .

2nd Centipede- Hold it ! Quiet ! I seem to hear some murmurs coming from that area of the square where those "no goods" were just a minute ago and I believe that they are still there : if we remain quiet , we might hear something .

1st Centipede - Do you hear them talking ?

2nd Centipede - Yes, I hear them talking and I believe that I can catch some words of what they are saying !

1st Centipede - Go ahead and listen, but, to me , paying so much attention to a couple of dark and shadowy figures in the corner of a square seems a lot of a waste of time! This waiting, this constant thinking and this continuous wondering at what anything or anybody could be or be up to, does nothing good but it only creates anxiety for none existing things and situation . What a difference, my dear Zantavius, with the mental outlook of Sir Alambert Piedileone of the Piedileoni of Valcoccola , at a full alert and shouting my anger at the tyranny of Giants and mushrooms and anybody and anything who would not like us ! Down with the tyrant Giant Trees, down with the Mushrooms, down with slavery and the arrogance of the "Giant Everybody"...Long Live Liberty !.....This, Zantavius, is my concern!

2nd Centipede - If you make so much noise I cannot hear anything they are saying, these two or four wretched vagabond tramps !

1st Centipede - Vagabond Tramps...???!!..But, Zantavius, what are you going to come up with next time...???!!

2nd Centipede - Yes, Alambert : vagabond Tranps , and that was what the Witch Queen used to call them when she was telling me about a time of great preparations for an expedition of several of those Tramps armed with powerful machines and with the purpose of exterminating a great number of Giant Trees in the nearby Forests and "liberate",and that is what she said : "liberate" the Forests from the tyranny of the Giant Trees , and that was what she used to call those Tramps ,just plain, good-for-nothing "VAGABONDS" .

1st Centipede - But I find it difficult to figure out the way of thinking of this your "Witch Queen" about the Giant Trees being "tyrannical" to the Forests ?!

2nd Centipede - In a sense, that is : you see, the Witch Queen was saying that the shadow caused by these gigantic Trees by preventing the sunlight and its warmth to easily filter in through the closeness of their bulky and massive built and the thick density of the foliage was of such an extent that, at least in her opinion, the world below those Giant Trees was languishing in a perpetual humid environment ,cold and depressing surroundings full of desolate and exhausted creatures who lived down there and that the time for a revolt against the Giant Trees was just in the making ....Oh!.. Listen, listen !...Oh! Yes, I hear quite well and these "Vagabonds" have started a conversation among all four of them,and they are talking now in a louder voice than they did before and until now, but I can hear them at this time , quite well..Strange ! Very strange ! Now one of them has raised one of his upper legs, or whatever they are, the ones on the upper part of their bodies , and seems to point it in our direction !!......Heavens forbid ! Could it be that they have discovered us ??!!....... Alambert ! I believe that we are in a terrible danger !

1st Centipede - No good panicking, Zantavius ! First of all I doubt that"pointing of one upper leg" somewhere and somehow in what it could have seemed to be our approximate direction ,did at all occur, but, even if that were the case , I do not see what the danger could be for us to panick.

2nd Centipede - Nobody is panicking , Alambert : just measuring distances and looking for the next move and , now , my dear Alambert , another one of those "wretched vagabonds", is pointing his upper leg in our direction and that makes two of them pointing in the same way and,THAT,does not seem to me to be pure coincidence, regardless of what you may be thinking .

1st Centipede - May be they just want to take a walk "that'a'way"they are showing with the leg !!

2nd Centipede - Listen ,listen ! Alambert , if you would keep quiet and pay more attention to what's going on, you could hear too what they are saying : do not forget that the smart Trones did make special electronic arrangements for us to be able to understand their talking .

1st Centipede - How could I forget such a wondrous feat??!.....The fact is that I am far from being at all interested in what they are saying !.....But, O.K., let's listen , if you take that so much at heart!

****

Meanwhile, the "vagabond Tramps", so called by the contemptuous and irreverent 2nd Centipede, and who were still standing at the corner of the square, were, actually, regular and well trained timber-men hired by a Paper Company to harvest trees, talking among themselves, and studying how best to begin the job and start working, ...at the same time, though, while the Electronic Wizards were working on achieving a communication liaison for the Centipedes and the unknown suspicious creatures at the corner of the square, these Wizards, by purely an electronic overlap of impulses , had also created a bridge of reciprocal communication so that the human creatures too could be aware of the Centipedes'language and expressions in a way that was not apparent or conscious to them , but fully and clearly perceptive , subconsciously , of the Centipedes'way of communicating , the inflections and meaning of their words and sentences and so on....strange, indeed...but true!!

****

1st Forester - Heigh ! You, blockhead ! Did you hear ?

2nd Forester - Hear ...what ?

1st Forester - That idiot, down there, on the other corner of the square, getting so restless and working himself up in a frenzy, yelling his head off and kicking up a fuss with all his legs up in the air and the plumes on his head sticking up like posts on a fence! But can't you see him ?!

2nd Forester - Oh! Yes, I see him now : so what ?.....It's only a large centipede . Big deal !

1st Forester - Big Deal, my foot! That enormous centipede is claiming to the top of his phonetic capability that he and his Braves and the Army of the Piedermi will march against the Mushrooms and the Giant trees !.....and soon !

2nd Forester - And let him march with all his friends !!...What is that to us ,anyway ?

1st Forester - You dumbbell, you never understand anything ! If that maniac is allowed to get into the forest to attack, as he so openly claims, mushrooms and giant trees, he will also drag behind him all that rabble of millions of insects that could produce some damage to our trees by boring into their wood and depreciate the value of the lumber : how does that grab you, genius ?

2nd Forester - Ah ! Now I understand : it means that it wouldn't be so good, right?

1st Forester - Wrong : it would be very good ! You, Ninny ! Why were you born so stupid ?

2nd Forester - I don't know , but, if you are really interested , I'll try to find out from some acquaintances of mine and from my own Parents : yes?

1st Forester - Forget it ! Don't try to be stupider than you already are : pay attention and listen , instead .

2nd Forester - Is it O.K for stupid people to listen ?

1st Forester - It is perfectly A-O.K , unless they are deaf .

2nd Forester - That , I did not know .

1st Forester - Good ! Now you know .

2nd Forester - Thank you , Metimoro .

1st Forester - Don't mention it , Orotimo.

2nd Forester - Still , I hear nothing : you had asked me to pay attention and listen .

1st Forester - So I did. Now, pay attention : we'll have to do a lot of cleaning up work before we can get going on the harvesting of the trees , and , first ,we need to get rid of all those vermins before they can get to the forest and damage the trees .

2nd Forester - Metimoro , shall we start now ?

1st Forester - Not yet, Orotimo : I have just sent word to Headquarter to provide us with the necessary pesticides and as soon as the truck arrives ,then , we'll be able to start .

2nd Forester - What shall we do until then?

1st Forester - We'll keep an eye on those insects and wait .

2nd Forester - That's fine : I'll just seat here on this rock and clean my chain saw .

1st Forester - That's a good idea , but don't forget to give a glance , now and then, towards those insects, and I'll do the same.

2nd Forester - O.K, Boss .

****

The two Centipedes, Zantavius and Alambert, have been listening to the conversation of the two Foresters and, now , they have no doubts that Zantavius' fears are proving themselves as a very dangerous and sad REALITY.....!!!

****

2nd Centipede - Alambert!!....We are doomed !

1st Centipede - Not yet ! I'll instruct the flying Beetles to rush to Headquarter and summon the shock-troop Squadron of the Queen Wasps to attack immediately the two Tramps.

2nd Centipede - Alambert : they call themselves "Foresters".

1st Centipede - Well , O.K , Foresters !....So, as I was saying, I will instruct the Squadron of the shock-troops to attack right away those Foresters and anyone else that would come along once the truck with the Foresters' offensive weapons is here .

2nd Centipede - But the Foresters, Alambert , will kill also the Queen Wasps with the horrible weapons that they have !

1st Centipede In war, my dear, there always is a chance of being killed, that's common knowledge , but the Queen Wasps' attack on the Foresters will buy us time to march on and get into the forest with our armored divisions before the Tramps do and launch our final assault against the mushrooms' fortifications and attack the Giant Trees .

2nd Centipede - It all sounds very good in words, but, Alambert , I doubt that we will have time to do all that before the truck arrives .

1st Centipede - That should not be a reason for us not to try it : many a battles , even wars , were won ,in antiquity, by one side persistence in "trying", while the other side, almost secure in the belief of their victory, would not believe that the other side would, actually, try again to renew the attack .

2nd Centipede - This all sounds very good and it looks impressive in the History books of those human Creatures , but, dear Alambert, Centipedes do not have History books to marvel upon , least of all any history to brag about in schools, associations, or in selected and eminent Clubs and they do not have either any "humacides" to spray those Foresters with or any "chain-saws" to cut their trucks, full of "pesticides", to pieces!!

1st Centipede - But they, those Tramps and their friends, do not have an Alambert Piedileone of the Piedileoni of Valcoccola, either !

2nd Centipede - Oh! Alambert !! Blessed be your naive conscience and your juvenile mentality ! I really, would have wanted to say "infantile Mentality" but, under the present dire circumstances I thought that such an address would not have been proper , not only proper but even somewhat cruel towards you, so forgive me for expressing my sentiments so openly and, sadly, may be even inadequaely !

1st Centipede - Thank you, Zantavius, but remember that words alone and, worse, if accompanied by a veneer cover of sentimental philosophy ,do not help much in situations like the present one!

2nd Centipede - Alambert ! Alambert !..... Look!!....The Truck ! The Truck !!..We are doomed , we are doomed , Alambert , we are doomed !!.....And were are the shock troops of the Queen Wasps ??!.......Alambert ! The truck has arrived ..!!!

1st Centipede - Don't you worry, Zantavius : the Queen Wasps will welcome it !

2nd Centipede - But, Alambert , I see no wasps , least of all any Queen Wasps !

1st Centipede - Zantavius, "shock troops" manouvre in total silence and secrecy and are not preceeded by a military parade band playing stimulating and heroic military tunes. You'll see them when they'll launch their fierce attack !

2nd Centipede - I only hope that that it would not be too long before they would launch their attack , Alambert !! Look, Alambert , how swiftly those Foresters are getting busy around that truck preparing their weapons . Alambert, I am afraid that our last hour has come !!!

1st Centipede - Even if it were our last minute , I , Alambert Piedileone, will not retreat or leave the battlefield , and Alambert will lead his legions to the attack and to victory in spite of any trucks !

** Meanwhile............**

**......meanwhile, the two spinster Sparrows, our two old maids , Celesre and Andrea, in the relative safety of the high branches of the Oak Tree , anxiously and , also , sadly, watch the developing scene on the ground below and wonder if peace will ever come again to the troubled Forest............. **

Andrea - Celeste ! The way things are shaping up it looks as if pretty soon we'll have to leave our native Forest and migrate to another one, in search of another tree and , most likely, not as comfortable and hospitable a tree as this old oak Tree is where we were born, you and I .

Celeste - But your Family, Andrea , lives in another Forest far away from this one and you had just come back from visiting them and warning them of the ongoing dangers, if I recollect your words correctly .

Andrea - That's true : you see ,shortly after my birth, here, my Family migrated to the other Forest in order to be together with some cousins and , of course, small and young as I was at that time when my Family left, I had to go with them, but, in my mind and in my heart, this Tree, this Forest are the places were I feel myself at home !

Celeste - And to think that even this good home may soon be no more,and all its memories!

Andrea - Where will you go, Celeste ?

Celeste - I do not know yet,Andrea: I do not have any Family left, they all perished when disaster struck our original Forest, long ago and I had remained the only survivor.

Andrea - And how did you come here from your destroyed forest ,left alone and without help , Celeste ?

Celeste - When the terrible wave of terror passed over, an old passerine Bird of the ancient House of the Turdidae , a Turdus migratorius in a direct and uninterrupted line of descent , a true to the heart Troubadour, really, an acting and singing minstrel with an enchanting ,melodious rhythm and who made a living with his impromptu poems and songs, and who had escaped the violence of that day , took pity on me and together we flew away from that horrible scene of destruction and he brought me here and made sure that I was settled safely and comfortably, out of danger .

Andrea - And what happened to your saviour and benefactor , Celeste, after he brought you here ?

Celeste - He stayed with me and cared for me until I was able to fend for myself, then, one day, he told me that he had seen that I had settled down nicely and that I was in no danger and that he had to do on on his way and see other lands, other forests and meet other minstrels like he was and that he might come back one day to see me, but his life was one of poetry and songs and he needed inspiration from other places, other lives , other creatures in this world ....and with a sweet song on his beak, he flew away ,one early morning, at sunrise.

Andrea - And did he ever come back to see you, Celeste ?

Celeste - No : and I never saw him again .

Andrea - I wonder what might have happened to the poor old chap !

Celeste - I was told by an old Owl , that he had died long ago, his death caused by a mysterious collapse while he was singing a ballade he had produced and which recounted the rescuing of a damsel from the ruins of a destroyed forest .

Andrea - Ah ! Celeste ! He must have been thinking of you !

Celeste - May be .

Andrea - And you, Celeste , did you ever think of him or remembering him from time to time?

Celeste - Yes, I did .

Andrea - So, that's why you never married !!

Celeste - I do not know .

Andrea - Did he ever marry ? Do you know that ?

Celeste - Yes.

Andrea - But, Celeste, what does a cut and dry "yes" mean ? Did you or did you not know if he ever married ?

Celeste - He did not .

Andrea - Ah ! Now I begin to see the light spreading on the whole story and now I begin to better understand your seeming indifference to current events, Celeste !!...Celeste you were in love with that minstrel who had saved you !!

Celeste - Andrea, why don't you take a look and see if anything ominous is happening down there ?....We must be ready, you know,to fly away if the situation worsens !

Andrea - I understand, Celeste !!....I am sorry, really sorry Celeste. ....and I did not mean to evoke past memories that might cause the pain and sorrow of events too close to one's heart, to be of any comfort !.....Yes, Celeste.....I'll take a look to see what's going on down there....right away !

ss

Celeste - Thank you , Andrea .

***

** ......While Celeste remains pensive and motionless , perched on the branch of the Oak Tree and Andrea begins to scout with her keen eyes the scene around the immediate surroundings of the Giant Oak Tree, the Foresters get very busy with the unloading of all the goods and equipment and the pesticides........and Andrea immediately reports the discouraging findings to Celeste..**

***

Andrea - Bad news, Celeste : the little creatures are hard at work unloading a large truck of all its goods which seem very similar to those mentioned by the old Witch Queen when , long ,long ago, in a rage of anger and of sorcerous fury, hired the same type of human creatures and sent them on to destroy a forest because she thought it was throwing too much shade on the little creatures below, making their lives miserable. This is no good, Celeste, the way it looks !

Celeste - We must, then, prepare to fly away.

Andrea - But, Celeste, you said that you had no place where to fly to : may be, did you remember a place ?

Celeste - Not sure . May be, faintly, a place far, far away from here where only wild and lonely creatures live and where no other creature has ever dared to tread foot because the undergrowth is so dense and hostile that the forest can only be reached by the flight of a bird.

Andrea- But, Celeste, would you remember how to locate that far away forest of which you seem to have only a vague knowledge of where it is ?

Celeste - I think I could , Andrea . Somehow I feel that I could fly there by pure instinct : I believe that it lies at that line of the horizon where the sun settles at dusk in all its glory .

Andrea - Celeste ?

Celeste - Yes, Andrea : what is it ?

Andrea - Celeste, is that forest the one where your Saviour Minstrel lived after he left you ?

Celeste - May be it is, may be it isn't .The old Owl had told me that it was .

Andrea - But, Celeste, how will you be there all by yourself ,alone, with no friends, no one you know and, may be, even no one left there to talk to, to converse with....you know, life can become very miserable and desolate in such a perpetual solitude and you may even become sick and, more, what will you live on ? Food may be scarce or become unavailable or difficult to obtain and if you would be sick or become incapacitated ,then, you could become a casualty of that forest too : food could become hard to find, even for a lonely bird !

Celeste - Memories, Andrea, are the lonely birds' nourishment and food .

Andrea - Celeste ! I am worried about you ! You are depressed and life is a pretty hard game as it is even for strong and steady folks, but it can be murderous to creatures on the edge of an abyss they most often are not even able to see or be aware of it . You need help, Celeste !

Celeste - That's what everybody says when running out of any sensible answer to life's real problems, hardships and well represented realities .

Andrea - That's fine, Celeste, but, in spite of your sentimental-philosophical mixture of life's representation , you still need help and I don't give a damn at what you are saying because I know , if ever my name is Andrea , that you cannot go there and live alone . That would be not only a sign of depression but of sheer madness , if you want to know what I am thinking of it .

Celeste - Andrea ! What has come over you ??!

Andrea - Nothing has come over me, under me or on either side of me ..I tell you what....

Celeste - What ?

Andrea - I'll come with you !

Celeste - To that far, far away forest at the edge of the horizon where the sun sets at night in all its glory ......??!....Andrea.......YOU are mad !

Andrea - Mad or sane, I don't care. Celeste: I am coming with you!!.....And we better hurry and fly away before we get caught in the approaching tempest .

** The two Centipedes, Zantavius and Alambert, begin to realize that danger has come very close to them and Zantavius, who, as we know, is the most prudent of the two, is begging Alambert to leave a situation that is quite clearly already lost even before it had a chance to start, besides the anxiously expected shock troops of the Queen Wasps have not shown up at all, so, as the picture of the unfolding events becomes foggier, Zantavius, again and again tries to get his friend out of that place and out of danger ....**

Zantavius - (the 2nd Centipede)- Alambert, but where are those shock troops ? Where are those Queen Wasps? Those Foresters are working at a pretty fast clip in unloading that truck and if they get that fluid in their spray tanks, Alambert we'll be all killed unless we leave immediately. Alambert, do you hear me ?

Alambert- (the 1st Centipede - Yes, Zantavius, I hear you loud and clear ! The first flying beetle returning from the mission to Headquarter says that the shock troops are on the way : they could not have been here just there and then because they had to answer another emergency request for help, but they'll be here, you'll see !

** In the meantime the Foresters are busy filling their tanks with the killing fluid and are getting ready to spray the ground on the square, the soil around the trees and the trees themselves, when.................................. **

1st Forester - We must work hard and fast and catch those fastidious insects before they can reach our trees and do damage to the wood . As to the mushrooms we hardly care anything about them, and, most often , they are poisonous anyway,so we do not have to be very particular about where and how we spray : we just spray to clear everything there is to be cleared .

2nd Forester - Which side shall we start from, Boss ?

1st Forester - I had thought to start on the other side of the square, first, where I had noticed that large centipede that was screaming and yelling like a maniac as he had been possessed !!....

2nd Forester - ....And may be he was ....

1st Forester - Then, if he was and still is, it's about time to calm him down .

** Suddenly, a swarm of yellow wasps appears as a dark cloud in the blue sky and prepares to swoop down on the Foresters............**

1st Centipede - Zantavius ! Zantavius !...We are safe, we are safe ! Look, look up in the sky...the shock troops are getting ready to swoop on the Foresters and destroy them ! Zantavius ! We are safe , safe Zantavius and free !

2nd Centipede - But,Alambert, the Foresters have already filled up their tanks with the killer liquid and they'll use it first on the attacking wasps and then against us ! Alambert, you just do not reason! Please, I beg of you, Alambert, please come away ,right now while we still can get away !...Remember : when everybody will be dead, there will be no one left to raise you a monument for your bravery.

1st Centipede - Here they come ! To death the Foresters ! Hurrah for Liberty and down with the mushrooms and the giant trees ! To the Palace , my braves, to the Palace !

2nd Centipede - O Immortal Gods , poor Alambert has gone nuts !

........meanwhile, the Foresters........

2nd Forester - Boss ! Boss ! Look at the sky ! a cloud of wasps just above our area : shall we get our hoses ready ?

1st Forester - By all means, and use the fog spray so that the insecticide can be spread wide and large and get all of them with one burst of our hoses.

2nd Forester - Fine, Boss : and here we go !......But, Boss, they are coming down on us fast and in a solid block....!!

1st Forester - Better so: as I said , it should be easier to get them all with just one burst of our hoses !

2nd Forester - Sacrebleu !!!.....á la grâce de Dieu.!!!.Boss !....They are coming down like a giant battering ram trying to hit us and the truck with the maximum possible and massive force .

1st Forester - Quick, now, Orotimo, open up the hose and let go at full power!!

2nd Forester - O.K, Boss : and here it goes ! ..The whole cloud of wasps caught in the dense fog of the spray hose !!....Phew !!...That was a hit !!!

1st Forester - Good work, Orotimo !

2nd Forester - The whole massive block of those vicious wasps got caught in the dense cloud of the powerful spray and I saw just a few escape and fly away: I do not see any more of them around .

1st Forester- Good ! Good work, Orotimo !...And now let's get started on those insects and we might want to begin the spreading of the insecticide on the other side of the square where that maniac of a giant centipede was "screaming" his lungs out and shouting war-like slogans against mushrooms and giant trees ! The poor fool !

2nd Forester - I didn't know that centipedes could be fools !...I was always told that people were fools .

1st Forester - Of course, Orotimo, and that makes sense, from the centipedes point of view, of course .

2nd Forester - Ah ! Then, I am not so stupid ,after all, and I guessed "right" about the people being the fools, didn't I ?

1st Forester - The centipedes will think highly of you, Orotimo.

2nd Forester - Oy...! Shucks ! I am speechless !

1st Forester - Well, now, Orotimo, get your speech back and let us start spraying those damn insects before they can reach the trees and damage them and let us shut the mouth of that shouting and yelling insane centipede that is still screaming his head off totally unaware of what's coming his way, the poor fool !

2nd Forester - But, Boss , centipedes do not yell or shout !!

1st Forester - They yell and shout in this story , Orotimo.

2nd Forester - Ah !....Then it's all right .

1st Forester - Is everything in order, Orotimo , and at the ready to start spraying ?

2nd Forester - Yes, Boss ! Everything is ready !

** The last anxious, agonizing appeal of Zantavius to Alambert, begging him to leave before doom befalls them !!!...**

2nd Centipede (Zantavius) - Alambert , in this almost certain last hour of our existence, won't you listen to my last pray and heartfelt love for you, dear Alambert, and leave this scene that will be witnessing a nefarious massacre of highly motivated creatures and the total , utter destruction of everything we had believed in, our beloved and glorious Nation of the Centipedes and the rightful strife for justice, liberty and honour . Alambert,I beg of you : let us leave now....the Commissioner of Supplies has left, Alambert, and he has sought refuge in a drain , here , just behind us , as he saw the complete annihilation of the Queen Wasps' shock troops and the loss, with their destruction, of any hope of success by our forces !.....Alambert, let us leave , now, immediately, and it is not a shame to leave now, but it would be if we stayed and provided the fun for the Foresters to use us as target practice.

The learned smart Gopher - Sensible words, compelling logic! How true is the heritage of history , any history, be that of the human specie, or of the specie of Agaricaceae, like our illustrious and Royal Minister friend here, Agaricus Campestris, our mushroom, now involved in the feverish defense of his real estate and that of the Trees, giant or not, under attack from the army of the Piedermi, or the history of the zebras, the beetles, the frogs ,the toads and the lizards and,not least,our Gophers' history too, how true, I was commenting, how truly history teaches us that strifes and struggles and battles and wars, during the assigned running lap of our individual lives, are, more often, won by use of common sense than by unsustainable bursts of ostentatious show of power and pride .

The learned Moth- I couldn't have said it any better myself .

The old Owl from a branch of the Old Oak Tree - Alambert, this is your friendly, neighbour Owl and I , together with all the other Owls in this Forest, love you, so, Alambert, your friend Zantavius is right in begging you to spare his life in addition to your own precious one ! Alambert, you should remember what you learned when you were at school , immersed in that mesmerizing and wondrous world of antiquity, when Gods from the mighty summit of Mount Olympus were shrouding their heroes in a cloud of dense fog to make them disappear and become invisible to their enemies or to impending danger, as they intended to protect and preserve the lives of these heroes destined for other and greater adventures and future feats of great significance .

2nd Centipede- Alambert ! You heard the learned Gopher, you heard the wise Moth, you heard the Owl : Alambert, listen to reason !!

1st Centipede (Alambert) - The reason is " MY REASON " ! The ones without reason are the ones on the other side and they are my enemies !...........Besides , I do not see any fog coming to shroud me from hostile injury, so , I shall charge the infamous mushrooms and giant trees and exterminate them all ! Hurrah for our victory and triumph !

1st Forester - NOW !...Orotimo, let the spray go ,at full power !

****

*** A large, dense cloud of lethal pesticide erupts from the large nozzles of several hoses with furious force and it engulfs the square... ***

****

1st Centipede (Alambert) - To the attack, my braves.!!.....attack ! attack.!....the Gods are with us and Thank You, oh! mighty and merciful Gods.....You DID send the shrouding FOG to protect all of us even when we did not beg YOU for such a merciful and righteous gesture towards us and we shall fight to our last breath of strength and on to victory for justice and honour.....to the attack, my braves and have no fear..to the..attack...the Gods are with us......with ...us.....with.................

2nd Centipede - Oh !...Lord have mercy !...The Tempest !!...I can't breathe anymore !..Alambert ! Alambert !!...He does not answer !....Oh ! My Lord have mercy ! Immortal Gods ! ....What do I see,,!!!!!......the Army of the Piedermi falling by the hundreds, by the thousands, engulfed in that deadly cloud ...!!!.....This is the.....this ...I cannot breathe......this.....is......this.....is.....is......Alamb...

The Centipedes' Commissioner of Supplies (hidden in a drain)- YOU !! DISGUSTING RABBLE...!!...Murderers ! Murderous vagabond tramps !! Two legged murderers , I censure you for your cowardice and infamous, vile and heinous act !.And I, Prophet elect by unanimous suffrage of the glorious Nation of the Centipedes , foresee your "cloudy" future as a deadly fog for your lust of destruction ,your only courage the use of lethal substances against unarmed opponents bearing the standards of liberty, justice and honour . Time will come, as it usually always does, that will repay you ten folds over for this brutal, horrid, sacrilegious slaughter !

1st Forester - Excellent work, Orotimo and, please, do not stop and continue to spray until the very last insect is in sight ! Once they are all "gone", then, they cannot do any more damage to our trees .

Chorus of the solitary Trees - We have some reservations about the positive statement, just made, of "our" trees, that would denote a condition relative to a contextual relation to "property". We are perplexed at this representation of the trees in a forest ,particularly when we are not aware or we had not even been informed to belong or to have belonged or to belong, in the future, to somebody : we believe that we belong to the Forest .

2nd Forester
(Orotimo) - This good drenching seems to have produced the desired effect : I cannot see any more insects crawling around and, even the tops of these big trees seem to agree with it by the way they undulate their tops .

1st Forester
(Metimoro) Orotimo, you cannot help to ever act silly with your stupid comments : trees do not have ears or brains or eyes, so they do not know, obviously, what we are doing, you silly old ninny .

2nd Forester - But, Metimoro, you had told me that everybody and everything here, in this Forest , has ears, mouths , lungs , eyes , brains and good vocal cords to yell and shout with !!.....Do they also have a thick beard and mustaches ?

1st Forester - Ah! Quit being so stupid and keep your mind on the spraying,instead : that'll do more good than your dry and insipid humour.

The Centipedes' Commissioner of Supplies (hidden in the drain) - Heavens above !!!....What a catastrophe ! What an unnecessary tragedy ! The entire combined armies of the Piedermi completely destroyed while these brave soldiers were trying to bring forth the standards of Liberty and Justice and mount a powerful frontal attack against the fortifications of the mushrooms and attack, also, the Giant Trees ! Oh ! What horror to see so many brave patriots fall for what they believed in as compared to other creatures' apparent indifference and even scorn for those sacrosanct values ! Probably these vagabond tramps would have been acting differently if this kind of ball-game would have been played in their own backyard !

1st Forester - I think that we can stop spraying now : I cannot see any more insects moving on the ground and the soils is still pretty well soggy from the insecticide condensing on the ground so we can expect some peace around here for a while, at least, and we can start the harvest of our timber . Orotimo ?

2nd Forester - Yes , Boss !

1st Forester - Orotimo, get all our chainsaws in order so that we can start working pretty soon .

2nd Forester - But, Boss, I am hungry ! I haven't had a bite of anything since early this morning and I am starving to death !

1st Forester - With that big belly of yours it's hard to believe that anyoine here is starving to death, but, O.K , let us stop for a moment and have a bite of something and, then, back to work.

2nd Forester - Oh ! Boss, tha's a swell idea ! Let us sit here,in the shade, and I'll let you taste my sandwich : you'll love it !

Chorus of the solitary Trees - It seems to us that the idea of a "property", per se, even if contestable, can still be an attractive prospective, particularly when sought after by these two legged nasty creatures,often referred to,by Worms and Centipedes,as "good-for-nothing", poor mixtures of hatred and suspicion, of murderous traits, unworthy of friendship, void of self respect, avid of everything that's not theirs, insidious and ambiguous in their dealings and in their thoughts , always ready to take the advantage of the bad turn in somebody's life for their own benefit ,as we have just witnessed in the case of the recent extermination of the army of the Piedermi so that they could get to us for a good "lumber-harvest" without the annoyance of those "infamous insects"..........We are, therefore, absolutely, uncompromisingly, unequivocally, disgusted .

The Centipedes' Commissioner of Supplies (hidden in the drain)- The violent tempest and the crushing rain appear to have ceased and I cannot hear any sounds at all : no cries, no excited voices , no stimulating shouting by the inflamed vigor of brave soldiers, no war chants resounding in the forest ,no sounds of marching armored warriors and there seem to reign a desolate silence in the entire Forest.......everything has fallen still ! Oh! Mighty and Immortal Gods, why such terrible evil had to fall on us, humble and undefended insects as we are? Have we offended you ? Is it because we did not offer you proper and timely sacrifices ? ....Oh ! Mighty Gods ,even if we might have, inadvertently, missed some due sacrifices, this one here, today, I assure you, will compensate more than a thousand folds for the sacrifices to your Greatness and Majesty that we might have missed in the past or that we might have missed recently or that we might miss in the future, in the entire length of our lives! ..And now, Immortal Gods, everything is silent : life is no more for the valiant and honourable Nations of the Worms and the Centipedes , and everything is silent, under the pall of death and the beautiful flame of Liberty and Justice is only a faint beacon that rapidly will fade away in the obscurity of only sad memories .

Chorus of the Wise Worms - The tumult, the thunderous shouting of war chants and the passionate expressions of jubilation by our troops prior to the perverse Tempest that fell on them , has so disturbed our minds, our thoughts and offended our ears that we feel immensely depressed and saddened by all the recent events. We may be considered wise worms but we cannot absolve ourselves from lamenting the loss of so many valiant young Worms, the flower of our youth, who so strongly and genuinely did believe in Liberty and Justice and loathed and despised Tyranny . To those brave and faithful heroes go our thoughts, our admiration and our profound sadness for the loss of so noble sons . A day will come, and we are certain of that, a day will come when our lost young warriors will be vindicated and Liberty and Justice will triumph and Tyranny will perish.

Chorus of the Wise Centipedes - Of the glorious people of the Centipedes we are the elected Elders and we are of a honest and open character . The disastrous events of the war, its confusion and fury, have taken us by surprise and we feel deeply saddened by it and, at the same time, also angry and very disturbed by the irrational and wanton aggressive attitude of those irresponsible and opportunistic two legged monsters , dedicated only to disrupt and, in the end, destroy other creatures' lives for their own way of securing pleasure, comfort and riches . The naive, the visionary , the idealistic creatures, as usual, were swept away by these two legged beings not even worth to be called "beings" ! And now , that beautiful aura of enthusiasm that seemed to have spread everywhere, has vanished and has left the poor, the innocent, the simple and honest creatures to bear the consequences of that conflagration, of true cosmic proportion, all by themselves, as it usually happens after conflicts and wars of all types and dimensions, creeds and greeds, and to bear that onerous weight without compensation of any glory attached to it : " Sic transit gloria mundi " .

The combined Chorus of the Wise Worms and the Wise Centipedes- We do not know or recognize that"caption" by some scholars of the Centipedes, and saddened and desolate as we are for the recent terrifying events, yet we are resolute in all of our intentions and we are moving back to our own lands, those safe shelters that Mother Nature has selectively and with great wisdom set aside for every single living creature in this Forest, where the tired and worn out creatures can repair the damage that they suffered by the heinous attack by those two legged sinister monsters with also a head, but its content still questionable, and we confirm and reconfirm, again and again , that a day will come when we will have recuperated from this disaster and gathered our forces together once more, then, that fatidic day, our renewed and stronger troops will go to the assault of those fine Castles and history will repeat itself , but, this time, at our own marching tune !

* The few Worm and Centipede Survivors of that terrible massacre begin to leave in all secrecy to follow the Group of the Wise Centipedes and of the Wise Worms back to their respective Lands. *

** Meanwhile, our good old friend, the Mushroom, relieved by the end of that tempestuous time of tumult and disorder, comes to his usual confident attitude and breathes more freely of that peaceful air pervading the Forest, and, along with him, all the other jolly mushrooms, glad that they did not have to get involved in a fight to defend their positions and ground, at the foot of the Giant Oak Tree.................................. **

Chorus of the free Mushrooms - As far as our limited span of vision permits us, we cannot see any offensive host approaching our fortifications, for quite sometime now and we therefore assume that the threatened and expected attack by the Army of the Piedermi is no more, so we can reduce our alert status to just moderate, let the possibility be of a stunt by some ill advised lunatic insect full of unwise spirit of futile heroism .

The learned Moth- Have no fear ! They , the Insects, are all dead !

Chorus of the free Mushrooms - But how could they have died ??!...We did not fire a single shot, least even seeing any of them near our fortifications !!

The learned Moth- Have no fear ! They, the Insects , are all dead !

Chorus of the free Mushrooms - We heard you the first time, Moth !!....Why are you repeating yourself ?

The learned Moth- To make sure that you understood .

Chorus of the free Mushrooms - We understand everything quite well, even when loaded with peevish sarcasm.

the learned Moth- I realize that you have a large head, but I wasn't quite sure of what's in it .

Chorus of the free Mushrooms - There is "plenty" in our large heads but we keep it a secret so creatures around us chat and gossip freely, feeling safe of not being interpreted in the meaning of what they are talking about, but...we know !!...And this silence ! It's frighteming !

The learned Moth- Why ,then, did you not know of the cessation of the hostilities and you only guessed the end of it, if you are so clever and understand everything ?

Chorus of the free Mushrooms - Understand everything, yes: that we do well..except sepulchral silence, of course.

The learned sweet Gopher- Congratulations: says an old proverb:"Words are made out of silver, but "silence" is golden " !

Chorus of the free Mushrooms - And why did you have to butt in , all of you , to talk nonsense and bother us ?

The Gopher and the Moth - What would life be without a little nonsense and fun, don't you think ?....Besides we wanted to test the "capacity"of those big heads of yours......simple, isn't it ?

Chorus of the free Mushrooms - If something is simple, that is the way your reasoning goes: you should know that our large heads are famous............

The learned Moth- We are aware of that.........

Chorus of the free Mushrooms - May be you are but not in the sense and value we attribute to them.

The learned Moth- That's something really new !

Chorus of the free Mushrooms - Indeed ! And,for our heads being so large we have acquired, through eons of time, two distinct features .

The learned Moth- Did you say "distinct" or "indistinct" ?

Chorus of the free Mushrooms - You don't ever give up, do you ?

The learned Moth- You know, it is in our nature, the way we were built, and that is "never cease to do anything we are doing" .

Chorus of the free Mushrooms - Like flying persistently around a light until you drop dead ?

The learned Moth- I have to give it to all of you ! .....You guessed darn right !...Pardon: rightly !

Chorus of the free Mushrooms - Well, as we were saying, Mother Nature has given us two"distinct"and important features..........

The learned Moth- I am dying to hear them..!!

Chorus of the free Mushrooms - Well, here they are! The first one, which applies not to all of us, but, nevertheless, to a large number of us, and that is of a delicious, appetizing disposition to cause several creatures to seek our companionship at their tables, and the.......

The learned Moth- The second, yes ?

Chorus of the free Mushrooms - Don't be so impatient !...Yes, the second one is a very large and wide head on which eminent and famous Gnomes sat and watched the goings in the Forest and offered to the passers by to read their future .

The learned Moth- ....GNOMES....??!!

chorus of the free Mushrooms - Gnomes.

The learned Moth- But that's history of times long gone by and they were popular figures in the grotesque representations and fantasies of the creatures of the Middle Ages, if you might happen to know what the Middle Ages were !

Chorus of the free Mushrooms - Obviously they were in the middle, of course, but of what , that's a different story, or should we have said : "that's a different History" ??"

The learned Moth- Heavens be praised , for the innocent and the simple ! They shall always be the choisest crop of Mother Nature !

Chorus of the free Mushrooms - We know that .

The learned Moth- Presumptuous too, ha !

Chorus of the free Mushrooms - Presumptuousness belongs to Nature: we were born that way .

The learned Moth- You don't say !

Chorus of ther free Mushrooms - We do say !

the learned sweet Gopher - But for how long do you all intend to carry on this stupid, insensate conversation?

Chorus of the free Mushrooms - For as long as this annoying, stupid, stuffy Moth will fly around us, bothering us and failing to mind her business .

The learned Moth- But that "IS" my business !

Chorus of the free Mushrooms - Oh ! We wish we would have a candle ready !

Chorus of the Candles - When lit, we spread a good light , for everybody and not only for the Moths, so, do not use our "attracting" luminescence for evil thoughts : a good, sobering rule of luminescence is let everybody shine for all they are built to shine for.

Chorus of the free Mushrooms - And what does that mean ?

Chorus of the Candles - It simply means, at least in our luminescent opinion, whatever its worth, that the light of a candle shows that the Moths know what's worth to look at in life or to be shown, by the light of a candle, the deeds, noble or base, of many famous and illustrious characters, as it was the case of a famous Swiss born creature, thinker , writer , philosopher ,who was born in the year1712 and died in 1778, when we, the Candles, reigned supreme in every household, be that of a pauper or be that of a King !

Chorus of the free Mushrooms - Did this famous Thinker and Philosopher live in the King's Palace, in the light of thousands of sparkling candles ?

Chorus of the Candles - No. Actually he happened to be in a garden, sitting at a small garden type table, set in a secluded yet comfortable and well attended shrubbery, and at the light of a simple candle, right in the open air and almost in the middle of the night, wrote one of the most beautiful passages of his imagination .

Chorus of the free Mushrooms - Is that why the moths fly so eagerly and insistently around a light ? Are they trying to come up with some inspiration, may be, and write some wondrous stories about the mechanics and meaning of flying around a light ?

The learned Moth- Pretty soon I'll fly something on top of your heads, just to give YOU some proper inspiration !

Chorus of the free Mushrooms - Nae, nae , now, let's not lose our cool in spite of the hot lit candles!! How about quitting "flying around" each other and each of us going our own way, along with candles, philosophers, writers and small tables recessed in cozy garden carrels ?

The learned Moth - I'll take you off the hook on that one and I am going to find myself an ancient candle, on a small garden table, in a small garden setting ,in a well manicured and cozy cubicle in that garden and hope to talk to the spirit of that famous candle !

Chorus of the fre Mushrooms - Atta, boy !.....Girl..??...Well, "Atta", anyway !......Now, that's talking !!

*** With some peace returned to the Forest, after the debacle of the Army of the Piedermi, the Giant Oak Tree and his Minister, our old Fabius, the Mushroom, find themselves still alive and spared by the horrible vicissitudes of war and revolt and happily renew their governmental ties which were so badly frayed by the inexplicable changes in the attitude and mental status of his Minister,old Fabius, the Mushroom, prior to the revolt...................and the Giant Oak Tree reacts to the annoying jabbering from down below ***

Giant Oak Tree - What is it that I hear blown to magnitude right to the top of my high branches, sounding like a cascading vortex of words upon words, sentences, refrains and more words on top of that and a continuous chit-chat down there, in spite of the hostilities being over....and, we hope!...for ever..!... and no word yet from Fabius, my trusted Minister, who exhibited some distorted and, possibly, pathological mental stress and strain due to the imponderable directions and uncertainties of war and revolution . Yet I would like to talk to him again, because he was very good and efficient at Government Affairs ! I wonder , now, if it could be him, to cause all that jabber down there !!

Mushroom (our old Fabius!)- Sire, it's nice to hear your voice again after all what happened, Heavens knows! Yes, Sire, I am your trusted Minister, down here, at the centre of your Kingdom, fortunately spared the devastating and gruesome horrors of a wide spread war !!... But , I am not responsible for the chattering noise down here !

Giant Oak Tree- And "hail " to you, old friend, and it is wonderful to hear your voice too, again, and you sound so peacefully and pleasantly disposed, an unbelievable , yet most welcome and joyful turn around of what your disposition had seemed to have succumbed to a dire reality of adverse times !.....So , I am "so"glad to hear you again !.....And you said that it was not you to favour all that noise down there, right ??

Mushroom - Right, Sire,it was not me. Actually ,believe it or not.........

Giant Oak Tree - Oh! do not worry , dear Fabius : the way things have been going on recently , I believe anything, I assure you !!

Mushroom - Well, the chit-chat was between our just discharged military personnel, our local mushrooms , and a petty and nosey Moth, supposedly learned and spirited in her aggressive social contacts, who teased the mushrooms and they answered back, causing the annoyance. Sorry about that, Charlie, but, perhaps, that candid debate on frivolous questions and statements gave them some relief from the stress and tensions caused by the war. So, no real major problem and, now, everything appears quiet and calm.

Giant Oak Tree - And a little bit of cam is what we really need after all that depressing sequence of , events !!

Mushroom - And I am glad to find you in good spirits and all through the agonizing hours of the impending assault of the army of the Piedermi, I was worrying if something of a disastrous nature might have happened to you : everyone knows when a war starts, hardly anyone knows why it started and, usually no one has any idea of when it will end, if it will end and what will the score if, eventually, it will end. So , I am really comforted to hear you again and in such a good mood, Sire.

Giant Oak Tree - Yes, I feel a lot better, now that the situation has calmed down and it makes me somewhat more confident in looking towards the future, yet I cannot help to perceive a strange feeling of premonition of something still hanging in the air, a sort of a foreboding of some nature, the exact nature of it not clear but persisting !

Mushroom - Yes, Charlie, I feel that way too in spite the fact that we all,You,I and all our folks in this Forest, are relatively well and out of any immediate danger now, but just by thinking back to the pronouncements made by the frenzied Worm and Centipede mob, slogans like : " hail to Liberty!", " Down with Tyranny ", " Death to all who oppose us!" , " Death to the mushrooms", and, do not overlook the fact that they included You too in the specific selection of their targets, shouting with all the energy left in them and over and over, again and again :"Death to the Giant Trees", "Down with Tyrants" and adding, just for completedness of their fair intentions:"Down with the Mushrooms, shamefully protected by the Giant Trees"! Charlie, and this is just like a little bit of "dust" on the bulk of the action !!

Giant Oak Tree - What kind of "dust", Fabius, are you talking about...??

Mushroom - Well, Sire, just a way to say that what I just said and the slogans so eagerly shouted by that mob were only a veneer of enthusiastic fervor, the hidden dangers behind it, not even known or even in the least perceived by that inebriated mob !!

Giant Oak Tree- But, Fabius, I do not understand : how could that"mob" be"ignorant" of what they themselves were promoting and hailing as their prime and prized yearning !!

Mushroom - Yes, Charlie, and that would be understandable if they,"the mob", that is, would have been and remained "just" "the mob", but they were ignoring, either because of pride or just sheer ignorance, and to even great danger for themselves, the presence of those two legged creatures, with two.........

The learned sweet Gopher - ....hands, two eyes, two ears and all these features packed in a bulky head gear, the inside of it, still highly questionable, at least in our personal Gophers'opinion!

Mushroom - Well, it's just amazing that some Gophers could see the problem while thousands of Worms and Centipedes and their Generals could not see it or perceived it ! And that is what I meant when I faulted the mob of the Worms and the Centipedes for being ignorant .

Giant Oak Tree - You may have something there, Fabius .

Mushroom - Something indeed, Charlie,and more!! Just think at the audacity and impudence of these hideous, loathsome Worms and their companions, those cock-sure, brazen show off braggars, the Centipedes, forming among themselves a league in order to muster a stronger force and attack and destroy me, just here, near your roots, and get a foot hold, the one hundred feet of the Centipedes would have achieved that kind of solid hold, and from there to attack you, Charlie, Your Sacred Majesty ! Just think of that, Charlie !!

The learned sweet Gopher- My dear and respectable Minister, Sir Mushroom Fabius, Chief of the King's Privy Council, I do not mean to be or bring forth any unthinkable disrespect to Your eminent Person, dignity or high status, but I feel that His Majesty should not be constantly reminded of the misery, the desolation, the untold suffering, the hardship and the depressing anxieties caused by the sinister spectre of this war and revolution .

The learned Moth- His speech and the enunciation of it are as bright as the flame.......Oh! shucks !...I do not even know if I should say it, but I'll say it just the same.........as bright as the flame of a famous old candle could have been !

Chorus of the Candles - Thank you .

Giant Oak Tree - Is that odious, annoying, irritating jabbering starting up again down there? Heavens forbid...!!

Mushroom - Fortunately not, dear Charlie !

Giant Oak Tree - But I just heard a lot of it, just now !!

Mushroom - Yes, but it was only the Gopher and the Moth trying to make a show of themselves by declaiming some stuffy sentences that rightly should belong to a style of times long gone by, when we, instead, and here now, in these present days, need fresh, engaging, strong new ideas and views for our future !

The learned sweet Gopher - In a simpler form as you had put it, of course, but that was what we had meant: precisely the last part of your remarkable speech, that is "fresh, strong, engaging new ideas".

Mushroom - But you had inferred, just before your speech, that the king should not be bothered with unnecessary lamentations about the war and the revolution.

The learned Moth- Precisely so,Sir Fabiuus.Why keep on hitting on what has been instead of thinking on a forward front for rebuilding what has been destroyed, reinforcing what's still standing and only slightly damaged and, in the process, fostering the confidence of the subjects of this glorious Kingdom ?! ....Of what has been , we all know: but it's what lies ahead of us that no one has a clear knowledge of .

The learned sweet Gopher - Demosthenes, the famous Greek stateman and orator,if still alive and present here, would probably be jealous of this"enlightened" exposition of facts!

The learned Moth - The above"enlightened "expositions , O Demosthenes !..wherever you are!..were not mine, as emphasized by our sweet and learned Gopher, but they were the famous candle's ones !....And I mean......that famous candle in the garden.......that kept the light shining in the middle of the night to allow a famous man to write...!!

Chorus of the Forest depressed Subjects - Strange !.....And it was only a few seconds ago that one of those jerks had just made a mention of wasting time flying around with a bunch of unnecessary words and talk , instead of thinking at practical and urgently needed matters !!

The learned Moth - That was only a way to give you an idea of what"flying around" really means .

Chorus of the Forest depressed Subjects - Wise Guys !

Giant Oak Tree - Fabius ! That annoying and constant jabbering down there does not seem to be ending at all !! Can we do something about it??!.....I can't stand it anymore !

Mushroom - I'll see to it promptly, Sire . But you must also understand that your Subjects down here in this Forest Kingdom of Yours, are anxious and fretful in the present post-war and confusion situation, that is one of want , lack of much needed basic supplies of everything causing considerable hardship secondary, as I had just said, to this tumultuous war-revolution combination-like catastrophe, and they find some solace by venting their concerns and anxieties........You see, Sire.......

Giant Oak Tree- I understand that, Fabius, but where are, then, the counselors, the managers of the supplies lines, the Government Coordinators, and, also, the members of the Forest emergency Services and the Police Department detachments, who, all together, should strive to bring some order and some stability in the general situation ? Where are they ?

Mushroom - Sire, there has been a war !

Giant Oak Tree - I am aware of that, Fabius !!....One reason more that those Departments should strive to do what they were created for : to reestablish continuity of function after a disaster. And their respective Chiefs should know better !

Mushroom - Sire, they are no more .

Giant Oak Tree - WHAT ??!!

Mushroom - Sire : they are all dead .

Giant Oak Tree - But how's that possible..??!!!...You and I, here, at the Centre of Government were relatively safe, how could they have been wiped out without anyone of us realizing it ??! This is terrible!!....Almost unbelievable !!

Mushroom - Sire : they were not here, within the Government relative safe enclave and its fortifications .

Giant Oak Tree - Ah ! I begin to understand now : they deserted, didn't they ?

Mushroom - Sire ; they didn't !

Giant Oak Tree - But, then , Fabius, you do nothing today but confusing me! Where were they, then? I wish you would come out with it, if You know the score of this puzzle !! These are no times for pranks or stupid jokes, Fabius .

Mushroom - No pranks or jokes, Sire . Let me explain : Sire, as you had ust said, You would have expected them to perform their duties, during these emergencies created by the war, the utter disorder and the violent revolution, precisely in the way they had been trained and they , Sire , did their duty as you would have wanted them to do and they went out, in the middle of that terrible confusion and danger, trying to see what best could be done under those stressful circumstances , to alleviate the pain and the hardship for those subjects caught in the destructive path of those maddening moments ! They performed their duties, Sire, admirably .

Giant Oak Tree - Ah ! They were heroes , then !! Oh ! Immortal Gods !.....Unknown Heroes !

Mushrooms - And they died like heroes , Sire !

Giant Oak Tree - Oh ! Gods !!

Mushroom - They were caught in the middle of the exploding hostilities and when the two legged creatures, the ones quite well known to the inhabitants of the Forests, those cruel and selfish ones with two ....

The learned sweet Gopher - .....hands and two.....

Mushroom - Enough of that , you impertinent little rodent : we are talking in the presence of the King !

The learned sweet Gopher - Sorry, real sorry ! But I was just trying to lighten the grim, depressing and sobering weight of the reality of what has happened .

Mushroom - Thank you, but enough of lightening reality efforts.......so, as I was saying, when the Foresters, yes, yes , those two legged monsters , opened up with the fury of their lethal weapons , it was like a "universal deluge" falling on top of them and they , unprepared as they were for that kind of warfare , were all caught by surprise by the sudden and powerful flow, an immense rolling swell of liquid from those innumerable spraying hoses and they were, all , swept away in the drain . No one ever saw them anymore .

Giant Oak Tree - Immortal Gods ! Thy Fury never ceases to humble the Creatures of this Forest !

Mushroom - They were loyal employees in Your Majesty's Governmental Force, Sire, and they were faithful to the sacred principles governing this Forest , faithful to You , to Your Kingdom and to their Land : yes, Sire, they were really heroes .

Giant Oak Tree - An official day of mourning shall be declared and a monumental tree, a Giant of Giants tree, will be dedicated to them . Fabius ?

Mushroom - Yes, Sire ?

Giant Oak Tree - Fabius,you will initiate the proceedings for the accomplishment of those declared honours , immediately .

Mushroom - Yes, Sire.

Giant OakTree - Thank you , Fabius , and at least it is comforting to realize that you are stiil here and able to help the Government with your expertise : I really do not know what I would have or, even, could have done without you after the terrible and disastrous events that we have gone through !

Mushroom - Well, Charlie, we can consider ourselves lucky, in a sense, for not having become involved in a direct fight as it had been originally planned by the combined Army of the Piedermi, that powerful Army that was formed when the two Generals commanding the forces of the Worms and of the Centipedes, agreed to merge all of their resources and "men-strength" together in one single armored unit under the name of the "Piedermi", that would stand for Centipedes and Worms combined army .

Giant oak Tree - A fancy name , indeed !

Mushroom - Indeed ! But, Charlie, what disturbed me most about their actions was the cheek and the contempt for a dismal lack of consideration for the Authority established by Mother Nature in regard to the various responsible and multiform functions of every being and creature in this Forest where we all live, more than their mean and pretentious desire to attack and destroy us all , unpardonably ignoring the very first rule of respect for the established sequence of priorities in the fulfillment of those allotted functions.

Giant Oak Tree - Indeed , an unpardonable and unacceptable breach of self respect and dignity .

Mushroom - Precisely, Sire , but, I am afraid that there is a lot more of an ominous content in that attitude ,very possibly a derivative contamination with the spreading way of seeing things in the Forests brought about by the greedy and insatiable desire of those two legged creatures, the human kind I mean, who don't think ever of anything else but to change things, modify things, distort things, and uproot things from the way Mother Nature had first put them all together .

Giant Oak Tree - A pretty stark and harsh assessment of the character description of those humans, Fabius , don't you think ?...... And are you sure about it ? Sometime, the worry,the anxiety, the very pitch of our perception, possibly shaken or deprived of some of its sharpness by untoward or unpleasant events, could distort the appreciation of things, of people and of facts .

Mushroom - Sire, not that I am trying or naively attempting to justify my "declaration", so to speak of, about the human creatures, but what I am saying is a direct "take" from the same human creatures slogans, when they began to clear up the ground from all those millions and millions of Worms and Centipedes, who were infesting the soil where they intended to go and work on the trees.

The learned Moth - Your Majesty, I vouch for Sir Fabius'declaration about the saying and intent of the actions of the human creatures, because we had heard those words too .

Mushroom - Sire, the interjection of the respectable learned Moth was not my idea, although, in a way, it represents the truth. It is true that we seem to have recovered from a situation of disorder and confusion and open warfare to one of relative calm and peace, yet by just examining the content or, as the human creatures call it, the significance, of what they were saying, the outlook for our safety and peaceful existence appears grim ,considering just one sample of their talk, like :" Our trees" and " Let us get rid of all those insects", meaning the Centipedes and the Worms and any of the wood-burrowing beetles, " that may damage OUR timber". and do not forget that emphatic "our" that implied a very dangerous trend in their intentions, Sire, and I felt that they were thinking of you and of all those beautiful large trees, Your faithful subjects, Sire !

Giant Oak Tree - My dear Fabius,be assured that I was not trying to question your thinking or your deduction in regard to the intentions and activities of those two legged creatures, the human beings, but I was only attempting to let a ray of sun and hope filter in the rarefied atmosphere of this present day, and, on the contrary, Fabius,I am very happy to hear your fears and that you confide in me about these worrying questions and I value your advice which I consider of vital importance to me because, tall as I am, I am too far away from the everyday happenings down there, where life stirs its course with its daily chores and it is difficult for me, if not altogether impossible, to follow closely all the aspects and events of life, on the very ground where you live and are exposed to the constant changes, happenings, news, gossips, trends and all kinds of thoughts of so many of our subjects .

Mushroom - Thank You, Sire, Your kind words mean a lot to me and certainly they do let a warm ray of hope filter through this sad day of mournfulness, yet my unabated concern about the intentions of those two legged humans are the result of my mental follow-up scrutiny of their own statements when they were saying over and over to each other how important it was to exterminate all of the insects before they started to "work" on the trees and get all "that good timber" before the insects could get to them and damage the potential value of "our timber", meaning You, Sire and all your other faithful trees.....and that Sire , is what's frightens me !

Giant Oak Tree - But, then, Fabius, this attitude,if true and correct in its meaning and interpretation is tantamount to a declaration of a revolution, an insurrection, including extreme violence and planned massacres , purely on the basis of a wicked and deplorable greed for affluence and wealth .

Mushroom - I would not be in the least surprised if that was "it", indeed ! That kind of refrain is one exclusive of the human race, Sire.

The learned Moth - Sire, we agree with the Mushroom, Your respectable Sir Fabius, Your Chief of Your Privy Council ,Sire.

The learned sweet Gopher- With utmost humility, Sire, I respectfully beg to be enclosed in that agreement .

A Passing Scholar on vacation from the famous University of " Gogetitburg" - The Historical Nemesis !

Mushroom - And what's that ?

Giant Oak Tree - Don't pay any attention, Fabius : it's an ancient doctrine .

Nemesis - But true , though .

Mushroom - Charlie, Sire:it has been a long day since the cessation of the hostilities! I see some of your subjects, the few remaining survivors of the onslaught of the war and disorder, slowly returning to their lairs to pick up what's left and start rebuilding some shelters for themselves, and , Sire, I feel very, very tired !!....Charlie, may we call it a day and a night and, may be, even two days and three nights.....!!.....to get some much needed rest and talk problems and politics tomorrow or even the day after tomorrow, just to be safe ??!

Giant Oak Tree - Fabius, you may take a full lunar cycle for resting, if you would like that, or you would want it, or you needed it ,all at your discretion ! It has been already great and good of you to have conversed with me and to have shared with me your thoughts, your worries and your ideas . So, go and have a good rest and, in the meantime, I'll listen out for you to inquiries that might come from our people.

Mushroom - Thank You, Sire . You certainly have a way to understand us , the little people !

Giant Oak Tree - Fabius , there are no little people in this Forest of ours and in this Kingdom under the immense sky above us : but only people .

The learned sweet Gopher - Wise words, Sire.

The learned Moth - Tut –tut , the wise Gopher !

The learned sweet Gopher - Well, why can't I be wise like, for example.......hm........YOU ??

The learned Moth - Simple : you cannot be as wise as I am because I am not wise. How's that for an answer ?

The learned sweet Gopher - Very stupid .

Mushroom - Now, now, Children! ...Time to rest a little and not throwing darts at each other!! Haven't we had enough trouble lately to waste time now in more trouble ??!.Calm down and act like proper Gophers and distinguished Moths !

The learned sweet Gopher - I agree, but I'm afraid it won't be easy for the other party.

Mushroom - Just try : O.K ?!.....And stop annoying us with your nonsense! Clear ?

The learned Moth - Clear as a mud pie, Chum !

Giant Oak Tree - Leave them alone, Fabius : they just "ain't" worth your, our, or anybody's time. Go and have a good rest instead .

Mushroom - Yes , Sire, and right away !

The same passing by Scholar on vacation from the famous University of "Gogetitburg" - Unimaginable as it may seem, yet the trend to hostility, animosity , confrontation and a "desire-like" mood to hurt, offend and denigrate , mentally , emotionally and even physically one another, appears imbedded in all created creatures as an instinct and, insensate as it may seem, an instinct clearly represented as a "need", like eating and sleeping . Strange, very strange, indeed !

Chorus of the strange Things - We may appear strange to you, likely, for two very simple reasons, not even catalogued in your famous University, O Passing by unlimited Scholar !

Scholar - I am not limited , for your information.

Chorus of the strange Things - First of all, Sir, we did not say "limited": we said "unlimited" .

Scholar - What's the difference! The way you said it was just a cover-up for really and wantonly say "limited"as you had thought but were cautious in saying it, and a deplorable, denigrating assault to my intelligence.

Chorus of the strange Things - What's that ?

Scholar - Ah ! Forget it ! You would not know the difference. Besides all that....who the Hell are you ??!

Chorus of the strange Things - Hell certainly not, for the simple reason that Hell is Hell and Hell is not strange, or it could not be strange even if you or anyone else would choose to look at it that way because, if it were actually strange, it couldn't be Hell, because "strange" denotes a questionable state of perception by the party who actually experiences that feeling and examines, probes and scrutinizes something or somebody. So.......

Scholar - You annoy me .

Chorus of the strange Things - And so do you, Mister : You annoy US too, you ninny! Do us a favour, Chum : go back to your University and "gogetit " the answers in your "burg".

Scholar - I resent that remark : rather personal, I presume.

Chorus of the strange Things - Not at all: that only meant go and get it at your Burg University , and, to the best of our knowledge, the name of your University was " Gogetitburg" University . Now, wasn't that the right name ?

Scholar - It is ,of course . Well, it was just a thought , and DON"T DO IT AGAIN !

Chorus of the strange Things - And how could you worry about us doing it again ,when the University is already done ! How could we possibly do it ?!!

Scholar - I hate these kind of vacations when instead of peace and relaxation you encounter, first a Forest ravaged by a recent war and revolution and, second, a bunch of idiotic inhabitants ! This is the most depressing environment in existence !

Chorus of the strange Things - There are worse ones, we assure you !

The Dean of the Gogetitburg Uni. Gentlemen! Gentlemen, please !!

The Chief of the strange Things - One of your scholars , Sir, has taken the advantage of the fact that, at least in his limited opinion, we are just "Things" and in doing so has caused us grivious pain and sadness and seriously affected our most deep-seated "sensitivity thing"and we, therefore, disdainfully reject your scholar's remarks about us .

The Dean of the Gogetitburg Uni. - I understand and I fully appreciate your well presented complaint, yet, in this Uni. and in the light of what University means, that is its Universality, we cannot or should not censure our Scholars for their personal opinions, except for having some reservations about our vacationing Scholar's appraisal of things, that being his personal opinion, of course . I , and with me the entire Staff of this University, wish to assure you, Sir Chief , that "WE" do appreciate things , very much .

The Chief of the strange Things - You do ?

The Dean of the "Gogetitberg" Uni . - But , of course we do ! We do things, we manage things, we think of things, we compare things, we devise things, we object to things, we dream of many things, we would like to have many things, we always wish for things, we hope to acquire things, we, sometime, dispense of things, or, conversely, we acquisition things, we even wear various things, we look at things, we imagine things too, and we get involved , often , in too many things and, in doing so, unfortunately, at times, we get all muddled up in difficulties, probably the same way our vacationing Scholar became muddled up in his better reasoning, and That , is another thing .

The Chief of the strange Things - We appreciate your frank, honest, educated, wise and appropriate response, Sir, and we consider that response a good thing. Now, in regard to your Scholar, we understand : he may have had too many things in his head and the juggling of all those things, that you probably would rather better describe as "ideas", might have affected his better judgement .

Chorus of the Judgements - He who has the best judgement, throw the first thing .

Scholar - You see, I am not the only one to pass a witty thrust at you !

The Chief of the strange Things - Yes,we understand that,but why to add more bad things to what is already known not to be a good thing to say ?

Chorus of the Judgements - That's good judgement, at least in our opinion .

The Dean of the Gogetitberg Uni .- Gentlemen and all concerned, it was nice to be with you, all of you, exchanging ideas and indulging in active and interesting conversations with all of you, Things, Scholars , Judgements and all and we enjoyed immensely the subtle exchanges of ideas and we acted in the light of that Universality that embodies itself in the Universal approach to thoughts, to thinking, to Things, in the form and aspect and substance of a University .We hope, now, that these here illustrious and respectable Things will be satisfied and will go along with us in advocating an old way of settling differences among civilized things as we all are, by saying"let's let bygones be bygones"and enjoy the fairness of the fine privilege of speaking freely, responsibly and in an atmosphere of conscientious conscience. And now, all this said and done, is nice for all of us to have a rest and go to sleep in an adequate manner, and that means "adequately"...... and.....

Chorus of the Scholars of the University of "Gogetitburg" - BRAVO !!

The Dean of the "Gogetitburg" Uni. - ......AND HAVE A GOOD REST .

Chorus of the Scholars of the University of "Gogetitburg" - BRAVO TWICE !!.....Hurrah..!..Hurrah !..."BRAVISSIMO"...!!

The learned Moth - People, generally, love being or pronouncing themselves in emphatic manners and foreign languages slogans, proverbs or just simple words, thinking that the lingo variation will add to their intended projection and effect of the meaning attached to it . Incidentally, "bravissimo" is the superlative form of "bravo" in the Italian language, and it means, probably closer than any other translation , "clever" or "smart", and in this case, "very clever" or "very smart" but , in the jargon of the Moths, it does not carry the same exact intended projected meaning as it does in the Italian language where it indicates something between"good, clever or smart" and, yet, not quite so, as it includes, in its expression and underlying subtle texture, the association of some form of "courage" in it, either because of the tenor of the presenting occasion or because of the character of the promoter of that enthusiastic exclamatory sensation.

The restful Dodger- Wisely spoken words, so , now, we can go to sleep........unless the ants will start to bother us !

Mushroom - Good Heavens !!...And where and when did you hear that ??!

The restful Dodger- In the land of Antaplenty, near the infested marshes of Pavengo , as I was making my way towards your Forest .

Muishroom - But, how did you learn of the possibility of the ants being up to some questionable antics , worth worrying about them ?

The restful Dodger - As I went through their land of Antaplenty,and reached the Capital of that Nation, the City called Comantcomall, the major avenues of that City, the façades of the main buildings, the large columns , were all literally plastered with large signs urging the population to gather together to watch a show and a parade of their best units of the armed forces on the occasion of forthcoming dramatic and far reaching announcements by the Queen and Her Staff , and there was a great coming and going of everybody as if something of unparalleled importance was bound to happen right there and then .

Mushroom - Do you suppose that they may be planning some expeditions in some far away lands or a voyage of discovery in some yet undiscovered lands ?

The restful Dodger- It is hard to say : besides the ordinary ant in the streets did not have any idea of what was going on except that they were all excited for the unexpected occasion and were hurrying in order to reach the preferential places to hear the news .

Mushroom - Did you notice anything else that could have suggested some ominous aspect of that excited atmosphere or it was just an enthusiastic appeal for the forthcoming of the Qeen's announcement ?

The restful Dodger- I really did not pay any attention to either of those possibilities : I only noticed the excitement and that was all and I continued moving on my way . What happened after I left, I do not know.

Mushroom - Thank you ,Mister, for your kindness and information and, may be, we won't have anything to worry about .

The restful Dodger - May be so . Good night .

Giant Oak Tree - Fabius, I heard you getting on in a tight conversation with somebody, so I did not want to interrupt you, while you were talking, but, now, you seem to be free, so all I wanted to tell you was to wish you a good rest and a good night rest : have a good rest, Fabius !

Mushroom - Thank You, Sire: I really need that rest and I hope that it will be"restful",because I have a vague feeling that something is brewing and that brewing may not be made out of the best ingredients.

Giant Oak Tree - You never stop worrying, Fabius, and that is not a good way for relaxation and rest.I noticed that whenever you talk to some strangers you always come up, later, with some fears and apprehensions purely motivated by an after thought of what information that stranger had shared with you : isn't that right, Fabius ?

Mushroom - Sire, I do not know much of "after thoughts", but it was what that stranger told me that made me worry a little, even if, I admit, unnecessarily.

Giant Oak Tree- Well, that's how it is, sometimes. But, Fabius, first of all, tell me, and I am sorry to delay your planned rest, but tell me : who was that stranger ?

Mushroom - Sire, he was the restful Dodger .

Giant Oak Tree - Restful Dodger ??!!....And where is this new fellow coming from ?

Mushroom - He does not remember that well, Sire.

Giant Oak Tree - That's rather strange ! Is he that old and sick that he is afflicted with a very poor mnemonic retention capability, or is he a little bit, let us say, touched in the head or something ?

Mushroom - No, Sire, that's not the case . The fact is that he is not particularly interested in paying attention to the names of places where he goes or travels through,like lakes or rivers or mountains and even cities and Nations he visits in his travels, except when something really unusual happens in those places that he travels through, as it happened just before he arrived to our Forest when he had passed through the Nation of the Ants and.........

Giant Oak Tree - Never heard of that Nation, Fabius , at least not in our immediate vicinity. As a matter of fact, I had never heard of it . Did the stranger recollect its name ?...And I wonder if he did, after what you told me about his lack of interest in those "tourist only" details !!

Mushroom - Yes, Sire, he remembered that, because, as I had told you, he would remember names of the places he went through, only if something unusual was happening in those places .

Giant Oak Tree - But, then, Fabius : what was the name ?

Mushroom - The name of the Nation, as he was told when he had asked for it, was Antaplenty, and he rested a while in the Capital City of that Nation, City of Comantcomall, a very beautiful City and, in that City , he saw some unusual and bizarre activities .

Giant Oak Tree - What unusual activities, Fabius ? Aren't we used to some of those"unusual" activities, here too, in our own Country ?

Mushroom - Yes Charlie, to some extent, but, and apart from the recent revolution, our unusual activities were of moderate size, scope and intention , while the display the restful Dodger saw in the City of Comantcomall , were specific with a clear referral to a military parade and an official announcement by the Queen herself, a rare and,indeed, very "unusual" event in the Nation of the Ants.

Giant Oak Tree - Well, did our glorious stranger listen to the Queen's announcement ?

Mushroom - No, Charlie : he couldn't be bothered with it and left before that happened .

Giant Oak Tree - But, then, Fabius, what is all this fuss about a situation no one seems to know a blasted thing about it ? We need facts, Fabius, if we want to formulate something positive out of only superficial observations by a ......vagrant Dodger !!

****

* Suddenly, a Guard bursts into the King's Chamber and cries:
" Sire, the Ants have crossed our Northern Border " .

Giant Oak Tree - Soldier, are you sure of your report, lest the fatigue of your dramatic run from the border might have confused you to some extent and caused you to misinterpret the real meaning of the errand you were given to deliver to me ?

Soldier(-lieutenant)
"Zphyr" - Sire, truly, I am fatigued: it was a determined, desperate run, but the message was and is still very clear in my mind : "Sire, the Ants have crossed into our Northern Territory and We ,at the border Garrison, had not received or heard of any orders from your Ministry in reference to the legality of this unexpected, sudden entry into our territory by a host of Ants and preceded by a powerful force of armored soldiers Ants and, that, in itself ,was the reason why the Governor of our Northern Territory sent me here.

Giant Oak Tree - But, couldn't have the Governor contacted us for directives and information?

Soldier(Lieutenant}
"Zephyr" - Sire, he tried, but all communications were down, we could not establish any contact whatsoever and we were left with no alternative but to send me here to ask for directives on this urgent problem, Sire .

Mushroom - Ah! The Dodger was right ! There was indeed something unusual brewing in the Capital City of the Nation of the Ants !

Giant Oak Tree - Quiet, in the Chamber !....Soldier....

Soldier(Lieutenant)
"Zephyr" - First Lieutenant Zephyr, Sire.

Giant Oak Tree - Lieutenant, did your Commander know of why and how had the Ants crossed into our Territory ?

Lieutenant Zephyr- Yes, Sire , and this is what he told me to report to you which is what the Ants had told him !

Giant Oak Tree - Go ahead , Lieutenant .

Lieutenant Zephyr- Sire, my Commander said a high ranking Envoy from the Queen of the Ants own personal Secretariat, had approached him bearing an official document signed and sealed by the Queen herself, declaring that Her Majesty the Queen, upon hearing of the violent hostilities erupting in our land , had decided to come to our aid with her powerful Army and help us defend our territory . It added that this help had an expected two way purpose, one to help us defend ourselves and the other to prevent an attempt by the Worms and the Centipedes, to invade their land , should have the Army of the Piedermi been able to break through our defenses and reach their borders . For that reason her Majesty the Queen had instructed her armored units of the Soldiers Ants to cross the border and come to our aid.This is what the Commander said and this, Sire, is what the Commander told me to report to You.

Giant Oak Tree - Thank you, Lieutenant ! You are excellent in expressing messages and I am grateful for the important information received .

Lieutenant Zephyr - Thank you , Sire .

Giant Oak Tree - One thing , though, perplexes me , Lieutenant .

Lieutenant Zephyr - And what is that, Sire, if I may help ?

Giant Oak Tree - It makes me think a little. The hostilities were over when the Ants entered into our territory from what I can figure out by your given report by matching mentally the probable time of their crossing and the annihilation of the Army of the Piedermi, who was attacking us, and it just dawned into my mind how could they claim that their crossing into our land was intended as a double edged action to help us and them at the same time, on having heard of the hostilities even when unable to reach us for informations, so, I am asking myself, how could they have heard of the hostilities and not of the cessation of them ? That's what's perplexing me !

Lieutenant Zephyr - This may be of help, Sire, and it happened just a couple of days before they started their crossing of our border, when two soldiers Ants were intercepted near the border who, when questioned, said that they were a forward patrol on the Queen's orders, to investigate and report to her of the developing situation since they could not establish any link with Your Ministry.

Giant Oak Tree - But, Lieutenant, weren't these two soldiers detained for further evaluation ?

Lieutenant Zephyr - No, Sire : they were let go because we had no orders or any instructions towards a situation of emergency in our Nation as we could not establish communications with your Ministry either, and the two soldiers' papers were in perfect orders, so we had no alternative but to let them through and go back to their quarters .

Giant Oak Tree - Then, they must have known of the cessation of the hostilities !!!

Mushroom - That is exactly what the Dodger had thought ! Very "unusual" activities, Sire !!

Giant Oak Tree - "Unusual" is too lenient and too accommodating a description for what it appears to be deceitfulness, wickedness, and a blatant, brazen, heinous act of treachery !

Mushroom - My feeling of premonition, Sire, unfortunately, is proving to be right .

Giant Oak Tree - Lieutenant : thank you for your magnificent effort in providing vital information to your King and its Ministers on the serious and ominous situation which is likely developing further in a darn dangerous situation, one of open and covert aggression and, after you shall have satisfactorily recovered from the exhausting expedition from our far away Northern Borders to our Government Sites , you are free to choose either to remain here with us and help us in planning the strategy to prepare for this new emergency or you may choose to return to your garrison at the Northern Border . Irrespective of your choice, I herewith and in the presence of my Minister and Chief of My Privy Council, declare you : " Captain Zephyr " of the border Guards and recommend you for the " Branch of the Forest" medal of honour for your bravery, courage,endurance under aggravating circumstances and your encomiable sense of duty .

Lieutenant Zephyr - Sire, did I hear you correctly? Did you say "Colonel Zephyr" ?

Mushroom – (to himself) - (Let us help this poor worn-out bugger!!) - No, Lieutenant:the King said :"General Zephyr".

General Zephyr - Thank You , Your Majesty ! Your obedient Servant.

Giant Oak Tree - Thank you, General .

Mushroom - A brave soldier, Sire, a worthy member of your elite entourage!

Giant Oak Tree - Yes, Fabius, our Nation is blessed with its brave soldiers. But, now, that we are faced again ,or so it appears, with new dangers, what kind of action can we take to overcome this new treacherous assault ?

Mushroom - Well, Sire, the way I see it we do not have a great many of valid choices at hand !

Giant Oak Tree- Could you name a few, right now, just out of your hat ?

Mushroom - Well, Charlie, although my hat is pretty large yet it doesn't hold inside a "mecca" of choices.......although, I guess, one of those possible choices could be to appeal to the two legged creatures, you know, the human creatures, and ask them to take care of the ants as they did with the Worms and the Centipedes, this, I am afraid , a very long shot, because I hardly believe that they would be greatly interested in doing it, even through appropriate incentives and WHICH incentives that being in itself quite a question, but, anyway, I seriously doubt that they might be interested on the basis that Ants do not constitute, really, a major problem or obstacle to their harvesting wood and, the other choice would be to welcome this invasion of ants, offer them hospitality, cordiality and friendship on the same level as they did with us by seditiously crossing the border and entering our land with armed forces on the pretext to come to our aid, offer them some incentives and try to induce them to undermine the human creatures and their cutting-equipment by infiltrating it and making it worthless, causing the two legged creatures to become furious and open up their lethal hoses and thus destroying all the ants . Now, which one of the two choices would be the more likely to succeed, that, really, I do not know or would dare to guess !

Giant Oak Tree- Brilliant idea, Fabius, brilliant .

Mushroom - Which one, Sire ?

Giant Oak Tree - Either one, Fabius. Brilliant, Fabius, brilliant.

Mushroom - Thank you, Charlie, but they might not work, in spite of their brilliance.

Giant Oak Tree - It would not matter,anyway. At least we are thinking, and we are not losing our cool, we stand united with brave soldiers with us and we are not in the throngs of panic . Therefore, noble Fabius, I declare you "Knight of the Super Forest" if your plan will work , a well deserved recognition .

Mushroom - Sire, I do not aim and I do not covet for honours that I feel I do not deserve : my thinking, planning and preparing are only guided by my patriotic love for our land, Sire, Your Kingdom and our national pride .

Giant Oak Tree - That alone makes it one reason more for you to deserve it , Fabius ! So, let us see if that set of choices will work . I believe that we should start with some covert contacts with high ranking leaders of the Ants, reaching, in the end, the Queen herself .

Mushroom - Yes, Charlie, Sire : a very good idea .I'll give instructions to our Secret Services to start the initial tentative contacts .

** Meanwhile, in the territory of the Forest just entered by the advanced armored Units of the Soldier Ants, an Officer addresses in all earnest the soldiers...................................... **

1st Officer of the Ants armored Unit - Soldiers ! I expect of you obedience, loyalty and dedication . You are in a land yet unknown to you, a foreign land, that has been ravaged by war and revolution lately and we do not know for certain if any remnants of the fighting Armies may still be at large .So , you must be on maximum alert and be prepared to respond in a well directed and instantaneous manner and with maximum force, if threatened or attacked . But if the atmosphere and the surroundings would, instead, prove friendly and peaceful, then put up your best comportment and show that you are "friends" and not "invaders" and then start digging into the rich ground : they would not know the difference !

Chorus of the armored Soldier Ants - Hail, Chief !

1st Officer of the Ants armored Unit - You, Corporal, signal the Queen's Staff and entourage that the mushroom appears to be mature and that orders will be given to begin the excavations as soon as we will receive the Queen's approval to procede .

The Corporal (reporting to the 1st Officer) - Sir, the Queen has given orders to attack immedely the roots of anything that has roots and of the thin fibres under the mushroom, particularly the ones of the large mushroom near the Giant Oak Tree, from gallery Number 2 . Simultaneously the orders are directed to the immediate attack to the lairs of the Worms and of the Centipedes, now that they appear either dead or in a deplorable state of confusion and semi-torpor or almost stunned to immobility. These were the orders, Sir.

1st Officer of the Ants armored Unit - Soldiers! You have your orders ! Long live the Queen !

Chorus of the armored Soldier Ants - Hail , the Queen !

*** As the soldier Ants begin to work and dig deeply below the ground, following the Queen's orders, the Mushroom reports to the King (the Giant Oak Tree..!), that his first contact with some leading Ministers in the Queen's own entourage were unsuccessful.He had been told that some serious situations existed at that moment at their border to the North where some turbulence and some form of a " protest-rebellion " type of uprising by the snails about the new taxes on their dwellings, had started and all the branches of Government were extremely busy... and to call later.......!! ***

Giant Oak Tree - Well, Fabius, were you able to make any progress in the tentative secret approach to some leading Figures in the Ants' Government ?

Mushroom - Yes, Charlie, and no Charlie !

Giant Oak Tree - That's a mighty strange report, Fabius..!!!!

Mushroom - I know, Charlie, and it really is ! ...And so was the laconic response from my first low contacts with some Agents in the Ants' Government Secret Services, quoting their Superiors with instructions to be given to me in ....

Giant Oak Tree - Mighty cautious and almost suspicious in their behaviour.....!!

Mushroom - Well, Charlie, and, here again, yes and no !

Giant Oak tree - The way you put it, Fabius, it sounds to me like a very strange acting kind of Government !!....Were they hostile, Fabius ?

Mushroom - No, Charlie, they were not in any way hostile or rude, but they said that they had their antennae busy at a maximal and almost dangerous vibratory pitch because of problems in their Northern Borders ,where the local Snails' Minority was causing a lot of problems .

Giant Oak Tree- !!........................Did you say........"snails"...Fabius??!

Mushroom- Yes, Charlie, unusual as it sounds but it sounded rather strange to me too when I heard about it, and ,even stranger, because undoubtedly true .

Giant Oak Tree- Unusual and intriguing at the same time! I did not know that there was a Snail Minority living up North, at the extreme limits of the Ants'Nation and, to a greater extent, what is so surprising to hear is of a "revolt" by snails because, slow as they are in every movement they do, it's hard to believe that they can "mount" any extra movements, least of all a......"revolt"...???!!

Mushroom - Those were the instructions the Government Secret Service Agents had received from their Superiors to be handed to me.

Giant OakTree - Well, you hear of something new all the time in this Forest ! But, then, Fabius, did they tell what was the reason, if they knew it, of course, for the Snails protest ?

Mushroom - Yes, Charlie, they seemed to have an inkling of what is causing that protest .

Giant Oak Tree - A serious matter, I presume .

Mushroom - It did not appear so, Charlie, as far as the Government had seen it, but, probably of great importance to the Snails.

Giant Oak Tree - Fine, Fabius, but, now, please, come out with it !!...With you, getting news, is like trying to uncork an old bottle without a corkscrew .

Mushroom - But, and "Usually", Charlie, those bottles have very good old-fashioned corks and they, the bottles ,the ones of course with those good corks, do not want to lose them .

Giant Oak Tree- Ha ! Ha ! Ha !....very, very funny, old chap !! but, now, try to be prompt in your answers and tell me :" WHAT were the Snails protesting about ??" , Fabius ?

Mushroom - It appears that the Snail Minority at the Northern Border is staging a massive protest over the recent increase on the taxes for their dwellings in the lands where they are located .

Giant Oak Tree - But, Fabius, the snails' dwellings do not sit on or occupy any ground ! How can it be taxed at all, in the first place, and worse still, the fee increased !!!!......It would seem something like taxing anybody just because they might happen to carry a backpack !!!

Mushroom - Of course, there is nothing anyone can do about it, since it is the Ants'Country and they make the Laws. Now, as to the wisdom of those Laws and of the ones who enact them, that's a different story .

Giant Oak Tree - How true , Fabius ! But, then, now , and apart from all that , what are we going to do or, rather, what CAN we do ??!

Mushroom - The way I see it , Charlie , there isn't really much that we can do.....except........

Giant Oak Tree - Yes, Fabius , ...except ...?!.....What..??

Mushroom - Except , I had just thought of it, now,...except for us to try to send some Envoys , secretly, of course, to the area up North where the Snails Minority , apparently, is up to some"no good"for the Ants Government but, may be, they could do some "good" for us, instead .

Giant Oak Tree - What do you actually have in mind, Fabius ?

Mushroom - Well, Charlie,when I received from the Ants'Government Agents that information about the protesting Snails in the place where they live, located close to the Ants Northern border, an idea came to me to see if that situation could, may be and in some ways, be turned into our favour and help us out of this stressful and injurious situation with the Ants.

The learned Moth- Our Golden Book of Luminescence, kept and guarded jealously in the deep caves of our Elders, tells us to always be wary of ants and snails, the former ,but too fast and furious, the latter, far too slow and placid .

Giant Oak Tree - This blasted Moth does not leave us or anyone else alone ! Why couldn't she look after her own damn business, instead of bothering everybody else'!

The learned Moth - "To bother or not to bother, that is the question"would have said a famous ancient poet, but, since that poet is no longer here and other existing Poets, at this time, have not bothered or can't be bothered to answer that question, I declare the harsh invective thrust at me by His Majesty the King a respectful, humble and totally void of any malice insult, worth of his Majesty's blessing.

Giant Oak Tree- Very well : be blessed and get going ! GIT OUTA HERE !!!

Mushroom - Well, Sire, the blessed Thing, the Moth I mean, does not know any better, so it's not worth it worrying too much about her .

The learned Moth - Oh , YEAH ?

The Peregrine Moth- Leave them alone, O learned Moth : they ain't worth a zack !

The learned Moth- But,You , peregrine Moth, whatever your name is, but what you just said "zack", is pure Australian slang !! How could you have known that expression ???!

The Peregrine Moth- My name is Matilda and I was born in the land by that name of Australia .

Giant Oak Tree - Well, Fabius, going back to our discussion about what to do or what we can do, in this dire situation with the Ants after the uncalled for and rather rude and stupid interruption of our conversation by an even stupider Moth,........

The learned Moth- Oh, YEAH ??

The Giant Oak Tree- If you don't clear out from my presense in five seconds, I'll have my Guards to put you in jail .

The learned Moth- Oh, YEAH ?

Giant Oak Tree - Guards ! Arrest this Moth !

Officer of the Royal Guards - Sire ! How can anyone catch a flying Moth ?

The learned sweet Gopher - Simple, by just catching "it" !

Giant Oak Tree- Idea ! Idea!

Mushroom - Sire ! I hope it's a good one !

Giant Oak Tree - Guards ! Arrest the Mushroom ! He has insulted me !

Mushroom - But, Sire, I was praising you, not insulting you !

The learned Moth - The Peregrine Moth says that the Big Tree wouldn't know the difference between insult and praise and that's why you have so many troubles in your land .

Giant Oak Tree - Guards! Arrest the Peregrine Moth !

Officer of the Royal Guards - Sire ! I do not have that many Guards around me ,sufficient in number to catch and arrest all of these Moths, Mushrooms and anyone else that might still come up for the same treatment !

Peregrine Moth - Pay no attention , Officer: your King cannot reckon numbers, people or situations, because, although a King, he is only a tree made out of wood, his head made out, of course, of the same material so he cannot think, conjecture or discern complex problems, that's why he constantly asks his Prime Minister, the Mushroom ,for advice, unable himself to think of any ,in any form, by himself .

The Learned Moth- ALLELUIAH !! Finally, some much needed wisdom from down-under !

The Learned Sweet Gopher - That assumption would not be valid, exultant learned Moth, because its meaning would be upside down, therefore incomprehensible by anyone in this Forest situated on the opposite side of the Poles ,of the Forests, of course .

The learned Moth - Incomprehensible my foot, wishing I had one, of course; anyway "foot" stays and marks my answer and it stresses the pure nonsense of what you just said ,you smart Aleck !!

The learned sweet Gopher - My talking is just plain reality, my dear elated Moth ! How could you read an upside-down message ?

The learned Moth - By simply standing on your head .

The learned sweet Gopher - That would be very uncomfortable and hardly achievable if you happen to be suffering from arthritis, old age or be in a very crowded place .

The learned Moth - But it is not necessary to go to all that trouble to read an upside-down script ! Did you ever had to stand on your head to eat an upside-down cake ?

The learned sweet Gopher - I give up !

Officer of the Royal Guards - Sire ! Shall I escort those two disturbers out of the Royal Chambers ?

Mushroom - Charlie, please, listen to me and I do not mean to imply that my saying is loaded with any significant or impressing meaning but , believe me , let us forget about Moths and Gophers and let us keep, instead, our sharp focus on the actual and pressing problems !

Giant Oak Tree - But, Fabius, these two crazy "skunks" are bothering us to the limit and they don't seem to have any inclination towards the idea of leaving either !

Mushroom - Sire , Moths and Gophers have been around for a very long time, since this Forest was born, and have lived in many ,many more Forests before this one was born and, to all practical notions available by scientific research today, they are expected to be around for a long, long time yet . We get rid of one and ten more will show up , so why don't we let go of all that almost unavoidable nuisance and, instead, pay serious attention to our problems which, at least in my limited opinion, are far more pressing, demanding and serious than to pay our attention to some verbal duets between a Moth and a Gopher that, although colourful, yet do not carry the essential ingredients to either alleviate or right out solve our present situation . Besides, Charlie, nobody really knows what their existence and the meaning of that existence really means .

The learned Moth- He has Spoken !!..Alleluiah !

Officer of theRoyal Guards - Sire ! May we return to our barracks ?

Giant Oak Tree - Yes, Officer, you may .

Officer of the Royal Guard - Thank you, Sire . We will still keep an alert and watchful eye on the developing story,Sire, and on the two Disturbers , Sire.

Giant Oak Tree - Thank you, Officer , You are dismissed .

Mushroom - Now, Charlie , back to the more important business of the Ants and Snails ! Finally !!!

The learned Moth - In our Golden Book of Luminescen............

Mushroom - Look here, Chum ! We.......

The learned Moth - Heavens above !!...He called me " Chum " !!!....The irreverence, the audacity of these times !!..".O Tempora, O Mores " would have cried out some famous old Roman of high civic status !

Mushroom - OK, OK, well ,listen here you Chum Moth.., I wanted.......

The learned Moth - Even Worse ! I'll have to fly away and find myself a more civil and gracious place to fly around !

Mushroom - Wise thinking , chap Moth ! Wise thinking , indeed , and let me add that we wanted to tell you and your partner ,the Gopher, that we love you like we love all of the citizens of this Forest, but, learned as you are, you should know ....and I hope to bring up to you some historical Biblical Recollections......so, as I had said, imbued as you are with all your knowledge, you should remember the old story of a certain old man of antiquity, of an antiquity of long, long and long ago, by the name of Job, who was well known and admired for his almost unbelievable endurance in exercising his patience regardless of the degree of sufferance, difficulty and pain and his submission to the will of his God in bearing all of those afflictions planned for him by his God , but, you see, I am not Job and, the King is not God , so my patience may not be unlimited and the king has already enough problems on his head to think of finding some more to try our patience, and , having said all this, now here is the moral of the story : if you have any salt left in your head, please be smart and take a hint and, if by some unknown reason, you should not know what a "hint" means ,then......" GET OUT OF HERE !! "

The learned Moth - "Hint" being taken, processed, analyzed and found valid . So, we, Moths, are displeased with creatures who do not like us and we have a distaste for flying in places which are inhospitable, and permeated with selfish prejudice and, based on that analysis, I decided to leave . SAYONARA !

The Learned sweet Gopher - Now is my turn to say "Alleluiah" !! ...and sayonara to you too , you old goat !

The learned Moth - I hope all of your teeth will fall out so that will fix you for good .

The Peregrine Moth- Do not worry, O learned Moth ! If this Gopher will persist in his uncalled for nasty attitude , I'll summon a pair of Tasmanian Devils and they'll take good care of him .

** The Moth and the Gopher are preparing to leave **

Mushroom - Sire , I believe that the Moth and the Gopher have ,finally, got the right idea and are leaving : for how long I do not even want to dare guess it ! Anyway they are leaving and we might have some peace at least, for a while .

Giant Oak Tree - Well done ,Fabius, well done !!....So, now, back to the Ants and the Snails .

The learned Moth - In the Golden Book of.............

Officer of the Royal Guards - Out with you, damn Moth, or I'll shoot you down !

Mushroom - She left !! Astonishing ! Sire , Your guards are good, resilient, quick thinking Guards !

Giant Oak Tree - Fortunately so, Fabius . In these trying times we need something " astonishing" every once in a while to prop up our badly sagging spirit .

Mushroom - Well, Sire, picking up from where we had left our conversation, discussing and thinking what could be done about the difficult situation in our Forest, created by the deceitful entering of the Ants through our borders and the uprising or protest by the Snails up North , I had come up with an idea about the snail situation and leaving aside, for the time being ,the ants, possibly taking care of them later , and on that account I had.......

Giant Oak Tree - A plan, Fabius ?

Mushroom - Well, Charlie , not really a plan right at this moment , but just an idea .

Giant Oak Tree - I am anxious to hear it, Fabius !

Mushroom - Well, Charlie, here it is : I have been thinking if we could , somehow , interest the Snails to continue their revolt and also increase the tempo and the intensity of their movement, even at the risk of some sacrifices, which, naturally, would be amply compensated by us, and it occurred to me that, if this approach were accepted and implemented by the protesting Snails, the developing subsequent situation in the Northern border of the Ants Land could become serious enough as to make it imperative for the Ants to send sufficient numbers of troops to take care of what might loom as an insurgency, requiring a significant amount of Force to control it, even suppress it, thus requiring, likely, the withdrawal of their troops from our territories, and I wondered if this plan could , may be, and , I repeat, just may be, have any chance of success .

Giant Oak Tree - It seems to me a plan, Fabius, that could really have a good chance of success, because it makes sense in the sequence of the possibilities that would develop within its impact : that is very good in its ideation. The only difficult section of its application would be the projected contact with the Leaders of the protesting Snails, their understanding of the plan and the assurances of our support and remuneration for losses and their willingness to go ahead with it, without counting the possibility of some negotiating overtures by the side of the Ants Government , which, if favourable and successful, would make it unnecessary for the Snails to continue their struggle, leaving us to hold the....sack !

Mushroom - I agree with you on all the issues, Charlie, but, then, what other choices do we have for us to become so cautious and choosey, while the Ants are going on with their excavations and it might not be too long, yet, before they'll reach us too !! There is an old foreign language proverb, Charlie, which I had learned at school in my Foreign Language class, that says, in its foreign language version:" mangiar questa minestra o saltar dalla finestra !", which, literally translated, means :"either eat this soup or jump out of the window " .

Giant Oak Tree - A rather clear cut proverb, Fabius , even for a foreign language .

Mushroom - Well, it wants to explain that, if someone is caught in a difficult situation and needs help to get out of it and the possible and, may be , even the only available choices come down to only one, in this case represented by the soup, and he does not want to eat it or take a chance with it, then the next and only alternative will be to jump out of the window,not a pleasant prospective, particularly if you would not know the exact distance of the window from the ground.

Giant Oak Tree- You , Fabius , would have made of yourself a fantastic promoter for selling goods!...Well, it seems to me that you are suggesting that we take the way of the Snails and try our luck with them .

Mushroom - At the moment, Charlie, I believe that to try this route would be better than "jumping out of the window",......" for sure " !

Giant Oak Tree - But, Fabius, do we have in our diplomatic arsenal sufficiently trained Agents that could infiltrate the Northern Territory of the Ants and try to make contact with the Leaders of the Snails ?

Mushroom - I believe so, Charlie. I know myself of some of my own family of mushrooms, able and capable chaps, skilled in the art of contrivance and disguise and experts in foreign languages and extremely able technician in the handling-dispensing of powerful contraptions and venoms. I believe that they could be successful in their covert operation .

Giant Oak Tree - In a general view, the plan appears desirable even if highly risky, yet, as you had just said..."eat this soup or jump out the window !!!", so the water is reaching the brim of "our jar" and it might flow over at any moment !.....Fabius, your plan may be the only way out for us from this complex and damn situation .

Mushroom - I have given a lot of thought to it and, Charlie, I agree that this appears to be, may be, our ONLY solution to our stalemate . Charlie: shall I give orders to initiate the covert operation ?

Giant Oak Tree - Yes, Fabius, with my full aprroval and support .

Mushroom - Very well, then , Charlie. Your orders will be carried out immediately .

Giant Oak Tree - And , Fabius , please do not overlook to inform the secret Agents that they have my full support, admiration and confidence in their skills, patriotism and love of Country and that this Kingdom, "their Kingdom", will be always grateful for their dedication to duty and the defense of the Nation.

Mushroom - It will not be overlooked , Sire, and Your wish, Charlie, will be carried out.

Giant oak Tree - Good .

^ ^^^^^^^^^^^^^

*** The Northern Territory ***
of
The Nation of the Ants

** In the heart of the enclave
of the Snails Minority Clan
two local snails are engaging
in an exchange of views, upon
hearing of the recent commotions
in their midst and abroad **

Ostanavia - Come back into the house, Slidenova : it is dangerous these days to stick your head out of your house and look and scout to pick up some visual glimpses of what's going on !........and I believe that "something" is going on , Slidenova !

Slidenova - The danger, these days , my dear Ostanavia , is just as real inside as it is outside , with so many ruffled tempers sliding around..!!.....Besides, how could you prepare yourself for building some protection from possible catastrophic developments or seeking a refuge , if you did not look around ?

Ostanavia - But you must have heard of the recent invasion of the Ants into the territory of the Forest, the Kingdom ruled by the Giant Oak Tree and his Minister, the Mushroom, Sir Fabius Maximus, didn't you ?

Slidenova - Yes , Ostanàvia, I had heard something about it but my mind and interest were primarily focused on the protest being staged by our Labour representations in the Capital , Comantcomall , about the proposed new tax on our dwellings,which we all consider outrageous, unjust and partial to our being a minority in their Nation .

Ostanavia - But what do our naive representatives dream of ? A handful of snails against the massive, coesive and interlaced system of the Ants'Regime?.To me,it just sounds like a very poor sense of perception, on the part of our representatives, like trying to attack an object that runs faster than them, as if they wanted to catch a ball fast running down a slope at the speed that we have been allotted to .

Slidnova - Yes, I understand what you are saying or trying to explain and clear up for me, but, I believe that there is more behind all this than just what the eye alone can see!

Ostanavia - What are you trying to say, Slidenova ?

Slidenova - Yesterday, after sunset and as darkness covered the ground , the watchman of the school of "The speeding Snails",you know,the one located to the far end of the territory and bordering with the extreme Northern border of the Forest of the Giant Trees ....

Ostanavia - Oh! Yes, I know where that is ! My niece used to go to that school, prior to the Olympics events in the land of the Lizards : she had a fixed idea that the snails, if properly trained,could favorably compete with anybody else in spite to my begging her to desist from such an impossible achievement, but to no use, because she kept on saying that there was an undercurrent of thought ,among her many friends at school, that the snails could win any competition if, instead to compete for the fastest run, the competition rested, instead, in competing for the slowest run and it was thought,without any hesitation,that the snails would easily triumph.

Slidenova - But this what the watchman saw had nothing to do with speed or competition for the Olympics or the Lizards, but it had something that he had never seen before and , in some ways, rather strange, almost with the appearance of mystery or some sort of secret meeting of some of our own Snails and, believe it or not, in the middle of a secluded, well protected patch of a thicket of trees, and talking, I am almost incredulous myself ....

Ostanavia - But, come on, Slidenova, come out with it !......Talking to whom..?

Slidenova - To some mushrooms .

Ostanavia - Are you serious ?....And where did these mushrooms suddenly come from ?

Slidenova - That's the mysterious part of the whole thing:it looks like a covert action . The first impression that our watchman had was of some mushrooms at the foot of some young trees . Even he, our watchman, a veteran of the Snails Scouts in his younger years and used to pay attention to details and to the unusual in the surroundings where he used to guide his Scouts, became curious of that peculiar sighting and,approaching it, could not find a soul there : no snails ,no mushrooms.

Ostanavia - But "somebody" must have noticed or seen something ! I have heard and, I am pretty sure that you have heard it too, that mushrooms , as the refrain goes, "grow over night", but.... Snails ?....Snails, my dear Slidenova, don't grow overnight, as best as I know, since I happen to be a snail myself and, apart from that, they also do not disappear or reappear out of a Cheshire Cat hat , so the whole thing is mighty strange indeed , unless..........

Slidenova - What ?

Ostanavia - Unless...the watchman was drunk.

Slidenova - I doubt it, apart from the fact that he does not drink alcoholic beverages, but, more interesting, the report of one of the free lance reporter of the "Liberty Press of the Toads", who, reportedly, saw the same thing the watchman did .

Ostanavia - What you say, if true, and, apparently it seems to be so, is terrifying !!

Slidenova - Not quite so, Ostanavia , based on what I have heard at the meeting, yesterday, of the wives of some of the Labour Representatives now engaged in talks with the Government about the new proposed taxes on our dwellings . Believe it or not, but I was led to believe that the presence of our Labour Representatives in the Capital, engaging in deep and serious discussions and contestations over the taxes, is only a cover in order to prevent those secret meetings between the Snails and the Mushrooms being discovered and they swore me to complete secrecy .

Ostanavia - Are you trying to tell me that we are engaging with the Nation of the Giant Trees in a covert movement against the Nation of the Ants to help us win our struggle for independence from the oppressing tyranny of the Ants ??!!....and did they tell you who those mushrooms were ?!

Slidenova - Yes, Ostanavia: are Secret Agents of the Forest King, here to sound our resolve .

Ostanavia - A King to ask for our "resolve" ?! Resolve for what? Slidenova, I do not like it !

Slidenova - I do not like it either and I am wondering where, actually , is leading to !!

Ostanavia - But, Slidenova, if the King is trying to find out the "consistency" of our resolve,it must be for some reason, particularly if he thinks that the strength of our resolve is so important to risk sending his secret Agents on a covert contact operation with us, in an apparent quite complex operation, don't you think so ?

Slidenova - That, Ostanavia, is what , in final analysis, it appears to be .

Ostanavia - But, if REALLY so, this situation , then , it is "NOT" terrifying !!

Slidenova - May be not, Ostanavia . At the present moment, of course, it is hard to tell if it is a good or a bad thing, but ,after a cautious, sober and considered thought, it may hold a flickering light of hope for our freedom, justice and independence .

Ostanavia - Slidenova , I have a feeling that the flickering light of hope will grow to a bright flame of luminous reality .

Slidenova - Let us hope so ....and that would be for us an impossible dream come true !

*** Meanwhile, back at the King's Chambers, the Mushroom informs the King that the initial secret contacts with the Leaders of the Snails Protesters has taken place and it is promising success............ ***

Mushroom - Sire , preliminary steps for contact with the Snails up North are under way : initial procedures examined by both sides, most accepted and will be implemented as soon as orders will be issued and reached by the protesting and rebellious groups of Snails, now organizing themselves into fast and agile fighting units under the command of Grand Marshal Rudolphfienolov , the Hero of the famous battle of Paris where the Snails had their glorious victory over the famished , starving folks during the French Revolution , who wanted to round them up and guillotine them for refusing to sacrifice themselves on their tables for the cause of the revolution .

Giant Oak Tree - It looks as if your plan, Fabius, may be working after all ! Let us hope that the Snails will maintain the momentum of their initial enthusiasm and resolve to fight for their cause, which is now becoming ours too !

Mushroom - Momentous times, Sire .

Giant Oak Tree - Fabius, what level of preparedness and training do these fighting Units of Snails have ?

Mushroom - Excellent, Charlie, under the direct instructions and guidelines of Grand Marshal

Rudolphfienolov .

Giant Oak Tree - Then, Fabius , we should let, now, some of our secret, elite, Reserve Guard Units, of our Main Garrison, now closed in behind fortified defense structures, to go out of their posts and, secretly, may be under the stealth of the night, as the Roman Legions did in the ancient history of the Republic ,when it was illegal for any armed bodies to walk or exit the City of Rome in full day light, and march up North by the uncharted route through the mountains, and join the Units of the insurgent Snails .

Mushroom - Under whose command would they be, Sire ?

Giant Oak Tree - If acceptable to our Commander of the elite Guard Units, it should be under the command of the Grand Marshal of the Snails, Rudolphfienolov, whose battle proven strategic and tactical skill would also benefit our own Guards .

Mushroom - It sounds like a logical proposal and I believe that our Commander will accept it : he is a good soldier and is used to obey orders and accept them when sensible and for a good reason.

Giant Oak Tree - Then, Fabius, give the necessary orders for the initial phase of the entire plan .

Mushroom - Yes ! Sire .

*** Back in the Northern Territory enclave of the Snails, some perplexing news are trickling down from the chat and gossip of old maids and nervous Gophers who are complaining about their tunnels and caves being run over by armed intruders heading towards the Northern borders.. ***

House Snail - Well, good morning, Nelly, how are you ?

Office Snail - Very well, thank you, Jeanie .

House Snail - And how are things at the office, Nelly, these days ?

Office Snail - Oh!, You know, we keep on going ,struggle on so to speak, there is some tension lately in the place and everybody seems a little on edge, may be the weather !

House Snail - Well Nelly, did you hear the latest news ? They were broadcast last night by the Chief of Communications, the white Owl , and what she said sounded awful !

Office Snail - My goodness, Jeanie, you frighten me !..Come, now, how bad could it have been?

House Snail - Bad enough, Nelly ! Bad enough, really , to cause great apprehension among us, defenseless creatures in our houses and it really scared the hell out of us !

Office Snail - But what "so terrible" did you hear, dear Jeanie, to cause such a terrifying fear ??!

House Snail - Nelly, it all started last night after the white Owl announcement that a revolution was being on the verge of erupting, here, in the Northern Territory, according to information trickled through the grapevine of some poorly identifiable sources .

Office Snail - Those sources, Jeanie, if not accountable for, are just as good as NO news,or even fraudulent news, sometimes put out by underground saboteurs to spread panic and cause confusion in preparation for something else . Besides, how come we, in the Office, did not hear anything about all that ??

House Snail - Nelly, I agree, the information was not an official Government notice, yet it mentioned, in an inquisitive form, that there was some reliable suspicion that the Kingdom of the Giant Trees might be behind it : I repeat, Nelly, I agree with you , that many a time these kind of curious news are proven, later, to be false, but, these ones, for some strange reasons and "feelings",seem credible , and that's why we, locked defenseless in our houses, became very, very worried about it all !!!

Office Snail - As I said, Jeanie, we, here in the Office, did not hear anything of that, but, let me tell you, in all confidence, that as far as I am concerned, I would not mind to take a peep at one, I mean to a revolution, just to see how it looks .

House Snail - You MUST NOT BE SERIOUS , Nelly...!!!!

Office Snail - My word, that I am, Jeanie !...I mean, SERIOUS !!

House Snail - How can you, possibly, say a thing like that, Nelly, or you must have forgotten that you are, just like I am, a SNAIL !!!

Office Snail - I have not forgotten anything and, in order to alleviate your apprehension about me preserving the ability to see myself and identify my image and specie, I can tell you that I "definitely" realize that I am a SNAIL and ,at the same time, I still would like to see a revolution, just to see how it looks.

House Snail - That's all nicely said and done, but you, dear Nelly, are overlooking an essential point in your desire to see a revolution, which, it seems to me, was prompted by the possibility of one erupting right here .

Office Snail - What am I overlooking, Jeanie ? I just told you that I fully realize that , I too, am a snail .

House Snail - You are "overlooking"the fact that, we snails, are able to see only the revolutions of the future .

Office Snail - What are you saying, Jeanie ??!!!..The Revolutions of the..FUTURE...???!! That's absurd, Jeanie !

paste Snail - Yes, Nelly, the Revolutions of the future and what I am saying is true and real .

Office Snail - I just can't believe that you can come out with a statement like that..!!

House Snail - More than a statement, my dear Nelly, is a reality because, you see, slowly as we are allowed to crawl along by Mother Nature's issued capabilities, the revolutions which occur today are already past and gone, as far as we are concerned , by the time we could reach and see them or partake in them .

Office Snail - Well, the way you see this whole thing it might work just fine because "this" revolution has not started yet, so, if I can get going now I might be able to arrive there just as it starts and, if not, well, Jeanie, we know how changeable and irritable most creatures are, so I will always be in time to see one, any one .

House Snails - Nelly, you seem to be made out of a mixture of happiness and pessimism, all at the same time. I wonder from where did you inherit that kind of character ?

Office Snail - I don't know, Jeanie . May be Traditions ? History ? Inheritance ? Experience ?.... Who knows ?

House Snail - So young as you are,Nelly, and boasting of experience ? Traditions, Inheritance, History, well I accept that, but "experience", Nelly, that seems to me a little far fetched , even for a snail !

Office Snail - But forget about "MY" experience : I was referring to the Experience, Traditions, Inheritance and History of my Ancestors .

House Snails - I grant you that interpretation which, at first, had just slipped through my mind, yet, even traditions, history, inheritance must have some positive links with a significant past to be of a demonstrable value, right ?

Office Snail - You are right, Jeanie, and let me explain why I said those things, if you are interested to know !

House Snail - I am, Nelly and I'd love to hear all about it .

Office Snail - Very well, then, Jeanie, you must know that my Great Grand Father and my Grand Father were both French, born in Paris and lived there all their lives and were there at the time of the famous French Revolution and died for its cause .

House Snail - Oh ! Nelly, I did not mean to bring back such sad memories with my preaching and warning about revolutions ! How could I have known of your heritage and past Family history ? You'll forgive me for this, won't you, Nelly ?

Office Snail - But, of course, Jeanie, and don't you even give a thought to it ! As a matter of fact ,I found some solace in talking about these past events, memories that you cannot share with anyone except very close friends and, Jeanie, I believe that you are my very best close friend .

House Snail - Yes, I am and I am very proud and happy to be your close and very best friend !

Office Snail - Thank you, Jeanie, and now I am going to tell you the story of my Great Grand Father and my Grand Father....

House Snail - Go ahead, please, Nelly, and do tell me !!

Office Snail - You must know, then, that my Great Grand Father and my Grand Father on that fatidic day of the 14th of June,1789, were having their usual walk along the walls of the Bastille, that famous and fortified old medieval castle that had been and was currently used as a prison for political prisoners, when the revolution erupted in all its ugly fury .

House Snail - Oh ! Terrible !

Office Snail - Yes, terrible and blood-curdling, but ,of course, not so for everybody because for the revolutionary it was a triumph of their long suppressed aspirations and a hope for reforms and freedom from hunger .

House Snail - Yes, Nelly, I remember when I was at school , our teacher explaining to us how, years before, some famous French philosophers and writers and one, in particular, by the name of J.J.Rousseau, had postulated ideas that reflected the serious social imbalance prevailing in those days that eventually exploded, literally, into a grisly orgy of blood !

Office Snail - Those were the dramatic days of the French revolution and its Terror, that seemed to have no end, until a soldier by the name of Napoleon, an artillery Officer, put a stop to it and took charge of the whole situation, but this, now, has taken us away from my Ancestors, so, going back to them, as the revolution.......

House Snail - Were they badly involved in it, Nelly ? Were they in a terrible danger ?

Office Snail - This might surprise you, Jeanie, but to the contrary !

House Snail - But how could they be out of danger when everything around was upside down and nobody, I think, really knew what was going on, as the whole thing started !!

Office Snail - You must know, Jeanie, that my Great Grand Father and my Grand Father, had some revolutionary spirit in them, simply because they were witnessing as special messengers for the Courts and various Government Offices, some frequent and high handed decisions in favour of the rich and aristocratic folks , while fairness and impartiality were often denied the poorer or the "lesser"! So, when the Revolution erupted , my Great Grand Father and My Grand Father, following the impulse of their hearts towards the ideals of that revolt against despotism and injustice, joined the revolutionary movement.

House Snail - Ah !

Office Snail - Unfortunately, when they arrived eventually to the Headquarter and the Offices of the Supreme Council of the Revolution, Roberspierre had already been guillotined and the Reactionaries were already on the way to turn things around ....

House snail - An almost incredible story, Nelly !

Office Snail - But true, Jeanie .

House Snail - What happened then ?

Office Snail - What happened then ? At the pace they were travelling, of course, when they arrived at the Headquarters , the revolutionaries were gone and the Reactionaries were already in.......

House Snail - Had they had time to realize that and stop in time before presenting themselves into those Offices ?

Office Snail - They were not sure, so they retreated into their houses and waited but the police became suspicious of them, took them in and they were recognized as revolutionary, summarily charged with treason against the State and condemned to death .

House Snail - How terrible, Nelly, how very terrible ! Were they guillotined ?

Office Snail - No, they were sentenced to be stewed, instead .

House Snail - Good heavens !

Office Snail - Yes,Jeanie, a real sad, dramatic end to the lives of good and better deserving men, but nothing sensible could be practiced in those days of no sense at all, with only the hope of trying to be above water in that ocean of madness, violence and total absence of any straight reasoning or fair play ! Their stewed bodies were thrown into the prison cells occupied by some supporters and sympathizers of Roberspierre, who were waiting execution, and these two Ancestors of mine were divoured by the prisoners who were starved almost to death , and to think that these prisoners, at the beginning of the Revolution, had been my two Ancestors' best friends,but, in the midst of that dire, devastating and dehumanizing condition, since those prisoners were humans, they had lost their sense of comradeship which always flourishes when everything goes well !

House Snail- Lor'an' Mercy ! What an infamous act !

Office Snail - Yes, dear Jeanie, that was a day that ,really, as a famous statistician and President of a Great Nation once said on the occasion of a similar deceitful and murderous event by enemies, " a day that will live in infamy", and so it was, but, looking back at it from our "distance", now, that so much time has gone by, may be it all boils down to one single word and that is : "destiny" .

House Snail - How true is what our teacher at school used to tell us little ignorant pupils, that words not only are well adapt at distinguishing and illustrating things and facts but they also can be monstrous weapons in their subtle and erosive power in the destruction, manipulation, alteration and falsification of facts and things,inclusive but not exclusive of even the most sublime instincts and achievements of living cretaures ,not to mention the vituperation of the dead ones too, and how very limited our intellectual resources really are when , after my long explanation of the power of words, we can only come up with a single word"destiny" to describe and identify a tragedy that not only affected two lives but that of thousands upon thousands in all ages of life in the known history of living creatures, snails included, of course . Words, harbingers of doom or glory, but we, snails, have not figured out ,yet, their true intrinsic value or need to be needed at all , in the first place .

Office Snail - You may have something there, Jeanie, because frequently , at work, people come out at you with such expression as"be careful what you say" or " watch your language"and, most preferred item in the vocabulary, "shut your mouth", so , I just wonder....who invented words ?

House Snail - Of one thing I am pretty certain !

Office Snail - And what's that ?

House Snail - We didn't .

Office Snail - And Heavens be praised for that, Jeanie !!

House Snail - Excuse me a second, Nelly : but what is this noise I hear ?

Office Snail - Noise ? Where ?

House Snail - Yes, Nelly, and it seems to come from the far edge of the Forest where the trees' line ends and the meadows begin : I can hear it even louder, now !

Office Snail - You are right, Jeanie, I can hear it too ,~~now and it seems to be getting stronger~~. What could it be ?

House Snail - The revolution ? Do you think ~~that~~ the revolution has started ??...Oh! Nelly !!

Office Snail - It looks that way, although I cannot be absolutely certain right now .

House Snail - Can you see something, somewhere that could give you an idea of what might be going on, Nelly ?

Office Snail - I am not quite sure, Jeanie : I can see some glittering in the far distance that may indicate the reflection of the sunlight on some shiny surfaces .

House Snail - You don't see anything else ? No movements of soldiers or transports or something ?

Office Snail - No, Jeanie, none of that, at this moment. Sorry !

House Snail - But there must be something ! Oh ! Nelly, I am so afraid !!

Office Snail - Don't be afraid, Jeanie, and I'll stay here with you .

House Snail - Thank you, Nelly, you are a real friend and I am so ashamed to be so worried and panicky but I have a feeling that something big is bound to come and fall on us !

Office Snail - Well, if that would be the case, then the example of my Ancestors'story and their fate did not help much to curb the appetite for revolutions, not even the stories of the Great Great Grand Father and of his Great Great Grand Father and of the great Great Grand Fathers of the Great Great Grand Fathers . These young, excited and innocent Snails are eager to see a revolution at all costs so as to appease their unexhaustive curiosity !

House Snail - But, my dear Nelly, you surprise me by saying that because, at the beginning of our conversation, just as we had met, it had seemed to me that you had a strong desire to go and watch a revolution yourself, one revolution, of course, that had not happened yet, so that it could have afforded you plenty of room to get there on time in order to compensate for our slow going, or, may be, did I misunderstand you, Nelly ?

Office Snail - You understood me correctly, dear Jeanie, and it is true that I had expressed that desire, but, in the meantime, I have changed my mind .

House Snail.- Why, Nelly ? What caused you to think it over and abandon your plan ?

Office Snail - Well, Jeanie, after telling you the story of my Ancestors during the Revolution, the French Revolution, I started thinking a little, somehow in a clearer mood after confiding in you that gruesome story as if, by letting you in that little slice of our and their existences, had suddenly lifted a veil off my mind and I felt that my perspective seemed to be a lot clearer after I had told you the story than before I did .

House Snail - Incredible, Nelly !! But, then, what are you thinking ? What are you going to do ?

Office Snail - Yes, Jeanie : "what am I going to think" and, "what am I going to do" !! Two very big questions. I'll try to answer the firts one, first .

House Snail - Oh! Nelly, I did not mean for you to take it seriously ! I was just wondering whether, may be. you had decided to see this emergency situation through right here and hope for the best .

Office Snail - Jeanie, I have decided to stay here . I realize that we, snails, are rather slow in our moving around, and that is to put it very mildly, but, conversely and contrarily to common public opinion, we are quite resourceful and speedier with our heads, proof of it our two exquisitely sensitive and finely tuned antennae which alert us instantly of any errors of interpretation, or of decisions thought or not thought or which we should have thought and we did not, or which we should have taken , the decisions, of course, and we did not , plus the perfectly trained sensitivity of those antennae that tell us if it is hot or cold , they warn us when it is safe for us to get out of the house and go shopping or on a date, or instead to stay safe in the house if it rains or snows or the wind blows too hard and also they,those antennae I mean, can also warn you if........a revolution may be just around the corner !

House Snail - My dear Nelly, you certainly show a lot of skill at getting out of a contradictory situation !

Office Snail - Common practice in our office, Jeanie, I assure you, but, I would rather classify it more as a "office acquired adaptability" than anything else ! All this is not important anyway at this time. Let us listen if we can hear anything else: shall we ,Jeanie ?

House Snail - By all means,Nelly ! Besides it is not just out of curiosity that we want to listen to some sounds or look for some signs that would tell us what's going on, but for our own safety !.......Well, I hope that I didn't talk too soon but, Nelly, I seem to hear some chatting and some strong and loud talking down in the street leading to the Esplanade : was is not from that direction that you thought to have noticed some glittering shining as if the sunlight had hit some reflecting surfaces ?

Office Snail - Yes, Jeanie, that was the general direction: as you said ,somewhere in the direction of the Esplanade . Let us listen .

******

In fact, a crowd of middle aged local snails, somewhat past their prime, yet still resilient and full of vitality as well as hope, were coming through the narrow road leading to the Esplanade where , they had been told, the new Army of the New Snail Soldiers, were mustering. As they were going through the road, they chanted patriotic slogans, expressing deeply felt thoughts about the new soldiers, and heading swiftly to the Esplanade .

******

Chorus of the old maids slightly past their prime - Ah ! Those glorious, wonderful boys, fulgent in their new uniforms and with a determined look in their eyes and countenance and the poised serenity of their whole personality..........Hurrah ! Hurrah ! for the new soldiers ! Hurrah for the revolution , liberty and justice and death to the bands ! We are the daughters of the revolution !

House Snail - Did you hear those Ladies, Nelly ?.......They are loud......ain't they ?!

Office Snail - Yes, Jeanie, quite clearly too : they were chanting something that sounded to me like a mixture of patriotic fervour and an invitation to some different type of patriotic enthusiasm, more on the emotional, enticing, seducing sliding scale than straight patriotism, although, I admit, sometime, in life, subtle differentiations are not always possible or practical or attainable .

House Snail - But they are marching towards the Esplanade, are they not ?

Office Snail - Yes, Jeanie, they are and they seem very excited too and the ones who by now are closer to the Esplanade and are able to get a better glimpse of the soldiers seem even more excited than they were when we spotted them marching in the narrow road . I guess, Nature is with us even during revolutions .

House Snails - But, then, Nelly, that glittering that you saw in the far distance must have come from the reflection of the sunlight on some type of reflecting surface, like, I guess, a weapon !

Office Snail - It is possible, now that we know that there are soldiers gathering there .

House Snail - I knew it, I knew that there was something going on and I felt it even if I could not put my finger on it, borrowing that expression from the human creatures, who, sometimes and in spite of lacking antennae, are formulating some effective vocabulary. So, there is a revolution on the march, Nelly !

Office Snail - I heard one of those passers by saying that among those soldiers is also the famous Grand Marshal Rudolphfienolov, the victor of the famous battle of Paris, where the Elite Legions of Veteran Snails defeated the counter attacking Reactionaries.

House Snail - Let's go to the Esplanade too, Nelly ! We must not miss this opportunity to see a real revolution as it happens without having to wait for the next one . Never in my entire life as a snail I saw so much vertiginous development of events, a condition rather unusual for the character of snails, generally, used as we are to taste events that have already turned into history .

Office Snail - Well, opportunity, usually, does not knock twice at anybody's house so let's go and take part in this momentous event.

****

*** Nelly and Jeanie take now to the narrow road that leads to the Esplanade , following closely the crowd of the middle aged,, past their prime, yet still vivacious old maids of the local Snail subdivision in the land of the Ants, whom they usually referred to as Bands, short for Bandits,in a derisive,derogatory way so that they could not be arrested and possibly charged for a public insult to the governing Authority of the Land, but they also used that word"Bandit" as a "code word" that would let one know if the "other one" was also a creature set against the Oppressors Ants, by the way the other one would react to it . Having taken that sensible and rational precautionary and wise measure, the vivacious old maids kept on yelling at the top of their voices.. (these snails, by special permission of Mother Nature, following duly submitted request, had been benefited by a temporary rule, to express themselves with the sound of voice, an unusual commodity for snails, that is "if" spoken word and voice do really qualify as a commodity, but, anyway, they were granted the temporary function of voice in all its steps of modulation, because of the incumbent great event of the revolution and, also, it was whispered, to give them a chance at being heard and ,may be, make a good , even an amorous impression on some of the soldiers, sparkling the endless flickering light of love in their virtuous hearts as well as in the yet unknowing hearts of some of the soldiers.......and as we were saying, these enterprising old maids, while swiftly approaching the Esplanade, had kept on yelling patriotic and inciting slogans and "hurrah" like volleys from a thousand cannons !..

" Hurrah,for the new soldiers!", "Hurrah for the Revolution!" " Hurrah for Justice and Liberty!", "We are the Daughters of the Revolution !", "Down with the Bands"! , " Death to the Bands !"..

Officer ,
(any type or kind of a regular Officer, turning to whom it appeared to be the vivacious leader of the vivacious,past their prime,old maids) - What Bands , Madam ?

The leader of the vivacious old maids- The Ants .

Officer - You said "Bands".

The leader of the vivacious old maids - No, Officer : we think that we said : "Ants" !

Officer - I heard you saying " Bands ".

The leader of the vivacious old maids- Sometimes we call the "Bandits", Bands for short so as not to scare the children ; I wonder if that's what happened .

Officer - Madam, there are no Bandits here .

The leader of the vivacious old maids - There are many where I come from .

Officer - Where do you come from ,Madam ?

The leader of the vivacious old maids - From the Land of the Bandits, Officer.

Officer - Is that why you left your country and came to the Land of the Ants ?

The keader of the vivacious old maids - Yes,Officer and we hope that this revolution will wipe out those horrid "Bandits"!

Officer - Yes, Madam, and we hope so too!The Bandits are horrible, deceitful,despicable and very rapacious creatures and, we are confident that ,one day, they will be wiped out .

The leader of the vivacious old maids - Officer, you sound as if you too came from the Land of the Bandits !!

Officer - Not quite, Madam, but Bandits are not living only in the land of the Bandits and there are plenty of them everywhere and anywhere, not really Bandits ,so to speak of, but some other type of criminals who might be right here among us in this here land .

The leader of the vivacious old maids - That is why we call them "Bands" so that no one what we really mean except for those who hate Bandits .

Officer - That is true, Madam : but I must go ,now .

The leader of the vivacious old maids - Why ?

Officer - Duty calls, Madam and there is a revolution on the horizon .

The leader of the vivacious old maids - A Revolution...??!..And how do you know that there is a revolution on the horizon?

Officer - It is no longer a secret at this time as preparations are accelerating and our troops are taking up positions and everybody in the Esplanade is fully aware of that.

The leader of the vivacious old maids- But, then , are they fully aware that they may be fighting the powerful Army of the Ants ??

Officer - Madam, we are going to fight the horrible, despicable and deceitful ....BANDITS, Madam !

The leader of the vivacious old maids - Heavens be praised ! .....YOU ARE ONE OF US !!

Officer - Not so loud, Ladies !! The battle has not started yet and has not been won either, yet. The place is full of spies and the Army Units of the Ants who had crossed into the Kingdom of the Forest on a despicable and deceitful pretext, are on their way back, by forced march, trying to reach the Capital before we have a chance of capturing it. And , now, I must leave you to attend to my command . I do hope that we shall meet again.......next time ! I'm sorry but we do have a revolution on our hands !

The leader of the vivacious old maids. - It must be a very small one if you can hold it in your hands !

Officer - It is a way of saying things when you are sure that you have a good, solid hold on something !....Something in your hand !

The leader of the vivacious old maids - Ah ! We too would like to have a good ,solid hold on something !.....Something in our hands !!

Officer - Do you want to join our revolution ?

The leader of the vivacious old maids - Well, what we really had in mind was to join you !

Officer - And be a...... soldier ?!!,,,Why, you could not make it even if you tried !

The leader of the vivacious old maids - TRY US !

Officer - O.K, then ! Come along and we'll make some good soldiers out of you, sweet Ladies !!

The leader of the vivacious old maids - Agreed ! And we'll make very good husbands out of you , glorious soldiers !

Officer - W.....What ...???!!

The leader of the vivacious old maids - You keep your word and make good soldiers out of us and we'll keep our end of the bargain and make very good husbands out of you soldiers !

Officer - You must be crazy !!

The leader of the vivacious old maids - We, "your sweet Ladies"....as you called us, do not think so . You, Officer and "one of us" in creed and political conviction, you are a Veteran of the glorious Battle of Paris and you were with the Veterans in the Napoleon's Army in Russia and most of the soldiers, in those times, had their wives accompany them, so that they could have their shirts washed, their socks mended and their...spirit lifted when down a little .

Officer - I knew it !!...... I should have known it and I shouldn't have fallen for it !...Yet, there is a war, there is a revolution, so, why worry about such an everyday thing like a marriage ?......Come on, Girls, and on to victory , on to......well, to whatever else that might come along...!!.....And you'll never know, these days, what might suddenly come along !

Chorus of the old maids past their prime but still vivacious - Hurrah, for the new Soldiers ! Hurrah for the Army of the Snails!! To Victory! To victory ! To justice and to Liberty and, if we are lucky, to a happy marriage too, time permitting!

*** The Officer rounds up the vivacious old maids who are, now, very excited and escorts them to the mustering area and sets them in, quite comfortably,in some makeshift barracks , while completing the necessary procedures for enrolment in the ranks....................................****.

***** By this time, our two wondering snails, the House One and, the other, the Office Snail, arrive in the Esplanade, having followed the chanting old maids, past their prime yet still vivacious, and with bulging, wide-open eyes (these snails do have eyes in this story), try to embrace the entire swelling scene of soldiers, arms and armor, Standards and Colors flying in the early morning breeze, an overwhelming sight they could not ever have imagined in their wildest imagination to be at all possible in the Land of the Ants, certainly not in their life-time . *****

As they watch the developing of the various actions under way, the commanders seem to go around in a hundred directions, giving orders, shouting signals of alert, mustering the troops and the soldiers prepare for the passing in review and to listen to the address of Grand Marshal Rudolphfienolov .

*** At the edge of the forest, in a wide open field, a host of snails armed to the teeth......well, to the.....antennae, that is, is gathering in order and military fashion under the supervision of several Officers of the covert Guard Units sent by the Kingdom of the Forest in support of the uprising of the Snails and under the direct and overall Command of Grand Marshall of the Snails, Rudolphfienolov . ***

Grand Marshal Rudolphfienolov - Veterans of the battle of Paris ! Soldiers of the New Army of the Nation of the Snails, I bring you news of freedom and glory at your doorstep .

The armed Snails- Hail ! Caesar !

Grand Marshal Rudolphfienolov - Today is the coveted day of liberty and justice come true and you are Destiny's chosen architects of it ! Be worthy of this prophetic choice !

The armed Snails - Grand Marshal ! We, the Veterans of the battle of Paris, we shall march to victory with our Destiny, for our Destiny, to our Destiny and the Colours of the Standards of Liberty and Justice and the spirits of our dead Veterans will march in front of us and guide us through the new battle to total victory.

Grand Marshal Rudolphfienolov - Officers, take command of each of your assigned regiments and initiate the attack: the advanced scouts have reported that some elite units have already secured the large bridge leading into the City ,destroying the little Ant garrison who was trying to defend it . Once in the City, give the assault to the main Government Buildings and Offices and Communication Centres ,but pay extreme care, and I repeat, extreme care, in sparing as much as possible the civilian population. You have my full trust and the Great House of the Snails may accompany You !

*** The various columns of the army of Snails begin the march towards the bridge linking their territory to the City of the Ants, the Capital, Comantcomall............ while, back in the Giant Oak Tree's War Chamber, the Mushroom informs the King that the war has started up North and the operations are in full gear..... furthermore, reports from observers of the King's Guards, indicate that relevant numbers of soldier Ants are in the process of leaving, headed North, by forced march and hardly any Ants are around.......***

Mushroom - Sire, latest coded flash news from the Northern Territory by our elite covert Guards indicate remarkable progress of the insurrection with the advanced Units of the Veteran Units of the Snails already crossing the Bingle-Dangle bridge and infiltrating the suburbs of the City itself, with some scouts of saboteurs already in some Government Buildings and in the sophisticated Communication Building, the proud masterpiece of the Ants' elite engineers, making sure that no contact will be made with the Army of the Ants now to the South and trying to reach the Capital by forced marches but, it appears, with a very doubtful chance of success, if any at all .

Giant Oak Tree - Fabius, this is more than we would or could have expected out of our tentative and daring plan ,but it appears that, at least from these initial reports, it might have a promising chance of success and , I mean, full success.

Mushroom - Yes, Charlie, and let us not forget that, as far as our Scouts here assure us, no Ants can be found anymore, except ,may be , a couple of sick ones or elderly and hardly able to crawl . That is what we were hoping for when we were planning our mode of action and, Sire, apparently, IT PAID OFF !!!

Giant Oak Tree - It certainly did and this temporizing activity will increase our chances to cement our partnership in the control of the Northern Territory with the formation of the New Nation of the Snails, the defeat of the Ants and leave us free, then , to combat any other dangerous situations that might occur in our Kingdom .

Mushroom - Yes, Charlie. exactly so and I almost cannot quite believe it myself that everything went on so smoothly, so effectively and so quickly, so that the Ants had hardly any time to think things over, readjust their tactics, reorganize their supplies and prevent the occupation of their Capital, now, firmly in the hands of the Veteran Snails and Grand Marshal Rudolphfienolov, as per the latest coded message just in !

Giant Oak Tree - Well done, Fabius ! This is your hour, because you did it with you keen and clear vision of facts, situations and intended projections and, Fabius, do you remember when, earler, we were threatened by the deceitful crossing of our border by these conniving Ants and we were discussing various plans of defense and I had told you that, if any of the plans would work I'll make you "Knight of the Super Forest". remember ?

Mushroom - Yes,Sire, I remember .

Giant Oak Tree - Well, Sir Fabius, RISE ! Thou art herewith declared "Kight of the Super Forest with the Golden Branches"and you will be presented with a diamond Testimonial for your service and dedication to your Country, to your fellow Citizens of this Kingdom and to the Kingdom itself, including its King . Sir Fabius , I will also have the Privy Council work on a Law to make you my heir, in case of my death , and my successor to the highest Office in the Kingdom, so, Fabius,you'll be King!

*** Great jubilation in Comantcomeall, the Capital of the Northern Territory of the Ants, long lines of Ants seen marching in the streets taken prisoners by the Veterans of the Snails Arm, the standards of Justice and Liberty flying on top of all the major buildings in the City and on the Palace of the Governor in the main square.Rumors were spreading around that some elite Units of the Veteran Snails under the direct orders of Grand Marshal Rudolphfienolov, were in an earnest search for the Queen's Royal Chambers, trying to intercept the Queen herself so that she could be made to issue a promulgation declairing the hostilities over and proclaiming the formation of the New Nation of the Snails, which will comprise a territory between the lands of the Ants and the extreme upper northern border of the lands of the Kingdom of the Forest, this arrangement constituting a perfect buffer zone of protection for the Kingdom of the Forest in addition of having at the Northern frontier a friendly Nation and, so , achieving the Grand Plan that had been envisaged by the Mushroom.

** However, among the jubilant crowds, some elderly Snails seemed to have some different ideas about the turning up of the recent events and had second thoughts about war, revolution, customs and attitudes and anything else . **

Elderly Snail - Things were different when I was young and there was more self restraint and more self respect than these young brats of snails are able to show nowadays ! What is the meaning of all this shouting, yelling, chanting and boasting when, I am pretty certain, the majority of them do not even know why they do it .

Solitary Snail - Life can be pretty dull under a changeless, uniform, monotonous sky .

Elderly Snail - And who are you, so young and so bold to allow yourself to come out with such a depressing statement ?.And in a day like this one when our soldiers are marching proudly in the streets of the Capital and the Ants have been defeated! Why don't you join them instead of crying because the sky may be monotonous and uniform!

Solitary Snail - I wanted to, but the military draft rejected me .

Elderly Snail - I am sorry . I did not know that . But why were you rejected by the military, may I ask ?.....It was not for depression, I am sure !

Solitary Snail - It was because I had only one antenna .

Elderly Snail - But I see two antennae !

Solitary Snail - After being rejected, I had an artificial one planted by a plastic Surgeon, so that I would not attract other snails curious looks and unsavory comments .

Elderly Snail - Sorry! Really sorry !....Sometimes Nature, in all its Might and Perfection, can also be cruel to some of us .

Solitary Snail - I know .

Elderly Snail - How did you then cope with your disability ? Did that abnormality affect you deeply ?

Solitary Snail - I became very depressed and very lonely and I realized that the way you are and look can prevent you to be and act like all the others who are normal, so I retreated in my house and never wanted to get out of it again .

Chorus of the solitary Snails - Birds fly, crickets stridulate, grasshoppers leap in a saltation frenzy, crocodiles lie in a soporific rest, cuttle-fish ejects black-like ink when in danger, pigs grunt, and cows moo........why must we always be silent and move around at a "snail's pace" and always behind everybody else's steps ?.....And why do we always have to live inside our house even when we go out to take a walk ? The mouse has his/her lair, the horse has his/her stable, the eagle its nest, the spider spins its web, Penelope did do and undo her famous web, everybody goes here and there, up and down and side ways too, and that is the most often preferred and highly skilled performance, so, we are asking, why do we have to stay in our house even when we go out for a walk ?

Elderly Snails - What the devil are you talking about ??!!

Chorus of the solitary Snails - What is a devil ? We have never heard of him or it or her or what !

Elderly Snail - If you haven't , do not worry about it . It looks like that since you say that you have never heard of him, the devil, that is, then it is quite likely that you have not seen him either and it would take a lot of time to explain to you what he really is and what it represents and a lot of time, if ever, for you to comprehend why he at all is talked about, represented in our everyday language and not always thought of as a nice guy. Why don't you, instead, unravel for me all that junk that you were talking about, spiders, horses, mice and eagles and Penelope's web, pigs and birds...and whatnot ??!

Chorus of the solitary Snails - The solitary Snail, O Elderly one, will tell you better than we could because she too spun her own web, long ago.

solitarySnail - I do not know if I shall be able to do it but I shall try, encouraged as I am by the recommendation and support of my sisters Snails and get to the heart of that question which, in the end, has something to do with all of us and not only me.

Elderly Snail - Thank for your good nature in agreeing to explain it to us, at least trying your best to do it, and I am grateful for that and I am "all ears" too, even if snails do not have ears, so we are told , but is a conversational expression of some value that emphasizes the meaning of an intention, so , to cut it short : I'll listen to you !

solitary Snail - You must know, dear old Snail, that I have lived all alone since the day I was born and that was a long time ago. Around my neighbourhood I used to be referred to as an old maid, old spinster, but I knew that that was purely an outburst spun by envy and jealousy because my house was always shinier than most of the others in the neighbourhood and, also, because I never went out of my house . Since I was born I stayed and lived in this area and, you'll understand that it would not have been easy to find a husband staying closed in my house all the rime.

Chorus of the solitary Snails - That was due, in our opinion ,to lack of initiative .

solitary Snail - The problem was not of "initiative", but of the "lack" itself , if you know what I mean .

Chorus of the solitary Snails - We do not know what you mean .

Initiative - Good on you, you said it well .

Chorus of the solitary Snails - But, now, 'who' said it well ??

Initiative - The one who said it well, of course ! You Ninnies !

Elderly Snail - I begin to feel that the World is starting to spin backwards the way snails talk today or I must be dreaming !

solitary Snail - Both, my dear !!

Chorus of the solitary Snails - You are talking through your hat, that is if you had one and, since you do not have one, you should try to get one, anyway your talk is just nonsense,you stupid solitary Snail . With your incoherent as well as absurd speech you caused us to lose the thread of our main story which tells us of the great event of the war, of the revolution, of the victory, of everything far more interesting and appropriate to discuss and talk about than your stupid antennae, depression and spinster status telling us your story which has nothing to do with us and with the happenings in the Capital now, and completely out of our sphere of interest in it . If you stayed hiding in yourself as well as in your house, that does not mean that you, now, can claim or expect the attention and sympathy of the other fellow creatures who did not choose to remain stuck in their houses or feel sorry for themselves as you did. The birds sing, the serpents hiss, the lions roar, the cats mew, the elephants do some peculiar sounds too, so, why do we have to stay home even when we go out for a walk ? ....

(.....A learned group of Snails from the local University of Comantcomeall, in the Capital, just pointed out to me , - ..the writer of this story -, that snails do not walk :they prefer to slide, reference would not be repeated in the future . I assured them that this writer will take their complaint to his heart and make certain that, from now on, all snails will slide instead of walk and, upon hearing my emotional and deeply felt declaration,and feeling reassured and satisfied of the results of the meeting, strong in their legitimate assertion and vindication of their means of locomotion, they slowly slid away in the direction of the main square where great celebrations were under way .) .

solitary Snail - You too seem to have lost your best sense of direction by talking so much and so emphatically that you seem to have lost your breath ! Why dom't you follow your own advice and join those festive soldier Snails who might restore your breath as well as your petulance , instead of bothering me and prying maliciously into my private affairs .

Chorus of the solitary Snails - We ? We interfering ? Interfering into your private affairs ??!....Oh ! Never would we lower ourselves to such a despicable act of animosity towards a fellow snail ! Never ! You see, we observe things, event, happenings, fashions, characters of creatures, their attitudes, their interests, their faults, their habits and we do that not only with creatures who look,"slide"or think like we snail do, but with every kind of creatures and, believe it or not, even with creatures which are not really creatures in the sense that they move, eat and sleep and everything else, but those built complexes that go under the classification of "bodies", be they celestial or just some forms put together by forces yet unknown to us, like mountains, rivers, deserts, oceans and other strange bodies like figs, carrots, potatoes, onions, celery, nutmeg, pepper, squash and lettuce: you see, dilly-nilly Snail, we are eclectic Snails!..... For us revolutions, wars, discussions, dissertations, promulgations, edits, ethics, extra marital activities, inter governmental activities, no activities at all, madness, knowledge, building and destroying, thinking and sleeping, eating and starving, laughing and crying, running or standing, sitting or getting up, do not mean anything in particular but we take interest in all of them in whatever order they might come to our attention and it does not matter when all of those named facts, activities or representations did occur because, at the speed we move, any of the above, today, tomorrow, yesterday or all at the same time, stimulate the same interest in all of us because we never know when anything begins and when anything ends so that at our "vertiginous speed", that is in a reverse form, every single fact, every event, every thought, emotion, feeling, instinct, fear, joy, despair, elation, pride, love, dejection, ambition, humility, meanness, gallantry, honour, betrayal, madness and sanity, friendship and enmity, and, also, a pinch of salt, fail to evoke our direct interest in any of them particularly, but because of our semi-stationary stand, we can embrace them all and all at the same time and, just at the same time, extinguish them in our memory for the lack of a positive reaction to it or to them or whatever, because without a direct impact of extraordinary magnitude, memories grow weaker and, soon, will go to sleep .

solitary Snail - And ,for heavens sake, what does all this muddled mix-up mean ??!!

lonely Snail who was just listening - True ! The solitary Snail is right . What does all that big, long, tedious talk mean ?

Chorus of the solitary Snails - No mix ups, no muddled up things : really the whole thing is rather simple .

lonely Snail who was just listenung - You should have thought of that before you went on that monotonous tirade full of nonsense, out of place, out of any significance: and you call it "rather simple ?

Chorus of the solitary Snails - Yes, simple and we say that with regret because, in its simplicity, everything that was becomes, ever so slowly but relentlessly, a fading image which, finally, will disappear altogether because the original partners to that image shall have passed away or no one directly connected with that image, at the time when that image occurred and still living, would have any particular interest in it, and that goes for the pinch of salt too .

lonely Snail who was just listenung - I can't make head or tails out of it : honest !

Elderly Snail - I cannot really understand a blessed thing of what they are talking about and of what they have running in their heads !

Chorus of the solitary Snails - Ours is the spirit of "intuitive initiative" .

Initiative - Now, we have heard everything...!!!!!

Chorus of the solitary Snails - Honorable Snails, we have grown tired of this prolonged conversation with all of you and we bid you farewell. Although we are solitary Snails, we are solitary not because of character dysfunction but out of our own choice which we consider a wise choice, nevertheless the occasion of this fatidic day appears overwhelmimg and we shall visit the square, the Governor's Mansion, the theatre, the gardens, the rallies and the parades in spite of any of these things making any difference to us because we can still be comfortably set in our house whether we go to a rally , to a wedding, to a war, or a revolution and we still are at home even when going out for a promenade . So , goodbye, be good and soon will be night and a restful sleep is good and desirable even for revolutionaries .

solitary Snail - Unbelievable...!!....The emotional confusion of disorganized mental excitement !

Elderly Snail - Disorganized ?...Perverted, I'd rather say !.....Immortal Gods, have mercy on us !! This is the tenebrous twilight of the era of the Snails .

*** In the Capital, meanwhile, the Snail Authorities are busy enforcing order among celebrations and festivities, keeping the hot heads in check!! ***

*** While in the Capital, Comantcomeall, now firmly in the hands of the victorious revolutionary Snails, festivities and celebrations were under way, in other strategic parts of the Northern Territory of the former Nation of the Ants, work was moving ahead in great earnest by positioning, in several lines of alternating depths, powerful contingents of armored Snail Units and several contingents of rapid engagement assault Units of the Veteran Snails, looking to the South from the Capital, ready to intercept and rapidly destroy, should the occasion arise, the possible attempt by the powerful Army of the Ants to regain control of their Capital City and the Northern Territory, that Army of the Ants that had been reported as returning North towards their land by forced march, that same Army that, several days before, had crossed the Northern border of the Land of the Forest in a "bravado" like gesture as well as a deceitful move intended to invade the land of the Forest under false pretext and take over its resources . However , the Grand Marshal Rudolphfienolov's Headquarter had received secret coded messages from their advanced Snail Scouts indicating that none of the several scout Units, spread in a wide semi-circle projection of intense search, had made any contact or sighted any regular armed Units of Ants and it was surmised that most of the soldiers in the Ants Army Units had disbanded in all directions in the countryside either by direct orders of their Commanders to avoid capture or just by personal decision of each soldier, after realizing the failure of their mission . In a way this fact was considered a relief for the defense of the City, but ,also, a hidden worry , lest the supposed disbanded soldiers would, now act as guerrillas and commit acts of sabotage and stealth activity to undermine and even destroy the gains of the revolutionary Snails. For that reason, the Grand Marshal had given strict orders of maximum alert and had ordered a termination of all festivities while intensifying the search for the Queen and her Chambers.

****

In the Kingdom of the Forest, now free from anxiety and fear from the failed invasion of the Ants, things seem to get back in some order and the population is gaining some more confidence in the management of the relief efforts on the part of the Government and are receiving emergency supplies of victuals as well as monetary bonuses to help repair or rebuild their premises . Under these favourable circumstances ,the mood of the subjects of the kingdom has improved and the general atmosphere is one of tolerance, patience and content and the Giant Oak Tree is assessing the general situation.........

** The Giant Oak Tree, reassured of the returned stability in his Kingdom after the many convulsive disorders which occurred in his Nation, rebellions, revolutionary trends, Invasion of the Ants and the savagery of the two legged creatures of the human specie, resume his communication with his faithful and clever Minister, now "Sir" Fabius, the wise Mushroom, and tries to explain to him the unusual behaviour of the birds on his branches..

Giant Oak Tree - Fabius, good morning : is it not a beautiful morning , this morning !

Mushroom - A most beautiful and peaceful looking morning too, Charlie !

Giant Oak Tree - How are things down there, Fabius ? I understand, from your reports, that the general situation has greatly improved, things are returning close to near normal and our good citizens are resuming their usual activities and there does not seem to be anymore scarcity of provisions, yet, at least up here, there is , this morning, a lot of apparent agitation among the throngs of the usual birds perched on my branches, who are acting in a somewhat different way than they usually do every morning, at least that is what it seems to me .

Mushroom - May be, Charlie, they are just jubilant about the returned peaceful calm to our land and are exchanging their favourable impressions at each other !

Giant Oak Tree - Yes, Fabius, that could be the case, but there seems to be a little extra excitement attached to that representation of satisfied appraisal of the improved atmosphere in our land, noticeable in the way they have increased by a tenfold their jumping from one branch to another in an almost continuous going and increasing the tone as well as the duration of their shrills, chants and chirping, in a way that I had never noticed ever having happened before: indeed, a rather bizarre behaviour, even for birds. They act in a way that I could almost identify as being alarmed at something that "displeases" them !!

Mushroom - If that were the case, Charlie, like : "something displeasing the Birds", it must be "something" really big, coming at them and threatening them, I should think .

Giant Oak Tree - Possibly, Fabius . Anyway, whatever it is, it's certainly disturbing them to an almost intolerable pitch of their chirping and the general agitation has also increased noticeably .

Mushroom - Charlie, sometimes birds become so frantic and loud if a suspected shadow of a hawk slowly circling in the sky above them is noticed and the birds, fearing it, give a signal and raise the alarm and warning by a show of increased agitation and jumping from one branch to another in repetitive jumps along with that altered behaviour and sharply increased pitch of their chirping .

Giant Oak Tree - Now, that you mention some possible shadow in the sky that could have alarmed them, just a while ago there seemed to be something in the sky that you could say it looked like a shadow .

Mushroom - As I said, likely a hawk .

Giant Oak Tree - Well, it could have been a hawk, yet it behaved in a strange way .

Mushroom - Could you at all make anything out of it, Charlie ?

Giant Oak Tree - I am not certain, Fabius , but what I think that I saw , might have been precisely what had caused and it is still causing so much excitement and wild flutter among the birds .

Mushroom - Can you, Charlie, make out a description of what you saw and what you might still be able to see now ?

Giant Oak Tree - Again, not yet !....Well, not quite !.....But it seems a sort of a vague silhouette against the clear sky that now you see it and next you don't and, to the best of my observation, it seems a rather weird thing, flying in a peculiar manner and in two different directions at the same time in a zigzag course in its trajectory across the sky, turning sharply at an angle and diving and climbing without any proper respect to the rules of flying and at almost vertiginous speeds !!.......Fabius, I have never ever seen anything like what I believe I am seeing now !!

Mushroom - May be that bizarre shadow in the sky is a very big bird just escaped from a Birds'lunatic asylum .

Giant Oak Tree - Apart from your usual humour, Fabius, has anyone down there noticed similar shadows in the sky as I have seen them up here ?

Mushroom - Yes, Charlie, in a way, you could say that what was noticed down here, might be similar to what you saw up there, but with a caution and warning attached to it, Charlie !

Giant Oak Tree - Caution..?? Warning ?? Lord have mercy ! Is that shadow so foretelling of doom ??!

Mushroom - Well, Charlie, down here and on account of what everybody thought that they had seen, there is a great commotion among the little people because rumour has it that the Witch Queen, reportedly the Great Grand Mother of that famous

Centipede Warrior, Alambert Piedileone of the Piedileoni of Valcoccola, who died on the battlefield during the famous battle of the Army of the Piedermi, this name identifying the combined allied forces of the Centipedes and the Worms, the name being the result of academic research resulting in the shortening and compacting the two long...........

Giant Oak Tree - Fabius, I did not ask for a lexical dissertation on the origin, intrinsic value and meaning of a word, but only if someone else saw what I did see .

Mushroom - I know, Charlie, and that was exactly what you had asked me to find out, but it would be also prudent as well as safer to pay attention to the relationships involved in this particular case, relationships that could "really ZIGZAG " if not properly understood in their right perspective since we, probably and, also, likely, happen to know who the "Zigzagger"actually is . So , Charlie, let me finish my "lexical" illustration of the battle of the Piedermi and, then, we'll go from there .

Giant Oak Tree - Ah ! What patience must Kings muster these days to accommodate the whims of so many !!

Mushroom - As I was saying, actually, trying to say before being interrupted........

Giant Oak Tree - You may dispense with that, Fabius .

Mushroom - Yes, Sire!..Well, the name of PIEDERMI was a shortening and compounding of the two names, Centipedes and Worms, " PIED" of the " –pedes" of the Centipedes '"pie-de" ,Italian for "foot"from where the name Centipedes, a hundred feet insect.....and "ERMI", again from the Italian word for Worms, as " VERMI, the academic brains successfully forging the name "PIEDERMI", the happy result of intense academic study and applied scientific expertise.

Giant Oak Tree - Fabius, I do hope that this is not the end of this extremely interesting and all encompassing study !

Mushroom - Oh , no ! Sire !.......and, yes, it was a memorable battle that of the Piedermi near the village of Dingbangboo which lies a short distance from the City of Boobangding...........

Giant Oak Tree - Fabius, it seems to me that you are rushing through your narration .

Mushroom - Sire, I don't know what you mean !

Giant Oak Tree - Well, in a properly and serious description of a passage or a situation or a location, whichever, and, in this case, you forgot to tell me how far was the distance of the village of Dingbangboo from the City of Boobangding! That, Fabius, was an omission the Academicians would not easily condone .

Mushroom - Sire ! Charlie, You'll forgive me, but I am serious now ! We better finish what I had started to say for our own good and I'll explain that a little later, but, now, ...now, we better finish what I had started, and please, Charlie, be patient and you will not regret my cautious and careful approach to this story, may be superficial and a bit silly to you, but damn serious in many other respects . So , Charlie, that of the village of Bingbangboo was indeed an epic battle and there died as a hero, Alambert, Sir Alambert, that is, and all of his braves, in the glorious belief of Justice, Liberty and Freedom from tyranny and oppression ....

Giant Oak Tree - .....From the Giant Trees !

Mushroom - Well, Charlie, you said it : I didn't .

Giant Oak Tree - Don't worry, Fabius, I can read you like a book or, more appropriately,like the veins in a vine's leaf, and I know perfectly well what you are talking about, so please do continue and finish your sermon.

Mushroom - Thank you, Charlie, and I knew that You would know it too, but I wanted to be sure that I would not be misunderstood in my efforts to be adequately prepared for a situation which is, Charlie, and you "believe you me", could be serious and even dangerous .

Giant Oak Tree - The Witch Queen ?

Mushroom - Charlie, we'll come to that later, if you follow me, but, as I was saying, unfortunately the battle was lost for the intrepid Piedermi because of the overwhelming power of the weapons of those two legged creatures, called humans, and so the battle was over in no time and all was lost, except their glory and their pride, that of the Piedermi I am talking about, of course.

Giant Oak Tree - But ,Fabius, aren't we straying away a little from our main subject with all this talking of the past hostilities in full details, except of course your missed information of the distance of the village of Bingbangboo from the City of Boobangbing, but, anyway, and the glorious demise of Sir Alambert fighting for Liberty and.........

Mushroom - Yes, Charlie, in one sense it may seem that way ,but not anymore if you let me finish the story and why I brought back all of those memories and emphasized them too.

Giant Oak Tree - Go ahead, Fabius, I will not object anymore, since I slowly begin to dig into your reasoning for saying all of those good things about the Army of the Piedermi and the famous battle near the village of Bingbangboo.

Mushroom - I knew it, Charlie,that you would see why I was going into all of those tedious yet historical details, but the reason for doing so was there and you understood it and that takes some worry out of me and relieves me because, Charlie, here, I mean down here, everybody is quite convinced that what you refer to as a"shadow", actually seems to be the real Witch Queen, the Great Grand Mother of that famous Warrior Centipede, Sir Alambert, whose death she is said to be determined to vindicate and she is flying around here where all the battles took place, trying to find a motive and or a pretext to punish those who caused the death of her beloved great grand child . I believe, Charlie, and ,now, I am almost sure about it, that the shadow that you saw flying wildly in the sky was,actually, the Witch Queen herself.

Giant Oak Tree - Coming just like that into my Kingdom, not even announced ?

Mushroom - She is very independent, from what I hear, and very capricious and abusive as well as pretty dangerous if antagonized or obstructed with her plans . Sire, you should be very careful should you come in contact with her or if she would ask for your help . Please, try to be courteous but not servile, firm but not hard and do your best to show friendliness and hospitality and willingness to help, or, if cotradicted, she could turn into a nasty and unsympathetic "shadow" !!

Giant Oak Tree - Thank you,Fabius : you are always there, ready to give me the best possible advice and provide me with up to the minutes warnings about important things in bad times and good times and I am, as usual, very grateful to you for that . I shall try to be very careful, prudent and cautious in my comportment and address to her should we meet and I shall remember your warnings !

Mushroom - Yes, Charlie, and not a minute too late, because I can feel the wind beginning to blow harder than it did just a while ago, as a matter of fact there was a nice, pleasant breeze a while ago and worm and gentle, but it is changing and quite rapidly and so unexpected and unforeseen with a clear, blue sky and no clouds and this sudden change, I am afraid, tells me that this could be the advance notice that the Witch Queen is in the neighbourhood and, may be, even closer than we would think or would like her to be . That is one more good reason to be on our most careful alert !

Giant Oak Tree - Are you certain that the increased blowing intensity of the wind is a sign that the Witch Queen could be around ? She or, shall I say, her shadow, at least the shadow that I saw, did not seem that massive or so gigantic to be instrumental in changing the prevailing force of the existing wind, don't you think ?

Mushroom - Charlie, she commands the winds .

Giant Oak Tree - Now I am beginning to wonder whether it might have been a lesser problem the Ants or this new "shadow" thatdoes as she pleases and even commands the winds and, on top of that, we are supposed to be obsequious and ceremonious towards her or face severe retaliation for failing to do so !!...... Humbug !!!

Mushroom - Well, Charlie, if that's the way You like to look at it, it's just fine with me : I have done my best to advise you, to warn you but, you, of course, have the privilege of the choice ! I, myself, have a different view of the situation and my assessment is matched and shared by the majority of the little people down here, who think a lot differently about the Witch Queen, particularly when she is out looking for something that interests her : at that time, Charlie, it's better to stay out of her way .

Giant Oak Tree - Why ? That contradicts what you had just preached to me and advised me about it, and that was to be pleasant , helpful and cooperative towards anything that she may ask for or want or desire to have..!

Mushroom - That is true : the problem, however, arises when she may ask for impossible tasks from little people or creatures who are not furnished by Mother Nature with similar or competing powers of the same level of strength and range like the witches have, expecting from them the same expertise and dispatch in carrying out the special and mysterious and occult and unnatural actions against the targets of her own choice .

Giant Oak Tree - Fabius: You are a mushroom, right ?

Mushroom - No doubt about it , Charlie !

Giant Oak Tree - Then, Fabius, your memories do not reach back in time as far back as mine do: right ?

Mushroom - I guess so, Charlie !.

Giant Oak Tree - Yes, Fabius, and you guessed rightly because you were born, as everybody knows, so to speak of, just yesterday, considering the supposedly fast growing speed of mushrooms, generally, as against mine of slow, long centuries: right?

Mushroom - If you say so, Charlie . But, Charlie, and this is just between You and me, what has all that got to do with the probable impending arrival of the Witch Queen ?

Giant Oak Tree - Fabius !......I don't believe she is a Witch and even less a Queen .

Mushroom - C H A R L I E !!!!!!!!!!!!

Giant Oak Tree - Listen, Fabius, what I just said about you being young, born of a rapid growth as against mine of long many, many years and even centuries, well , what I wanted to tell you with that comparison was that I have seen a lot more history going by than you have and I still remember, well printed in my hard and ligneous memory, innumerable images of past events that embrace large periods of time like the 12th Century famous adventures of Robin Hood, or, as another example among the many,the tragic march of the Roman Consul Varo and his Legions through the treacherous Forest of Teutoburg in the year 9 AD, and I can tell you, Fabius, that witches were imaginary representations of the confused and uneducated minds born and raised in the twilight of the Dark Ages' intellectual sleep, and dark they really were in their attitudes except, may be, in their unconscious yet surviving instinct of unity in the light of the still pervasive and extensive use of the language of ancient Rome . Anyway, Fabius, I 'll say it again, they were wilful creations of the imagination,perhaps in an attempt to absolve the "graying"of the human intellect and the starvation of its resources in that dark period of the history of the human kind .

Mushroom - Charlie, thank you for the interesting glimpse of past history, something that everybody seems to forget quite easily along with the instructions inherited from those event and "reminders" of its realities that no one ever "remembers" but do not forget that we too in this story are a fruit of the imagination and we talk, we think, we plan, we fight, we love, we laugh, and we entertain many episodes of various creatures' lives and aims and hopes and tragedies as well as joys : Charlie, if we are real, why couldn't the witches of the Dark Ages be real too ?

Giant Oak Tree - Because, Fabius, I believe that stark reality and I mean a reality of gloom and doom like the one of the witches was, is void of favourable stimulation, a sort of an invisible block to the mind to proceed any further, remaining stagnant in its own quagmire for failure or fear to reinforce its intellectual pillars. So, I do not believe in witches , that's all .

Mushroom - I hear you, Charlie, but let me add a little to your explanation of the witches' saga : somebody in those dark days of the human intellect must have still been able to "think" something even without any supporting pillars for his sagging intellect in order to figure out the idea of "witches" and all the incantations about their doings and must have had a considerable advance premonition of things to come, like flying for example, by providing the witches with a very convenient,very economic means of transportation by placing at their disposal a broom stick, a cheap commodity even for those very Dark Ages .

Giant Oak Tree - That's a different story, Fabius : we cannot change easily what someone else thinks or prevent him, her ,even it, if acceptable, permissible and questionably appropriate, to think or wishing to think, or dream, or fantasize about something. As far as I read from the books of the mighty thinkers of days past it is not easy to stop a thought and, apart the many theories and the potions invented for that purpose, and the artifacts of dictatorial Institutions to prevent "any thinking" adverse to them, a thought cannot be stopped, at least as far as we understand, and as a matter of fact we do not know how "something" does become a thought and comes out as "something" that we, actually, had thought not even realizing how it became represented like that, a thought, and, most intriguing , why it did so, at all !

Mushroom - But, Charlie, this Witch here is not a thought !!.....and ,Charlie, our Witch Queen is not a dream or fantasy of the Dark Ages' tepid and senescent imagination , she is REAL, Charlie...... she is a reality and.......a REAL ONE too !!

Giant Oak Tree - I'll check on that when I'll see it........this REALITY !!

Mushroom - All my sympathy to you, Charlie, and don't you call on me if you should need assistance : because I shall be invisible at that time !

Giant Oak Tree - You pay too much attention to old fables and stories, Fabius .

Mushroom - And I would listen to them even more if they were just fables and ordinary stories, but........................CHARLIE !!!

Giant Oak Tree - What, now ??

Mushroom - CHARLIE !!...... LOOK , LOOK.....!!!!

Giant Oak Tree - Look WHAT, Fabius ?....What is it, Fabius ?..Are you trying, by any chance, to give me an unrehearsed performance of Medieval Times' surprise impersonation out of the fantasy of your "senescent" imagination ....?!!

Mushroom - I wish it were just a"senescent impersonation",Charlie,but this"Medieval impersonation" is no impersonation at all but is the real THING that goes under the name of...........

Chorus of the Little people of the Forest- THE WITCH !! THE WITCH !!.......The WITCH QUEEN is here!!!...Run! Hide !....The Witch Queen is here...!!!!

Giant Oak Tree - Is that it, Mushroom ?

Mushroom - I do not know about "it", Charlie, but if you mean by "it" the Witch Queen, then it is a resounding " IT, YES ", and you better take care, Charlie !

Giant Oak Tree - But, Fabius, I can't see a thing !

Mushroom - You will and soon !

Giant Oak Tree - Is she riding on a broomstick ?

Mushroom - She is riding all right !.....As to the broomstick, that's up to anyone's imagination and to the suppliers of brooms, in general .

Giant Oak Tree - Is she coming this way, Fabius ? How is it possible that the little creatures on the ground down there can see ,of all things, a Witch coming and I don't ??!!

Mushroom - At this moment, Charlie, even the little folks down here cannot see the Witch Queen , but.........

Giant Oak Tree - ......But, but....always but....and truly, Fabius, this is preposterous !! How can folks, regardless whether they may be small, large or medium, see things that are not there yet, and, Fabius, to remember that the age of Electronics has not come upon us yet .

Mushroom - We know that . The little folks know that, but....(and here, Charlie, is another"but"...!!) .... we are at this moment in a semi-enchanted and occult atmosphere, where Witches reign supreme and, with them, the prophetic images of the future in their crystal ball .

Giant Oak Tree - But.........

Mushroom - Hm.......!!!

Giant Oak Tree - O.K , O,K ., I'll leave the "but" out : happy, now ?

Mushroom - Extremely so, Charlie,....."but"....all I wanted to do was to draw your attention to your expressed annoyance at all those repetitive"but"used in our conversation. As far as I am concerned , I really don't give a darn damn ! Sorry, Charlie, for this interruption...........and you were saying...?

Giant Oak Tree - Yes, and I'd like to know how these little folks can tell things ahead of them ! Are they also using a crystal ball ?

Mushroom - The folks down here, Charlie, can tell of something unusual coming their way and, in this case, being able, by previous experiences, to identify the arrival of the Witch Queen, by the intensity, force and sequence of the gusts of wind caused by the bizarre and violent motions of the bushy end of her broomstick and her unorthodox flying patterns, which you yourself had previously noted .

Giant Oak Tree - I see ! Interesting . She is probably approaching us hoping to see me and ask for help in regard to some information about her adored Great Grand Child, Sir Alambert, and looking forwards to a natural relationship of address between two Royal Figures .

Mushroom - May be you'll be the one needing help, Charlie, if engaged in that type of "natural royal relationship" !......That "Queen",Charlie, is far from being "Royal"!

Giant Oak Tree - And why,then, is she called a "Queen" ??

Mushroom - Because she is very "high up" in her turpitude , Charlie !

Giant Oak Tree - May be she'll calm down a little in the presence of my legitimate and authoritative hereditary royal posture .

Mushroom - Good luck, Charlie !......I wish you all the best and I hope that everything will go your way or, shall we more realistically say, that everything would go the way you would like it to go ! Whichever way, Charlie, please, do not forget my advice and do not ignore my warnings !

Giant Oak Tree - Do not worry,Fabius, I will not forget or ignore anything ! Yet, I wonder, here there might be a golden opportunity for me to solve my Kingdom's deep seated problems and clear up the mystery surrounding the confusion and the turbulent commotions of these last events, inclusive of the ultimate and unprecedented violation of our Northern borders by the deceitful invasion of the Ants and the unfair, purely greed-motivated attack and destruction of the far corner of our Forest by the two legged creatures !

Mushroom - Charlie, this "Queen" is hardly interested in solving or mending political, or emotional or economic problems : she is interested in causing them !

Giant Oak Tree - Well, Fabius, compare the evil doings of the two legged crearures, the deceitful invasion of the Ants, the rebellious attitudes of some of my subjects about what..... I still do not know, and I wonder, how much worse than all those bad things that happened to us can now her supposed "horrible" character be ? She could turn out to be, instead, a God-send help for me !

Mushroom - As I said before, Charlie, good luck and I wish you all the very best, ever !

Giant Oak Tree - May be the solution could be a lot simpler if seen afresh from a different perspective that would be clear of the petty restrictions of understanding of local interpretations, likely being able to see things in a wider scenario and with a less partisan attitude. Well, whatever the result may be, I still think that it would be worth the attempt. The question now : how to get her attention !!

*** ....The Witch Queen now flying in wide circles above the wooded area, the pattern of the circles wide and slow, at first, then, gradually, becoming narrower and narrower, picking up speed, and converging faster and faster like a corkscrew motion into a cork, towards a single point and sweeping down towards the centre of the Forest, while ominous dark clouds rumble in the stormy sky holding hands with thunder and lightning and the wind howls its sibilant, terrifying message of desolation and destruction and befriend the sardonic smile on the contorted face of the Witch Queen ...... ***

The Witch Queen- The wind, the rain, the thunder, the lightning ganged up with the snake and the raven, in the creation of a powerful empire but, following a discord among themselves, death befell them in the struggle for supremacy and I, having discovered their remains, ate them, drank their venom, drenched myself in the violent rain, dried myself in the implacable wind, spread light on the gruesome scene with the lightning and belched with the thunder.Ah!The Forest!This must be the Forest where my poor Great Grand Child,SirAlambert the Warrior, met his glorious yet untimely death ! Thunder and Lightning, I perceive problems down there in that obscure thicket of tall trees and I can well anticipate a great abundance of delicious flat-breads and flat-cakes out of all those stupid, insignificant creatures...Oh!..And what a good time I shall have and what a marvelous binge is waiting for me ! Thunder and Lightming do act and announce me !

Thunder and Lightning - Giant of the Forest ! The Queen is here ! Pay homage !

Giant Oak Tree - Your Majesty,We, the Kingdom of this Forest, wish to extend to you our most and deeply felt welcome to our land, and I am the Giant Oak Tree, the King of this Land and of this Forest. WELCOME !

The Witch Queen - And who is this idiot who is welcoming me ??!....It must be a Giant Stupid One if he is so naive as to call out to a witch and welcoming her !!....Let me get a little closer and have a look !....Ah ! It figures ! It is a Giant Oak Tree and he calls himself a King !....Shucks !

Giant Oak Tree - Your Majesty, it is customary in this Land to welcome Visitors whoever they may be and, in this particular instance, it is our pleasure, honour and joy to have You here among us and our Welcome is tenfolds its usual intensity !

The Witch Queen - Come to the point, old man, or whatever you are !......What do you want ?

Giant Oak Tree - Dear Queen, for some............

The Witch Queen - And don't you "dear" or " Queen "me, you big , fat, Giant wooden stick . The name is DAGA , and don't forget it either .

Giant Oak Tree - Very well and I won't forget it . But here, now, is what I had intended to ask you in regard to some problems that occurred in my Kingdom over a period of time, causing serious distress and civic commotions .

The Witch Queen - A rather common handicap these days, my good old man,......tree, I mean.....

Giant Oak Tree - Common, may be, but it degenerated in an open revolution which failed only because of the prompt help from a neighboring Forest who had sent powerful Army Units to reestablish order.

The Witch Queen - Strange ! That action would have been alien to my way of thinking .

Giant Oak Tree - Really ?!

The Witch Queen - I would have sent in even more soldiers to "increase" the disorder and foment more revolutionary furor .

Giant Oak Tree - Yes, Daga, I understand, in a way, your point of view, but the situation was becoming very difficult for me and for the basis of my foundations, pain and anxiety for the proper balance of living conditions for my subjects, associated with an ever increasing difficulty of communication with the ground roots of my many constituencies, some coperative and, then, some others offering resistance to any of my suggestions and Laws, and some becoming apathetic with no energy or initiative, a dead weight to the economy of the Nation . My contacts with the all important root environment were becoming weaker every day, the relationship almost painful at the very roots of my very feet almost unable to carry me, sustain me and guide me. Those were the conditions, I believe, that led to the unhappy commotions and all the troubles. In your fine perception of things and situations, Daga, what kind of advice could you offer me in this reference ?

The Witch Queen - If the trouble is at your feet, your roots, I mean, try to see a chiropodist, You know, one who makes a business of caring for the feet .

Giant Oak Tree - But you do not seem to understand me, Queen Daga !

The Witch Queen - I am not interested in feet problems .

Giant Oak Tree - But they are the very basis for the balance of my Kingdom, and when, at times, this Kingdom seems to shake and totter it causes great concern to me and I am anxious to find out ,if possible, its cause.Am I now asking too much?

The Witch Queen - Well. listen here, good old man, at the moment I am on vacation with full approval of the Syndicate of the Witches International and I have no desire to get down to work for some trees and unknown trees on top of that, come up with suitable advice for their problems and in the middle of a thick and dark Forest.....well....I just thought.....unless....unless....Oh! Nothing...forget it !

Giant Oak Tree - My dear Daga, and my sheer anxiety will justify the addition of "dear" to your name..!...but you, who are so clever and inexhaustible in your endevours, finding constantly new ways to increase the load of human worries just as a form of healthy exercise to keep their safeguards in full alert status, couldn't you, really, give me some advice, even if only requiring a few seconds out of your vacation, with the possible intervention of some remuneration.......unless you would think otherwise, but possibly ,shall we say, enticing remuneration ?

The Witch Queen - Hm..!!...You certainly know how to get your own grist to the mill, you lucky dog of a tree!....And that in spite of being all a solid piece of wood ! Well, let me tell you, big overgrown Giant, that the essence of everything is in the make of the pie, or, I'd rather say......well, I really prefer to say the main point of everything is in the making of the bannock !

Giant Oak Tree - A.......bannock ?!....Are you serious ??!

The Witch Queen - Yes, You precious dupe, I said "bannock" .

Giant Oak Tree - Daga, I do not mean to harass you or doubt you but what kind of relationship could "pies" or, as you call them, "bannocks" have in the problems of my Kingdom ? Daga , there are severe complications in the everyday functioning of the State Burocracy and many conflicts exist down below in my roots and among my laborious yet impoverished subjects, something has to be done!

The Witch Queen - Listen to this wooden stick!!....talking about his " subjects" and his"Kingdom" and His failing "burocrasy" and doesn't even know what's going on below ,in his"roots".....!!!....Well, yes, "you little giant of a tree",....bannocks, bannocks, those are the only remedy for all your problems and those of the rest of the World .

Giant Oak Tree - What is the "world" Daga, Queen ? This is the first time I ever heard that word around here: in this part of the land we call our land "forest" and we have never heard of world forest . I do not think that there are any in our area.

The Witch Queen - And you don't know how lucky you are not to have ever known the World! Bannocks, Bannocks, my dear, you need bannocks in your land and plenty of them !

Giant Oak Tree - I believe, Daga, with my utmost respect, that you are making fun of me !

The Witch Queen - Oops-a-daisy !..Eventually you came to it, my giant wooden stick ! You understood !!! I really congratulate you for your extraordinary intellectual power in penetrating the meaning of a sentence and in the correct sense too!! I had wondered if you'd ever come to it, dear stick of wood ! However let me tell you that I was not joking about the bannocks . .

Giant Oak Tree - I am surprised .

The Witch Queen - Surprise is not a feature of knowledge but of ignorance, according to the Academy of Sciences of the Institute of Knowledge of the Faculty of Wisdom of the Department of Occult Endevours and of the Office of the Credentials for the elite corp of the Witches of the World....OUR World , of course .

Giant Oak Tree - Now, I am not surprised but simply amazed.

The Witch Queen - Good on you, old boy. And now, back to the good old bannocks.

Giant Oak Tree - So, I see: apparently you really were serious about them and you really meant it when you said that you were not joking about the bannocks !

The Witch Queen - But of course not : Witches never joke about anything, not even about jokes. Bannocks, my dear glorious dupe, bannocks are the universal remedy for all!!

Giant Oak Tree- Then, the way you say it, these bannocks must have some very powerful as well as occult identities to be so effective in all kind of problems !

The Witch Queen - But of course, you butt-head, and this is an excellent recipe for a delicious and very appetizing bannock : " Livers of newly born sparrows, and.......

Giant Oak Tree - Do sparrows have livers , Daga ?

The Witch Queen - I don't Know . But what does it matter ? The recipe says so .

Giant Oak Tree - Right .

The Witch Queen - Just don't you interrupt me anymore, you butt-head : clear ?

Giant Oak Tree - Very .

The Witch Queen - Now, then : as I just said, livers of newly born sparrows . If these not available, say you are at the North Pole, then you.......

Giant Oak Tree - What is the North Pole, Daga ?

The Witch Queen - One more stupid question like that and there is where I am going to send you and all your friends in this damn Forest and so"that"would be one way of taking care of your problems . Now back to the bannocks . So, if the livers of newly born sparrows would not be available.....for whatever reason!!.....then the livers of oxen would do just fine, add milk of Lacertas Viridis, the green lizards and.....huh, huh.....don't ask....I do not know, but the recipe says that those lizards do have it, besides, should they not have any, it is perfectly safe to use any milk and, so , put that to cook until midnight.......the recipe says that you must start at nine o'clock.....then add a poisonous mushroom and half a cup of finely powered glass, mix it all while keeping the whole mixture on the fire, then add two putrefied eggs ,some parsly, one spoonful of sand and a teaspoonful of finely minced toad skin, stir gently but thoroughly and , as soon as the whole mixture thickens a little, then you can pour it in a container of the finest available majolica covered earthen ware and wait for the arrival of your worst enemy whom you had invited for dinner a little earlier and, as he came, welcome him with the sweetest compliments and praise him for all his deeds, and once the dinner is served and dutifully attended to and the feeding terminated , your enemy will have been terminated too, will not be able to be an enemy anymore because dead people, usually,are not considered dangerous anymore not even to regular trees or giant trees, so , I have given you a fair hint of what can be done for straightening out your forest problems, I have done you a good service and ,now, I am out of the whole mess .

Giant Oak Tree - But Daga, my gracious Queen, I have no enemies to eliminate !

The Witch Queen - Then the problem is a lot simpler: eliminate yourself and ALL will be fine !

Giant Oak Tree - But how could I come to resort to an action so dramatic with all the responsibilities that bear on me for my subjects down there on my large roots, the very base of my entire State and Kingdom ?

The Witch Queen - Responsibilities..??!...This darn idiot talks of responsibilities in times like these !!!....You are too tall and your wooden head lives in the clouds, so you are like a water melon full of colour in your imposing image but just water inside your head . Responsibilities !!!... The darn idiot talks of responsibilities and does not even register that things have changed in this World.....well, that would justify his ignorance since he did not even know what World was!! You, poor ignoramus !!.....And you think to have responsibilities still when no one else does, not even knowing what they do represent in men's lives, that is their value and their lofty posture in guiding men's tremulous adventures ! It is almost as difficult these days to find that famous needle in the hay stack as it is to find an honest and responsible body anywhere in this World !!

Giant Oak Tree - What you are saying, Daga Queen, seems to reflect a total rejection of today's life's essential ideals, yearnings and hopes by denying even a little glimpse of morality still lingering among the human specie ! I disagree with you, Daga, because in this Forest, although ignorant of Worlds, responsibilities and all that, I and my fellow Giant Oaks, still produce abundant acorns and feed sumptuously thousands of squirrels and discharge our responsibilities towards Nature's dictates quite accurately, assiduously and ...."responsibly" !!..What you are saying, Daga , looks to me as being ludicrous and, still with my greatest respect for your ideas and beliefs, also somewhat senseless .

The Witch Queen - Sense, He says, senseless reasoning!And what kind of sense would you like to suggest to have or to use in these days where confusion, unrestrained violence, unscrupulous, unprincipled elements and their questionable claims of honourable deeds, are so wide-spread and rampant ??!...Under these prevailing times, my dear stick of wood, all senses have seen their better days and they seem to have just and simply vanished ,except ,of course, for those who never had them naturally, and, now, these fledgeling beacons of the new morality are trying to become the leaders of a new World, which they themselves scarcely undestand.

Giant Oak Tree - In a "sense", I guess, I may be following your way of explaining the new trends in the lives, interests and endevours of the new generations of the so called human beings, who look different from us in the aspect and form of the body but not so much in the intricate mechanisms of function that make us, I a tree and the other a man, and you might have misinterpreted what I actually had intended to say about the meaning of"senses", the one senses that I..........

The Witch Queen _ Which University did you attend in your younger years, genius ? Was the name, by the way, that of the "Uni. of the Acorn" or, may be, the "Uni. of the Unicorn"?

Giant Oak Tree - None of them, Daga, but the Uni. of the Forest, the one that does not fly too high among the clouds of fantasy and controversy bat stays well and solidly planted in the good old soil of Mother Nature, from where it draws its nourishment .

The Witch Queen - I had to expect an answer like that from a wooden stick ! What else .....??!!

Giant Oak Tree - May be, Daga ,Queen, may be there is something "else"that, may be, is even quite solid in its meaning and message as a wooden stick would be and that............

The Witch Queen - Like a ully grown "stick" like you,....you dumbbell ?! What a big baby you are , so big and so stupid !

Giant Oak Tree - With all respect, Lady Queen Daga, but it occurs to me that your choice of words does not seem to carry the selected taste of Royal discretion .

The witch Queen - My discretion may not be Royal in the real sense of the word, but it goes right to the point.

Giant Oak Tree - As You wish,Daga, and I do not intend to argue with you, but I still want to finish what I had started to say about the senses, those senses that we seemed to have some different views about them and I want to agree with you that some of them are the expression ,many a time, of anger, rancor, jealousy, and even inexplicable hatred, but I meant the less common,sometimes even absent notions of them,like the perception of righteousness,honesty, sincerity,honour, liberty ,justice and, above all freedom of thought. Those.... well, I really mean, these are the senses that distinguish the highest vertices of our thinking and of our existences and in which I firmly believe with the stubborness of a wooden stump .

The Witch Queen - You'd better leave alone all your big "perceptions" and get down, instead, to more practical and smaller "perceptions", like growing up, not in size that you are already too big, but in the size of your brain, if one is available among all of those thick and twisted branches and come back to earth, to the ground where your roots are and leave those pale thoughts of yours where they belong, in the heads of creatures that can think, that where they belong and not in a crazy creature like you who claims to be a king and does not know how to govern and has to ask advice, believe it or not, from a Witch!!.... Incredible and ....very, very depressing and sad , even for a Witch .

Giant Oak Tree - But, even leaving aside my lack of intelligence so well represented and illustrated by you, tell me, Daga, to what end are you still denigrating and chastising the deeds of present days World of yours, inclusive of almost any aspect, expression, motive, yearning, that your World is capable of producing, and I said"almost"because I thought that you would excuse yourself from that category of creatures and from an abode in that World that you said I was lucky not to have known it .

The Witch Queen - Aspect ? Expressions ? Motive ? Yearning ? Oh ! You ninny, haven't you found out yet that this is a world that does not follow the strict rules of eighteenth century's sentimentalism ,least of all reasoning, but pride itself, instead, of being a pitfall of forces fighting among themselves, each of the interested parties tightly barricated in their own unmitigated and unmitigatable concepts and faulting everything else the other camp would offer, while prejudice, rancor, hatred and, at times, even perversion of fundamental ideas of regular living and being, become entangled in a choking hold of forces difficult to explain even to a tree, as giant as he can be. It is a mad world, Chum, and you consider yourself lucky to be just a tree in its midst !

Giant Oak Tree - You haven't answered my question .

The Witch Queen - Witches don't have to answer if they choose to do so .

Giant Oak Tree - But, real Queens, Daga, they do.

The witch Queen - What a quotation, what a quotation !! My dear spindleshanks, what a quotation !! But don't forget that Witches, Queens or no Queens, are part of the whole creation, like good and bad, like you and me, not that the particular sequence would match our virtues, but just to inform you that I belong to it just as you belong to it and, if you preach freedom of thought why can't I think what I want to think about this World ?

Giant Oak Tree - You are not thinking : you are cursing! You are cursing this World of yours and you also do your utmost best to force it on me ! Is that why you are so bitter against it with your eyes of a panther, yellow and green, your tusks protruding over the lower, flaccid lips, your hair of serpents and worms and your face in a contorted sardonic and evil smile, is that why you are so bitter against that world,precisely THAT world that banned you from its midst? And what kind of right do you have to attack, beat, deride, condemn, insult, contradict ,chastise and curse everything that comes within your grip ?

The Witch Queen - What kind of rights do you have? The right, may be, to carry on a miserable form of government ?

Giant Oak Tree - The right of Nature which I earned in my long,long growth from the goodness and pristine essence of the soil on which I live.

The Witch Queen - Well, good on you, sucker, so well stuck in your good and pristine soil . As far as I am concerned, my dear old spindle, I really do mot care to go over what is already past and gone:I am looking forward to new enterprises, new dumb folks to follow me, a few more "bannocks" here and there, some thunder,and a dash of lightning, and to enjoy all that power !

Giant Oak Tree - And, in the process, let your conscience get sour .

The Witch Queen - Conscience !...Damn the Conscience ! That's the problem of the world today: too many retrospections , innumerable deliberations, too many vituperations...

Giant Oak Tree - Just listen who is talking...!!!!

The Witch Queen - Of course I'm talking!.....And you better listen too, you pulp-wood head!..Too many of everything and too many conscience problems ! Fortunately, I managed to stay away from the problems of the so-called "gentile"people who make me laugh about their extreme kindness that, more than it is usually believed, kills,destroys and concocts all sorts of mischiefs and troubles like any other bugger does, but they do it with discriminating kindness. You, big fat Giant, look after your own conscience!.As to mine, I take care of it myself.

Giant Oak Tree - But, Daga Queen, are you ever assailed by a feeling of uneasiness or of anxiety about your deeds, particularly the ones of the "bannocks" which you so highly praise, which may cause you to have scruples ?

The Witch Queen - Scruples ? and WHAT are they ? Are they a medicament to be taken by mortals before going to bed at night to secure a good rest ?

Giant Oak Tree - Scruples are not medicaments and are not edible ,Daaga,...and......

The Witch Queen - What are they, then ? You asked me if I ever have "scruples" : I thought that they were something like doughnuts or truffle or strudel . There isn't such a word in the Witches'Dictionary.

Giant Oak Tree - Scruples, Daga Queen, could be described as a moral uneasiness over the validity of actions that were taken or that are being contemplated for implementation, a sort of a mental disquietude in judgeing the efficacy versus the deficiency of an action even if such state of uneasiness and anxiety would not, really, be necessary or justified .

The Witch Queen - Interesting . And, by the way, do these scruples, also, carry some added value to Royal Dignity ?

Giant Oak Tree - In ancient times they did but, as times went by, customs changed, minds were embarking on different roads of perspectives, the authority of Royal Patronage diminishing as other tiers of power were beginning to emerge from the lower classes of the populations and industrialization, large range commerce and goods exchanges world wide and no longer restricted or limited to one city to another, but, now, extended and extensible with great earnest all over the known world ,taking the upper hand of direction and financial organization, the Royal Authority slowly diminished ,although its Dignity remained unchanged and respected in those countries where its Members had retained the principles of ancient Chivalry and had remained faithful to the Code of olden aristocratic virtue and smiled upon the new, fast and growing world . So, under these prevailing and newly born circumstances, scruples are now left the sole property of..........

The Witch Queen - ....Mushrooms....Giant Trees....and ....Idiots , right ?

Giant Oak Tree - Of those, yes, I believe so and of all the other honest, laborious and virtuous creatures, at least in our Forest, but I do not know about that world of yours and cannot vouch for it since I do not know it, never seen it, never would want to see it either : it's all yours to enrich it with your malice, hatred, intrigue and violence, all of which seem to have taken excellent and promising rooting in an apparently extremely fertile soil .

The Witch Queen - Livers of newly born sparrows, my dear, livers of newly born sparrows, are the the answer and your own liver, I mean, you big chunk of compact, compressed wood, your own liver, silly!...that is, your "guts" are needed to govern, lead, obtain respect and be feared . If you want to govern, if you want to lead, if you want to command you must know how to display a gracious smile, a solemn but decisive firmness in eliminating enemies, and the ability to never hear, officially, anything at all .

Giant Oak Tree - That kind of gubernatorial posture and philosophy does not and could not very well be applicable in this nation of ours, in our Forest, I mean , since it is quite obvious that I cannot smile and, least of all, graciously, the only performance remaining available would be that of being firm as, obviously again, I could not do anything in a different way, planted solid as I am in the ground and, as to the"never hearing anything officially,that, also, would be out of the practical on account of the almost unbelievable noise caused by the chirping of hundreds of birds on my branches, sometimes, not even quieting down in the night, or if the birds are quiet then the owl begins to grace us with her monotonous, petulant song . How do you expect me to have "guts" up here when I can hardly see what's going on down there on my large roots ? What do you think I asked your advice for, Daga , you, the Witch Queen ?

The Witch Queen - To tell you the truth , ...Charlie.....didn't I hear your trusted Minister, the Mushroom, address you in that manner of speech as I was in the neighbourhood a while ago ?

Giant Oak Tree - Yes, he calls me that when we are at ease and not engaged in any official ceremonies or activities of Government.

The Witch Queen - Well, Charlie, the truth is that I am not in the least interested in the peculiar and disorganised state of your wobbly form of Government and I am also tired of this ,shall we say,"going nowhere" chit-chat, which has now become slightly boring, painfully tedious and unbearably dull. I am not inclined toward long discussions about things and situations that have hardly anything to do with my character and mode of action. I like "bannocks" and the gullibility of my World with an added pinch of perversion, intrigue, malice and treachery as well as an adverse turn around of destiny, is enough to satiate me fully.To you,I leave philosophy, sentimentalism, virtues and stupidity and your duty to the Spring cleaning of your house,well, I wanted to say, your Government . Charlie, it has been interesting, anyway, chatting with you, though for a far too long period of time, and ..." Ah is going, ducky !" , and good luck to you !

Giant Oak Tree - It's easy for you to be and act so bold, my dear Queen Daga, when you are on the outside of a situation which has no particular or specific interest for you or is totally extraneous to your life and does not require attention or worry should anything go wrong. In a way, Daga, I envy you, although I'd never want to change places with you !

The Witch Queen - "C'est la vie, mon cheri" !!

Giant Oak Tree - ...And by saying it in French does not add to it a single bit !

The Witch Queen - I know that . You know it . The Witches know it too, and so do also the French people . But what the heck : it's French !

Giant Oak Tree - Yes, of course . Anyway, dear Daga, I understand your desire to move on but, in spite of the different path of our ideas, I would like to ask your opinion about something else before you leave our Forest and, since you are a well versed creature in the many aspects of your World that, I suspect, might even include our own Forest, and I..........

The Witch Queen - ....And it does !

Giant Oak Tree - Even better, then, if it does, so it would justify my asking you for a favour before you leave us : would you be willing to listen to what I intend to ask ?

The Witch Queen - But of course ! I know that it is getting a little late, we did talk for a long time, you know, and soon it will be dark, but, then, I like to fly in the night sky and there is going to be a beautiful full moon, so I shall be able to fly right on its brightness against the dark sky on my wonderful broom .Go ahead,Charlie, I'll listen .

Giant Oak Tree - Just a while ago, as we were talking, I began to realize, following your representation of the World, your World that is, as a mixture of good and evil, honesty and dishonesty, kindness and brutality, falsehood and truth, all of them going hand in hand in a strange combination of efficient way of life, as I said, I began to realize that my Government needs an adjournment of its structure, the present one being too open, too simple, too naive, too honest to survive the new ideas and it dawned on me that I said to my self " well, Charlie, here you have an opportunity of a life time, don't let it slip away from under you ..." !!...and I immediately thought of you, who, as a maverick of the frailty of the average creature in the World which you tell me includes also our Forest, well, to make it short........

The Witch Queen - That would definitely help !

Giant Oak Tree - Well, I'll make it even shorter, and I wonder if you would be willing to help me in setting up a first class Government that would be pliable and resiliant enough to take its place among the rest of.......well, yes.....the rest of the World and all of its new ideas, good, bad, mediocre, brilliant, insane or just plain stupid, but 100% modern and up to the best of any possible best . And here, I rest my case.

The Witch Queen - It is wonderful to take a rest now and then, and we really needed some rest, here, my dear big fellow, to think things over . First of all I have to thank you for the compliment of having thought that I would be the best adviser for the formation or rectification, reformation, or whatever you want to call it, of your aging government set up, as it is standing today and I see that you are taking a sensible direction in the choice of your advisers by asking me to be one of them or, I would even suggest, the only one....of them!...In addition, your request and the compliment that silently followed it, is such that it would be difficult to turn it down .

Giant Oak Tree - What you say,Daga, is a great relief to me. Thank you .

The Witch Queen - But wait : I am not finished yet. You must know, then, that Witches have a brain and they use it regularly, the only difference form all the other available brain rests in the extreme rapidity our witches'brain works, a significant difference from, for example, the brain of some ligneous creatures who live in thick Forests and constantly need someone around to help them to do things,like a few I happen to know .

Giant Oak Tree - Anybody in this Forest that I may know, Daga ?

The Witch Queen - I am not certain but, I believe, he or they should not be too far away . Well, that's something else, and, in regard to your invitation to be part of your new Government as an advisor, I thought it over and I accept your bidding effort since you almost seem as imploring me to accept it ! However, my dear Forest King, there is something that needs to be clarified before we can start our mutual partnership .

Giant Oak Tree - Name it, My dear Daga Queen, and it'll be just as good as done .

The Witch Queen - Well, there is a French proverb that goes like this:"Les petite cadeaux entretien-ment l'amitie, mais c'est l'argent que entretient notre maison "....compri ?

Giant Oak Tree - It is not difficult to understand that , be it in French or Chinese or Hindustani : these days , it is the language that everyone understand : MONEY ! Nothing goes on anymore just for the joy of giving for a just cause or reason , so, Daga, what is your price ?

The Witch Queen - I like your straight approach to businesses which provides me with an encouraging sign of profitable work together and, in regard to my price,well ,you know nobody works for nothing these days or any other days and that includes the days gone by, because I am sure that even in the so called "golden days of our lives", people would not want to work for nothing, although many hoped that they would ! So, what does His Majesty plan to offer ?

Giant Oak Tree - I thought that, if you will be successful in the reformation of my Government, I shall name you Vice Prime Minister .

The Witch Queen - Ha!ha!ha!ha! You are always the same ! Hard as a piece of wood, in the head that is, Ha!Ha!Ha! You really make me laugh,You,Big Boy, a real master at diplomacy and a masterpiece of gubernatorial science !..But what do you think, Big Fat Boy, a Vice Prime Minister is in your Kingdom of pieces of wood when you, yourself, have to appeal to the services and the advice of a Witch, even though of Royal Heritage, to prop up and mend his government affairs ! You do not play games with me, dupe, and if you try your throat will be cut but, since you do not have one, you will be cut nicely and neatly right at your roots !...... So, be careful at making any "faux pas " !

Giant Oak Tree - You are blackmailing me !

The Witch Queen - Tit for tat, dear wooden stick . And what you think you are doing ?

Giant Oak Tree - Are you by any chance insinuating that I make recourse to blackmailing to ensure my survival ?

The Witch Queen - Yes, I believe so .

Giant Oak Tree - Careful, now ! I am the one now to tell you that I am no game and for you to watch your language, your steps and your behaviour !

The Witch Queen - You frighten me none , you big wooden stick, with a mushroom for a Minister and afarid of a couple of ants ! A fine King you are !.....And, yes, I believe that you are doing something wrong to your subjects, may be not really blackmailing but certainly short-changing them when instead of a doctor to cure their wounds, you choose a...Witch to do it !! Just think of it....a Witch ! You are a coward ,dear boy, standing there and crying instead of placing yourself at the head of your people and risk danger, even death, for their safety, progress, well being and prosperity and, above all, LIBERTY ! And to ensure all that that apparently you feel you cannot do yourself, you turn around and hire, of all the odds, a Witch !!...Poor naive Giant, don't you realize that the World today needs Leaders, solid, straightforward leaders, who will risk every thing to achieve an equilibrium in the World, now in great danger of being offset by many contrasting ideologies . Liberty is the yearning of the majority of the creatures on this World, yours too, the one you call your Forest, Liberty to believe in themselves, liberty to profess honesty, love of Family, love of Country . People do not want to be slaves and you, foolish Giant, who were a king, and you still are one, ruling over a people still free but you chose to become yourself a slave of fears , ghosts and childish preoccupations instead of confronting your State problems like that famous ancient Greek who, confronted with the task of finding a way of undoing a famous knot thought to be impossible to be undone, drew his sword and cut it open . You need to be resolute in you actions and in your deeds and you have been uncertain in your steps, causing your subjects to lose confidence in your way of governing, therefore became restless, intolerant and eventually moved into a revolt when the realization of poverty and stagnation gave way to insurrection, possibly thinking, apart from interfering malice from clandestine sources mixed with the honest, genuine subjects, that even a tragic end would be preferable to a continuing agony .

Giant Oak Tree - You certainly can come out with some good talk, dear Witch Queen, even you do not like me to address you with those titles, but you sure can talk with majestic eloquence and deliver a strong message for this "world" of ours, this here Forest, where we live in one way or another and, the latter, not always comfortable or serene, but it is easy for you to express yourself with so much candor and without any consideration for a possible disgraceful reference to whomever you may bring offense since you are riding on a broom and you can slip away in a flash should things not work out well or not work at all !

The Witch Queen - Only at night, my dear, only at night and at full moon .

Giant Oak Tree - Can't you fly during the daylight hours ?

The Witch Queen - During the day I'm busy making magic potions .

Giant Oak Tree - To poison the World ?

The Witch Queen - Now, listen here, you precious dupe, enough of this stupid talking back and forth, that's beginning to annoy me.

Giant Oak Tree - Would it be, perhaps, to say : " We believe that our verbal exchange has had its merits and a pause would be most welcome" ?

The Witch Queen - To hell with you and your verbal exchanges and I have grown tired and sick with this inconclusive blabbering, so , I am going to fork my broom and get out of here.

Giant Oak Tree - But, Daga, it is daylight . Didn't you say that you fly only at night and at full moon? Besides, tonight, there would be no full moon!

The Witch Queen - Well, if no full moon, that gives me some extra time to see what else you can come up for an offer in return for my services and may I remind you that down at your roots, the rumble of discontent may rise and from a rumble change into a thunder and from there into a conflagration and ,at that stage, nobody can predict the outcome of anything, not even a Witch could. So , the offer, ...well I do expect a "Royal size" offer !

Giant Oak Tree - Half of my Kingdom ?

The Witch Queen - You really make me laugh, you precious dupe, a naive of the naives of the naive trees !!...... Half of your Kingdom ? Are you crazy ? A bunch of some tall trees in a forlorn forest , infested with worms, centipedes and, lately, I hear, with ants and having an impertinent mushroom sticking itself into everybody's business, while just nearby those two legged creatures are at their best in destroying everything in sight , that is worms, centipedes, mushrooms and ants and all these trees around here just to make a fortune and all at your expense . Not even an entire Kingdom would be sufficient to repay me for my services, you ninny . What value can your Kingdom have when even your own subjects seem to refuse to live in it !

Giant Oak Tree - That's all I have : have no other, except my own self, Witch Queen.

The Witch Queen - And that is my price : YOU .

Giant Oak Tree - Damned witch !

The Witch Queen - Decide !

Giant Oak Tree - if only I could, if you'd let me.....

The Witch Queen - Decide !

Giant Oak Tree - But, in the name.....

The Witch Queen - Decide or die !

Giant Oak Tree - Damned you, revolting Witch ! I see your sardonic smile and you win ! What is it then that you want from me ?

The Witch Queen - Absolute submission.

Giant Oak Tree - But...... my conscience ?........my conscience...!!!

The Witch Queen - ....And unquestioning obedience to orders .
Giant Oak Tree - To.... what orders ??!

The Witch Queen - Mine ! Furthermore you'll have to worship me as your Saviour and Benefactor. You know, some time, even I need some ......moral support ! Ha! Ha! Ha! Ha!

Giant Oak Tree - Oh! Heavens !! The towering specter of wickedness and deceit !

The Witch Queen - You are wrong, dupe, and by saying that you show that you must have lost the thread of your reasoning, why, it was you who wanted me to save you and your subjects, these dark ligneous silhouettes in this dense and damp forest, and protect you and them from the sharp ax of those two legged creatures and, when I agree to come in and help you by throwing a magic spell, mysterious and griesly over this fortest so that no one would dare come in the Forest and cut down all the trees, you suddenly seem to turn around and feel sorry that you went into this agreement with me, accusing me of wickedness and deceit ! I am asking now, "what kind of logic does this King posses ? ", granting that he possesses one !! "

Giant Oak Tree - I din't know you well, then !

The Witch Queen - Don't blame me, my dear, because it was not me to call you, but it was you who very insistently courted me and begged me to help you. You, my dear King, you have a very short memory .

Giant Oak Tree - But I called you in good faith.

The Witch Queen - I answered in good faith too . Of course, there might be some slight variations from your good faith and mine . Mine is the good faith of a witch, of course !

Giant Oak Tree - I should have known it !.....Dear Me!!...I should have known better !!

The Witch Queen - But wait a darn minute, You King Royal Stupid Oak, no need to become so dramatic ! We are not rehearsing a movie scene, you know, but just talking plain business and who told you that your faith may be different or less "faithful"than mine ? Who told you that or where did you get that notion from?

Giant Oak Tree - Common knowledge , Queen Daga, just plain common knowledge !

The Witch Queen - Listen to him, a King who gets his information from "common" knowledge ! No wonder his Government is in a shamble !!

The Secretary of the Common Knowledge Institute....................- "Common", dear Queen Daga, in "OUR" understanding as well as in the registered reference study of the word, printed in our most valuable literary works, does not carry an assumption of "inferior", or, "undeveloped", or of "lesser value and taste " expression, but it indicates a knowledge of "many ", shared by "many " and compatible with realistic, down to earth, common identities of "many ".

t

Giant Oak Tree - Oh! Mister Secretary, Sir : do not pay any attention to her because she is not really interested in it or anything else except in what she is interested in and that, well, I would not want to elaborate any further.

The Witch Queen - But " I " would like to "elaborate" somewhat "further" into the issue of the meaning of "common"...!!

The Secretary of the Common Knowledge Institute....................- Your Majesty,King Oak, if for nothing else but for the sake of desirable fairness, the Witch Queen should be welcomed to express her opinion, I believe .

Giant Oak Tree - It is the choice of privileges of noble and fair people to be almost fastidious about the right of embracing and revere fairness in all its splendid candor .

The Witch Queen - High sounding speech, big words of majestic aspect and opulent meaning and content, typical of that famous proverb that says in reference to someone like the Giant Oak,the King, that it is advisable in that case"not to practice what he preaches" !

The Secretary of the Common Knowledge Institute....................- But, then, Your Majesty, Witch Queen, you had something to say......

The Witch Queen - Yes, Thank you : about "common" and about "faith " if the former is of a lower choice and the latter of a lesser value than his .

The Secretary of the Common Knowledge Institute....................- We praise your willingness to comment over those issues, Your Majesty, and never there should be any obstacles to free expression: so,.....if I remember correctly, You had expressed a desire to comment further on that "controversial" interpretation of the "common" contained in that phrasing of "Common Knowledge " : am I right ?

The Witch Queen - Yes, Sir Secretary, I really would like to add some of my comment and interpretation to that word, as well as to the other word "faith",which I had already mentioned .

The Secretary of the Common Knowledge Institute...................- This Institute and its Faculty will consider it an honour to listen to an open comment on issues, regardless of their origin, intention or purpose of meaning, since ours is common life's training ground .

The With Queen - Thank you, Sir Secretary and distinguished Faculty and I am elated at your highly praiseful foreseeing ability in the scrutiny of what is considered common or, may I venture to say, even uncommon,when that scrutiny is one of a WITCH.

The Secretary of the Common Knowledge Institute...................- That's only a name, and creatures only carry it .

The Witch Queen - Your keen and almost universal understanding of facts of life seems to progress deeper and deeper and.........................

The Secretary of the Common Knowledge Institute..................- Oh ! Not any deeper than a hole in the water, Queen Daga !....Our understanding comes from the simple roots of common knowledge, in a way very similar to the knowledge of the instinct of preservation among the many other natural instincts that anybody can observe everyday in all sorts, kinds and forms of creatures ! So, everything has his, her, its, their place and, now, we are anxious to hear your comment !

The Witch Queen - Thank you ! But, now, I am confronted with a difficult choice ! Shall I start with "common" or shall I start with "faith" ?

Giant Oak Tree - I would suggest to start with both of them at the same time................

The Witch Queen - I beg your pardon !!

Giant Oak Tree - Well, dear Queen and, purely by "common" and "simple" power of deduction, an explanation of those meanings, that is 'common and faith', formulated by you would carry, sadly, the same meaning for both of them, for all you care !

The Secretary of the Common Knowledge Institute..................- Your Majesty, King Oak, pardon my intrusion at the end of your spoken royal word,but may I humbly remind Your Majesty, purely out of the rules of common protocol, that Royal etiquette as well as the far more preferred and lauded aura of lofty and majestic dignity, Royal magnanimity, require gracious, respectful and sympathetic attention to the opinions of others and their ideas and feelings too, or shall we abandon the rare and splendid gift of discernment given to some chosen and deserving creatures by our indulgent yet thoughtful and purposeful Mother Nature ?....Sire !....Your Royal comment on the issue will be considered a great honour for me !

Giant Oak Tree - And honour you deserve, Sir Secretary !....and here is my comment : "Proceed, Queen Daga, in your voiced comment, if you'll be Royal !

The Witch Queen - To be Royal or not to be Royal , we heard of that, but "common" is the question!

The Secretary of the Common Knowledge Institute..................- "That", I think, has already been said, some time ago, somewhere, I really do not remember where but I know that it had been said somewhere, some time ago, by someone . Now, why it was said , well, don't ask me , but I feel pretty certain that we could find the answer in one of our innumerable scripts of our Common Library . Anyway , it sounds just as good now as it probably did when it was first announced some long time ago, proof that it must have been made of solid fiber if it sounds so good even now which is a long, long time from then, I think, but I am not entirely sure, so don't take my word for it and, if possible, ask time to help you.

Time ....- I cannot help anybody because I do not have a watch, besides , I am only a word . In spite of my long searches I have not been able to find any watches of some significant value anywhere in the Universe and from every shop I visited I always got the same answer to my request :" We have no watches and, even if we had them, they do not seem to be good enough because they only tell you the time for a limited period of only 24 hours and then they go back to the beginning and start again the same merry-go-round, and that's one thing. The other is that to check the time in the Universe you would have to have, that is if at all available, a rather large watch, so large, so big and so cumbersome that it would be very difficult to wear either on your wrist or waistcoat, if you were a human creature or in your brain , if you were not a human creature . In addition to that, I am having nightmares, at night, of course, when I wake up in desperate distress and ask myself, almost choking in my throat " Am I real ? " and, since I never get a sensible answer, actually, no answer at all, usually I go back to sleep.

The Secretary of the Common Knowledge Institute...................- Well, that's that! No Watches ! So, what comes next , Queen Daga ?

The Witch Queen - Next.........I should beat the living daylights out of this Royal Timber who keeps bothering and interrupting me , teasing and snaring me into going in a scrambled pattern of contradictions by his artful and contrived high handed posture at everything I say , so , what I am going to say , right now, is that HE , our big, giant Oak , our "Royal Timber" that is , actually HE is the"common no-Kowledge" jerk , big, tall and fat arborous Quercus robur and rubra of the genus fagaceous and cupuliferous trees, good for nothing but bearing acorns and making furniture, and, in saying this , I have made my differential appraisal of the word "common" , as contained in the phrasing of "Common Knowledge" and that fully, completely and unequivocally encompasses the whole width, size and height of our good, old and very stupid Giant Oak Tree .

Giant Oak Tree - Sticks and stones.....

The Secretary of the Common Knowledge Institute..................- "That", I think, has already been said, by someone, some time ago, but I do not remember where or exactly when and by whom, but the meaning is the same: regrettable, indeed, regrettable, but unavoidable when two heads fail to reason and disastrous and destructive when many more heads fail to reason : indeed, a rather unfortunate but common event. And where does this flourishing elucidation lead us now, distinguished Illustrators ?

The Witch Queen - One more item needs to be elucidated , Sir Secretary, one that was mentioned earlier and which had a signifioant part in our diverging opinions , the King's and mine, and which carries, also, some practical as well as historical values and I would like to further comment on it .

The Secretary of the Common Knowledge Institute..................- That would be an excellent idea ! Besides, if I remember correctly, we had already understood that the item you are mentioning is the same that was supposed to have been examined after the completed examination of the item under the name of "common": right ?

The Witch Queen - That is right, Sir Secretary .

The Secretary of the Common Knowledge Institute...................- ....And, if I am not mistaken, it was about the noun "faith" : right ?

The Witch Queen - That's right, Sir Secretary : it was a question whether something that our Giant Oak Tree had said and I had also similarly said, that caused some verbal as well as some emotional distress .

The Secretary of the Common knowledge Institute..................- Yes I do remember : you wished to comment on the word "faith", which word, apparently, had brought forward a question about its value when used in contest with diverging opinions : right ?

The Witch Queen - Just right !

The Secretary of the Common Knowledge Institute...................- Well, Queen Daga, the Forum is open, the podium is yours : we are anxious to hear your voice and your speech .

Giant Oak Tree - I am not .

The Secretary of the Common Knowledge Institute...................- Sire ! Noblesse oblige !

Giant Oak Tree - I guess it does, particularly when it suits somebody's mischievous aims! So, let's hear it and, hopefully, Noblesse will forgive us .

The Witch Queen - Thank you, Sir Secretary, and your renewed invitation for me to speak and conclude my appraisal of the last item in question couldn't have come a moment too soon following the remark of our Giant Tree which pinpoints exactly the essence of our last item .

The Secretary of the Common Knowledge Institute....................- Oh!,Yes, I understand: the"faith"item .You do mean the faith item ,don't you?

The Witch Queen - Well, yes, in a way,yes, and I'll comment on that later, but, right now, I am referring to our Giant Tree's latest sentence when he said......"when it suits somebody's mischievous aims..." and that is precisely the melting pot of our explosive disagreement .

Giant Oak Tree - I'd love to listen to that !!

The Secretary of the Common Knowledge Institute....................- I am somewhat confused , Queen Daga, and find it somewhat difficult to correlate "faith" with "mischievous aims", because in our common, everyday understanding , we just "ain't that complicated", but I am still willing to hear what you have to say, so , please, do not let me interrupt you anymore !

Giant Oak Tree - I'd rather throw her out if I'd listen to my better self , but, since I cannot move, may be Noblesse will have a better idea than mine about it all !

The With Queen - The king appears furious !

The Secretary of the Common Knowledge Institute....................- Well, the king is somewhat upset, but that's understandable , However I believe that he has agreed to listen, so, please, go ahead , Queen Daga .

The Wich Queen - Thank you, Sir Secretary, and I am going back in time, several centuries ago, when I met by pure chance one fine day of Spring in old Florence,in the beautiful land of Italy, a Florentine man, already famous in his own time and a writer, a politician and a thinker of "summa cum laude" fame, and whose political philosophy inspired me at times when trying to achieve a difficult task given to me by chance or requested by the whims of the intemperance of some creatures and, with that word"intemperance", I mean the lack of tolerance for the ideas or desires or yearnings of other creatures, so that when toiling with difficulties while trying to reach that planned goal, I went back to read of his works and where his political philosophy appears to concede that " the end" justifies "the means ",and our good old Giant Tree just mentioned,now,in his last sentence, indirectly, of course, that by closing one's eye to the mischievous machinations of somebody while making an effort to get the end that is desired and using "all and necessary ,adequate means", to get it, is not an honourable cause.

The Secretary of the Common Knowledge Institute..................- Is that where the notion of the word"faith"comes in to cause your disagreement?

The Witch Queen - Not quite, and it was mostly a question of poor trust in each other when we were protesting to one another that our answers to questions were in good faith and ,of course, some question arose whether the faith of a "Quercus genus" King, our Gi-ant Oak Tree, was as good as the faith of a witch, even if Royal ! Personally, I believe that the whole question rests on "whose" faith we are talking about, because"faith",in itself,is always good in its abstract meaning, but it might change in its meaning, interpretation and intent depending on the character of "WHO" is using that faith. But, of course, once started, we kept on spiting at each other and this spiting, more than anything else, brought about our disagreement .

The Secretary of the Common Knowledge Institute................. - From what I can understand from your explanation of the sequence of words that caused your mutual misunderstandings, it seems to me that it was not worth, after all, even talking about it .

Giant Oak Tree - Agreed . But it's not the "talking" or the "discussing" that causes the problem ! SHE is the problem..!!

The Witch Queen - And HE is too and even worse than a problem !! You see, it is easy to converse with you, Sir Secretary, and it is a relief to hear your assessment of various things, but talking or discussing or making plans with that giant chunk of wood is a real pain on account of his unabiding, uncompromising attitude on almost anything, yet he expects results for what he is after and, at the early beginning of our acquaintance, when I started taking steps to achieve that "end" that he so much desired, by using any available and effective "means", there he suddenly turned around and suffered from some convulsive emotional outbursts about his CONSCIENCE!

The Secretary of the Common Knowledge Institute..................- Not an uncommon case, Queen Daga, and most often it stems from an emotional condition due to fear of impending doom or from a severe distressful anxiety about an undefined situation that could develop into something bad or adverse, even though no definite pattern or warning has yet surfaced . Not an uncommon case, at all, Queen Daga.

The Witch Queen - Case or no case, anyway, it makes it very difficult for anybody to do anything at all with people of that kind of disposition.

Giant Oak Tree - I too happen to know "somebody" with that kind of disposition may be even a notch over the one I am accused of having, but the difference rests on the fact that the "somebody" just mentioned can fly away on a full moon if things go bad or are not as satisfactory as originally planned and hoped that they would be, while I, regardless of good or bad tidings,have no choice but to stay here planted solid on this ground :.....the same old story....nothing looks ever so bad from the other side of the glass !....and here I rest my case .

The Witch Queen - Did it ever occurred to you, big chunk of wood, that your inability to move around might represent a safety measure by our all-thinking Mother Nature when she concocted you so as to make sure that your stupidity could not be spread around but stayed in one spot for ever ?

Giant Oak Tree - But allowed your venomous turpitude to fly around to all corners of mountains, oceans and forests, including this one of mine, you abominable witch, spreading fear, disaster and terror to peace loving creatures just to satiate your thirst for lust, savagery and wickedness.

The Witch Queen - You heard the vague refrain of olden days, my dear, that advised you, or whoever else, when fearing the unwanted, to touch.......wood...touch yourself? You..... are made of wood, are you not ??!

Giant Oak Tree - Witch !

The Secretary of the Common Knowledge Institute................- Distinguished Exponents of divergent opinions, I ,The Secretary of basic,simple, easily assembled and disassembled opinions, notions and creeds, as well as in my capacity of the disinterested party to all this exchange of interesting points of view,I have, reluctantly, to disagree with the Queen Daga's statement on account of the known fact that our Giant Oak and all of his predecessors since they were created and the ones that will follow, have actually spread and can spread themselves by the very reduplicating mechanisms provided by the all thinking Mother Nature or whoever for her, as the case may be. So, I believe that time has come when this contrast and denunciation of notions, opinions and character colourful descriptions, should now come to its conclusion and terminate the entire engagement of wits, from both of you, You Revered Royal Exponents.

The Witch Queen - The Secretary is right! This long drawn and rather "contents thin" and very silly, childish like in appearance and motive verbal duet, has done nothing to clarify those issues being evaluated and contested and it has only worsened our attitudes towards one another and THAT is not the result of good, straight forward reasoning . I believe that we should listen to the Secretary's advice and follow his lead . Don't you think so , King Quercus ? King Quercus of the famous Quercus Fagacee Cupuliferous Trees, the majestic Giant Oak Trees !

Giant Oak Tree - Noblesse Oblige, dear Queen Daga, even under duress.Very well, then, let us bury the hatchet !...and that move, in itself, will be a wise pre-empting and cautious step forward . I am also ready to quit this nonsense altercation .

The Witch Queen - Well, it looks like we are in agreement on something, at least and at last!! And look, Big Giant Oak, how you have changed in this meantime!...From a tempestuous attitude and confrontational posture to one of more accommodating and reasonable inclination, all of which goes to your credit of Royal gracious amenability.

Giant Oak Tree - Thank you, Queen Daga.

Witch Queen - Yes, and you may call me now like that, as that initial seemingly vexed attitude of mine at your calling me Queen, has now subsided in a more friendly and open embrace of communication: you do remember, don't you, at the beginning of our encounter when I told you, quite sternly, not to call me Queen ?

Giant Oak Tree - I do remember it, distinctly.

The Witch Queen - Well, now, you see, my dear King, I'd really like for you to call me that way and yes, I would much prefer for you to call me Daga and I would love to call you as your Minister, when off official appearances, calls you ....

Giant Oak Tree - ....Charlie ?

The Witch Queen - Yes ! Yes...that's it : Charlie ! May I call you that.......Charlie ?

Giant Oak Tree - Yes, Daga, you may call me Charlie and I'll call you Daga . After all, haven't we talked enough together that we may know each other a little better and , in some way , even closer in our expressions and attitudes ?

The Witch Queen - Honest to goodness, Charlie, how true that is and how amazing it is, also, the way you have relaxed in an almost unbelievable friendly approach towards me!! Something I would never have guessed possible, after our initial confrontations!!

Giant Oak Tree - I have noticed that too, Daga, and it surprises me a lot, particularly so,because our confrontations, after the initial meeting, were far from what you would call them affable and courteous .

The Witch Queen - Yes, Charlie, and I fully agree with you . You see, Charlie, witches, once seen closer and talked to and understood in their way of speaking and thinking and in the way they go about their own lives, are not, after all, as repulsive, abominable and perverse as people, often, in their misgiving of interpretation and because of utter and wide spread ignorance, had represented them in pictures and held them in contempt in their restricted, prejudiced and super superstitious minds, people, I mean, who, may be, do not look the typical image of the usually pictured witch but act and think very much like one, probably hating me and you too, seeing in you a rich source of revenue, and then you see them turn around, as innocently as ever,and set their interests and aims in much the same way that witches would which,at times,and that is more times than often, is not that much more honourable than mine .

Giant Oak Tree - Have I, then, due to this indoctrinating process, become, shall I say,a bewitched and enlightened King of an enchanted Forest ?

The Witch Queen - Not so, Charlie, unless you want to see it that way. As you just heard from my story, it is more the suggestive evocative imagination of an old maid yarn and zealots' fantasies than anything else that makes you look towards the witches as being perverted creatures possessed of the devil, particularly so when the unattended imagination of a simpleton or the willful malice of a perpetrator shrouds them in the imaginary role of using abominable incantations and unhealthy practices when trying to reach the desired goal for their intended business .

Giant Oak Tree - How different the world of my Forest is today than when I was just a little seedling ! I liked it a lot more, then !

The Witch Queen - And Charlie, if you go and dig a little deeper ,you'll discover that "witches" is just a convenient "cover " name under which a great number of creatures thrive in their dubious deals in our own and everybody's lives today, as they did yesterday and they will do tomorrow . Charlie, it is the real, stark and realistic world of everyday where we all live and where we all try, in one way or another, some good, some bad, some objectionable, some criminal or unlawful, but all aimed in one simple direction and that is to make a living for ourselves, himself, herself or.....well, Charlie, aren't you trying to secure a good living for yourself too? Isn't it so why you wanted to hire me to "fix" your......"living" ? You see, we are all connected and, again, in one way or another,"WE ALL".....WITCHES inclued, need each other !!.....and that is.....whether you like it or not !!

Giant Oak Tree - If I had a choice I'll certainly opt for "not". And that's " for sure" !!

The Witch Queen- Charlie, dear Charlie, you should not think that way and you should not go back to those old memories of centuries ago and those absurd ideas of witches and bewitched creatures roaming the world, something similar to simple Folks seeing cheese on the moon !

Giant Oak Tree - No cheese on the moon ?.....Well, I declare....!!

The Witch Queen- No cheese on the moon, Charlie, and forget about enchanted Forests, too : there are none and there have never been any that I can remember and I have been around a long, long time!

Giant Oak Tree - And that's a real pity !

The Witch Queen - That I have been around a long time ?

Giant Oak Tree - Not that, the pity is that there are no enchanted Forests! I still remember ,when I was a little seedling,my Grad Father telling me stories of Gnomes sitting on toad stools under large, tall, enormous oak trees : I loved those stories!

„The Witch Queen - Yes,Charlie, in a way I agree with you and those stories do hold your imagination tight to the plot and their mysterious surroundings fascinate your fantasy, but our daily lives require something more than just fantasy and we are forced to leave the enchanted forests to the Gnomes and Goblins sitting on a toad stool and pay more attention, instead, to our daily bread !

Giant Oak Tree - We have come a long way, Daga, and all is fine, but something still puzzles me.

The Witch Queen - And what's that, Charlie ?

Giant Oak Tree - Well, if you say that a witch is just a "cover" for a person of dubious credentials, but otherwise just another "one of us", why then, when you first appeared to me, you showed up in such a dramatic fashion, shouting thunder and issuing bolts of lightning, flying at a vertiginous and chaotic speed on your broom stick while threatening the world around you of terrible and unimaginable consequences, if the world and everyone in it did not obey your orders to the letter ?

The Witch Queen - Well, Charlie, in this competitive world of ours, a little advertising is a most necessary tool to attract business, you know .

Giant Oak Tree - Well !.....I declare !!

The Witch Queen - Charlie, the world has changed , and so have the forests and.........

Giant Oak Tree - I begin to believe it.:!!

The witch Queen - Yes,Charlie, the World, the Forests have changed and they have changed a lot, but, at the same time, you have to keep some sort of a guarded balance between reality and modernization, conditions and appearances of local trends, distribution of local wealth, important representatives of local authority and civic status, influential lodges and associations, boy scouts schools and the various hospital Services in the event that you would become sick, then add a little bit of imagination as well as a dash of good luck and you may start building, producing and sustaining some form of a business paying attention to adapt it to all of the existing circumstances as mentioned above plus any other that may come afterwards, after becoming settled in that particular area, so, Charlie......

Giant Oak Tree - And why, dear Daga, are you "chanting away" with such a detailed performance about something of which I didn't understand one single syllable with that multitude of prevailing factors and circumstances and, more puzzling, what on a cucumber has all that to do with the changing of worlds and forests, wouldn't you, please,wouldn't you tell me, please ???!! May be I am too old to follow your mysterious like introduction in the business building process and I am not inclined for business anyway, in the firstplace and, secondly, I do not understand all of those steps to be followed in the seeming subtle game of makimg business work ! Dear Daga, centuries have seen my green leaves !!...I AM too old !

The Witch Queen - An old saying, Charlie, which I heard repeated over and over by countless creatures throughout my long existence and particularly treasured by abiding good folks through countless generations, clearly emphasizes the fact that "you are never too old to learn", so, I believe..................

Giant Oak Tree - And you can say that again, and.........." ain't I learning things..." !!!!

The Witch Queen - Not really so much more than you already knew : don't you remember, Charlie ? Have you forgotten it ?

Giant Oak Tree - What is it that I have forgotten and that I should remember ??

The Witch Queen - You were having a war and a revolution on your hands, Charlie..... well, I should have said on your branches,anyway there was a war and a nasty revolution going on in your Forest , Charlie, not too long ago : remember ?!

Giant Oak Tree - That was water long flowed under our trees, Daga ! I do not even want to talk about it : it displeases me .

The Witch Queen - Many are the"things"that displease folks all over the world and in all the Forests of this world, Charlie!.But you cannot be so dramatically and emotionally disturbed to the extreme point that you cannot even talk about them !!...and ,if that should be the case, Heavens forbid, then you are bound for a quick trip and a more prolonged visit to the local Mental Home, a step, this one, Charlie, to be avoided at all costs even to the extreme of accepting the standards rules of normal thinking, acting and behaving . Well, Charlie, at that time, when I first met you, you were ravaged by war and revolution......................

Giant Oak Tree - O.K ! O.K !...So I was !And what has"that"got to do with such emphatically projected trips to mental homes and dramatically embracing normal behaviour codes and so forth and so forth...??!!

The Witch Queen - Simple, Charlie, and as I was telling you just in a few words earlier, in order to ensure a fair success in business it is necessary to adapt to the conditions prevailing at the site of your planned business adventure, so, I adapted myself to the fury and threatening posture that both, a revolution and a war, usually command.

Giant Oak Tree - Oh! Those difficult times of war and revolution , so much liked by some and disliked by others, but you, Daga , did a real good job and performed an excellent business approach to the situation that fits perfectly well with what you just illustrated to me about how to conduct businesses ! I believe, Daga, that I might have misjudged you , in the beginning.

The Witch Queen - It is a normal first "Instinct" among the various creatures in the world and the forests of the world, Charlie, to be cautious and mistrustful, suspicious I'd rather say, of any new comers, particularly the way I came in !!...Besides I had also some other worries on my mind and I was very upset about some of my personal affairs. No wonder I must have looked a rather unfriendly and unapproachable type !!

Giant Oak Tree - Yes, indeed, the first impression was not very encouraging or favourable,but, instead, rather disturbing, and there were rumors going around about the reason for your arrival in our Forest that made your appearance even more ominous and threate- ing .

The Witch Queen - Yes, it is true that I had something on my mind that was disturbing me too, but I did not want anybody else to know about it. What did the rumors say, Charlie ?

Giant Oak Tree - Well , those little folks down there on the ground, where my roots are, run their mouths like water from a waterfall and news, impressions, opinions, gossips and all sorts of rumors reach them with the speed of light !....Almost incredible, and for one thing, they knew that you were nearby and that you were angry long before I or my Minister, the Mushroom, realized it !.

The Witch Queen - I must have caused quite a commotion, then, didn't I ?...And, again , what did you say the cause of it was ?

Giant Oak Tree - Rumors were going around that you had come to our Forest to revenge the death of your Great Grand Child who had died in the battle of the Piedermi during the last war and it was reported that you were furiously violent and with a ferocious look on your face and looking for those two legged creatures who had caused your Great Grand Child death .

The Witch Queen - And indeed I was ,Charlie ! And I assure you that on the outside it might just have been a rumor but it was wide open and bright reality to me !!....Yes, I was very upset and I had come to vindicate the death of my beloved Great Grand Child, Sir Alambert Piedileone, of the Piedileoni of Valcoccola ! A great soldier!

Giant Oak Tree - Did you find those two legged creatures, Daga ?...You know, those two legged criminals who had caused the death of your Great Grand Child,The Sir Alambert Piedileone, were also the same ones who had destroyed the Northern part of my Forest !

The Witch Queen - No, Charlie , I could not find them but I was able to work something else out that satisfied me just the same .

Giant Oak Tree - Really ?

The Witch Queen - Yes, Charlie, I worked things out in a foreign country, actually, in two foreign countries , who did not quite sympathize with one another , and I was able to foment so much mistrust, dislike and aversion to one another, always using the same business formula about businesses, that I had just explained to you earlier, and I purposefully manipulated that formula with added vigor of lust for revenge to the point that serious unrest followed shortly afterwards and the two Nations came to such short terms with each other that caused soon hostilities to break out and flare up into a disastrous , cruel, highly destructive war that practically destroyed everything that was there to be destroyed .

Giant Oak Tree But, that kind of attitude on your part, Daga, leaves me a little surprised and, also, disturbed, because why to destroy two Nations, innocent bystanders to a grief and lust of revenge on your part on two criminals responsible, actually, for the, shall we say,"accidental"death of your Great Grand Child, when those two Nations were not directly responsible for it, that enterprise of yours against them does not satisfy, in my opinion, an honourable cause !

The Witch Queen - The two legged criminals were citizens of one of the two Nations, Charlie : they were drafted at the breaking out of the hostilities and were sent to the front and no one ever heard of them ever since !......."THAT", Charlie, satisfied my lust for revenge . That's it and I do not want to talk about it anymore !

Giant Oak Tree - I understand you, Daga , and, as a matter of fact , I feel the same about my past experiences and problems and I can fully sympathize with you .

The Witch Queen - Thank you, Charlie, you are kind !

Giant Oak Tree - Thank you to you, Daga, for allowing me into your most secret personal history! Daga, you seem to posses universal Powers !!!

The Witch Queen - Charlie, no powers and not universal either !.....Just the right connections and the "proper" manipulation of the right business formula !!

Giant Oak Tree - I guess, you may be right. A guarded, cautious manoeuvring of well chosen steps in the right direction without any bombastic preludes, can bring faster and more reliable results than a blaring threatening posture and no skill behind it !

The Witch Queen - And there is a little more to be added to your excellent representation of reality check, Charlie, and that is that today Witches favour quite a different representation of themselves than the macabre image of olden days : they carry now flamboyant testimonials and have discarded the cheap means of transportation provided by the old style broom stick and opted for the more comfortable means of flying with the newly introduced aircrafts, and they sail undisturbed and respected everywhere they go and keep alive and running the old precepts of that famous Florentine politician and writer and thinker.....do you remember,Charlie, what I was telling you earlier about that famous Italian man ?

Giant Oak Tree - Ah!........." the end justifies the means" ?............
The Witch Queen - You are right on the button ,Charlie boy !!

Giant Oak Tree - Oh ! Yes, Daga, and I remember what you said quite distinctly ! And how could anyone and, I say, even a simple tree, even an Oak Tree, overlook the depth of those precepts which are just as good today as they were in those recently past centuries and still practiced in certain enclaves with unscrupulous astuteness.

The Witch Queen- Yes, Charlie, I have noticed that too, and I guess, it is because it does not come easy to forsake old habits, particularly when they bring good results !!

Giant Oak Tree - Undoubtedly,and,now,I feel totally bewitched, fully enlightened and comprehensively rarefied .

The Witch Queen - You are doing fine , Charlie, and you seem to posses the coveted gift , precisely, of comprehension and tolerance which, when combined, give a creature a commanding stature in the world. So, Charlie , now I really know : YOU ARE A KING !......and you are not just number one in my book , but you are first in my book . Congratulations !

Giant Oak Tree - I am number one and I am supposed to be "first" too ? How do those two descriptions go together ? Is that, by any chance, part of the enchantment I am supposed to be benefiting from ?

The Witch Queen - No, Charlie, it is a lot simpler than that !

Giant Oak Tree - I am glad to hear that and I feel relieved !

The Witch Queen - You see,Charlie, in our world, the world of witches that is, as well as of magicians, goblins, leprechauns and enchanted frogs waiting for a beautiful princess to get them out of their misery , "first" answers to a significance of somebody occupying a position of superiority, even absolute superiority due to special circumstances of birth or heredity or a privileged position whether deserved or not, while number "one" could be "anyone"and does not carry the devastating image of anything of extraordinary luminosity . So, Charlie, in the world of the Witches you are FIRST !

Giant Oak Tree - Well, although I am experiencing some slight difficulty in following your sharp reasoning about numbers but also praising your intuitive expertise on the values and aspects of cardinal and ordinal numbers, but, at least in my simple ligneous mind of just an old Oak Tree, I guess that restricting greatness, talent, ability and selective heredity to a number it would have the advantage of making it a lot easier for people to recognize and appreciate those qualities in other creatures other than themselves, particularly for those folks who cannot count, not even on their fingers, or their paws, or their claws or their talons .

The Witch Queen - You'll be surprised,Charlie,but many cannot even read number one on anything!

The Numbers - We are the beginning of everything, inclusive of Witches, Giant Oak Trees, Kings, Princes and Princesses and enchanted frogs waiting to be rescued from their misery by lovely Princesses and we were, also, the mathematical equations that made it possible for Pegasus to achieve its numerous flights transporting, on its winged mathematical-wonder of engineering marvel for those ancient times, Bellerophon in his attack on the fire-breathing monster Chimera, and making it possible for Perseus, riding on graciously winged Pegasus, to reach in the nick of time the rock to which Andromeda had been chained to be sacrified in appeasement to the famed Sea-Monster, and save her from being devoured by that monster, considering that Andromeda was Perseus's wife, but, apart from all that, no one needs to read numbers because, contrarily to the recent assertion by the Giant Oak Tree about folks counting on their fingers or claws or talons or paws, counting on fingers being a common popular pastime, up to ten if they have fingers and enough of them to accommodate that number or, those creatures who do not have fingers or, if they do and do not know what they are or what they are used for, or even not enough of them to count to ten, usually, do not give a damn to count anyway whether the counts starts before one or after one or before or after any other number that might come after that. So far, we have noticed that only the human creatures seem to have an "emotional number complex" and go bats over numbers of all sizes ,dimensions and mysterious interminable lengths and are known to go into a frenzy when they succeed in adding more numbers to the long lists of "them" numbers, they already have.

The Representatives of the "first"and the"one"- We resent the representation of our individuality by a bunch of ordinary numbers suspiciously driven by sheer jealousy at being just numbers and not of first ordinal status or cardinal sequence.Therefore we censure their statement as one lacking mathematical correctness and geometric precision

The Geometric Pyramids of Egypt - We tower over the immense desert in our geometrical precision and our mathematical correctness . We also know how many grains of sand are in any given receptacle and we know that in order to count them we begin with number one.

Number One - Folks, do not get yourselves drawn into counting grains of sand: that's nothing more than just a gimmick of the Pyramids to show off and, also, stop worrying about counting on your fingers or on somebody's else fingers and be amazed by a bunch of "loose" numbers !....Can't you see that all they are doing, those loose numbers that is, is talk loud so that they can be heard and noticed, that way, may be, being able to be taken into a logarithm and so being elevated from their base to the given number, a number that they could choose of their own stock! How avidly and possessively Jealousy and Lust for Power can induce creatures,even the numbered ones, to vie for impossible dreams, these days!

Chorus of the Logarithms...- What a nonsense ! These days no one ,number or no number, who cares anyway what they are, can count what those numbers are adding to their brains !

Giant Oak Tree - You know, Daga, those Logarithms may have something there !

The Witch Queen - Charlie, in all my long existence, I have not found anyone yet who does not have something "there" or somewhere .

Giant Oak Tree - How true ! How true! Indeed ! And life seems so repetitious in all its forms! But, now, Daga dear, we better go back to our original encounter and the crucial point of that encounter when we had assumed a rather confrontational attitude towards each other!

The Witch Queen - Indeed, Charlie ! Indeed ! I read you like a book !

giant Oak Tree - I believe, Daga dear, that my quest for a reconstruction and stabilization of my troubled and severely tried Kingdom, during the recent painful and deleterious effects of war and revolution, is a legitimate one and an urgent one and now, that we have established a closer form of understanding and communication between the two of us, let me ask you if you have come up in your mind with a good, reliable and productive blueprint of a solid project to achieve our goal .

The Witch Queen - But of course, dear Charlie , of course ! Am I not here for that purpose, Charlie ? But of course I am ,Charlie !.....And you have nothing to worry about , now that we understand each other so well..!!

Giant Oak Tree - Dear Daga, you must excuse me for appearing excessively insistent in this quest of mine,but, after all the tragic events which did occur on account of that revolution and war, any slight delay or hesitation in the reconstruction depresses me greatly.

The Witch Queen - Ah ! Don't worry Charlie! I understand you perfectly and I appreciate your anxiety, but wasn't I, by the way, the one who ran to your side to help you out of you dire situation in order to save your Kingdom ? I had no hesitation in doing that, didn't I, Charlie ?

Giant Oak Tree - Yes, you did come to my aid, even if with some rough approach, at first !!

The Witch Queen - I was tired of the long trip from the other side of the Earth, then, and I was not in the right mood to talk. But, now, we need to pause and reflect a little over the situation and be calm,very calm,lest a hurried up action would jeopardize our very best efforts .

Giant Oak Tree - I understand that, Daga dear, and I hope that a clear appraisal of the present conditions will lead to a satisfactory resolution and I hope so very much, Daga.

The Witch Queen - But of course you do hope, Charlie ! Don't we all constantly hope in our lives ? Well, do not worry about anything anymore, Charlie, and you need not have any anxiety or fears about your Kingdom:leave everything to me and I shall resurrect your Kingdom and guide it to safety, prosperity and glory !

Giant Oak Tree - Those words sound like a prophetic omen, Daga, and the pale vision of a dream about to come true ! But what about the plan and the means to achieve it? That is what preoccupies and worries me !

The Witch Queen - Oh! Charlie,you amaze me,really! Why, didn't we talk about that precise subject for about half a day??!! Don't you remember, Charlie ??!.......The "Means"you say !.....Well, Charlie, the end will justify the means I will choose to do the job and I assure you that I will not be very fussy in choosing the right means to do the job!.....Charlie, you make me laugh.....ha!ha!ha!.....Just don't you worry !!

Giant Oak Tree - I am not really worrying about your ability in choosing the right "means" to do the job, Daga, but do I detect a strange and faint echo of your past appearance in the way you have been acting and talking during these last few minutes ?

The Witch Queen - Do you really think so, Charlie ? Why, I am not aware of it, Charlie ! And what kind of acting and talking on my part made you feel that way , Charlie?

Giant Oak Tree - Daga, you seem to have somewhat changed in your posture , in the tone of your voice, in the more forceful expression of your attitudes towards the present situation and your acting, which has assumed, so it seems to me, a more resolute type of address to questions and situations. That's why I brought this subject up and, please, forgive me if this disturbed your feelings.

The Witch Queen - I understand, Charlie, and don't you worry a bit if you perceived some changes and construed them as you have described them to me. If that is the way I appear to you, it's just all part, I believe, of the business : in other words, it conforms to the compelling need to get into your best possible form adaptable to the selected job to expedite the business ! Nothing serious, Charlie ! Ha ! Ha ! Ha ! Ha !

Giant Oak Tree - I suppose you are right, but I cannot help being worried !

The Witch Queen - Worried about what ?That I cannot, may be,bring the job to a favourable conclusion ?...Ha! Ha ! Ha ! You Simpleton, You !...Just look and wait ! Ha ! Ha ! Ha !

Giant Oak Tree - I shall look and I shall wait, but what shall I do in the meantime, Daga ?

The Witch Queen - You may call me Queen, now, Buster and, as to your "act" in this job, all you have to do is rather simple : " OBEY " .

Giant Oak Tree - Oh !!..." That " !!

The Witch Queen - Yes," THAT ", and I mean : "THAT" ! You also will realize that failure to do so would incur in my displeasure with all the attached unsavory consequences .

ant Oak Tree - But...Daga !!...You.......

The Witch Queen- You may call me Queen, now : I just told you so !

Giant Oak Tree - But....but ...why such a change.....Queen Daga ??!....We were calling each other by first name just a few minutes ago..!!!...Why...I....

The Witch Queen - This is business, now, Buster, and the rosy interlude has had its useful and usable time: now, is back to real life and real ME, Giant Oak !!!.. Ha ! Ha ! Ha!

Giant Oak Tree - Immortal Gods ! This is a dream, a terrifying dream, it must be a dream or I must have gone mad !

The Witch Queen - It is not a dream, you credulous nincompoop, and you have not gone mad either, at least for now ! This is reality, plain and dry, Ha ! Ha ! Ha ! Ha !...You haven't learned your lesson yet , stupid chunk of wood, but, as we know, there is always time to learn !!!!.......Isn't there ?!...... Ha ! Ha ! Ha ! Ha !

Giant Oak Tree - Oh ! You mighty Gods on that awesome Olympus Mountain, why can't you free me from this ruinous ,destructive condition and utter misery ? Have I offended you ? Have I failed to make proper and deserved sacrifices to you?If I should have failed in my obligation towards you ,if that were the case, if I had erred, then,Oh, Mighty Zeus, why didn't you send one of your winged messengers to warn me of such irresponsible and unpious act on my part ? Have I ever failed in my devotion towards your Might and universal powers ? Oh ! Zeus, have mercy on this Oak Tree and his Kingdom...!!!!

The Witch Queen - Prayers are futile, O credulous chunk of wood, once the dyke is broken and the water gushes out with the thunderous power of your Mighty Gods !...Too late, then......even for a King....!!!....Just think, you Giant Of a Ninny !...and think hard ! ....What other choices do you have ?

Giant Oak Tree - Is this, then , the PRICE , Daga, You,.... Witch Queen ?

The witch Queen - Yes, Big Oak, this is the price, but far worse and higher if you quail .

Giant Oak Tree - Oh ! Gods , what is, then, wisdom worth when pitted in the conflict of righteous creatures and perverse souls?

Thw Witch Queen - Worse than that,is your weak and wavering mind,you simpleton of royal greatness!!...When in cahoot with perverse creatures, the same ones that you yourself were appealing to for help, at least you should have the courage to become perverse yourself !Your path is clear in front of you and back you cannot go anny more or the lightning will strike you, the rain will drawn you, the wind will tear apart your limbs, the hurricanes, the tempests will dilacerate, mangle your body and the sinister sound of thunder will accompany you to your grave.

Giant Oak Tree - Then I see, it's all over for me !

The Witch Queen - It's a point of view ! Ha ! Ha ! Ha ! ha ! Ha ! Ha !....You really make me laugh, Charlie boy ,you really do !

Giant Oak Tree - You called me CHARLIE again, Daga ! Does it mean that we, you and I , are back again as we were, friendly and in pleasant harmony with each other and planning for the best furure for my kngdom ? Oh! Daga, I do hope so very ,very much !!

The Witch Queen - Listen, crying boy, "Ah ain't just in the right mood for fun", and you either shut up or get lost, this latter feat hardly achievable by you alone unless I'll ask for some help and have you removed . What kind of nonsense are you talking about, you ninny ?!

Giant Oak Tree - I had thought.....I thought that you ....might have changed your attitude and become........

The Witch Queen - Watch it , Buster, "Ah ain't becoming anything that I never was", so You are bothering me, now, and you have disappointed me and I believe that I have spent already too much of my valuable time with a useless creature like you . You have had your way, in past times, now the hour is mine : your subjects are mine, now and you do not have to worry about their welfare : just look after your own, from now on! Ha ! Ha ! Ha ! Ha !...and wait for my return and whenever I do, I always carry the latest news that so much attract the interest of everybody . And don't you worry about a thing: you are in good hands with my many subordinates who always follow and execute my commands and wishes to the letter , in the same way as you will learn to do, unless you would be so ill advised as to ignore or criticize my orders and run into my displeasure,and that really, would be a pity.

Giant Oak Tree - But where are you going Queen Daga ? Why do you have to leave now when your presence here is more needed than ever, to save my Kingdom and set it right and prosperous again ?

The Witch Queen - Kings and Queens, the real ones I mean, have many subjects and a multitude of duties towards their subjects as well as towards the country of which they carry the distinguished symbol of pride, justice and liberty : how can you be so presumptuous, big chunk of wood, that you can entertain in your mind the notion that a Queen could or should stay here with you for an unlimited period of time??!! I advise you to attend quietly my return, whenever that will occur, think carefully over the mistakes of the past and forget about plans for the future, Big Oak, because you have none. That future, your future, now, belongs to me. Ha ! Ha ! Ha ! Ha ! Ha ! Ha !

Giant Oak Tree - Not the future, damn witch, but is the present that comes crashing down !

The Witch Queen - Not only you are a dramatically inclined creature and a slow tree in churning your lymph in deep thoughts, but you are also far too big for being comfortable in company with other creatures : in other words ,you are stupid . You have compromised your right to exist with your presumptuous attitude which and because of its very appearance reflects your real mind and image. As I have already told you, don't dream of impossible exits from your doldrums, because the future has no more value for you, dear King of some lost Forest .

Giant Oak Tree - I may not be a King to you, but I am a King to myself, if to nobody's else and it is in this capacity of mine, by birth, by right and by Nature's mighty will, that I TELL you, abominable witch : GET OUT on your broomstick, now, with or without a full moon, and don't think of ever coming back to stir up your empire of ill-will, treachery and deceitfulness ! Time will come that your name will go down in history as a despicable, hideous, disparaging symbol of hypocrisy, horror and unscrupulous intrigue, despised by everybody and everything, inclusive of the most magnificent and regal Forests in this Forest world of ours ! Now "Git" or I'll summon my still loyal and faithful Praetorian Guards and have done with you ! GIT OUT ,damn witch ! Git out of my Kingdom !

The Witch Queen - I see and I hear, you dumbbell : the last utterance of desperation !! What do you think you can do stuck as you are in your deep sunken roots ? Are you going to brandish a sword, may be several swords for as many branches that you have and try to scare the daylights out of people, that is, stupid people ? It looks to me that you have not learned your lesson yet and it's high time to put a definite stop to your unimaginable stupidity and let this lesson be a good reminder to all who may feel a need to be haughty with me !

Giant Oak Tree - The will of all the Forests will condemn You !

The Witch Queen - Damn You ! Damn all the Forests ! I am Daga, the Witch Queen, the Queen of Queens and of all the Kings in this Universe of Forests : I summon you, evil spirits and malevolent creatures ! To me ! To me ! I command you ! Wind, Tempest, Thunder and Lightning, To me! To me ! This is my order ! Dash your fury down there where the thick forest thrives with all its giant trees and the young shrubs aiming hopefully for the sky and where the confusion, the despair and the misery reign supreme at this moment, and accompany me in the savage onslaught that so well identifies my personality and the Regal Mantle of my Royal Identity .

Lightning and Wind
Tempest & Thunder – Daga, O Queen of Darkness, Malignity and Rancor, your orders are our wish .

The Witch Queen - Then GO !.....Destroy, kill, incite dissidence, disorder, hatred, arouse fear and spread terror, and warp all of those creatures' minds, obliterate judgement and common sense and incite to rebellion and against each other, whoever they may be . GO ! That is my order ! Destroy, ravage, spare no one, not even a blade of grass, a puff of pollen, or a clear and shiny dewdrop.! GO !

to Wind, Lightning Thunder & Tempest - Your orders will be carried out, O mighty Queen Daga . Your orders are our coveted reward and our pride !

*** ....As the Witch Queen departs, the Thunder, the Lightning, the Wind and the Tempest set out to expedite their assignments among the creatures of the Forest Kingdom, causing catastrophic distortion of thought and behaviour and producing an avalanche of undescribable insane acts and weird attitudes in the bewildered little creatures of the Forest Kingdom and intense, widespread destruction of tangible assets, while with defiant shouts of overheated hatred and obscene invectives against each other, the confused and irrational hordes of all kinds of Insects and small creatures are swirling around, aimlessly, in the Forest, totally unknown to them why they are acting that way........................ ***

Chorus of the Snails - Time is up! Revenge inflames our spirit! Our Hearts, should we posses one, beat the rhythm of our war song ! Down with the mushrooms ! Down with the Tyrants, whoever they may be and wherever they may be or wherever they are or could be or would want to be or not to be at all, to us it makes no difference, because we are snails and snails know nothing about Tyrants,so"WHO CARES"!! Down with the puppet Tyrants of all the Forests ! Down with everybody !!

Chorus of the Worms - Long live Liberty ! Death to the Snails !

Chorus of the Centipedes....- Hail to the glorious survivors of the Army of the Piedermi ! Long live the flame of justice and freedom for all except for the abominable mushrooms and the despicable Giant Trees ! The fallen Heroes have risen from their graves and are leading our quest for total victory ! Death to the mushrooms and to the giant trees ! Death to the snails ! Death to the lizards and the vile asparagus plants!

Chorus of the fugitive Ants - What's the use of being frugal in times of utter ruin, discord and confusion when the best of everybody's thinking ability has been shattered into a thousand and one pieces and reason sent to smithereens in this whirlwind of unbridled violence and hatred and uncompromising madness !!....HAIL ! MADNESS !, then, and let us forget to gather the fruits of the land to bring them in a secure storage area : that should be the work of our future slaves, the mushrooms and the giant trees, that is, and not for us to do such humble menial duties ! Therefore it is herewith declared that our destiny lies with the revolutionary forces of all sides, colours and creeds and with our joining ranks with them while, at the same time, embracing the inveterate chaos and unforgiving violence ! Down with everybody and everything that stands up! Down with everything that stands anywhere! Death to the asparagus plants and the sugar beats ! Hail, triple Hail, quadruple Hail to our Queen !

The combined voices of Lizards, Sugar Beats and Asparagus Plants -Idiots! Has anyone ever wasted any time in teaching you some manners ?....Or are you all fishing for a punch on the nose ?

The Insects - We know about punch and we can brew up some mighy good beverqge of it,but we have never heard of a " punch of the nose ". What kind of spices do you use in making it ?

The combined voices of Lizards,Sugar Beats ans Asparagus plants - The most commonly used ingredients are a firmly clinched fist, a fast swing of the arm and a well directed trajectory of the wrist and an idiot at the receiving end : that makes an excellent punch .

The Insects - Quite interesting . We'll have to try it sometime: may be we'll invite you to our house and we'll welcome you in with an excellent punch on the nose, made fresh just for you .

Giant Oak Tree - The horrible Witch is gone but the Weather has turned unpredictable and it appears as changing into a violent storm with an unending peeling of ear-shattering thunder : the sky has turned very dark, menacing like, and rain has begun to pour down with violent force spurred by sudden gusts of stormy winds, and incessant lightning ! The poor little creatures are scrambling for some shelter, wondering why such an unusual tempest should have come upon them, so suddenly, so devastatingly and out of the blue !!..........Oh ! Oh ! Lor' have mercy on us ! What is this ? The rain has picked up with fury and it is so dense, so fast pouring down that's like a solid, continuous sheet of water and I can't see an acorn in front of me ! The fury of the Wind is tearing the branches off me and the other trees and the lightning continues to strike everywhere, relentlessly!!!.....This is the worst tempest I have ever seen in this Forest since I was born !....That wicked Witch!! But a day will come when the World of all the Forests will take this infamous Witch to reckoning of her hideous deeds !!!......Oh! How right the Mushroom was, old Sir Fabius, my trusted Minister, when he was warning me to be afraid of creatures bearing presents with a sardonic smile on their faces!...Heavens ! The screaming ! The cursing ,down there !....Shouting and threatening "salvos" of hostile words uttered in a crazy, disorganized, senseless sequence that makes it sound as if everyone down there on the ground of my Forest has gone out of their minds !!.....It is the evil, malevolent, heinous work of the devil Queen, the Witch Queen !!......and she has no religion !!!!....Oh! Omnipotent, Mighty Zeus, stop this unjust fury !

**** While the vengeful hatred of the Witch Queen is tearing apart the Kingdom of the Forest,the World begins to note some changes in his personal health which he cannot readily justify but, based on the outsiders'view of some old and knowledgeable Asteroids, from the Galactic University of "Twinkle Little

Star", his indisposition, of the World I mean, appears to be ,at least for a good measure, the result ,yet unknown to him, the World I mean, on account, firstly,of the turmoil caused by conflicts of natural interests among various insects, birds,trees and greedy two legged creatures and, secondly, of the reeling from the recent turbulence managed by the wickedness of the deceitful Witch Queen and her spiteful accomplices and accomplices subordinates, the Wind, the Rain, the Lightning, the Thunder and the Tempest and, as a consequence of these distressful and aggravating circumstances, our poor World has become depressed, somewhat somnolent , tired and disenchanted of his surroundings and is beginning to give some serious thoughts about slowing down and that would be a terrible thing to happen, if for nothing else but for the very existence of himself and everything else on him!!...So , as he was ruminating all those possibilities and conditions and circumstances, he starts reasoning to himself .... ****

The World - For some reason not quite clear to me yet, but I feel somewhat hot, rubicund and a little sweaty ! Should I be alarmed at this unexpected change of my physical stamina or am I to understand that my end is near ? Well, how could that really be true? I am still so young and full of vigor, at least I was just yesterday, then, early this morning, the trouble started and I became hot,irritable,a little tense and felt, also, annoyed with myself which is a ridiculous feeling big as I am and having been around the Sun for quite a while! Never the less I need to do something to correct this sick feeling and restore myself to better health and I am planning to ask those two Asteroids that cruise around here in my neighbourhood if they have any new knowledge on how to take care of ailments like mine according to the latest studies and experimental research at their University of galactic renown, the famous " Twinkle Little Star " University . May be they might have the answer, at least I hope so !

**** ......as the World continues to ponder over his indisposition and wondering what could have caused it and also planning to ask for a scholarly advice from some University Folks from a nearby galactic University, down in the Forest Kingdom things seem to have somewhat changed .The Tempest and her close friends are almost at the end of their destructive assignment and are satisfied that enough evil has been delivered and are preparing to halt for awhile and wait for some further orders, some uneasy quiet seems to be spreading across the land and the Forest and, as it usually happens in the vicissitudes of ours and everybody else's lives on this world, a solution for almost any trouble always seems to appear out of nowhere, somewhere, and

often , from the least expected or anticipated sources and begins to mend what war and revolution had undermined in the fragile fabric of the Kingdom and "things", eventually, calm down and life resumes its normal rhythm and it alleviates the former problems and prepares for the new ones which are sure to come !! So,"things" started to settle down in the Kingdom and the little people have begun resuming their normal activities, while some learned and scholarly old wise Wizards among them take pride in declaiming in public squares and in schools and in private Lodges of learning the poem on :
"La quiete dopo la tempesta",which translated into the local vernacular would approximately sound like: " The peace (or the quiet)after the tempest",a poem which had been written by a noted Italian poet , and the children were playing in the streets, in the gardens, in their homes .
However, this, of course, has nothing to do with the intent of a dialogue, particularly one between a Giant Oak Tree and a Mushroom, therefore we leave "things" here as they are and take a broader view of the scene in the Forest where it seems that the Thunder, the Wind, the Rain, the Lightning and the Tempest have accomplished their assigned task which caused widespread damage to persons and property and desolation and horror in a wide scale a short while ago, sending the little creatures scurrying in all directions desperately seeking a refuge wherever they could find one! Now, the five Apocalyptic Messengers who had been sent by the Witch Queen to terrorize and destroy the peace and the estates of the Forest Kingdom in order to teach a lesson to the incredulous and resentful King, the giant Oak Tree, these five Monsters,now having diminished their fury, prepare to leave, having been called away by the Witch Queen and assigned to some other high priority and urgent work in other far away lands and Forests and, as a result of their departure, the sky begins to clear up .

The Giant Oak Tree, somewhat relieved at seeing some peace returned to his people, at least a tenuous glimpse of it for the time being but an overwhelmimg joyous reality right now, is churning in his head how to get in touch again with the Mushroom, Sir Fabius, his most trusted Minister, from whom he had become separated when he entered in a sort of conversational engagement with the Witch Queen and Sir Fabius, being opposed to that meeting and having warned the King of the possible nefarious consequences stemming from it, had left the King and departed for an unknown destination, fearing the true intentions of the Witch Queen .

**** While the King is trying to figure out how to send word to the Mushroom to come back and join him in the laborious task of reorganizing the shattered and gravely impaired functioning of the Government, something out of this world appears in the now clear sky .... ****.

Chorus of the little Creatures............- LOOK ! LOOK !....IN THE SKY!!.....IN THE SKY..!!!

Giant Oak Tree - What's now??!......More troubles..??!!!.....Another WITCH on the Horizon ??!

Chorus of the little Creatures............- THE SKY !!.......THE SKY...!!!!

In the clear sky a large Comet has appeared, slwoly and majestically moving in the limpid aer and the World, still slightly indisposed, spots the Comet.................................

The World - Oh ! Look ! What do I see ??!......A passing Comet..!!!..That's good luck for sure !....Well...well....I'll ask her if she might have heard of any ailments such as mine going around . She should know, travelled as she is and so wide and large . ....Oh ! Here she comes !

Stella, the passing Comet - Hi ! World !.....And how are you this century ?

The World - Oh! I cannot complain, not too bad, really, considering the slight tilt of my side, but it will straighten up again, I hope .

Stella, the passing Comet - It will. It will....it might take a little time, you know, everything goes so slowly lately in this empty space but, eventually, everything falls into place . But, tell me now, how are things with you?....You seem a little reddish and it looks like you are sweating some : do you feel sick or unwell ?

The World - Not really sick, dear Stella, but a little under the weather, you know, may be just a cold : who knows, anyway thank you for asking .

Stella, the passing Comet - Oh !Yes, it could be a common cold . I heard a lot of complaints about that annoying ailment as I went by here and there and, in every place I visited, I heard the same complaint and I heard a lot of sneezing too,that's why I always try to hurry away from those places, lest I should catch a cold myself !

The World - Did you hear of any good medications for it, for the cold I mean, as you were passing by those other places with the same complaint as mine ? I am no doctor but I believe that some proper medicament could alleviate my discomfort and suffering .

Stella,
the passing Comet - Well, not really of anything outstanding, but I over heard some Asteroids who were frolicking around in the area where I was travelling through, just a short and uneventful couple of centuris ago, and were indisposed with the same problem as yours, and they were talking about going to bed on one of the planets around and have a good rest after taking a glass of warm milk and a couple of shooting stars and, if no improvement, then, in the morning they would call the Galaxy on duty call and ask for further advice.

The World - That sounds good, but, dear Stella, where would I get the milk from ?

Stella,
the passing Comet - I am surprised at you, dear friend !.....But have you, by any chance, overlooked the fact that you live and have permanent residence in the Milky way ?

The World - Well, of course I know that, and who wouldn't, but where is the distribution Centre ?

Stella,
the passing Comet - Ask Jupiter : he has the franchise of the business .

The World - Well, that's just fine : I get the milk from Jupiter's shop, but where shall I get it warm ?

Stella,
the passing Comet - Simple : just ask your Mount Vesuvius . His range is always ready and hot , he'll warm it up for you .

The World - I'll do that, Stella, and thank you for your timely advice ! You see, Stella, I was and I still am, a little concerned at my ailment lest I might pass it on to the other members of the Family, you know, Saturn, Jupiter, and least for last, Mars, Venus and Pluto and all their cousins Moons, but the ones I am most concerned with are Jupiter and Saturn, my Mother side cousins, so I was told by a Magician, who could turn themselves into a real menace when they sneeze, so big as they are !....Well, I'll be in bed in no time with a warm water bottle coming from Mount Vesuvius hot tap, and I'll drink the warm milk as soon as a shooting star will bring it to me.......A...a...aaa.........ap....ap....chieu !!! Oh ! Those two cousins of mine must have got the bug too !!...There is nothing much else anyone can do in cases like this..!!!...How true it is that you need a lot of patience in this world !

Stella,
the passing Comet - Well,dear World, I hope that you cold will soon be over with a little comfortable rest and a good glass of warm milk and you,I am sure, shall feel a lot better, but I cannot stay here any longer and I must continue my itinerary or the other Stars and Planets and Asteroids will be worried lest something had happened to me ! So, bye, Old Friend, and I want you to know that you are my preferred and

best looking guy in the sky, so colourful, so neat and so different from the many others I visit ! So , take good care of yourself and I hope that you'll be feeling better very soon . Goodbye, now!

The World - Bye, Stella, thank you for coming by and stopping for a while to chat with me. Have a good journey and come again and let me know what's new around .

Stella, the passing Comet- I will, Old World, friend, and, as you know, I always bring good news .

The World - I wish I could say so of myself !!

Stella. the passing Comet - Why ? Something wrong,again? I thought that you said that it was the cold that was bothering you : is there something else ?

The World - I am not sure but since yesterday but diminishing this morning, I had a persisting and irritating itching on my side.........

Stella, the passing Comet - Which side, old Boy ?

The World - The left side, Stella. Why did you ask ? Is "which" side so important ?

Stella, the passing Comet - Well, not"so"important in the real sense of "importance" but it is the side of the heart, therefore connected with passion, emotion, affection, moral nature and moral nature of conscience, courage and enthusiasm, it could have been some conflicts of all those properties clashing with equally adverse ones as I see it occurring frequently in other places while I travel trough those areas. Nothing to worry about, really, it that were the case, so do not over worry over it !

The World - Well, by the way you mentioned that, in your experience, is there anything good or useful that can be done to get this extra discomfort under control ?

Stella, the passing Comet - Well, old Boy, according to the Galactic Centre of Internal Studies in regard to similar cases, they are due, most of the time, to some form of indigestion and a few burps and a generous throw-in of some additional type of laxative and even purgative, like a mixture of Moon dust, regular sand, and you have a good supply of it in your Sahara desert, mixed together and cooled with Martian ice, will, usually, promptly relieve the problem . Well, I really must go now, so, see you again sometime, old Boy, I believe in a couple of centuries and I'll see then if my recipes did help you . Bye, now, and take care .

The World - Bye ! Bye ! Stella, and come again ! I'll be waiting for you ! Have a good trip ! (now, talking to himself)........May be Stella is right : a few burps and a good laxative and I might get rid of this indigestion !.....So, I'll give it a try and may be I'll feel again as good and happy as the brightest Star ! ....)

*** Meanwhile, down in the Forest................***

*** While the Comet and the World were engaged in their conversation, the little creatures in the Forest could hardly absolve themselves from taking their eyes away from that celestial sighting and had kept on gazing at the sky as if mesmerized by that unusual sight.................................***

The little Creatures - The Sky !....The Sky !....A Comet !....A Comet...!.....A Comet...!!!!

The Elderly little Creatures - We have never seen such a majestic Comet in our entire lives !

The little Creatures - We are afraid !

The Elderly little Creatures - Afraid of what ? That Comet, big and awe-inspiring as it looks, is so far away it could not even see you in a thousand years.

The little Creatures - But if it cannot see us and we cannot watch it closely and touch it, why is it there ?

The Elderly little Creatures - Nobody knows, except that everybody knows that they are there. No wonder, really, because there are so many controversies about our very selves and so many explanations of that ,except, as it is for the Comet, everybody knows that we are here. Anyway, nothing to worry about : she is so far you couldn't touch it even if you tried..!!!!

The little Creatures - Not even with a very long stick ?

The Elderly little Creatures - Not even with your wild, wilder, wildest imagination and most willing imagination !

The little Creatures - But, dear and respected Old little Creatures of the Forest, we are poor people, we have very little of everything and we have not one ounce of imagination in our pantries, we never had any and we would not even know where it could be purchased, should we want some, or if there are any stores in the Forest selling it .Besides it may be a luxury item ,affordable only by wealthy Creatures of leisure who can spend time searching for shops selling imagination, but, we are sure, it would be too expensive for us, poor creatures.

The Elderly little Creatures - Imagination is free, dear little ones and anyone can own some, should they wish to have and enjoy some .

The little Creatures - Then, it must not be worth much if it is given away free for anyone who may want it !

The Elderly little Creatures - About its worth, it all depends on which way you like to think of it .

The little Creatures - Oh ! we didn't know that this stuff called imagination is something to think about : we thought of it like something that can be eaten : that would be something we could really use.

The Elderly little Creatures - Well, no, it is not edible stuff but, in some cases, it has provided good food for people who used it extensively.

The little Creatures - Oh ! Where did they get it ?

The Elderly little Creatures - Well, it is something a little personal and kept under discreet understanding, but it has been observed that Mother Nature is able to get it at a reasonable bulk rate price and when it has gotten enough of it in the store, then distributes it around to first come first served, so nobody knows for certain at the time of birth of all of us ,who gets it and who does not .

The little Creatures - Strange way of doing business, if you ask us .

The Elderly little Creatures - Well, as we alredy said, it all depends which way you like to think of it : some folks like to imagine things even without imagination and some other folks don't like to imagine things even if they have imagination, most of the time, not knowing what it is there for. Then, some other folks would like to be able to imagine things or anything else but are unable to do so because they were not the first ones to be there in time at Nature's distribution Centre to get some, or, if at the very end of the line, might have gotten only some left over little crumbs that would have been very difficult to even imagine them as being able to imagine anything and, then, some who were the first ones in line and were given a good supply of fresh and wholesome imagination, not always imagine, in a fresh and wholesome way, good, sensible and honourable imaginable things.......so........

The little Creatures - Yes, we understand that, but we have no money to even manage to think, let alone imagine things, should we, may be, have been in the last line of the distribution process and got just a few imaginable crumbs, so, we just look at the Comet and think of nothing : just looking . Even that , "just looking", we do as the result of a pure chance of circumstances because, if we were asleep or some where else, or blind, we could not have seen the Comet and, THAT would have been IT , imagination or not........we would have missed the sight of a beautiful thing but that, again, is debatable as to its inherent importance of being seen, because a born-blind creature could never have seen it and to that person a Comet would have been just a Comet, just a word .

The Elderly little Creatures - But if the sighting could be described to them,they could still see it in their imagination, the only question, though, would they be at all interested to know it!

But that, again, is another question and something out of the ordinary : we should always try to navigate in the middle lane, where waters are usually safe and that, again, is another question .

The little Creatures - Tell us, O wise old Creatures, how many questions does anyone need in order to be able to imagine things ?

The Elderly little Creatures - As many as you can imagine or, shall we say, as many as you may be willing to imagine . You see, that is another question .

The little Creatures - We see.....well, actually, we don't see how that works but we take your word for it : we are certain that you must have seen a Comet before in your lives, may be not as big and bright as this one, but, may be, a tiny little one that you might be able to touch............with your imagination ???!!

The Elderly little Creatures - We did not see any Comets before this one but our Ancestors, centuries ago, saw a magnificent one, so big, so bright, that people, by just looking at it, changed their lives and history changed with them too . We still think that a Comet is a beautiful sight, an unusual sight at that, even if we do not know why it is there, why it comes by now and then and why it looks that way as it does, with a long, long tail and so different from the other stars, but, it is there, so why can't we look at it with our stupefied eyes and wonder......

Chorus of the Wonders - Wonder, per se,is just a second rate expression of ignorant perception of events, phenomena and sundries, unless supported by an inner impulse to try to explain its awe inspiring magnificence and mysterious composition .

Giant Oak Tree - As usual, give somebody something to look at and everybody jumps up ready and willing to throw in his, her, its or their grain of salt and I am tired of it all ! Actually, I am tired of everything after going through a revolution, a war, an invasion and a squabble with a vicious Witch, a deceitful, treacherous Witch, a real fiend disguised as a witch, and I wish that the Comet would chase her out of our Forest, for ever.

Comet - I heard you, Giant Tree and King of the Kingdom of the Forest, in spite of my distance from where you are located, but it is amazing what Comets can do.... ....well, we do not have to go into that right now, so, as I heard your lamentation and your proferred wish, I looked this way and I saw the bland, serene and peaceful look in the eyes of your little Creatures down there and that candid look made me feel good, really good and it touched my heart with an impulse of love right in the middle of my core, and I thought : " Gee, what nice people live down there ! They do not speak, they do not shout and they do not point their finger towards an unreachable sight : they just wonder !.......And that, dear Giant Tree, is just beautiful, at least from a celestial point of view . Because of those little creatures down there in your Forest and on account of that simple, clear and unbiased look on their faces, I will grant your wish and the wicked Witch will never ever be seen in or around or under or above your Forest and in any other Forest where simple, candid, honest and sincere people live . It was nice having known you, Your Majesty, and peace be with you,.............always ! Farewell !!

*** The Giant Oak Tree, waking up.........***

Giant Oak Tree - OH ! What a dream !!...And it is late...this morning....my O my ...how could I have slept this long ??!...What a dream ! What a Dream !!...and it looked so real.....!!.........Oh! If I could only fall back asleep and dream up the whole thing again..!! ...But, dear me, this is terrible ! I was trying to find a way to send words to the mushroom, my trusted Minister, to come back and join me again, when I must have fallen asleep ! I have not heard from him since we separated on account of that no good Witch and I, really, should have followed my little Mushroom advice and run away with him avoiding the Witch until she would have gone away and left the Forest ....but what am I talking about..??! For Heavens above !...It was a dream, Witch and all and I know that I am fully awake now and I know that I had an unbelievable dream....but WHAT a dream! Well,now, how to reach the Mushroom ?...But what a dream! What a dream..!!

Gnome - Mali, Mali, Tum, Tum, Tum . Mali, Mali, Tum, Tum, Tum .

Giant Oak Tree - Scarabello , is it you...???....Is it really you?...I hope it isn't another deram...!!!!

Gnome - Mali, Mali....Mali, Mali ...

Giant Oak Tree - Well, this is a surprise !!...Scarabello, I know that I can hear you and I am pretty sure that I am awake now, so I am not dreaming...tell me: have you heard anything about the Mushroom, you know, Sir Fabius, my trusted Minister ?

Gnome - Tum,Tum,Tum.

Giant Oak Tree - Heavens above ! But how could it be possible ? And I not being able to hear a thing about it !!! ....Could that be true, Scarabello ? .....Are you sure ?

Gnome - Mali, Mali .

Giant Oak Tree - Oh ! Great Gods ! My poor little Mushroom, my sharp witted mushroom , my Minister, with all of his illusions, good intentions and a lot of common sense, and so young !

Gnome - Mali, Mali, Tum, Tum, Tum .

Giant Oak Tree - But, I do not understand, Scarabello !..What about all of my subjects, I just saw them going back to their chores and putting their lives back together again....yes, Scarabello, I just saw them picking up from where they had left and get back on their feet......well,....or....on whatever they had been on before....I saw,them, dear Scarabello, just a short time ago.......I think I just saw them....or....Oh! Gods!!....where they, may be......oh !......were they....just in my dream...???!!....... Tell me, Scarabello, what happen to therm ?

Gnome - TUM , TUM, TUM,.

Giant Oak Tree - What ??! They too ??! I cannot believe this ! If this what you are trying to tell me, Scarabello, you wise little gnome of this Forest and known to me for a long, long time, and I trusted you in the past just as well as I trust you now, that what you are trying to tell me is true it would be a tragedy that even the damp of history could not tone down !..... And I was led to believe that after the horrible fury or war, revolution, tempest and all wicked insults to our way of living, things had turned up for the best and gone back to normal, slowly, yes , but on the right direction. !

Gnome - Mali , Mali.

Giant Oak Tree - Oh! Immortal Gods ! You supreme arbiters of human escapades judgeging our actions and planning recompense or doom for our actions, look and see what your sanctions of obedience and devotions to good and right might,sometime, be misinterpreted by some and misused by others or taken alltogether and thrown them at somebody with vengeful hatred. Is that your way, O mighty Gods, to repay and praise honesty and faithfulness to your Laws of decency and truth ?

Gnome - Tum, Tum, Tum .
Tum,Tum,Tum .

Giant Oak Tree - What's now, Scarabello ?

Gnome - Mali, Mali,
Mali, Mali.

Giant Oak Tree - Oh !Yes ,what's the use of wisdom unless there a sword behind it to protect or to make it work ! What would you have done, Scarabello, had you been in my place ?

Gnome - TUM, TUM, TUM.

Giant Oak Tree - To make a clean sweep of everybody and everything, right ?

Gnome - Mali ! Mali!.....TUM ! TUM ! TUM !.

Giant Oak Tree - But how to set out in those brief and lightning instants of panic, furor and madness the honest creature from the perverse ones and hit only the bad ones?A Government of civic and civilized heredity cannot dirt itself in innocent blood......or can it ??.. I do not think so, ...well ....I do not want to think so, although there might be circumstances where the malevolent intent of the assailants might distort, on purpose, the meaning of their attack and make it look as a preposterous legitimate issue out of a perverse and purely criminal act for personal, selfish and greedy aims to power and riches . Yet what would be or is the use of acivilized complex of people if it is not teaching the art of winning by the use of intelligence and reason ?

Gnome - Mali ?.....Tum ! Tum !

Giant Oak Tree - I know : it was used some time ago : the famous century of "reason" and the fiercest battles took place in tha period !! So, it seems mighty hard to say who is right or who is the wiser. Again, what would you have done in my place ?

Gnome - TUM ! TUM ! TUM ! TUM ! TUM !

Giant Oak Tree - Force, violence, destruction, ruin, annihilation, is that right ?

Gnome - Mali. Mali.

Giant Oak Tree - I do not feel as being convinced about it as you seem to be, wise Gnome, and I am not quite certain yet if you are saying what you really think and feel about it all! Tell me, Scarabello, do you really believe in what you are telling me ?

Gnome - Mali, Mali, Mali !!

Giant Oak Tree - You seem to overlook, dear Scarabelloo, in your emphatic affirmative tone the sort of the Mushroom and of all my subject , vanished in the unscrupulous, savage onslaught bythose two legged scoundrel who wiped out at the same time the Northern side of my Forest ,purely for the greed of riches and to put more weight into their miserable pockets ! What advantage, I am asking myself, could force and violence have in the peaceful coexistence of all living creatures when the violence of force, even when used in the defense of righteousness and justice, will kill and destroy the perverse along with the good one , instead of crushing the former and glorify the latter with the arts and civic virtues of civilization ?..... Tell me, wise Gnome , is this that I am saying not true ?

A solitary Bee - The wise Gnome has fallen asleep, O giant Oak Tree : he is not used to such a prolonged chatting on subjects that he has little interst for ! You know, his primary duty is to guard the inner treasures of the Earth, a real job of responsibility and not in direct dependance of what goes on the "surface" of the Earth .

Giant Oak Tree - That's rather strange !

A solitary Bee - Why do you say that, O big Oak Tree ?

Giant Oak Tree - With all respect for our wise Gnome, who is also my personal friend, but, in all truth how can he be a guardian of the treasures of the Earth by being fast asleep?

A solitary Bee - That is one of Mother Nature's wonders that gives some special senses to certain creatures and not to others and, in this case, the wise Gnome can hear and see all that is necessary to be heard and seen , brought right to him instead for him to go around and look for it . He is asleep but his senses are wide awake !!

Giant Oak Tree - Well, if that is so, and I have no doubt that it is, why then didn't he answer me?

A solitary Bee - That's why he is a Gnome !

Giant Oak Tree - He is a "Gnome" because he does not answer me ??!!!.That's a mighty strange way of being anything, I would say !

A solitary Bee - It may not sound very "mighty" but it is very "wise", sometime !

Giant Oak Tree - And what are you doing in this Forest ,dear solitary Bee ?

A solitary Bee - I am on vacation from my apiary and I came here to visit with some old friends. As a matter of fact when I stopped by your friend, the wise Gnome, and you, I was on my way to see some of those friends in their Apiary and see what they had new to tell me .

Giant Oak Tree - Have a good vacation and when you see your friends say "hi" from me too and tell them that in my capacity of King of this Forest I give you and them my most sincerely felt welcome in my land .

A solitary Bee - Thank you, Your Majesty : I did not know you were a King but I somehow suspected it because of your imposing figure, the majesty of your foliage and the sincerity of your address. I will remember and treasure this encounter . Bye, now, and thank you for talking to me.

Giant Oak Tree - What is this chanting I seem to hear in the distance ?

A solitary Bee - The chanting, your Majesty, comes from the Apiary where my friends are and they are singing the praise and the prayers of the day to their Creator who was so munificent in bestowing on them so much of good things .

Giant Oak Tree - I am so glad to hear that, particularly these days when creatures tend to forget the good things they have, taking them for granted as if "due" to them !

Chorus of the Bees - Nature did not give us eyes and mouths in an ostentatious form, but was kind and solicitous enough to provide us with antennae, wings and the will to work . We forage on the corollaceous envelopes of floral leaves , we suck the nectar of those flowers but we are not deceived by their gaudy colours and we are rich, useful and frugal . We are envied by many other creatures because of our unique assets and wherever we go we are always welcome in special lodgings and there are very many different flowers around for us to inspect and to nurse, and we are organized, politically, under the aegis of a Government of highly sophisticated social organization and under the protection and majesty of a Monarchy, but we keep all these trappings under close secrecy, this giving us the coveted ability to be deaf and dumb to vane prides and glories so loved by infatuated folks,but it empowers us with a sturdy, sharp and highly effective sting to daunt foolish and meddlesome creatures .

Giant Oak Tree - ......(turning to the solitary bee....).... Now, do your friend chant their prayers like that every day or only on certain specified days ?

A solitary Bee - Every day, every hour, every second of every and each day for each day, each hour, each second of their natural lives, King Oak .

Giant Oak Tree - Remarkable ! Pity Mother Nature didn't build the same safety valve in all of us!!

Chorus of the Bees - Look around, Giant Oak Tree, you are living far away from this changed world, whether a Forest world or any other world, and the time it took you to reach maturity and experience was a very long time because it take a very extensive and slow process in your growing from a seedling into a giant tree and the pitfall of your destiny lies in the unquestionable evidence that,once achieved full grown status and you are large, powerful and very, very tall, you will be left too far away from that world that Mother Nature had destined to remain small and bound to be born, to vegetate and to die in a short period of time, and your newly born little ceratures at the time when you were, like them, just a little seedling, will be there no more when you will fully grown and you will be surrounded by total strangers, a crowd of new beings with new ideas, new aims, new customs and new intentions and creeds who will look at you as someone, with an indifferent mind and a disinterested desire for past history, would look at a dusty old monument and think nothing of it .

Giant Oak Tree - Kind and laborious Bees, is perhaps your sermon prompted by pity for me ? But, if your saying means just that, why to linger on facts that strictly belong to Nature's Laws and which Laws no one of us, you, I or anyone else born in this Forest can change or try to evade . Your representation of the real development of life's intriguing steps would be of no comfort to anyone or it would not explain why you felt it necessary to explain it . I am old, dear Bees, and tired and saddened by all the recent unhappy events and I am also grown tired to talk, chat or argue .

A solitary Bee - But you were not old ,some time ago :weren't you ?

Giant Oak Tree - What kind of a question is that ? Of course , it is well known that "ANY" time "ago"means just that, so if you are old now you must have been young some time before getting old, right ?

A solitary Bee - I guess so.

Gnome - Mali, Mali .

Giant Oak Tree - You see, dear solitary Bee, even the wise Gnome agrees with me .

A solitary Bee - But I have heard some old folks, while chatting among themselves, saying that being old means being more experienced, more alert to pitfalls and "illuminated" by wisdom acquired over so many and almost interminable years of growth .

Giant Oak Tree - Fine !......And then be looked upon as a derelict object from the past,out of touch with the realities of present days,just as your friends in the apiary were just chanting and preaching it to me??!!......You, probably, little solitary Bee, may not be fully appreciative of the inner conflicts of some old creatures, the life's vicissitudes, the anxieties, the anguish,the fears, all of them piling on your conscience like a stone of formidable proportions !

A solitary Bee - Remorses, may be ?

Gnome - Mali, Mali .

Giant Oak Tree - Remorse, You say !!.....I have been a just Ruler and I have loved my little subjects as if every single one of them would have been my own son or daughter: I have no remorses, my dear !

Gnome - TUM ! TUM ! TUM !
TUM ! TUM ! TUM !

A solitary Bee - Apparently someone has second thoughts about your fervid statements, Giant Oak !

Giant Oak Tree - The gnome, yes, he is wise and he is my friend too, but he may not know every thing of somebody else's life .

Gnome - TUM !!

A solitary Bee - You see, Giant Oak, the Gnome contradicts you !

Giant Oak Tree - Contradiction is but an incongruous logical assumption of somebody's personal assets or statements or personal life's events, therefore I consider it worthless as far as your pointing to a subtle feeling of weighty remorses. I'd rather think of all that just as memories of events which could not have been prevented or anticipated in sufficient time to be prevented . Just memories and they can be weighty too !

Chorus of the Remorses - Memories... ?!...Memories...?!....We roam in the depth of the night bent to find and choose the bad creatures, and to instil in them the bitter recourse of shady memories or gruesome, reproachful memories and cause discomfort, apprehension and even fear.....Memories...memories...and it was just the past night when you, Old Oak,in a desperate appeal, called to us while the Witch Queen was destroying your Forest and your little innocent creatures. Remember...??!

Giant Oak Tree - Mine was wrath of anger at such destruction, fury and malevolence against me and my people, by so meaningless, perverse, murderous powers for the pure pleasure to inflict pain, horror and desperation all around them .

Gnome - Mali, Mali,.......Mali !

A solitary Bee - Oh ! Listen! Listen!,,,Something big, something very important is about to happen...listen..!!

Gaint Oak Tree - I cannot hear or see anything at all that would indicate such an important forthcoming event or if one would be coming at all : how can you tell that ?

A solityary Bee - May be you do not know, but we, dear Giant Oak, were richly endowed by Mother Nature with highly specialized mechanisms of communication apt to allow us to keep in touch and translate gathered information to and with each other,and I know now that something of major importance is about to happen !

Giant Oak Tree - You should consider yourselves very,very fortunate creatures for having received so much consideration by Mother Nature and you should bear sincere gratitude to her for being so imaginative and generous with you .

A solitary Bee - We are, O giant Oak Tree, we are !...And so that we can make our gratitude visible and tangible we produce large quantities of sweet materials that really delight all creatures in this Forest and also another manufactured item that is soft, pliable,and adaptable for many purposes of use which, among them, one that if slightly rubbed and polished, shines like the rays of the sun or, if compacted into a more solid consistency, it acts as a perfect seal to secure materials contained in any receptacle. This we do to show our gratitude, a rewarding work that many creatures can derive pleasure and enjoyment from it .

Giant Oak Tree - Those enviable gifts from Mother Nature must cause your night to be serene, placid and restful, free from memories, guilt or remorses !

Chorus of Remorses - Memories ! Memories ! Good or bad, seldom can be forgotten, overlooked or gently and unconsciously fogged . Of the unhappy,depressed and desperate creatures we are the assiduous companions, we are the liberators of the good who had turned bad, we are the Judges of the wicked creatures and the Persecutors of the fiendish soul . Remorses and Memories ! Ah ! Those bulky rocks of forbidden ascent, unclimbable mountains of perennial anxiety and distress. We roam the depths of the nights to choose and pick those unfortunate creatures and instill in them the unending desperation of the wrong that was done and can be mended no more, but only tears are left to lightly attempt to rinse its obscure image .

Gnome - Tum , Tum , Tum , ...

Giant Oak Tree - Yes, I feel the subtle and insinuating swishing of their passing by, but I do not take notice of their presence anymore ! My heart is old and has suffered enough, a mere wisp of drama could stop it for ever, but such an event,would not really preoccupy me to any reasonable extent : I might even be willing to welcome it. and the passage to a different time would be a relief from the present unhappiness !......Time !...When I was a little seedling time seemed to me as an immense space and a far, far away object, but, now, in my old age, it appears so quick paced and short lasting . But what is the use, as the human creature say, to cry over spilled milk ? It has been spilled, it cannot be put back unto the pail, what has been spilled will not, then, be a disaster or a ruin for the entire Family, so , get back to work, milk the cow again, she would not mind almost certainly, and get the pail full again, only a little caution.......

A solitary Bee - Really ? ! ...And what would it be ,Giant Oak , that little caution ? /!

Giant Oak Tree - Don't spill it again.

A solitary Bee - It makes sense .

Gnome - Mali .

Giant Oak Tree - I believe that I have bothered everybody here long enough with my old age attitudes,sermons and sentences,and it is time to leave all of you alone and in peace. I wonder how did you fare, dear Scarabello, during this prolonged chit-chat of mine : did it disturb you ?

Gnome - Tum,Tum,Mali.....

Giant Oak Tree - Well, apparently you took it in stride, nevertheless you seem to me a little upset .

Gnome - MALI , MALI , TUM! TUM ! TUM !......

Giant Oak Tree - Immortal Gods, this seems to be something serious : is it really Scarabello ? Listening to you everything should always go wrong : " Tum,Tum,Tum "!!......Well, Scarabello, what's happening now that's so attention-getting ? I do not seem to see anything so eye catching or so threatening to cause such an alarm: do you ??!

Solitary Bee - The Queen ! The Queen !!

Giant Oak Tree - Oh! That's why there is so much excitement around here ! Not another "Queen", I hope, like the one of past sad memories !....I guess it shouldn't be, because, if it were, the bees would not become so favourably and joyously excited about her appearance . So, it must be a different type of Royal Majesty, may be and, hopefully, more Royal than the first one of good memory ! Heavens be merciful on us!!!!

Gnome - MALI ! MALI ! MALI !

Giant Oak Tree - I mustn't have been too far wrong, it seems !

Chorus of the Bees - The Queen Bee has flown fast and far to choose her spouse. Our Queen is good, laborious and very helpful to all of us, she is also very versatile in the performance of her many activities and she can give us good, efficient "workers" bees whenever we need them, govern us wisely and assiduously and dies when the time comes : what more could any bee want ? Besides, dear Old Giant Oak, to be noticed that we are not very attractive types of creatures as insects and, certainly, not very beautiful or lovable and we do not deck ourselves with those gaudy and ostentatious personal adornments so lavishly exhibited by many other types of creatures and, yet, no one offends us, or conspire against us, or shows any undue or violent disdain at our presence somewhere, on the contrary, almost everybody protects us ,while, in contrast, unscrupulous and callous hunters always kill without mercy the most beautiful specimen among the most beautiful creatures .

A solitary Bee - By a thousand wasps !! Good show !

Gnome - Mali ! Mali !

Giant Oak Tree - Oh ! Your talk is fascinating, dear Bees !....Unfortunately it does not help me or my kingdom very much, at this time! I appreciated , anyway, very, very much your sharing with me the important aspects of your existence and the priorities of your life and I will preserve in my memory the wise and solid representations of how your life produces good, serviceable and practical things. But, before you resume your work and your activities I would like to ask you a favour : you seem so kind and helpful that I thought you may not mind helping me with some information, or am I asking too much ?

The Secretary of Queen's Chamber - You are most welcome, Sire, and Your Majesty will receive all the possible and available information on that to be requested that may be in our knowledge or possession . What does Your Majesty require information on ?

Giant Oak Tree - I was wondering if any news might have filtered down as to the condition and whereabouts of my former Minister, Sir Fabius, the Mushroom, who had separated from me on account of some disagreement in the emergence of a critical situation in our Forest,and I have never heard of him anymore and I am grieving over this loss of communication and separation : do you, by any chance, have any information on this Mushroom, Sir Fabius, my trusted Minister ? I thought that in your wide travels you might have been able to pick up some news or heard some news about him !

voThe Secretary of the Queen's Chamber - Your Majesty, up to today, our ofiice has not received any information on your Minister,Sir Fabius, and no news or relevant suggestions to the possible or probable whereabouts of your Minister, Sir Fabius, were reported by any of our scouts . We sincerely regret our inability to be of some productive service to your Majesty and your Kingdom,Sire !

The solitary Bee - "His" Kingdom...????!!

Giant Oak Tree - Mot a very friendly atmosphere, I see. Well, may be, you, Scarabello, know something of my Minister and my people, or don't you ?

The solitary Bee - "His" Minister ! 'His" people !! Now I hear it !!

Giant Oak Tree - I would not consider the answers of the solitary Bee and of the Gnome exactly friendly ! I begin to realize now, how much deeper the commotion caused by that Witch has penetrated in everybody's minds and hearts, distorting opinions, counterfeiting long established beliefs and fomenting a spirit of rebellion not only against a government, which in certain cases could even be understood, but against common, solid and decent REASON itself ! Oh ! Die we must,all of us, one day or another, so why worry too much over people's erratic loyalties and sentiments. May be the Bees in the apiary might be able to tell me something more : I'll take a chance and I'll ask them. If I get the same answer as I did from the solitary Bee and the Gnome, it won't hurt ,being used to it !

Chorus of the Apiary's Bees - Your Majesty, Sire, Royal Giant Oak Tree, we heard you and we followed your regrets over the poor reception to your enquires to the solitary Bee and the Gnome about your missing Minister, Sir Fabius, the Mushroom.

Giant Oak Tree- (softly , to himself.......) Oh! I almost cannot believe that some civic manners have survived in this Forest but do not let me "wake up" from this dream-like feeling, before it vanishes from my memory !.........(...then , turning towards the apiary and the bees inside it........) ...Thank you, dear and respectable Bees, and I wonder if you might be more leniently inclined in answering my question, or, if refusing or unable to do so, at least parting with a less stressful attitude .

Chorus of the Apiary's Bees - Your Majesty, we will tell you the truth and we do so not in the least fearing a hostile response from you if the information we'll give you and if its content may not ne pleasing to you, because you are a King and we have great respect and devotion for our Royal Image of Trust and Dignity, so here it is, Sire .

Giant Oak Tree - Thank you, gentle and courteous Bees, you are worthy of Royal Command !

Chorus of the Apiary's Bees - Sire, here is all that we know of your Kingdom, your people and your Minister! Your subjects, Sire, and your Minister, the Mushroom, known also as Sir Fabius, although still part of your Kingdom, yet they are not the same, inclusive of your Minister,the Mushroom, all of whom you knew before the devastating events which occurred in quick succession on your lands and which caused so much destruction and desolation for all who lived there .Those subjects, Sire, succumbed during those terrible days of confusion and terror , the Mushroom the only one known to have survived the massacre, and we were told that since then he had made contact with you again and that things seemed to be improving .

Giant Oak Tree - So far ,what you are saying is very correct , and I am grateful to you .

Chorus of the Apiary's Bees - Very well, then : and here is some more . The descendants of your old subjects, the new seedlings and the young shrubs as well as the new mushrooms, are still here,on this land that you identify as "your Kingdom".You must know, then, that, usually, in the story of our and anybody else's lives, after the tragedy comes the comedy and, after that, the curtains come down and the show is over and, with that, the lights go out too, and the new generations spring up, most of the time completely ignorant or hardly interested in the affairs, problems or diffculties of the previous generations, just looking forward to the future even if in doing so they show a rather sad and poor knowledge of what may lay ahead. Regardless of all that, in the end, the new generation will not be too much different from the one who had passed away .

Giant Oak Tree - Thank you,gentle Bees, this is very good historym but did you hear anything about the Mushroom, Sir Fabius ? Is he still...alive..or.....

Chorus of the Apiary's Bees - Yes, your Highness, he is alive and well, and, more important of all he is a lot wiser ! Actually he is very wise, more so than he could have ever been before, and he, Sir Fabius and all the new, young subjects areregretting that light and wisdom took so long to come by their shores !! In spite of that regret they are all happy that they have peace now and , may be, can look forward to an even happier old age. As you see, Sire, we have told you the truth.

The solitary Bee - Nothing, absolutely nothing but the truth !

Giant Oak Tree - But why, then, if all this new life and young new subjects and Mushrooms are populating again my land and seem to be happy and satisfied, why, then I receive no news, no information,no demonstration of happiness from down there where my roots are and my subjects live and, apparently, flourish. If things were as you just described them to me, this icy silence around me should be melted by chants of joy and excited voices and the rumble of frantic new activities by a people in the effervescence of a new life and new horizons !

The solitary Bee - Precisely .

Giant Oak Tree - But...then, ...I do not understand ! I hear nothing and dead silence all around me!

Chorus of the Apiary's Bees - It all sums up into "experience", Sire . Experience passed along to them by the fate suffered by their ancestors who, when they turned to you for help instead of wise and prudent policies by you and your Governmemt, got the services of a Witch and from that day on they learned that when THE CHIEF is himself a worse slave than the little people could ever be, then all trust is lost in that Chief. Too wise and cautious they have become these new generations and they dare not even showing themselves to you for fear that, may be, you may be inclined to get another Daga Queen to help you and them, as they learned the worse of their lives when the old Witch Queen came to administer them !!

Giant Oak Tree - Gnome, you wise Gnome, tell me is it then true what these gentle Bees have brought to my ears ?

Gnome - Mali, Mali .

The solitary Bee - The Gnome is wise and the Gnome knows the story and the Gnomes know the story because they do have a predilection for sitting and resting on the large umbrella of the mushroomsso they are well informed of all that goes on around the....neighbourood !

Giant Oak Tree - But if everything is then as you are presenting it to me now, well, at least someone could or should be able to tell me if my old Minister , Sir Fabius, the Mushroom, is still alive and around ! After all, he himself is also partly responsible for all the changes,events and troubles that have plagued this land ! I remember but too well when he had become very bellicose and stubborn and wanted to do this and do that and off with somebody's head and many more things I do not even remember any more what ! If Sir Fabius would still be around this land, somewhere, why couldn't he talk to me ?I would be very happy to talk to him again !

Gnome - TUM ! TUM ! TUM !

Giant Oak Tree - What do you have in mind to tell me, wise Gnome, with that negative rumble? Have you found the Sir Fabius ? Tell me : have you found out where he is ?

Chorus of the Apiary's Bees - But, Giant Tree, what good would that information be to you ? The Mushroom, that very Mushroom of the olden days, Sir Fabius, your trusted Minister,never more will he beseech you for anything, or will he ever talk to you again. Look. look down here where your roots are and see for yourself: the wise Gnome is sitting on the Mushroom, the same old Mushroom, your trusted Minister who,now does not trust...YOU anymore ,and the Gnome answers all questions and whatever else for him, avoiding any unhealthy involvement and compromising himself.

The solitary Bee - Very wise precaution.

Gnome - Mali, Mali, Tum,Tum,Tum.

Giant Oak Tree - Oh ! Miserable fate of our existences, how many a time the simple beginning of almost irrelevant circumstances could lead, in the end, to tragedy and despair !

The solitary Bee - A common ailment, apparently . Several mentions of similar "circumstances", were made in antiquity by eminent and learned men, philosophers, writers and poets, who had witnessed or had heard of tragedies of recent vintage or of ancient times and several writings flourished out of those"circumstances".

Giant Oak Tree - Is this, then ,my fate, that I shall live the rest of my old age in a world deaf, dumb and blind ? ....All around me destroyed and taken away and only some feeble and thin seedlings scurrying around as if totally ignorant of the past tragedies ? Is this really my destiny ?

Chorus of the Apiary's Bees - Because you are seen as the symbol and impersonation of the Ruler who sees everything painted with a rosy colour and believes that everything goes well even when it does not and fails to look deep into the problem in order to modify it or improve it or change its impact altogether, naturally, in acting that way, he alienates the confidence of many and their interst in bringing up the problems for his attention. That is a bad trait for a Ruler and an annoying one, and, since it is an almost unchangeable fact that all things that annoy live the longest time on this Forest of ours, it goes that you, most likely, will live a long, long time. There is no doubt then, that, as time goes by, you will most likely hear again the voice and the clamour of young voices and the busy going of activities in "your"forest, because those new seedling will have forgotten the past by then , because "experience", even if lived for a while, will eventually lose its freshness and, besides, since experience is not "hereditary", will be pretty soon taken over and smothered to death by the Vices who are, instead, so much more pliable and adaptable to all kinds of "experiences " and "circumstances" .

The solitary Bee - Interesting, but was it really necessary to say all that ? I just wonder !

Giant Oak Tree - If they said it, it means that they felt that, at least in their opinion, it was necessary to be said, I guess . But, THAT, of course is of secondary importance. What counts is the foretelling of the coming back to life and joy in the Forest at some point in the future of this land, I guess, when the seedlings will take up a more substantial role in the activities and life in the Forest, and I disagree with the prediction of doom, because the new generation will know better and wiser.

Chorus of the Apiary's Bees - This may be true . However what is it worth having an area of ground when the will of its inhabitants to cultivate it has been lost ?

Giant Oak Tree - The inhabitants may loose or might have lost the will to cultivate that land, dear and gentle Bees , not so the ground itself : its resourcefulness is unlimited and it's Nature's own dictate .

The solitary Bee - Are we starting another two parties debate.. ???.....Lord have Mercy.....I couldn't stand it...!!!!!

Gnome - TUM ! TUM ! TUM ! TUM ! TUM ! TUM !

The solitary Bee - Good on you, you old Mushroom ! May be, after all, "experience" helps a little!!

Chorus of the Apiary's Bees - All we wanted to say was simpler than what you might have had in your mind, Giant Oak .We wanted to point out that, figuratively, if the will to look forward to a better future wanes, then every other form of expression, be it mental, emotional, intellectual, physical, intuitive or diversified into a million other expressions, the germinating wonder will cease or become dormant, preventing or retarding the flourishing of what is beautiful, precious, useful, intriguing and high in its meaning, purpose and intent , while, in that torpor of decadent inactivity, perversion, animosity, hostility, debauchery, hatred, all compelling attributes, always, following internal commotions, will spin a web of indifference and apathy in the hearts and minds, sparing no one, father, son, daughter, spouse, the intelligent and the stupid, the wayward and the agreeable, the saint and the devil. You will be left alone, giant Oak Tree, alone to wonder !.....And we have said enough .

The solitary Bee - Enough, indeed and a Golden Appraisal of ...."enough" !!!

Giant Oak Tree - If destiny is for me to be alone, so be it . Better to be alone than surrounded by diminutive beings, impregnated with resentment, displeasure and feeling sorry for themselves . If I was wrong, if I am wrong, if I shall be wrong again, I am a King and, I am STILL a King and in this capacity bestowed on me by Mother Nature and not granted to me by my begging for it, I herewith declare this land of mine, this new and to be Forest of mine, to be my Kingdom Forest and let every creature around know that there is no wrong in our lives that could not be made right if the wrong was made either by naiveness, faith or love .

Chorus of the Apiary's Bees - As we just have said, we have said enough, even too much that would be of any value.

The solitary Bee - Oh ! the unbelievable power of natural resilience, even in a simple Bee !!

Chorus of the Apiary's Bees - The Sun has risen high in the celestial mantle above us and at this time great are the hopes of the great and the humble as they always were, throughout the life of this Aviary of ours, the great Queen Bees and the intrepid Drones, so naively fearless of their predestined and declared fate, and we wish for you that the Sun's warm rays will warm your limbs, your conscience, your heart . We bear no hostility or hatred towards anybody, great or small, and we believe that there is not a tragedy so sad or hideous that can surpass, in its finality, that of death, and there, every tragedy, every torment, every illusion or disillusion will vanish as by sheer magic.

The solitary Bee - You don't say !!

Chorus of the Apiary's Bees - We do say, you smart Aleck of a bee !.....And, please, do not bother us anymore!

The solitary Bee - Yes, Sir !

Chorus of the Apiary's Bees - Good ! Time has come for us now, dear Old Giant Tree, to go back to our business, and desisting from using so much of our precious time in chatting about well known and worked over phenomena and ideas , so.......

The solitary Bee- Wise move .

Chorus of the Aviary's Bees - We had told you not to bother and not to interrupt us anymore !

The solitary Bee - I forgot .

Chorus of the Aviary's Bees - We declare...!!...Well, dear Old Giant Tree, Sire, we need to go back to our work and make all the necessary preparatins because the Queen is about to return to the Apiary and great is everybody's expectation. As you certainly know, her return is very important . Farewell, then, Sire, and Nature's coveted blessing be with you, always .

Giant Oak Tree - Farewell, gentle Bees, so laborious, so tenacious, so good !.....And what else has been left out but to say "farewell" ?....Oh !You mighty, powerful immortal Gods, how very shallow, miserable and frail is then our existence !

Chorus of the Apiary's Bees - " OUR " Existence ? Do you mean"your"existence ? ....What about the existence of everybody else's ??! Is, then, somebody else's existence different or less important than yours ? We had thought that you could have been able to think a little higher than that.

Giant Oak Tree - I am tall enough to think as high as I see fit or deem to be fit and I am tired of this constant retorting to anything that anyone says ....Bees ! You had just said that you had to go back to work, expecting the arrival of the Queen : well, permission granted !.

The solitary Bee - Atta boy ! You are coming in good, lately !

Gnome - Mali, Mali, Tum,Tum,Tum.

The solitary Bee - Bye, Bye, good, wise Gnome, and I'll miss you when I'll be back in my home ! Do you have anything to say, before I leave ?

Gnome - Mali,Mali, Tum, Tum, Tum .

The solitary Bee - Well, my dear Gnome, is that all ?

Gnome - Mali, Mali, Tum, Tum, Tum .

The solitary Bee - May be that looks like " it is all" !! I wonder, I just wonder, if the Mushroom might have found out what the meaning was of the whole story ? I just wonder !

Gnome - MALI ! MALI ! MALI ! TUM ! TUM! TUM !

****

The End

DIALOGUE
of
The Peasants and the Machines
with the participation of a pair of old mud-shoes and the Spirit of invention .
(narrated in a personified form for its protagonists)
****

1st Peasant (Gaelec) - Why didn't they think of it a lot sooner, instead of letting me sweat it out every damn single day of my life and getting nothing or near nothing out of it....!

2nd Peasant (Nagic) - What are you talking about ? Think of "what"...??.....And "Who"...THEY... ??!

1st Peasant - Who..!!...Who...!!...Somebody, that's who !

2nd Peqsant - I don't get it !

1st Peasant - You never do and you never did......blessed your pious soul !

2nd Peasant - But you didn't say who !

1st Peasant - Ask your Grand Mother to explain it to you .

2nd Peasant - I don't have one : I am alone .

1st Peasant - Then. you.....you should really need a who !

2nd Peasant - Would he or could he help me understand what the hell you are saying ?

1st Peasant - I don't know: sometimes, I do not understand myself what the hell I am saying !....... Leave alone someone else by the name of "who"....!!!

2nd Peasant - But, then, why did you seem so upset about someone not having "thought of something" long ago ...??!

1st Peasant - I am old, now, my youth wasted in endless labour with miserable rewards at doing something that now a child can do by just pushing a button ....And "who" wouldn't be upset just thinking of that ?

2nd Peasant - I have not seen any children pushing buttons, Gaelec !....Ceratinly not around here .

1st Peasant - It's a figurative speech, Nagic . It just means that everything is so easy these days that even a small child can do it by, figuratively, just pushing a button...!!!

2nd Peasant - Really ?.But "WHAT", Gaelec, is so easy, these days that wasn't the previous days ?

1st Peasant - Eating is one, for example .

2nd Peasant ... Eating ...???!! ....But I never had any difficulty in eating and I do not have any now, only not always enough of it or as much as I would like to have, sometime........ but is eating much different now, do you think, than it was when we were young kids and always hungry ?

1 st Peasant Food has not changed much, hunger has remained about the same, young kids will always be hungry, not everybody has what it really needs and the weather can playa heavy hand on the availability of food as well.....

2nd Peasant - Anything to do with the swallowing of food? Did they or whoever was there in ancient times have to chew their food in order to swallow it ?

1 st Peasant Hard to tell: probably so, unless they were so hungry and just swallowed it as they could for fear it would leave them.

2nd Peasant - Terribly anxious times those must have been L.And how did they get their food?

1 st Peasant With difficulty and at the risk of their own lives by hunting wild beasts.

2nd Peasant - Oh! No shops, apparently, where to buy food, right?

1 st Peasant Quite right: there were no shops.

2nd Peasant What's so different now about food: you said it was easier......... how easier ???...I do not understand what you mean.

1 st Peasant Because it is manufactured, now, to a much larger extent than it ever had been in previous times, so that, comparatively speaking, you can eat today, by simply pushing a button: it's already cooked and all you have to do is warm it up, if you so desire.

2nd Peasant - Does the food come ready with a button?

1 st Peasant No : the food is pre-cooked and frozen to keep it fresh over long periods of time and, after purchase, is placed in a machine, a button is pushed and "pronto" !....... the food is ready to be eaten!

2nd Peasant Ah ! I see what you mean !Y ou are talking about canned food, prefabricated food, machine confectionary and all that modem stuff: I call it mechanized food and my wife likes it . She says that it is a lot easier to prepare a meal these days than when she was just a little girl and saw old women sweating it out in front of a fire even in the middle of Summer, on hot days, and prepare a meal from scratch for the men when they came back home after a hard day's work in the fields!!

1 st Peasant The intense Family life of those days, though, that kept people together, under one roof ! .

2nd Peasant - One roof is fine, when there was one, sometimes, just a tent or a thatched roof and no rest or hope for the miserable souls inside, when the doors and the windows were closed and hope was left outside .

1st Peasant, - Better now, you think, everything automatic, push-button, electric, computerized, hard to distinguish whether you are eating a preserve or a wing-nut or a staple or a meatloaf of some unspecified formulated and engineered ingredients as against a robust piece of deer meat or a real carrot or potato .

2nd Peasant - But women, or, for that matter, anyone else, women or men preparing a meal, do not become as tired as they did in the old days while labouring around a meal and, some old stories have told us of terrible tragedies which occurred in some ancient kitchens !!

1st Peasant - Folkclore has always had a flare for dramatization of even simple events in ancient times, since they had nothing else better to do or think in those days, particularly poor peasants like us .

2nd Peasant - No, Gaelec, it wasn't a silly story or a fantasy or a fairy tale, but a real event of very sad consequences and all because of food .

1st Peasant - Did it have anything to do with an angry husband beating his poor wife for having spent too much money at the market, may be ??

2nd Peasant - No, Gaelec, nothing like that but something far more serious and very very sad that caused even the famous prince, the Great Conde', Louis II, in 1671, to become very distraught on hearing of that totally unexpected tragedy, and all on account of food !

1st Peasant - My dear Nagic, the way you are presenting your case, your story I should say, is so mysterious, so priming in its anticipation, that even Job would probably lose his proverbial and famous patience !.....Courage, my boy: how tragic did the tragic tragedy came to be.....??!

2nd Peasant - It happened during a hunting expedition, when the Great Conde', stopping for some rest during a hunting party with the King Louis XIV, offered a dinner at one of his castles nearby, where the famous cook of Conde' was at that time.

1st Peasant - My dear Nagic, you must have either a strange sense of the nature of a tragedy or a total misconception of its meaning and representation . Why ! I don't see anything tragic in all this, at least........I grant you....at least not so far !!!

2nd Peasant - That is "precisely" what everybody thought and felt at that time too, resting at the sumptuously laid tables, jesting and bragging about the hunting and having a good time,when the news,suddenly,spread that Vatel,the famous cook of the great Conde', not having been able, at such short a notice of that unexpected stop of Conde'and the King at that castle, to find and prepare any fish for the usual one of the entries in the customary sequence of dishes presentations at such an important assembly of personalities and, unable to bear the disappointment that such a failure would cause to the Great Conde', Vatel......committed suicide .

1st Peasant - Why didn't you tell me that a Royal hunting Party would lead to such a deleterious conclusion, just because a famous cook could not find some fish for such an important impromptu Royal dinner ??

2nd Peasant - How can anyone tell ahead of anybody's planned suicide ?

1st Peasant - Well, now you want to make a joke out of it .

2nd Peasant - No, it was you who thought that my story was a "joke" !

1st Peasant - So, we are square now, and, apart from any jokes, where did you hear these extraordinary stories ? Was now the one you just told me one of your Grand Mother's bedtime stories ?

2nd Peasant - No, Gaelec: it was taught to us at school .

1st Peasant - I did not know that you had been through school !

2nd Peasant - Yes, Gaelec, I went trough some grades, passing from one to the next because my teacher was a sentimentalist and it would break her heart to see me lost in the same grade, year after year....!!

1st Peasant - Sometimes it is helpful in life to meet someone with a heart .

2nd Peasant - Yes, it does and I was lucky , because, although I am not bright yet, at least, I am honest and my teacher used to tell me that to be great, really great, very great in life, the first ingredient is to be honest .

1st Peasant - Ah ! That's humanity's most arduous task !.....Some people think that it is only necessary to be honest in one thing and not necessarily in everything, like judging one's self, for example .

2nd Peasant - I do not know about that , but my teacher used to say that to be honest, and she meant "really honest", very, very honest in all your actions as well as thoughts and endeavours, was a virtue few creatures ever possessed in all its parameters, and those who did were often ridiculed, shunned and even killed .

1st Peasant - Perhaps they failed because they were not eating the right food or they were eating the so called modern type of manufactured foods .

2nd Peasant - Gaelec,I am afraid that you are entering into something that I cannot follow you in...
1st Peasant - Do not worry, Nagic,....Ah ain't going nowhere ! Just peasants' talk !

2nd Peasant - Good: that makes me feel a lot better: it is very distressful for me to have to think!

****

*** While the two Peasants go about their talking *** and attend to their chores , some machines , nearby, after listening to the two Peasants' chatting, turn on their power, engage their gears and begin talking to each other .

****

1st Machine (Sinope) - What are those two idiots talking about, I am asking myself, and I cannot make any head or tail of it . I heard them jabbering for hours ...!....What about, I really don't know !!

2nd Machine (Ophelia) - I heard them too, Sinope. It seemed to me that they were talking about some buttons: whose, I don't know .

1st Machine - One of them looks like a button himself, ready to be pressed into his stupid head .

2nd Machine - Yes, it looks like he has a "button" complex ! The poor thing !.....Strange way of thinking, if you ask me .

1st Machine - That's my opinion too, Ophelia . People seem to have lost their heads in recent times and particularly so since the day when we came around .

2nd Machine - Yes, Sinope, I see what you mean . People, certainly, appear to act differently than they did before we came around and seem a lot more nervous, excitable, impatient and grown a lot more demanding and insufferable of any waiting, losing their patience faster than they ever did in the good old days of "horse-and-buggy days"when, getting out of your house door in a beautiful Spring morning, anyone could stop on the door-step and slowly breathe in that balmy, good and fresh air and look up at the bright sky without running the risk of being hit and killed by a running away automobile .

1st Machine - And you, my dear Ophelia, would have fitted into that celestial atmosphere splendidly, may be even turning around from your door-step and going back to your lounge and write a poem about it all .

1st Machine - I am glad you are in a good mood and making jokes, but.......

1st Machine - I am not making jokes, Ophelia, or am I trying to ridicule you but, really, those were the days when time went by at a reasonable clip, without any race-course type of accelerations, and it afforded some precious time, also, for some thinking........and....

2nd Machine - I konw what you mean, my dear Sinope, I understand perfectly well what you are getting at, and it is true that things have taken a faster route of different and multiple directions, dragging along with them willing and unwilling folks who will follow the new race anyway just in order not to be left behind and lost in the dust of a "horse and buggy"serene trottting...........yet, I wonder.....

1st Machine - Now, what ??!.....Have you lost some of your safety-pins and have second thoughts about those gentlemen Earthlings, the button-pushing enthusiasts ?

2nd Machine - No, Sinope, all my safety pins are O.K., but I was wondering whether the Earthlings might have found, after all, a better way of living by inventing those buttons ....Just a thought, you know .

1st Machine - They, probably, would have if they had planned to use them judiciously .

2nd Machine - Yes, I understand what you are saying and, in a way, you have a point there : yet, at the same time, we must recognize, even if unwillingly so, that they created us .

1st Machine - A selfish feat , if you ask me . They didn't do that art of creation for us : they did it just for their own selfish interest .

2nd Machine - Yes, in a way you are right, Sinope, but just think of all the constant attention we get every day with cohorts of concerned Earthlings taking exhausting care of us, pampering us and worrying by the minute about our life and performance !.....Do you think that they would do all that if our birth had been envisaged purely on a basis for just extra amenities and fun for them ?

1st Machine - I see your point of view, Ophelia, yet I am not completely satisfied with any of the explanations, so far .

2nd Machine - No one ever is of anything, particularly if it is something he does not believe in .

1st Machine - This, my dear Ophelia, does not seem to me a matter of belief in something . This is a straight forward consideration about some actions, by some creatures, whose reason, purpose and aim for that particular action , is missing in the perspective of my thinking .

2nd Machine - Have you tried to give some attention at the living conditions of now-a-days as compared to the life when water had to be brought to the homes from a far away river or pulled up with a rope and a bucket at the end of it from a deep well, or when the roads were melting with mud and stones after a heavy rain and even carriages could hardly travel on it to get to the near village to get the necessities of life, or the oil in the lamps had drained out and you were in the dark ?

1st Machine - You have a flare for dramatization,my dear, a mixture of sentimentalism and romantic junctures in your mechanisms that encourage you to view ordinary facets of casual life as ethereal representations !

The Spirit of invention - I disagree .

2nd Machine - Who said that ?....Who said THAT ???!!

1st Machine - Calm down, Ophelia, no one said anything ! You must be hearing things, overworked in your obstinate defence of those mysterious and unorthodox Earthlings .

2nd Machine - But I heard something and quite distinctly , I did ! Somebody said " I disagree " !..... and I heard it quite plainly , I did !

The Spirit of invention - Of course, you did ! I said it !

2nd Machine - Now it's clear: now it is very, very clear!Somebody....somebody said "something"!!

1st Machine - May be is a little new device invented by the Earthlings and implanted in you to make you hear things when they want you to hear them !.....Give you orders or instructions, through them, and..... keep a check on you....!!! That's what I think .

2nd Machine - I don't know what to think of it: I never had any troubles in hearing things, whether things were there or when they were not !.......So, "something" is going on and that is not my imagination or, as you tend to suggest, my dear Sinope, due to secretely implanted devices !!

The Registrar of patents - Why to be so excited and awed at a secretely implanted device, even if that were the case in this particular instance ? You are wrong at being aroused by the mere assumption that some secret device has been "secretely" implanted in you ! My dear Lady Machine of the 2nd order, nothing is secret : only unknown . That "something" which seems to agitate and worry you, by its very nature might have been floating around for ever in the foggy mist of our comprehension and whose notion was only recently caught by somebody's fervid imagination, and why to bestow so much honour and praise and wonder, by Earthlings' customary and beloved practice, on those who do stumble across a discovery, often unintentionally and, many a times, by pure accidental coincidence of purpose, when the revelation of any new inventions, creations, or enlightments is nothing more than a finding of something that had been always there for anyone to find, since the beginning of time ?

The Spirit of invention - I partially agree with it, Officer, and, yet, was that"something", really, always there? Sometimes, simple thinking facilitates the comprehension of what..."was always there".....as in this case of "examplary" deductive intuition by you, an Officer of the Registry of Inventions, who sees inventions of "what was always there" day in and day out, year in and year out, even when He Himself, happens not to be "there" to register those"always there"inventions. And, yet, I wonder, are they there, those "somethings", just to test our comprehension skills or just to taunt us ?

2nd Machine - (....now, Ophelia, turning to Sinope, the 1st machine.......).....Sinope,I must tell you something .

1st Machine - You must have been impressed by the redundant speech of that inventive talker, calling himself a spirit and bragging about inventions of some"somethings": is that what you want to talk to me about ??!....I really hope this not to be the case !!

2nd Machine - Not that, dear Sinope, but just that I had felt a lot more at ease when listening to the two peasants talking together than I do now,trying to keep my rivets and screws firm and tight while listening to this conversation of some show-off ghosts !

1st Machine - I don't believe that there are any ghosts, anywhere, except those "man-made" ones .

2nd Machine - Ah !...The Earthlings, you mean ?

1st Machine - The Earthlings, yes, I do mean the Earthlings .

2nd Machine - But how did the Earthlings or, for that matter, how did anybody come to think of "Ghosts", if they do not exist ??!

The Spirit of invention - That is the time when I come in .

2nd Machine - A little presumptuous, isn't he ?

1st Machine - A ghostly presumption may not have that much value, anyway .

2nd Machine - I hear you .

*** A lonely couple of insulated mud-shoes, used to be worn while doing heavy machine work, were lying by the side of one of the machines and had an urge to feel their own oats and enter the conversation, because,as they later revealed, they wanted to show their own shoelaces........!!....... ***

Insulated mud shoes - Would we be allowed to enter this conversation and say just a short "something" ? Or are we, may be, "pressing the button" of our presumption too hard ??

1st Machine - Hardly at all, dear shoes, particularly so when intriguing ghostly entities are trying to steal the centre stage !

Insulated mud shoes - Ah ! Those ghostly characters ....well, they do not bother us as we are well insulated and well adapted to find and maintain our right way even into the mud of any path, be it a weather produced mud or a quagmire produced by ghosts .

2nd Machine - Excellent ! A really solid demonstration of the usefulness of insulation from the many and far too insidious hazards of today's World, unfortunately !

Insulated mud shoes - Oh! Thank you ! No one has ever honoured us with such a rewarding attitude !

The Spirit of invention - First the peasants, then the machines and, now, some muddy shoes ! What a combination of really"ghostly" appearances they are !!

Insulated mud-shoes - No need to be so upset and, I would say, so annoyed, apparently, by my entry in this interesting conversation, dear Spirit of Invention !

The Spirit of invention - I am not upset and I am not annoyed : I am disgusted . Does this clarify your wondering about my attitude, you stupid pair of muddy shoes ?

Insulated mud-shoes - Muddy may be appropriate, since we were built, then manufactured, to be a tough competiror with mud, but ...stupid...well, I am not so sure . You see, we have some very good shoe-laces, which keep all of us well tightly wrapped up so that no mud can penetrate inside us, regardless of the mud conditions, whether natural occurring mud or some "imitation" mud, produced by inadvertent and casual creatures .

The Spririt of invention - Mud is mud, dear mud-shoes, and stupidity is stupidity, each in its own merits and, quite frankly, I do not fully grasp your analogy with your "shoe-laces" or shoe-strings, whatever !

Insulated mud-shoes - We meant no"analogy", whatever that may be, anyway, since we do not even know what it means, but we wanted to point out that ....WE IS NO STUPID SHOES .

The Spirit of invention - To stupidity you may, now, add " audacity " .

Insulated mud-shoes - Stupidity, audacity....what else, we wonder, may inspire you, Sir, in your exquisite address to our personality ?

The Spirit of invention - The absurd equation of : "stupidity and audacity = no brain" .

Insulated mud-shoes - That one, Sir, is a highly debatable equation since, to begin with, it has been known for a long time that stupid people can be audaceous or, vice versa, audacity can make fools of already stupid people, and those with no brain, they do not exist, since evryone that moves or crowls has one, size apart .

The Spirit of invention - So they say, folklore wisdom !......Besides, who cares or gives credit to an old pair of old muddy shoes and their.....

Insulated mud-shoes - Pardon the interruption, Sir, but we are not "muddy", we are insulated against mud entering and "muddying" the feet of our wearer .

The Spirit of invention - Fine, but the fact remainsthat your brain is hard.....I would have rather said"muddy", but substituted the appellative in a more subdued and acceptable descriptive image by identifying it as"hard" and "leathery", and you would not be able to go very far if somebody's feet would not take you somewhere .

Insulated
mud-shoes - The way civilized feet have become these days, they would not go very far either, without shoes and, even worse, if on a muddy road !

The Spirit of
invention - And "you" would not move either if tyhere were no brain, slightly up higher, to move and direct those feet with you at their heels !!

Insulated
mud-shoes - Nor would the brain go very far either if it didn't have legs, feet and shoes to carry him or, ...is it...carry"IT" ?

The Spirit of
invention - So what !.... A brain does not have to walk in order to cover distances and, it was not made for the purpose of walking to start with, dear Shoes of mud .

Insulated
mud-shoes - Sometimes, we are wondering about that . You see, in our experience, and that goes for millennia of time, we have never been able to observe a brain leave anybody's head in order to go somewhere, and we are talking about the fellows whose feet we did provide with comfortable and protective foot wear .

The Spirit of
invention - A purely allegorical formulation .

Insulated
mud-shoes - And we doubt that anyone would or could go very far with "purely allegorical" foot wear, paricularly in this civilized and weakened world where you need all sorts of apparels in order to live, exist and partake of the "main" mainstream, including foot wear .

The Spirit of
invention - Appropriate, compatible, representative or elegant footwear may be of some interest in a civilized society, but a pair of mud-shoes, large, thich and heavy, hardly ever elicit an enthusiastic response or awe at their sight......particularly so if soiled all over with mud !

Insulated
mud-shoes - Well, there is an old Italian proverb that goes like this:" Scarpe grosse, cervello fino", which, translated, would be something like: "Thick, rough shoes, but a sharp mind and subtle brains", so what would you say to that , Sir Spirit ?

The Spirit of
invention - Humbug the thick shoes, humbug the subtle brain !

Insulated
mud-shoes - How true it is and I see it plainly now, and how easier it is to mechanically change or improve on things that we can see and touch, and how painfully slow it is and disconcertingly resistive it is the ameliorating or the changing of an existing trend of thought in the brains of various creatures, always provided, of course, that "amelioration"of the various creatures'thinking was, at all, Mother Nature's primary intended notion......in the first place...!

The Spirit of invention - That is precisely what I thought !...You are thinking with your brain in your shoes and your shoes, being...BIG and THICK, do not seem to help you very much in the hard road to fame and glory, your thinking barely treading at street level while mine can reach the Heavens with the power of its fire, as a famous old poet once had said!

Insulated mud-shoes - May be so, may be so ! Invention can figure out an unimaginable amount of things, stories and notions, some verifiable by even a limited amount of comprehension, while others, if not of any intelligent content, may not reach...well, shall I say.....the highest heavens of...YOURSELF, ...I mean , of INVENTION .

The Spirit of invention - I was not meant to be understood by underprivileged receptive brain assemblies .

............The machines, which had been quietly listening to the ongoing chatting of the Mud-shoes and the Spirit of invention , turn to each other and comment............:

2nd Machine (0phelia) - A little presumptuous that Guy of a spirit....didn't I tell you so just a while ago ..??!

1st Machine (Sinope) - Yes, you did . I also remember saying, in answer to your comment, that a "presumptuous attitude", even of a Spirit of invention or a Ghost of some sort, may not have that much value, anyway .

2nd Machine - You are right, Sinope, and I remember it now, you had said that !...And, more than just saying that , it was, also, quite appropriate, I believe ..

Insulated mud-shoes - I believe that I heard your mechanical comment, respectable Machines, and, in spite of my leathery brain, I even understood the meaning of your comment and I most sincerely praise you for that lucid and timely comment .

The Spirit of invention - That's, really, some news : a "lucid and timely comment"... by a machine...!!!....Has today's World lost its marbles ?

1st Machine (Sinope) - Well, I do not know about that . We may lose a couple of screws, or a bolt, now and then, a belt, sometimes, or a few teeth in a gear, but "marbles " ??....Well. the only marbles we are aware of are the ones our friendly and caring operators use for fun, when playing games : are those the marbles you are referring to, dear Spirit ?

The Spirit of invention - Not quite those antique, ancient and historical marbles which even Julius Caesar used and cast when crossing the Rubicone river in Northern Italy,but the"marbles"in people's heads !

2nd Machine (Ophelia) - They must be quite some powerful heads, those heads, to be able to hold marbles . Do you happen to know the fellow who had manufactured those heads ? Most certainly, he must have been a very good and skilled artisan , I guess .

The Spirit of invention - That skilled artisan who created them was, in my opinion, more of an optimist and a trusting mind rather than a skilled manufecturer, and those vulgar heads, not appreciating the value and the hidden power of that labyrinthic poultice in their heads, thought that the weight of marbles was more valuable and marketable than a brain.

1st Machine - So , they lost the marbles ? ....I mean... so....did those heads lose their marbles ? But you had said that you were wondering if the World had lost its marbles ! How many marbles are there around ?....I don't understand .

Insulated Mud-shoes - Allow us to answer this one : incredible numbers of them are widely and heavily distributed throughout the World and we know it well, because we carry them around, every day!... Now, how they may become lost, this particular instance we are not familiar with .

The Spirit of invention - Absurdity upon absurdity and an extra serving of stupidity to keep company to the absurdity . They call it "The Century of the machines !!"...Bah ! Humbug !

2nd Machine - Ah ! Is that the name of the marbles' Manufacturer? Is it Absurdity or Stupidity ?

The Spirit of invention - I live the guessing and the choice to you, but, personally and, confidentially, Stupidity is what I would consider a sensible chioce .

2nd Machine - Thank you, Spirit, ever so much, and I had figured it out that way myself too, since that was to be expected of you, but I wanted the legitimation of the name Stupidity coming directly from you as your preferred representation of general comprehension, including....your respected one, of course...!

The Spirit of invention - Bah! Humbug !...You do not even seem to know what you are talking about, you little scrap of junk-yard metal ! What did you intend to say with that big speech...??

2nd Machine - Nothing much, really : just stupidity....in order to keep pace with yours .

The Spirit of invention - Bah ! Humbug ! I , really, do not care, or , to keep up with your level of reasoning... "FRANKLY, I DON"T GIVE A DAMN " .

Insulated mud-shoes - Please, Ophelia, don't pay any attention to that old bugger and let him mumble to himself, but, as we were saying, it is difficult for us shoes to figure out those phraseological subtleties like"loosing something as heavy as a marble"which, apparently, is sitting in somebody's head, because we.......well.....because we....we never lose our shoestrings......and............

1st Machine - Same with us : we seldom lose any of our components or ...should I say "marbles" ?

Insulated mud-shoes - Precisely, but, you see, marbles, being round and prone to roll, could push one another in a fiercely contested, confrontal and highly intellectual"Spirit of invention" type of a fulgid episode andcascade out of a head full of marbles, that head, probably, being slightly undersized and unable to contain and retain the sublime magnitude of that intellective explosion produced by the lofty Spirit of invention, waving its magic wand.

*** the peasants, who had been silently listening to the ongoing chit-chatting, do not seem either happy or convinced about the content of that blabbering .... ***

1 st Peasant Gaelec) I am telling you, dear Nagic, things have been going on too fast since those push botton machines have come along! Even their chit-chatting is almost insufferable and it gets under your skin and gets your nerves in a quandary !

2nd Peasant (Nagic) Well, Gaelec, you need to be patient with new things, new gadgets and ftesh developments, before expressing disapproval or discomfort with them: you need to give them the benefit of the doubt of their usesefulness and try to allow a reasonable time of trial to prove their claimed new benefits.

1st Peasant - May be you are right, Nagic. But, can you tell me why you think so?

2nd Peasant - Well, Gaelec, I have been reading something about it in an old Farmers' Almanac and it was written that it was discovered, recently, a substance in some plants that seems to be the cause for the green colour of some of those plants.

1 st Peasant - You don't say!.....And has anyone found out what gives us the colour of the sky?

2nd Peasant - More than that, Gaelec : it gives the plant that carries it the advantage and privilege of self-nourishment, permitting it to grow.!

1st Peasant - Phenomenal!! I wish our good old Mother Nature would have thought of something similar for us, poor sweating labourers as we are, in our daily chores! !

2nd Peasant - But it did, Gaelec ! It really did

1 st Peasant - I don't believe you !

2nd Peasant - Y ou'd better believe me, Gaelec, and it may not be exactly the type of substance that gives the green colour and permits nourishment to some plants, but another substance, probably just as good if not better than the one for the plants, but powerful, very powerful, the Almanac says, and specifically provided for us .... well, let me rephrase that............specifically good for "thinking", so that good things, new things, improvements, can be achieved like these machines near us and make our work a lot easler.

The Spirit of invention - Yes, dear Gealec, your friend, Nagic, tells the truth: it is the magic of a process that enables creatures like you to.........

1st Peasant - But we is only peasants, dear Spirit ! Who would want to bother to think for us ?!!

The Spirit of invention - Ask the mud-shoes...they will tell you !!

Insulated mud-shoes - No one will think for you, dear peasants, because "thinking" is free, does not belong to any particular Agent, Nation, Consortium, or special geographical places : it belongs to the one who is thinking and, that one, could be anyone, even one of you .

2nd Peasant - Ah! That's what the Almanac is saying !... But then, when I was reading it by myself, I coulnd't quite catch its full meaning ! Now. I understand: .....and it says too that that thinking gives rise to some thoughts and energises them with a lot of strength to enable them to expand , to enlarge and branch out to reach for the heavens !...The"HEAVENS"...it says..!!!

1st Peasant - That's kinda scary, I guess !

Insulated mud-shoes - Not so , if you keep your shoes on, while thinking !!

The Spirit of invention - Well I do not think "that" particular rule to be an absolute requirement : as long as you avoid the mud......in your thinking, that is .

Insulated mud-shoes - Don't we know....!!!

The two Peasants - Tell us about ..!!

The Spirit of invention - Do not pay excessive attention to their exclamatory sentences : those shoes suffer from a mud-complex mental preoccupation .

The two Peasants - We too, then, must be affected by the same disturbance as we have to deal with mud quite frequently in our daily work, particularly in Winter time . So, why do you think that those shoes suffer from a complex ? To us it seems pretty natural .

The Spirit of invention - A lot depends on how the mud is dealt with, addressed to and avoided or controlled or disposed off . How do you deal with it, when you encounter it ?

The two Peasants - We usually fill up the place where it has formed with large gravel rocks, so that we can walk easily on it .

*** On hearing that , the machines increase their pitch, rev up their motors, tense their belts and address each other.......... ***

1st Machine - Ophelia ! Did you hear that ?

2nd Machine - What was I supposed to have heard, Sinope ? You seem so agitated !!

1st Machine - Ophelia, do you recollect, a liitle while back, when the Spirit of invention complained of the World having lost its marbles ?

2nd Machine - Of course I do, Sinope, and he appeared quite annoyed and irritated about it too !!

1st Machine - Well, Ophelia, I have great news for you !

2nd Machine - For Heavens above, Sinope, I am worried : I hope the news are good !

1st Machine - Not only good but excellent ! Ophelia, I know now where the lost marbles of the World were actually lost,yes, the ones the Spirit of invention had complained about.

2nd Machine - In all sincerity, dear Sinope, I had, really, forgotten all about it ! Is that so important to know where they went..????!!

1st Machine - I believe so, yes, because by knowing it, I now know why the World is in such a poor shape .

2nd Machine - You do ? Why ?

1st Machine - Because those marbles are in a mud hole !

2nd Machine - Astonishing .

1st Machine - Indeed.........and what's the score ? Depressively, a big fat "ZERO" .

2nd Machine - What's up with you Sinope ?? This kind of talk is not your usual one ! I am beginning to worry about you !

The Spirit of invention - A natural and casual occurrence, the one that our respectable Sinope may be experiencing in this Age of automation, push-button gadgets, instant this and instant that, all for a rush to somewhere without a map, any idea of direction, only obsessed to...get there !...And where there ??! Personal dreams of fortunes ? Careers' glories ? Notoriety ? May be even Immortality !!!!....And, in the end, nothing much changes from one day to the next, one year to the next, one century to the next until, eventually, the whole process will age and will die and, with that in mind, all perplexities and hesitations, misconceptions, nebulous instincts and even sorrows will dissipate but to return, on schedule, for the next generation in line.....I have spoken....!!!!!

Insulated mud-shoes - You can say that again ! For sure !

The Spirit of invention - Yes, I will say it again and listening to it , it's optional .

Insulated mud-shoes - You can't be serious..!!!

The Spirit of invention - Very serious, just as serious as the great writers of all times, ancient and modern, who have written over and over of love and adventure, of happy days and dark days of happiness and despair, catastrophies, rare events, fateful expeditions to unknown lands, glories and triumphs, death and life, history and politics, to what use, no one really can tell for certain, except the urge of being heard, because at the end of even the most formidable pen.......everything is always the same ......

**** The Peasants, who had been listening, are puzzled at the remarks of the Spirit of invention and enter the coversation.. ****

1st Peasant - Yes, we agree with you, dear Spirit, because we see that happening every year : don't many trees and various plants grow and lose leaves exactly the same way, year in and year out, season by season, with uncanny timely sequences and coordination?

2nd Peasant - Gaelec, I don't think that you should have answered our respected Sir Spirit the way you did, as your statement tended to place you on an even platform with the Spirit himself which, I believe, could have been interpreted as a disrespectful attitude to his superior knowledge and issue .I think that you should correct that and apologize .

the Spirit of invention - No need for that, dear Nagic : though distinguished, yet, those attitudes of unconditional respect are no longer applicable to today's living trends and realities and "Haughtiness", still a favourite Chimera for some, is becoming less and less of an issue in place of efficiency, honesty and personal values without ostentatious malice. Then, there will be no longer a need for ostentation and haughtiness, pride and prejudice.....not even for myself !!

Insulated mud-shoes - By George, by William and by Cocchinilla, if those words had not come out of your mouth we could have sworn that they had come from our shoelaces, so heavily loaded with enlightened wisdom !

The Spirit of invention - You are one step behind my supposed wisdom, encomiable shoes! Wisdom is not loaded, lent, enlightened or borrowed : it is earned .

1st Peasant - You know, Nagic, I...........

2nd Peasant - I don't, Gaelec .

1st Peasant - Well, let me put it this way: "...Nagic I wanted to tell you something". Is this better?

2nd Peasant - Much better .

1st Peasant - Good. Then listen, and all I wanted to.....

2nd Peasant - I am listening .

1st Peasant - Good. Then , all I wanted to tell you, Nagic, was that I..................

2nd Peasant - Yes, Gaelec, I am listening to what you are wanting to tell me and you had just said that ....but you didn't say what...!!

1st Peasant - I would have, if you had let me, you ninny !! So, as I was saying , I ....

2nd Peasant - Go ahead, dear Gaelec , I am listening.......

1st Peasant - One more wise-crack from you and I'll clubber you on your head .....

2nd Peasant - No comment .

1st Peasant - That's better : now, I was going to tell you....and DON"T YOU DARE INTERRUPT ME......that I believe that we must have put too much fertilizer into this soil because the response we have had, has been beyond what anyone would have expected , an explosion of bountiful crops of all kinds, some even resembling a legitimate expression of some form of communication !....Very, very strange !

2nd Peasant - Strange can be anything unusual but not so strange if justifiable, I think .

1st Peasant - You may be right, Nagic, but I have a lingering feeling that someone, something or somebody or "many" bodies, were actually talking and chatting and arguing among themselves , even getting us two into their conversation.....is it not quite strange, Nagic ?

2nd Peasant - Strange is not the right word to use, dear Gaelec : unusual, I'd rather say and, as your Grandmother would have told you, don't tell this to anybody, keep it to yourself and, may be, some of those folks will talk to you again if you'll spread some more fertilizer on the soil .

1st Peasant - I hear you . Well, it's time to go back home : it's getting dark .

2nd Peasant - It is getting dark : let's go back and have some supper !

1st Peasant - Right : back home and to a good supper .

The Spirit of invention - Have a good rest and a good night, fellows, and thank you for the excellent fertilizer! It was encomiable of you to have treated this humble soil with unselfish generosity of purpose, Thank you .

2nd Peasant - Gaelec, did you say something ?
1st Peasant - I didn't .

2nd Peasant - But I heard something !

1st Peasant - May be you inhaled some dust while spreading the fertilizer , so , now, you are hearing things....!!!!

2nd Peasant - May be, but the spreading was done early this morning and I heard something now !

1st Peasant - Don't worry about it, Nagic : in the long run of anything in life, including our own, it does not really matter much if you think that you heard something or that you are hearing something or that you might be hearing something : because no one, really, knows the real meaning of that, although many have trtied to explain it . Frankly ,I would not pay much attention to it . It's getting late, Nagic : let's go back home and have a good supper .

Insulated mud-shoes - An excellent idea !!

2nd Peasant - But...I think.... that I.......

1st Peasant - ......I know !...I know !.....That you heard something...???!!...I diddn't hear anything, dear Nagic, but I smelt the delicious aroma coming out of the kitchen in our house !! Let's hurry home, dear Nagic, and have a good supper. That might make us hear some sweeter things and more delightful music .

The Spirit of invention - I'll bet it will !

2nd Peasant - I heard it ! Gaelec, I heard it ! This time I heard it, distinctly ! Oh ! Boy, didn't I hear it !!!

1st Peasant - Yes, now I know for sure : there is a warning on the sacks of fertlizer that inhaling the fine particles from the dust, while spreding it, can cause some hallucinations, unless you wear a mask , so it is necessary to hurry home and wash the whole thing down with a good supper .

Insulated mud-shoes - Atta boy !

2nd Peasant - Gaelec ! Gaelec !...I......

1st Peasant - I know, Nagic, you heard it and I hear you ! Come, now, and let's go home : you need some rest . It was a long. long day !.....I may need some rest too !!!

The Spirit of invention - We all need some rest, I believe, dear Gaelec .

1st Peasant - Well, sure we all need some rest.......what on earth am I saying..???!!....Am I getting dizzy too, hearing voices and what not ???!!.....But, somebody called out my name! Nagic, did you just call me ?

2nd Peasant - I don't think so , but I heard your name called out too : may be Rosabelle, from the house, shouting at us to come home and have supper .

1st Peasant - Next year, one thing is certain : I'll have the fertilizer spread out for us by a machine: that will take care of all of our problems !

1st Machine
(Sinope) - The poor things : next year will be the same and, simple and naive as those two are, they will probably hear our motors humming and they'll take it as a speaking guest from another planet !

2nd Machine
(Ophelia) - And why not ?

1st Machine
(Sinope) - OPHELIA.....!!!!!!!!!

****

THE END

DIALOGUE
of
The Squirrel and The Turtle

******

Squirrel - Hey !,,,Look who's here !!...A Turtle !...Oh ! I want to talk to her in spite that I am so busy right now, but I think that I should be able to finish my work in plenty of time before she is able to reach my tree : she's moving so slowly.........!!!

*** The Turtle slowly and very leisurely inches closer to the tree where the little Squirrel, a wiry bundle of energy, keeps up jumping from branch to branch and up and down the tree in a seeming harmonious cadence with his tail, and spots the Turtle, now quite close to his tree................. ***

Squirrel - Good morning, Turtle, what a big surprise to see you here ! Quite a rare sight for a turtle to venture into these woods, but a very pleasant one for anyone lucky enough to meet you !! ......Well, how's that for a heartfelt welcome, Lady Turtle ?

Turtle - Oh! Thank you ! Thank you ! You really make me feel welcome in these here woods, dear Squirrel, and if I had carried along with me a big cannon I would have returned your friendly welcome with a twenty one salvos from a single gun...!!....But, since I do not carry a cannon with me, all I can manage to work out is just a simple nod of my head and a deep sigh !!

Sqirrel - No need for guns, cannons, sighs or nods, dear Turtle : your being here is reward enough for my welcome, honest !

Turtle - And my most heartfelt salutations to you too, dear Squirrel : and how are things with you, these days ? Enough time to look around, rest and sleep and enough food to eat ?

Squirrel - I cannot complain, really. So far, I have been able to get a good portion of all of those good things you just mentioned and some peaceful existence too : hardly anyone ever comes by these woods .

Turtle - So I noticed on my way to this forest : you know, I have always plenty of time to observe things around me at the speed I travel. I hardly ever miss anything and I did notice an almost majestic peace and quiet among these beautiful trees with a lot of shade and a cool breeze.

Squirrel - Yes, I agree, this is a blessed portion of real estate, as my broker Agent is used to say at our weekly meetings of the "Concerned Citizens of the Forest" when projecting the estimated values of properties in this area. But now, back to us ,dear Turtle, and how are things with you and a most beautiful morning to you, AGAIN....!!

Turtle - „„„And I believe that your wishing of a beautiful day, today, is a good omen so that I may look forward to an auspicious day of travelling in front of me !

Squirrel - Yes, my dear little Turtle, yes indeed this beautiful day carries a very good omen : no rain, no violent weather like thunder and lightning or hail, or impetuous wind shears good enough to tear you apart, but just pleasant, all around weather in front of you !....I know it and I sense it .

Turtle - I'm amazed !.....And how can you do that, you amazing little Squirrel ?

Squirrel - You see, dear Turtle and I hope you'll be so tolerant as to excuse my liberty in addressing you so confidentially, but you'll relieve me of a great burden if you would do so, sparing me the trouble of conventional and appropriate technical approach to the phenomenon of weather , but, as I was saying, I know when the weather changes and I sense its variability as I jump here and there and run up and down and side way and even upside down and all the variations of the air that I encounter at all different levels where I jump and run, I am able to retain them impressed in me and, when instinctively and by hormonal deduction these impressions are being analyzed, I am able to synthesise them into fair or bad weather .

Turtle - Now, I am even more amazed than I ever were before ! Extraordinary, indeed ! It is a great natural privilege to be endowed with such refined and sophisticated warning system ,dear Squirrel !

Squirrel - Yes, we Squirrels think so too. As a matter of fact, I always remember my Grand Parents telling me, when I was a little kid squirrel, that some other types of creatures who cannot climb and jump on trees as we and some other creatures similar to us do, they need some special instruments and complicated calculations and extensive observations in order to predict the weather and, even with all that apparatus, still most of the time come up with nothing as accurate as we can . .

Turtle - Quite interesting, dear Squirrel and, do you know what ?

Squirrel - No : what ?

Turtle - Well, since we first met we haven't been talking of anything else except the weather !

Squirrel - And how right you are and you are really coming in, my dear Turtle ! ...Yet, I am not surprised at our talking about the weather; a famous writer once said:"Everybody talks about the weather but no one does anything about it " !!!

Turtle - Yes, I remember when he said that as I was slowly making my way along the shores of the mighty Mississippi !...That was a long time ago ,dear Squirrel !

Squirrel - You are right, dear Turtle, time goes on and leaves only memories behind . I have no time to stop and think of the past as I am constantly overtaken by the present , looking for the daily necessities wherever I can find some!

Turtle - Oh! Dear Squirrel, that is just fine and you don't have to pay any attention to me or to my passing by and you keep on with your chores and activities and you need not be distracted by passers by like me ! You are a fast moving creature, full of vigor and extremely agile and I have heard many stories about your kind of people in my travels , so you need not explain to me anything !

Squirrel - I hope that what you have heard about our kind is good!

Turtle - Oh! Of course it is good and it is interesting too !

Squirrel - My O my, what did you hear so interesting about us, I wonder !!

Turtle - Well, for one I heard that you are buddy-buddy with the beetles, for another that you are in cahoots with the lizards and, most interesting of all, there are rumors that your kind has an inclination for flirting with the butterflies !

Squirrel - But where on Earth, and I am saying this because we live on it and I heard of it from the Wise Owl , and again...BUT WHERE ON EARTH did you hear all those unbelievable stories ?

Turtle - It appears to be common knowledge, dear Squirrel, just everybody seems to know and to agree on that ! Well, as for myself, those beetles and the lizards and the butterflies are very frivolous creatures, dear Squirrel, without a fixed residence, here now, there tomorrow and, then again, there and here and here and there, without a point of reference for their identities. They do not seem to have or care for any thoughts or problems or intentions of any kind ! Well, in a very simple way, this behaviour is understandable because their lives are rather short, so their seeming carefree attitude may be justified to some extent, except for the lizards.

Squirrel - Oh! My dear Turtle, you seem to come down hard on those little creatures, who are my friends ! But, you see, I am going along "fine" with them because often we engage in competitions to see who can run faster or jump higher : it's a lot of fun, dear Turtle, and you have certainly heard of the old refrain that all work and no fun is bad for your health : haven't you ?

Turtle - Yes, I have heard of it, but the refrain is not quite complete just as that !

Squirrel - Oh! Not complete ?! What else to be added to it? It seems to me quite self-explanatory as it is !

Turtle - Well it does not quite indicate clearly what "kind"of fun .

Squirrel - Well, my dear Turtle, let me tell you an amusing story about fun and its interpretation among "creatures of this world" as the Wise Owl is always saying, a story that has become famous and has given origin to a most coveted Order of Chivalry and Distinction in the civilized World, following an amusing yet highly didactic example of the interpretation of "fun" by a righteous mind .

Turtle - And, dear little Squirrel, won't you tell me this amusing story, right now ?

Squirrel - Of course I will! I am going slowly about bringing it to your ears so as to increase your interest and your anticipation for it .

Turtle - I assure you that you have both of them !

Squirrel - You must know, then and, I am certain , you must have heard of that famous "Admonishment" pronounced by that famous King at that famous Ball about a famous Countess whose famous garter had fallen from her famous leg, supposedly the left one, while dancing and the famous King's polite and respectful reinsertion of that famous Garter back onto the famous leg of that famous Countess, of Salisbury as we know, and that famous King's cute but forceful remark to his Courtesans whom the King had noticed laughing while He was performing His courteous and chivalrous act which the Courtesans were construing in a totally different way with a chuckle in their throats and an irreverent representation of that act in their lascivious smirking minds, the King, turning to these lesser gentlemen, pronounced His famous verdict:"Honni soit qui mal y pense" .....which could be translated, perhaps, into something like this:" Disgraced be those who think of evil "....or ......,may be.....as:" Shame on those who harbour bad thoughts " ! ......In other words the "fun" I meant was a good, wide open fun !

Turtle - I heard of that interesting episode as its repercussion in the aristocratic and chivalrous world reached this side of the Channel, when I happened to be in France......

Squirrel - But.....but...Turtle...!!!??!!.....That episode happened in the year of 1349, in Jolly England ! How could you have been there at that time and, at the same time also along the shores of the mighty Mississippi to hear the words of Mark Twain about the weather ???!!....Or do I have to absolve my mind in believing that you are not a live Turtle but just an apparition of a ghost Turtle ??!

Squirrel - Don't worry, dear little Squirrel, I "AM " a live turtle all right !.....A real turtle and not a ghost of a turtle !.....You see, I just know and " sense " things just as you do the changes in the weather : simple, isn't it ?

Sqirrel - Simple, may be yes, but not so simple in understanding it !

Turtle - Have you ever tried to understand how you can "sense" the changes in the weather ?

Squirrel - Not really : I take it as a natural inclination of my make up, like eating,sleeping....

Turtle - Well, so do I and I think nothing of it....... That "sense" ......well, it just comes naturally.

Squirrel - And indeed it does.....that is coming in naturally, ,dear Turtle ! Extraordinary and quite interesting this specialization of our species, almost unbelievable if you put your mind to it and try to figure out its mechanism and.......

Turtle - It does not seem to me that extraordinary and almost unbelievable as you say : why, dogs can smell an underground fungus very far away from its actual location, geese can travel a thousand miles and longer dead right on their destination without any compass or charts or maps or radio waves, homing pigeons do their travel in an amazing display of that precise "sense" that we are talking about, so we are not the only ones privileged by Mother Nature's benevolent gifts !

Squirrel - Yes, I agree with you, Turtle, we are not the only ones to brag about our finely tuned natural gifts, but it was the way you talked about that special"sense" and the way you seemed to have figured to yourself the actual event that it sounded as if you would have actually been there yourself when it happened !!

Turtle - And I was .

Squirrel - Well, now, aren't we going too far with the help of imagination, even if only the imagination of a squirrel and a turtle, or, may be, you are taking me for a fool or just having a good time making a fool out of me, may be both !??

Turtle - None of them, dear Squirrel, none of them . You see, our slow temperament in everything and, particularly, mental and physical attitudes, the latter including locomotion, enables our kind to absorb and store everlasting impressions of the surroundings when we happen to be at one particular given spot and time and, when something is seen and registered, its imprint remains in our memory and it goes from generation to generation .

Squirrel - Turtle, what you are saying now it sounds even stranger than when at first it appeared to be !!

Turtle - Well, my dear Squirrel, not so strange or stranger because, as you probably have heard at school, nothing's new under the sun, somebody said that sometime ago, and, ...by the way, how did you know about that famous episode of the famous King, the famous Garter and the famous Countess who lost it ??.....Where you, by any chance, there when it happened ?

Squirrel - My dear Turtle, I haven't lost my mind, not entirely yet, and, of course, I wasn't there ! Our teacher at school had told us the story and he was very fond of historical anecdotes .

Turtle - We are also fond of everything and we learned about all those anecdotes of history at school too, those historical events were so vividly and realistically described that the texture of the unfolding event or drama or happy , even triumphant glimpse of a glorious deed, got us all wrapped up in their intricate followings as if we were there ourselves and a living part of it !

Squirrel - I remember those days at school : the learning of so many good things , some of them seemed so far away from us and yet,...yes, Turtle, you may be right, their interesting and, at times, fascinating, even intriguing mixture of the thoughts and customs of times gone by, did really catch our attention and carry us away to those days, to that particular event ,and we felt as we were there witnessing the event..!!...As that famous Poet said in one of his Plays : " O , for a muse of fire that would ascend the brightest heavens of invention, a Kingdom for a stage and Princes to act and Monarchs to behold the swelling scene", ...just as you said, as if we were there ourselves..!!

Turtle - Yes, dear Squirrel, exactly so ! And why , don't we all know of the ill-fated Antony and Cleopatra's interlude, of old Moses, of glorious Julius Caesar and of the Count of Montecristo and, not least, of the sad circumstances of Madame Bovary's life ?..Yes, of course we do and we talk about them as if we were there with them just as we read news in the papers about events in our daily lives! .....and, yet, some of them were thousands of years behind us !

Squirrel - You are a funny sort of creature, you are, dear Turtle, but one thing you are forgetting about it all !

Turtle - And what would that be ?

Squirrel - Well, my dear and historically inclined Turtle, we all can tell or know about the past and we can bring back and revive in our consciousness those instants of past lives and events as if they were there for us to observe or if they were there because we happened to be there too, whichever way their glow might have influenced us, depending on the intensity of that mysterious "perception"of yours, or pleasure, displeasure of that particular event, and that is just fine with the past, but no one, my dear Turtle, can tell a thing about the future !

Turtle - But, of course !...What's so strange about it ?

Squirrel - My dear Turtle, I feel that you are beginning to confuse me and I begin to wonder whether the house that you carry with you may be too heavy and its weight may be causing some fatigue to your mind , judging by the way you say certain thing and the way you represent them ! Now, don't you think that it is strange for creatures to be able to see and revive the past but not to be able to see the future !??!!

Turtle - But of course it is NOT strange at all ! Tell me, now, dear Squirrel, how can anyone see or tell of something that is not there yet ?

Squirrel - A minute ago I was complaining that you were beginning to cause great confusion in my mind and, now, you have completed your task : I AM confused !

Turtle - And so am I !

Squirrel - I'll be ....

Turtle - Well you'll better be:"I'll be.....".. whatever you meant to say but I can guess easily what you wanted to say just the same even without you completing your sentence as I "completed" your total confusion. And who wouldn't be confused when talking so much nonsense and at such leisurely pace? But, tell me, now, little Squirrel, do you like music ?

Squirrel - Do I like.......WHAT...??!!

Turtle - I just asked if you like music .

Squirrel - Music ??!...And what's that supposed to be ?..Ah!....Is it a special type of acorn ?

Turtle - A special type, yes, but not quite like an acorn .

Squirrel - Then, it's no use to me, whatever it is!

Turtle - Well, it is not an acorn but an accord .

Squirrel - And what can you do with it ?

Turtle - I'll tell what can be done with it : for one thing you can listen to wonderful sounds that soothe your mind, fortify your spirit, and restore your appetite .

Squirrel - Oh! Turtle dear, please...!!....do not talk to me about appetite ! That's the worst curse that can be brought on anybody's head and a distressful responsibility for a large family of squirrels !

Turtle - I understand, but I assure you that squirrels are not alone in regard to that predicament !

Squirrel - Tell me, Turtle, could those accords of yours that you just mentioned, help with the appetite problem ?

Turtle - You mean to curb it or to do away with it altogether ?

Squirrel - May be a mixture of both, if that were possible...........

Turtle - Possible is just a word and facts, sometimes, do not go hand in hand with words, so,in your case of the appetite question and whether the accord could help the appetite equally or better than an average acorn, it is hard to say, because , to begin with, it would require a prerequisite of perception, mental that is, and also spiritual, so...........................

Squirrel - Turtle, you may be slow in your locomotion but you certainly can go by leaps and bounds when it comes to exploring and explaining things !!

Turtle - Oh ! Dear.....!

Squirrel - But, then, these accords must be hard to come by or they are difficult to be put to any good or practical use for our everyday living: isn't it ?

Turtle - Well, in a way yes, my dear Squirrel, because music is not a ready source for procuring abundant victuals to those who answer to its melodious and enticing call and compose it, but, rather, only offering food for their spirit, for their imagination and for their sentimentalism, but not very satisfactory, in practical terms, as a food for quashing the cramps of hunger .

Squirrel - Are these music writers squirrels ?

Turtle - I do not think so . Why do you ask ?

Squirrel - Because the way you describe them, as being hungry, I imagined that they must be looking like me when I search desperately for acorns for myself and for my family .

Turtle - They are not squirrels, but like anything in life, it's most of the time a matter of perception .

Squirrel - Perception.....whatever that is..... of WHAT ?

Turtle - This may be hard, now, for you to understand, little Squirrel, but, sometimes, any logic explanation of things that happen in our lives depends in the way creatures , all sorts of creatures, different types of creatures that is, look at things that happen in our daily lives. Among these many and varied"things", food is one of those "things", and, for some creatures, "food"is just a generous amount of something tasty, plentiful and edible, while, to others, food is represented as a symbolic reward to their mental, spiritual and sentimental achievements .

Squirrel - Turtle ! Turtle !....I think that I am losing you in your jumping from one lower step to a higher one and keep going up and down, sideways and downwards with your loquacious tongue and I feel a bit easier and more at leisure when I jump from branch to branch in search of my beloved and most needed acorns .....

Turtle - But don't you see, little Squirrel, that you are just playing music doing as you do in your jumping from branch to branch and from tree to tree, in your daily continuous search for the acorn that gives you life, while you write music doing so !!

Squirrel - What..... did you say....??!!....I , writing music...???!!!!

Turtle - But of course, with your imaginative and unimaginative jumps and runs and your spirited and fast runs across the paddocks, dear Squirrel, your acting is just like writing notes.

Squirrel - Turtle, what you are saying is not only extravagant but altogether absurd : I do not even know what "writing" is or means...!!!

Turtle - No need for that, dear Squirrel : music writing is different . Why, the notes do just as many jumps and as many spirited as well as unspirited runs on their branches, you know,those linear long lines where they are constantly running and climbing up and down trying to catch and hold those precious "acorns" of their own called "accords" and, in doing so, producing those wonderful melodies while flying on those branches in awesome spasms of emotional fire for power, for love, for glory and dreams or crash majestically in a mournful lament of sadness, of desperation, or of the hopelessness of fateful Destiny. ....You, Squirrel, are an accord Squirrel !

Squirrel - I'll be.....!!

Turtle - You'll be a genius, a musical genius, if you only could write some notes ! Why, with all those jumps and ascents and descents up and down the trees and the balancing acts on the branches of those trees and your impressive flights from one tree to another , that could produce exciting music, a dance, a minuet or a classical ballet or even an unforgettable symphony .

Squirrel - Turtle, how do you write music ?

Turtle - Usually, with musical writing instruments .

Squirrel - Oh ! I see . Well, what kind of instruments?

Turtle - In the world of music maker Folks, these instruments are called in many different and various names .

Squirrel - You don't say ! Did I hear you mention "many" of those instruments and different too ?

Turtle - Yes, Squirrel, and each one is used in different ways depending on the inclinations, properties, talents, feelings and imagination of the ones who use them for writing music .

Squirrel - Turtle, this seems extraordinary interesting, but can these instruments be eaten too if someone becomes hungry, or must they be put aside somewhere while writing music and then eaten later on ?

Turtle - That has been the eternal dilemma in writing music, dear Squirrel : sometimes, it is possible to eat after writing some music provided the writing instrument and the one who employed it did write the right note, otherwise, and often, they starve .

Squirrel - Oh ! I see !....Then, dear Turtle, my "acorns" are somewhat more rewarding than your "accords", so it seems to me, anyway and it does not matter if my jumps and runs do not hit the right branch or the right tree, I still get my acorns and rarely I do starve, regardless of my jumps and runs "hitting" or "not hitting" the right note !

Turtle - I see your point, dear Squirrel, and I understand the way you interpret what I was trying to explain to you about music, the music makers and the instruments to make that music come alive, but, and here I'll say it again, it all has to do with a matter of perception.

Squirrel - Is that, may be, that what you just said, "perception", is more edible than the musical instruments ?

Turtle - Well, in some way and in some hypothetical form it can be ignored, swallowed, digested and eliminated altogether and, here again, depending on the fibers a given creature is woven into, perceptions may vary .

Squirrel - I tell you something, dear Turtle, I.........

Turtle - Fine, I'll be listening, but don't you want to hear an answer to your question about the edible qualities of "perception" ?

Squirrel - Oh! not much, really : all I wanted to tell you was that you are getting me off the track all the time, first helping me getting into it and, then, coming out with some other unbelievable stories and off the track I go again !

Turtle - Nothing of the kind, dear Squirrel, and you yourself are using perception every day while searching for your acorns, nothing more than your ability to instinc- tively recognize the right tree that bears the good acorn for you from an ordinary shroub that does not, with the only difference that you are blessed with the ab- sence of the genie of obsession for greatness and glory, so much pervasive, in- stead, in so many other perceptive creatures, here and there .

Squirrel - There you go again, my dear Turtle, using words that I have never heard spoken to me before ! Why can't you talk normally like we squirrels do ?

Turtle - Good point, dear squirrel, good point, indeed ! The problem, however, rests on the inalienable fact that creatures do not think or act or fantasize their dreams in synchrony with each other, some seeing things one way, some seeing things a different way even when "the things" are exactly the same , so, some creatures like to starve in order to fulfill their "hunger" for recognition, or for praise, or for fortune, while others keep on living just in a dream-like aura of imaginary expectation of grandeur without ever seeing it or achieving it and yet believing in their inflated perception , to have achieved it and those are the arid beds of brooks gone dry .

Squirrel - A strange world that must be! I would not like it, I believe.

Turtle - Dear Squirrel, it does not seem to be a question of whether anyone likes that type of world or not : it just happens to be that way for some creatures and it does not for some other creatures . So, it is a varied situation , a different "accord" for each creature looking for something to eat, searching, in their own respective worlds, for some "acorns" using the gift of their own specific "accords", sometimes making it and making it good and, sometimes, making it modestly or poorly or not at all ,this situation causing a "dissonance" in their lives, possibly but not necessarily, caused by a simultaneous combination of several adverse happenings .

Squirrel - I still prefer my acorns .

Turtle - And you, little squirrel, may be the wisest of them all !

Squirrel - I BEG YOUR PARDON !!!

Turtle - No offence, dear Squirrel, no offence ! Among the blessed creatures with an inbuilt anxiety for grandeur, that expression categorising you as a "wisest " person, is a compliment, not an offence to be getting skittish over it like a horse!....Actually, I was praising you for your way of saying things : in a way that is simple, clear, straight forward, natural and always very adherent to the core of the subject discussed or talked about . Really, I am thinking, how fewer and fewer "dissonances" there would be in the lives of all creatures if they would be able to use your way to look at things !

Squirrel - I do not look at things, Turtle : I just grab them when I see them, those acorns I mean, and eat them !

Turtle - If only life had just acorns to be dealt with !

Squirrel - I am sorry : I didn't hear you, dear Turtle...were you talking to me ?

Turtle Oh ! No, dear Squirrel, just ruminating something to myself. Nothing really important, I assure you . Please, don't worry !

Squirrel - We had a long talk, dear Turtle, and I am wondering now if I have detained you be-beyond a civilized exchange of time in pleasurable chatting , preventing you to continue on your way to wherever your travelling plans would have taken you .

Turtle - On the contrary, my good friend, I enjoyed talking with you and chatting on many things even if in a loose and lighthearted way, but nevertheless a very pleasant interlude in my extended travelling itinerary ahead of me.

Squirrel - Are you planning a very long trip, turtle, or just moving to a different abode?

Turtle - Yes, I am "moving", so to speak of : as a matter of fact I am on my way for a trip around the world .

Squirrel - Ask a casual question and you get the answer you deserve !!..Well, that's something, my dear Turtle. Are you kidding or are you serious ??!

Turtle - Serious .

Squirrel - May I ask you why would you want to get into such a laborious task of travelling around the world ?

Turtle - I am not quite sure. Sometimes I become a little depressed, sad , in my lonely house and I thought of moving around a little and get my mind off the chores of everyday petty life. May be I'd like to inquire about the"accords" of other creatures in the world and find out if they have found the golden solution to all problems or are they still working on it like we do.

Squirrel - I wish I could come with you, dear Turtle !

Turtle - It would be very nice to have you as my companion in this long voyage but we have to be realistic in making plans in our existences, dear Squirrel, and although we may like each other and get along wonderfully together on a temporary and courteous short engagement, a long haul may prove straining and more onerous for both of us if nothing else, just for the disparity of our speeds while moving ! So , you belong here, dear Squirrel, in this forest, and to your tree and to your trees and to your acorns : I may be a gullible turtle for my search of "accords" !

Squirrel - No, dear Turtle, I disagree about our incompatibility in a long, long voyage like the one you are planning to undertake because with my fast speed I could be a good scout for you in providing information on conditions ahead on the way, keep you company and, if I should become tired or sleepy I could take a nice nap on the roof of your house, while you would still trot along . I believe that there would be no "dissonance" in our...."accords"...!!

Turtle - I really enjoyed the way you portrayed our trip together but I still think that it might not last for the whole trip around the world : You see, dear Squirrel, one thing is doing something for fun or for something new and different and another is doing something to appease your somnolent lease on life or to alleviate your mind of untowards thoughts. You belong here, Squirrel, and you are very alive, fast and active all the time and you do not need to go around the world to look for something else:you have, here, everything you need, want and desire.You see,there may not be acorns along the road or,if any available, how would we know if they would be safe and good enough for you to eat ?

Squirrel - Well, no problem about that, dear Turtle ! Why, I would just eat then some "accords" .

Turtje - Touche !!...Well, my dear Squirrel, you are learning fast and you do not need to go around the world to learn anything more : somebody, sometimes, somewhere said that knowledge is important in providing creatures with good balance in their life's decisions, but too much of it could favour a hint to presumption in certain analphabets . Squirrel, as I have already mentioned it to you, repeatedly, YOU BELONG HERE, in this forest, among your beloved trees !!

Squirrel - Turtle, you are sapient, or I'd rather say sagacious, and either one you master well in your peaceful mind, which does not rush to quick answers or indulge in long, futile questions . May be you are right : I probably would be more of a burden to you in the long, long trip once the initial excitement of a new dimension is ingested, digested and ejected . What shall I say, dear Turtle ?

Turtle - How about:"Goodbye, hope to see you again, soon, on your return from the around the world trip, take care and, if you should have a little time to spare, now and then, send me a post-card from some unusual or interesting places that you might encounter on your way " ....How's that ?

Squirrel - You make fun of me, Turtle, thinking, perhaps, that my fast moving, acting and reacting, is a good indication of my ability to grasp notions . Very well, then, if this is the way you like it, goodbye, send me a couple of post-cards, take care, see you soon and get lost .

Turtle - Ah! Go on! Come off it !....You little rascal !...You know, Pia, the match-maker Lizard, told me that you are very busy these days trying to organize a large expedition, comprising a large number of squirrels, to far away lands in search of the Golden Acorn : is that true ?

Squirrel - And how did you get in touch with that.......well, with Pia, the lizard match-maker, anyway?

Turtle - I.met a lizard on my way to this forest along my planned trail, that's how, and I had stopped for a little time to rest close to some country stores on the side of the road which happened to be in the shade of large and tall trees, when this lizard approched me, asking if I felt well or if I needed some assistance.

Squirrel - How exquisitely sweet of her !

Turtle - Yes, I thought so too. Anyway, after I introduced myself and she introduced herself, stating her name as Pia and being one of the local Civic Couselors and, after I had assured her that I was fine and just resting, we engaged in a little conversation about nothing, as it is the usual outcome in these kind of encounters, but she took great pain in warning me that, should I have needed help while travelling through the forest which could be seen in the distance from the stores and down the trail, may be, a couple of miles away, I probably could not have been able to summon any help at all because the squirrels, almost the entire population of them in this here forest, were supposed to have left the forest on a very perilous journey on their way to far away lands in search of the Golden Acorn .

Squirrel - The Bitch !

Turtle - Oh! Squirrel !! Why ?...Has she given me the wrong information, may be ?

Squirrel - The impudent match-maker of a lizard, that Pia ! She did everything she could to get me involved with her daughter once she found out about my plan to go after the Golden Acorn, so that she could get the benefit of that bounty if I were successful ! The Bitch !...........

Turtle - And I had been under the impression, when planning my trip and the best places to travel through, that this forest as part of that itinerary, would have been the most pleaant, the most attractive and the most amenable to friendly folks ....was I wrong..??

Squirrel - Not entirely, but certainly so as far as the lizards are concerned, dear Turtle .

Turtle - And why would the lizards be singled out, I am wondering, from all the other creatures of this forest and surrounding lands ?

Squirrel - My dear Turtle, you have no idea how nasty these here lizards in this forest can be ! When they heard through the grapevine of the forest of my planned expedition to find the Golden Acorn, they became very envious of my plan and angry that I had not offered them a place in the organization of my expeditionary force, they tried to discredit me, they tried to lure me in unsavory deals which, fortunately, I was able to outskirt, and then went on trying to set up all kind of obstacles for me to make it difficult or even impossible to achieve my goal, unless I married the daughter of the match-maker, Pia, the mean, conniving, deceitful, unscrupulous lizard,....the Bitch !

Turtle - I believe that some referring signs and warning signs should be added to the maps of this area : " Mean Lizard country, please, detour ! " .

Squirrel - As a consequence we don't see eye to eye anymore with the lizards since that sequence of events and after I declared the lizards of this forest as enemies of my Clan .

Turtle - But couldn't it have been possible to come to more friendly terms and reached an........"accord", before letting things deteriorate to the point of no return ?

Squirrel - We tried, but those lizards are something else.They are strange creatures,full of themselves, overbearing, presumptuous, aloof and do not tolerate anyone disturbing them when they do not want to be disturbed, or interfering with their periodic spells of rest and "good repose" and, in their brains, or whatever is left in their heads of it, they seem inclined to think that it is the world that revolves around them and, should they desire to do so, they could stop it from turning around them or anybody else's . I just can't stand these kind of pocket-size Super-Novas, I am a free creature and love my freedom as well as I respect the freedom of others, and I detest the disturbing qualities and tendencies of some........well....of some other creatures to pretend that they are made of privileged stuff and claiming, with questionable logic, a privileged status!! .....that Bitch !

Turtle - Alas.....it isn't easy to get along on an even keel with everybody seeing that there are so many differences among all of us ! Perhaps nobody worries about me or annoys me because everybody knows that I live longer than anyone else and that I will not go very far anyway to be in anybody's way . Because of that, I guess, I live in relative peace . But you, squirrels, are too much active, spirited and agile and enterprising, and everybody, therefore, is jealous of you and fearful of your potential predominance .

Squirrel - I know that you are wise, dear Turtle, and a good observer of characters and situations, probably facilitated in this keen discernment by your calm and your slow attitude that afford you more time to look at and decipher more clearly the essential qualities of creatures'actions as well as of the development of situations and happenings, never perplexed at difficult problems and persistent, patient and enduring in your every day existence, yet, I cannot understand why would a lizard be fearful of a possible predominance of our specie over theirs when I stay most of the time on my tree, jumping from one branch to another, bothering no one and only occasionally straying over an adjacent tree to pick up some extra acorns .

Turtle - You did not fall for "sweet" Pia's daughter and you failed to marry her !.That's the problem!In her mind you are a squirrel that is preconceived against lizards and looked upon as a predominant character . She'll never forgive you for that !

Squirrel - Someone else will marry her "sweet"daughter, and I'll have a good squirrel laugh when that day will come ! After all, we are not the arbiters of our lives, there is something beyond our reality that guides our existences, and not very accurately either, in some instances .

Turtle - Destiny ??!..May be ! ??

Squirrel - Who knows !

Turtle - Do you believe, dear little Squirrel, that everything in our existences as well as in the existences of everyone else, inclusive of rock formation, love, fortune and disaster,is under the auspices of that famous entity called Destiny ?

Squirrel - And who knows !?...I guess we should ask Destiny about it: he should know, unless he, himself, is under the auspices of another Destiny of some sort, and would have to ask his own Destiny first, before answering to our inquiry, the whole thing becoming a little complicated and , in final analysis, questionably worth of losing time and sleep over it .

Turtle - True . But, now, dear Squirrel I must get back on my trail and keep going : I believe that I can still go some distance before night fall.

Squirrel - Yes, I believe so too, and it will be at least a couple of hours before the sun will disappear beyond those hills at the end of the trail in the forest : is your plan still the same, dear Turtle ? Are you still on your way for your trip around the world ?

Turtle - Yes, dear Squirrel, I have not changed my plans . Indecision is a bad habit or a poor form of character, it always leads to uncertainties, inconvenience and confusion . What's important is to be sure of your thinking in making plans, but, once everything has been duly studied and analyzed , then it is advantageous to stick to the plan .

Squirrel - I envy you for your determined way of seeing things and I am so much tempted to come with you and see new places, new squirrels, new forests.........

Turtle - May be, even new lizards.....why not !!

Squirrels - That remark spoiled everything, dear Turtle ! With that possibility flashed in front of me, all my enthusiasm for coming with you has disappeared that very instant you said that !!

Turtle - Squirrel, you are much too fast in coming to conclusions : you seem to turn on every subject,sentence or thought with the same lightning response as you do when you perform your acrobatic acts on the branches of your tree !!

Squirrel - Destiny ??!

Turtle - I am more inclined to think in terms of excellent muscles and exceedingly well tuned nerves .

Squirrel - Yes, you may be right, again, I am a little too fast, but then I could direct the same criticism at you for being too slow, so , given and taken, we are square ! But, this is not what I wanted to mention to you before you left ......

Turtle - Oh ! That must be interesting ! What is it, dear Squirrel ?

Squirrel - As I was busy working on my plans for the long voyage to search for the Golden Acorn, I was told that in some lands very, very far from here, there are trees that in some moments of sadness or distress actually shed tears, and the extraordinary aspect of that unusual behaviour for a tree is that they cry not only for their own problems but also for the sadness or distress of other trees that are not able to cry !

Turtle - Squirrel, who told you that story or from which source did you get that information?

Squirrel - It was some time ago when one day, while I was idling for a while on a branch of my tree, that a passing bee stopped on that same branch where I was and asked me if she could take a little breath and a short rest because she had just had a very, very long and exhausting flight and needed to stop for a while before reaching her aviary .

Turtle - I hope that you let her stay: didn't you ?... The poor thing !!

Squirrel - Actually, my dear Turtle, she didn't turn out to be either a poor or exhausted "thing" due to heavy work or fatigued for lack of nourishment or something else !!

Turtle - Who was she, then , and, furthermore, why was she flying around by herself without an escort and on the verge of collapsing on your tree !? Did she give you her name or, at least, introduce herself ?

Squirrel - That she did : it turned out that she was the Queen Bee on the day that she, by that natural instinct that distinguishes those valiant and laborious creatures, having dutifully attended to her numerous would-be-lovers and having successfully accomplished the elimination of all the eager suitors but one, the strongest, the perfect flyer, the one overcoming with ease and grace the overwhelming and difficult long distance cruising speeds and endurance, that natural and charming duty of hers excellently performed , she, the Queen, as I said, thought of taking a little rest and go gleefully over her significant avchievement . Her Majesty's name was Aurora . Quite a bee, that Queen !...She.....gives ORDERS.........when she intends to be loved !!!

Turtle - Apparently, being a Queen, offers some significant advantages .

Squirrel - Would you have liked to have been born a Turtle Queen , dear Tuirtle ?

Turtle - Not at that speed .

Squirrel - I agree . But, then , let me finish the story about the crying trees, and the Queen told me, also, that there is plenty of water in that land, and long ,majestic rivers and lakes and mountains with snow covered peaks and also several inhabitants there and, among them, a tribe of splendid squirrels, highly civilized, she said, who live happily and without any fears or fights and, best of all, not one single lizard around !!

Turtle - But, my dear Squirrel, in that seeming enchanted land, so appearing at least the way you describe it and as it was represented to you by the Queen Bee in her voluptuous and exciting nuptial flight, even the lizards, if there would be any around, would very likely be just as peaceful and adorable as the civilized Squirrels thriving there, ! Don't you think ?

Squirrel - That would be a wishful thinking even in an enchanted land and in a fabled story ! But, on that subject I have some reservations because life without stress , without fights, disappointments and or confrontations, likes and dislikes, joy and sorrow, is a little poorly represented and underscored in its true values, particularly so when that knowledge is gained through information provided by a bee, as bees are well known for using forced labour, forced love-making, murdering all the males when their use is no longer needed and becoming really nasty and aggressive if you go bothering them in their houses .

Turtle - You are really hard on those poor bees, dear Squirrel...!!

Squirrel - Oh ! Just talk, dear Turtle...probably the bees themselves have some reservations on me and my fellow Squirrels when we go too fast from tree to tree and on the paddocks, disturbing the pollen on their flowers ....so....not much use wondering about other creatures' problems....don't we have enough of our own, dear Turtle ?

Turtle - I think so . But, now, dear Squirrel, is that the land to where you plan to guide your people ?

Squirrel - May be, although I am not certain yet, but the lure of a new "something", a "something" never seen before, even if just the same as the one where you live every day, but "somewhere" else, is always something you look forward to even if no one there is waiting for you .

Turtle - That gives me some comfort and some courage too, because by being very slow in getting anywhere I give plenty of time to myself and any other creature to see, to absorb and to ponder on what "anything" is really best or just good or altogether negligible . Anyway, thank you for the story about the crying trees and.......well, now, just thinking about it, I heard that story about the crying trees, back home, where I come from, and they have a strange name that sounds just as sadly crying as the trees themselves ....

Squirrel - Oh! Dear Turtle, please, tell me how those trees are called in the land where you come from : I am very, very curious !

Turtle - That's strange : for such an active, enterprising and forward flung spirit that makes you a squirrel, this apparent longing curiosity for a sadly looking and crying tree seems somewhat mismatched .

Squirrel - My dear Turtle, even if so that my curiosity might be mismatched to my character and way of living and acting, well, I wouldn't be alone in this world to qualify for it my dear Turtle : your spirit and your yearning for seeing the world seem to me two qualities quite mismatched to the way Nature built you !

Turtle - That's rather personal, dear Squirrel !

Squirrel - Not intended that way at all, my dear Turtle ! Not at all !! I only wanted to emphasize that a physical aspect of a creature, any creature, or an abstract interest in "something" by that creature, even if that "something" or that "interest" is poorly identifiable with that creature's character or image,will not have any bearing on that specific creature's normal and effective equanimity of his, her, its, their intellectual expression , function and ability .

Turtle - Amen !!.....None, whatsoever, and I fully agree with you, my dear "didactic" Squirrel !

Squirrel - I really did not aim so high, my dear Turtle, to the point of becoming a didactic old squirrel !!.....I am contended and plum happy when I can reach as high as I can on my big trees to catch some acorns or ..... shall I say.....some of your ..accords !!??

Turtle - Well, my dear Squirrel, the quality of being modest that reflects so well in your expressions and attitudes, is a fairly good representation of a soaring intellect, simple but eager and honest, in its effort to reach as high as possible to catch an acorn of invention .

Squirrel - Shucks !! I am speechless !

Turtle - ....And very well represented, like the old saying :" the word is made out of silver, but silence is made of pure gold !"

Squirrel - Ah!.....Those metals !....I would starve to death even if I had tons of them.!!........But, my dear Turtle, while indulging in the midst of all of these "intellectual" and "didactic" acorns ....you forgot to tell me the name of those crying trees, how they are actually called in the land where you come from .

Turtle - You are right, dear Squirrel, we got carried away on some silly remarks, whose memory and print of their significance will not come up to even a heap of beans ! So, here is the name of those crying trees as they are referred to in the land where I come from: the name is : " Felix babylonica " ..but.........

Squirrel - Thank you, Turtle, thank you , and now I know why those trees are crying ! Anyone with that name could not do anything else but cry .

Turtle - But, generally, are referred to as weeping willows.....

Squirrel - The poor things !! Nature, sometimes, seems to be totally insensitive to the personal feelings of various creatures as well as rather indifferent in the distribution of her assignments and incongruous prescriptions for certain creatures' life-codes and "modus vivendi" !!

Turtle - You are telling me !!!!

Squirrel - Well, at least you don't cry over your cumbersome bulky shell !

Turtle - Life will be life, dear Squirrel, regardless of how much time and effort we will or we would spend in trying to decipher its meaning and its reason to be as we see it now or how it will or could be in a hundred and thousand years from now or even longer beyond that target !

Squirrel - Well, that's debatable, I should think.........

Turtle - For all the lizards in this world, my dear Squirrel, you never fail to amaze me with your intuitive speculating initiatives almost reminiscent of the sayings of that famous Latin philosopher, who wondered how poorly would generations, centuries from his age, judge his age knowledge of "things", mysterious and almost occult at his time but, probably, common place and common knowledge at theirs .

Squirrel - I never thought of it that way, dear Turtle : too complicated for my little brain . Tell me, was this philosopher of yours a famous squirrel ?

Tutle - Famous, yes, but not a squirrel . Now, if that makes any difference, I really do not know .

Squirrel - Oh! It's not that important . I just thought that if he had been a squirrel, he might have had some educated ideas of how to get better and more plentiful acorns : that was all .

Turtle - And " all " is, indeed, a large chunk of reality even if only as a "was"......well, it's getting late, " tempus fugit" said someone with a flare for the latin language, long time ago, so I want to tell you that I had a great time chatting with you : it refreshed me, it inspired me, it will help me in my projected voyage around the world, but now it's time to say goodbye and get on my road, with a pinch of regretfulness and a dash of sadness .

Squirrel - Now, here, Turtle, just make sure that you'll stop by this tree when you'll come back and tell me all about your trip, your experiences about it and all the wonders that I am certain you'll be fortunate enough to see and alert and eager enough to retain a good representation as well as a clear memory of them .

Turtle - Yes, dear Squirrell, I will do that provided everything will go well during my long voyage and, if so, when I'll be back here I'll come by the tree and I believe that I'll be able to recognize it and find it still standing and big and full of leaves but, I am afraid, that I might have to tell the story of my adventure and of the wonders that I might have seen, not to you, poor little squirrel, but, perhaps, to your grandsons because, at my pace, it may be a very, very long time before I would be able to be back and to come by your tree !

Squirrel - I understand, dear Turtle, and I am not surprised at your " calculation" about the time span! Life is like that . But I will tell to my Grandchildren, anyway, about you so that they will be able to recognize you and bring you my personal welcome home by the way of them . What would be the difference, anyway, whether it would be me, in person, or them : they are squirrels too . Goodbye, Turtle, take care and send a few post cards whenever you can, enjoy yourself and.......

Turtle - ....Shall I complete your departure farewell by recollecting some rehearsal farewell a while ago and add......: " get lost " ??!

Squirrel - I should have expected that ! you never fail to intrigue my imagination, dear little Turtle ! Anyway, "Adieu", my good Turtle, and genuine " squirrel speed" to you!!

Turtle - Thank you, dear Squirrel, and.......well....it just dawned on me....may be you would want to think it over about sweet Pia's charming daughter, when I am gone....right ?

Squirrel - NEVER !!

Turtle - Bye, Squirrel : see ya ! Sometime !

Squirrel - Bye, Turtle !

*** THE END ***

DIALOGUE
of
the Thought and the Reason
******

(Beginning with the soliloquy of the Reason)

**

Reason - Well, thanks Goodness !....After my long promenade I am finally back home!! ....But I seem to feel somewhat more tired than I would have anticipated, well, may be nothing of major consequence, or I might have inadvertently either walked a little faster than usual or, lured by the balmy weather, extended my walk of a couple of yards, taxiing mercilessly my limited capacities of "track running"...!!!....But one thing is certain and it is good....: I AM HOME !!!.....And my favourite lounge-chair is right here waiting for me...Aaaaah...!!...Thia is wonderful....and it seems to be even softer now than it ever was ...!!.....And my poor aching feet.....they seem to be on fire! Now, let me take off my shoes and my socks.....here......OOOOOOH....what a relief.... ......what a relief......what a fantastic and pleasurable relief and now I can stretch my legs and.....this is life at its best.....ah!...how wonderful !....Here....well, yes, my house maid Camilla, she is so wonderful, so efficient and she always leaves a ready kettle with warm water near the fireplace, just close enough to the fire so that the water becomes just warm and not too hot and ready to be poured into this basinette here, near my lounge chair, to rest my weary feet and let indulge in the relaxation provided by this delightful, soothing bathing and relaxed soaking......while I shall enlighten myself with the latest news from our local paper and, soon, it will be time for my supper and, just thinking of it, it makes my mouth water and builds my appetite, reinforced, as it already is, by the generous prod from my reinvigorating.....walk !!...Ah!...This is indeed life....at its very best....and how else could it be if not at its very best ??!.....At least, that's how it feels to me this late afternoon and I shall make no comparisons with previous afternoons or guess of possible improvements in future afternoons, I am just going to enjoy what I have at hand and be happy with it..........yes, I am happy and.....well.....but where is my dear Camilla ? I do not hear a sound from any part of the house or from the kitchen where she usually is, busy at this time preparing supper........and, another thing that just comes to my attention this moment, I see that she did not seem to be home when I arrived back from my walk........I was more tired than usual and I did not pay much attention to that situation, eager and anxious as I was to get on my lounge chair, get my shoes and socks off and plunge them into that basinette of warm water......but, definitely, she must not have been home because, usually, she comes around and asks me how was the walk, if I was tired, how was the weather and if there were many people around, did I meet anyone I knew, or did I need anything special right away or was I comfortable enough to wait a little while for supper to be ready and a few other vernacular expressions of everyday use trown in casually just before retiring to the kitchen to apply the final expert touches to the fabulous supper........but, thinking back, this time I did not hear a sound anywhere and from anywhere !...A little strange.....well, may be, she is still in the garden picking up some choice leaves of endive for the supper or, may be, she had to hurry to the market to pick up some last minute needed supplies.......Oh! Well !....She should be home soon, anyway, and no need to worry about it ......yet, if she had thought to be late, she would have left, most likely, a note warning me of that delay, not that she had to, but it would have made sense doing it, since it represented an unusual situation, or, even if she had not thought of it or had had no time ti leave one for me to see, the Gardener, then, would have done that, possibly so instructed by Camilla before rushing to the market, warning me of Camilla being late, before he himself left after his day's work......well, she'll be here soon, I am sure.....although this is the first time that such a thing has happened ...!.....Oh! ...What's the matter with me, making a mountain out of nothing....!!!...Let me relax and everything will be all right, Camilla will be back home, my supper will be served , I will eat it and, after that, a couple of nice puffs on my pipe and soon will be time to go to bed and get a good night sleep !....In the meantime, while waiting for Camilla to come back home, I'll have a good chance to relax and enjoy the wonderful feeling of being home.....home, sweet home !!....In my own home and in the placid atmosphere of my cozy parlour, considering, after all, that this might be a rare opportunity to savour the anticipation of a gourmet supper!.......Adding to it the realization that not a single moment of my promenade this afternoon was wasted combining the excellent effect of the actual walking and the successful shaping of my new shoes, adapting themselves smoothly to the shape of my feet, on the outcome of this most pleasant and enjoyable outing and on my general well being, all achieved without an inch of a problem or inconvenience, just perfect, I would say.......or, on second thought, I wonder if it might have been my feet adjusting to the shape of the new shoes, instead of the shoes to my feet......considering the fiery feeling of my feet when I took my new shoes off, it gave me the impression that neither of "them two" adapted to anything at all...!!! Anyway, this warm water is a very pleasant treat to my aching and tired feet!.Ah.. I was going to forget to clean my new shoes...!!!!...Do not let me forget to do that, Heavens forbid.......these days, with prices so high, you cannot afford to buy yourself a pair of new shoes whenever you get in the mood for it, so, you got to keep what you have in good shape and repair, clean it and not using it unnecessarily, particularly if the weather is bad , rainy and muddy and, in that case, you better get hold and wear an old pair of shoes which had seen their better days . Well, I'll have to get my feet out of this basin full of warm water first, dry them and then I can start cleaning my shoes,,,,now, I need a towel.....now.....Oh ....the wisdom of my dear Camilla, how far-sighted and provident she is, anticipating my possible needs, and here is a beautiful towel, the one I really need to dry my feet, slip on some warm socks an slippers, all of which I can already spot neatly arranged on the floor within my easy reach.....Oh....this wonderful Camilla, she is....she is the best of everything ...!!!.....And here is the brush and the shoe polish ....ah!...so well organised and ordered.....everything in its proper place !....Even the brush was laid with the bristles facing up so as not to become warped by some heavier object leaning on them, and placed even at some distance from the can of the shoe polish so that the brush could not run the risk of becoming contaminated should, by accident, the lid of the shoe-polish can become loose ! Perfect !....Just Perfect! Really, a surprising logical sequence of arrangement, quite unusual and unexpected in a relative simple and uneducated person like my dear Camilla is.......Well let me correct a little that remark, as I did not and I do not intend to undermine the excellent gifts of Camilla's ability at anything she engages in, her mastery in cooking and, in a general sense, in her overall ingenuity and resourcefulness as a house maid and these enlightening facts are indeed as refreshing as my awariness of her talents . A really good woman, my Camilla : I do not konw how I could manage my life in this house without the constant help and attention and dedication of her good disposition and that without considering the extra benefit of her superb cooking art and skills !.....Well, so it is....so it is.....and here, now, are my brand new shoes,clean and shiny again, just as they looked in the windows of the shop, where I bought them . I am glad that I took time to clean them after I returned from my promenade because I firmly believe that, in general, it is important to take good care of things, anything, and particularly so when those things are your own but and, I repeat it and feel very strongly about it, but this attitude and habit should not be intended and practiced as an egoistic, selfish tendency to safeguard your own property only, disregarding the properties of others, instead of being also watchful and considerate towards the belongings and property of your neighbours and any other people at large because, if everybody would take good care of his own property or of the property that one is empowered of as a trustee, or which belongs to dependents, friends, employees, and so on, it follows that the properties, as a whole, would well kept, in good order and secure . But what on earth am I talking about ??!....Here I am waiting for my supper and we go on a tangent talking and commenting on how to keep up properties, keep things in order, keep them secure for your own sake and the sake of your neighbours and fellow humans, and it is already six o'clock in the evening and no sign of Camilla !!.....But what could have happened, I wonder !!....Why is she not here yet !....This is very, very strange and it worries me, now, lest something bad would have happened to her, may be, a fall or feeling bad or an aggression on the street on her return from the market......well, I'd better take hold of myself and stop guessing about situations which might not even exist......and it is also highly unusual for Camilla to stay out this late in the evening or to be late or unpunctual for anything !.....What could have happened,I wonder !!....And to be out of the house, towards evening, when it will slowly turn dark enhancing the apprehension of being caught in total darkness, out of your home, because, in these here times we live in, you may never know whom you might meet in the streets , at that time of night, in total darkness !.....Times of uncertainty and instability these dfays are and full of shady characters whose only wish and endeavour are doing harm to whomever may happen to cross their way , not that I pretend to assume the high seat of imparting a critical picture of present days morality, no, Heavens forbid, not at all, and, certqinly, not me, yet I cannot help realize that, out there and, particularly, hiding in the protective darkness of the evening and even the deeper darkness of the night, there may be some valiant people ready to practice their best talents in attacking honest folks and cut their throats and even their heads as a trophy of their noble skills, whether physically proper or purely demonstrative of their achievements, resorting to those methods because,these days,no one likes to be reasonable,that is to use their reason to work out their problems, difficulties, unexpected set backs, adversities or just plain misfortune,and they do not even want to listen to reason when good and benevolent people around them, if they would be so fortunate has to have some around...... well, would try to help to think some ways out of the present trouble, not only that but they even seem to be, believe it or not, they even seem afraid of it, that is to use reasoning, and unwilling, therefore, to practice it ....And why is it so , you might ask me.....well, I'll tell you why : they just are unable or unwilling to use reason, to reason things out, because they have lost that old-fashioned common sense and they seem to comprehend and hold high above anything else only their own way of thinking and their own way of interpreting things as best it suits them and are weary of others professing different ways of action and attitude even if these other peoples' ways are better than theirs ! On this account, of course, they cannot entertain to acknowledge any reasoning at all, for fear to lose their prominence, their privileges or the upper hand in their demanding codes of social and general life styles and activities!......Scoundrels they are these would be Scholars ! ...What is reasoning worth if the willingness to adopt it and the common sense to utilize it have been neglected and lost ?......Well. I'd better keep quiet and stop ruminating on all those thoughts and, instead, be myself . Afterall, I am Reason, that's my name, not that a "name" you were given at birth enpowers you to follow and take advantage of its properties, but it so happens that I am actually interested in reasoning things out ! ...Now, whether that is a blessing or something and, most likely, more just a "something" than anything else, I cannot say because, so far, no one has been able to predict the future so I cannot tell what that "something" will do for me during the rest of my life, so my best advice...to myself !!....is to keep quiet, don't bother anybody, if possible, be tolerant of others intolerance and enjoy your existence and keep your reasoning to yourself and, above all, try your best not to tread on anybody's....shoes !!....Besides, what is the advantage or what would really be the advantage, I ask myself, to reason with these"savvies" ,when all they are interested to hear or.......well, let me say this....or what they are at all capable to understand is what is favourable and fruitful to them and.....well......why am I talking to myself so much !!......I hope that I have not lost my....."reasoning".....Heavens forbid !!...No, nothing so dramatic, just a leisurly digression a simple, innocent digresssion just to change subject and avoid slowly slipping into a self-recriminatory sermon that would lead nowhere !.....And, besides, the whole thing would not stand to....Reason!!!..Why ! I am here waiting for my delicious supper refreshed as I am now after resting some following my promenade ! I can already anticipate the sight of a beautifully appointed table, like my dear Camilla always manages to prepare, shiny silver candelabra with white, brilliant candles to cast their warm light on a nitid and embroidered table cloth, fine silver ware neatly arranged on it and dishes of fine chinese porcelain, which look at you with such exquisite appearance as if begging you to pick them up, hold them gently in your hands, admire them and praise them for their extraordinary beauty and then seat down with them and enjoy the taste of some excellent food laid on them for your pleasure and as a trait of esteem for and prize and recognition for their useflness !..Well, they certainly are useful ! Now, some philosophers would say"not necessarily so"....!!...Agreed......in a strict sense, may be acceptable, meaning that "nothing", really, is necessary in order for "anybody" to be able to eat, since we, as humans, have hands and, tomtbe exact, we are not theonly ones with hands but, apart for that observation, hands have fingers and fingers can grab the food and bring it to the mouth, even to think that some creatures in this world do not have hands and fingers and, yet, eat regularly without any difficulty, then, on the other side of the coin, man, whenever possible, likes to seat in a comfortable chair and at a well appointed table and those utensils, I mean the expensive silver ware, the exquisite porcelain dishes, the fine table cloth, embroidered serviettes and so on and so on, certainly add to the pleasure of the table, of course, not a prerequisite to eating and, in some quarters of our Societies, the delights of the table are not considered a proper way to virtue and a waste, however delightful those delights might be, as well as an excess that offends the hungry . Diogenes acted rightly, they claim, when he tossed aside his wooden bowl he used to gather water and drink from it, after observing a youngster drinking at a water spring by making a cup with his hand.!...Diogenes!! ....Oh !!....But where have I come, this evening, talking and talking to myself of I do not know what , from the shoe polish, the brush and the shoes and all the way to...Diogenes...!!!.....And to think that, in all probability, Diogenes would have thrown the shoe polish, the brush and the shoes too...!!....Well,he might have been quite right in doing so and also justified for rejecting those apparels and the leather shoes and all !! ....He might have argued, what good is it to have our own skin under our feet and to what purpose it is there if we, instead of putting out own skin under our feet to good use, are using someone else's skin to place under our feet ! Well, this may remain a point of personal "liking"and "habits"and the question will still remain unanswered about why is it necessary to wear shoes on our feet, or, place our feet into some shoes, weakening, in doing so, the natural strength of the skin of our feet, furthermore, who told us to wear shoes, was it in order to run faster and negotiate more difficult terrains, reach destinations quicker than you could have done bare-footed, considering that, as far as we know at the rate of present knowledge, nothing is going any faster than it did the day before or the year before, or some centuries ago or even several thousand of years before then, so, in simple words:" what's the hurry ?", and is the going faster on perilous terrain, wearing shock-proof shoes, bringing us faster, richer rewards than if going along at a slower pace and bare-footed ? Of course, the cobbler has to feed his family, he needs to make shoes, the farmer has to sell his animals to make ends meet ,support his family and make a profit too, if possible, and those skins will make excellent leather for the soles and the otal shape of the shoes, so, it all seems to me to boil down to the realization that this world moves around only because of shoes and it does not make any difference if our head has no shoes since it never walks that far, anyway . I really do not know how did I get into all this nonsense talking and we could reason and argue for ours about feet, shoes and "head-less" shoes, claiming that several creatures walk bare-footed, some others with very large, enormous shoes and smaller heads, and slander, thin, elegant shoes adorning the provocative feet of nervous female silhouettes, walking fast but surely in the direction of their choice, and many more cases of shoes and feet in our lives, some leading nowhere, others walking the path to glory, and many getting stuck in the muddy subsurface of crime and turpitude, neglect and despair, elation and disillusions, greed and waste, selfishness and prodigality, but all, nevertheless, wearing shoes , and we could discuss the matter for hours, for days, for weeks,for months, for years, may be, even for centuries, without coming to a satisfactory or correct conclusion or agreement of principles resulting, perhaps, in the persistent presence of the real interesting subject, perfectly and happily unaware that all the reasoning about that subject is, of course, the ubiquitous nature of shoes . To be further considered that, to be truthful, these shoes would have a pretty good reason to be totally unaware of all the reasoning about them, even not at all interested in all that chatter and, perhaps, remain silent, after a few shortly after birth little squeaks, and indifferent but self-assured, though, of the traditional importance reserved for them by the well being of a multitude of feet, yearning for some protectors in their lives and daily existences so close to this Earth of ours..... Well, talking about shoes, it just comes to my mind an old proverb that, more or less, goes like this:"Large, solid, bulky shoes......sure indication of a fine brain".... but this dogmatic proverb and the tenet in its interpretation have never been analysed, I guess, to elucidate whether "fine" means a "veiled" thinness of the cerebral substance, indicating some deficiency in the constituent matter, or, instead, an astonishing finesse in the substance of the cerebral composition as opposed to the enormous, stompy size of the large shoes, which would indicate and represent stability and, as a consequence, the ability for a well balanced existence of equilibrium and judgement. But, as we read history, this was a well known proverb in the past and, to our dismay, that knowledge did not seem to help much in the general application of that equilibrium and judgement if we consider the constant turmoils this world did go through, is going through and, most likely,will go through, in the foreseeable future, not that I want to be a pessimist but only adopting some small town reasoning to the facts that are going around these days, and, partly, at least, this depressing view of the world might be the result of my supper being late : even the rosiest sunsets may look like the fires of hell on an empty stomach.!.......And my usual supper time is long past and no sign of Camilla, yet !!......An awkward situation, where all I can do is look at my new shoes, "brand" new and shiny and how nice and elegant they are......well, just to think of them, I wonder if there ever was a proverb that said:"fine shoes, and a bulky brain", because "that" is how I feel right now !....And I wonder if, may be, in those days when the proverb of the feet and the brain, rather, of the shoes and the brain, was first promulgated, people, then, knew their feet and shoes very well and the brain very little, or vice-versa, as they say now:" whichever comes first " and that, of course, would presupposed a"second"and, not being aware of one existing, we''ll leave it there to sleep. Anyway, I was reading, yesterday, that a famous man of wisdom and reknown had said :" Man usually recognizes what he has knowledge of...", so I could say, also, in the end, that I was right when I felt and I reasoned that I wear shoes on my feet because I "knew" that my feet performed a lot better when walking inside some shoes and "recognized"the very important value of that arrangement, proving, beyond any fastidious doubts, that the famous saying by that famous man passed the magic threshold of veridicity and applicable theory to practical reality and I am sure that, in some way, not yet easily explainable, my feet will agree to the old proverb by the famous man . Oh!......I do not know what came upon me this evening that I am talking so much and....to myself !!!......I have even forgotten to take my feet out of this water that, by now, it's almost cold ! I got to get my feet nice and dry and then put on my warm socks...I wonder whether there ever was another proverb that said:"warm, well knitted soaks, well hewn brain ".......but this may be a redundant entry even if talking to myself ! So, here are my socks, warm and soft, well fitting asround my feet and here they go past my ankle and half the length of my calf and then, here right into my new clean and shiny shoes and it is also "HIGH" time, by Jupiter and Juno, to find out what could have kept Camilla away from the house for such a long time....Most unusual, most unusual, indeed..... my goodness....it is already a quarter to nine .....almost "night time"!!!......Bed time, I should rather say, and Camilla is nowhere !!....I'd better take a look outside to see if anything out of the ordinary is going on in the streets this evening......these days, you'll never know what could happen...........

(Mr. Reason prepares to descend in the street to look for any signs of anything unusual in the sreets that could have caused Camilla to be so late.................)

Oh ! Oh!.....But....WHAT am I seeing...????!!!.....By Jupiter and Juno.....I can't believe it.......for Goodness sake and all the heavens above I believe that I can see Camilla standing at the corner of the next street from ours and talking in all earnest with that trifling, shallow, concocting, contriving, vane, good for nothing Mr. Thought !....Oh !...of all that could have happened...this is the worst !!...Some people refer to him as "Sir Thought"with deference , but certainly not I ! I know him better than that, being my closest neighbour..!!....Oh! this, now, is too much to bear, even if I put forth the best of me, that is my progressive and steady reasoning !......I'll have a few well chosen expressions to praise him with, and let him know what I do think of him other than being my closest neighbour !....That blown up gas-brain of that deciduous thinking bag of tricks and ploys and high handed circomlocutions just to satisfy his stupid ego.........the whole sight of him talking to my naive Camilla and probably trying to take the advantage of her good and simple nature ,may be, to try to get her to come to his service and leave me!!! I know these words Manipulators, trying to fool everybody.....Ah!.....this.really, I wouldn't have expected to happen to-night, or, for all it matters, any night or day or ever !!......And myCamilla is too polite and considerate to cut him short and leave for fear of affending him, as she is well aware that he is my neighbour and that we exchange greetings whenever we meet somewhere.So, it is an embarrassing situation ! This, really, irritates me and the best intention of my reasoning, just seeing him or looking at him.....well....but, then,......well....no....that wouldn't work well after all and I'll better calm down and, to a second thought and a little reasoning, there is, really, no reason why my dear Camilla and Mr.Thought, that devil of Sir Thought, I mean...!!....Oh! well, I shouldn't have said that "that" way, it just slipped out of my mouth, inadvertently, ...well....back to the right track, so, as I was saying, there really is no reason why my dear Camilla could not talk and chat with Mr. Thought, if they so desired and under favourable circumstances. After all, they are standing in the open and at the corner of the street. No harm in that, really, May be I am a little selfish in expecting almost a military like compliance with schedules and arrangements! Well, then, let me reconcile myself with myself, even if grammatically and whatever other way incorrect, but with the same meaning, of course, and so, I am going to meet and see them in the street and welcome them, just to show concern, interest and apprehension!...Who knows? May be they are talking about something important, something interesting and of some value, because our neighbour, Sir Thought, sometimes, has sparkling ideas on certain days, not often, though, yet, some, sometime.... Oh. well, may be something unusual or unexpected happened in the village, or news came around of a cataclysm in a far away land, or the conflagration of a war erupting somewhere, or an invasion by something or somebody.....I'll better hurry up to them and see what's going on.

****

(So, Mr. Reason leaves the house and proceeds with a leisurely gait towards the street corner where Camilla and Sir Thought were standing and chatting, just to the opposite side of the very large square, one of the largest squares ever built and the most beautiful one in the village....)

(In the meantime, while Mr Reason was talking to himself in the house and before deciding to go out to see for himself about what he wondered that might have been going on, Camilla and Sir Thought, were engaged in a lively conversation)

****

Camilla - My! My! Mister Thought, oh! It are really lovely to talk to you and to hear you talking to me, me poor, simple maid, we does not know all them good words, like important folks say, , you knows, like Sir and Lady, Squire and Lord, we just go about blabbering something to say something to someone we like and we pay respect , as youse, Sir, that I always like to hear talk to me, a poor ignorant girl, and does not know nothing about youse idée with illumination and the going of the astralis, you has studied all them things, but we, poor ignorant folks, does not know anything about the transmission of the illuminated idée, like you tell me now, or of the sending of the astralis.....Oh! Oh!...Dear, dear Me..!!! Sir, it is so late..!!...Late, late, Sir, that I is become so confused about the illumination and the astralis, and ah has forgotten about to get ready the supper for my Master..! Oh! Dear! Dear Me...!! Mr Thought, what was I to tell my Master about being so late..???!!...Oh! Dear, dear me!!!

Thought- I don't think that you need to worry so much, Camilla, about being a little late this particular evening, and even if once in a while something is a little late, the world will not fall off its orbit, I assure you, even if this evening you were a little late in preparing his supper. Apart from that little detail, I want to tell you and I want to assure you that I have the greatest respect for you and your intelligence and that I have never doubted it .

Camil;la - Ah ! Yes, you is good, Your Eminence, a kind man, you really is !

Thought - But, mydear Camilla, I want to clarify some of your words that I just heard you saying, if you will allow me .

Camilla - But, Your Eminence, you is very welcome to clarify all them words that I said,but what do "clarify" means ??!

Thought - Nothing really important, Camilla . It just sets the orthography of the words in the proper order and perspective so as to represent teir correct and intended meaning . So , for example, as you were saying....................

Camilla - Oh , you is so kind to talk to me, poor ignorant maid, and I understand only nothing or something of what you say, but I listen anyway, and I like your voice......

Thought - Very well, then : what I usually say or talk about are not"astralis" but abstract ideas and they, these ideas, have no relation whatsoever with illumination like lanterns but they are meant to enlighten people and encourage them to think .

Camilla - Oh ! That sure must be the thing because I sure remember now to think about the dinner for my master and that I is to run home as fast as I can and prepare supper ! My master will be very upset by now ! Oh, my, it is so late !....What is I to do..??! Your Eminence, I must hurry home !

Thought - I am sorry, Camilla, to have kept you talking when you, actually, are in a hurry !

Camilla - Ah ! Your Eminence, that was all right ! I always is very happy when I can chat withYour Excellency, but all that illumination of those things, whatever you call them things, do not cram themselves easy in the heads of we poor ignorant people and I is only a house-maid and Youse , Your Eminence, talk to me of illuminated astralis, but I does not see any light except except the one from the house of my Master , you know, Mr. Reason, and by now, save my poor soul, he sure is angry and upset ! You is to excuse me, Your Eminence, it has been very good talking to youse, this evening , but I must really run, now . So, my respect and deference, Your excellency, I must run now, and good evening !

Thought - But, Camilla, calm down ,you seem too much agitated just for being a little late : nothing serious, in my opinion ! Anybody can be late, sometime, no specific reasons or problems, just like our case, we met in the street and exchanged a few words and a couple of minutes, more or less, do not amount to a great deal of time and, sometime, there is a pertinent justification for being late .

Camilla - Ah !.....Your Eminence....That is the type of penitent mistification that I would really like to hear, to save my soul ! My Master sure must be mad and angry now!

-

Thought - Justification, Camilla, J-u-s-t-i-f-i-c-a-t-i-o-n.......NOT Mistification...!!

Camilla - Ah ! Your Excellence, that youse must excuse we poor, simple, ignorant people..... we does not know all those difficult words and cannot figure out them different vocals. Your Eminence, does youse be so kind and excuse our poor people ignorance of those difficult vocals........Oh ! My, My......it's late, it's late, what will my master think ! My master must be very, very upset now !

Thought - Very well, Camilla, I will not keep you any longer and I understand your anxiety but, just one more thing .

Camilla - Yes, Your Excellency ?

Thought - Camilla, at what time does your Master wish to have supper ?

Camilla - At eight o'clock, on the dot , every evening and no excuse !!! I , slowly, worked the time out for him, because he, my master, would have wanted the supper earlier and earlier, every day !!

Thought - Really ?

Camilla - "Really", Your Excellency says ?......REALLY !!...Says I , too !! You cannot even imagine it, but my Master lives on the points of the hands of the clock, youse know, one of those small clocks that fit into a small pocket, and straight to the minute in and out that clock seems to go all the time, the entire day and I is not surprised at all if he did not do it during the entire night too !...You too, Your Excellemcy, would go by the minute if you was to live with my Master...!!!

Thought - Camilla, I understand the problems and the difficulties that you must be facing every day, living with your Master, but that situation does not enter in the daily or nightly experience of me, because I do not know or perceive time and I , as a thinking medium and time as a coadjuvant , interlace with one another in an eternal continuity, continuously, revolving, without an end in memories, visions, thoughts, that have been and those which will be, because that is my Naturae and, for me, a thought has no past no present or a future because is there, timeless in its conception . Time is in my thought and, ifso understood, travels with it : think of it as a passing cloud in the sky .

Camilla - Lor'...an' Mercy !!Your Eminence, please, that you was not to talk so loud about clouds because, then, it might start raining !....And when it rains it pours and it comes down cats and dogs and, when it rains like it, my Master.......Oh....Lor' an'Mercy , he gets so nervous and sees them seconds and minute on that clock as if them was double !!!!

Thought - Camilla, my good woman, do you, then, believe that by just saying one thing , as you just noted about the clouds, that "that thing" will in fact happen and materialize, just by mentioning it ?

Camilla - But, what is Your Excellency saying ...??!....Yesterday, as I was bringing the soup to the dinner table in a hurry because my Master had grown impatient, I was hoping not to catch my foot in the carpet in front of the parlour door that gives into the dining room, becasue I is going too fast, and, believe it or not, I sure caught my foot into that damn carpet and spilled a lot of the soup on the floor to the great uproar of my Master !!......But I really does not understand everything that Your Excellency says !

Thought - It is not really difficult to understand what I am saying or I am trying to say, dear Camilla, or even what I am thinking , really. All I was trying to find out, Camilla, was if you could believe that our thoughts could be transmitted in a particular way, to a distant area or place or person and persons so as to cause a certain wish of ours to be received and perceived and understood by the person or persons or any other entity to whom our thoughts were directed , by purely "thinking" of it and thinking intensely to that end . Did you follow me, Camilla, and, if you did, do you believe in it ? It was just a second ago that you said to me not to mention "clouds" because it certainly would bring rain: didn't you ?

Camilla - But,Your Excellency, you just said that them clouds and the rain does not bother you none, and Your Excellency does not even carry an umbrella !

Thought - You are right, Camilla, and it is true that rain,wind,sun,tempest,or thunder do not disturb me at all .

Camilla - Lucky you, Your Eminence, that nothing bothers you !! My Master, instead, and he also knows a few things, is always upset and disturbed for what he thinks that goes through my small head, if anything at all and if I is able to think about doing things....pity on me!....That he thinks there does not be any brain inside my head !

Thought - Your Master, Camilla, is not quite right thinking in the way you just said he does and, apart from all that, it is not absolutely necessary to have a large head and a compatible matching size of brain for that particular size of head, in order to be able to think : some people think, at times, in such a way that they give the impression to have a rather small brain or, even, no brain at all, so to speak, and a brain is no exclusive commodity of any specie of living creatures, inclusive that of your Master .

Camilla - But, what is your Excellency saying..??...My Master has no brains ???!

Thought - I did not say that, my dear Camilla, all I said was that a brain is present in many living creatures, now, whether all of them can think or whether they cannot,that is something else. Your Master,sure he has a brain,or he couldn't get so upset when his dinner is late or the soup is spilled on the floor...!!!

Camilla - Oh!,Lor'an'Mercy, I was to think that I was dying , that day !!!

Thought - Well, that's lies in the past, nothing to worry about now, my dear Camilla .

Camilla - If only my Master would think like youse does, Your Excellency ! He tells me all the time about that mess and looks angry at me !!

Thought - A sour-puss, your Master, isn't it ?

Camilla - Your Excellency, me does not know much about sour things, but my Master sure is bitter when he gets mad about something !

Thought - Well, may be so......anyway, what's important is the way or the mode by which they, I mean these brains, can be enlightened, that is encouraged to perceive the meaning of any particular thought .

Camilla - Your Excellency, ah is a humble woman , a maid, and I cannot see if ah has a brain or not, and if ah had to illuminate it with a candle to see if it is there or isn't, it would burn right away whatever is there !....So, ah has better leave all those astralis and illuminations that Youse Excellency was talking about to Your Eminence and my Master, and for me, little ignorant woman, rush back to the house and prepare supper before the house would come down !!!

Thought - Camilla, simple and ignorant as you claim to be, yet your representation of possession of a brain is almost equal, in its splendid and spontaneous simplicity, to an expression of pure essence .

Camilla - Ah does not know what to say, your Excellency !When ah think of pure things me think alawys of condiments, salt, pepper, flour, oil, butter, and good wholesome veggies tomake good and finger-licking-good dinners and suppers for my Master and soups and sauces and Gran'Ma' s old recipe Ravioli !!......And, My oh, my...! lost as ah is, youse see, Your Excellency, that Your transmission of those astralis with illumination, brings to my poor mind with no brain, my Master's supper and the ravioli I had prepared for him, to-night .!....And all the rest ! Mercy, how late , how late, my Master will be plum mad by now...!!!....I must run !

Thought - So , it seems to me, Camilla, that you must believe in the transmission of a thought , if you said what you just said !.....And "that", Camilla, is a"thought" and not an "astralis"..!!

Camilla - Well, Your Eminence, ah only knows about the transmission of some mysterious thoughts, as people in love does all the time ! May be ....Oh !....Oh !....Your Excellency !......Ah cannot believe that youse Eminence......well, that your Excellence...that you...well...ah cannot believe it!..ah cannot believe it....Lor'an'Mercy!

Thought - You cannot believe what, Camilla ? What were you saying about people in love ? What did you want to say ?

Camilla - Oh! Your Excellency, you is also gentil, I says, and kind, and ,then, you believe that ah has a brain too,and I has already right understood your under the table astralis, in the same quick motion that I taste my food and see whether I should add salt, or water or pepper and now youse come in with a lot of pepper you....you ....you naughty you, Your Excellency !

Thought - "NAUGTHY BOY".....?????!!.....Camilla !....What are you thinking ??!!

Camilla - Oh!...Come, now, Your Excellency, you wants to say as as the ones in love says, that he says :"What does you think, my love ?" and she, the girl that is, the answers:" ....and what does you think, my love ? " , and he,then, answers again:" I think just what you are thinking, my love"........and, then, they look into each others eyes, intensily, for a while........after that, they fall into each others arms and everything and kiss each other !!....Oh ! Youse is a clever boy, Your Excellency is, a naughty, naughty boy, but ah is a simple, ignorant and naive girl, may be just a little bit more than a girl, ah passed that road some time ago, youse knows, age gone by......fast, youse knows.....Ah!....to think of your Excellency transmitting those naughty astralis and illuminations into my head....!!!....And at my age, that ah is no more a young girl !!.......Naughty, naughty Excellency...!!!

Thought - My dear Camilla, the evening chill of this cloudless night must have caused you to lose control of your most primtive instincts and to utter such daring thoughts on the intimate natures of lovers, but I MUST TELL YOU THAT YOU GOT EVERYTHING UPSIDE DOWN.....!!!!!!!!!

Camilla - That looks purdy straight to me, Your Excellency, and ah see you standing straight like a lamp post, and my eyes is purdy good, they is !

Thought - What I meant with that expression, Camilla, was that you misunderstood the actual meaning of what I wanted to say .

Camilla - Oh ! That Your Excellemcy did not worry, but ah did understand very well what the meaning was !!!

Thought - I don't believe you did, Camilla, honestly or you wouldn't have come out with all those ironic and annoying comments, and I'll prove it to you.....You see, I deal exclusively in serious thoughts and not the frivolous ones like the Lovers might use or other senseless persons indulge in, and then I analyze the content of those thinking expressions and try to establish some value for them, if any value is at all there to be at all analyzed, of course, and do study the origin of its imprint and then strive for an unbiased definition of their worth, purpose and consequence for the enlightened appreciation of their true meaning to be absorbed and used by any one who would seek my wisdom or just be hungry for elightenment......And, now, how could you at all think that I was trying to become affectionately audacious towards you ...!!....Camilla !....I am surprised !!...Not even for a thousand and one thought !!!

Camilla - But, look here, now ! Listen, Your Excellency, that now you is retreating from the advance and start a rear march !!!....Eh!...I really see how really is quite handy not to have a brain, like ah is, because what you says or what you hears, it don't make any difference, goes out one way, comes in another and goes out again and no problems.....Men !!...Men !....All is the same!...Them rascals, them always knows how to wigle out of everything and right in the middle of it !!....Oh !....And me figuring that Your Excellency.....Oh....ah had in my mind that Your Excellency is trying to tell me...well...something!Oh!...You cruel, naughty Excellency, to make fun and take advantage of a poor, ignorant maid ,weak of heart and melting with sweet affection and you, Youse Excellency.....you cruel, cruel and naughty Excellency...!!!

Thought - Camilla, my good woman, what has so suddenly come upon you ? Why are you so upset and frantic about something that I do not even know what you are complaining about..???!!!

Caamilla - Oh ! Your Excellency, nothing, nothing, really !You does not need to worry about me talking, tonight, a strange night, and you really does not need to worry a cent about me talking, tonight, and every night .

Thought - But, my dear Camilla, you look so upset, even irritated and, by what reason, I cannot really figure it out !

Camilla - Oh, nothing, really, nothing : with all those astralis and illuminations.........

Thought - Camilla, I alredy reminded you, several times now, that it is abstract ideas and enlightenment and not "astralis" and "illuminations"; and, if you keep on thinking and talking that way, nothing would ever make any sense to you !

Camilla - Oh!Your Eminence, it makes no sense to me anyway with illumination or in darkness, with those transmissions of ideas and thoughts that Youse talk about, ah become some confused and a little unsettled : us poor women without a brain and still poor even if one is in our head and, ah hope, ah does have one, us poor women cannot think of anything of all them things that youse Excellency talks about, one thing gets through from one ear to the other ear on the other side of the head and nothing stays there because there is nothing in the middle from the ears, tyo keep it there ! We is weak and sentimental and we believe right away to the nice things that anyone tells us ! My Lor'an'Mercy, Your Excellency, now is really late and I has still the ravioli to cook and the condiment for them, prepare the fine dish with the truffle, a very special dish that is for my Master, and the fine veggies and put the icing on the chocolate cake I had baked this early morning for tonight's supper!And how is I going to do all that,at this late hour! Lor'an'Mercy, dear Your Excellency, I plead with you, please, not to say a word to my Master of all this chatting with Your Excellency , tonight !!

Thought - Do not worry, Camilla, and rest assured that I will not mention an iota of our conversation to your Master, Mr. Reason . Besides, we may not even see him tonight and, tomorrow, all will have been done and forgotten .

Camilla - Thankee, Youse Excellency, really, much obligated, Your Excellency.

Thought - Good, Camilla, I am glad that my answer puts your mind to rest : you see I never talk about my chatting with friends and acquaintencies and I never think of these little transactions of superficial thinking and light conversation nor of food, however appetizing it might be . Food is for mortals and is not a preferred victual for my life style and need .

Camilla - But, Your Excellency, you must eat, sometimes, does Youse not ? Or is You just living out of thin air ? At the beginning of our chatting, Your Excellency seemed interested in my cooking , but now, after talking to me about the astralis and the illuminations, Your Excellency start talking about the portals and the victories and ah has become even more confused than ah is before !

Thought - Camilla !...I said"mortals", not portals and "victuals" and not victories !

Camilla - And what's them, Your Eminence ?

Thought - Ah! Never mind, Camilla : just a way to describe various situations . A way of saying things .

Camilla - But, Your Eminence, what difference do it make to Yopur Lordship, if it is mortals, as you says , or portals, as I says it, and no one has a brain to understand it, so , I believes, one and the other says the same thing , but if them portals or them astralis with all the illumination that's gone with them, is really working in the every day life of us poor, simple people, why does you not, Your Eminence, try to send some of those astralis, or mortals or portals and illumination to the head of my Master so that he will feel strange and funny and may even invite you tonight to have supper with him, a fine supper is going to be, Your Excellency, ah has prepared....

Thought - Camilla, you are tempting me, in spite that food is not my primary concern , but, for instance, what shall we have for supper tonight??! I remember you mentioning ravioli, a special dish of truffle, selected vegetables and a chocolate cake, am I right ?

Camilla - Your Excellency , you is just about right and you have a good memory remembering what I must have said earlier !...A poor, simple woman ah is and jist a maid, but, to me, my supper looks better than jist astralis,portalis and victories .

Thought - It sounds like a very tantalizing supper and appetizing too, the way you describe it, and it may be really worth of trying my experiment of the transmission of a thought and, at the same time, a salubre experiment in the identification of the influence of various edible ingredients on the power and proficiency of thought transmission and thinking, in general .

Camilla - Oh ! You, most Excellency, you must try it ! There will be also two capons, two quails, a roasted eel and oysters.

Thought - A real challenge for the study of the behaviour of thinking under those circumstances .

Camilla - And my Master always brings to the table the finest selction of wines, to accompany the various foods .

Thought - My dear Camilla, based on what you are saying, it looks like that thinking will have to tread lightly on all those perilous scenarios .

Camilla - That Your Excellency does not worry a bit about anything, my Master will take care of it ! He do not care about anything and attacks food and drinks with almost violence until everything is gone !.....And Your Excellency must be quick in grabbing some food and drinks before youse will be left with nothing to eat and drink !

Thought - At a second thought, I am not so sure anymore whether accepting your Master invitation for supper, should he offer one, would be a good move, if the supper would be such a savage occurrence .

Camilla - Oh! I says it just to say that my Master loves my food and the more I does the more he eats !....And, tonight, the ravioli are freshly made and plenty !

Thought - That's more reassuring, now !

Camilla - And the truffle, that is a present, and my Master do not like it to be told that way, but he got it and the two capons too, as a return for certain favours to a friend .

Thought - So , capons, ravioli, truffle, eel, quails and the chocolate cake . Any fruits and wines ?

Camilla - Of the very best and imported from France .

Thought - The fruits too, from France...???!!

Camilla - No, Your Excellency, ah is a little confused and I gave you the wrong impression: the wines is from France . Your Excellency, does You know where France is ?
I is curious about France but I is afraid to ask my Master for it .

Thought - Camilla,you should never be afraid to ask legiyimate questions, regardless how simple or innocent they might be or seem to be . Why ! No one knows "everything" that there is to know in this World and beyond, so you should not feel poorly in asking questions. I tell you where France is ....

Camilla - Yes, yes, Your lordship, that ah is madly curious to find out where France is.......

Thought- Well, to begin with, France is where its name locates her : that is, she is in France.

Camilla - Lor'an'Mercy, ah would have never thought of that, to save me life !!...And that's for sure !!

Thought - But, wait, Camilla : there is more .

Camilla - Is there more than one France, Your Eminence ??!

Thought - No, Camilla, there is only one France, but she is located in a far away area of this World, on the other side of the ocean, so...............

Camilla - Now, do that means that she is under water ???!!

Thought - No, again, Camilla : it just means that it is a place far away from where we live and it is part of a far larger extension of land that accommodates several other large countries .

Camilla - Like is many potatoes in a sack when I go to shop at the market .

Thought - Oh! Yes, they grow potatoes too, over there, along with excellent wines and other savory confections like large varieties of extraordinarily tasty cheeses, salami, sausages, and an infinite variety of sweets of all sorts and different tastes to please the demanding and discriminating tastes of millions of people and, above all, they produce what, in my opinion at least, is the "piece de resistance"...the famous "marrons glaces"...!!.......Ah !.... Ils y a un gout delicieux !...........

Camilla - I is a little confused, Your Lordship Eminence, is this France a country made of chesse, salami and marglasses ?

Thought - Ah ! It is certainly a country with a sweet taste, tastier than its cheeses, salami and sausages and sweeter than its sweetest "marrons glaces "....indeed, she is just that, my dear Camilla !

Camilla - But, Your Eminence, that Youse Excellency would excuse me, but Your Lordship is not saying where this France is !!

Thought - Yes,Camilla: " you "is" absolutely right"..!!!, And I did not tell you where France is . Well, it is located in Europe and is one of many other Countries contained in that vast extension of terrestrial domain .

Camilla - And does those other countries make also good wines and sausages and cheeses and marglasses like France do ?

Thought - They do, but never as so perfect and delicious as the French People can .

Camilla - Sweet people French People, I figures !

Thought - The sweetest on Earth : it is said that they invented Love .

Camilla - Oh ! There is Your Eminence again at your naughty game ! ...Has Your Eminence ever visited France ?

Thought - I came from there, originally, dear Camilla. Great People the French People with large thinking capacities, who even overshadowed the opulence of their cheese, wines and salami, with the awesome power of their brains, and there was so much thinking in those days when I was born that space to accommodate all of it became so scarse that I had to venture across the ocean and landed here to breathe some fresh air and......who knows,,,,may be, with some luck, even run a good chance of tasting some ravioli and roasted eel, and capons and truffle and chocolate cake..........all in honour, ofcourse, of the Great French Folks .....

Camilla - Ah ! Lor'an' Mercy....!! That I is forgot again that it is late, late, late and supper is not ready yet...... !!!

Thought - So, Camilla, you said that the wines come from France and, now, you know where France is, but the fruits ? Where do the fruits come from ?

Camilla - The fruits is coming from Spain....and ah is to wish to tell your Excellency that ah knows very well, this time, where Spain is !!

Thought - Really, Camilla ? Ah! That's wonderful ! And where do you think Spain is ?

Camilla - Where it rains, Your Eminence : so eveyone says .

Thought - And in the plains, Camilla.....do not forget the plains !!

Camilla - I is not going to forget nothing, Your Eminence ! This time everything is very, very plain to me, poor ,simple and ignorant house maid as ah is, where Spain is !

Thought - And those fruits from Spain and the wines from France should really make a sumptuous appearance at your Master's supper table .

Camilla - ...Oh!...Your Excellency, Your Lordship should see my Master's table when it is all ready for the supper !!

Thought - A real banquet, I guess .

Camilla - It is a surprise for my Master, the supper is, tonight . My Master do not know it yet , because ah did not did tell him yet !

Thought - My dear Camilla, that's just right, because if you had told about it to your Master, it would not have been a surprise anymore .

Camilla - Well, You see, Your Excellency, that Your Lordship has brains and can figure out the thinking of the astralis and illuminations of the people but, I too, that ah has no brain, or, may be, just a little bit of it, is able to put some thinking in it and come to the same conclusion and told nothing to my Master about the surprise supper , so that it is a surprise . You see, Your eminence, I too thought of "that" and without the help of the astralis or any illumination .

Thought- Camilla, I am proud of you ! You are, really, coming on fast in learning the transmission of thoughts and your interest in it and your quickly acquired knowledge seems to stimulate, in a strange and inexplicably subtle way, my idealistic interest in your tantalizing and, really, mouth-watering supper exposition of its contents and their exquisite as well as enticing"composition",all, of course, purely from a study point of view of the influence of such conditions on the human thinking process, to such an extent that I feel ever more encouraged to try the experiment of the transmission of thought to your Master,the Honourable Mr.Reason, not because I would appear to vie for an invitation to his succulent supper, but purely for the experimental and scientific essence of the experiment itself, the transfer of a thought from one person to another, another person, that is, that has a brain in the head, of course

Camilla - Really good,Your Excellemcy, and the experiment would be good also for a sample of experimental eating of the food, really eating it, as an extra kick of the experiment of thinking .

Thought - Good thinking, Camilla ! You really "has " come a long way !

Camilla - Sometimes, us poor, simple, ignorant people can also see the minds of other people not by any illumination but just by looking into them eyes that tell long stories and thoughts that even he who have them do not want to tell anyone .

Thought - Intuitive genius of simplicity !

Camilla - Ah! That You, Your Eminence,do really understand us simple people with simplicity ! ...Sometimes ah wish so hard that my master would wish so simple too, but he is so complicated, so rigid, so regulated to reason and that only, that make me feel depressed sometimes.......and ah is plum afraid that my Master will be very, very angry at me being so late for his supper!! My,oh! My, what shall I do ??! I have never been so late as ah is tonight, that Heavens will forgive this poor maid !

Thought - He might decide to come out to see for himself why you, Camilla, were so late this evening, in preparing his supper !

Camilla - And I is to die of shame if my Master is to show up right here, and regret for being late and failing to prepare the supper for my Master!...Lor'an'Mercy! .....What shall I do.....what shall I do....!!!!

Thought - I believe, my dear Camilla, that you will have nothing to do, so do not worry !

Camilla - Why do your Excellency says that ?

Thought - Because, just now, I got a glimpse of your Master coming directly towards us at a pretty good clip !!

Camilla - Oh ! My poor woman that ah is, caught chatting with a stranger at the corner of the street, in this late hour and supper waiting to be prepared for my Master !........ What shall I do....Lor'an'Mercy...What shall I do !!!

Thought - Do not fret, my dear Camilla : I am here, with you, and I shall take care of whatever situation might develop .

Camilla - Oh! My goodness ! ....Your Excellency ! Here come my Master ! Poor me, he will be mad at me ! Please, please, Your Excellency, does you not tell anything to my Master about our chatting, tonight, or ah is afraid he will does something rash !

Thought - Camilla : do not fear ! You can count on me .

Camilla - Oh! Mercy! Here comes my Master !!

**** Mr.Reason arriving to the corner of the street where Sir Thought and Camilla were standing , after a quick walk from his house and addresses Camilla who, on Sir Thought advice, had , in the meantime, moved herself apart a short distance from him , so as to avoid some embarrassement, should her Master have burst into a rage.. ****

Reason - Camilla, for goodness sake, what is the idea of staying out so late in the evening, these days when you never know whom you are going to meet or pass by in the semi-dark streets, with so much crime going around that not even a Knight in shining armor would dare go out, and you exposing yourself to possible trouble by some ill-intentioned rascal or criminal ! I was really worried and, as time went by and I did not see you , I became anxious and decided to come out and see for myself what might have happened that caused you not to be home as you usually are : that's why I came out of the house in search of you !

Camilla - Oh! You, Honourable Master, I beg to forgive this poor, simple maid, me, that I is so late in preparing the supper for your lordship !

Reason - It isn't really the supper that I was worrying about : it was you, Camilla, lest something ight have happened to you at this alte hour of the evening and you not showing up anywhere and any sooner at the house !!

Camilla - Oh! Thankee,your Lordship, for youse kindness and worry for me, poor, simple maid, and ah hope that your Lordship have forgiven me for the late supper !

Reason - But, of course, Camilla, don't even think anymore about it : it is good to have found you in good health and in no trouble !

Camilla - I is really sorry for being so late but I got myself talking and talking, youse knows how us poor simple women is, sunk in the kitchen all day in front of a hot stove, cooking, and cooking, and fixing this and fixing that, that when we bump into somebody that talks good and is kind and.....so thoughtful... we like to listen to them sweet words and thick thoughts and we forget everything else !

Reason - That sounds very important! An encounter of some extraordinary importance, I guess, for making such an overwhelming impression on you, dear Camilla !

Camilla - It sure does you over to listen to that kind gentleman when he talk , and he can make your head swim in confusion with all the funny things he talk about it !

Reason - Did you recognize this gentleman, Camilla, and was he someone that you and I know too ?

Camilla - Sure we does and You, Your Lordship, does too, and very well !....Our neighbour, just a few blocks down from our house : His Eminence, Sir Thought !

Reason - Ah !!..I should have suspected it...that good for.....well...not tonight....let's keep it peaceful..well, Camilla, what did he want from you that.....that....gemtleman to keep you out for such a long time and getting dark ??!

Camilla - Ah ! Your Lordship, you should has hear from him, he talk so high, so important that the mind of us poor ignorant maids can not knows what to do, ifto look here pr there or the the right or to the left, that you loose the mind and see nothing anymore and time is no matter anymore !

Reason - I am not surprised at you, Camilla, because, and I am certain, that you didn't want or even dare to interrupt him and cut him in his talking for fear of being disrespectful to him, since you knew that we knew himand that he was our neighbour....that good for....wel....that good....neighbour of ours....but where did he go now? Did he leave you when he must have realized that I was coming? Leaving you here, all alone and at this hour, that wouldn't have been a good idea! Besides, I doubt that he could have done that by the way you describe him !

Thought - I couldn't agree more to it than I do, Honourable Reason, Sir! Allow me to say good evening to you and to assure you that your devoted Camilla was not left alone not one single minute !

Reason - Ah ! What a surprise ! Indeed, Sir Thought, good evening, indeed to you too and glad to see you and see that everything is fine and that my dear Camilla is safe and sound and in your good and respected company .

Thought - Thank you for your kind remarks, Honourable Sir Reason : your gracious maid and I met at this corner a short time earlier and, since we had not seen each other for the past several days, engaged in the usual few vernacular salutations and, then, since when we met the hour was still young, we kept on talking about some more news and one thing led to another and time flew by without we even noticing it. I am really sorry if this inadvertent delay in the return of your gracious maid to yur house, has caused any undue stress and discomfort .

Reason - Nothing of that, Sir, nothing of that for sure ! On the contrary, I believe it was a fortunate turn of events that made it possible our encounter too, this evening : it had been several weeks since we last saw each other , if my memory does not fail me !

Thought - Precisely so, Sir Reason, and in spite of you and I living so close to one another , just a couple of blocks away and on the very same street !

Reason - True : sometime, the realization that something is at hand and easily reachable , makes it less compulsive the motive to reach it, leisurely confident that it is there, anytime, whenever one would want it . Apart from that empiric explanation, I am very pleased to have met you and seen you tonight ,Sir .

Thought - Same here, with most deeply felt regards .

Reason - Well, now, Camilla, I believe that it's getting darker and I believe it to be safer to get back into the house and, may be, there is a good chance that something can be done about my supper !...I really missed my supper at the usual time, this evening, while worrying and becoming more and more anxious about you and if something unpleasant might have occurred, since you were not home and, more than that,you were not home so unusually late !! May be a good supper, even if late, will restore my sagging strength !

Camilla - I is running back home, Sir, and, tonight, there is a lot more to a supper than Your Lordship can possibly imagine : some astralis and illuminations has come around and prepared a big surprise for your Lordship!So,I say good night to His Eminence, Sir Thought, and take leave and run home to fix the supper by the transmission of thoughtt .

Reason - Camilla,are you all right ? May be you are tired,even exhausted.Are you sure that you can walk home by yourself ?

Camilla - Sure as a fiddle can be, Your Lordship, and with all that illumination in front of my astralis, and the trasmission of thoughts, the supper will be great .Good night !

*** Camilla leaves and walks quickly towards home, while the two gentlemen stand together a little longer, exchanging conventional discourse, just before leaving.. ***

Reason - Strange talking of Camilla.......she must have heard some weird news in the village, while shopping,this evening , I guess .

Thought - I wouldn't worry about the way of her expressions, Sir Reason : there has been some talk going around in the village, lately, about intercepted communications with alien creatures from outer space and the interference of their presence with the efficiency of our thinking. You know how these kind of news become easily distorted in the minds of everyday folks, eager to talk and change a little the monotony of their daily dragging lives .

Reason - May be so, May be so....there is so much hearsay these days running in the streets, in the shops, coffe houses and markets, that's no surprise some people become overwhelmed by the absurdity of certain news. Well, the hour is getting late, at least it is late for me, and I say "good evening", again, Sir Thought, and it was a real pleasure to have had the opportunity to see you tonight .

Thought - The pleasure is all mine , my Esteemed Sir, and it is indeed a real chance to see you outside your house at this late hour .

Reason - Yes, indeed ! Indeed you are quite right, Sir : it is very unusual for me to be out at night !.....My reason advises me not to be out late in the evenings, claiming that the night is meant for repose, rest and sleep .

Thought - And I fully agree and I never questioned the wisdom of that assertion .

Reason - Thank you, Sir, and my saying appears almost as superfluous as ,instead, I should have made a better use of my usual logical reasoning in formulating my expressions and thoughts .

Thought - Nothing, really, to worry about, Sir : I understand perfectly well. Instead, I feel gratified at this rare opportunity, so unexpected , that seems to favour, perhaps , a good chance to exchange a few words , tonight, with such a respected and pleasant personality, like Your Honourable self , and so comfortably, just before supper !

Reason - You, dear Sir, do appear to be even more reasonable than I , by reminding me of my supper, that,hopefully,waits for me at home, provided, of course, that my dear

Camilla could have possibly reached my home safely and speedily and started working in all earnest on that ....overdue supper of mine !!

Thought - I am sure that she is working on it, right now, and even trying to make up for the lost time !

Reason - Thank you for your encouragement, Sir, and I beg of you to excuse my seeming anxious attitude about the late hour , so being that, at the approaching of night, I retire early, have an early supper,......this, not seeming to fall into that schedule tonight.........but, customarily, I have, as I just mentioned, an early supper and, then I go to bed shortly after the supper is over and, it would have been the same sequence of steps tonight, if it had not been for our over-talkative Camilla, so that at precisely this time , I would already have been in bed ...!! Besides, it seems to me that the temperature is dropping some and turning a little cool, isn't it, Sir Thought ?...And, Sir, do you plan to retire to your home soon ?

Thought - No, not right now....I feel also this cool, light breeze and I have in mind of to take a little walk, really just a few leisurely steps a few blocks down that road that leaves from the other end of the square and is flanked, on both sides, by brightly illuminated homes and beautiful front gardens full of flowers . The evening is full of mystic shadows, dispersed, vague and strange silhouettes, subdued whisper like muffled sounds that may recall the early dawn of the spirits of the past

Reason - Ah ! Really intriguing your saying ,Sir, and a stimulating thought ,so well adapted to this late hour : but, wouldn't you, perhaps, consider a more pleasant setting for a night like this one, that in front of a friendly fire dancing in an inviting manner in a warm fireplace and, may be, even the benevolent embrace of a well stacked library, to relax the mind after the pleasure of the indulgence in a good, refined supper ?

Thought - I really would not know, dear Honourable Sir, I really would not know how to answer that question adequately or appropriately . At this moment, I do not have a clear answer to that enticing and extremely well formulated proposition and, as you certainly know, it is in my nature to tend to dissociate myself from the inherent inconveniences so permanently pervasive of the fragile human body and from the physical laws that restrict its horizons to a mediocre expansion, in addition to the acquired customs and systematic habits which render the human specie slave to a code of behaviour and function, ignoring it causing significant disfunction in the everyday process of life avtivities . That is why, my thinking encourages me to alienate myself from all and everything that is physical and . dedicate all of my energies and intuition to thinking and deductions of principles, whatever they may be,......of course .

Reason - I follow your general concept Your honourable Sir, but alienating yourself completely from anything and everything of a physical nature , does not seem to agree with the Laws of Physics . Actyally, don't you think that "Pure" Physics is also a "thought"....?

Thought - You may have some justifiable leverage in your assertion, Sir , and, as you appear to imply, it is, indeed, a "pure" thought, the thinking into the Physical Phenomenon. I agree with that , of course, limited to the ability of my intellectual resources. .

Reason - But, then , that is one more reason, in a way, even to be considered a good, viable scientific reason, that to practice the"thinking into the phenomenon", like that great philosopher and mathematician once said, and..................

Thought - ....Sir Isaac Newton, if I am not mistaken.......

Reason - You are perfectly correct and, what better way of looking into that phenomenon than by thinking about it in the company of a warm flame flickering in the fireplace, looking at it and following the dances of its variable flames and admire it in that extraordinary exhibition of the chemical-physical reaction of the combustion of combustible materials ?

Thought - The sparkling flame in the fireplace is, indeed, very attractive and inspiring utter comfort and promoting relaxation by just looking at it while enjoying the warmth emanating from it , but, at the same time, so it may seem to me, betraying a concealed sign of selfishness !

Reason - SELFISHNESS.........??????!!

Thought - Yes, I think so. Have you ever noticed, my dear Sir and respected Friend, how the flames seem to strive all the time to reach the opening at the top end of the chimney as if attempting, in their fulgent furor, to escape their confinement and, even against those vane and highly improbable odds, to leap, in a burst of repressed agony , out of the chimney and into the free air ?.....And as the intensity of their flaming furor roars in the narrow confines of the fireplace , so does their yearning for freedom ?

Reason - Well, now, Sir, those flames are nothing else than an expression of some odd pieces of dried wood , bone dry, that is, for that particular purpose, and good for nothing much else but burning, same as if we were to feel guilty for stopping abruptly the flow of the waters of a mighty river in front of a gigantic dam and force them to go through the intricacies of several turbines to produce electricity for our selfish use, totally forgetful of the freedom of the fishes swimming in those waters, before finally releasing them back to the rightful owner ! I believe that there should be a sensible and discriminating approach to any pliable thought, before proclaiming one as the right one . Don't you think inclined to feel that way, Sir ?

Thought - Sensible thinking, discriminating thinking, scrupulous thinking, guarded thinking,

Thought - (cont.) responsible thinking, all of those projections have always been my most coveted ways of thinking, I assure you, Honourable and respected Sir and Friend, but, sometimes, emotional nostalgia overhelms our frail firmness and mental configuration .

Reason - Nostalgia can be the cause of depressive thoughts , rarely of hapyy ones, most often of unnecessary ones, buried in the past and uneasy at being woken up from their peaceful rest in the oblivion of what was and need not be resurrected again . Sir, Your Honourable Sir and respected Friend, I wish you would take my advice and build yourself a nice fire in an even nicer fireplace and you'll never regret it , I assure you !......Oh ! My ! It is nine o'oclock already and I am afraid that I will fall sick with all these delays!!........Sir, I beg your kind understanding but I must bid you good night and, regretfully, take leave of your pleasant company , but it is frightfully past my time for supper and bed time !!

Thought - By all means, Sir Reason, and, please, do not let my presence detain you unnecessarily outside, in this cool night, and away from your supper and your night rest, but let me touch, briefly, on your comment about the fireplace, the flaming wood and the comfortable appearance of that representation but, in all truth, that representation of comfort is nothing more than a psychic illusion, the fireplace, the flames, the warmth generated by the flames, you see, what I mean,....well, looking at it , seeing it, of course, we feel warm, comfortable and relaxed even by just watching the jolly good old flames dancing happily in sparks and leaps, while in the midst of that soothing torpor we forget to warm up our spirits and just out of laziness, so induced by the relaxing atmosphere of the fireplace, we do not even try to release, instead, the same burning flame in our spirit, in our minds, in our thoughts, and, instead, content ourselves only with the disturbing and simple sight of the burning wood

Reason - Do you think, Sir, that early man, after discovering fire, was so discriminating in the way he was looking at it ?

Thought - I was not there, at that particular time, to assess the implications, and, at a second "thought", I wish that I had remained at that primordial immense simplicity .

Reason - Come, now, Sir and my respected and dear Friend, no time now for regretful"thoughts" ! Time lies unlimited in front of us , to use it, or misuse it, no one can ever tell, no one was ever able to tell in the primordial times or in the more sophysticated times of recent times !

Thought - A very thoughtful recreational armamentarium !

Reason - Sir, I follow your words as accurately as I can and, in spite of the late hour, I would like to continue to enjoy this rare occasion to be with you , but, as I said , it is very late already!However, we might still have a little time to spare and I would like to answer your last remark and, at least in my opinion, to the point where you seemed to confuse two important factors and I beg you to forgive my audacity in using these type of words in my approach , meaning no offence whatsoever with it, or rebuff , but, purely and simply, an honest comment for the sole purpose of an open , free discussion , so, as I was trying to say, and I just said, I feel that you, Dear Sir, maybe confusing two important factors .

Thought - Really ?

Reason - Indeed ! At least in my opinion and, the two,are very different one from the other.

Thought - To say, for example ?

Reason - Well, to begin with, our spirituality, our thoughts are inherently tied to a constant physical reality which is represented by our own body and, when the weather turns cold, spirit or no spirit, thoughts or no thoughts, our "spirituality"needs to get some warmth and fast, in order not to die from exposure or freeze to death, whichever comes first as it is expressed in modern jargon, and, with it, spirit, thoughts, arguments, ideas, pretentious mental locubrations and intellectual masterpieces, will freeze to death too, along with everything else, unless something is done fast like reviving the whole process with some quickly assembled warming essentials so best represented in happily dried wood and its warm flame will revive the splendor of those lofty thoughts, spirit and spirituality and everything else, and wood, Sir , is a physical entity.

Thought - I follow and I praise your precise way of expression in projecting your definitions, Sir and Honourable Reason, and your particular character and natural tendency to reasoning, those traits highly distinguish you .

Reason - Thank you .

Thought - However, I need to point out that our brain, and I mean the brain that is supposed to be located in the head of so many creatures and causing, sometimes, some disconcerting hesitation in believing that it is, and I mean in some creatures who act as if they did not have one at all, anyway, and apart from this tedious digression, as I was trying to say or, more correctly, as I was trying to point out, is that our brain is a physical entity too, at least that is how our anatomists describe it and pathologists describe it which, on the other side of the picture, the philosophers appear to express different points of view, and when I inquired about the thinking mechanism, they wouldn't even let me in and hear me, in spite of my knocking at their...."door"..., so to speack of, of course, and all they said was that, at times, they "thought", this special, unique, circumvoluted mass becomes violently agitated , inflamed even, they keep on thinking, when, seemingly, out of the blue, a thought comes out of it....and I had to laugh when they said that......and how and why, still a mystery, they said !

Reason - Did these honourable scientists, say anything more about the "thinking process" ?

Thought - They seem to suspect, that an initial spark, probably and, or, possibly, produced by a violently inflamed brain secondary to an unusual and yet unidentifiable type of extraneous stimulus of unknown origin, this spark, then, prods other sparks to ignite and a consequential flow of sparks to follow , causing, in a final burst of joyous exuberance, some kind of thought .

Reason - What did you make of it ? How did you feel about this research in "depth" ?

Thought - I felt very "deeply" perplexed because I never saw a spark near me, either normal sparks or joyous sparks, and I was always under the impression that thinking was just as a simple equation as walking, eating, sleeping, loving, working, building, studying and reading or, at times, slightly deviating from the average path and go the wrong way, becoming crazy .

Reason - I am perplexed too about these scientific findings because, on that basis, "reasoning" should also go by sparks, debatable yet as they might be,whether simple, regular or joyous, but, I guess, that "reasoning", in itself, being somewhat unpopular among avearge folks these days, does not need any sparks for advertisement. May be, it is only the "thinking mechanism"that needs sparks to ignite the famous candle that burns long into the night in deep, laborious studies.

Thought - My dear Sir, no one has seen it burning .

Reason - Really ?

Thouhgt - Sir, right so !.....At least.......not yet .

Reason - It is said, however, that it has been seen flickering somewhere, a little here and a little there, with no fixed paths, going on spreading its glow at random, at times brighter than on some other occasions, but to turn, frequently, less luminescent and with an increased flickering as if the little flame were buffeted by unfavourable breezes, the general luminosity becoming slightly hazy,losing its natural bright colour and appearing somewhat darkened as itis not able to burn well and it begins producing a lot of smoke that spreads everywhere at the inconvenience and disconfort and confusion of anyone that would chance to be in the vicinity, causing those unfortunate creatures to cough and get tears in their eyes.

Thought - Nobody ever told me this that you just said !

Reason - And it is not all ! Nobody , so far, has ,really, figured out how this happens and why it happens, but it is suspected that some brains get all worked up and become red hot due to the excessive friction of the vocal cords talking excessively and interminably with high pitched sounds, the intensity of which may reach unusually high and dangerous level of strepitus-like shouting, and the improper use of all these mechanisms does not allow the brain to burn at a "thinkably reasonable rate"and with a clear, sustained and well formed flame, but ,with so much smoke it has no other way but to rise as high as it can into the air and there it is said that tremulous and foggy as it is, that little flicjkering flame loses its bearings in those immense,uncharted and unexplored regions of thinking, does not know where to shed its light and nobody knows what happens to it next . I am sure that you are well aware of that phenomenon, Sir .

Thought - I do not intend to contradict you, Sir Reason, but, in all truth, I have never had the fortune or the pleasure or, even, the misfortune, to visit those unlimited, immense and uncharted vast expansions of ranges up in the air , but I will be honest with you and I have seen in my long existence, a few secondary extensions, possibly some elegant extensive thoughts of little expansion .

Reason - I guess, once out in the open air, even smoke dissipates .

Thought - Good observation, Sir .

Reason - Thank you .

Thought - Frankly, Sir, You are reknown for your good reasoning and I intend to be honest with you by saying that, really, I do not know how to refrain myself by formulating my assertions as a contnuation to the discourse between the two of us .

Reason- Sir, it is I who feels humble at the ample compass of your vision and comprehension, the majesty of your intuition .

Thought - Thank you, Sir and Honourable Reason : such compliments and recognition do not come easily to little known intellective representation, like the one I happen to be, just a thought.......but that is not what I was going to continue saying and my very nature has made me so that I have no sight for objects or entities but only a sense of intuition , a feeling, I would say, for an exquisite sensitivity to whatever stimuli I may be able to perceive under varied circumstances and...........

Reason - That is the nature of the invention, of the inspirarion, of the fervid imagination of the creative genius of the........

Thought - I never reached that far,Sir, sorry to disappoint you, but I was barely able to maintain my sanity by following simple rules of discipline, mental and spiritual, and striving to remain just a good, simple, straight forward thought .

Reason - All to your good-standing among righteous creatures, you, Sir, Honourable Thought .

Thought - Some more of those exclamatory praises and I will run out of my limited supply of "Thank you's.Anyway,in reality,I am acting as if I were blind and, sometimes, reacting to something that feels good or that feels bad, moving aimlessly in a void world , full of uncertainties , with no fixed address, no cozy fireplaces, well appointed dinner tables or helpful maids in constant attendance but......................

Reason - I do not want to appear as if I were contesting your saying but, sometimes, lack of "something" is the expression of personal, subjective tendencies and selective as well as elective ways of living, all of which, of course, are just as good as any others if so desired and enjoyed by the user of them, I would surmise .

Thought - Yes, surmising is one thing, but, enduring its gloomy landscape is another.

Reason - But then and, foremost and at the same time and incessantly, the free spirit of free thinking will always be held as the finest expression of anything that is expressible, Sir and Honourable thought, maid or no maid in constant attendance !

Thought - Are you surmising that too ?

Reason - This time is a step slightly ahead than just surmising, because....WHY....should we cry upon the way we are when we are the way we are, not that we wished to be the way we are but purely because we are what somebody made us the way we are and no way to change that by crying about it . Surely, while floating aimlessly in that great void of the imaginary and intuitive world, there cannot be only sad, gloomy and depressing places, but,......I would surmise.....there might be also, as in our evryday life, some more salubrious and friendly, cozy and comfortable places, even if only on an occasional basis .

Thought - Wishful thinking seldom marerializes the wish, so, peregrine I continue my odyssey without repose, sometimes heiled as a revelation, sometimes derided as fatuous nonsense, sometimes even persecuted for not conforming to the existing prevailing standards and always looked upon with diffidence, particularly in regions where the circulation of air is stagnant .

Reason - The description of your personal existence, Honourable Sir, poses a serious handicap in the desire and willingness to at all embark in any process of thinking, however innocent, by any brain .

Thought - Many a times I have been dreaming of having a fixed abode , comfortable and inviting, where I could entertain all brains in sympathetic discipline of manners and formulations of expressions of revered respect for the personality of thinking. But, now, Honourable Sir, please, tell me, where is this brain, this entity that you are talking about ?....And where could I find it , because I would be quite interested as well as anxious, to entertain it and engage it in serious, sustained and proper study of the head that, you seem to indicate, houses it .

Reason - You should have tried to do that,as probably some of your Ancestors did, at the time when peregrine thoughts were quite happy and lodged in very spacious, comfortable, even elegant, palatial enclaves, an enclave surrounded by harmoniously crafted colums, called peristylium or peristyle, basically an exquisite architectonical marvel, so powerfully, yet pleasantly, inviting to the rigorous, discipli-ned and fertile mechanism of thinking .

Thought - Are, by any chance, some of those "harmonious" enclaves still available ?

Reason - Yes, but their role, these days, is mainly that of a tourist attraction, where people of all sorts go on a cruise, get here and there, are told by some Guides that here and there some ancient people used to walk, leisurely, with their heads in the clouds...thinking . After that, they leave and there comes the next crowd of tourists and are told the same thing and nobody thinks anything of it .

Thought - Ah !....There is where I can find that brain !!...

Reason - Where, Sir ?

Thought - Why !...You just said it : in a head in the clouds !

Reason - Well, yes, most of the time it is found in the heads of most creatures, and not necessarily when in the clouds, unless they would happen to fly through some of "them clouds", and that condition aplies, of course, to those creatures who have a head and those which happen not to have a head ,the search for the location of the brain is still on going, although some investigators have suggested various other possible locations, but some of those other and possible locations may not be in step with pure, selective and scientific research. Studies, though, are still pursuing that elusive characteristic.This is what is being learned from books written by serious investigators and by records from historical events of some follow up . .

Thought - And, kindly, Honourable Sir , please tell me : do these learned investigators use their brains when they write those books and when they explain their theories ?

Reason - It is suspected that they do , although no one is ceratin about it .

Thought - How can you say that and, more, on what ground do you place your certification of their doings ?

Reason - There seem to have been times when certain activities occurred of some rather strange character where certain groups of heads with some brain in it and embo-died with specific views on the way other heads with brains should live, or die or conducting businesses, decided to find out about it by embarking in a laborious and persistent as well as persuasive endeavour by gathering as many heads as they could place their hands on and cutting them off in one of the largest brain finding experiments ever conducted in the History of the Human Specie,if I remember correctly, during a revolution, I believe,by the name of French...revolution...and....

Thought - The famous French Revolution of the seventeen hundreds ??...But that is impossi-ble !!.....France is the ultimate in civilization !!

Reason - Probably so : they were claiming that in order to find out what civilization and the spirit of proper, civil and patriotic feeling were, it demanded that as many heads as possible be analyzed to determine the origin, the trend, the effectiveness of the thinking of the brain and to capture its thinking so as to be able to study it and comprehend its mysterious implications, but, unfortunately, they could not find anything in those cut-off heads, least of all any clue of the "thinking machine"or an inkling about it from the rest of the body from which the head had been cut off, "thinking" that, may be, when the head fell of the body, the "thinking" might have tried to find a refuge in the body that was not cut to pieces : a very discouraging situation, indeed .

Thought - And where could have that thought gone to ? Did they ever figure it out ?

Reason - I don't believe they were able to and nobody really knows : not even those who had their heads cut off .

Thought - A real pity ! So many cut-off heads without any thought at all and.....no thought at all in those heads that had been left were they usually belong . I don't believe that it would be a desirable abode for me to live and to dream in those brains to be, may be, after a while, cut to pieces by some zelous investigator looking for answers .

Reason - Sir Thought, we have come already quite a distance from my home while chatting and pleasantly discussing upon various notions, without even realizing it...!!! I admit, all interesting subjects and enjoyable too, at least to the two of us, but it is quite late, I would almost dare say, alarmingly late, at least for my habits, and I must really part from your company and hurry back home : you know how our gentle women are , and they could become upset at my late appearance, after I remonstrated to her for "her" being late...!!!!

Thought - Please, do not be surprised, Honourable Sir, at my naive countenance but, in all truth and frankly with you in all friendship, I have not the least knowledge or insight in the ways of thinking by the people you seem to be referring to as " our gentle women " !

Reason - No problem at all, Sir , no problem at all ! It is just a time-honoured way and not necessarily a good one either, of referring facetiously to the gentle sex and, not so gentle either, sometimes, and not much different than trying to comprehend the flight of a bird or the eruption of a volcano or a solar eclipse .

Thought - But, Honourable Sir, those comparative phenomena to the physionomy of the gentle sex, are sequences in Nature of extremely complex accuracy as well as fascinating beauty and mystery !

Reason - Precisely so,Your honourable Sir and respected Friend, precisely for those reasons I chose them as comparative representatives of the gentle sex !

Thought - I have the impression that you, Honourable Sir, have made a study in depth of the "gentle sex" phenomenon .

Reason - The reason for that knowledge is derived from an unescapable realization of continuity among living creatures, extremely well understood and strictly followed in its parameters but totally unknown as why and how . This last deduction, of course, not impairing in the least its overwhelming and enthusiastic approval among all living creatures .

Thought - Interesting: that might explain, in some way, certain interpretations in the thinking of this........did you mention ;"gentle sex " , if I remember correctly ?

Reason - Yes I did: and why, may I ask, are you wondering at such curiosity ?

Thought - Oh! Nothing ,really, of major significance, only a strange way of coming to conclusions on certain subjects or just simple sentences as interpreted by this so called"gentle sex".

Reason - But....."Your honourable self had just pointed out his lack of knowledge about this gentle sex"....!!! How, then, could you, yourself, Sir, make now a comparative referral to some "characteristic" of this genetic characteristic of our sweet creatures?

Thought - Simple : by chatting with your devoted house maid, this evening !

Reason - Ah !!...Camilla...!!!

Thought - Yes, quite an interesting opening of my mind into the labyrinth of her peculiar way of interpreting ordinary, general discourse and adjusting whatever meaning she intended to give it to satisfy what she might have anticipated out of it, regardless whether it was right or wrong but, anyway, satisfactory to her .

Reason - Well, that leaves me relieved from explaining any further the mysterious intricacies of the creatures'intricacies and that stands to reason in as much as we are what we are and about what we think, Juno and Jupiter, help us !!

Thought - I praise you, Honourable Sir and respected Friend, for such restrained expression about our thinking and thinking in general and it has always been my coveted effort that of cautioning folks not to think, unless their thoughts were directed towards something good or of value or of appreciation for something done righteouisly .

Reason - Thank you, Sir , and it stands to reason, for me, to reciprocate your praise in support of your incentive to use the thinking process judiciously, appropriately and with utter sincerity, and not as a viable bridge to ostentetional showmanship of poorly deserved fame . The hour is late and, regretfully, I must take leave !

Thought - So, I will have to deprive myself , Sir and respected Friend, of the privilege of a prolonged promenade with you this evening, surrounded by the pleasant atmosphere of our spaciously encompassing discourses and vagrant speculations on so many notions and then some, very relaxing, indeed, to the pathways of our minds.

Reason - Well, Sir, one one hand the refreshing breeze of this pleasant evening would wisper to me some encouraging incitement to accept your prospect of a prolonged promenade but, on the other hand, my pocket watch and my well-engraved habits advise me to decline this promising invitation and, instead, to choose my way home ! The state of things of all of us and any single one of us, Honourable Sir, appear to identify itself in a well defined and individualized "destiny" like pattern, that often over used invocation about our frailties or something of that sort !

Thought - Quite interesting to hear from you that your destiny is tied up so intrinsically to a well controlled and fixed time like that of a watch .

Reason - Well, perhaps, I said it in a redundant and, certainly, not in a clear explanatory way . What I really meant was that I am bound , by natural tendencies, and by almost devout belief, to a reasonable regularity in the rhythm of my life and the activities connected with it and, more or less in a "joking" way, I refer to it as if programmed and sanctioned by our individual "destinies"......or something of that nature !

Thought - Yes,excellent, indeed ! ....And I understand your earnest desire,Honourable Sir, to return to your home and I also comprehend that you really believe in "thinking" that way but, at the same time, allow me to take a slightly different deviation from your assertion and wonder whether "Destiny"may think that way too, or, may be, within itself, think quite differently .

Reason - Well, I do not have an answer for that, except that, as far as I know, no one has expressed an opinion or passed a judgement on "Destiny", to wonder, then , wether this Destiny has a thinking mechanism of its own or just a set of ready made programs to be allotted at random, first come first served like fashion .

Thought - Pre-ordained, do you believe ?

Reason - Alas ! Sir !....But your simple question carries more of a turbulent wind of inquietude and its terse presentation is apt to stir already treacherous waters into a raging tempestuous ocean and alley all intentions to sail forth on our tremulous thinking into those infuriated and waves .

Thought - All waters, Sir, and all air, soil and wind are treacherous, yet real and part of ur daily living, so, we shouldn't be hesitant or afraid to enter in what we think is "the unknown " or we....."surmise".(.!!..)...to be treacherous ! ....Actually, I believe that there is no such thing as the unknown : only that we have not thought of it , yet .

Reason - I, usually, do not venture into those deep and tantalizing questions, unless there are some problems of a direct meaning or importance to me personally, and that, of course, is not only rare but it would be almost an inpossible eventuality, anyway !!....And the"unknown", ...Oh! Well....as far as I can tell, it is and it will remain where it is, wherever that is and still unknown !.....But one thing is clearly known to me !

Thought - Really ? And, I beg of you, what is it ?

Reason - My pocket-watch is .

Thought - So , as a compliment to what is known and to an adieu to what is not, could I make a suggestion ?

Reason - And why not ? By all means your suggestion will be more than welcomed, saturated as it probably will be with deep and lucid deep thinking !.....By all means, Sir, and am I guessing widely in speculating on your proposal to be, if that would be an invitation to a little longer promenade ?

Thought - Well, for one thing, I am certain that after a nice and invigorating walk , your supper will seem even more appetizing and tasty and palatable than ever .

Reason - And, may be, you are right, provided, though, that I would not become over tired .

Thought - My evening promenades, Honourable Sir , are usually short and comfortable, done on the spirit of the moment, here or there, without a fixed or methodical direction or goal, so , I keep on going whenever I feel like to move, may be one day this way and, another day, another way because Sir, and I must be honest with you, I have no sense of direction as If I were a locomotive on well established and fixed rail-tracks, but I have no fixed itinerary or path and most of the time I stary somewhere and I haven't the slightest idea to where my walking will take me !

Reason - But, Sir , don't you ever think and I beg of you to pardon this somewhat unfortunate expression of mine as I know quite well that you think all the time, but has it ever occurred to you that such an inclination could expose you to some untowards reactions against your chosen paths and, sometimes, even involve you in dangerous situations ?

Thought - May be even disastrous situations if I happen to miss the main road and finish up in a cul-de-sac at the end of a lonely trail !..But it is difficult for me to direct myself, so fluid, variable and expansive my nature happens to be!

Reason - However, Honourable Sir, according to history and the chronicles narrated and recorded in its books , it appears that many a learned and valiant minds in the past as well as in the present, did manage to harness the power and influence of pure thought and put it to work towards good,just and illuminating causes without getting caught in a cul-de-sac at the end of their thinking"promenades !

Thought - Really ?

Reason - Certainly and you , Sir , should be the very first one to know about it !!

Thought - I must confess to you,Sir, that often I feel very sad and depressed for my failure to share the company of those who thought of me and followed my paths and promenades and did not finish up in a cul-de-sac as I often do when I am wondering on my own and not accompaned by a solid mind to keep me from deviating from the trodden path ! When I think back to the ancient times, how easier it was then to keep the thinking concentrated along those comfortable and inviting peristyles, and enjoy the company and the trust of those ponderous minds who really shared my dreams and, of course, my most coveted thoughts and aspirations and who were my friends and who respected me !

Reason - An unrewarding existence , yours, Sir, you seem to describe to me ! A world without love, affection, friendship or happiness, in your constant roaming in search of understanding and in an endless run to promote wisdom !

Thought - Yes, and so it seems and so it is too ! A constant , unsettled, restles and, most often, even ignored wanderer !

Reason - However, Honourable Sir and highly respected friend, always going back to the chronicles of history, as I have already mentioned before, it appears that there were several periods in the existences of the human specie,the one specie,I guess, that we are currently approving with the possession of a thinking capacity, and that in those periods of seeming fertile production and growth of the tree of wisdom, there lived great men who respected and valued greatly the existences and the work of other lives dedicated to the enjoyment of your company and learned men of thought who, in turn, praised , used and respected you with great veneration and enlightned work .

Thought - May be it is or, it was, as you proclaim with so much sincerity . However, I , personally, do not know, or, better, I am not aware of human history, unfortunately, or , for all it matters, I am not familiar with any other history at all, not having been able to stop anywhere for any length of time and become knowledgeable of the surroundings and of their inhabitants , never stopping on anything or anywhere and subject as I am to sudden changes of mood, direction and style ,sensitivity and sensibility and grade of depth, depending on the variable winds of creatures's conscience and desires, sometimes good, sometimes mediocre, sometimes not so good and, occasionally, even bad, seldom brilliant and, sometimes, and that is the most frequent of times, nothing at all : dead silence !

Reason - By Jupiter and Juno, you are so right, Sir! Are you, by any chance, thinking of the, of the Dark Ages..??!

Thought - Those were, indeed, the times when I felt extremely depressed and my very soul left me .

Reason - Oh ! Well, do not be so pessimistically minded, Honourable Friend, in this pleasant evening: as you see, I am still here with you, not that I am aspiring at some glory related to the days of those famous and glorious "peristyles" but obviously interested in your talking and your company and to prove my sincerity, I will stay with you a little longer and try to cheer you up !

Thought - REALLY.....??!!! Oh ! This was the best sentence I have ever heard through the eons of my life ! A pleasant evening in company of Reason ! Well, then, will you honour me by continuing our leisurly promenade a little longer and allow me the rare privilege of sharing and configuring my thoughts with a well directed reasoning measure .

Reason - I believe that my reason will be the most rewarded entity in the overall of our promenade and to consider the unprecedented concession to this extra distraction and unusual circumstance by my....pocket watch , with no protestations !

Thought - I feel certain that, tacitly, your pocket watch will enjoy the promenade too, something different from the usual routine . Sometimes, a little something different, is just as good as a sumptuous holiday .

Reason - More over, as you had mentioned it before, after a little prolonged promenade , the supper will certainly taste more succulent .

Thought - I thank you,Sir , for your courtesy : it will be a real pleasure to converse with you in this refreshing evening breeze, in anticipation of your well attended supper .

Reason - You, Honourable Friend, have succeeded in convincing me of the refreshing advantages of a promenade in the evening breeze and preparatory to a follow up supper to the point that, as it happens, I am actually walking with you, almost against my own good and sober reasoning !

Thought - What a pleasant feeling , Sir , to be in your company ! It is so rare for me, indeed, to ever enjoy the satisfaction in realizing that I am appreciated and valued and ....may be, one day, I may even find for certain also the reason for my very existence .

Reason - A good and solid reason was, undoubtedly, that which moved those ancient and valiant minds of glorious times to seek your patronage and esteem, through the centuries .

Thought - Ah !..The famous perystiles..!!!.The solid minds through those colonnades did not have evil thoughts,they did not dash me against a stone if I was slow in solving a riddle, or I did not have to ride on the back of a lizard to go to the thought market to buy some fresh produce of ideas : they were srpringing all around me like a million jets from a million fountains, centuries ago!

Reason - But, please, Sir , just reason it out : at the moment you are with me, "passeggiando", (an Italian friend of mine used to say that, meaning "walking" "promenading"), so, it stands to reason that you , at least at this moment, are not being bashed against a stone by some impatient thinkers or cursed by an evil intrigant, or by the mind of an evil thinker and, most certainly, you are not riding on the back of a lizard on your way to the market, but, let me say this again, you are with me and, furthermore, I believe that what I am saying is quite reasonable and, please, pardon my facetiousness .

Thought - Very well, but, even so, who would believe it ?

Reason - But what is there not to believe ...??

Thought - A thought and a reason walking together ?.........Unheard of !!

Reason - This fact, our being together,would seem to me, instead, to be precisely one more reason for you to feel satisfied that you actually have many more friends and admirers , wherever you go .

Thought - Even among the rocks or on the back of a lizard ?

Reason - Even on the back of a dragonfly or of a beetle ! In final analysis what difference does it make where a thought , particularly a good thought , eventually rests ? The importanrt thing is that it stays firm, solid and useful, no matter where it seats .

Thought - Interesting your interpretation !I wonder what the dragonfly and the beetle would think of it . It would be probably interesting to hear their opinion , an extra opportunity to avoid my loneliness in the evenings when I walk slowly alone and had it not been for meeting your sweet maid Camilla, I would have passed another evening in my seemingly perennial solitude .

Reason - Sometimes, my respected and trusted Friend, solitude is just one of the many modes of our existences and not necessarily an affliction . Just think of the mountains , always alone, silent, and the higher they are, the loftier they are, the less green grass or sweet and tall trees they have to keep them company, the more solitary they stand in solitude but they do not complain and do not think of becoming sad or depressed, on the contrary, they roar their might with the vorticous winds and snow tempests at their own will .

Thought - I did not know that the mountains could be capable to realize their physical condition and rationalize about it .

Reason - Either do I and, I guess, so do the mountains too, that is ," to be able to think and have the ability to rationalize !!!......But, if they did.....they would be a superb example in the magnitude of geniality in their majestic silence .

Thought - Silence! Silence! When you talk about silence it brings to me a sense of torpor , so real and so persistent , because in silence and in the peace that it creates, it is possible to hear even the most veiled whispers of many, many things, although I do not see them .

Reason - Ah ! A ray of poetry, Sir , and I really envy you for your ability and agility to find motives, inclinations, emotions, ideas and sentiment even when in the middle of solitude .

Thought - Yes, my respected Friend and honourable Sir, yes solitude and silence and many, many things, all being considered and thought at the same time , good and bad, fruitful and disrupting, honourable and disgraceful, and so many distortions! Really, silence, sometimes, seems to be the only refuge fo a disillusioned thinking...

Reason - And to think, Sir, that not only those "many things" are actually an immense myriad of thoughts, very actively practiced by the human specie, but also a potentially explosive reservoir of irrationality, if misused or misinterpreted by the untrained scholar or the arrogant up-start . You mentioned, a while back, about the risk of your personality being bashed on a stone or having to ride a lizard to the market, and I mentioning dragonflies and beetles......well, I cannot verify whether the same occurs among the stones or the lizards or the beetles and dragonflies, but, I guess, they must have their problems too .

Chorus of the Stones - The lizards rest on us but do not cause us any troubles .

Chorus of the Thoughts - We firmy support our reknown Sir Thought, whom we greatly esteem for his Universality with respect to all there is, inclusive of stones, rocks, lizards, dragonflies and beetles, and for his amazing resiliance in being always ready to think about everything there is to think about, inclusive of silence, desolation, depression, and several other oddities that can be found here and there .

Mr.Silence - I would like to ask the respectable representative of the thinking enclave, Their Eminencies the Thoughts, to please be quiet : all that vociferous noise disturbs my restful peace .

Lady Envy - I am not surprised at Mr.Silence's request for quiet all around him, because who could possibly notice him if there is so much noise all around? He is insufferable of sound .

Mr.Sound - Certainly not I, Lady Envy, not I could possibly be the cause of Mr.Silence's discomfort, since I too need silence around me in order that my sound be heard . Besides, I , really, do not exist .

Mr.Silence - That is the stupidest, most idiotic declaration of non-existence, that I have ever heard !!!

Mr. Sound - To the contrary, Mr.Silence , Sir : to the contrary . You see, I exist only as a complex of sounds or, to be slightly more specific, I exist as a sequence of harmonic vibrations of extensively wide latitudes and, really, some of my higher sounds cannot even be heard .

Lady Envy - What a silent fracas...!!

Mr. Silence - I love solitude and silence and that's myself .

Chorus of the Stobes - We have not the slightest interest in any of you . In addition to that, your stories have no interest or any appeal at all .

Chorus of the Lizards and the Beetles - We feel just the same .

Mr.Silence - Then....SILENCE....please !

*** Meanwhile, the conversation between Sir Thought and Sir Reason continued while the aroused other entities were squabbling about their own affairs...... ***

Thought - I am enjoying this leaisurely strolling and in such unusual, unexpected and so very pleasant company like that of your personality, Sir Honourable Reason .

Reason - I am surprised myself as well as almost incredulous at finding myself promenading at this hour of the evening and registering no ill effect, on the contrary, may be a feeling of well being and alertness !

Thought - I am really glad that it turned out this way . At the beginning of our walking I became a little worried, should my exhortations and encouragements have caused you an undue effort and a disagreeable effect on your well being, but I rejoyce now, that I see the promenade is having an excellent effect on you.!

Reason - And indeed it has and all to your good advice anf general knowledge .

Thought - As to your reference to my good advice and general knowledge, it brings to my mind the words expressed by a reknown philosopher and literary man who, one day at Court, when approached by some members of the Court hinting at the good salary that the Crown was paying him for his vaste knowledge, replied :" If the King would pay me for what that I do not know, the treasures of the Empire would not be sufficient !", so, anyway, thank you for your kindness, as always ! ...

Reason - But, anyway, it really was because of your timely advice that I am here, now, enjoying this beautiful evening which, had I given in to my "stale" and old-fashioned habits, I could never had experienced . Tha's definitely a "big PLUS"..!!

Thought - Thank you, again, Sir Reason . But, I would still like to indulge, briefly, of course, over some points of our past conversation where you intimated, quite cursively, of the existence of several human creatures, who, through the lapses of time and through the centuries, esteemed me and even loved me, and whom I would like to be able to see, although I cannot see, but, at least, delineate their characters and spaciousness of their far reaching minds with my refined sensitivity .

Reason - Yes, some love and esteem you and, yet, some have apprehension about you !

Thought - Apprehension....about me ????!!.......And of...WHAT , I wonder...????!!!

Reason - Yes, my dear and respected and honourable Friend, apprehension about your versatility about moods and enthusiasms as well as a real fear to dare think .....!!

Thought - I am astonished by what you say and I cannot believe it to be true !

Reason - In a way it can be explained because, to think, it implicitly reqires a strength, both of mind and spirit, the thinker must have enthusiasm and freedom of sentiments, honesty and high ideals, at least for what regards the human race and, not always, these qualities exist all combined in the same individual . When they do, usually a new Era begins in the historical Saga of humanity and, "that", is no common event .

Thought - Now, I am more surprised tha ever ! ...If "to think" is an extraordinary event, possible only by extraordinary conditions of perception, sentiment and idealism, what, then , "common" thinking comes under, if "under" antything at all....???!!

Reason - May be under the stones and the lizards sitting on top of them .

Chorus of the Stones - The lizards and the beetles sit on top of us, but they cause us no problems . They do not think either whether they bother us or not .

Chorus of the Lizards and the Beetles - The stones are hard .

Mr.Silence - Quiet, please !

*** Meanwhile, Sir Thought and Sir Reason conversation, continues.......................... ***

Thought - You know, Sir and honourable Reason, Friend, I believe that the Lizards and the Beetles must or, at least, are able to think .

Chorus of the Lizards and Beetles - Really ?

Reason - It could be, if you think so .

Thought - Well, don't they have to take care of their lives, to think about food, shelter, defensive postures against predators and so on, and, also, about the ever so demanding urge to reproduce ?

Reason - Well, it would seem reasonable to be inclined to think that way, if you pardon my audacity for thinking so, but I was referring, really, to a different type of thinking.

Thought - I am not aware of "different" types of thinking .Well, may be.........let me think! You may hinting, probably, at different types of brains having different types of thinking , right ?

Reason - Not quite that way, although your impression could be quite viable. What I actually meant was more like abstract thinking .

Thought - Astonishing .

Reason - I realize that you might be perplexed, even amused by my saying but what I had in mind was that the lizards, of course, may be thinking in an instinctive way, just the same, probably, as a river chooses to go down a slope and, eventually into the sea or a lake and not the other way around, back to the slope from where he came tumbling down originally, but, as I said, what I had in mind was abstract thinking, and I wouldn't be surprised if you were to come out ,again ,with your "astonishing" exclamation in a sarcastic mood....

Thought - Oh! No, never I would do such an astonishing thing !

Reason - Touché, mon ami !.....Well, back to the source to finish my masterpiece discourse this impeccably perfect evening ! So , as I was saying.....yes....abstract thinking , those thoughts so elegant , so exciting and, at the same time, so mysterious and so complex, that they do compell several other human brains to start vibrating and rush to seek knowledge and wisdom . That kind of thinking I was thinking about and it seemed a reasobale thinking to my personal way of reasonable thinking .

Thought - And a reasonable way, indeed, to interpret certain "reasonable thinking" procedures, particularly so when practiced with reasonable dexterity, but, I wonder, why would any elective brains want to partake of my solitude and wandering, just to obtain some knowledge and wisdom ?

Chorus of the Stones - Please, do not ask us about it .

Reason - Well, for one thing,before being able to collect information of what kind of knowledge is desired at any particular point, it is necessary to think of its specifications, first, then, it will be necessary to start a research of where from to collect them, and, once collected, absorb them, digest them, and, finally, and hopefully, retain them in our brain and, while thinking, knowledge is, then , acquired .

Thought - I did not realize that the whole rigamarole was so complex and twisted .

The Wise Elders of the Lizards' Clan We didn't think so, either .

Thought - Is, then, this venerable knowledge such a very important item?

Chorus of the Lizards - Is not important to us .

Beetles,Stones and gofers - Not to us, either .

Thought - Sir, Honourable Friend, please tell me : is, then, this knowledge a very important, shall we say, necessity ?

Reason - To the human specie, it has always been at the very roots of its existence as well as of its evils, from time immemorial . They figured it into their motivation for life .

Chorus of the Stones - Modus vivendi .

Mr.Silence - Please, be quiet, you hard stones ! Stop talking loud about sentences and maxims of which you do not even know the significance of the meaning carried in them!

Chorus of the Stones - We disagree with your remonstration, Sir . We saw it sculpted on one of our boulders and on many other stones, like us, therefore we know what's written on us .

Mr.Sound - This affirmative reply appears to have a good affirmative sound .

*** Meanwhile, Mr.Reason and Mr.Thought, continue to carry on their conversation.. ***

Thought - I am very pleased to hear from you, Sir and Honourable Friend, that this Gentleman by the name of Knowledge, I believe, is sympathetic towards me and, apparently, uses me and considers me as his friend . He is a....boy.....isn't he ?

The Wise Elders of the Lizards'Clan - What difference does that make whether"that"Knowledge is a boy or a girl ? If it's a good knowledge, it's good : PERIOD !

Reason - And the Wise Lizards are right: Knowledge has always..............

Thought - Did you hear some lizards.............talking ??!....Don't tell me, now, that you heard some lizards saying something...!!!....Or I'll begin to think that the evening air is having an adverse effect on you...!!!!!!!

The Wise Elders of
the Lizards' Clan - Do not worry, he's only pretending : it's just a "way of speech" of the human creatures, like, for example...." Jiminy Cricket " or " raining cats and dogs", " Geronimo !" and " leaping frog" and several others ...!

Thought - NOW, am I supposed to have heard what someone seems to have said ?

The Wise Elders of
the Lizards' Clan - Of course, you do ! Isn't this whole affair a confabulation between two non-physical entities by the name of Thought, one and, by the name of Reason, the other ??

Thought - Well.....yes, in a way we may be considered non-physical, whatever that means, anyway, besides, we are within the physical framework of a fully formed physical entity, so we must be part of that physical aspect as well, don't you think?

The Wise Elders of
the Lizards' Clan - We don't. And "do you" think, now, that ,may be, spectators in a theatre, listening to music, are musicians too, just because they are sitting in the theatre ?

Thought - I don't know what you are getting to or trying to get to. By quick and ready evidence, it seems to me that you are trying hard to advertise the apples in your basket.........you know.........just as a way of speech........

TheWise Elders of
the Lizards' Clan - Quite an impossible task : we do not have baskets, let alone apples. But one thing we have : we like to sit on stones and gather as much sun-light as we can and the sun's warmth : you see, everything is clearer in the full sun light than in the darkness of the night where you are now, that is why you cannot understand anything and you are even mocking your companion, Sir Reason, who seems to have heard and understood us! You, dummy, can't you understand that, sometimes, the subconscient of something, if there is at all such thing available anyway, or of somebody, may substitute its fine, mysterious and uncanny instinct to the rigid and restricted perception of the mind....you know....that thing where you are supposed to be................

Reason - And rightly so....the reason why, sometimes, a thought, even if solid, good and useful is.......................

Thought - And here we go again....!!

Reason - Pardon me !.....Where ?

Thought - Oh ! Never mind ! .....Just a way of speech !

Reason - I see. Well, as I was saying, the reason why, sometimes, a thought, even if solid, good and useful, is rejected by some but to be, at the same time, embraced by others, rests on the civic pride of a population. But, if at any time a misunderstanding about its meaning would occur, a conflict may ensue among the promoters of that thought and the opponents of it, an unnecessary event that could have been easily avoided had the various parties utilized some"thinking"at the very beginning, all working together, eliminating what might have seemed superfluous or redundant and unnecessary, in the contested thought, instead of making of it an occasion for hostility and dissession .

Thought - And why there must always be some uneasiness and complications about a thought which is only an expression of a form that cannot even be seen, or looked at,or touched for consistency and strength, is a notion that really baffles me, irritates me and displeases me, greatly!

Reason - It's an everyday occurrence, my dear Friend !.....There always is a veiled presence of ambiguity and uncertainty in the thinking process of the human specie : some may like and embrace the thought, some others revolt against it, some might show complete indifference .

Thought - What a pity ! That ruins the beautiful feelng of this superb evening ! But, Honourable Sir, do you posses any reasonable knowledge of the cause of that behaviour and its effect ?

Reason - My dear and respected Friend, you are asking me for the reason of the peculiarity of the human way of thinking : if only there were one, even if very small and, in all my existence, I have never been able to come across one !.....May be, my dear Friend, a possible reason lies in the fact that human experience is slow to develop and for a thought to assert itself it's a slow and subtle endeavour, may be covering years, even centuries, because, following a constant and unceising, deductive reasoning, any one given thought could be accepted or repudiated or even forgotten altogether .

Thought - An interesting bunch of creatures, this specie .

Reason - They think so too, my Friend . Anyway, it has also been recorded in the evolving history of the human specie that many a times a thought that had been previously discarded or even derided , ridiculed, or given no attention for centuries , would become popular again and dominate several on going ones , if we are to believe some of the reports and trust their authors .

Thought - Incredible .

Chorus of the Stones - Not to us . We wonder, though, about the authenticity of those historical reports. Our Elders have checked some ancient stones and found no evidence of those reports .

The Lizards Elders - That does not necessrily annul the veridicity of the report .

Chorus of the Stones - And why not, wise Elders ?

The Lizards Elders - Because, in the long intervals of time, some of the stones might have rolled over due to rain, or earthquakes or mudslides and what might have been written on one side would have turned over and not be able to be seen again .

Wise Gofer - Always "if"s but never anything definite : conjectures, that's all that can be said, thought and done, when solid evidence is not there . However, for the sake of accuracy, to consider that some of the truth would rest on the amount of stones on shich something was inscribed .If very many, then less likely that physical natural events would have wiped out the entire evidence or every single inscribed stone, but, if only a few stones were inscribed, then, the chances of total absence of proof would be greatly diminished ,if not entirely lost .

The lonely Lizard - *Much' Ado'About No'thing*.......much *!!!* ...... wrote an Old Poet...!!!!

Thought - All that I have heard, so far, gives me the impression of some perplexing confusion in the way the human specie goes about at interpreting the function of the thinking mechanism. It seems to me that the way it is learned and practiced, it is more of a worrisome anxiety than of a helping hand for their problems .

Chorus of the Stones - Not to us .

Reason - Sometimes, ithas even been recorded thata certain thought that that had been previously discarded ,ridiculed and even condemned, was reaffirmed and accepted with great honours, even by those same officials who had originally condemned and ostracized it !

Thought - I am appalled .

Wise Gofer - Insufferable hypocrisy .

Reason - Honourable Friend, did you say....something ? Something like...hypocrisy ?

Thought - No,I didn't,but you can be sure that I thought of it and I might have just been thinking aloud !!

Reason - Yes, it might have been that ! Anyway , even if it was hypocrisy , surprisingly enough, in those days, those governing Officials did not think so !

Wise Gofer - A shameful about-face, if you ask me !

Chorus of the Lizxards - No one asked you ! Get lost, you idiot !

Wise Lizards Elders - Oh ! For the sake of ants and frogs, please all present, abstain from scurrility !

Wise Gofer - I still insist on my opinion that the behaviour of those..well....whoever they were, was a definite shameful about-face !!

Chorus of the Mountain Range - We could never do that , even if we had ever thought of doing it : we are firm, immobile, determined and always facing one way .

The lonely Lizard - Interesting . Enpowering .

Mr.Sound - I like this harmonic "crescendo" of this interesting developing discussion .

Thought - A real pity that the embodiment of a thought, My dear Friend and Honourable Sir Reason, would be left wide open and unprotected from the assault of the prevailing ideologies of the time and from some Agents of debatable intellectual valor .

Reason - And to think, my Honourable Friend, that those"Agents", the ones you seem to be referring to, were, actually and truly, real Princes , both lay as well as ecclesiastical Princes...carrying on those unfortunate policies and promoting them too..!!!!

The lonely Lizard - We, lizards, would never do that : we do not even know what "princes" are .

Thought - Just thinking at that disturbed and undignified attitude of those responsible Authorities, in those sad days of iniquitous corruption, gives me a knot in my throat !

Chorus of the Stones - We do not have a throat therefore we cannot have a knot in it, but our will is as hard as a rock and we stand firm behind Sir Thought !

Chorus of the Lizards, the Beetles and the Frogs - We too !!

Wise Gofer - When general consensus is at hand, everybody jumps on the bandwagon !

Reason - As I was saying, those were times of peculiar attitudes in almost every single site of the human activities, physical and intellectual, not readily explanable with just a direct answer and, worse, even draped in a thousand and one contradictory reasons for being that way !

Thought - Reasons ! Reasons !....And more reasons !....Why there always has to be a reason in order to think, whereas , I believe , the process of "thinking" should not be either secondary or an inconsequential sequence to some....shall we say...."reason to be."....?.......Is this trend , perhaps, by any"reason", a human habit ?..I wonder!!

Chorus of the Stones - Indeed, we couldn't have said it any better ourselves ?

Mr. Sound - That's a distorted sound.

Wisw Gofer - Nevertheless, a sound .

Mr. Silence - Quiet, please !!

Reason - I really could not say, my dear Friend and respectable Sir, if a reason is needed prior to conceive a thought and if that were a habit for the human specie for anything and everything that required some form of thinking, be it a bad reason or a good one, borrowed one or stolen one, ridicule or serious, loving or hating or edified, it is really hard to pin point its real bearing on human tendencies and interests, since it ....

Thought - Ah ! There is, then, a reason.....!!

Reason - Not so sure about it or how to call it, since, as I was saying, it appears that a most regrettable habit of most humans is, on one side, easy forgetfulness, almost bordering negligence of thinking,or, to put it in a more plausible form, unwillingness to care too much about problems and dig deep into their origin and formation, unless of a real direct and dire nature and, usually, by then , it is most often too late to even "think" about it .

Thought - How strange !......In my World, it is not so difficult to think .

Chorus of the Lizards - "Neither" in our World, it "isn't" !!

Chorus of the Gofers, the Beetles and the Frogs - Neither it is in our World, and "THAT""s " for sure "...!!

Reason - Of course, my dear and respected Friend, your World is a privileged one, where thinking reigns supreme, free and fertile,no "Princes" of any denomination around to contest, distort or condemn your purity, your glory reserved only for those free thinking exponents of unbiased principles in the human race .

Thought - I see . Now, from what you are telling me and the way you describe the oddities of this human, shall we say, way of living, being and thinking, it seems to me that there are,also, some human beings, these creatures you call so fondly “odd”, who appear to make a respectful pledge among themselves, of thinking with a serious intent, and that is a comforting notion, but tell me do these beings use a”reason” as a prescribed initial start in their thinking Itinerary ?

Reason - Well, your question could be considered in different ways : I........

Thought - Why in different ways ? All I asked was a simple, single and straight question : didn’t I ?

Reason - Of course you did, but its answer implies two different aspects of representation in the arsenal of the types of human “thinkers”

Thought - That is even more complicated that I ever thought it could be and even”beats” my own thinking !!

Reason - Not really and not so dramatically, my dear Sir, but this is the way I see it and, generally,among the common folks,the rare human specimens who“think”and“pursue”only the purest form of abstract thinking without an a priori reason for thinking it, are considered crazy people, sometimes the appellative graciously tempered with a more benevolent form of representation like “odd persons”, and then,...........

Thought - I never suspected that I could be considered a freakish or eccentric entity, fantastic and bizarre to the point of considering crazy the folks who rejoiced in my company !

Reason - Capricious can human search be in his path of thinking, not always constant or loyal in its “affections”. May be the right representation of that particular aspect could be represented by the word :” fickle “, I guess .

Thought - I thought that I thought that I had been thinking that I was thinking, but this is the limit !

Reason - There are no known limits, dear Sir Thought, in the human changeable and unstable character . However, there is another type of humans who choose to use a specific reason from where and for what to start a thinking process .

Thought - Ah ! That’s why at the beginning of this explanatory talk you hinted at two different aspects of representation for my question : right ?

Reason - Yes, but, really not to be so strictly necessary or mandatory only just more orderly in its representation ! So, then, as I was saying there is another type of human who chooses a more direct approach at explainng thoughts, associating them with a specific original purpose or reason,whichever you like to call it,to start a thinking process and these type of thinkers are, then, called "intellectuals" not any different than the pure thinkers, but with one eye to the thought and the other eye to the world in which they live, just in order not to be carried away in the interstellar space . Of course, the original reason may fade away, in time, once the thinking becomes tired along the way .

Chorus of the
Lizards,Beetles, Ants and Frogs and Stones - Hurray !!

Thought - I heard something like a rustling sound in the vegetation on the sides of our walk : we may have some admirers hiding in there and unseen by us who may be agreeing with our discussions and may also not !!

Reason - Do not pay any attention ,dear Friend, it's only the wind . It may blow one way today, it will blow the other way tomorrow or the next day . Unfortunately,that is very similar to the way,often, the humans think: "as the wind blows", as they say ! Of course, you know, this is only said in a facetious way !

Thought - The more we talk about humans and thoughts, the more I begin to believe that humans have a strange way to perceive the essence and the purpose of "thought" !

Reason - They do have other preoccupations also, that they have to deal with,a great number of them quite far apart from a priviliged situation of "absence of need",as we talked about a little earlier and, just thinking does not bring groceries on the table!

Thought - And the reason for that......and with that I mean no reference or impropriety to your precious personality,Sir Reason, because you are a thing apart, but latching on to the groceries on the table, pure thought loses its full, comprehensive taste when it becomes almost destroyed by systematic and not always educated analysis by the different points of view of its innumerable students, just the same way as a Chef in a prestigious restaurant does with "pure food",by dividing, cutting, mixing and diluting in several diverse forms and sizes, so as to appeal to the discriminating taste and preferences of his patrons .

Reason - But, Sir, it is not possible to live with pure thought alone ! At leasrt, not on this Planet !!....I trust, dear and respected Friend, that you might agree with it !

Thought - Sir, and dear Friend, although I fully appreciate your reasoning, yet I must tell you that pure thought does not agree with anything or disagree, either : thought just thinks. Now, whether its thinking goes the way some wish it to go, it's fine, and it goes and everybody is happy but, if not, well, the thought will keep on thinking , regardless of anybody's need for victuals .

Chorus of the
Victuals - That jerk must be crazy.If his ideas would take hold in some people's imagination our catering business would be ruined !

Chorus of the
Stones - Never mind what he says : That thinking Jerk is so blind, all wrapped up in the clouds and fantasies of his thinking that he even keeps on bumping into us all the time, wherever he travels !

Chorus of the Lizards,
Beetles, Frogs and Mice - We need victuals, not thoughts !

the learned
Moth - "Panem et circences" cried the Roman Populace , centuries ago, shocking the elite Roman Enclave !

The Lizards'
Elders - We knew that part of old history.We also feel that it has nothing to do, whatsoever, with the present topics .

The lonely
Lizard - What's a topic ?

Mr.Sound - Cheap skate .

The lonely
Lizard - What's a "skate" ?

Mr.&Mrs Skate - That's Mr. Sound's real name .

Mr.Silence - Quiet , all of you ! Don't you have any sense of decency and civility ?

Chorus of the
whole crowd - We don't .

The Lizards'
Wise Elders - Oh ! Tempora ! Oh ! Mores !!.......What times !....What attitudes !

Wise Gofer - Do you mean, "customs" ?

The Lizards
Wise Elders - Yes, that too : just an expression of disapproval of that improper behaviour .

Wise Gofer - But that remark was made centuries ago, at the times of the ancient Romans ?

The Lizards'
Wise Elders - Has anything, really, changed that much ?

Thought - My dear Sir Reason, I keep on hearing some rustling on the greenery along the sides of our road and it even seems to be louder than the one I heard a while ago !

Reason - May be the wind has picked up some strength !

Thought - But, my dear Friend and respected Sir, ...there is no wind ! Not even the slightest breeze !

Reason - Then, may be, some lonely Ghosts promenading like us and commenting, on their own, on our discussion....!!!

Thought - Do Ghosts care to think too, Sir Reason ?

Reason - Perhaps , but it's hard to tell .

Thought - Perhaps ! Perhaps ! Always and every time perhaps for everything that's being thought ! Do you think, Sir, that....."perhaps".......I should assume a more concrete form than that of just an imaginary entity considering that I am being used by concrete forms, humans and various others, I believe, and divest myself of my traditional invisible cloak ?

Reason - I am not a judge of abstract behaviour, my dear Sir Thought,but only a humble reasoning creature, who believes in almost the unbelievable , provided that the bewilderment would be a relatively"reasonable" one !

Thought - I imagined, a priori, that this would be or could be your answer! But then, if I wanted to change my aspect and absorb some realism in my abstract essence, I doubt that I would be successful, because, right or wrong, excessive or[impractical, aloof or detached, I would not be anything else, anyway, because I only am a Thought !

Chorus of the Lizards - Noble Words !

Chorus of the Stones - It would really be hard for us to deny it !

Chorus of the Beetles - The usual way out of an impossible situation .

Mr.Sound - A lot of noise, for an empty bag .

Mr.Silence - Quiet, please ! Go away and think somewhere else .

............meanwhile......................

Reason - Well, I have to admit, Sir Thought, your reasoning was quite reasonable .

Thought - Yet I cannot help having some reservations about my supposed and desirable change !

Reason - Any change involves considerable amount of moral strength, fortitude of spirit,determination and desire to succeed and honesty of purpose, but and above all, a clear understanding of the reason for it .

Thought - The reason was already appreciated, but the actual change, from abstract thinking to a more practical one would, by necessity of purely needed adaptation, require a fractioning of my simple, solitary and universal thought in many thoughts .

Reason - I am sorry, dear Friend and honourable Thought, but I don't follow you !

Thought - Oh ! Nothing really hyperbolic, only a down to earth considerationon on the effect of my projected change .

Reason - That might help !

Thought - Indeed !...Well....and, simply, as many as there are human beings scattered around almost everyehre, there ought to be as many, if not even more, thoughts patterns available in order to be practical and useable and accommodate the appetite of so large and diverse crowd as well as the level of comprehension at so many different levels of interpretation, that would contradict and weaken my resolve to absolute purity .

Reason - But, my dear Friend, isn't it precisely what your projected change would be supposed to bring about, a more practical and useable thinking approach and implementation of its fruitful results, and wasn't the idea of thinking of a change the basic reason for it in the firstplace ?

Thought - Of course, it was ! However, it would stand to "reason", I guess, for me to be allowed a little room for my comments and I can already see some difficulties delineating on the horizon, like the hardship on me to partake and follow so many different ways in all directions by such a large multitude of multiform minds,and it would be a real loss of fruitful time to disperse my energies in so many directions just to satisfy the practical intellectual whims of these little capricious Creatures .

Reason - CAPRICIOUS.....???!!!!!......That's the best I have ever heard on human consistency !!!

Thought - Oh ! Just a lucky interjections ! Sometimes, in the distant fogs of the imagination, I feel as if I "were" and if I "were" not .all at the same time, just an invisible nothing and a ful whole, again, all at the same time !!!

Chorus of the Lizards - That jerk of a Thought tries to play "hide-and-seek" .

Chors of the Beetles - It figures !

....................meanwhile........................

Reason - A difficult existence,Yours, Sir Thought, I would venture to say, to be an invisible nothing and a full whole, both at the same time !

Thought - Difficult is a human expression but, to me, is meaningless because I, really, am ignorant of anything since I only practice the stimulus to think : what the thinking, then, leads to, that escapes my initial effort .

Reason - Could you, please, give me if possible, a slightly clearer example of what you just said ?

Thought - But of course, and with great pleasure .

Reason - I will be listening with renewed interest, I assure you !

Thought - If I become entangled in a fully formed body, or, should I rather say "mind", like that, for example of a living creature, I , then................

Reason - A man, would you say, Sir Thought, a human creature, I mean .

Thought - Not becessarily : I mean a living creature and, of course, it could also be that of a human being, naturally, but, as I said, not necesaarily so, and capable of some transformations .

Reason - You'll pardon my intromission in your explanations, dear Friend, but and as far as I am aware of, humans do not seem to transform themselves quite readily except, of course, when they die and change shape, look and substance, volume and consistency .

Thought - I understand your observation, Sir Reason, and I praise your interpretation because I esteem your vigorous way of reasoning .

Chorus of the Stones - And they call that "reasoning"...???!!

Chorus of the Lizards - To us they appear as idle people, having nothing else better to do, and trying to explain what has already been known since time began .

Chorus of the Beetles - Who told you that ?

Chorus of the Lizards - Common knowledge .

..............................meanwhile............................

Reason - Thank you, Sir Thought, for your gratifying recognition of my reasoning, but, really, my reasoning is far from deserving any praise, since I still have some difficulty in following your recent claim that"difficult"is just a human definition .

Chorus of the Stones - This Jerk of a Thought, he does not know what he's talking about ! Difficult, he says, is just a human definition...!!!....Shucks !!....That Thought doesn't have the slightest clue about the terrible and trying difficulties we have to go through constantly with those living creatures that he is talking about, treading on us all the time in one way or another !

Reason - Sir Thought, did you say something ? I am sorry but I couldn't catch it quite clearly !

Thought - No, Sir Reason, I did not say anything, right now. May be, it's again a light breeze in the shrubs .

Reason - May be. But, then, what about your final explanation ? I am interested .

Thought - There isn't one, really, that could logically associate itself to the concrete reality of the visible lifeand its"difficulty": you see, what I am talking about is something that, actually, does not exist, cannot be seen but can only be imagined and portrayed in a thousand and one configurations and multiple of that, and built into a colossal palace of vivid and amazing splendor of intellective endevour, just as it could be wiped out altogether in less than a hundreth of a millionyh of a second, if your mind so desired .

Reason - Oh ! This is fine, but it does not seem to explain to me, yet, the relationship of the human"difficult"expression and your ability to build and wipe out whatever thought might have been envisaged, in no time at all .

Thought - And why not ? Can a beaver build a dam, can an ant build an anthill, can a man build a castle or a World and then, wipe it out of existence in no time at all,without even leaving the slightest trace of what had been envisaged and thought in the first place ?

Chorus of the Stones - This fellow Thought is not only a jerk, he is plum crazy ! Why ! Many castles and other things have disappeared without a trace due to the work of time and the erosion by the elements .

Wise Gofer - But not in the split time of a hundreth of a millionth of a second , I guess .

Chorus of the Stones - What's the difference ?

Wise Gofer - Substantial . A Castle or anything else, cannot be built in a hundreth of a millionth of a second and wiped out "within" that same time that it was built, but a thought can .

Chorus of the whole crowd - Are you "Fer or agin us ?" ?

......................meanwhile.............................

Reason - I begin to see a little more clearly what you meant when you said that the word"difficult" is meaningless to you and only........

Thought - As you see, thought is infinitely rechangeable, therefore, for me, it poses no difficulty .

Reason - How wonderful that would be if all the various factions in the human arena would be so highly spirited as to allow the human mind the freedom of pure thinking .

Thought - But, my dear Friend, there are already several areas in this World where that proposition is in force and followed correctly and unanimously !

Reason - True, but frown upon, obstacled and even persecuted in large parts of our living World , still !!

Thought - It is probable that the disparity in the distribution of those policies among humans which favour the complete freedom of thought, are due to the constant uncertainty pervading the existence and function of their lives, therefore restricting, under the adverse influence of that psychic anxiety, a free and spacious flow of thinking and producing a gloomy, introspective tendency to look into one's self, instead to free the mind and the spirit. And you, Sir Reason, my dear Friend and respected neighbour, you represent exceedingly well that part of the World of free mind and free spirit .

Reason - Yes, that could be a reason for the disparity as mentioned, the uncertainty of the fate of our lives: uncertainty is, indeed, synonimous with the very living,I believe.

Thought - In a way,yes.Yet, it does not seem to reflect, in another way, the style of your life! Just look at yourself , for example : you have a good, comfortable life, I should have said, perhaps, a reasonably good life, and you are well, you feel well, you enjoy succulent meals, followed by a restful sleep until the next morning when the anticipation of a similar good and joyous day will clear your mind of any worry !!

Reason - I do agree with your description of my daily living representations but all of that is possible on account of the skills and the outstanding performance of my excellent maid Camilla, who makes any possible effort to please me and go along with my habits .

Thought - A very trusted maid, indeed ! I envy you for the fortune you have to be taken care by her ! I guess, by now, she must have readied your succulent supper !

Reason - Indeed, she must have !!.....Meanwhile, our interesting talk has taken us away from my house while promenading in this peaceful and delightful evening ! Do you, Sir , feel, may be, a little tired ?

Thought - Not really, I am used to this evening walk and I enjoyed greatly being with you .

......While the two Gentlemen continue their leisurely walk, silently pondering on the meaning of their lengthy discussions, Sir Thought begins reflecting within himself the lonely and disconsolate existence of pure thought !........

Thought - (talking to himself.......) - ....And I, solitary and insipid poor "me", a lonely whiff of something which only a few odd creatures vie for its possession and its friendship......I have to starve just to keep faith and be true to my image of pure thought and supremacy over material things !.....A real hard bargain in the natural selection of chain of events !!...Oh ! How much would I too enjoy the culinary attentions of that sweet Camilla...!!!...Particularly so after her mouth-watering description of the grand supper to be and the effect of this invigorating evening promenade !!

Reason - Sorry, my dear Friend, but did you say something ? I was just walking and thinking something else and I thought I heard a sort of a whisper, but I wasn't sure whether it was my imagination again, or, maybe, a "whiff" of an evening breeze, or just nothing of importance !

Thought - I did not say anything, Sir Reason and, confidentially, even if I had wanted to say something, I should have desisted from doing so because we have already said "eneough" for one evening ! Don't you think so, dear Friend ?

Reason - That was exactly what I was thinking about when I was just walking, saying nothing and ruminating within myself about the amazing volume of talk that we have managed to put together this evening, something that will stand as a monumental wonder in the history of the convenient process of reasoning and the enticing process of intellective thinking and, this delightful evening, is a blessing for both of them...!!

Thought - Of course !.....And a good reminder that the evening is slowly parting ways and is welcoming the night to the scene of our oratory and, with these late hours, rekindling a desire for the comfort of home, a joyful fireplace and a succulent supper . Ah ! I wonder !.....How good must that be, the life of material concepts !

Reason - Well, in a certain way it corresponds to that kind of concept since creatures of all sizes, shapes and functions are made up of various materials , some with an extra pinch of salt in the brains which belong to the presumptuous and overbearing "genus humanus ", so, as I was saying, these materials have a right as anything else to claim some attention which, for them, usually comes in the form of food .

Chorus of the Lizards - Hurrah..for all material things,from stones to victuals and everything in-between!!

Chorus of the
Beetles - We love those materials' left overs ! The more, the better .

Chorus of the
Lizards - We understand that too . No big deal, though .

Chorus of the
Beetles - It may not be to you,.....you Sun-whorshipper Reptiles of the sub-order Lacertilia Sauria, but it means a lot to us !

Chorus of the
Lizards - Such remarks can only be expected from waste-loving Beetles .

Chorus of the
Beetles - You mean to say that your long sittings on a stone absorbing the Sun's rays is no "waste" of time ?

Chorus of the
Lizards - That's no waste, you"wasted"Ignoramuses : that's what we must do by the programmed mechanisms in us .

Chorus of the
Beetles - Same here, you ignorant reptiles of the sub-order Lacertilia.

Mr.Sound - Same here for the harmonics : they are built in me .

MrSilence - I wish that "silence" were built in all of them !

Chorus of the
Stones - We too ! We too !!

Wise Gofer - ..." We to! We too" !......what ???..You Ninnies !!

Chorus of the
Stones - We meant: " we too, comprehend the need for the Lizards to sit on us to absorb the sun's warmth and that we too comprehend that we are stones and lizards sit on us ".....and that's what "we too" meant , you "go fer....." gopher of the genus Citellus !!!

Chorus of the
Beetles - But you, stones, mineral and material earth boulders, you had not said "whom" or "what" with did you plan to identify yourselves, by just saying " we too" !! Do you have any idea at all to whom you wish to identify yourselves ?

Chorus of the
Stones - Who knows ?

Chorus of the
Lizards - Senseless kind of talk .

Chorus of the
Stones - Senseless if for creatures that have no "sense"of.....direction : we can go any other which way.

Chorus of the
Lizards - We can go straight up, straight down, side way and upside down : try that for a change .

Chorus of the
Beetles - Enough of this nonsense ! Haven't you had enough yet of the chatting of those two"chirping birds",competing with the magpies mischievous chattering and chatterbox consistency, walking and talking as if they were facing an audience ?

Chorus of the
Lizards - But we never saw anybody around listening to those two magpies !

Mr.Sound - Excellent ,harmonic sound : I rarely hear such effective orchestral sounds !

................meanwhile..

Reason - Yes, Sir Thought, my Friend and respected Neighbour, by just going over and back to your representation of the existing conflicts within your , shall we say,"representative self", the embodiment of pure thinking is what I wanted to say, well as I was saying, I believe that I am able to.........to recognize and understand too your anxieties and plight about the difficult and harduous work of continuously distinguishing between pure and material sensations as they keep on forming in the mind, well, in the brains of all sorts of creatures .

Thought - I do appreciate,really, your concern as well as interest in that most peculiar status of my composition .

Reason - My dear and respected Friend, I do that with good reason .

Thought - I thought so .

Reason - Often, as you certainly have noticed, we ask ourselves the same questions over and over again, then we roll them upside down in our minds, we examine and re-examine them, scrutinize them, then we get tired of them, we forget all about them but to claim them back soon from our memory and drive ourselves crazy with a thousand and one questions,arguments,conclusions, contradictions, totally dissatisfied at the very end..... and........for nothing !

Thought - It's amazing how these material situations and wordly problems and conditions can be so far away, almost totally separated from the realms of pure thinking !

Reason - May be not so much separated but only slightly dissociated due to unavoidable preferences of the various brains in going about the daily business, some time satisfied, some other times dissatisfied, but nonetheless always anxious in seeking an answer to the as old as the World question of who are we, where did we come from, why are we at all as we are, why are we living on this planet , why do we have a brain and why some do not, and why is it good for us to eat a balanced diet, avoid excessive sweets and the abuse of alcoholic beverages. YES ! Sir Thought , how well I understand you , believe me !....And with good reason !

Thought - Sincerely touched ...!!

Chorus of the
Questions, Arguments and Conclusions - It is really great fun rolling in the minds of those living creatures ! A lot of fun, believe you us !!

Thought - And furthermore I am really glad and encouraged at the realization that you, really understand me . Thank you, and that is a deeply felt feeling for me !

Reason - Truly, My Friend and Sir, I do understand you .

Chorus of the
Questions, Arguments and Conclusions - We do not, for sure !

Chorus of the
Stones - It is very hard for us to understand anything, let alone questions, arguments and conclusions ! ....What are they, anyway ? Any connection with the magpies ?

Chorus of normal
Lizards - That the stones are hard enough not to understand anything, that's quite natural because it is a Law of Nature, but we are not certain about the connection with the magpies, although that name had been mentioned before .

Mr.Sound - "Dura Lex , sed Lex", were saying the Old Romans, when confronted with hard decisions about some pending issues when, sometimes, facts may have been contradictory to the case causing the Judges to wonder about the application of a Law.....but " a severe Law, nevertheless a Law ".

Wise Gopher - What has that got to do with what is being talked about ?

Mr.Sound - I am not sure but it might have had something to do with the mention of the"Law of Nature" and I thought that the Romans would have thought the same .

Wise Gopher - And you feel that your explanation justifies the interjection of your comment into the general content of the present conversation ?

Mr.Sound - I do .

Wise Lizard - Of all the impudence.....well....this is the limit !!

the "Choir" of
the Laws - The stones knew that: they are very hard and consistent and durable and firm, just as a Law should be, if at all a Law .

Chorus of the
Stones - Interesting .

Chorus of the Lizards
and the Beetles - We do not see anything at all that interesting in all this .

Chorus of the
Stones - Party Poopers !

The Legal Representative
of the Lizards and the Beetles - Better watch your language !

Chorus of the
Stones - We do not have one .

The Legal Representative
of the Lizards and the Beetles - Then you better get one and, then.....SHUT UP !

Wise Gopher - Oh! Tempora ! Oh ! Mores !

The Wise Gopher's Son - What does that mean, Daddy ?

Wise Gopher - Insufferable bad manners, in my own mind, but, by sheer translation from the Latin it means " What times ! What customs ! ", hinting at a sort of deterioration of manners and civic standards .

The Wisw Gopher's Son - Where did you learn Latin ,Dad ?

Wise Gopher - My ancestors were assigned to the inner and secret chambers of the ancient Roman Senate and had access to all the tablets, papayrus scrolls that were rejected or no longer needed and learned the language well: they really digested it.

The wise and
lonely Lizard - Nothing is new under the sun or over the stones .

Reason - But, now, my dear Friend, we must make a decision because the evenng is late, so much later than I would have ever expected to EVER come to experience !! It is, really, the beginning of night and we have come a significant distance away from where we had started from !

Thought - Your are right, Sir Reason, and, to be frank with you, it is a little late for me too as this evening my walk in your company and while chatting so pleasantly over a million and one things ! So, shall we turn back and walk home ? It isn't, really, that far so we should be there just in a few minutes . It looks as we did walk a long distance but that impression came about because we talked so much and we paid no attention at the ground we covered .

Reason - And, indeed, we covered a lot of ground, if not exactly with our feet but, certainly, with our imagination, from pure thinking to pure matter to the intricacies of innumerable relationships of thought, of matter, of creatures, of minds, and whatever more we did discuss....indeed, my dear and trusted Friend, our deductive discernment of the various subjects was, in my opinion, simply............well..... yes, brilliant !

The Splendid Choir
of the Diamond Club - That Jerk talks nonsense ! May be he sounds as he would even be able to convince everybody that the Moon is made of green cheese ! What kind of brilliance is he talking about, we wonder !

Chorus of the
Stones - It is really hard for us to follow any reasoning and understand it too. For us, to understand , we always need very hard evidence .

Mr.sound - You don't say !

Chorus of the
Stones - But we do, you idiot !

Mr.Sound - Oh! Tempora Oh ! Mores !!!

......................Then.........

Thought - Now, Sir Reason, to complete your last sentence about thought, matter and mind and so on, or, as we had discussed earlier, completed and incompleted forms and all that stuff , like unfinished matter that becomes finished,so to speak of, and you understand, I am sure ,what I am talking about... like, for example, in the case of finished matter, and just in order to be practical in my explanation, referring to every day occasions, as the appearance of trufle, ravioli, capons, trouts,eels,cakes and all of them well arranged , of course, always in a proper and correct sequence with respect to atoms, cells, of course, substances, various numbers of them, on a beautiful decorated dining table, over flowing with many and diverse entrees, that would, naturally, be an exquisite example and even a practical proof that our theory of unfinished matter becoming finished, is, indeed, formulated on a very solid, positive and.....substantial......platform !

Reason - But what a droll you are Sir and respected Friend, quite amusing, indeed, and I admire your versatility in keeping such a well balanced equilibrium even in your own thinking !!

Thought - Thank you for your generous esteem, even if I am only a thought .

Reason - Yours, my dear Friend and illustrious Neighbour, is an unnecessary demureness ! You shine even in total darkness !.......And even more so, now, that you have found some open roads leading you to the"practical World "of every day life,from the excelled and yet foggy and austere peaks of pure thinking, after our walking and deambulatory strolling while challenging the unknown, this enchanted evening !

Chorus of the Stones - What's this mambo-jambo of peaks and deambulations and the hullabaloo of this trump up challenging of the unknown in an enchanted evening, of all places !! Big Deal, really !!!...There you got an invisible thought which, just after a few leisurely steps, becomes not only visible.....and "that", in itself, is already a lot of disappointment......but, also, solid as a rock, taking shape from "not-settled" to "fully settled " status and acquiring, in this extraordinary descent from the austere peaks of pure thinking to the plains of the human valleys, all the aggregate perceptions of world liliving, inclusive of the olfactory sense, and all the other noble attributes of that infamous mankind that keeps on treading and trampling on us, splitting and breaking and muddling us up in all kind of muxtures !......And,now, we ask ourselves :" Will these humans ever listen to us ??? "

Thought - And, my dear Sir Reason and Honourable Neighbour, I have to add that I feel a little guilty and selfish in having kept you out of your house and away from your long established and honoured habits of an early supper and early bedtime ! I just wonder what that sweet house maid of yours, the gentle Camilla, might think of me !!

Reason - Please, my dear Friend, my illustrious Friend, do not even think of it !! Camilla, I am certain, will always think the World of you and she will be glad that I did get some needed exercise on account of your persuasive insistence that I accompany you in your usual evening promenade. I consider it a priviled and a great ,unexpected, unanticipated pleasure that of having spent some time in your precious company and in the embrace of so many enticing discussions !

Thought - The pleasure was mine too, noble Friend, I assure you !......

(then , softly, to himself....: " If he only guessed what's behind my effort in entertaining him , he, probably , would not be so pleased anymore ! ....What I mean is my attempt in a purely purest "thinking" way to get an insight and , if lucky , even an invitation to that fabulous supper ,sweet Camilla, mentioned to me, a while ago........!!!)

Chorus of the Stones - That jerk petrifies us !!

Reason - Pardon me, Sir, but did you say something ? I think I heard something like a whisper but I was not paying attention and I might have missed something !

Thought - Oh ! Nothing, nothing of importance,Sir Reason......just an erudite digression and a furtive and belated return......home .....to some well worn abstract thinking and comparing it to the enchanted evening we spent together like a mantle of mystery embracing us with a giant fireplace raised between the sky and the earth, you know, the planet where you and Camilla live, and thinking that I may be lighting a match to set forth the warm flames of the fireplace to enlighten my thoughts and warm my shallow feeling of a lonely, vagrant, and forgotten thought .

Reason - Then, is it so that you, Sir, by just stimulating your thinking, can overcome sadness, tiredness and the "shallow" feeling in your body ?

Thought - ....Body....??

Reason - Oh ! How unreasonable of me !!...I was just talking without "thinking" !! But, of course, we all know that you, Sir, as a pure thought ,do not have a body although you have the ability to make yourself known in a very positive and perceptible way whenever you decide to have an idea of your particular choice to be carried to a succesful end and, "that"often observed sequence, is well known among the thoughtless mortals . All I was saying was just an attempt to represent in some form your image in such a way, that it could be seen and measured as a comparison with other forms around us .

Thought - Don't you think, Sir, that this anxious instinct of the human forms to always and constantly wanting to compare anything with anything else available , tends to be a form of suspected prejudice ?

Reason - I do not really know how to answer your question , Sir, but , let us say , this apparent tendency or habit of the human specie to wanting to compare everything that can be compared , is , in all truth, a favoured and most diligently practiced activity of that specie , particularly so when they elect to think .

Thought - Humans ! Humans !....Always Humans...!!!! Isn't there anything else around to compare things with ??

Reason - Sad as it may seem , my dear Friend, Sir, but they "is" here to stay , to show off, to tell stories and to propel themselves to the forefront of everything !

Chorus of the Stones - We too are here to stay, we also show ourselves off on the peaks of the highest mountains and we are the basic "stone-steps" in any construction the humans start building .Yet, no one thinks much of us : they look at us just as ...." Oh ! A stone" and kick us out of their way . "

Chorus of the Lizards - We sit very regularly on the stones to warm up by absorbing the sun's rays ! We think a lot of the stones, which we consider our best friends , after the frogs .

Thought - Your are a fortunate creature , Sir , in being able to present and explain facts as well as phenomena, because you are a fully completed form at the end of the chain that started originally somewhere, and you, of course and therefore, are the validation and confirmation of the final and completed achievement of that original starting point . For me, though, it is different because I am only a thought, simple and isolated, void of any substance unless caught by sheer chance by an open and pristine mind who was looking for some company . Most of other times, I am neglected if I ever stick around, most of the time unrequested and most often not even tolerated . You see, as I have said before, I am only a thought .

Choir of the assertions,
Questions and conclusions - He claims himself a victim of prejudice, this elite Sir Thought, and a simple pawn in the indifference arena of mankind, but he thinks lightly of all the serious problems that his thinking may cause all over where civilized thinking occurs and is being practiced, so many problems, so many more dissensions, so innumerable conflicts, so many more controversies and contradictions than there are grains in a pinch of sand !

Reason - Your claim of being"just a thought",my dear Friend and greatly esteemed Neighbour, is a valid and genuine assertion, but, then, many other entities are also standing alone like mountains, oceans, lakes , forests and they, also, could very well claim to be"just a mountain" or "just an ocean " or "just a potato or a carrot ". I do not mean to be facetious, only , by human standards, comparing claims to the evidence of facts .

Choir of the assertions
Questions and conclusions - I'll bet anything that this elite and thoughtful jerk will come out with some incomprehensible stuff and with tepid content .

Thought - But would a simple creature ,without educational priming, or without any inclination to study and/or thinking , believe in the idea and even accept, at all, the idea or the thought that the agglomeration of an infinite number of invisible particles actually materialized into concrete forms, like the petals of a flower , the bark of a tree, the tree itself, the mountains, the rivers, the lakes, the oceans, and even he, himself, who does not catch the idea of it all, that "HE" himself materialized ..... from all that...??

Reason - Not only a "simple" creature, my dear and respected and illustrious Sir, but even a more "complex" creature, may have some difficulty in embracing and capturing the immense idea of that beginning and how it must have been before it started .

Thought - Just Matter .

Chorus of the Stones - And who would believe, simple or complex, that we are the end result of an idea smart enough to put together innumerable numbers of invisible Particles and make us look like we do !

Mr.Silence - Your silence, dear"pebbles".....is far more eloquent tha your forms .

Chorus of the "Pebbles" - We deeply resent that unfortunate and very personal reference to ordinary stones by using our appellative in an indirect and suspiciously sarcastic mode . Not that we have any adverse sentiments towards the stones or rocks or boulders, generally, but purely on the basis of heraldic decency .

Mr.Silence - No intentional harm done . My "intention" was one of an"intentional" form of affection .

Chorus of the Pebbles - Thankyou, and that clears our minds and, in the spirit of solidarity which well applies to rocks and boulders, we express our approving message that ...;" your silence , dear cousins Stones, speacks more eloquently than anything else you may have ".

Reason - My dear Thought you just said a very terse.." MATTER ", to describe how "IT" all was before it started . That is fine, and, I am certain, that up there where you float freely and aloof you must perceive and encounter explanations of things that we, down here, cannot readily afford to even "just think" about ! But, then , how does it happen ?.....Or, may be, you think that my asking is almost puerile or altogether preposterous ?

Thought - Not at all . No one knows anything about all that, so, it makes really no difference whether you ask a simple question or a complex one : the answer will always be a vague, pale, ineffective, unsatisfactory answer, because no one really knows, but only.....presumes .

Reason - But how would they..."presume", then , for it to happen ?

Thought - Synthesis of various matter, sometimes like the formation of the amazing subterranean creation in the form of the ascomycetous fungus of the Genus Tuber ....

Reason - No wonder hardly anybody knows anything about all that ! How can you get to work and discover things if you have to escavate and wander under the earth in subterranean meanders...??.......And what on Earth did you say about that new discovery in subterranean caves....did I hear you mention something like a..fungus??!

Thought - Oh ! Nothing really of an extraordinary importance except for its culinary applications .Yes, Sir Reason, a very special type of fungus . Very special, yes, indeed, but well known to your sweet maid, Camilla . As a matter of fact, she had mentioed to me, just before.........

Reason - My dear Friend, Sir, did you, by any chance, refer to that special Fungus that grows around the roots of some special oak trees in very limited and well demarkated areas in the World, and which goes under the common knowledge name of "truffle"..??

Thought - Precisely, Sir Reason.and I hope that your gentle and reasonable nature will pardon my digression ! I must have been a little absent-minded !

Reason - Oh ! Please, no need to worry about such trifling things ! I understand perfectly well that the pure nature of Thought and its faithful accompianist, Master Thinking , are , by the nature of their being, often absent-minded and distracted .

Thought - Yes: in a way . However my thinking,at that time,was somewhat of a frivolous nature , and I am sorry .

Reason - The PHENOMENON of SYNTHESIS ....a frivolous thought ....????!!!

Chorus of the Stones - Not the blasted Synthesis, you idiot !......The TRUFFLE !!!!

Thought - My dear Friend and noble Neighbour, not the Synthesis and its associated phenomenon !.....I meant the truffle .

Reason - The Synthesis of.......the truffle...???!!

Thought - But certainly: the everyday occasions and happenings , meaning that the saturation of ingredients into a form could be accelerated by stimulation .

Reason - Really ?

Thought - Yes, Sir, and respected Friend, and this Synthesis.........

Reason - Of the Truffle, you mean ?

Chorus of the Stones - But, of course ! You Ninny !!

Thought - Yes, my dear Friend and illustrious Neighbour, I did mean the Truffle, but just as one of the many things that can become visible by sheer force of synthesization, like it could be with poultry, fish, sugar,chocolate and any other products that usually make honour to a good and well attended dinner table, I guess !

Reason - How good and accurate your description, Sir, of those material entities, so far removed from your way of living that I am really surprised that you at all could even just imagine them to be as they actually really are !!!

Thought - I wish, Sir, that I could reason as you do ! How simpler would be my existence and how happier my itinerary in life .

Reason - Why not try it, my Trusted Friend and respected Neighbour ?

Thought - Would it be worth the effort, Sir ?

Reason - It is a common practice among humans to constantly scrutinize, analyze, criticise someone's intelligence or ability to interpret things, as you just did, while praising their own, and give sparing recognition to somebody about some accomplished endeavours, while, of course, enlarging on their own, being very careful to recognize the good on their side and assign the bad to the other side, to exalt and exttol someone to the skies ,but to dash him or her down to the abys, the next time around, and all this, sometimes, even without any plausible or serious or righteous reason . My dear and respected Friend, I do believe that you could certainly improve on all those infamous scores !!!

Thought - Are there, may be, some other types of humans , around, on the planet ?

Reason - Yes : now and then, some outstanding human creatures with fine intellects and spacious minds and keen , profound, elective power of perception and understanding ,have appeared on the human horizons, but not all were welcomed, several were ignored, many obstracized, several even killed, so the tally is dismal as far as righteosness among humans is concerned !

Thought - No close keen folks ever found or contemplated for some better cooperation among all ?

Reason - Some Scientists thought of some types of Apes, but, after several studies and various attempts at socialization, the Apes refused to cooperate .

Thought - Oh ! A dismal world, indeed, that of the humans, Sir Reason ! And there does not seem to be a way to escape it, either !!

Reason - It is a strange world ! Something exists, something does not exist, something goes this way and, then , it suddenly goes the opposite way !.......And the funny part is that.... there is no escape from that set up...!!!!

Thought - (...to himself) - (but something. I know, does exist, and Camilla said so, like the truffle, the capons, the trout, the eel, the ravioli, the cake and, of course, the very Camilla, herself...!!!)

Reason - You were saying, Sir ?

Thought - Nothing, really . However of one thing I feel guilty of !!

Reason - And what reason would that be, Sir Thought ? I hope not an unpleasant one !

Thought - Oh ! Nothing of that nature, for certain !! I am suspecting to have forced you, may be and in a sense, to accompany me this evening in my promenade and this against your well set habits !

Reason - Oh ! Not at all, Sir Thought, not at all ! It has been, instead, a real pleasure. After all I do not seem to be that "misanthrope" and a "walking clock", as people depict and descri- be me !! Not that I really choose to be alone but, the way I regulate my life, it creates difficulties in finding other creatures with the same tendencies and habits, but, for one evening and in such splendid company, I am willing to make an exception and i did and I do not regret it a bit of having done it !!

Thought - It is very refreshing to me and also rewarding to me to hear you say all those good things about your"unusual" walk this evening, but it certainly relieves me of some of that guilty feeling I was talking to you about.

Reason - Well, you are too kind .

Thought - Thank you and I am glad that you appreciated my relief at the realization that nothing actually caused you undue discomfort . You see, sometimes, the interpretation of my meaning has such a wide radius of comprehension, that not all creatures have the power or the intellective means to correspond with me .

Reason - Well, I feel pity for those unhappy creatures who cannot converse or partake of your interesting company, but, as far as I am concerned and ,also, as a "reasonable" representative of collective reasoning among this human specie, I feel that I have been endowed with the horizon of wider horizons while chatting with you . Besides, interestingly enough, while still chatting and remostrating to each other the pleasure we experienced in being together this evening, we retraced our steps and we are almost exactly where we had started from : my house !!!

Camilla – (running out of the front door of the house and addressing her Master, Sir Reason ......) - But, Sir !... where have you been all this time ???!! The supper was ready long ago and on the table.....but where have you been all this time, that the food has almost gone stale by this time....!!!

Reason - Here I am, here I am Camilla, please do not worry, here I am and all in one piece !

Camilla - Ah does not worry, Sir !! Ah is not at all upset ! Says you, Sir honourable Master! But it was youse, Sir Master, who was urging me , jist a while ago, to get back in the house and prepare the supper and scolding mefor being late and chatting with that good for nothing........

Reason - Not so loud, Camilla, please...!!

Camilla - Well, even in a low voice, I should not be upset after almost breaking my back by working like a mule in the kitchen, not that I is seen any of them mules ever working in a kitchen but jist for way of saying things, and trying to prepare a supper and now Your Lordship becomes upset because I is upset ! Oh! Mercy,oh,Mercy, how unjust the World can be with us poor maids that we is always chastised for doing something, even when we does somthing good !! Mercy, oh!....Mercy!....How unjust this World can be !!....Whichever way it goes .

Reason - Camilla, please, don't get all worked up for a little thing like this ! After all I am back and invigorated with an extraordinary appetite !

Camilla - Oh ! Yes, I says, a good appetite and everything is cold on the table !

Reason - (turning towards Sir Thought, who had been waiting patiently to say the parting "good-night " before retiring..........) - Please, Sir Thought, my dear respected Friend, be so kind and excuse us for our little Family squabble ....You know how women are annoyed when something doesn't quite go the way they had planned it to go !

Thought - Oh ! Please, please, do not worry about anything, Sir, and my trusted Friend, I understand everything perfectly well and I am perfectly all right too ! No problems! Now, as to your mention of women's attitudes, unfortunately I cannot be a good judge or a consummate connoisseur, because I do not know how women are, whether they are in their role of superlative cook-wizards in the fine art of preparing gourmet suppers......(.....then , to himself, softly..." but don't I know them, though...!!!) ....or whether they...............

Reason - Nothing of importance, Sir Thought, it is a common habit among humans to always pick on each other about silly and superficial faults and peculiarities !

Thought - I see ! Well, now I am wiser than I was about the women's issue !!...Yet, I wonder whether they could represent the materialization of a thought , a culinary thought or a thinking process that has the potential to become a visible and tangible supper by purely thinking of it and transmitting it via material particles , that is, formed entities, like truffle, capons, trout, eels, phesant, ravioli and, for those mysterious intricacies of Nature's bewildering ability in the wondrous art of manufacturing, also a gorgeous cake ....

Reason - Well, I am glad that I was able to give you a glinpse into the wordly mechanisms that so closely affect our daily lives, and I am quite familiar with these things and I know that my sweet Camilla could become upset , even offended, were I to cause a poor outcome to her precise preparations for food !

Thought - Hard to find, these days, such a conscientious house helper !!

Reason - Quite so, I guess ! She wants to have everything perfectly arranged and neatly presented, and, should I ignore those extenuating preparations, I am certain that my next meal would be just a pinch of salt and pepper served on a silver plate and half an herring on a small piece of stale bread. And "that", for pure spite !

Thought - I understand the situation, my dear Friend, and I feel somewhat responsible for the supper"time" confrontation with your sweet house maid Camilla, because it was I who kept her talking far longer than courtesy would customarily allow !!

Reason - Oh! Sir thought, nothing really of such consequence to even be worthy of being discussed !! I am certain that my sweet Camilla enjoyed that unexpected and fortunate chance to exchange some converastion with you !

Thought - I certainly did enjoy it and I hope that your sweet Camilla did too.

Reason - Did she inopportune you with her simple talking and empty sense of expressions and what did you all talk about ?

Thought - Oh ! We touched lightly on several subjects of the day, occurrences in the Village and we also talked about the weather .

Reason - Extremely interesting and catchy subjects those must have been and I feel certain that it was something different and simple and lighter than the effort of a ponderous conversation .

Thought - And, indeed, it was : a pleasant few words, just prior to a succulent supper .

Reason - Succulent.....SUPPER ? And.... how did............

Thought - Well, nothing dramatic, but, while chatting about one thing and another, your sweet Camille, was telling me of her work in the kitchen, preparing dinners for you and the way she described them, they seemed not only cooked to perfection but even as if "painted with gold " !!

Reason - Indeed she really seems to have her hands "painted with gold" when she attends to some of her culinary masterpieces !!!

Thought - Well, my dear and trusted Friend, the hour is getting late, particularly so for you, so the time has come for us to say Goodnight and part our ways and you to return to your house and to your supper that, I am sure, has been now waiting for you for quite a while. So, Goodnight and thank you, again, for your pleasant company.

Reason - I suppose, you had your supper already, right ?

Thought - No, I have not yet, really, but ,please, do not take cause about me because I will manage all right: it so happened that I forgot to prime the stove, before leaving my house, but as soon as I go back I'll have it working again in no time .

Reason - I hope it will work well again too.Anyway, I hope that you would accept the remark that I am going to make, graciously !

Thought - Go right ahead ! Nothing, really, bothers me ! Besides, coming from you, it might even sound funny !

Reason - Don't you ever have some remorse for the burning of that wood to keep your stove working and in all those fiery flames ?

Thought - Your remark was, indeed, remarkable, and I have to admire you and praise you, my dear and respected Friend, for your undaunted courage in making that remark!

Reason - What I meant with it was if you felt sorry for violently destroying what might have been the recycled particles of another creature, the ones present in the wood that you were burning .

Thought - Not really, Sir Reason, because if those particles were the ones from another creature, they would not have been in the make up of the burning piece of wood, according to the wise selection of purpose of the so called, all wisdom, Mother Nature . I assure you that they were "wood" particles !

Reason - And one more good reason for praising you for your witty acceptance of a joke which reminds me of a similarly silly one, in ancient times .

Thought - Really ! It would be interesting to hear about it !

Reason - It occurred several centuries ago : do you still want to hear it ?

Thought - I would like to hear it : was it recycled ?

Reason - It was repeated over and over several times, since then!!!

Thought - Well ? How did it go ?

Reason - It's about a well known ancient Italian Poet by the name of Dante Alighieri who, being at that time a guest by a famous Family by the name "Cane", whcich in Italian means "dog",and, one day, being at the table, the Sir Cane, just for a joke, had instructed, secretely, his servant, to gather all the disposed bones from the meats, which, as customary in those days, were thrown under the table, and pile them all up at the feet of the chair where Dante was sitting . As, shortly afterwards, some of the servants pointed at the huge amount of bones near Dante's chair, Sir Cane, then, rose and pointed out, laughing, at Dante, ridiculing the enourmous amount of bones and all the meat that Dante must have eaten ! To which Dante, simply replied : " Had I been a "Cane" (a Dog), you wouldn't have seen all those bones near me ", and Sir Cane, the Prince, then honoured Dante for his good humour in accepting jokes on himself !....There you are !!

Thought - Curious incident, in those far away days ! Is it a true happening or just folklore ?

Reason - It is one of the many anecdotes surrounding the figure and the life of this famous poet and it is difficult to separate with veridicity true from false .

Thought - That's nothing unusual ! It seems to be the very norm every day around us !

Reason - And so it really appears to be ! Something like one thing goes out of the door and,then, it comes back again .

Thought- Something like it, I guess !

(.....then, to himself : " this neighbour, Sir Reason, must be a little "touched" , I am afraid...!.....)

Reason - Well, Sir Thought, now, I wouldn't want to be inopportune to the point of interfering with your programs and activities and your personal habits but, if you would like it , I would be very honoured to have you as my guest at my dinner table and in my modest home: all I can offer is a simple supper , in all honesty, but offered with sincerity .

Camilla - (...overhearing her Master comment about the "simple" supper offered to Sir Thought ....!!!...)
.....Simple supper !!!....Modest Home !!....Sir, you call what I prepared tonight and placed it on the table a....SIMPLE supper ???!!....What about the truffle, the capons, the eel, the trout, the ravioli and the cake ? Is all them, now, a simple supper ? Oh ! Mercy! The ingratitude of high up people !!

Reason - Camilla,You misunderstood the whole thing! None of anything that you suspect ! None whatsoever !!.....Please, do not become agitated because there really is no reason for being so !

(.....Then, turning to Sir Thought ......)

Well, Sir ,would you like to dine with me , this evening ?

Thought - Really, very kind, extremely kind of you, Sir , to ask me to sit with you at your dinner table but, really, I would dread to cause you and your sweet house maid, Camilla, any undue concern, but, on the other hand, I would not want to seem impolite and unappreciative of the honour of being invited to dinner , by declining such a spontaneously and generously offered invitation and be guilty of an insufferable hesitation in accepting it .

Reason - Oh ! Please, do not ever think for a moment about all those little hesitations ! My invitation comes straight from the heart and I am certain that my sweet Camilla will be proud to have for dinner such a reknown guest like you . It would really be a pleasure to share my supper with you , Sir Thought .

Thought - Very well, then, and, thank you, Sir. Your kind invitation is gladly accepted and with great pleasure and this congenial episode will mark a most serene end to our evening promenade .

Reason - That was good and it is going to be a refreshing evening for both of us. However, please, do not build up your hopes for an "out-of-this-World" type of supper,most of the time it consists of "in-this-World" type of supper ! .

Thought - Even a simple onion would taste as good as some truffle while in good company ! Besides, is the thought that counts !

Reason - Then, there is only one thing left to do !

Thought - And what, may I ask ?

Reason - But, Of course ! Toget into the house !

Tought - Excellent reasoning !!

Reason - But I overlooked to add two more things to the first one !

Thought - Really...??!

Reason - Yes : to sit at the table, number two and, have supper, number three !

Thought - Sir, you never seem to want to miss an opportunity to poke fun at any given situation !

Reason - Perhaps the evening walk primed up my appetite and I am anticipating what has not happened yet, and that is the actual supper !....So, then, Sir Thought, please, this way......let's go in....

Thought - I'll follow you, Sir !

Reason - Oh ! No ! You first, Sir !

Thought - You are the King , in your Kingdom, you ought to enter first !

Reason - But you are my revered Guest ! You ought to enter first !.....The"King"...after...!!

Thought - Thank you, "SIRE " !

(......upon entering they , inadvertently, bump into each other ......)

Reason - Oh ! Pardon me !!

Thought - Sorry ! I am so awkward !! You see, I am not used to be in other people's houses, particularly at the time of meals being served, when no one wants to have any thoughts about anything at all, except the food !.....Did by any chance, step on your shoes ?

Reason - Oh! No ! Well, the most important thing is that we are in and ready for a nice supper : aren't we, now ?......Camlla !.......Camilla !....But where did she go now ?

Camilla - (......coming back from the kitchen, with a steaming soup-turreen full of unbelievably heavenly flavour smelling ravioli.....) ....Here I am, Your Lordship, here I am, bringing in the just reheated ravioli...!!....You know, they had been on the table waiting for your coming back, got cold, so Ah has been, gone and done and warmed them up again !

Reason - Oh! That is wonderful, Camilla, but you need to set another chair and silver ware and plates for an extra guest, tonight !

Camilla - Is that so ?

Choir of the hidden, and invisibleThoughts - ....Believe it or not, it is so ! .....(....But nobody could hear them) !!)

Camilla - Really, a special Guest, Your Lordship ?

Reason - The most special there is, Camilla, and I am sure that you will like him !

Camilla - Oh ! Your Lordship, that he does not keep this poor ignorant and frail maid on a suspension agony ! Who is this special guest , your Honour, please ??

Reason - The Guest is Sir Thought, Camilla !

Camilla - Ah is misbelieving that that is true, your Lordship ! Why ! This is really something!! And He, Sir Thought , is right when he says that he was experimenting with the illuminations and the transmissions of the astralis !! Oh ! My, my...this is really funny !

Reason - Camilla, what's now ? What are you mumbling about ? Do you feel well ?

Thought - Hem...! Well....now, Lady Camilla is trying to say that ....

Camilla - Ah ! Sir Thought, Your Excellency,....uh!uh!....Don't you say nothing, please,that Ah is making a surprise, a big, big surprise for my Master about the discovery of the trasmission of the astrali !!

Reason - Camilla! What's come upon you !! What on Earth are you saying ??!..Trasmission of the.....astralis..????!!....Do you feel well, Camilla or ,may be, it was too hot in the kitchen and you worked too hard at preparing the supper !!

Thought - But, my good Camilla.............

Camilla - Ah ! Sir, Thought, Your Excellency, that you allows me to say what Ah want to say! Ah is very, very happy at this happening ! Very happy and very excited !
(........Then , turning towards her Master, Sir Reason......)
You see, Sir, Your Lordship, this whole scene is entirely magnificent !!

Reason - But, Camilla, my good woman, what is so mgnificent ???!!

Camilla - Your Lordship, Sir Thought is and everything that he experiments with, is too !!

Reason - Camilla, I do not understand a word you are saying and I am increasingly worried about you: may be you do not feel well and you are trying to cover it up by being over alert and talkative, isn't it ? Well, I hope it isn't !!......With all that is going on, the ravioli will be cold again if I don't sit at the table right now and start "ingesting" them !!

Camilla - Oh! Master, that Your Eminence do not worry! Your Camilla feels fine and *fully enflowrick* when thinking at how many........

Thought - Camilla, did you, perhaps, intend to say: " fully euphoric", did you ?

Camilla - Ah sure did that *enflowrick* word, I did! We, poor ignorant folks, has not the brain of Sir Thought, but only *worn out* shoes and *hard heads.*

Reason - "Rough boots"...!! Camilla, not *worn out shoes!* " *Scarpe grosse* ", in Italian, and "*cervello fino* ", that is "sharp mind" and not Hard heads!, So, in Italian, it goes this way: "Scarpe grosse, cervello fino"!..."*Rough boots, but sharp mind*" !!

Thought - Interesting. Is that why we are having ravioli, this evening?

Camilla - Yes, but no, Your Excellency, but them ravioli are not Italian: I just made them!

Reason - Never mind, Camilla: you are fine! Here, now, Sir Thought, the finest ravioli...!.

Camilla - Oh! Master, Your Excellency, You is too good to talk such fine talk to my ravioli! It is all happening, you knows, just because of all those *illuminated astralis..!*

Thought - "Enlightened abstract ideas", Camilla..!! **NO** *astralis*, and not *illuminated*, either!

Camilla - Oh! I understand. Ah is no good at putting words together, with no education, but Ah is still good at *catching happenings, you knows*, so...the *ideal extracts* have arrived..!

Thought - Ideas! Ideas, Camilla, not *ideals*, not *extract* either! ABSTRACT IDEAS, Camilla!!

Camilla - Thank you, Sir, for that! **Ideal...no...ideas**...but just the same, the two has almost the same sound....anyway, the *abstract idees*, as Sir Thought calls them, can be sent from one person to another just as birds do when they fly from one branch to another, so, as he says, if someone thinks of something, like: "I want this or I want that", Sir Thought thinks and transmits the *astralis* to another person's head, so that..........

Thought - Please, please, Camilla! Not again! "Abstract Ideas" and not ***astralis...***!!!

Camilla - Well, one or the other! Youse transmits them, anyway!....So, that person, do and goes as the other person *want* him to go or do with no problems. Is that not magnificent?

Reason - Camilla, I begin to wonder whether you might have worked too hard preparing supper and the heat from the stove must have caused you to become weak and distracted !!

Camilla — Oh! No, your Lordship! Ah is no weak and no sick IOn the contrarily, Ah feel as good as is Sir Fiddle, as they say.

Reason — But, Camilla, what kind of fantasies are you telling me at this hour of the night, instead of keeping on serving the follow-up dishes that you said had prepared for the supper?

Camilla — But, Sir Master, Your Lordship, would you rather listen to it from the mouth of Sir Thought, who is the one who was experimenting?

(... Then, turning to Sir Thought.....)

Sir, Your Excellency, would you, please, tell my Master about your experiments with the astrali and that it was you who was experimenting?

Reason — I hope, my dear friend and respected and most precious Guest, that you will be so kind as to forgive this intrusion of my sweet Camilla and this unexpected inconvenience! My Camilla is an exceedingly good person but, at the moment, she probably is afflicted with tiredness!

Thought — Oh ! Sir, please, do not worry for this negligible encounter which, instead, has pleased me ! Your Camilla is a good sweet woman and, as she was saying, a thought can be anywhere, therefore even in your Camilla's head !

Camilla — But, that you excuse me, Your Excellency, but you were asking me about the truffle, and the capons, and the ravioli and at what time my Master took his supper and all them things and I would tell you to see if Your Excellency could trasmit all those goodies, the thought of them goodies, I says, into the head of of my Master so that he might get the idee and invite you for supper in order to find out how you done it and tell him about the transmission of the astrali .

Thought — My good Camilla, experiment is a way by which we try to put a thought to good use, by testing it first and, if that original thought was good, then, slowly, precisely thiough the work of the experiment, it gradually will take hold and will be seen producing good results .

Camilla — Oh! Yes, Ypur Excellency, the experiment is quite sure producing good results and is having a very good function, as your Excellency will allow, becauseYour Excellency is now eating at my Master's table...!!!! Oh ! How excited Ah is ! Ah is in love with the experiment!

Thought — But certainly, Camilla, Certainly!

(.....Then, turning to Sir Reason..........)

You will excuse, I hope, this slight deviation of discourse with your sweet maid, while remembering our encounter, earlier, at the comer of the street, just when you came to find us.......... sometimes, things are interpreted in confusing ways by people not used to practiced thinking. Don't.ypu think so, Sir Reason?

Reason — Of course I doL.And do not worry about it and let us enjoy the rest of the supper!

Camilla - Yes, Your Lordship, and here comes the follow up to the ravioli but, I was to say, anyway, that youwill excuse me too for being so talking so much, but all Ah was wanting to do was to surprise your Lordship with the magnificent experimentof the transmission of the astrali, but I probably got things a little confused !! We poor ignorant kitchen maids , we never knows where to begin to tell things from the beginning....!

Reason - And where and when to end .

Camilla - Yes, Sir Master, what does you say ?

Reason - Nothing, Camilla : did you, by chance hear something ?

Camilla - No, but Ah is not sure : but I thought I heard some sound .

Thought - Perhaps a propicious sound, just in time to dissipate a little cloud that was threatening the approaching of some possible bad weather and was slow in clearing away......!!!

Camilla - Well, it is always like that, we poor ignorant people does not even hear anything, even when we is hearing something : no one believes in our ways and they all ignore us . But He, His Excellency, that sly Sir Thought, he talks again about clouds as when we was chatting at the corner of the square.....!

Chorus of the
Stones - Poor Camilla !

Chorus of the Questions
Affirmations and Conclusions - We are aware, at last, that, fortunately, we are close to a con- . clusion, tonight, and if they would keep on eating instead of talking so much, we could even look forwards to a good rest tonight !

Camilla - Here is the salad, Your Lordship, and I will follow soon with all the other dishes!

Thought - Ah ! The truffle and the capons, perhaps, Camilla ?

Reason - Truffle ?! Capons ?!...And, my dear and trusted Friend, but.....how did you know?!

Thought - An educated guess, just a trained thought .

Camilla - Yes, Sir Master, and You sees, now, for Yourself ,that I was right when I was telling You about the transmission of the astrali of His Excellency, Sir Thought !!

Reason - For goodness sake, Camilla, please, forget about all those stories or the supper, I am afarid, will be spoiled entirely !

Camilla - But, Master, excuse us, but ah was not trying to be disrespectful, believe you me, but the Truffle and them capons, was all that Sir Thought was telling me, that he was trying to transmit them thoughts to your head!

Reason - Yes, Camilla, Sir Thought had already explained to me during our evening walk, the synthesization of the subterranean ascomycetous fungus of the genus Tuber, and which begins to be formed by invisible particles called i-toms, which, when fully visible as a completed fungus, have been given the name of "truffle", by the common folks.

Thought - Pardon my intrusion, Honourable Reason, but I meant "atoms", not i-toms.

Camilla - Ah! The transmission of the *astralis*...!!

Thought - Camilla, the ravioli were excellent, the very masterpiece of a superb cook!

Camilla - My respectful thanks, Your Excellency! You really is able to judge that!

Reason - Very good these ravioli, Camilla. May be, just a little more......forse, solo un po'piu'di sale e pepe......I mean, just a little more of salt and pepper.

Thought - Your illustrious Master wants to show his command of the Italian language that he acquired when visiting that beautiful country.

Camilla - Does Your Excellency, Sir Thought, desire some more pepper and salt?

Thought - No, thank you, Camilla. To me, the ravioli tasted very good as you had served them: excellent aroma and taste. A real delight, Camilla, along with the buttered truffle!!

Camilla - Ah is very happy that *youse* is happy too: Sir Excellence.....and your *stimbactization* of the truffle from them "*i-tom partaclies* "!...Oh! You sly devil, you, Sir Thought!.

Reason - Camilla, please, do not forget to bring that claret wine that's really so palatable!

Camilla - Right up, Your Lordship: that good claret wine!

The Conclusions - If only some salt and pepper would follow, that would be"a conclusion", but, with the added claret wine, a conclusion of this charade is just a wishful thinking.

Chorus of the claret wines - We will induce those two jerks to fall asleep: Lordship and all...!!

The Choir of the Conclusions- Halleluhija!And blessed be the Lordship and the claret wine!

THE END

DIALOGUE
of
the Twig and the Flower
(*narrated in a personified manner for its protagonists*)
The Flower - The Twig - the nearby Oak tree - the foraging Bee - the Lady Beauty
****

Flower - Hey !...Twig...!!

Twig - Yes?

Flower - Yes, Twig: do you think that I am beautiful?

Twig - But, of course! You **ARE**...beautiful...!!

Flower - Thank you, Twig: you are very kind.

Twig - Flower?

Flower - Yes, Twig.

Twig - And how do I look to you?

Flower - A little skinny, may be?

Twig - Not only a little bit, but very skinny, I would say and very, very dry too, lacking any distinctive colours that would make me an object of attention. Like I am, I cannot possibly appeal to anybody, not even the bees, I guess...!!

Flower - Well, I think that you are very attractive to me: I see you thin, svelte, stylish and manly, without frivolities of adornments. You look very masculine...!

Twig - ....And very sad and depressed in a.... very masculine way!!

Flower - Oh, do not worry: that feeling is but a passing stage. Sometimes, along our separate roads, we all feel that way for a multitude of reasons, but, then, the dark cloud passes over and the sun shines again.

Twig - Thank you, dear and gentle flower, for your encouragement, but, you see, sunshine is good for beautiful creatures, yet, darkness is more appropriate and more protective for unsightly things like me.

Flower - But you are also beautiful: after all, beauty is what anyone wants it to be.

Lady Beauty - Did I hear someone calling me? I heard distinctly somebody mentioning my name. Somebody must have talked about me, but I don't see any soul around.

Flower - Of course we did call you. What's so strange about it?

Lady Beauty - ..."We"...did somebody say: "WE"...?!...We ...WHO?... I still do not see any soul around here...!!!

Flower - But, dear Lady, you are not looking in the right direction: just straight in front of you : can tou see us now? Of course, you do! I am a flower in company of a twig and, yes, we were talking about you. Did we, by any measure, bother you?

Lady Beauty - Oh! Gentle flower, not at all ! You and your precious friend did not bother me at all.....not at all... !!! I was just wondering who was he or she, who wanted to call me, because, usually, no one ever calls me: they, and "they" means whoever is there thinking that they see beauty somewhere!!....Anyway, they just stay there in awe, any time they see something they perceive as being beautiful and gaze and stare and look and sigh, but no one ever talks to me. That's why I appeared startled when I heard my name called out and I couldn't see anybody around.

Twig - Apparently we share a common fate! No one talks to me either!

Lady Beauty - But you just called me. Did you not?

Twig - I did not.

Lady Beauty - But then....WHO...?

Twig - May be the flower did.

Lady Beauty - "May be" the flower! But why doesn't he say so, if he did?

Twig - Search me! Everyone has his or her own ideas.

Lay Beauty - I hear you.

Twig - Good.

Lady Beauty - Thank you.

Twig - Don't mention it.

Lady Beauty - I thought so too.

Twig - So did I.

Flower - But what is the meaning of this silly talk, like kids in "kinder garten"! Why don't we, instead, invite Lady Beauty to converse with us and keep us company? After all, that would be the correct address, after mentioning her name...!!

Twig - Yes, I believe that your suggestion would be very nice, but I wonder if anyone and, of all creatures, Lady Beauty, would at all enjoy the company of a distorted twig.

Oak Tree - Stop complaining about your imperfections, twisted Twig, and look around, if you can, and you will see that you are not the only one in this world of ours to have some problems, whatever they may be.

Twig - I hear you, mighty tree, and I can go along with your admonishment only to a point because, you see, say, for example, that something would be amiss with you for whatever reason, there still would be a large amount of you left over to compensate for any fortuitous loss or any imperfection. Now, just look at me: all I have is misery, ugliness, dreariness and nothing more to compensate that sad picture with.

Foraging Bee- Ah! I should have known where those lamentations came from! A twig…!!...Just a twig..! It figures.

Twig - Well, what's so strange about a twig? Of course, I am a twig, you dim-wit of a dumb bee…!

Foraging Bee- I say, see one twig and you see them all! Besides, nothing to gain from them, not even a sniff of perfume that would promise with anticipation a possible source of good stuff and sumptuous nourishment, and that apart from the incivility of their vocabulary.

Twig - You are a selfish complainer, you stupid buzzing insect, all wrapped up in yourself just because you can produce wax and honey and, I bet, you do not even know that you are manufacturing that extraordinary production, you dumbbell of a buzzing bee, you…!!!

Foraging Bee- Actually, we do know, but we do not tell that to anyone, not even to our Queen.

Twig - And why not? As your Queen, I think that she should be entitled to know everything that goes on in her kingdom.

Foraging Bee- May be she is entitled to know all is there to be known in her kingdom and we agree with you on this, but we are afraid that, should she fully realize it, it might go to her head, and she would want to look around and aspire for more romantic and adventurous Don Giovanni's type of suitors than just our insipid drones.

Twig - Foraging Bee, do you think that my clean cut, tall and dark figure and my mysterious aspect, could interest your Queen?

Oak Tree - And how could that be…??!

Twig - Well, for one thing, it would be different, image wise, at least.

Foraging Bee- It would be different all right and very monotonous indeed your aspect rather than mysterious, and depressingly monochrome, I'd say!

Twig - Monotonous, monochrome, may be, yet, different, steady and enduring.

Foraging Bee- If you say so.

Twig - And, yet, you noticed me, recognized me for what I represent and you realized and were able to tell yourself that I was not what you were looking for and disappointment encouraged you to make disparaging remarks about my appearance, usefulness and productivity, because I just did not or could not satisfy your voracious appetite for your foraging. Yes, dear foraging Bee, yes, I am different.

Foraging Bee- You can say that again…!!...And you may also add : " And I am ugly too" !!

Flower - Gentlemen, gentlemen, please! And you, gentle foraging Bee, don't you know that variety is the spice of life?

Foraging Bee- I guess it all depends on what kind of variety.

Flower - On the contrary, dear foraging Bee, on the contrary! Variety does not depend on what kind of variety it is, because variety is variety and does not go by way of "what kind" of variety it is or it might be.

Foraging Bee- You don't say !

Twig - She does.

Flower - Look at me, gentle foraging Bee, look at us flowers: so many of us, so different, so colourful, so endowed with aromatic scents, and, then, look at anything around you and look at…….

Foraging Bee- I am looking and I was looking and I had been looking, but all I could see was an ugly, black coloured and shapeless dried out insignificant twig.

Twig - Watch your language, you impudent buzzing Bee, or I'll report you to your Queen. .

Flower - Foraging Bee, just listen to me, and never mind the Twig, because he is upset and you just listen to me.

Foraging Bee- O.K.

Flower - As I was saying, just look at anything around you, look at the jagged rocks of the mighty mountains : would you say that they are ugly and jagged? Of course, you wouldn't ! Why, creatures even risk their lives in trying to reach them and admire them!

Foraging Bee- Well, about those daring creatures risking their lives, I believe that, particularly in this case of jagged rocks and mighty mountains and unlike the flowers, we most definitively have a ***kind of variety*** among those daring creatures, in spite of what you had said about *variety*, insisting that variety is variety and no special "kind" of it. One thing is clear: I sure wouldn't want to go to those jagged mountains.

Twig - I saw your Grandmother foraging on scented mountain flowers on those jagged mountains, last year, you silly Bee!

Foraging Bee- There always is one in a crowd.

Flower - But listen: and what about +the vast oceans with thundering waves and turbulent tempests and, would creatures say that the oceans and the seas are dreadful, horrible and ugly? Of course, not, and they place themselves at their mercy, defying the ever presence of danger and death while justifying it with the infatuation of adventure.

Twig - It appears to me that Lady Beauty is able to penetrate and permeate the souls of the mighty oceans and the mighty jagged mountains, but it can capture the soul and the imagination of the flowers!.....Sheer fantasy, to me!

Lady Beauty - And why not, dear unbelieving friend? Fantasy relieves the worries of the day and it helps the mind to liberate itself from the boundaries of sadness and depression, I believe. Tell me, little Twig, has that ever occurred to you?

Twig - Hardly! You see, I am also figured as representing all of that !!

Lady Beauty - "*All of that...*" ??...What do you mean, dear friend?

Twig - Yes, Lady Beauty, exactly *all of that* !! Sadness, depression, despair, and a frigid, uneventful expression of nothingness!

Flower - To be depressed may be a natural inclination, at times, but it needs not be a ruke.

Twig - You may call it an inclination anything that just does not go quite right, but what should I say about my twisted, blackened limbs that Gentle Mother Nature bestowed on me? Should I say: "An inadvertent slip of the magic wand?", or " An unfortunate act of neglect ?", or " An unavoidable pay-off to accommodate someone else's fortunes ?". I just wonder.

Lady Beauty- Twig, you should not feel so down hearted about your unsightly limbs! They are beautiful! Anything is beautiful ! It all depends which way you look at things and in what kind of spirit you may be at the time thatyou are looking at something, but, most important, I believe, is whether your mind is inherently contoured to seek beauty, and embrace ***ME***.

Twig - Thank you for your encouragement, Lady Beauty, but where are the ***inherently contoured creatures,*** desperately seeking beauty in my not so glorious black limbs?

Lady Beauty - Why, many painters of Nature became famous after discovering you, admiring you for your unique looks and painting you into remarkable portraits, representing your slender, twisted and enigmatic profile of your limbs!

Flower - It is true, dear Twig, and those painters, now famous, stole the attention of the Art World, by representing you with the fascination of a beauty not ever imagined possible, decades before they started painting you.

Lady Beauty - The Flower is telling the truth, dear Twig!

Flower - Very, very true, indeed, dear Twig, and Lady Beauty speaks the truth, and it is so very true to the point that, for a certain period of time, these famous painters even neglected to paint flowers, in spite of their beautiful design and forms and variable soft shades of colours as well as bright vivid colours, and the great variety of their subtle hues, so different, so enticing, so captivating, but, instead, they rushed to paint you and immortalize you for ever, so much more favouring your dark, rigid and intriguing form, rather than our sensuous and suggestive lines and kaleidoscopic colours.

Lady Beauty - So, dear Twig, you see?!

Twig - Yes, I see, and I realize, also, while seeing it, how thin and foggy-gray must be the boundaries which confine the thin veil of vanity in the *enticing and colourful* world of flowers!

Lady Beauty - No, dear Twig, and I believe that, here, you are wrong.

Flower - I think so too, really. As a matter of fact, I think so too, "honestly".

Foraging Bee- The Twig misinterpreted the flower's redundancy in comparing the appealing beauty of a flower to that of a dry twig as a reason to explain the painters' rush to represent a twig instead of a flower.

Twig - I also see how different interpretations can be, depending on the nature of interest that various parties may have in interpreting and misinterpreting issues and declarations!

Lady Beauty - What do you mean?!

Foraging Bee- Undoubtedly, he means what he means with the conditional attachment that what he means may not be as clearly represented in his mind as it is in his diction.

Twig - All against me, right?

Lady Beauty - On the contrary, we are all bound and dearly interested in helping you!

Twig - Helping me!! That some news! Are you trying to make me sprout like a new seedling or embellish me with a bouquet of *sensuous and enticing, colourful flowers* ?

Lady Beauty - We are serious, Twig, and we don't play games and what we are interested to do is to show to you that your interpretation of your looks is not proportionate to the gravity that you seem to assign to it. That's what we are trying to do.

Flower - She is right, Twig. Lady Beauty told you straight and from the heart what we think of all this situation and I feel that you should take a careful heed of it.

Foraging Bee- That may be a difficult step for the Twig to take, his mind barricaded in a mood of no acceptance of any reason, possibly influenced by contacts with humans in his younger days.

Lady Beauty - Yes, Twig, why don't you tell us something more about yourself?

Twig - Something more…!!! Something more…WHAT..?...I am a twig: right? I am ugly: right? I serve no useful purpose: right? My limbs are dry, dreary and distorted: right? ….What other ***"something more"*** about my story should I add to myself…???!!

Foraging Bee- The real story.

Flower - The foraging Bee is right, dear Twig: the Bee is right and I can tell you why.

Twig - Why?

Lady Beauty - Go ahead, gentle flower, but use your fulgid colours and your inherent passionate, ardent and inspiring way of expression, that way of expression that only beautiful flowers can inspire, and tell the Twig the inalienable right to anybody's birthday and personal story.

Flower - I will.

Foraging Bee- There always is a personal story, just as there always is a birthday, of someone, somewhere, sometime, and the birds know that too.

Twig - I am waiting.

Flower - I thank you, dear Twig, for accepting our offer to try and shed some light into the obscure vision of your existence and thank you again for accepting my simple and humble approach in delivering that beam of light to you, simple and weak as that beam may be, yet, genuine and straight from the heart.

Twig - I am waiting.

Flower - Well, then, how is your memory, lately, Twig?

Twig - Very good, I think.

Flower - I am wondering, though, because by the way you mention things, something seems to be missing.

Twig - I wish there were many more ***things*** missing!

Flower - Well, for one, you keep on complaining about your distorted and dry and blackened limbs, but you never mention anything at all about the days of your early childhood, when you must have been all nice, fresh and green, before becoming an old, distorted, black twig in your old age.....right?

Twig - Ah! My childhood! Flower, never mind my childhood!

Flower - Twig, you seem to be too hard on yourself ! Every creature in this world of ours, has had a childhood.

Twig - Not I.

Flower - But how is that possible? May be you have forgotten about those times.

Twig - I wish I had forgotten: nothing, really, to be remembered.

Flower - But, dear Twig, at least, and I say, "***at least*** " , you must have remembered your Parents, at one time or another!....Or…may be, your Parents were not good to you?

Twig - I had no Parents.

Flower - WHAT…..??!!!

Twig - I had no Parents.

Flower - But that's impossible…!!!!!

Twig - Dear and perplexed Flower, my presence here should be confirmation enough that "that" ***is possible.***

Foraging Bee- Our Queen told us, one day, that, in this World of ours, many things that would seem at first impossible, oftentimes are possible.

Flower - Possibilities exist in our lives and that's true: we all are well aware of that and we see them happening every day, but events that defy the inalienable strict code of natural sequences are not governed by sheer chance of possibility.

Foraging Bee- Our Queen didn't elaborate on that point.

Flower - Twig, you probably do not remember and there is a chance that you might have been taken away from your Parents while still a fledgling seedling and never saw your Parents again, but you must have had some Parents, Twig…!!!!!

Twig - I had no Parents.

Lady Beauty - Do not be so pressing, dear Flower, with your bewilderment at our little Twig's answers: you just upset him more by acting that way and you may rekindle memories that might hurt his feelings and his pride.

Twig - Sometimes, a little ray of light can find its way through dark clouds.

Lady Beauty - Sure, and we will not bother you anymore, dear Twig, but I want you to know that we only meant well and that we were honestly concerned about your sadness.

Twig - Thank you, Lady Beauty, thank you for your understanding, and I, also, want you to know that what I said about my Parents, is true.

Lady Beauty - I believe you, dear Twig, and I respect your saying, but you should also understand that your answer created some unreconcilable confusion about that kind of issue.

Foraging Bee- Our Queen never brought up the issue of confusion: we seem to know very well where to go, always, without fail.

Twig - Smart aleck.

Flower - I am sorry, Twig, if I upset you with my inquisitive surprise at what you had said, but I respect your silence and we'll leave things as they are and let them fall asleep.

Twig - That is precisely what I would like to do, many a times: just fall asleep and forget all about my past.

Lady Beauty - That might help a little, some times, but not always if the past is still hard set in your memory with a tight grip and a tireless perseverance, like the issue of your Parents. But, there again, clouds are only shadows, soft or menacing, at times, but, eventually, they'll float away.

Twig - My clouds never did.

Lady Beauty - May be you didn't want them to float away, dear Twig!

Flower - Now, who is *pressing* our little Twig??!

Twig - Dear Flower, Lady Beauty spoke well and I understood what she said to me and how she tried to explain things to me and I did appreciate her trying to help me and this recognition does not limit my appreciation to her alone but I fully extend to your interest in trying to find out the possible cause hidden in my past, as being the possible cause of my terseness in my answers or in no answers at all, but, what I said and what I did keep on saying, about having no Parents, is true.

Flower - I understand, little Twig, and I thank you for showing kindness to me and you need not say another word about it all and I wont ask any more questions about it.

Lady Beauty - You are kind, little Twig.

Foraging Bee- When things go his way, of course.

Lady Beauty - I don't think so, Foraging Bee, and you shouldn't have made such an untoward remark because our little Twig, now I know, may definitely have some personal and sentimental reasons, distressing as they may be, and, yet, unable to escape the grip on his mind, memories, perhaps, which disturb him deeply and, likely, have disturbed his normal life for quite sometime.

Twig - And, *again,* thank you Lady Beauty for your judicious intuition, and my past, indeed, disturbed my existence and it still pains me now.

Lady Beauty - Life has its pitfalls, its pinnacles, its abysses an its lofty mountains and regardless at which of these locations it encounters you, it will always carry an entry fee to those premises, totally unconcerned of which one to whoever will come by. Your location must have been one of uncharted waters and left alone to fend for yourself.

Twig - And so it was, Lady Beauty.

Lady Beauty - I am sorry, Twig, if, and quite inadvertently, I brought back to you sad memories with my unwary comments.

Twig - Sad memories belong to the past. The reminiscence of the facts connected to those memories, that reminiscing is what creates the sadness.

Lady Beauty - Oh! Dear Twig!!

Twig - Yes, the reminiscing is what creates the sadness.

Lady Beauty - Oh! my dear Twig, if I could only be able and even try to alleviate that distressing and constant reminder of what must have been a tormenting disappointment or an unfulfilled expectation in your memory…!!!! If I only could know its dark secret…!!!!

Twig - No secret, Lady Beauty: I was an illegitimate branchlet. I never knew my real Trees.

Flower - Oh! Dear Twig! You make my petals fade away and wither!!

Twig - Don't blame me for that, fading Flower!....I did not ask you to investigate my life.

Flower - But , now that I did with the encouragement of Lady Beauty and the foraging Bee, I feel better and I feel closer to you than I would ever have suspected it possible before.!......Oh! Twig!....You make my petals fade away…!!!

Lady Beauty - On the contrary, my dear, on the contrary! It is love that colours your petals and your proclaimed love for our unhappy Twig will restore and enhance the colour of your petals with even more varied and brilliant hues.

Foraging Bee- Our Queen never ever mentioned anything like that to us, ever!

Lady Beauty - And, yet, she must have known something about it, by the way her subjects are able to produce such extraordinary sweet nectar.

Flower - Perhaps, for the Bees, an explanation is not necessary about love, because they may be just the expression of it, I guess.

Twig - Love! Yes, Love! That state when the mind becomes obscured by the brilliance of an infinite joy and vacillates between reality and a dream world! If only I could have experienced that even for one single moment!

Flower - But your single moment is right here, now, dear Twig, among all of us, with the love that we all feel for you! Even the foraging Bee will concur in this expression of sincere sentiment for you, dear Twig. I….I, dear Twig, feel so distressed about your past!!

Twig - Don/t feel so distressed about me, little, gentle Flower: I am not alone in this state of affairs, and I am in a very good company, sadly and unfortunately, of many like me, and you can ask the foraging Bee!

Foraging Bee- Sentiment and sympathy, yes and may be, but as to illegitimacy, not me, not us..!! We are always very careful in our visiting assignments to prospective Parents and siblings, in our scouting of flowering trees, flowers, various other plants and so on, and so on, always very careful to pick on the right and secure path. We, actually, are socially and legally propense creatures

Twig - No blame is passed on to you, dear little foraging Bee, no blame at all…!!

Foraging Bee- Twig?

Twig - Yes, foraging Bee?

Foraging Bee- Twig, what's a "branchlet"…?

Flower - Yes, I was wondering too about that word!

Lady Beauty - And so did I but, under these circumstances of sadness and discouraging reminiscing, I hesitated to inquire about it, but, I too, am curious about that word!

Foraging Bee- Please, Twig, wont you tell us what is the meaning of that word , so that I can refer to our Queen on this extraordinary encounter?

Twig - But, of course, I will: nothing so difficult or strange, really, The word me……….

Flower - May be not so strange to you, but very much so to us, because we have never heard it spoken in our midst. What does it actually mean?

Twig - The word "branchlet" means a ***small branch growing from a larger one***. It was in use in years past, in a land called England, where the English language is spoken.

Flower - Ah! Interesting!

Twig - You, possibly, could call it an"offshoot".

Foraging Bee- That's why you call yourself an "illegitimate branchlet"!!... Now I understand!

Lady Beauty - Foraging Bee, your comment was not appropriate, in my opinion and it was not rewarding for the kind and open-hearted openness of our dear Twig, who was mentally and emotionally generous enough to confide in all of us his most personal feelings. Sometimes, dear foraging Bee, inaccuracy in the correct answer to a sudden perception, can be crueler than a direct affront, because it underscores ignorance of somebody's inner feelings.

Foraging Bee- Our Queen never lectured us on this subject. I will report to her immediately about this new interpretation on the pollination of things the moment I shall return to my domiciliary and, thank you, Lady Beauty, for bringing to me this interesting aspect on communications.

Twig - I can't stand these ignoramus nincompoops types of creatures…!

Lady Beauty - Don't let that upset you, dear Twig: just a sharp curve in the long road of our existences.

Foraging Bee- Twig?

Lady Beauty - Foraging Bee, don't you think that you have already aggravated our dear Twig enough, to impose on him again with something else?

Twig - Oh! Dear Lady Beauty, let the little Bee ask what she wants! At this stage of our conversation, I feel that I have reached a more relaxed feeling about myself through your kindness and your interest in my past story. So, I do not mind being asked questions, anymore!

Flower - That's very sweet of you, dear Twig. It really is!!

Twig - Thank you, gentle flower and……and I just happen to note that your petals are not faded, on the contrary, are brighter than ever!

Flower - The intrinsic intensity of your story did it, dear Twig! …And I would like to hear some more and let my petals become the brightest ever in all the world of ours.

Foraging Bee- Twig?

Twig - Yes, foraging Bee?

Foraging Bee- Twig, may I ask you one more question?

Lady Beauty - Foraging Bee!! What did I just told you???!!

Twig - Lady Beauty, please, do not feel uneasy about the loquacity of our here friend, the foraging Bee: he is just curious and he has never been exposed before to such circumstances, therefore he has become anxious to find out the meaning of all this new environment and, most probably, in the end, much to his disenchantment.

Lady Beauty - Very well, then, if that pleases you, dear Twig, and I will not interfere anymore.

Foraging Bee- Twig?

Twig - Yes, foraging Bee: what is it?

Foraging Bee- One more favour, Twig, and I'll be on my way, but could you, please, explain to me the meaning of that word that I used while defining myself and my genus?

Twig - But, of course I will try, dear foraging Bee! But, why did you use it at all, if you did not know its meaning? That is what " **I** " would like to know…!!!!

Foraging Bee- An old Savant Bee, friend of the Queen, used to say that word while instructing us young bees in the fine art of well organized social behaviour, which would produce unimaginable wealth through the free effort of everybody in the community.

Twig - And what was that word, dear Bee? I don't quite seem to recall it right now!

Foraging Bee- It was "propense".

Twig - An old word, again, but perfectly correct, except being, now, classified as "archaic".

Foraging Bee- Thank you, Twig, you are very kind, indeed, and what.....

Twig - I know! And : "What does archaic" mean!!...Right?

Foraging Bee- I wouldn't have dared to ask, unless you had come up with what you just came up....!!!!

Twig - "Archaic" means something marked by the characteristics of an earlier period. That is the classification given in major dictionaries that I have used in my school days. I guess, you would say, in today's usage, "antiquated".

Foraging Bee- Thank you, Twig.

Flower - I have to admire your seemingly inexhaustible patience, dear Twig, and so graciously versed in kindness towards others!

Twig - I learned kindness when I was very young, a small child, yet, and lonely and yearning for a sign of tenderness and friendship and attention and even love, if anywhere available...!!

Flower - And when did all of that come your way, dear Twig? When did something, or some happenings, or someone, show you the silent and inherent power of kindness??! Did you call out for it, crying, may be, or did a **magic wand** wield the elusive world of make believe into coming true?

Twig - It was simpler than all that and much more of a normal, everyday type, natural way. You see, I grew up alone in my childhood and early infancy and survived an uncertain existence only because a gentle, sweet and pleasantly richly green Ivy, one day, came very close to me, liked me, came ever so closer and, one day, she embraced me in her tender spires and protected me from the fierce sun with her generous leaves.

Flower - Oh!! Twig...!

Twig - From that day, and on, we became very close friends and, one day, we decided to continue to live our lives together and we then grew together in that wondrous embrace.

Flower - Oh! Twig...!!!

Lady Beauty - Twig, you did find, then, love, friendship and affection, and that was wonderful and I feel so happy for you, but, dear Twig, my happiness is somewhat damped by looking at you here all alone: what happened to your beloved Ivy? Did she leave you? I could hardly even think of that!!

Twig - In a way she did: she died.

Flower - Oh! Oh!!....Twig…!!!

Lady Beauty - It saddens me to hear you announcing her demise, dear little Twig, and I know how distressful her departure from your side must have been for you, now alobe again, old and forlorn! Oh! Twig, how cruel our existences can be!

Foraging Bee- Such departures happen all the time in our house but we do not pay much attention to it: there are so many of us around, a few more or less are ever hardly noticed.

Flower - I believe that the time is getting a little late, dear Foraging Bee, so I would think that now would be advisable for you to leave your rendezvous and return to your lodgings: you will certainly have a lot to tell to your friends there!!

Lady Beauty - Flower, why don't you let our little foraging Bee and her inherent inclination and propensity at showing off the commentator-type of erudition and take a pause while, may be, picking up a few more morsels of your nectar and then you could send our foraging Ambassadress to…….to the Beehive, I guess, where she most satisfactorily belongs to.

Foraging Bee- Yes, is getting late, indeed, and we all must have lost the track of time, while engaged in our animated conversation, and an important and revealing conversation that was!!

Flower - But it seemed to me that you had failed on several occasions, during our conversing, to appreciate the issues at hand and their correct meaning. How could you, now, focus so sharply on them by proclaiming their importance and worthiness…??!

Foraging Bee- Nature has, yet, unidentifiable ways of explaining certain procedures, in certain creatures, in diverse situations. Well, yes, is getting late, folks, and we, as a rule, are early to bed and early to rise type of beings.

Lady Beauty - A very healthy habit that is, dear foraging Bee and we would really like to prolong this interesting conversation but it is getting late for us too, so , the logical thing to do would be to say goodnight and retire for a good night sleep. Don't you think?

Flower - But the foraging Bee has not answered my question clearly, yet….and in full !!

Twig - I am sure that she will, so much inclined as she is in sophisticated commenting!

Flower - I don't care what kind of commenting that is or could be: besides, my dear Twig, your sadness, your recriminations about your childhood and your old age, do not necessarily give you the license to be so persistently critical of our foraging Bee, and why you keep on doing it, even after helping him in understanding the meaning of words, is incomprehensible.

Twig - Habit.

Flower - And **ALL** I was asking was an explanation of the foraging Bee's sudden change in perception, a feature she had not even come close by a million moons throughout our conversation: **THAT** is what I am extremely curious about and I would hope that the foraging Bee would give it to me: an answer!

Foraging Bee- The answer, my dear flower, lies in my Beehive.

Flower - Foraging Bee, I was hoping to hear something from you and not from a Beehive.

Twig - I told you so…!!

Flower - But, my dear foraging Bee, please, be reasonable and a little cooperative: how can a Beehive, possibly, give me an answer…???!!

Foraging Bee- I didn't say that the Beehive would give you an answer. I said that the answer **"lies"** in **the Beehive and <u>not</u> that the Beehive will give you the answer.**

Lady Beauty - Foraging Bee, our little, gentle flower, may be a little confused, probably tired, so wouldn't you try to help her and answer her so much desired question and explain it to her?

Foraging Bee- But, of course I will, and I will consider it an honour and, more than that, a pleasure, to do so.

Lady Beauty - Thank you, foraging Bee.

Foraging Bee- Beehives, of course, my dear Flower, do not speak and do not think, but they buzz with the incessant activity of a great number of bees, by the genus of Apis Mellifera, busy bees, those indefatigable workers, who produce wax, honey, eggs and the essentials of life.

Flower - But, foraging Bee, what kind of an answer is this to my question of your amazing and sudden sparkling surge in your ability to perceive notions, after an initial appearance, in our conversation, of a seeming intellective torpor on your part?

Foraging Bee- Dear Flower, I just told you and I repeated it twice as well:" the answer lies in the

Beehive, didn't I…?

Flower - Yes, you did, but I am not really able to fully grasp its meaning, dear foraging Bee!

Foraging Bee- You cannot "grasp" its meaning…!!...And WHO can…???! And neither can I, nor anyone else can. How are you going to explain with absolute certainty the process of wax making and honey producing by small little winged insects of the genus Apis Mellifera by the simple use of some nectar that we pick up from flowers like you?

Flower - But there must be some form of mechanisms inside the Beehive, which will take care of the manufacturing of the honey from the materials that you gather and bring into the Beehive, right?

Foraging Bee- There are no manufacturing machines in the Beehive, my dear Flower, and there are no chemical facilities to distill, to separate, to amalgamate, to combine any materials or the primary one that we collect from flowers like you, and that goes without mentioning the geometrical precision in building our premises and storage areas for the honey and the eggs.

Flower - That is fine and it is a wonder, we all know that. What intrigues me is your sagacity, suddenly springing to life from an apparent initial indifference.

Foraging Bee- Keen perception, I guess, is proportional to anyone's specific interest. Had I been more interested in your topics in the conversation, probably my "intellective torpor", as you describe it, might have woken itself up to my present *sagacity*…!!

Flower - But you didn't even seem to show any affectionate or even a simple emotional response to the sad story of our little Twig and the sad departure of his dearest companion, didn't you?

Lady Beauty- Flower! Don't you think that you have already taxed our little and kind foraging Bee enough with the somewhat anxiously uncivil request of yours about someone else's way of thinking which, in this case, it reflected our foraging Bee's "thinking", by criticizing her questionable response to Twig's sad story…??!

Flower - I am always accused of causing untoward reactions to various creatures, be those reactions joyful, mournful, sensuous, provoking, reminiscent, sentimental or none of the above, but always inducing some sort of an unusual reaction to the recipients by my sudden appearance, either as a single unit of me or in a bouquet, or as a commemorative wreath, these last two arrangements made up of many and varied images of "like-me" samples..! I am sick and tired of this kind of stereotyped representation.

Foraging Bee- Do not irk yourself over this little detail, dear gentle Flower: you see, you may be right, Lady Beauty may be right and our friend, the Twig, may be right too! And, I am asking, who is here among us, so mighty to tell anyone what's wrong or who's wrong?

Twig - It sounds something like Judgment Day!!

Lady Beauty - Please, Twig, won't you try to abstain from picking at our little foraging Bee at a time when everything seems to come into shape and into a pleasant, fruitful and sensible conversation so that a good memory of it could remain in our minds? After all, it is nothing more than a token conversation.

Twig - As our foraging Bee just said "you may be right", so, Lady Beauty I'll bow to your kind reminder and I'll desist from this silly habit of mine which I had picked up since my companion died and left me alone, leaving me desolated and irritable.

Lady Beauty - That's understandable and many of us, probably, would have felt the same under those circumstances and in view of your background, but, since we have rekindled now the old memory of your sad past and the demise of your faithful and loving companion, tell us, dear Twig, if you would, what did your existence turn out to be after the lovely Ivy passed away?

Twig - Oh, yes! What did my existence turn out to be…! Miserable, indeed, dear Lady Beauty, an existence of loneliness, depression and sorrow, so that, slowly, I became sick without her protection and I aged prematurely, became old, lost all my leaves, all of my skin and turned out to be the unglamorous figure that you now see of myself.

Flower - No, Twig, you are not unglamorous: you are grand in your sad history and you have now assumed the clear cut image of a well delineated figure standing sharp against the sky as a source of inspiration to suffering and enduring with your dark, distorted limbs proudly standing there, witnesses to your courage and love.

Twig - The courage and love were the blessings of my beloved Ivy's treasured disposition and celestial affection: mine was just her blessing upon me.

Lady Beauty - And blessed are your words, dear Twig, that Ivy inspired in you.

Twig - I loved her. I lost her. I still love her very much.

Flower - Oh! Dear, dear Twig…!!!!

Foraging Bee- No further comments from me, dear folks, because, when the subject reverts to the quick sands of the unfathomable land of love, the average mind seems to lose its bearings and reason fails.

Flower - But we should still be able, at least, to say goodnight to one another and wish all the folks here present the best for the next day and do so before we might run the danger of losing our bearings and run afoul with our reason.

Foraging Bee- It sounds reasonable, although it is not the general practice in our midst. I will go along happily, though, with your proposition, dear Flower, since this has been a most pleasant interlude in my busy day-work schedule and, I am certain, just as pleasant for all the other partners, this evening, in our conversation.

Twig - Hear! Hear!

Lady Beauty - But you had promised, dear Twig that........

Twig - I really meant "HEAR", this time, but **NOT** in reference to what the foraging Bee had just said, but because of a loud buzzing noise coming from somewhere.....and look!.... look! Do you all see that cloud coming towards us..??!!

Flower - A cyclone? A tempest? but I heard no thunder and saw no lightning! A dust storm, may be??!....Oh! This is terrible...!!! And all my companions here, these beautiful flowers!..Oh! What will happen to us..!!...We will all be destroyed...!!

Foraging Bee- Please, please, Folks, do not panic like this and do not anticipate doom before you know that doom is imminent!

Flower - But....but....that threatening cloud...???!!

Twig - The cloud is getting closer and the buzzing has increased by a hundred fold...!!!

Foraging Bee- There is no threatening cloud, dear Flower, but only a scout of foraging Bees from my Beehive, flying here to pay homage to all of you Folks, for having been so kind in entertaining me in your conversation and, most particularly, to make the personal acquaintance with you, dear Flower, and with all of your flower companions in this perfumed and delightful garden.

Flower - This is astonishing, dear foraging Bee, but how on "earth" did these foraging Bees from your Beehive, know that you and we were here and that we were kind to you...???!!

Foraging Bee- Because, my dear Flower, the answer is still in that Beehive.

Flower - I really begin to believe it, now!!

Foraging Bee- Goodnight, Folks, may be we'll see each other again, sometime.

Twig - Goodnight, foraging Bee.

Lady Beauty - Goodnight, foraging Bee.

Flower - Goodnight, foraging Bee.

Foraging Bee- So long, dear and gentle Flower and I'll be back, sometime, may be even very soon. I am very attracted to your beautiful colours, your soft petals and your nectar, dear Flower and you look superbly beautiful in your magnificent garden.

Flower - But isn't it a sign of love? Isn't it, dear foraging Bee?......Foraging Bee?.....Please, foraging Bee, answer me!

Lady Beauty - The moment he heard you pronounce that word, "love", she took off at an unimaginable speed as if startled by an impending danger! I wonder why.

Flower - Yes, and I know why....the quick sands of the unfathomable land of love!

Lady Beauty - What are you talking about?

Flower - Nothing, really: just a glimpse of an old story, known since the beginning of the world and, who knows, may be even before the beginning of the world. Goodnight, Lady Beauty.

Lady Beauty - Goodnight, Flower.

****

THE END

DIA LOGUE

of the Patience and the Arrogance with the Young Tree
with the participation, also, of Tolerance
(beginning with the soliloquy of the Arrogance)
(and personifying the various characters .)
****

Arrogance - Ah ! What a beautiful day !....What a Beautiful day...and I could reiterate my exclamatory effusion on and on and still not quite fully paying justice to this glorious weather !....It's Spring time, I know, and the pines on those far away hills stand out so clearly and neatly against the blue sky !...And the sky is so blue !! The air is saturated with the intense perfume of a thousand flowers that almost overwhelms the very breathing !...The sun, the glorious light, the gentle breeze bring about to me a feeling of happiness and I cannot refrain myself from gazing over and over, again and again, at all this glory of Srping colours and sights, to the far away hills and to the wide plains that spread out from the end of this forest and stretch farther as the eye can reach to the folds of those far away hills . Ah ! So serene and pure is this day, so luxuriant of vegetation and new life bursting un-impeded with a majestic embrace from all sides that I cannot spare myself to miss even a single instant of all this glory !...It is, indeed, a very pleasant day, the weather is mild and the temperature is not hot, just enough warm to lull anyone into a gentle relaxation and to seek some shade and enjoy the gentle breeze that seems to solicit you to stop and rest a while but, at the same time, does not discourage you to continue your leisurely walking should you so desire instead to stop and rest . Really, a beautiful, or, I'd rather say, a magnificent day !! So, let me get back on the road, and I believe that I have rested long enough to be walking efficiently on my journey . I seem to see a small farm cottage a short distance from the edge of the end of these woods and on the bank of a small river that seems to wriggle its way between two small hills as if they were trying, but unsuccessfully, to kepp it all to themselves !......But, now, before leaving, what shall I say to this here little tree that sheltered me from the sun in its comfortable shade ,while I was resting in the middle of my walk through this forest ?....Shall I say, in an effusion of loving gratitude :" Oh ! You, simple and mute creature of Nature, slender and shady, I wish you could hear my talking to you and my giving you Thanks for restoring my strength in your refreshing shade in the middle of my long walk..."......and this expression of my revered appreciation would, anyway, be carried away by the gentle breeze, I being the only sender and receiver of that kind formulation, in essence a self-proclaimed recognition of my exquisite sensi-tivity,so well embodied in my personality that even I, myself, am very proud of it, even if such a deduction might encounter some opposition at being recognized as such.....in a civilized World !....So, you simple and mute creature of Nature, slander and shady, I shall depart from your comfortable shade and I will say to you, regardless whether my words will be carried away by the gentle bree- ze, I will still say to you :" So long, gentle tree, born happily in this forest , green and shady,and doomed to die,one day, along the path of your earthly life, a day yet far away but, even then, Nature did not seem to have granted you the faculty of speech, whether that is a gift or a curse it is still hard to define, nevertheless a way of expressing oneself, unless the rustling of your leaves is your natural speech and, if so, a gentle and more pleasant form of speech, indeed !........In a way, Nature was wise not to provide you with a mouth, a throat and vocal cords !....Too many of them has Mother Nature already produced of all forms,sizes and resonances and the amplification of their sounds debatable , to say the least ....!.......Well, so long, young little tree, with your gentle rustling of your green leaves in the evening breeze : slender as you are, yet you provided a wonderful shelter for me from the sun's rays and so you deserve my respect and my affection : so long, then, and good luck to you !

Young Tree - Thank you, O vague wayfarer, and best wishes for your travel !

Arrogance - Ah ! How stupid of me...!!....I should have remembered that according to the Little People's stories and the fables of ancient times, Old Spirits dwell in trees in the vast, obscure and mysterious forests and that trees have, also, a soul as confirmed by Gnomes and Leprechauns who live and have lived in those forests for thousands of years....!!.........

Young Tree - Yes, they have lived amomg us for a very long time and they are our best friends .

Arrogance - Well, I am glad, in a way, dear little tree, that you have reminded me of the soothing echoes of those far away times when some consideration was still fashionable for courteous address among living creatures,You and I included, of course, and so different and disheartening from the prevailing anxieties of modern times and the unbounded fervor of expediency in lieu of a more relaxed and distinguished expression of politeness..................

Young Tree - It is not only I, O vague wayfarer, that feels that way : the entire Forest does too !

Arrogance - What I meant was the alienation.......well, the disenchantment, I mean, from the fascination of the forests of old with their alluring images and the suggestion of tantalizing thoughts mixed with that eerie feeling of mystery of that fantasy that was so pervasive of ancient ideation and folklore ....Yes, my dear young and little tree, I am deeply impressed with your kind answer in acknowledging my farewell greetings to you as I was preparing to leave and I praise your linguistic skills and well reserved and polite answers, yet.........

Young Tree - Thank you, O vague wayfarer : you are kind...........Sorry to have interrupted you ! Really sorry !!

Arrogance - Oh! Do not worry about that : your appreciation of what I had just said to you was more than worth its weight in return ! But, yes, what I was just starting to say was that yet I cannot help wondering about your soul, provided that you do, indeed, harbour one within your wooden frame and I do not seem able to reconcile myself at the thought of your soul, as I said, if you do have one, being kept so tightly inprisoned in your hard frame, denied any freedom of movement, without any emotional expression, except in the waving of your branches in a gentle breeze or in the stormy weather !

Young Tree - It never occurred to me to think that way .

Arrogance - That's probably why you are made of hard wood : I surmise .

Young Tree - May be , but no one ever told me about it . Probably, they just forgot .

Arrogance - Oh ! You little innocent tree, I was just teasing you ! Besides, don't you ever forget that creatures never ever miss a good opportunity to tell nasty things to other creatures...!!.....And, trees are no exception !.......Anyway, I was going to add that my sister...you know......Lady Impudence, would probably refer to your blessed soul as a : " damn of a soul ", but, of course, everybody knows that , unfortunately, she does not have any sense of decency and, probably, after having caused such an insolent rudeness towards you, she would turn around and casually say : " Oh ! Dear little tree, catch me, if you can..." !!!....Really shameless, my Sister, I tell you !...And "shameless" is putting it gently !

Young Tree - I do not know your Sister, o vague Being wandering in our forest and I have not heard of her, ever . You see, news seldom come to these vast and solitary wooded lands and those which might occasionally reach us are easily dispersed among all those leaves and branches and no one ever hears of them anymore .

Arrogance - A miserable existence without news, dear little tree, I would guess .

Young Tree - Oh ! No ! A peaceful one, instead , I believe . To your way of thinking it may sound a little bit naive of me to say that, but, in this Forest, that's how we feel .

Arrogance - Well, I can tell you one thing : my sister Impudence , she certainly is not on the naive side of things, and that's "for sure".....!!!

Young Tree - I hear you. But, then, if that is how she is, let her be herself : obviously, she could not be anything else becase she already is what she is , so , there must have been a good reason for her to be as she is and it does not really matter if the reason was a good one or a bad one for her to come out as she is, because the fact stands by itself that she is as she is , so , why worry about her ?

Arrogance - Nobody's worrying, you simple little wood, we just bring up and out things about various creatures and comment on their "critical" specifications......and that is a pretty normal attitude and disposition among all sorts of creatures : the ever tempmting tendency at criticizing and belittling everyone and everything , but one's self .

Young Tree - That condition is not familiar to me, o vague traveller .

Arrogance - I see !....You,"vague" little piece of wood , still in your green phase of adolescence....!!.....But, tell me now : is there anything at all in this Forest that "might", just, just might, be familiar to you...??!......And I wonder !

Young Tree - Yes, o vague Traveller, there is : actually, there are .

Arrogance - You don't say !!

Young Tree - I realize that you may not be interested or at all care to listen to what is familiar to me but, since I have nothing else to do, the day is fine and I am here to stay, I'll tell you anyway and listening to it will be entirely up to you since you can walk and do not have to stay here near me .

Arrogance - On the contrary, little Tree : now that you have put it that way I have become curious to hear your side of the story : how about it, then ..?

Young Tree - Ah!Then, to me the fresh, pure air flowing through my branches, the chirping of thousands of birds,my leaves and branches accompanying their chanting with broad ondulations, and, then, the nourishing rain, the invigorating sun rays, the.......

.Arrogance - Fabulous, indeed !....But tell me, now, you little chunk of wood, are there any poets among your "familiar"....representations that would be able to express in mighty rhymes "the swelling" scenes you just decsribed, like that ancient great Poet did, if I recall correctly, in Jolly Old England when he was jotting down his "familiar" impression of Henry the Fifth ??!

Young Tree - I am sorry, O vague Traveller, but I am not able to follow you in what you are saying and the names you are mentioning : you see, there are no schools in this Forest, no teachers come here to teach and, if they do come, it is only to rest under the shade of one of us trees, just as you did .

Arrogance - I can see : an immense forest of ignoramus Trees .

Young Tree - I don't know that name either, o vague traveller, or the ones you had mentioned before about something being jolly somewhere: would there be other names "familiar" to me which I might recognize and , so, be able to answer your question ?

Arrogance - Ah ! Forget it !..." I "am the one who is fast becoming "familiar" with the prevailing intellective atmosphere of this Forest !!....So , let's change the subject or go back to what we had been talking just a while ago : shall we ?

Young Tree - But of course, traveller !...Why not ?....And I do remember what we were talking about, then : wasn't it about your Sister ?.....Right ?

Arrogance - I am surprised at the accuracy of your memory, my dear green piece of wood, and so right it was what we"was"talking about : my Sister, exactly!!...........Oh! She is really something else, I assure you, and insolence, rudness and brazenness are just heavenly characterizations when compared to her barefaced audacity !

Young Tree - Those are big words you are saying, o vague Traveller, and my branches are not spread out wide enough yet to catch those words'meaning and weight as they pass through . I believe, though, by the way you are representing them, that they must be important in your life .

Arrogance - Not in mine, you ninny of a green tree, but in the life of the many stupid creatures who roam the surface of this planet .

Young Tree - Planet....??

Arrogance - Don't tell me, now, that you are not even "familiar" with the place where you live!!!

Young Tree - Oh ! I know that ! I am living in a forest : is Planet, now, the name of this Forest ? Strange . I never heard it mentioned before by any other travellers .

Arrogance - One thing I am asking myself and that is how and why did I have at all to come through this forest and rest here !!!

Young Tree - Are there better forests than our, o vague traveller ?

Arrogance - Smarter, yes and that's "for sure " .

Young Tree - Are they far away from here ?

Arrogance - They are all over this planet .

Young Tree - Now, there you go again with difficult words . Oh ! I wish we would stay on the original simple subject about your Sister !

Arrogance - That subject is not simple either, if you knew the entire truth about it .

Young Tree - There is, again, another word I am not familiar with: is this word,"truth", something similar to our evening breeze?

Arrogance - Most of the time it appears to be and unobtrusively blowing in from nowhere and most of the time....at the wrong time too...!! It is not a type of breeze that you would welcome as a pleasurable relief from a hot day and it is not a popular item among living creatures with two legs supporting a small sized brain, and it is easily dispersed as a "breeze non grata"...and happily so ...!!

Young Tree - Ah ! That's neat !.....Now, as that breeze flows through, does it bring some welcome relief to those two legged creatures' branches ?

Arrogance - Hardly ever : it only brings trouble !!

Young Tree - That breeze must not be as good as our is . Is it a morning or evening breeze ?

Arrogance - It has no specific timimg and comes along swiftly, sometimes, and even blowing with unrelented fury .

Young Tree - That's a hurricane.....!

Arrogance - To some, it's even worse : it is then, when insolence, rudness and brazenness explode in a furious pandemonium of frantic efforts to lie about the truth . Ah ! That's the moment that my Sister is waiting for and charges into the fray with boundless glee....!!

Young Tree - Does your Sister also uses those big words you just mentioned as she charges into the fray ?

Arrogance - She uses them and she practices them exceedingly well and consistently: "Insolence , Rudness, Brazenness " are Her business credentials ! After all, isn't her name Impudence ?

Young Tree - Inconsistencies and deviations, from the ususally accepted normal, are facts in everybody's existence, as we learn in the annals of the chlorophyll for what concerns matters in this Forest and, I am sure, in some other form of chlorophyll in other creatures existences, yours, theirs and your Sister's too..........

Arrogance - No doubt at all about her CHLOROPHYLL...!!!!!

Young Tree - Well, as I was saying, in all those existences and in a moment of lost sanity or when the lymph of life may be running in the opposite direction to the right one, all kind of things can happen, but here in this Forest we have a system that levels off losses and troubles and there always seems to be a viable alternative to all kind of things that appear or happen in this Forest and, I believe, in many other forests .

Arrogance - How happy would my sister Impudence be in hearing you talking like this, dear litle green tree, and she, probably, really would like to tease you, just out of her inborn gift of civility, with the challenge for you to....catch her, if you dared and, of course, if you could ......!! ....Does that sound brazen enough to you ?

Young Tree - Now, then, o vague traveller, wandering through this forest, why should I worry at the possibility of being teased by your Sister with a suggestion for a clearly "logical impossibility"...?....I do not have legs but only roots which keep me firm and solid on the ground and I was not meant to be a running champion on a coveted race track.

Arrogance - You'll be amazed, young tree, but my Sister Impudence loathes Logic .

Young Tree - It does not matter : whatever she may like or dislike, it's all the same to me . But of one thing I am sure and that is that I am glad that I was born in this forest . I don't think that I would have liked the type of breezes you just described, accompanied by a distressing feeling of suspicion or guilt by those two legged creatures with a thin brain........no.....you said something else.......oh!.....yes, with a small brain on top of those legs .

Arrogance - Now, now, little Tree, what kind of talk is that ? What kind of reasons are you trying to bring up ? Do you happen to know who is standing here near you ?

Young Tree - I don't think so . I , really, do not know, o gentle passer-by, because I cannot see you and even if I saw you, it would not change my opinion on those turbulent and insiduous types of "breezes" that you just described and which flow, from time to time, among those two legged creatures .

Arrogance - Ah!You bold and brazen piece of wood, how dare you talk to me like that? How is it possible that you can hear but not see , if, according to the old folks stories and the ancient Wise Men, you have a soul and you know how to express yourself in a normal language ,or, let me correct that,you are just able to talk and just talk, meaning proferring vowels and syllables without even knowing why they go one after another or so , just, just talking because, as far as to "know" a language, you are or you may be quite a long way from that skill, my little wooden carcass...!! And, you,..... measly little tree, you want to give me some " reasons" for not liking my "breezes "...???!!...That's tantamount to straight forward, irreverent, impertinent, disgusting self conceit.......and a wooden type on top of it !

Young Tree - Dear gentle passer-by, I did not intend to give you the wrong impression as to some of the reasons I was going to bring up to properly and dutifully justify my inability or even my reluctance, if you, by chance, might have interpreted it that way, to run after your Sister , but purely to clear up to you why I would not want to do that and the reason why : that was all that I had intended to tell you, but, you, unfortunately, interpreted it as an unfriendly approach .

Arrogance - Well ! Well !....That's better . Go ahead, then, and feel free, now, to tell me your reasons, in full !

Young tree - All I had wanted to say was that I cannot run after anybody because I have a system of support under my body which keeps me, as I have already told you, firm and solid on this same ground where I was born and I am talking about my roots .

Arrogance - That's not a reason : that's a known fact to any living creature .

Young Tree - But there is more to it, o vague and gentle wanderer in our forest, because in addition to giving me stability, strength and secure standing on this ground where I was born , my roots bring me the daily nourishment necessary for my growth and well being as well as the wisdom of the good nourishing soil as an extra stimulus to my growing clean and vigorous and ample so as to embrace as much of the good air that permeates this forest, and, this, I was told about when I was still a young seedling and................

Arrogance - You have grown a lot since, haven't you, dear green stick ?

Young Tree - Some,I have, indeed, and my Elders were always telling me that the good nourishment always comes from the inside of the soil and, particularly so, very beneficial to the trees in this forest, which, then , can grow strong, straight up and lofty and proud of their roots where they were born . For "these" reasons, o vague passer-by, I do not run after anybody and I prefer to remain here, where I am, with my roots .

Arrogance - And you call this long drawn out sermon a "good reason "to justify the fact that you are tied down by some ordinary roots, the existence of which all creatures, even those with half a brain, are aware of, and that's why you cannot run...??!.. Oh !....For Heavens above...!!.....Of all the stupid things that afflict our existences on this Earth of ours..................

Young Tree - O vague and gentle traveller, I wish you were using less of that sophisticated language of yours, mind you, with all my deepest respect for it anyway, but more, of our wooden, solid and all encompassing forest jargon so neatly compressed and expressed in our ring-shaped circular inner and outer circles , there, then, I might follow your reasoning more closely !

Arrogance - I wonder........but, dear fledgeling green piece of wood, what's the problem, now ?

Young Tree - I am not sure, really, but I seem to have heard you saying, just now, "this Earth of ours", and I had never heard that expression before: you see, all I hear is:" this forest of ours ". I never heard any of our Elders ever talking about something like "this earth of ours"...did you, by any chance, mean the actual soil, the actual dirt we live on ?

Arrogance - Even stupider than I thought ! Anyway, let me finish my saying, my little arboreal simpleton, and time has come for me to teach you a little of something because it appears to me that your learning and tuition is in dire need of help, void as you seem to be of any tangible aspects of well constructed, oriented and refined knowledge .

Young Tree - Oh ! That's wonderful !

Arrogance - Good . So , listen and listen really good and I am going to tell you many valuable things and......

Young Tree - To me...?....Only to me....among all these big trees, really ??!..I'm so happy..!!!

Arrogance - I am sure that you will.......well....yes, that you will be very happy and mark my words ! ...But, also, in the process of telling you the many good things, I will let you know whom you have standing here near you, a real special entity of venerable and indisputable authority even if I have to proclaim it myself, by myself and about myself, and a flamboyant entity of great influence and ascendancy on the minds of those who think that they can say the same of themselves in their uncultivated heads . Anyway.........................

Young Tree - Oh ! That's wonderful !....Wonderful !....A wonderful present !.....You see, o vague passer-by of indisputable importance like you is a great event around this forest !!....Usually, hardly anybody, important or not , ever goes by these woods and, if any ever do, be they special entities and venerable authorities or just simple folks void of any authority, unworthy of awe inspired reverence and totally lacking impressive dignity, they never stop to talk to me ....So , please, please, just tell me who you are !....What's your name , o famous Traveller ?

Arrogance - Well, if you really want to know my identity , then, listen and listen good .

Young Tree - I am all ears!.....Oops....that was not quite appropriate for a tree like me to express myself in that way: it was just a recall from a fortuitous hearing when some two legged persons were passing by through this forest, some time ago, and were chatting among themselves and I picked up some of their jargon....well, I should have rather said:"Your Excellency, I am all leaves and bark", but, in the end, how I will listen to you has little importance: what's important is to know your identity so that I can be very proud and tell my roots of such a famous encounter .

Arrogance - Let us hope that you will still be very proud of this encounter once you learn of my true identity . Now, then, be quiet and listen and don't let me repeat it again ! ....I am ......

Young Tree - Very well : I will be very quiet and I'll be listening .

Arrogance - One more time you interrupt me and I shall leave and tell you nothing: understood ?

Young Tree - Sorry .

Arrogance - Good : and shut up . Now, then, I am Arrogance, the Temptress Goddess, who defied my arch rival, Lady Reason, and I am the one who destroyed my worst enemy, Lady Candidness . I am the one who causes Nature to blush and I am the one who lures humanity, you will remember, I am sure, those two legged creatures with a small head on top of them...........

Young Tree - Huh !...Humm......

Arrogance - Yes, indeed, very small heads on top of those long legs and, so , as I was saying, I am the one who lures those creatures to vie for such wuthering heights to where Nature had never intended them to rise and then, once there, I dash them down with a sordid laughter . Is , now, my introduction viable and clear ?

Young Tree - Oh ! Thank you, o vague stranger travelling in these woods and stranger no longer since you have divulged your name clearly and forcefully to me and it was very kind of you to do so..........

Arrogance - Don't mention it .

Young Tree - Yet I still cannot know with certainty who you really are and, please.....please !.....I beg of you, do not misunderstand my preoccupied incredulity even if at first thought it my seem so, but, o vague and gentle traveller, as you well know, I cannot see, only hear, and so by reason of the cruel ways and unkind doings practiced by some devious minds towards the creatures who do not possess the blessings of vision, you could really be anyone entity, as you like to call yourself, who could pretend and claim to be anyone to fit any given or desired situation . Have I alienated your esteem, now, by professing such a guarded representation ?

Arrogance - Oh ! Listen ! Just listen to this youg stick turned counselor and advisor:"I could be whomsoever"...says he !!! The audacity of today's youth..!!..It's incredible ! It's preposterous !......Well, my dear stupid tethering stick, even though you cannot see me, yet it seems that you can hear me well enough to grasp what I am saying , so listen carefully to my next sentence and here it comes :" I believe that you are a very stupid creature, a real, rough and solid wooden head "....Did you get that , you measly stick ?

Young Tree - But, my dear eminent Traveller, apart from stupidity, what other kind of head could I ever have since I am made of wood ?

Arrogance - A sensible explanation .

Young Tree - You see, o vague and noble traveller through these old wooded lands, Your exquisite Eminence, I should have rather said.....anyway, whichever applies and, as I was saying, there is no denying that I am made of solid wood, only wood, nothing else but wood .

Arrogance - Your abilty to stay the course on logical explanations, obvious as they could already be, impresses me greatly, regardless .

Young Tree - Thank you,Your Eminence, I do appreciate your support in my trying to"explain" ......myself..!....Well, so, as I was saying......

Arrogance - "As you were saying"... and I wish you would say it, finally, and get it over with ! Your talking is a good forerunner of the possible length of your future branches...!!!

Young Tree - I understand and justify your impatience with my seeming slow pace of narrating facts and events, but this trait is an integral part of our very being, since we grow slowly out of the soil and aim upward .

Arrogance - That's, indeed, very good and fortunate too: your birth would have been rather uneventful if you had been growing deeper and deeper into the soil instead of ....upwards......!!

Young Tree - May be so : however, if that had been Nature's blueprint, it wouldn't have made the slightest difference which way we would have grown, I guess . Anyway, as I........

Arrogance - I am waiting !!!

Young Tree - Yes...true..!!!...So, my roots, also, are made of wood and they are solid, strong and tenacious, boring their way into the soil to help me keep erect and as straight as possible and firm and solid and strong to enable me to withstand fierce winds with courage and determination , but in no way...........

Arrogance - Encomiable endowments, courage and determination are, indeed, and not widely distributed or available either .

Young Tree - I am sorry, but I do not know about that: what I was referring to was the usual make up of our kind, as we come up from our roots . Anyway....as I was saying....

Arrogance - But, of course !..........You.......were saying....??!

Young Tree - I was saying that in no way, my respected Lady Arrogance....... and this is the way my better judgement advises me how to address you, in no way I would try to compete, or pretend to be of any comparison, with certain creatures, or entities, as you like to express yourself, who keep on trying endlessy to appear with different and more impressive heads that Nature had granted them, and.........

Arrogance - ....Amen...!

Young Tree - ....And enlarge them in many and multifarious ways beyond any reasonable measure, to the extent that, in the majority of cases, they experience difficulties to fit their heads through various doors and risk tipping over and lose their balance with such enormous heads !

Arrogance - I see that you are beginning to dissipate the fog around my personality, although in an almost timid way, probably, I presume, to protect yourself from a more furious wind of rage from my real self and letting you know with adequate accuracy who I am !....

Young Tree - No timid way, noble traveller : just a respectful address to your eminent Entity .

Arrogance - That's nice !......I have also noticed or so it seems to me, that you must have had the opportunity to meet some of my devotees, since you noticed their outsized heads, so overloaded with wisdom and authoritative expressions, that, apparently, had some difficulty to walk and keep their balance on the right side of the road, so to speak, with such enormously inflated heads precariously balancing on those two long and thin legs !!

Young Tree - Yes, I have seen a few of those large round heads floating around, but what I said was just my simple, unrefined and uneducated way of describing casual happenings, scenes and facts of everyday occurrence, and nothing much to it, either . But, what I was going to point out was that my head is quite different from the heads of your devotees, what I mean is that.................

Arrogance - Your portrayal of your head is a masterpiece of lucidity, indeed .

Young Tree - Well....what I meant, really, was that my head is far simpler and rather modest in appearance by comparison with the large, well inflated, all rounded and gleaming heads of your devotees, which condescendingly oscillate left and right and front and back in an authoritative nod of patronaged gentility, uncommon ascendancy and superiority of instinct, those heads, indeed, large enough, to accommodate all of those astonishing gifts and.................

Arrogance - Go on: I am curious to hear the conclusion to your dissertation .....

Youg Tree - Oh ! No big deal about it, Your exalted Eminence, only that my head is spread wide open and wide with fragile limbs and tremulous leaves so as to perceive and allow all the whisper of this forest to come and go, to rest and linger, if so desired, or to fly away if of no definite useful purpose and retain only what's essential in a reasonable distribution of information , sensitivity and selective discretion and, in this way, it enables it, my head that's it, it enables it to...................

Arrogance - Yes, I heard you : it enables your widely spread simple head......go on !

Young Tree - Oh ! Yes, really so !......It enables my widely spread and reaching head to receive and absorb all the whispers that might come this way from all parts of this forest and by virtue of the very configuration characteristics of my head with the relative dispoisition of my branches and leaves, it affords a good stimulus to remain balanced, alert and responsive in a solid ligneous way to the surrounding events .

Arrogance - Just as I thought! A head lost between leaves, branches, and a lot of rough bark trying to catch the "breeze" of a thought from this enchanted forest, that is if even by a sheer chance a tremulous thought would suddenly spring forth in some subdued glorified semblance, but to be soon dispersed by the wind ! What good is it to you, , I wonder, to have a head, anyway, when, after all, you could not even norture a "seedling of a junior thought"....!!.....provided, of course, that you could think of one !

Young Tree - You think so ? And why couldn't I ?

Arrogance - Because, you silly ligneous young tree, thoughts are very special products of very special heads.....

Young Tree - Ah ! I see ! ....Those out-of-shape, enormous heads that tend to fall at any minute: are those the "special" heads you are referring to ?

Arrogance - In a way, yes, but not the"out-of-shape" ones, as you suggest, but enormous head, yes, in a way, as a practical representation of their "enormous capabilities" rather than size alone, adequately furnished with very special substances, it is believed, so specifically formulated to give birth to those thoughts and the more sophisticated and refined these substances are, the better the outcoming thoughts, it is believed, expanding and...............

Young Tree - It must be an excellent form of chlorophyll in those substances mixture, I guess .

Arrogance - Not exactly the chlorophyll you are thinking about, but one,probably, just as good if not better than the one running in you, a type of mixture that gives those thoughts the energy and the strength to expand, to enlarge and branch out to reach for more thoughts .

Young Tree - Strange !....That's what we do all the time, regularly, from seedling to fully grown tree : " expanding, enlarging and branching out", precisly as you just said...!!

Arrogance - Not quite, you ninny of a green stick, the expansion and the branching out, is not a physical process but a form of an intellective mechanism, the way it is displayed, the true nature of its existence and its possible and probable ingredients to make it "be", are yet unknown, neither do the scientists know anything about such a mixture of ingredients, if any at all......and if it is at all a mixture or ....anything ....!!!

Young Tree - Why do they talk so much about it, those scientists, then, if they do not even know if the whole thing is " anything"...??!

Arrogance - Listen, just listen to this stick of wood !!!....What's the use of teaching on deaf ears ? !!

Young Tree - You are not teaching on deaf ears because we have none . Besides, you are teaching things already well known to us and not new : any seedling in this forest knows about expanding, enlarging and branching out and that's nothing new !!

Arrogance - Is that so ...?

Young Tree - What, instead, puzzles me is our lack of information of the location where those enormous forests of expanding and branching out thoughts, are! O vague and distiguished traveller, are those forests very far away from our forest ?

Arrogance - You ninny of a young green tree, those forests are nowhere and everywhere and are invisible : only..........

Young Tree - INVISIBLE....???!!.....To.......whom....??!

Arrogance - To those large heads on two long thin legs, you silly tree!Those thoughts are invisible to them but perceived as a beneficial breeze that elevates the spirit of the two legged creatures or, at least, so they think .

Young Tree - I didn't know that those two legged creatures with large inflated heads were blind.

Arrogance - Itis not a physical invisibility , dear little tree, but a specific perception of some meaning riverberating in their heads and expressed in thoughts : their eyesight is regular , barred the usual handicaps of shortsightedness .

Youg Tree - Imagine that : invisible thinking forests.......!!!!.....Incredible ...!!

Arrogance - And there is more to it than just meets the eye and those.......

Young Tree - But, my respected and honourable Eminence, you had just told me that those thoughts were invisible !!

Arrogance - Never mind that : just one of innumerable expressions among large heads which only tend to emphasize a given thought . You are fortunate and a lucky entity, dear silly and green young tree, for being so ignorant and so naive . I guess that is the reason why forests are so shady and restful .

Young Tree - Not "so" restful during a tempest .

Arrogance - A tempest ! The stimulator of powerful thoughts !

Young Tree - I am not familiar with that expression . What's next, Your Eminence ?

Arrogance - Casually and, I am pretty certain, quite unknowingly, you inquired what was or could be the continuation of our discussion, and that reflects the ever lasting, perpetual journey of life and, unaware as you are of its meaning, yet you expessed it spontaneously in its unending continuity . My answer to your inquiry is : nothing any different than it was before or that shall be in the future .

Young Tree - May be it is as you say, but I cannot follow you on that path : it is out of reach of my branches .

Arrogance - I understand . Well, you are very young yet, and, when you'll be growing up and become a large , majestic tree, then, at that time, you'll understand more things !!

Young Tree - Ah...!. Does, now, your type of learning come by as you grow bigger and larger?

Arrogance - "Over eating" does that more likely than "learning" would, dear young tree!! But that is not what I meant : what I wanted to explain to you, even if in vain, was that, sometimes, wisdom comes with old age . Some luckier creatures obtain a glimpse of wisdom in earlier life, but those occurrencies are rare .

Young Tree - But, then, o famous traveller, what's the use of this that you just said, I believe it was......wisdom?, Right ?.....Yes, wisdom....so , what's the use of getting this wisdom when you are old and ready to die ?......Or is it so that it can be willed to someone else, younger, for safe keeping in one of those invisible forests of thoughts ? Tell me, now, what do your scientists know about all this ?

Arrogance - There is the time when I come in and start raising everybody's chin, causing frowns from disapproving foreheads and promoting steadfast looks towards the philosophers while disputing the whole mystery among themselves as well as with the Mystics, and other various groups interested in that matter and, usually, never reaching a definitive explanation of the process .

Youg Tree - I really cannot understand why it is so difficult to explain something that everybody is able to observe, realize, feel and think about it, as you mentioned, since those scientists and philosophers, those mighty heads, regardless of size, DO think, ...don't they...?....I believe they do, I surmise, and that means that they are practicing"thoughts",so,all of"them savvy scientists"should know all about thoughts and be able to explain it, and whatever else goes with it and why and how .

Arrogance - Does every seedling in this forest know why they are growing out of the soil ?

Young Tree - But of course they do !!

Arrogance - You don't say !!

Young Tree - Of course they do ! Why wouldn't or couldn't they know it ? It is a very simple mechanism : nourishment is furnished by the soil, the sun furnishes the warmth and the rain keeps the soil moist so that the nourishment can be absorbed by the roots . Every seedling knows that . Besides, we do not have any scientists or philosophers, whatever those entities might be .

Arrogance - And that is a pity !! No scientists and no philosophers to discuss your origins ! That is why, I guess, all you can do is to grow into large chunks of wood !

Young Tree- I understand that, o eminent Traveller, but our large chunks of wood do produce, in addition to the actual wood, also a large amount of leaves .

Arrogance - The frail and light leaves of your ligneous thinking in this forest are but a fatuous expression of a thought destined to be swept away by the wind or to fade with the withering of those leaves .

Young Tree - But, Your excellency, those withering and falling leaves, once on the ground, are capable to produce excellent supplemental nourishment to the very soil on which they fell, prompting the sprouting of new leaves and seedlings all over the forest .

Arrogance - Thank Goodness about that !!........At least they are good for something and their tremulous fluttering "thinking" turned into a practical aid and nothing going to waste ....!!

Young Tree - Oh ! Yes, Your Highness ! Nothing, nothing is ever going to waste in this forest, I assure you ! ....Not even a tremulous thinking leaf, as you just said .

Arrogance - And that is a "Pity"...!

Young Tree - Pity...???!!

Arrogance - Yes, definitely a Pity , I say !

Young Tree - In all honesty, distingished traveller , I cannot see any substantial reason for your commiseration about an happening, like ours"nothing is going to waste", this happening being a most natural and fortunate transition in the evolvement of our daily existences . It should be welcomed . It should be praised .

Arrogance - The way I see it is quite different and it may not agree at all with your idea .

Young Tree - I don't see why it doesn't !

Arrogance - Apart from your....Grammar.....well, for one thing, some waste would clean up so much garbage, because I feel certain that there must be a lot of garbage in a forest where there are no schools, no universities, no teachers, no professors, no scientists and no philospphers to keep the atmosphere above the illiterate level in this thicket of wooden heads !......My young green stick, I happen to know better and even more !

Youg Tree - I have no doubt of that, Your Highness, yet, my Elders.......you know, those large, great and tall oaks.......always tell me that waste is a commodity, not an encombrance and that many creatures derive an excellent source of remunaration for disposing of that waste in addition of that waste to be, also, a good source of nourishment for many other little creatures............

Arrogance - If I were not Arrogance, I would probably cry listening to your sentimental journey of the waste...!

Young Tree - You need not feel that way, Your Highness: it is just an everyday occurrence, because,as far as I remember,my Elders always told me that there has not been a case yet of anybody's existence where there was no waste .

Arrogance - And you said that there are no scientists and philosophers in your forest ?

Young Tree- None : if there were or had been any, my Elders would have told me so . Yet, I even doubt that because we, in this forest, have never heard of those entities and we do not know what they are or represent, really .

Arrogance - "Really", is the right answer, dear little green stick, because, really, I am bewildered at the opacity of the understanding process in these thick woods !

Young Tree - I fully sympathize with your dismay in realizing the hopeless response from our thick wooded forest to your superior knowledge, yet, our vastly expanded branches and innumerable leaves seem to perform a strange function, at times...........

Arrogance - It may seem strange to you, ninny of a green stick, but hardly to me, I assure you !

Young Tree- All the better so, then, Your Highness, its meaning will be clear to you and what seems so strange to me is the extraordinary way those branches and leaves react when they are confronted by a blowing and unforgiving wind bearing some form of"waste"across this forest ....

Arrogance - The word must have gone around that this forest is a good place to dispose of garbage...!!!

Young Tree - But what's curious is what my Elders tell me , that this unwelcome, displeasing "waste bearing breeze"appears to be caused, most of the occasions, by some lonely and discarded thoughts, probably some solitary thoughts like the ones you just described to me, and they strain, rather, filter, that is, this waste, probably, as my Elders suspected, being some thoughts sprang forth from your disciples.........

Arrogance - Ah ! Yes, my supreme disciples...!

Young Tree - Spme fragile thoughts. perhaps, which came and went, grew and expanded, probably, beyond measure so that no big enough head could be found to accommodate them and must have finished up desolate, depressed and, eventually, sad and......wasted.......we suspect ....Of course, they accumulate with all the rest of the....garbage,,,,we suspect .

Arrogance - Poor, little tree, slightly annoyed at my remarks on the forest garbage and waste! But, none of my thoughts are ever depressed or desolate : they are refulgent !

Young Tree - I have no doubts about the excellence of your intellective activities, o vague being that wanders in this forest, I have no doubt at all about it or the slightest hesitation in admiring the intrinsic power of your thinking, but, you see...............

Arrogance - I see...!

Young tree - I am glad that you seem to be paying attention to my talking and that makes me very proud and, all I was trying to do, was to emphasize that my thinking is not of the same "shape" and "consistency" of the kind of thinking that you profess, but it displays itself in a very different way and.........

Arrogance - Thank Heavens for "that" difference.....!!

Young Tree - And it lacks the embellishment that you so leisurely indulge on your followers with an ostentatious and presumptuous attitude, and I hope that Your Ladyship will pardon me for being so bold in my expressions, but, as I was saying, my thought is different and......................

Arrogance - Thank Heavens, again and again for"that"difference....!!....For a moment I thought that your speech was going....... to waste !!

Youg Tree - Even if it did or if it would have gone to waste, my dear traveller.....oops..!! forgive me, Your Excellence, ...even if it had gone to waste, Your Highness, no damage done or any loss suffered, because many more young little trees would have been"speaking"just the same and"thinking"just the same, so, my "speech" would have still been viable , picked up by innumerable seedlings and carried on in the cool shade of this forest : and.......no waste !

Arrogance - Hallelujah !! About time you stopped your insensate rhetoric! I am getting a little sick with your stupidity, low grade imagination and a litany of choice nonsense .

Young Tree - Well, even if my type of "thinking" is tedious, unimaginative and lacking intelligent choices, it is my thinking, nontheless, and difficult to alter or change in this old forest of "solid" stand and firm ground and deep rooted feelings of simple but straight forward responsibilities .

Arrogance - Excellent...!

Young Tree - On that basis, I'd like to finish my "speech" before it would go to waste as You had feared, and then you may leave me and continue on your journey and forget all about my encounter : would you be agreeable to this ?

Arrogance - Agreed !.....And that would be a salubrious relief !

Young Tree - Yes, my dear and revered Highness, my thinking is different and it consists of a steady and continuous exp..............

Arrogance - Are you by any chance planning to go through the entire litany of the previous highlights about the forest, the waste and the garbage and the "who knows what next" pedantic rigmarole long list of nonsense...???!!

Young Tree - No. That is not what I intend to explain, Your Excellency . All I was going to say was that my thinking develops in a continuous expansion of active, well coordinated circles of expression in its forming, shaping and.............

Arrogance - Ah ! Now we come to the point ! Now we understand why your talking never seems to have a proper beginning and a suitable or sensible end ! Why, of course, it goes around in circles.....!!!.....And it never ends....!!.....Poor,little green tree !

Young Tree - May I correct that, with Your Highness blessing?...It is not a circular motion but a motion of circles .

Arrogance - Were I not Arrogance, but a Professor at a famous University, I'll make you Professor Emeritus of Trigonometry .

Young Tree - Thank you, o vague and illustrious traveller through this forest, thank you, indeed, for your kind thought, and I am very sorry and I wish to apologize for not being able to absorb all of the potentially wonderful feelings produced by your generous offer, but, in this forest.................

Arrogance - Is the proximity to so many other old and younger trees that makes you feel somewhat embarrassed at receiving and accepting compliments ? You should see how more inflated and overbearingly insufferable some of my disciples become after receiving a compliment or a praise .....!!!

Young Tree - That is fine for your disciples, because it is part of their make-up, but here, in this forest, we do not ever hear of Universities or Professors or trigonometry, unless, as I have already mentioned to you earlier, they come by just to have a rest and relax in our shade and tranquillity . But, then, several other creatures do the same, on the ground, on our roots, in our branches, so it is a little difficult to identify and figure out all of them .

Arrogance - After your answer conveyed to me with such a brilliant speech, I have changed my mind and, instead of nominating you Professor of trigonometry, I shall make you Lecturer Emeritus of Pedanthood at the University of *SINE QUA NON*.... !

Young Tree - Why bother to do all that, your respected Eminence, when I could not go there or anywhere, since I am firmy rooted on this ground and I have some serious reservations about anyone's compelling desire to hear the whisper of my leaves....unless...........

Arrogance - Ah ! Are you changing your mind about your investiture of a Lecturer Emeritus at the famous University of "sine qua non" ??!

Young Tree - Oh,no ! I was going to say ....unless a tired Professor....."sine" consequence, may be, would casually stroll along and let his ......"pedant" teaching have a rest .

Arrogance - You know what ?

Young Tree - I, really, do not know "what" !

Arrogance - Well, let me tell you, then . At a second thought, your last remark had a good sound to my perception, almost as good a sound as one that my acolytes could have formulsted.......it was spomtaneous and beautiful.......and you had said...:"unless a tired Professor, may be the type of "sine consequence".....would casually stroll along and let his"pedant" teaching have a rest...." ....!....Just beautiful! Arrogant and contemptuous : Bravo...!!.....You little silly green stick !!

Young Tree - Why such a commotion about a simple observation,Your Highness ? I don't quite follow you .

Arrogance - Because your statement had some substance in it that made me wonder , for a moment, that is, whether, after all, you could become a good disciple of my Club. ....May be !......But, now, Emeritus , what about those circles ?

Young Tree - Oh !...Yes, the circles !...I wonder, though, whether Your Highness would be at all interested to hear about any narrative about circles, particularly so, since they are part of this forest, which Your Eminence does not seem to sympathize with because of its lack of excellence in imagination and sharpness of intuition .

Arrogance - That was a while ago, you silly stick : now I want to hear some more about those circles . So, what happened to the circles ?

Young Tree- Nothing much : they are still there, of course .

Arrogance - Come on ! What about those circles ? We haven't got the whole day, you know !

Young Tree - If you'll excuse my audacity, Your Highness, but those circles do have the whole day and all the days to come !

Arrogance - Fine, fine, finer and finest humour, old fashion style, annoying rather than irritating : come on, now, finish up your story, it's getting late, I am tired, I want to find a decent place to sleep so hurry up and let get it over : shall we now ?

Young Tree - Yes, Your Highness : we shall . So, as I was saying, my thinking, so different from yours, develops in coordinated circles of expression, shaping and advancing towards the outside to the light and the warmth of the sun while, at the same time, it florishes by progressing inwards in an introspection of similar circles,year after year, without any applause or servile adulation but........

Arrogance - What a pity ! Just like a concert would sound without the musicians ..... !

Young Tree - I do not know about concerts, Your Highness, but I know that our type of thinking will grow endowed with ,with a solid, stable and fertile disposition, very patient, but steady and observant in its making, without..........

Arrogance - How monotonous and insipid your type of thinking is shaping up, you silly green tree ...!!

Young Tree - For one thing, if you allow me,Your Highness, our thinking will not suffer from so many interruptions like my narrative is experiencing now.........or any impediments, hesitations or contradictions, but with a constant and well weighted expansion and expression and well programmed patient and laborious geniality from within outward and from within to the inner most enclave of our lymph by that imponderable will given us by our Mother Nature . And now,Your Highness, you have the assessment and the story of the circles . We hope that those circles didn't make you feel dizzy .

Arrogance - Not dizzy at all : sleepy, may be, for the astonishingly interesting sequence of events of what it looks like some sort of "circular thinking", indeed an altogether new style for a form of mental lucubrations, with which I am not overly familiar, although I have heard of it .

Young Tree - We are not familiar either with this form of mental locomotions and.......

Arrogance - Lucubrations, dear little green tree....lucubrations!Oh! Well, I guess that, locomotions or lucubrations, it does not make a bit of difference in a forest of this size and composition : the trees will grow happily just the same, regardless of the two appellatives .

Young Tree - And we are not familiar with the type of "circular thinking"that you are talking about : we just think in well defined movenents of circles and not one of our thoughts becomes distorted or lost in a tangential shoot-off .

Arrogance - Some tangential spin-off would, probably, improve your spirit....well....I should say" your lymph" and make you a brilliant forest .

Young Tree - The Sun brings enough brilliance to us, o vague traveller, and we do not need words arranged in elegant speeches to give us luminosity : the best brilliance of anything, my Elders tell me, is the one that reflects from spontaneous, natural causes and not from artificial arrangements of enhancing artifacts .

Arrogance - Excellent observation : golden words , indeed.........indeed......yes, and so it is that every creature justifies its own deeds by the intervention of the "Imponderable Will of Mother Nature " !!...That's an easy way out should something go wrong in the application of that " Imponderable Will "....!!............Anyway, your type of thinking was a formidable expression of yourself and an illuminating one and, further more, I would most emphatically add a "glorious sparkling" and, altogether, a rather warm "representation" of your thoughts, perhaps a subconscious foreboding of your final "glowing expression".......in a "brilliant" fireplace!! !

Young Tree - It is not a sign of distinction , ...and Your Ladyship will forgive me for saying so,...........to mock the Laws and the Rules and the well-planned stepping stones in the work of Mother Nature, that Nature that created me and, I am almost sure, created you too, and, probably, did that during a day of bad weather and not quite sure if she really wanted to do it.........and I wonder whether you have ever given some thought at what your final end will be .

Arrogance - As a matter of fact, I haven't .

Young Tree - Why are you, then, interested in the probable end of others, prophesying the event in "brilliant" details, when you, apparently, do not even care or want to know about your own ?

Arrogance - Why should I ? My type of being and its attributable attitude, are mainstays in the life of everyday creature and it includes, in its complete structure, the entire World and the whole of the Universe: don't all these parameters seem outrageously arrogant to you in the way they exhibit themselves?They certainly do not seem to worry a bit at the way they act, at the way they carry out their cataclysmal mishaps with a total disregard at anybody in their way, or the way they look, and how are they looked upon by others ! So, why should "I " worry ?

Young Tree - That is the most outlandish attempt at an explanation of a fully established reality, that of our end, that does not need an explanation, at all, simply because we have not an explanation for it .Your"crescendo"highlighting speech on the subject fell dead on all of my branches,...........Your Ladyship .

Arrogance - So much, the better : so we won't have to worry about talking about it anymore !

Young Tree - But you had just condescendingly suggested that kind of attitude to be an "easy way out", should things prove different from what they would have been expected to be, or anticipated or contrversial . So, I am a little confused, Your Highness .

Arrogance - You have to make up yourself an explanation for what's missing in a statement and, sometimes, statements are made unintelligible, precisely so that no one understands what they really mean or, even worse, are meant not to have any meaning, just a show of vane rhetoric, and my disciples are masters at it .

Young Tree - And may I be allowed to ask : " What is the usefulness" of such a practice ?

Arrogance - Inspire a feeling to lesser folks that there are folks skilled in craftier undertakings.

Young Tree - But that tantamount to deceitful representation of intents....!

Arrogance - Details ! Details !.....Always looking at little details! No much ground can be covered by stopping to analyze any minute details.....just always aim high, improvise, boast, enlarge and even embellish what may not be so good to be embellished at all, if you want to get somewhere, you silly, naive little green stick!.. My advice to you : be arrogant ! And why not? Everybody is, in one way or another, sometimes acting that way without even realizing it, but it is almost impossible to delete, from the minds of several creatures, the crave for notoriety and superiority, in spite of how utterly despicable that attitude can be . Now, how "does that grab you ?" , you silly little green stick ?

Young Tree - "To grab, grabbed, grabbing", is not, really, a way of understanding among the simple creatures of this forest, o vague spirit that wanders in these woods, but I do understand you, in some way, well adapted as I am and we all are in this here forest, firmly attached to this soil and quite used to hear of everything a barrel...!

Arrogance - That what you just said, dear green stick, sounds like one of those statements that have no meaning at all! I just wonder how you could roll a....barrel of anything !!

Young Tree - Your Highness, please, pay no attentiom to what I just said : it is just "one of those statements" that have no meaning at all and I am just practicing, as you had suggested, only a little while ago .

Arrogance - Hard and ligneous as you are, still, you seem to be learning fast ! But don't let this resiliance fool you in thinking that you are "just IT " like all the other poor illusioned advocates of my teachings, so anxious to practice the alluring way of showing off : it is necessary to digest the matter very well first, before even thinking of having tasted it, and that takes a long, long time .

Young Tree - How long did it take you, Your Eminence, to master it ?........I mean, to taste it ?

Arrogance - I did not master or taste anything : I was born by it . For my devotees, of course, it's a different story .

Young Tree - Yes ! So it is, my dear and respected wanderer in our forest, so it is, indeed, and so much tolerance, so much patience in this forest is constantly practiced every hour, every day, every month and every year in order to accommodate the "rationale" of those growing thinking circles, and..........

Arrogance - You certainly need that"rationale" to justify the unperturbable snail-track type of thinking of those "famous" circles...!

Young Tree - That is why we try to provide a refreshing surrounding in these woods so that tired travellers may find some rest for their tired minds and reorganize their thoughts according to an inviting atmosphere of peace and tranquillity in a congenial reciprocity of freedom of thought among so many innumerable trees, offering an abundance of "branching" ideas from those majestic trees, along with the notion that there is plenty of patience and limitless tolerance available for their individual thinking .

Arrogance - Impressive, indeed, even if a little artificial .

Young Tree - I am certain that you know what the Ancient Wise Folks used to say about large forests in the old and ancient times : don't you ?

Arrogance - Yes, of course : that they are, indeed, very large and have trees in it .

Young Tree - That was not a necessary remark, Your Excellency . I am trying to adapt to your way of acting, thinking and explaining facts, but I receive no support or encouragement from you or any praise.But, it doesn't matter:how true it was, then, what our Ancient Folks used to claim : a refreshed traveller will know the right road !

Arrogance - Patience, he says, patience ! Tolerance ! Ah! My little green and silly tree, patience is good for those who have it, practice it and wait, patiently, of course, for the next best thing that may come around or it applies to lazy creatures or to creatures able to do very little of anything useful of anything ....not for me, my dear, just not for me....!!!

Young Tree - Have you ever tried it ?

Arrogance - What..?....Patience or Tolerance ?!

Young Tree - They share a lot in common .

Arrogance - They do not share anything with me, for sure . I am always in earnest to overtake everything and everyone, always first and always in front and, certainly, never behind anything or anybody, as several creatures do by playing the game of life by waiting passively and "very patiently" and "very tolerantly"for "Auntie Fortune"to come by and caress their expectations . Bah ! That's, certainly, not for me !

**** It just so hapened that, at this precise time, Lady Patience and Lady Tolerance were passing by this area of the forest as they were returning from an important mission of mediation and reconciliation among diverse parties, who had become involved in a bitter dispute about the ownership of some large tree tracks, in a far away tropical forest. As they were approaching the scene were the Young Tree and Lady Arrogance were chatting away, they had overheard Arrogance last preaching sermon to the Young Tree and, their curiosity aroused, they decided to stop and introduce themselves ....****

****

Young Tree - Look...!....I believe somebody's approaching !

Arrogance - At this late hour in the day ?....Probably some lost travellers trying to figure out a way out of this dense forest .

Young Tree - It could be , but they do not seem agitated or looking here and there for clues, just walking casually, and only slighty changing their apparent original course after spotting us and turning in our direction .

Arrogance - I still think that they are lost tourists and having, luckily for them, spotted us, they are trying to come to us and ask for help.

Young Tree - The way they look to me from up here, in my higher branches, they seem more likely ready to offer help rather than ask for it, by the way they comport themselves, apparently self-assured and steady with a firm gait and pleasant look on their faces reflecting no anxiety or perplexity : a lost person would show some emotion and some distress, but these creatures seem very much at ease and in full control of themselves .

Arrogance - It is difficult from a distance to tell about the status of ceatures . Sometimes, it is even difficult to recognize a creature's real make up at a much closer range !

Young Tree - They are almost here...!!....And they do not seem alarmed a bit ! I wonder who might they be, and at this hour, and in this forest..???!!!

Arrogance - That's quite obvious, little green Tree : they are here because it so happens that this forest is here, this is the direction that they had chosen , they must have been returning from a business trip, may be, they were on their way back home, saw us as they passed by, bored perhaps of the long trip that they might have had, thought of stopping by, say "hello", exchange a few words, ask about the weather, smile and part again, towards their homes and to have a good rest .

Young tree - Here they are...!!!

Arrogance - Hello, strangers ! So late down here in these woods ! Is anything wrong or do you need help ?

Young Tree - Good evening, travellers, and welcome to these woods !

Lady Tolerance - Good evening, everybody : how nice to meet you in these dense woods ! We are on our way back to our homes, not too far a distance from here, and this way trough the forest shortens significantly the length of the walk, which would have taken considerable longer time had we gone around the forest, skirting it, on the main route .

Lady Patience - Being a little tired, the shorter way was very appealing to our tired limbs !

Young Tree - You must have come a long way from your original destination, dear and gentle Ladies : is your final destination, your home I mean, still very far from here ?

Lady Patience - Not really : not more than half a league, may be even less than that and it can be covered rapidly with a fast walking clip if you are not tired .

Young Tree - Then, since the evening is not that advanced yet and the daylight is still going to be clear and available for a while, you could still have time to rest before resuming your walking towards your homes as you would still arrive at your destination in daylight, while a little rest will restore your....worn out limbs !

Arrogance - Young Tree, you shouldn't embarrass these noble travellers by offering a suggestion that they may find it difficult to either decline or accept, because I trust that their make up is one of gentility and of distinction .

Young Tree - I was only formulating my offer on the basis of what one of them had just said about the distance to their house from here: "really, not a long distance if you are not tired", implying, I guess, that they were tired! Earlier, they had complained of their "tired limbs"! That's why I came up with my suggestion that they rest for a while, because the evening was young and they could have reached their final destination still in day light, but more refreshed .

Lady Tolerance - But of course, we understood perfectly well, dear Green Tree, what you really meant and you should know that I am talking on behalf of my travelling companion as well, because my companion and I share our mutual friendship as if we were dedicated sisters, endowed with similar, even if not strictly identical motives and beliefs . So, thank you, dearly, for your offer, for your considered suggestion and your kind thought and concern .

Young Tree - Ah ! Dear Ladies, I am not worth that much of attention and praise, my tendency to such an attitude comes to me from the teachings of my Elders who tell me all the time that anyone should always be considered of the possible needs of others .

Lady Patience - Salubrious teachings, those of your Elders, indeed ! And a lot of praise to you too, young tree, for listening and adopting those good counsels . In our existences and in the life of any teacher of merit and respect, it takes a lot of preparation, mentally, and a lot of patience, emotionally, in order to impart any enduring significance to any form of teaching.You are a very good disciple !.....And my good travelling companion urges me to accept your kind and courteous advice !

Arrogance - Ah!Yes! Strange ! This young green tree and I were just talking about the art of patience and how poorly such an approach to a life style would suit my needs . That is quite interesting that you brought up the subject, dear Lady !

Lady Patience - Why is the art of being patient so adverse to your liking or, rather, why is patience so unsuitable to your needs ?

Arrogance - Madam, my nature demands constant action and does not accept delays or accommodations of compromise like patiently waiting for something that had not come right away hoping that it will still come .

Lady Patience - What's wrong with that ? Isn't every creature on this planet always waiting for something that more often than not will ever come ?

Arrogance - Losers, misfits, insecure creatures, depressed creatures, deprived creatures may feel that way, but Arrogance and that is my name, is neither of those definitions !

Lady Tolerance - Ah ! What a surprise ! To think of something that we could have never thought: meeting Lady Arrogance right here in the middle of these dense woods ! This is, indeed, an extraordinary occasion !

Lady Patience - Indeed, an unusual sequence of events to cause all of us to join here together in these woods !

Arrogance - I am charmed at your open and friendly expressions and, now, may I ask who Your Ladyships actyally are ?

Lady Tolerance - But, of course, you may ! I am Tolerance, and I have a fair and objective inclination toward those entities whose opinions may differ from one's own . In simple words : "....freedom from bigotry....." !

Lady Patience - She does possess an unequivocal liberal spirit towards the views and actions of others...!!

Young Tree - Indeed, a liberal and undogmatic view-point of the prevailing spirit of a dense forest .

Arrogance - I don't believe that this is really ....happening.....!!!!!

Lady Patience - You don't ?! But it is happening, in spite of the dense forest ! I am Patience, and we have had already a little conversation together ! I have the ability to suppress restlessness or annoyance in waiting for things to happen and I can bear misfortune or provocation without complaint, loss of temper, irritation . In other, simpler words, I possess an unequivocal ability to self-possession in trying circumstances .

Arrogance - Well ! Well ! Well ! Look who is here !!!....Indeed, an unexpected apparition: none others than Lady Tolerance and Lady Patience, themselves !!!....Or should I have, rather, addressed you as....."Your Highnesses" ? I believe that

"Your combined" composure and self-possession would allow both of Your Highnesses to absorb all of those titles and redundant attributes quite.....leisurely....!!

Lady Patience - Indeed, my dear Lady Arrogance, indeed, you are absolutely right in your choice of elevating me and my companion to such high honours of reverence because it did always take in the past, as it does take in our present days and, undoubtedly, it will take, in the eons to come, infinite, incalculable, exponential powers of tolerance and an entire magnitude of high and higher and highest degree of patience in order to have any reasonable discourse with you.

Arrogance - I am flattered !

Lady Patience - You'll be even more flattered when I am finished with my comments.......Your Highness...!!

Arrogance - The more the better, it is commonly proclaimed .

Lady Tolerance - It does not sound like you yourself the way you say that ! Is there, may be, a shift of your attitude in the wind ?

Arrogance - The wind is fine and appropriate but, may be, not quite the way you would expect it to blow .

Lady Tolerance - Hesitant about your own tendencies ? Or just not sure of their consistency ?

Lady Patience - Dear companion and dear Sister Tolerance, shouldn't you give our illustrious new acquaintance a wider berth of accessible answers to your question instead of pressing her into a narrow edge of an explaining process ?

Arrogance - Oh ! Do not worry about any of that ! As a matter of fact, I like direct questions, down to the point . No problem, at all ! What I had in mind to say was that, talking about the wind Lady Tolerance had just mentioned and conveniently acknowledging it and applying its meaning to strengthen what I had originally thought of saying......that was.....the more "wind" comes out of Lady Patience's mouth, the sooner we can forget the whole thing for what it is worth !.

Lady Patience - "Worth", my dear, is an expression that hardly fits you: your thirst for an absolute and incontestable recognition of superiority has the devastating effect to run dry any free flowing brook of good will of anyone who would genuinely and truthfully attempt any comminication or association with you .

Arrogance - Oh ! Well ! Now that you had your chest, mind and heart relieved of what you think of me, expressed in an open, sincere and clear figurative description, why don't we rest for a while and tell me, instead, what good turn took you to this neck of the woods,other than just shortening the walk back to your home.

Lady Patience - Why not ?.....Good idea : a little rest is beneficial to anybody's limbs and mind as well, and it encourages reason to poise itself and reexamine the mental landscape .

Lady Tolerance - Yes, the landscape of the mind, not always a well tended and manicured flower-bed, the weeds stealthily creeping up almost as if jealous or just intolerant of beautiful flowers .

Arrogance - Ladies.! I did not mean to enter into a poetry contest on the worthiness of rest ! My idea was just one of relaxation !

** At this point, The Young Tree, which had been silent and reserved while the three ladies, Patience,Tolerance and Arrogance, were exchanging views and talking in earnest among themselves, took suddenly courage and introduced himself into the conversation of the three Ladies, although he had not been invited to do so, but he had become most anxious and agitated after hearing Lady Arrogance's quest to find out if there were some other reasons for the two Visitors, Lady Patience and Lady Tolerance, to come through this forest, other than shortening their walk home and our brave and young tree, deep in his wood and in his tremulous leaves, felt that he knew why better than anybody's else as his Elders had taught him and the forest had always implied it, and that he had the right to say it and the joy to proclaim it ,lest the negligent and disrespectful attitude of Lady Arrogance would diminish and even ridicule the real meaning of the two Visitors presence in the forest, and particularly so, LadyPatience !....so ....****

Young Tree - Please, dear All, honourable Ladies, I beg of your liberal magnanimity to excuse me and my audacious appearance in bursting so irreverently into your conversation, but I, suddenly, got an inner feeling, almost a compelling feeling, to throw myself into your discourse with such an impolite impulse, but I felt the urge to answer the question by Lady Arrogance to you, who, apparently wished to know more and, more directly, from Lady Patience herself, of any other reaosns for coming through this forest, and mine is just a genuine, inner feeling, spontaneous in nature but well nortured by the way of life of the forest, and I would hope that neither one of your Ladiships would mind or object me doing so or feel offended by it .

Lady Tolerance - Child !......Let us hear your side of the story ...!

Young Tree - Thank You, Lady Tolerance, you are a great lady and I am grateful to you for your understanding of my impromptu quest and I feel certain that your intention is fully shared by Lady Patience . You, certainly, are more than familiar with those unmeasurable inner feelings that float from time to time within our material frames and which request no specific acknowledgement but they never do absolve our mind from ignoring them, so close their significance is to the very being of one's own existence .

Lady Tolerance - Go ahead, child, and let us hear those floating inner feelings .

Arrogance - Hear ! Hear!......Our new Solomon "of Wooden Stock" resurging and dramatizing the impending judgement with sentimental insolence .

Lady Tolerance - You should not prod so harshly this little green tree, inexperienced and unaccostomed,yet, as he is to the rigors and pitfalls of unguarded communication in the dense and misty forests of our existences .

Lady Patience - Yes, and I agree: let this young tree vent his feelings, for no one should feel offended, or annoyed, irritated or embarrassed by someone elses's remarks or opinions, if the listener is crystal clear in the mind .

Arrogance - Golden precepts, indeed, worth of sculpturing on some marble tablets for posterity to ponder upon and wonder, but I am talking in present times terms and, I'll say it again: the young green tree quest just makes me sick !!

Lady Patience - There is nothing "offensive" to either the sense of smell or the sense of understanding in what the Young Green Tree is asking : all he wants to say is his side of the story about us and, by the impetus of his sudden desire to talk about it, it seems to imply an intrinsic comprehension of it .

Arrogance - As to my "prodding" of the little green tree....this little green tree's audacity is what sickens me, particularly with his prolonged, highly monotonous explanation of why he, suddenly, desired to intervene into our conversation as if so directed and compelled by a higher apocalyptic immensity of superior knowledge.....out of a solid, very solid, hard as "wood"......... cauldron of wisdom!

Young Tree - Dear Lady Arrogance, Your Highness, let me explain, if I may. You see, we....

Arrogance - You certainly may and......you'd better !.....Am I a lesser listener than the two gracious Ladies ?....Of course not ! So , little green tree, proceed !

Young Tree - Thank you, Your Ladyship, I most sincerely thank you for allowing me to proceed and Your remark appears to indicate a willingness on your part to listen to me like the two other Ladies, in spite of my impetuous indiscretion in interrupting your discourse with Lady Patience and Lady Tolerance, but, you see.....I.....

Arrogance - Are we, by any chance, being marshalled into well aligned ranks and prepared to go through, again, with your recent, monotonous, repetitious talking, sounding like a recital and almost slipping into some sort of mumbling resembling more the like of a supplication rather than a talk, and that just to explain some simple matter along with dispersive and utterly stupid thoughts ?

Lady Tolerance - Be reasonable, Lady Arrogance, and let this young green tree tell his side of the story the best way he can in his own way ! After all, with the many branches that he has, it is not an easy task for him to coordinate all of them into a single voice all of a sudden and it is necessary to have patience and wait and listen when the time is right .

Arrogance - Ah !....And here we go again with the ever présent monitoring of patience ! Well, I'd like to inform you, respectable and honourable Lady Tolerance, that I have no patience at all, I do not practice one, I do not want one, I am not waiting for one : to me patience is tantamount as wasting time .

Lady Tolerance - Well, dear Cousin, if that is the way you feel about this situation, I and my sweet companion, Lady Patience, would not hold you to any strict social etiquette by detaining you into our company and you, we are quite certain, feel absolutely free to act your own way, the way that best suits your way of thinking and you, therefore, should not feel obliged to remain in our company.

Arrogance - Excellent explanatory round-up of telling someone to "get out of here"and not to bother "us" anymore !.....Well, I have some news for all of you, the green young tree included : I am going to stay, I am going to listen and I am even going to encourage our young green tree to come forth with his story ! After all, he is the one who burst into our conversation with a rather sudden expression of an impending emotion , or so it sounded like . That, of course, given that trees would have emotions . So, little green tree...go ahead..!!..and .. please........make it short..!!!

Young Tree - Thank you! Thank you most sincerely and to have the approval of all three of Your Ladyships, makes me feel good and serene.

Arrogance - If you are going again into one of your melodramatic recitals I might feel inclined to revoke my approval !

Yiung Tree- I have no intention of playing any melodramatic recital, whatever that is, anyway, and I will just talk as my Elders taught me and all the other trees .

Lady Patience - Dear cousin Arrogance, please, do not argue anymore with the little tree : it just delays his speech, and we need to reach our home before it gets dark.
(.....then, turning to the young green tree........).........Go ahead , dear little tree and tell us why you felt such a sudden urge to get in into our conversation with Lady Arrogance and we all shall listen to you .

Young Tree - Thank you ! Thank you, indeed, all of you, most gentle Ladies !.....Well, our Elders always told us that that trees are not mnotonous, rather they are steady, in their projections. Trees are not reciting prayers, like litanies: they just murmur with a rustling sound in the wind .

Arrogance - A high spirited lyric in a forest sonata in "wood flat-moderato andante".

Lady Patience - Cousin Arrogance....please.....!

Lady Tolerance - Is it so difficult to be serious, even for a few moments...........Cousin ?

Young Tree - Furthermore, trees are not repetitious, they are not pedantic and they do not practice pedantry, or pedantism, whichever you may prefer to adopt for your discriminating and listening ears.!

Arrogance - Hear ! Hear !

Young Tree - ....And they, dear Grand Lady Arrogance.....and they are not audacious as you had seemed to intimate a while ago on the occasion of my sudden intrusion into the discourse between Your Ladyship, and Lady Tolerance and Lady Patience.........no, they are not audacious : they display their feelings just as simply as a response to the good nourishment from Mother Nature .

Lady Patience - The perplexing and infinitely patient miracle of growth, in its perenniеal elusive course !

Young Tree - Lady Patience, of that aspect I have never heard a mention by our Elders and I am unable to perceive or understand your sentence, but we trees know how to respond to Nature by displaying a good coat of foliage, robust branches, and a continuous desire to grow higher, to breathe and see the majesty of the sky . Trees, besides, do not have the same advantages as other creatures have, for example, you know, like the.............

Arrogance - Like......like me, for example ?!

Young tree - Oh !..No, I did not have Your Ladyship in mind, I assure you,Your Highness! Not at all !!

Arrogance - And why not ?

Young Tree - No,Your Ladyship: I was aiming at the advantages that certain other creatures have, creatures that I cannot see, that we, trees, cannot see but whom we can perceive for their advantage by reference of their attitudes towards us, individually, and, as a whole, by the entire forest, to the disadvantage of other creatures, by the gift of speech so that nefarious actions can be justified by meandrous mental configurations, that no one else can contest .

Artrogance - So what ?....What you are talking about, my dear hard wood philosopher, is meaningless, probably, not in your wooden....core, but to the perception of anyone else's intelligence..........and what has all this got to do with your story about the presence of Lady Patience and Tolerance being here, I just wonder....??!!

Tolerance - Cousin..!..Please, let the poor little tree go about his own way in coming to it !

Arrogance - " Patience !!" ??.....Right ?!!

Patience - You said it .

Arrogance - I said that purely out of desperation, mental, that is. One thing is quite clear in my mind: I could never be a tree, not even an arrogant one !

Young Tree - Oh ! We have a few of them too, here, in the forest ! They are trying to outdo every other tree in size, hight and foliage ! It's a well known anomaly recognized throughout this forest .

Arrogance - "ANOMALY"...???!!.....You just watch your language, you junky piece pf hard wood !

Lady Tolerance - Cousin, your attitude is out of proportion to the present issue !....Why, hard wood is a most solid piece of wood, well representing its own appellative of "hard ".

Young Tree - Oh ! Yes, very true, and also quite well known for their difficulty to work with and to finish...!!

Arrogance - If this nonsense talking continues, I am not sure who might be in the ...."finish"....!!

Lady Patience - Now, now, all present, a little "patience", here, should be welcomed, rather than becoming embroiled in a petty sparring match of dubious intellective sustance, meaning and purpose : by calmly evaluating the trajectory of our conversation, it seems to me that we have deviated significantly from the originally intended talk .

Young Tree - I am not tall enough, yet, to be able or justified to pass a personal judgement or opinion on the subject, but my wooden instinct would go along with Lady Patience comment, and it is quite clear that we have lost the very primary reason for our intended original talk!...Weren't we supposed to have discussed the reason why Lady Tolerance and Patience, had come to these woods ?

Lady Tolerance - Precisely so .

Arrogance - More likely : " Unfortunately ...so " !!

Lady Patience - Regardless of our sweet cousin Arrogance questionable displeasure about it,it is obvious that we all finished up in a tangled and totally detached discussion about audacity, monotony, litanies, pedantry and tall trees, hard trees, arrogant trees, instead to stick to the main and intended subject of why LadyTolerance and I were here in these woods as interpreted and strongly felt by our little young and green tree !

Arrogance - And that last "interpretation"was what I was afraid of...!!

Lady Tolerance - Why ?

Arrogance - I dislike simple stupidity, unless embellished by the clamour and resonance of purposeful and roguish stupidity .

Lady Tolerance - That's restricting your view of "interpretation" of the various phases of the infinite modes of intellectual perception where there is even some wisdom in a jest, as the old adage still goes .

Arrogance - To me, life, is a jest .

Young Tree - Oh ! That's strange : I had never heard that life had two names .

Lady Patience - Little Tree, Take our Cousin's remarks with a grain of..."saw-dust"..... for he's always out to tease and challenge, and he does not seem to know any better .

Arrogance - Had you been a tree and not my cousin, I'd had you answered in the appropriate fashion with an unfriendly remark, but, under the restrictive circumstances, even a prince, like I am, must show restraint......at times !

Lady Patience - I did not make any disparaging remarks, particularly about life, but you did, so, no need for you, dear cousin, to force yourself into any "restrictive restraints" and just join all of us in a peaceful, patient and tranquil attitude and listen to our young green tree's story .

Arrogance - What else more glorious, more superb, more rewarding could any creature wish for than the unbelievably fortunate opportunity to listen to the enchanted narration of a stupid tree's confused and troubled emotional constitution ? I'd dare say : none, whatsoever !!

Young tree - I heard your comment, and the best way to alleviate the displeasure of your ....impatience.....is for me to come out with the remarks I had originally planned to make, if I shall be allowed to continue .

Arrogance - You had that permission long ago, dear stick of wood, and we most emphatically reaffirm it here and now : so, please, proceed and, as I had said originally, "make it short " !

Young Tree - I am sorry about these "unplanned" delays, but even trees, sometimes, have feelings and want to express themselves . Our Gnomes know that well !

Arrogance - Oh,No !!....Not the Gnomes, now, into the scene ! Between the two possibilities, You or the Gnomes, You and your story may be the least damaging to my ability to listen and pay attention. So, please, do proceed and if you bulk at this renewed invitation ,I will not listen anymore .

Young Tree - My story, indeed, and, more than a story, it is a clarification of that story, an event that perpetuates itself indefinitely in our existences .

Arrogance - Not in my existence, for sure, whatever this mysterious "clarification" may be!...Go ahead : what else is new ?

Lady Patience - The Young Tree will go ahead, cousin Arrogance, and shortly, but, in the meantime and, just to "clarify" and express my feelings about this mudh talked about of my and Lady Tolerance being here this evening, I have to say that I am mighty glad that I was born of a patient and tolerant heritage, two key features that help any creature to ford the uncertain river of our exsistences. .

Young Tree - Right ! Right !....Very ,very right, Your Ladyship, and that was exactly what I had in mind to tell to all here present, when, and I admit , I burst so rudly into the on going conversation, without the civilized and expected appearance of, at least, a polite, even if marginal, invitation !

Lady Tolerance - Among civilized creatures, or any creatures that feel that they may be civilized, whichever comes first, no one needs a specific invitation to ....join into an on going conversation, to which conversation the one desiring to join in was already part of that conversation, like you were .

Arrogance - I liked it more the other way : to burst into a conversation "totally uninvited" and just for spite .

Lady Tolerance - I like the old adage, too, that went and still goes like : " It takes all sorts to make this World " .

Young Tree - If I were not solidly planted and firmly secured to this forest ground, I would feel like sliding on a slippery path, back to the bickering we thought we had decided to leave behind !!!

Lady Tolerance - A wise...interjection and, at the appropriate time, indeed ! Thank you, little green tree !

Lady Patience - Shall we, then, proceed ?.....Or, rather, shall we let our little tree proceed and tell his story ?

Arrogance - With so many deviations, circumnavigations of the main subject and hesitations and bickerings and what not, I wonder if there would still be any substantial interest in a stupid little green tree story or opinion of a story !!!

Lady Tolerance - Unfortunately, what you just said, Cousin Arrogance, reflects the reality of today prevailing thinking among simple and not so simple creatures throughout our little forests, the perplexing inability to weigh facts ,events and ideas with patience and dedication, before committing the destiny of millions of trees to faulty conclusions .

Young Tree - But the two legged creatures who roam our forests. they do not seem to care about the destiny of anybody else, except their own and, sometimes, in their blind dash to power, glory and riches, they even seem to forget to care about themselves, let alone the trees in a forest !

Lady Tolerance - Those creatures, the two legged ones with a small head at the top, are hard to reach, difficult to communicate with and impossible to engage in any sensible and coordinated dialogue : they only speak their own language which, sometimes, they even forget to understand .

Young Tree - I am glad I am a tree, with many branches, so that I can see the world around me in many different ways and aspects, a solid coat to protect me in the Winter and a hard, well contoured body for strength and support.

Arrogance - So well equipped as you claim to be, little stick of wood, why don't you tell us, now, why Lady Patience and Lady Tolerance came by this forest today ?

Young Tree - That is exactly what I want to tell you, Lady Arrogance, and that was the reason for entering, uninvited, your conversation : the two sweet Ladies presence here and their passing by, today, is not an unusual event, but a true representation of our very existences : that is, at least, as far as we trees are concerned .

Arrogance - Dear little green stick, if you are so well synchronized with Lady Patience and Lady Tolerance, why, then, don't you try to adopt their remarkable brevity in expressing thoughts and elucidating their content, particularly Lady Patience!

Young Tree - Brevity is a concept difficult to adpt for trees as we are bound, by natural causes, to expand .

Arrogance - May be with a little effort and imagination you could do the same and you must certainly remember how Lady Patience,just a while ago, during our endless conversation about nothing at all, had clearly established her identity claim in just one simple, neat and terse sentence.....if you do remember...she said : "I am mighty glad that I was born of a patient and tolerant heritage...."...Etcetera, etcetera.....!!....While, until now, you have said,virtually, nothing in spite of your use of innumerable sentences, explaining nothing and boring me greatly . You talk too much , too prolix, your sentences are empty of any conclusive substance, full of unnecessary words and vague passages .

Young Tree - But,Your Highness, Lady Arrogance, I cannot help it while expressing myself!.....You see, and just look how many branches I have and how many leaves : what do you expect...??!!....And all those branches and all those leaves , all of them have a right to express themselves in their verious ways and feelings and show enthusiasm in doing that and yet, in spite of all those branches and leaves, I am not as garrulous as certain other creatures who have only two standard branches and no leaves.....or shall I say.....who have only two vocal cords .

Arrogance - Dear little stick of green wood, you'd better tell your branches and your leaves to stop acting like small children and try to grow up and be more reasonable in their expression preferences, to be more like trees than impromptu philosophers, so that all creatures can enjoy their real potentials like the gentle rustling of the leaves in a placid breeze as well as the refreshing shade and not to be bored, instead, by the endless monotony of your redundant and....shall I say....."branching" explanations !!

Young Tree - Lady Arrogance..!....You just hit the right key, you just did !

Arrogance - I am not surprised : don't I always ?

Young Tree - I have no doubt of that, but your saying, just now, opened up my mind to what I was going to tell you about the two sweet Ladies walking into our woods, and............

Arrogance - Oh ! No ! Not again !

Young Tree - Have no fear, Lady Arrogance : this time it is short and straight to the very middle of my tender trunk !

Arrogance - Heavens above is witness, o little green tree, and you had better be true to your saying, this time !

Young Tree - I promise !...Now, you want me to tell you why are Lady Patience and Lady Tolerance here today ?

Arrogance - Shoot...!!!....I am dying to know !!!

Young Tree - Well, they are not really here today, because.........

Arrogance - I beg your pardon.....!!!

Young Tree - Oh ! Lady Arrogance, Your Highness, please, do not let my seeming sibylline quotations startle you : they are just introductory assertions because, when I say that Lady Patience and Lady Tolerance are not here today, I , really, mean to say that for the two Ladies among us here, today, in this Forest, there is no today or tomorrow or when or why, or before or after......

Arrogance - .....Or a flip of the coin.....heads or tails ??!....Heads I see them, tails ...they ain't here !.......Come now, boy, you are stretching it too far !

Young Tree - No, no, Lady Arrogance, Your Highness, not the way as you seem to understand it : it's not a game, but reality .

Arrogance - Reality...!!...Humbug ! Reality for me is a solid , effervescent , unconditional, unsurpassed, unchallenged and unchallengeable proof of superior splendor and overbearing on stupidity so well distributed among young green trees in the forests of our planet !...Why don't you try to talk some sense, sometimes ?

Young Tree - I am trying and I have been trying and, in the best of my ability, I am still trying, but Your Highness doesn't let me complete my sentences to their full extent therefore causing confusion and misunderstanding : what I was going to say, was that.......

Arrogance - ......And here we go again on a monotonous, senseless, dreamy like sermon...!!

Lady Patience - How about letting the young green tree talk ? Don't you think ?

Arrogance - But of course !

Lady Tolerance - Shut up, then, irreverent cousin !

Arrogance - The audacity of such an unwelcome remark !

Lady Patience - But quite natural: even tolerance, sometimes, has its limitations when confronted with shallow responses .

Young Tree - Oh ! I am so sorry to cause so much controversy and discomfort among all of you, gracious Ladies, and I wish to apologize for my slow coming to definitive and "conclusive" conclusions, but, my reasoning and the forthcoming of the substance of my sentences, are bound ,by Nature's will and dictate, to follow the slow flow of my lymph ,from my roots and up and wide to my trunk and branches, but, I shall try my best, now, to complete my saying, to please Lady Arrogance .

Arrogance - It's all the same to me : now, later or never . What do I care to know the whereabouts of creatures who do not even know how to introduce themselves and lack the ability of boasting about themselves, wherever they may be !!!

Young Tree - You expressed the "reality" of the situation quite adequately, Your Highness !

Arrogance - Listen who is talking !......What ...."reality situation" are you coming up with, now, stupid chunk of green wood ?

Young Tree - The "reality" of what you just said.....:" Wherever they may be "...!

Arrogance - So..??

Young Tree - You see, Lady Arrogance, Your Highness..........They are here all the time !

Arrogance - Now, what !!

Young Tree - They never came, they never left : they have always been here !

Arrogance - My young boy, I say, you need to have your branches examined ! What kind of nonsense are you trying to sell me, when you yourself, some time earlier, had spotted the two Ladies coming into the Forest and were pointing them out to me !

Young Tree - I wasn't sure, then, if you would be receptive to such a reality, that of them being here always, and their coming in the forest, a pure illusion of time .

Arrogance - And creatures at large think that "I" am a flamboyant architect of indiscreet and petulant dispositions!!!!.......Boy !!....Have I found some competition ,,,!!!

Lady Tolerance - Not an idle asset in this world of multform forests .

Lady Patience - Indeed .

Arrogance - And a pain in the......neck, when dealing with an idle brain of wood !

Young Tree - I do not know much about brains, Lady Arrogance, Your Highness, particularly the ones made out of wood, the comprehension of that notion is, really, not so important to our existences, since Mother Nature thinks for all our needs and thoughts, but this is what I had intended to explain to you, Your Highness and.....

Arrogance - Not a prolix explanation, PLEASE !!

Young Tree - A very brief one, Your Highness..........They are here all the time !

Arrogance - The mighty Universe, I am certain, may not be as complicated and "boxed in" as this forest is. Young tree : the tedious and empty conversing with you has led me to become quite adjusted to the imponderable, for me to be wondering, now, of a sensible explanation . So, go right ahead and I rest my case !

Lady Patience - That last statement, distinguished cousin, is a monumental confirmation of the inalienable right of all creatures to be able to express themselves freely, whether they are made of wood or some other substance .

Arrogance - Thank you . Someone wrote something like that about a wooden puppet who could think and, in the beginning, he had a little of my character. Oh ! Well : nothing new under the sun, said someone else, as well !!

Young Tre - And thank you to all of you, too, from ther bottom of my roots for being so condiscending, finally, in hearing my explanation which, so far, appears to have caused some bewilderment and confusion, but I'll soon remedy to that, so,............

Arrogance - That's a comforting promise...!

Young Tree - And I'll keep to it too ! So , as I was saying, going back to the point of contention, that point that had caused some mental discomfort and the disdain of Lady Arrogance at my terse and self-assured proclamations about Lady Patience and Lady Tolerance "being here all the time...!!".....Yes, Lady Arrogance, Your Highness, going back to that point, really, I feel very confident in confirming that truth, that they are here today, just as they were here yesterday, just as they have been all the time since I was born..!!!

Lady Patience - Dear Child...!!

Young Tree - Since my Parents' seeds were spread, since this forest was born, Lady Patience and Lady Tolerance have always been and always will be near us, very close to us and to our spirits, in the midst of us little trees and will keep us company and encourage our growth while we slowly develop into larger trees, a process that Nature programmed since the beginning of time, long and slow in its progress and, for us, a long, slow development beacon in front to the horizon, yet a well determined and controlled path always supported and encouraged by the unending help of Lady Patience,"patiently"tutoring our long travel from a tremulous seedling to a sprawling tree...!!

Lady Tolerance - Oh ! Yes !!....We know !

Arrogance - "..Oh,yes "....I say that too and what a sweet sequence of cause and effect to stimulate and enhance the sentiment and the intangible emotions of a wooden stick !!

Lady Patience - Quiet, ...PLEASE !

Arrogance - .....O...K...!!........Old Spinster .

Young Tree - .....And Lady Tolerance ensuring and guaranteeing our hesitant and unprotected growth by infusing an atmosphere of tolerant expectation among the other surrounding plants, so that we could grow unimpeded, until we would reach maturity and, at that point..........

Arrogance - ......And, at that point, you will be relieved of your "patient" itinerary with your spirit nursed by these wonderful and undefatigable Ladies, when an axe or a saw will be applied to the base of your trunk to turn you into something more useful in a faster and more exciting existence as planks to build good furniture or for seasoned wood for a warm fireplace !

Ldy Tol;erance - An unnecessary and frivolous comment, Lady cousin, on the serious nature of life, any life that is, and well conforming to the old adage that...:" the fox sheds its coat but not its vice "........A good reference, here, to our distinguished cousin, Lady Arrogance.......!

Young Tree - Dear Lady Tolerance, your"distinguished"and questionably questionable appellative of "cousin" for a sarcastic creature of the stature of Lady Arrogance, if you will excuse my own arrogance in saying so, is , at least in my limited opinion, derogatory to your exaulted stature in the spirit of enlightened living!!

Lady Tolerance - That kind of attitude is not even worth of a half ounce of my attention !

Young Tree - But this " cousin" of yours, instead, delights in choosing sarcasm as a way of expression forged and coined by creatures with the kind of twisted taste that is so well palatable among "HER" Followers........I am proud of my nature and of the "message" Nature has assigned to me, for me to carry it during my exsistence in this forest and, after that, in whatever form Nature would have decided upon. .

Lady Arrogance - A "message" in a wooden stump.....??!!...I declare !!....How exciting !

Young Tree - Not so much exciting,Your Highness,Lady Arrogance, but, rather warming!

Arrogance - Atta boy !!....That's exactly what I had just predicted for you, young stick of wood...a warming embrace in an even warmer fireplace...!!

Lady Tolerance - Incorrigible...!!

Young Tree - Please,dear Lady Tolerance,do not worry about Lady Arrogance's comments ! You see, I believe that what is in one creatures's nature, cannot, really, be erased just because some one may not like that particular disposotiom since, in my limited opinion as a simple stick of wood, the trend to an arrogant behaviour, displeasing as it may be to a discerning taste, still is part of a natural phenomenon, beyond our power to decipher and comprehend, so let me answer Lady Arrogance expressed point of view !

Lady Tolerance - By all means, dear child : go right ahead !

Young Tree - Thank you, Lady Tolerance, and each of my young branches will share equally in the opinion of my expressions, I promise you ....

(then, turning to Lady Arrogance, who had been standing there totally aloof and with a disgraceful sneer on her lips, and addressing her........)

Lady Arrogance, Your Highness, I really do appreciate your insufferableness for these leisurely conversations, probably of no interest at all to your richly endowed superior sense of understanding, but and for the record of good explanatory matters, I have to disagree with your impression of a"warming" experience, as you had just mentioned and described /

Arrogance - Hear ! Hear !

Lady Tolerance - Incorrigible...!!

Young Tree - Your impression, dearLady Arrogance, is not quite the way you envisage the "swelling scene", and not quite so amusing as represented by your devious and sadistic partiality to what partains to your personality and existence as adverse to the existences and endevours of other creatures . You see, as a matter of straight record, I was given by Nature the clear mandate to carry a double message .

Arrogance - Don't you think that one would have been good enough ?

Young Tree - May be : but it is not for me or any of the other trees in this forest to question Nature: as I said, I was given two messages. The first.......

Arrogance - A good "spare"one for the road, I presume !

Lady Tolerance - Oh ! Incorrigible !!

Young Tree - I don't know about that and I don't know what"spare" is or means but, as I was saying, the first one message.....to give shelter and shade . The second, to warm the heart of the weary creatures with a glittering fire, so that nothing would go wasted of my nature, a green abundant spread of foliage when alive and a warm, affectionate embrace of light, warmth and comfort at the end of my existence . .

Arrogance - How thoughtful of Mother Nature !....Indeed...!!...Don't you think so too, Lady Patience ?

Lady Patience - Has it ever occurred to you, dear Arrogance, that Mother Nature may not have intended, after all, to be so "thoughtful" about your nature ?

Arrogance - For sure, it never occurred to me . So sorry about it .

Lady Patience - The trees have very useful lives : they contribute to our general well-being and, even in their death , theywarm us up and give us light and comfort and ask for nothing in return from us . What do you think about it, dear Arrogance, and what is your return for all the empty pride you instill on so many empty consciences ?

Arrogance - For your information, dear Lady Patience, distinguished cousin, I do not need anybody to do any "thoughtful" thinking for me .

Lady Patience - May I remind you, dear cousin, that a similar attitude had been tried in very ancient times and, in due time, it failed because Nature had not planned it in its long range message for the creatures of this planet, so that only thoughtless and, I would add, arrogant creatures, with inclinations very similar to yours. if I may say so, had the extravagant as well as the naive audacity to overrule Nature and its sobering "Laws" and set out to build something.

Arrogance - Probably those creatures had overlooked to apply for a building permit .

Lady Patience - Their arrogant attitude would not allow them to ask for any permit from anyone, least of all from Mother Nature, whom, probably ,they didn't even think it existed or, even if they did, they certainly didn't seem to care about it !

Arrogance - Blockheads !

Lady Tolerance - Had they been such, at least that condition could have atoned, in some way, for their recklessness !

Lady Patience - Anyway, those people set out to build a tower that you, probably, might have heard about in the history of this world, a story of those far away times in the lives of those forests of the day, a story that talked about a now lost town by the name of Babel and the tower that those arrogant people had set out to build, taking the famed name of the "Babel's Tower", the Jewish name for the ancient town of Babilonia, "bell" in ancient Syrian meaning "confusion", and so the tower remained unfinished for lack of sober and considered intention.

Arrogance - What's the connection with our young green tree, here, in this forest and your permanent presence in here, too ?

Lady Patience - None whatsoever .

Arrogance - And I am supposed to be arrogant ?

Lady Patience - Yes!The difference: you"ARE"while"I"am only pretending. Besides, it has a reference to the present talking: your reluctance to recognize others'values .

Arrogance - If other creatures have "Values", then good for them: I certainly do not care as, I am pretty sure, they do not care about mine ! So, you still didn't tell me what connection theTower of something had to do with our present talking ??!

Lady Tolerance - She just told you, dear cousin : " none whatsoever" .

Arrogance - And what kind of an explanation that's supposed to be ?

Lady Patience - The same type that you have been using when talking or answering our young green tree .

Arrogance - May be the young green tree was planning to build another tower, somewhere...!....So , I was trying to "confuse" him....!!!

Lady Patience - So, you had heard or learnt about that famed tower ?

Arrogance - Yes, I heard of it : it's common knowledge . They, those "arrogant"creatures, wanted to build a tower so tall that it would reach the Heavens and the higher it went the more confusion it created, rather then satisfy everyone . Oh! yes, I had heard the story, dear Lady Patience : it's common knowledge .

Lady Patience - Well, doesn't that tell you something ?

Arrogance - You mean......another message, perhaps ?

Lady Patience - May be .

Arrogance - Well, my dear cousin, it is not my fault if those ancient engineers and architects were a bunch of nincompoops !

Young Tree - But, my dear Arrogance, Your Highness, they, those audacious and irreverent creatures, must have had you in mind and as well an inborn propensity for your unusual and overbearing inclinations when they started building the tower, did they not ??

Arrogance - I doubt it : had they, they would have let some other nincompoops build it .

LadyPatience - Your remark, dear cousin Arrogance, is not even funny or amusing and, cert-tainly, not even witty !Why can't you be more congenial and discuss things on an even level rather than ridiculing eveything and everybody and ignoring their intrinsic historical and foreboding intent ?

Arrogance - As to"foreboding", really, I have no time and the least of interest in it . Now, in regard to"intent", I am only interested in one aspect of it : to excell above everybody and everything, takes what it takes . In that kind of foreboding and intent I place some of my interest .

Young Tree - Of all the odds !....Now I understand what our Elders Trees were telling us, young growing and aspiring seedlings !....They were saying, on as many occasions as they could, ...:" beware of strangers and of those with a loud mouth...!", because the lack of concern of these creatures for others and their inborn skepticism of anything orthodox and affable, makes them dangerous to trees and forests and, just as it happened in the Tower of Babel, they only seed confusion and, where confusion reigns, disaster soon follows .

Lady Patience - We all hold this to be true and clear in this forest and in all other forests made of noble timber in this world, but I doubt that Lady Arrogance would agree to it !

Arrogance - And why should I ? Stupidity is not my cup of tea, you know ! Emotionality, not even my cup! Philosophy not even worth of one sip, in my book ! Action, climbing, reaching as high as possible, as high as impossible, without regard for the means to achieve it and...........

Young Tree - Oh ! Yes ! I remember now what our teachers in high school were telling us of a great Man of Antiquity, an eminent statesman and Writer, who was advocating reaching"results", regardless of the means used to achieve the desired results !...If I remember correctly, his name was Macchiavelli .

Arrogance - It looks like to me that your"teacher" might have needed some extra schooling himself !

Young Tree - Why do you say that, dear Arrogance ??

Arrogance - Well, "Machiavelli" is spelt with only one "C", to begin with .

Young Tree - Are you sure ? May be there were two Machiavellis : one with one "C" and the other with two "Cs", no ??

Arrogance - Of course, the world is full of copy-cats and I am not surprised if someone, out there, did or does like I do . Anyway..............

Lady Tolerance - Incorrigible...!!

Arrogance - ....Anyway, some dumb sticks of wood, trees, I mean, will not stop nor try to correct or change my way of thinking, acting or living, insignificant as they are to my welfare .

Lady Tolerance - Oh !.....Incorrigible !!

Young Tree - Lady Arrogance's defiant standing tends to wither my beautiful and tender new, young green leaves !

Lady Patience - Do not worry about all this nonsense, dear little green tree: our our Forests are full of that kind of loud-mouths,contemptibly silly in their expressions and pitifully dedicated at the building of innumerable Babel's Towers of all shapes, heights and...consistencies and........

Young Tree - Please, excuse me interrupting you, dear Lady Patience, but I do not see any Towers !

--Lady Patience - As in the far away times of antiquity, dear little green and young tree, the present Towers lie hidden in many creatures'uneasy minds, in their own over-extended infatuation, tepid convictions but ebollient impetus to outdo every-one one and everything, without restraint or any use of common sense !..You do not see them, those Towers, I mean, because there cannot be any of them in a real material form, but they can reach the sky in the confused intellects of many creatures .

Young Tree - I believe you, Lady Patience,I really do and very much so, although my branches and my tender leaves are too young yet to be able to absorb with competency all that you have just said . May be, Lady Arrogance did understand, I guess .

Arrogance - Bah ! Humbug..!!....I do not waste time in second hand deductions about ancient times old women's yarns and their incomparable riddles of history .

Lady Tolerance - I was expecting such a comment !

Arrogance - Besides, I only see one way and that is to reach for the s`tars at any cost and even with contempt, when necessary, if necessary, in my subtle judgement, of course, of any rules of arbitrary-made convention attitudes and customs or of historical or emotional codes of observance in the intellectual shadow of ancient traditions , so well brought forward by the impassionate interpretation of them by our dear Lady Patience, with a veiled foreboding of vague representations . A foreboding of what ??!....Ah ! Humbug...!!

Lady Patience - Of doom, dear Arrogance : ...of doom !

Arrogance - No need to always dramatize situations : doom is an unfortunate episode in the existences of all creatures, in equal measure for the smart ones and the stupid ones, and through the entire scale of creation of living things , so there is no need to make a lot of fuss about it, dear Lady Patience, just a natural occurrence, unforeseeable and unpredictable !

Lady Tolerance - A rather simplistic way of looking at things....of various intent .

Arrogance - I don't think so and every creature knows that : but it is not a "stopping" stone, but, instead, a "stepping" stone to look at "why" and "what" went wrong about "something", that could not have been anticipated or more carefully thought, programmed and actuated .

Lady Patience - You contradict yourself, Cousin : you had just claimed that doom was a natural occurrence, unforeseeable and unpredictable.......what "stepping" stone are you talking about ?

Arrogance - May be lack of premonition or lack or preparedness, or, may be, just simple negligence, this last one so common a fault in any forest that I happen to know.

Young Tree - Oh!...Yes...I remember our Elders telling us, young fledgeling seedlings, something about this"doom"that you all seem to be talking about , when they were warning us of the incursions in our woods by the two legged creatures !

Lady Tolerance - What do you say to that, now, dear Cousin ?

Arrogance - Of course,"doom",is a "personalized"perception of it, its meaning strictly guided by individual intellectual and principled emotional intents, its "cause and effect",or,more specifically:".there is no effect without a cause.", admirably described by "Master Pangloss" in a well known novel by an eminent philosppher and writer.

Lady Tolerance - ...."Arouet" , by any chance ?

Young Tree - François Marie ..!!

Arrogance - Bravo !..Our little ..Genie or...genius in the forest !!.But of course: Voltaire !

Lady Patience - And what does all this mean, dear Cousin ?

Arrogance - Oh ! I do not know, but I heard people of some respect, talking about it, so, I guess, it must have some meaning . Anyway, "doom" should not prevent creatures to look at it square in the face, fight it , neutralize it and throw it under their feet or....well.....under their... stumps....!!...Well, sorry about it, but, anyway, always be on top of everything and even be irreverent in the face of doom . And I am not talking about " courage ", here, in the face of adversities, but just common sense in the evaluation ofa common denominator .

Lady Patience - Remarkable effort, indeed, but not always applicable .

Young Tree - I agree with Lady Patience : its applicability is questionable .

Lady Tolerance - I believe that Lady Patience and the young Tree are reflecting a logical assumption .

Young Tree - Thank you, Lady Tolerance, and let me add this : you see, dear Lady Arrogance, Your Highness, how could I avoid doom when and if coming to me or even just " face its face", as you suggested, when I am stuck solid here in this soil, even unable to turn in the direction from which the doom would come, to "face it"..??

Arrogance - As I always preach, and as I always practice, and as I always proclaim, it is not my fault if some aspects of Nature were to be made up of incapacitated creatures, that is, physically handicapped and, also, more often than seldom, of mentally incompetent creatures . It must have been a fortunate turn for my luck to have escaped such a gracious natural recognition of form and status !!!

Young Tree - What Nature made, Your Highness, dear Lady Arrogance, whatever Nature does or did or will do, is not to be criticized for the simple reason that she cannot talk back to us and explain , except, of course, in the form of what she does or does not, and this, Dear Arrogance, Your Highness, in my limited ligneous opinion and only in the limited projection as the extension of my branches can reach and no further....!

Arrogance - Of course ......

Lady Patience - On the contrary, dear Arrogance ! As a matter of fact, I believe that the little young tree said something worth of esteem, considering his solid ligneous input and the "branching" out of his insight to the outside world , yet demonstrating a courageous expression of his sentiments in a civilized manner, in a civilized World and in a discreet accentuation , and so do I believe .

Arrogance - My, oh ! My !....You don't say !!...A "civilized" World...!!!...Well, you must be certainly referring to some planets somewhere else in outer space, certainly not OUR World !!

Lady Patience - Much closer than you think ! As a matter of fact , precisely OUR WORLD, unfortunately the very same World that we have to share with types of creatures like YOU !

Arrogance - Am I to understand, perhaps, that we, that is all the gentle people who are here today in this assembly and company, am I to understand as I was saying, that we have to share that part of the World which is more to my liking, of course, and void, shall we say, of wooden stumps or exceedingly boring and"patient" creatures, like you : am I right ?

Lady Patience - You may think as you wish , dear cousin : after all, thinking , whether openly expressed or jealously locked in one's mind, is born naturally free and only altered if unguarded when exposed : sometimes, it is well disposed, some other times it may be questionable and, some other times still, and those are the most often times, it is confused, uncertain, inconclusive, vague and ill-constructed . This, of course, does not and should not prevent anyone from thinking !

Arrogance - That's what I thought !

LadyTolerance - And so did I: don't we all, now..??!

Lady Patience - Indeed, we all do!...Thinking, that is !.....And everyone is free to interpret matters to their own wishful interpretation although, in some far away forests, I am told, free thinking is at a premium and its practice has cost several trees their existence, but, then , let us look at the brighter side of things and, fortunately, our forest is still free : thanks Heavens..!!....So I believe that what the little green tree had said a while ago was not to be ridiculed . After all, he is only a little young tree and has not seen much of the World we all live in .

Arrogance - To tell you the truth, I have even forgotten what he said a while ago .

Lady Patience - But something should have remained impressed in your "adorned" head, dear cousin! You were talking with our little tree !

Arrogance - Hold it right there, my dear !....Just hold it a picking minute !! That little green tree is "YOUR" little green tree ! ...NOT "OURS" and, most certainly, not mine ! I would not want a piece of wood among my followers, I assure you af that !

Lady Patience - Think as you wish, but you must remember something that he said , just a little while ago .

Arrogance - Your patience, my dear, is just as fastidious as your very name is boring and your insistence annoying....Oh ! Well, what did he say, this wooden philosopher of...."YOURS" ? Nothing worth keeping for posterity, I presume !

Lady Patience - Oh! no ! Nothing, really, so dramatic, for there is no need for POSTERITY to be informed or reminded or be enveloped in an aura of golden majesty about something that even a small pebble, somewhere, knows quite well, except you, so it seems !

Arrogance - I have the least interest in pebbles .

Lady Tolerance - Likewise the pebbles in you, I am pretty sure .

Arrogance - And what do you expect to achieve or to arrive to, with this highly intellectual exhibition of pebbles dramatization, to put it quite blandly ?

Lady Patience - Only to remind you of what the little green tree was telling you about Nature, that ridiculing or contesting or criticizing it and its work, is no pedestal for anyone to be on it and preaching absurd conclusions on Nature's work , and that would have been what the little young tree would have told you , had you only had the "patience" to let him finish his saying !

Young Tree - And that is true, because it is not for any of us to criticise Nature ! After all, we do not even know what "Nature" really is......well, shall I say...at least, we trees do not know : we just act for her , I guess .

Lady Patience - Now......should I enlarge upon it , dear cousin...??!

Arrogance - Hardly necessary, illustrious and very patient cousin ! Instead, I begin to think and, I am thinking, really thinking, fervently thinking, unequivocally thinking, that, at this pace of your telling me what the tree was telling me, we will either forget the thread of the whole thing or go to sleep and dream of what the little young green tree was going to tell me and, once we wake up from the salubrious slumber, we will remember what the little young green tree had told us in the dream that we will have dreamt and we all shall be very, very happy, indeed....!!........And how true it is that "old adage" that it takes all sorts to make this World !

Lady Tolerance - And I couldn't have said any better myself, dear cousin, if you know what I mean !

Arrogance - I know very well what you mean and I don't give a hoot about it either . But, at the same time, how true it is the old "common knowledge" that a lot of patience is needed with slow witted creatures, always waiting, exceedingly patient, for a glimpse of furtive light to illuminate their dim intellects .

Young Tree - And, in this instance, I give credit to you, dear Arrogance, because you said it rightly: "patience", monotonous and unexciting as it is, yet, this legacy of "patience" and our Lady Patience, herself, ultimately will always be able to bear and, eventually, to put behind one's back the many difficulties encountered in our daily existences. I guess you might have heard that famous proverb of ancient times, in a foreign forest, that goes like ....

Arrogance - There are no foreign forests for me : I am well accepted and embraced everywhere there are creatures whose instincts push them to higher and higher grounds without without a specific reason for doing that, only moved on the cognizance of their own ignorance, much to my enjoyment of the theatrical performance and my contempt for their insignificant superficiality . Does this, now, answer your question, or query, or curiosity, dear little and young green tree ?

Young Tree - Oh ! Dear Lady Arrogance, Your Highness, I did not mean to even doubt for a fraction of the length of one of my leaves of your immense recognition so widely spread everywhere in the living World, that world that is still poorly known to me , young as I am, but all that I was thinking reguarded Your high posture and standing and............

Arrogance - Now you are talking, Boy !

Lady Tolerance - Oh !...Still incorrigible...!!

Young Tree - And, as I was saying, just because of that high posture and eminent standing you might not have been interested or might have been even bored by taking notice of a simple proverb, so popular in that foreign forest that I had just mentioned, so, without any intent to upset you or to even ventilate the slightest doubt about your Universality in this World, it all boils down that all that I wanted to recollectwas............

Arrogance - Courage, my boy, SAY IT !! We haven't got the whole day, you know !

Lady Tolerance - Oh !....Hopelessly incorrigible !

Young Tree - Yes, of course, yes, your Highness, here it is what I was going to say or, rather, recollect was a well known proverb, so very popular in that foreign forest, and it goes like this.......

Arrogance - This alien forest must be very, very far away from us if it is going to take such a long time to be heard, my dear tree ! How long do you expect me to pay attention to your historical recalls from very far away forests ,who knows, may be in a very far away different World !!

Lady Patience - What difference would it make, anyway, even if it were a different World ? To its inhabitants, if any, it would mean exactly the same as it would here in our World, I guess and, if not so, then, I doubt that it were a "World" .

Arrogance - Dear Ladies, I do not know much about "other" worlds, my interest is strictly focused on this World which I can appreciate, feel and touch and work my wonders and, I hope, this "famous proverb" to turn out to be a local product and not a shooting star across the sky !

Young Tree - Oh! No, Your Highness, it is not up in the sky and it is not so far away either, but, actually, useable and practicable even righthere in this forest of ours ! It is, indeed, a very common saying but one that carries , at least, one ounce of reality living and it goes like this : "...Ge.....

Arrogance - My,Oh1 My ! What do I hear !!...." REALITY LIVING..." !!!!!!!...Ohi! Ohi! I can't believe my damn ears !!....May be, your far, far away forest has brought you back, in your historical enthusiasm, to the lands and forests of the ancient mighty and wise Gods, who lived on a high mountain and tended to the destinies of the various creatures living at the foot of that great mountain and told them what to do and what not to do and, if things went wrong, they were always there, those mighty and, yet, benevolent, Gods, ready to give good advice and a helping hand to those awkward two legged human creatures!

Young Tree - I have never heard anything about those forests on those mountains and......did you say.." Gods" ?.....on those mountains or mountain or shooting stars in the sky, all those mountains and Gods helping everybody......incredible....did they help trees, also, when they needed help and protect them from the greedy notions of those two legged awkward creatures ?....But I assure you thatI have heard of that famous proverb, yes ,Sir, a known proverb ,very popular in that foreign forest and it goes like ....

Arrogance - You have said a thousand times before to be ready for that proverb to" ..go like this...." and it has not come yet !.....So , little silly tree, speed it up and tell me this famous or not so famous proverb of yours , before I will get tired of waiting and leave you and this stupid forest ! As you, probably and, yet questionably, might have realized by now, I am not the type of creature pleasurably inclined to wait for other creatures' comfort .

Lay Patience - In my book, "comfort" is synonimous with some relief of affliction, consolation and solace or a state of ease and cheerfulness for your neighbour !

Arrogance - I don't know or even guess what kind of books you read : it certainly is not my book !

Lady Tolerance - It shows .

Arrogance - Oh ! Enough of all this nonsense ! Where is this damn proverb ,damned who thought of it and damned all this wasted time and my gullibility waiting to hear it !

Lady Patience - A little patience, dear cousin, will smooth even the longest vigil .

Arrogance - That, my dear cousin, would apply to stupid creatures who so stupidly wait long vigils for something they will never be able to achieve except their own death !

Lady Patience - And aren't we all waiting ?.....And, I mean, stuipid and not so stupid and utterly stupid creatures, all waiting for the same thing, quite regularly and, for the smart creatures, they do not need any long vigils to know about their own death, well aware of it long before any of the stupid peoples do .

Young Tree - Ah !..That's a depressing thought !

Lady Tolerance - So unnecessary too, in the contest of this conversation .

Young Tree - Dear Lady Arrogance.....Your Highness, do you want to hear that famous proverb now ?

Arrogance - A little longer in this forest and I'll become balmy by just listening to the incredibly muffled and circumvolutory talk of these makeshift savants!! I even begin to believe that all this that's happening around me, is not really happening or really true !

Young Tree - I'll tell you the proverb, right now, just to prove to you that "all" that's happening around you, here, in this forest, today, is really true !

Arrogance - You are not kidding, are you ?

Young Tree - Not at all !! This long chitchat that has been going on without a speedy conclusion, about a lot of nothing, well conforms to another old proverb that.......

Arrogance - Oh ! No ! No! I couldn't bear it ! Not another proverb !!!

Young Tree - But this one is harmless, Your Highness !

Arrogance - Does that mean that the first one is ?

Young Tree - Not necessarily : only if you do not agree with it .

Arrogance - That's an imposition! How dare you, stick of wood, suggest such an impudent remark to my exalted majesty !

Young Tree - With my utmost sincerity, Your Highness, I did not mean any offence, outrage or disrespect to your exalted majesty but, it is a very common happening, when talking at length among various creatures, to talk more than is really necessary as, I am certain, you must be familiar with the old adage that one thing leads to another, so, it just led me to another proverb, that was all !

Arrogance - One more explanation and I leave without giving you the satisfaction of saying your proverb : clear ?

Young Tree - Clear it is and the proverb says : " Geduld überwindet alles " .

Arrogance - Is that all ?

Young Tree - Yes .

Lady Tolerance - What else did you expect, cousin ?

Arrogance - A proverb, I was told .

Lady Patience - And you did get the proverb .

Young Tree - Yes, I just said it . You must have heard me saying it, Your Highness, and there was no wind going through my branches and rustling my leaves, to muffle the sound of my speech .

Arrogance - I heard you saying it but I had never heard it before..besides,it is in a different language and I do not even know that language ! What kind of joke is this ??!

Young Tree - Heavens forbid, Your Highness, this is not a joke ! ...And why would I want to play a joke on your eminent person and for no reason at all !!!

Lady Tolerance - And why should everything that does not meet your approval , dear cousin, be now a joke ??!

Arogance - Call it a joke, a riddle, a child's quiz or a ridiculous statement, at this stage of the game and, by "game", I mean our conversation, I cannot..............

Lady Tolerance - That, what you just said, "that" is a real joke !

Arrogance - You may be right, dear cousin, a real joke among JOKERS and, very confidentially, that is exactly what I think of all of you .

Lady Patience - And why ?

Young Tree - May be I said something that offended Her Highness, Lady Arrogance ! Did I, now ?

Lady Patience - I do not think so : some creatures do not have the necessary gift of patiently considering all the various aspects of an equation, before coming to a reasonable, negotiable and productive conclusion .

Arrogance - What kind of a cockeyed statement that is, dear cousin:only dim-witted creatures need to spend eons before coming to a conclusion even about elementary issues .

Lady Tolerance - Well : have you come to a conclusion, yet, on this issue, dear cousin ?

Arrogance - Long before than you had even figured it !

Lady Patience - Interesting, but intriguing : I, nor Lady Tolerance, or the Young tree, had figured anything beforehand .

Arrogance - But "it figures" exceedingly well with me, as your answer is typical of undecided brains, unable to counteract an unapproacheable reality .

Lady Tolerance - I like that .

Arrogance - Like that...what ??

Lady Tolerance - The "unapproacheable reality ".

Young Tree - Ah ! Yes! Yes !.....Reality living..!! I had thought of it !

Lady Tolerance - But "my" reality was in reference to our cousin, Lady Arrogance, indeed the personification of an "unapproacheable" existence for a creature that would like to carry a meaning for itself.

Young Tree - I don't understand the tenor of this newly developed conversation : has this got to do something with my proverb ?

Arrogance - What anything has to do with anything : words are not tied together in a link sequence like sausages on a chain........they travel, instead, freely by themselves under their own individual power, the strength of that power proportionally equal to the brainy capabilities of the individual, something like your cryptic proverb is.......in an unintelligible language ! Are you trying to confuse creatures by mumbling some artifacts, their meaning, probably, even unintelligible to the "mumbler" himself, unable to grasp and explain the dimlit meaning of what he had just said !

Young Tree - Uh ! Is that so ? And what does all that mean, dear Arrogance,Your Highness?

Lady Tol;erance - In all probability it means that she, Lady Arrogance, does not intend to listen to your proverb .

Young Tree - Such a simple proverb.......our little seedlings know it by.....lymph and heart !!

Arrogance - Simple or not, I have never heard of such saying and I do not even know that language, that is if it is a language .

Young Tree - I am surprised at you, Your Highness, because you claim superiority on everything anywhere and everywhere you go or travel through, so you are expected to be, at least technically, famous and brilliant in anything there is in this visible and audible World, languages included, of course, or did the limited extension of my young branches prevent me from anticipating this little gap in Your Highness "all-wrap-around" universal knowledge ? Or would it have made any difference if I had translated it in our "FOREST LINGO", the way they teach it to us in school, to us seedlings ?

Arrogance - Spare me !

Young Tree- Or would I guess, should I have guessed, would I dare to think to even guess that a translation would be needed and, would that have made any difference....well, I really do not know...........

Arrogance - Either do I , I assure you.....!!.......As for you, that's understandable.......

Young Tree - But, for an eminent personality like Yours, who can climb the vertiginous heights of universal knowledge and where the majestic winds of perennial wisdom flow supreme, a simple, humble translation in an obscure dialect of an even more obscure forest, would not suffice to replenish your demanding ego! ....But, coming back to the point..............

Arrogance - To the POINT, indeed !! And your subject explanation combined with the intense significance of your wisdom and logic laden sentence, is so expanding and so vaste in its magnitude, that it would almost be impossible to think of it to be able to.....drag itself to a ....POINT...!!

Young Tree - In spite of the limited expansion of my young branches, dear Arrogance, yet, I understand your surprise and your impatience and your dismay and your disapproval of my lengthy explanations of situations that could be summarized, may be, in a few simple words or, may be, even better, not summarized or even ever said in the first place . But, now..........well !...REALLY, coming to "the point"...!!....Would you like for me to translate it to you ,Your Highness ?

Lady Tolerance - Offering to do what you are not requested or asked to do, without the ability or certainty to be able to anticipate whether your offer would be or could be appreciated or even desired, is not a wise approach in the everyday existence of creatures of this world and, most certainly, a suicidal one when the interested parties happen to be a silly, young, tremulous and naive tree and a...... .....Juggernaut of an impudent creature of the type of Arrogance .

Arrogance - And my most sincere and profoundly felt juggernautish thanks for that enviable compliment to my unique personality .

Lady Tolerance - Don't mention it .

Young Tree - Shouldn't I mention it , then ?

Arrogance - Ah! Of all the absurdities in this cockeyed world , innocence is limpid and transparent, well counterbalanced by solid, dense and stubborn stupidity! So , dear little and innocent tree, let me tell you something : no need to translate that proverb to me, because I know it very well and I happen to know it in all the languages, dialects and vernaculars of this world as well as of other worlds, should there be any around.......

Young Tree - But....but....Your Highness..... you had said that...............

Arrogance - Never mind what I had said : I just tricked you, you silly ninny ! I just delight in teasing and tricking creatures by causing them to think that they may hold an edge on me and my knowledge and authority, but to dash them into dust with a snap of my wit !

Young Tree - But that, Your Honour, Your Highness Lady Arrogance, that would be tantamount to deceipt for simple creatures, looking up to your authority and your aura of accomplished greatness, regardless of how accomplished or obtained, of course, and trusting your majesty as an inspirational incentive for their daily chores and the ever lurking danger of the unexpected, which can be joyous, at times, dubious, some other times, and, rarely, a happy one .

Arrogance - Do not be surprised, dear little green tree: too green are you to match my wit! You see, I happen to know that proverb very well, but, at the same time, how "brilliantly inadequate" of you to make a reference of it to my personality when, instead, and more appropriately so, it should have been addressed to our dear Lady Patience .

Young Tree - And why, Your Highness ?

Arrogance - Simply : proper character identification .

Young Tree - With all due respect, Your Ladyship, but a proverb, to the best of my simple and limited knowledge, has no specific address for anyone in particular : it's just a logical reminder of,of one of the many realities in the everyday life of everybody or anybody .

Arrogance - No need to be worried about my statement, young piece of wood : I only suggested that because our sweet Lady Patience is so much more closely iden-identifiable with " Geduld " than I, myself .

Young Tree - "Patience", you mean, which in the German language is " Geduld" ?

Arrogance - Precisely. And, as a consequence, if"Geduld", patience,that is, does overcome, in the final end, all and everything, and that is exactly what the proverb says...." uberwindet alles"....overcomes all.....don't you think that it would refer more appropriately to our precious Lady, standing here, near us ? I mean, Lady Patience or........should I rather say our:" sehr geehrte gnadige Frau Geduld "...which, in your forest lingo would probably and tentatively translate into something like :" A kind and considered Lady Patience"...!??

Young Tree - Well....as you wish, dear Lady Arrogance !....You see, I am too young to be familiar,yet, with all the various and multiform avenues of understanding of the proper aspects of character identification that best and most distinctly represent a true and unbiased representation of that particular character in any given creature and not being adequately mentally resourceful, yet, with the amount of lymph reserved for me at this age of my development, it is harduous for me to comprehend the difficult and complex intellectual processes needed to achieve a proper, correct and serene interpretation of that character, so......

Arrogance - I do not know of what kind of "various and multiform avenues" you are talking about ! I only know of one good avenue : MINE .

Young Tree - Oh !...Well..!!...Let me say it my own way ! What I mean is that the interpre-tation of all that mumbo-jumbo which seems to delight the cultured enclaves of the disciples ofYour Highness' High Society Entourage, actually leaves lit-tle or no room at all for my simple way of figuring things out or appreciating subtle variations in the tense of a peregrine thought or the passage of a flighty idea .

Arrogance - My boy, you are not talking, nor expressing yourself, not even discussing the issue : you are just talking a lot of nonsense !

Young Tree - Unfortunately, I cannot be a judge of that and.....

Arrogance - ...."And"...fortunately so !

Young Tree - Little and young as I am at this stage of my growth, my spirit, mind and soul are still far too fluid to be pressed into a definite form and stamped with a ticket of travel for a certain direction in my allotted existence , but, apart from that, I wanted to tell you that the reason for.....

Arrogance - Oh ! For all the heavens above ! Here we go again with some reasons, as if I had not had enough of them already !

Young Tree - Do not worry, Your Highness, I am not going into lengthy details.....

Arrogance - That's encouraging .

Young Tree - All I wanted to explain, by bringing up and mentioning that proverb, was that precisely because of our Lady Patience's..... patience....well, yes, because of her patience, we can grow slowly but steadily and she attends to our needs very patiently because, in our nature, the train of our existence runs very leisurely ....

Arrogance - Not in my existence, and that's " for sure" !

Young Tree - May be so, but I only know of ours, Your Highness . So, it also runs in circles, one circle at a time, one inward and one............

Arrogance - No wonder they cannot make any sense of what they are saying !

Lady Tolerance - Oh ! Incorrigible !

Young Tree - You are missing the point, dear Lady Arrogance, Your Highness, if you think so disparagingly of circles ! Why, all the greatest Institution of learning in many Forests of this World, and I cannot talk but of THIS world ,of course, have circles where great ideas are born and consequential thoughts are germinated ! We are proud of our circles, they tell us many, many things.

Arrogance - Except they fail to tell you the most important thing .

Young Tree - And which one would that be,Your Highness ? I really would like to learn it because we trees carry within ourselves an inborn message of adaptability to variable circumstances that favour our growth and insure our existence.

Arrogance - To "shut up" .

Young Tree - Your Highness...!!!

Lady Tolerance - Oh ! Despicably incorrigible !

Lady Patience - That's where I, usually, come in, to calm the stormy waters . Patience, courage and understanding ....even of offending foes, so do the Elders, in this Forest, teach the young seedlings, cousin Arrogance and, to the best of my patient examination of your character, you fit quite adequately in the thick files of the offending foes .

Arrogance - I didn't perceive any offensive intent in what I said : I just expressed my opinion . Is this a "free" forest or under a dictatorial Regimen ?

Lady Patience - Nothing to do with Regimens, dictators or restrictive Societies, dear cousin : only with tact, sensitivity and good manners .

Arrogance - Do you plan to go back to the days of crinolines and pompous wigs and hand - kissing Casanovas along with daring ballroom heroes ? My intent was purely a comment of strict, practical reality in regard to a situation : that's all what it was !

Patience - The intent, may be, but the thought that preceded that intent, was not of the honourable type .

Arrogance - You can say what you want and see it your own way : but I do not agree with it, at all

Young Tree - To be patient, our Elders always taught us little seedlings, at school, is a privilege, so precious a privilege, that only few creatures are ever endowed with it, as it is well known that few are the selected ones whose patience encourages positive thinking, sensible thinking and useful thinking, that type of thinking that while not conceding anything to chance or dubious choice, yet is sober enough to calmly ponder issues, discuss alternatives and apply common sense to any reasonable solution of presenting problems . Dear Lady Patience, by unanimous and universal consent of us trees of this Forest you are elected our most trusted and beloved Fairy GodMother !

Lady Patience - Oh ! An undeserved recognition !

Young Tree - You richly deserve that recognition .

Arrogance - I am touched by these expressions of unbounded sentimentality, but why am I still sitting here among these peculiar characters, that is, really, hard to explain, even to myself . Am I , perhaps, in an enchanted forest, where weird situations usually are known to develop ?

Lady Tolerance - If anything is weird around here can be easily located and identified in someone who just wondered about "developing weird situations ".

Arrogance - Are you talking about yourself, Lady Tolerance, dear cousin ?

Lady Patience - I believe that she was referring to you, dear cousin .

Arrogance - Is that so ? Well, I am tired of all this and I do not want to listen anymore to this soggy and second-hand philosophy so petulantly proclaimed by creatures of peculiar properties, particular to their own characters, but none of them like me ! Now, of course, it is not mandatory that anybody should be exactly the same like any other body but, this World is wide enough to allow sufficient space to be placed between unsavory subjects and myself .

Young Tree - Your Highness, with all due respect, but I happen to have overheard your loud denunciation of the present situation that has and is confronting you while sojourning in this forest and which has left you wondering why, at all, you had to stop here and listen to our talking, which, it seems to me, is not pleasing you .

Arrogance - What do you mean by all that, young green stick of wood ?

Young Tree - Well, I just thought that this forest has no fences, no boundaries, no guards, no laws requiring a documentation of residence or of transit through it, so, with all due respect, why do you persist in staying here, Your Highness, when the surroundings and the creatures around seem to displease you ?

Arrogance - Of all the immense sequence of talking that has been going on between all of us in this forest, today, at this hour and at all the previous hours, this what you just said, is the BEST of all I heard so far !

Lady Tolerance - Doesn't he, now, our little green tree, speak wisely about the innumerable variants of our daily existences ?

Arrogance - Indeed, he does, in its genuine simplicity, and I have to recognize it for his sake . But how perennial and how very true the old saying is that you should always stick to what you are made for, like in my case, that I was made to be above any other creature and look here what happened ! My, oh! My !,I allowed myself to be taken in by a " wooden" philosopher and taken, literally, for a ride !

Young Tree- What is a "wooden philosopher", Your Highness ?

Arrogance - You .

Young Tree - Ooo !!...I thought I was a tree : my Elders never told me any different .

Arrogance - Forget it, little green tree, and let your Elders go their way ! I am tired of this silly, half serious, half senseless, never substantial, always repetitive, pedantic, indefinite, "childishly" puerile, aimless and volatile, rather restricted and stupid talk among partners who have a lot of "patience" to sit and listen to all this gibberish nonsense, and a lot of"tolerance" to accommodate the pathetic representations of fantasies, fables and fairy tales !......

Lady Tolerance - Forests seem to have a specific disposition for that .

Arrogance - For that..."what" ?

Lady Tolerance - Fantasies, fables and fairy tales .

Arrogance - Oh! I am really mad, I am furious, infuriated, that is, and I shouldn't have ever listened to all of you and gone along my way !...Too late, anyway, to regret it now, so, why don't we talk about something else and more pertinent to the occasion like, for example, the real meaning of your two Ladyships being here without all the "trimmimg" of mysterious appearances and foreboding messages to the trees of this forest : how about it, Sweeties ?

Lady Patience - I do not know, really, how to answer your invitation, for one, because you had just said that you wanted to get away on your road, tired of all this"nonsense" and, secondly, because we had already told you why we happen to be here and, what you were told, was the real fact with no trimmings of any kind, shape or colour . In simple words : we are here ....because we ARE here .

Arrogance - And you wouldn't call that statement a "trimmimg", wouldn't you, now ?

Lady Patience - I wouldn't .

Young Tree - Your Highness, if you will be so kind as to reflect on what I had mentioned to you some time earlier, Lady Patience and Lady Tolerance, have been here all the time . I am certain that you can recall that conversation .

Arrogance - You mean , they never came, they never went, they never left, they never did anything resembling some form of locomotion , just hovering "patiently", of course, on the immensity of this forest, just to see you grow. An encomiable act of forestal appreciation , I surmise .

Young Tree - Oh ! No, Your Highness, they are extremely useful, actually, almost essential to the slow process of our growth and that is why they are an essential and integral part of our development which requires a considerable amount of time and steady, methodical, uncompromising and very patient sequencing of acts, in order to achieve our progressive development from a fledgeling seedling into a powerful tree. You see, Your Highness : Lady Patience and Lady Tolerance are our very soul .

Arrogance - Now !....Now, I am really seeing and hearing everything !! A flair for sentiment and, perhaps, even a whiff of poetry for the mystic forest of majestic trees, the beauty of wood combined to its strength, glowing in the perpetual embrace of love of Lady Patience and Lady Tolerance, to enable its ligneous malleability to make innumerable great things....out of itself !

Young Tree - No, No ! Your Highness ! I believe that you got it all wrong, if I may be daring enough to utter such an "invocation" !!..........

Arrogance - Even if I had construed everything wrong, it is not surprising : how can anything come straight from this coskeyed forest of yours ?!

Young Tree - I meant no offence, Your Highness, truly!! Just my way of talking ! You see......

Arrogance - I don't...!!

Young Tree - Your Highness ! Why doesn't Your Eminence ever try to give this little young tree a chance to speak forth and the benefit of a friendly ear ??!

Lady Tolerance - I'll answer that : may be, our selective cousin, is jealous of your adamant wisdom .

Arrogance - I , most certainly, am not jealous of your pitiful comments, sweet cousin Tolerance .

Young Tree - Oh ! Please, please, illustrious and refined representatives of the World's Elite Society : no more fruitless squabbles !.........But, lend me your ears, instead !

Lady Tolerance - No doubt that the seclusive aspect of forests are an invitation to thought, meditation and reflection .

Lady Patience - Yes, I agree ! Even a famous ancient Poet felt that way !

Arrogance - The poor thing ! He must have been very depressed !

Lady Patience - Indeed He was !

Arrogance - To me, the forest and, particularly, this HERE forest, gives me the creeps and encourages me to get out of it and never to come back !....As to the thoughts and the wisdom....well...millennia of "it" have not changed life a darn bit !

Young Tree - Your respected and honourable Ladyships : no one is wrong, everyone is right ....in his own way ! Why, feelings are a subjective matter, and their expression a multiform and caleidoscopic avalanche of representations ! So, why worry so much about something that...well,,,shall I say....comes natutal ?

Arrogance - And I fully agree with the astonishing brilliance of our young green tree intellectual vivacity that comes quite naturally too, as does stupidity .

Lady Tolerance - Dear cousin, do you happen to know what the noun" incorrigible" means ?

Arrogance - Yes, I do . According to the available grammars it is classified as an "adjective ": am I right ?

Lady Tolerance - Very well, dear cousin : now, do you know its meaning ?

Arrogance - Yes, I do .

Lady Tolerance - I am surprised !

Arrogance - Why ? No big deal, really, as the intonation of your initial approach seemed to indicate ! "Incorrigible", really, means something or someone that cannot be easily modified, changed or corrected from an existing form or appearance and that is exactly me : I am an incorrigible arrogant guy . Really sorry, for not allowing you the satisfaction of a hit and run venomous remark towards me , old Buddy !

Lady Patience - Why don't we lend our ears to the young green tree, instead of "hitting and running" volatile remarks ?

Young Tree - Thank you, Lady Patience, you do understand the world of the forests !

Arrogance - So do I and how true it is that it takes all sorts to make this world, and not only of the forests !

Young Tree - Since I am firmly planted on this soil, in this forest and I am not very conversant with the "other sorts" or "other worlds", my opinions, my feelings and my propensities are strictly local and I leave the universality of interpretation of things to more universal minds than mine !...So......

Lady Patience - "Local" is an expression not necessarily limited and restricted to a "forest", since even in the mighty Universe, I surmise, a "local" spot will be ceratinly found when describing a "locality" in its expansion .

Arrogance - Unbelievably complex, vertiginously compelling, utterly fascinating, intellective "anticipation" of a yet to be answered less vertiginous and less complex answer to the "universal" presence of stupidity .

Young Tree - Stupidity should not be ridiculed or scoffed at : do we ever mock a water brook ? Do we ever laugh at a blade of grass ? Do we ever jeer a lame duck ? Well, why should you treat stupidity any differently than a brook, or a blade of grass or a lame duck , since they all occur naturally ? So does stupidity : it's a natural occurring condition and I doubt that its real meaning and purpose has been correctly identified ,yet .

Arrogance - I am pretty sure of that, possibly , because there have not been enough great or greater minds in this forest yet to decipher the riddle !....Do you, wise and young green tree, suspect that one day, may be, a great mind in your forest will answer to the great call and solve the riddle of stupidity ?

Young Tree - Yes, I feel pretty sure about that possibility and eventuality : it could be even very soon .

Arrogance - How soon, genius ?

Young Tree - As soon as you will leave this forest .

Arrogance - Why not while I am still here, if it is "soon" ?

Young Tree - They might be apprehensive of your violent reaction in hearing their verdict and their opinion .

Arrogance - On the contrary : I would welcome a dissertation on the subject, once the great Mind of your forest would have come up with his identification of the "reason to be" of stupidity .

Young Tree - I seriously doubt that you would be that intimately interested .

Arrogance - And why not ?

Young Tree - Because you would be the "reason to be ": that's why .

Arrogance - The insolence is not even on a par with any reason since it betrays the independence of the intellectual scrutiny of the matter by being personal. Bah !

Lady Tolerance - An excellent intuitive perception of the present, projected into the future .

Lady Patience - The present, so far, has been deficient sufficiently on its own without worrying about the future:let a little bit of sunshine penetrate this tenebrous attitude of insensate talking . Young Tree, you were saying....?

Young Tree - What I was saying ? Well, all I was anxious to point out was that our seeming enthusiasm is not indicative of a superfluous explosion of dressed up sentimentality but, purely, a recognition of a vital function of our very life .

Lady Patience - Very good .

Young Tree - You see, our very slow mechanism of growth is ideal for thinking, meditating and fostering the teasing of the mind into producing thoughts, so that the entire process of our growth is, actually, a constant introspective study of that same growth and sotell us our Elders and our lofty Brothers around us .

Lady Tolerance- Very good .

Arrogance - Senseless talk, if you ask me .

Lady Tolerance - No one asked you......dumbbell .

Arrogance - Dumb..hardly. Bell, yes, and very resonant .

Lady Patience - A good mnemonic recall of your school days, I presume, dear young green tree, to cause you to mention such specific definitions of intellective activity like the "introspective"study and so on !!

Arrogance - I am glad someone picked up the unorthodox formulations of a young green tree!!

Young Tree - Oh ! That !!.....No big deal, really : just remembering what our teachers used to tell us about great thinking Men and one, in particular, who, when asked how did he discovered the famous Laws of gravity, simply answered : " .....By thinking into the phenomenon....", so , we apply that principle to our growth .

Arrogance - Armchair philosophers in wooden cloaks, I surmise !

Young Tree - We do our best with what we have !

Lady Tolerance - Attaboy !! You said it

Arrogance - Dear little green tree, whatever you say it matters not, I assure you . As to the wise, solid and ligneous personalities of your older Brothers, those majestic trees all around you and looking at you from the mighty, lofty height of their foliage, you need a most urgent reassessment of their status, including your own, so necessary an alignment of reality, particularly when you and your Brothers, fully grown and mature, will be spotted ....

Young Tree - We all, young, mature and older, we all know that : it is an everyday assessment of observations, measurements and expectations, part of a natural routine of unfolding events, not very different, indeed, from the same expectations lurking around the corner ready to "grab" the same ones who are trying to grab us ! Someone, in times past, had called the life's fray: " life's merry-go-round.".

Arrogance - And, being "spotted", is just the easy beginning of a more sordid follow-up, you naive little green tree, when these strange two legged creatures, called humans, begin walking through this forest not on a chivalrous quest for wisdom, or an introduction to the essentials of life, or the exhilarating spirituality of a poem praising the ultimate Universal Plan of Mother Nature, but, purely and solely, interested in practical, immediate, material gains .

Lady Tolerance - But, that kind of outlook in life, should not be a strange custom to you, dear cousin, isn't it ?

Young Tree - I would have liked to hear Lady Arrogance complete her saying about the strange two legged creatures because it reminds me of something we learned at school .

Arrogance - Not really much more to say about the humans, except that they will cut you down pretty fast along with your tall Brothers, expressing, in doing so, their exquisite consideration towards you by not causing you to feel singled out, in that massacre .

Young Tree - Is that, then, why so many soldiers are being killed in a war, so that no one would be feeling singled out ?

Lady Tolerance - Wars, dear little green tree, are not forests, but are often fought for possession of those forests, but why they are fought, is still a mystery. May be it has something to do with volcanic activity, when humans need to give out their compressed or repressed steam.

Arrogance - And there would be no special ceremonies to celebrate or commemorate the event and not a single thought about the inherent philosophy at the basis of your beginnings and your and your Brothers growth and no regretful memories of the ancient times of the old flourishing cedars on the shores of the Mediterranean Sea, since they cut them down too, without mercy.

Young Tree - Were those cedars at war, with somebody ?

Arrogance - I believe that the strange two legged creatures were the ones who actually had declared war to the cedars

Young Tree - How terrible !

Arrogance - And, once cut down, they'll make nice pieces of wood out of you for a cozy fireplace, or shape you into some fine planks to make furniture of all types, inclusive of those types that will have a"poetic" look, or a romantic shape, or an artistic expression so as to please the passionate exigencies of the strange two legged creatures . So , little green tree, do not forget that "that" is your Destiny!

Young Tree - O vague being, dear Lady Arrogance, who are visiting this lonely forest, where I slowly grow, year after year, and keep up adding circles around my body, so that one covers me on the outside, while another one, on the inside, works its way in unison, o vague being , please, tell me, seriously, do you really know my Destiny ?

Arrogance - I do, and I am not the only one to know it : it's common knowledge .

Lady Patience - Indeed, if I had not heard you, Arrogance, talking to the young little tree and claiming to know its Destiny, I would have thought of it to be a rather arrogant statement . But, coming from you, it is understandable .

Young Tree - Her Highness said that she knew my Destiny !

Lady Tolerance - Poor little naive green tree, so wide open to unscrupulous vagrants of creatures's frailty .

Arrogance - But, of course I know its Destiny !...And my knowing has nothing to do nor has any reflection with the appellative of "arrogance", so freely and indiscriminately bestowed on me, since it is common knowledge among creqtures what the destiny of trees is, unless they grow in the clouds .

Lady Patience - What if they would ?

Arrogance - Then, if you are so inclined as to even ask such a question, I feel that I have lowered myself low enough among certified morons and, furthermore, since I have lowered myself even lower by accepting to engage into a conversation with a piece of wood, but to reach the point of exasperation gealing with your slow intellectual grasping capacity and your habitual pedantic and somnolent disposition about almost everything, Destiny apart, of course, but you seem even more ligneous than the wood itself !

Lady Patience - How very kind of you ,dear cousin ! But you have not told me, yet, how you happen to know the Destiny of our little green tree : or have you forgotten ?

Arrogance - Oh! Dear! Oh, dear! I can't believe it ! Just as if you did not even hear or pay any attention to what I had just said about you !....Pedantic, pedantic, pedantic and pedantic, again and again !! It just does not seem real !!

Patience - Dear cousin : it seems very real to me . Didn't you hear me saying to you :"How very kind of you" , in answer to your deposition on my virtues or not so virtues ?

Arrogance - Yes, I did, but you came around with that darn question about Destiny, again, and I could not make any sense with it !

Lady Patience - It does not matter, really. However, mine,is not pedantry or pedanticism or pedantism and you have the choice to pronounce which one of the three you may feel more comfortable with, but, really, a simple and timely explanation of how did you know, of this little tree, the actual Destiny, would be very interesting to me . That was all I had asked of you .

Arrogance - And yet, I am pretty sure, you may know the little tree Destiny better than anybody else ! Why, didn't the little green guy, that little young tree of yours, say,just a while ago, that you were the elected Fairy Godmother of the forest ?

Lady Patience - Of course, he did ! And so did all the other trees in the forest !

Arrogance - And, then, simple folks say that "I" am arrogant ???!!

Lady Tolerance - There is no "arrogance" in the limpidity of truth, dear cousin . Our sweet Lady Patience is the promoting essence of this forest . The Fairy Godmother title is an honorary recognition of her ever unyielding patience in the slow growth of the forest .

Arrogance - But, "of course", then, and, since it is said that Fairy Godmothers know a lot of things, even unknown things, it figures that, with quite some certain certainty, our"beloved Fairy Godmother, cousin Patience ".....should know about the many and various possible and probable projections of the lives of everybody and everything : right ?

Lady Patience - Wrong . To a certain extent, it is possible, I guess, to figure out, from sheer experience, some basic sequences of possible and probable events in our daily lives but, Destiny, is a complex and elusive representation of the human mind, in its perpetual search for an answer to the very being of everybody and everything, an unexplained and ,likely, unexpainable phenomenon out of the reach of comprehension for me and even for a tree .

Arrogance- I couldn't have said it any better myself, dear cousin, I really couldn't have . So,we haven't made much progress in the search for the definition of destiny'. What shall we say, then, to the young green tree ?

Lady Tolerance - The same things that everybody, usually, says about destiny .

Arrogance - And what's that ?

Lady Tolerance - Nothing .

Arrogance - I'd rather opt for " the same things that everybody usually says",which are the closest to the definition of destiny than any other probable philosophical or scholarly interpretations, and that is that the life of a tree will end either by natural deterioration and disintegration on the ground due to old age or struck by a tempest, or cut by the two legged timber creatures for firewood or wood for furniture, or for work of art , to satisfy the many pleasantries of the human specie : rather simple, I think .

Lady Patience- Oh ! Yes, simple, indeed . Most often "things" are simple, when made to suit our own preferences, wishes and ideas .

Arrogance - Well, look here, now: who is resorting to some form of subdued philosophy ? Of all the odds, you, my dear cousin, coming out with subtle remarks , or, should I rather say, with "patiently" constructed remarks...!! Nevertheless, we must confront the inevitablein the life's course of your young tree which, once cut and taken away from its birth place, will make it necessary for you in all earnest....and it just tickles me to think of you to do something "in all earnest...!!.....anyway, once the tree is taken away.............

Lady Patience - Sorry interrupting you but I just want to identify, correctly, the meaning of "earnest" : not an indication of a specific measure of "speed", as you seem to point out, but an image of puroseful endeavour, according to the best of Lexica of ancient wisdom .

Arrogance - Well, whatever ! Anyway, once the tree is taken away, you'll need another home to settle in , patiently and diligently, and that translates into you needing another tree, provided, of course, that you could find one which would not have a Fairy Godmother already in it , so you would have a lodging problem on your hands, but, I guess, with some"patience " and perseverance....and I almost choke while saying this...!!......well, with some patience, you'll never know, another lonely seedling, just out of high school, could welcome you in and I would really like to watch the incredible event .

Lady Patience - Please, do not become over worried about my abode under those tenebrous circumstances: you cannot even imagine how many places there are around our existences that desperately need a lot of patience just to be able to get along, and that without any apprehension of being cut down ! But, tell me now, dear cousin, what would become of you, should Nature ,quite suddemly, bring about a mutation and make all of your arrogant followers change into penitent souls ?

Arrogance - My disciples turned into penitent souls....???!!!..Lady, how patiently naive you must be to even just think that way !!....This World, this forest....the Worlds ,the forests and all of the immensity of the Universe may fall apart, but not the insolence of arrogant creatures!....I assure you !

Lady Patience - So, I would have to miss an interesting show . Really, a pity !.....But, then, we tend to overlook the motives that Mother Nature might have had in the formulation for all the various and almost infinitely multiform types of exsistences and, reluctantly, we are forced to admit of our depressing ignorance about Nature, about Destiny, about almost of everything, so little we know of anything!

Arrogance - We have heard all that before, dear cousin ! But, do not confuse denial of supremacy over Nature with the false humility of ignorance : Nature did ot coin words but built mechnisms and there is nothing wrong or presumptuous on our part if we try to investigate and decipher everything about those natural means by which so much useful wonders are produced and learn from them .

Lady Patience - I did not say that we shouldn't look into Nature's masterful wonders : I just said that we have not made much progress in understanding it . Nothing new, really, and nothing old, really!.......And,yet, still foreboding to our existences .

Arrogance - My, oh! My !....What a conference of subtle knowledge!...And, then, the word goes around that I am arrogant, presumptuous, haughty, because I say similar things, may be with a different tone of voice and withiout previous representation by a notable official of a local club ! I begin to wonder whether I am called "Arrogance" by creatures who may not even know how to read or write their own names and are just jealous of my versatility .

Young Tree - (......suddenly, breaking into the conversation of Lady Patience and Arrogance, uninvited, but prompted to do so upon hearing Lady Arrogance mentioning the word."jealous").... ....Oh! Why do you say that, o Arrogance, and, incidentally, please, pardon me for bursting, uninvited, into the middle of your conversation with Lady Patience, but I became aroused by...........

Arrogance - Oh ! Not at all, dear little tree !...It just seems a compulsory trend for you to do so !

Young Tree - I know and I well remember not too long ago, in the early beginning of our conversations,that I suddenly got into the"fray"of a subject of which I was not a party, but moved by a sudden inborn interest in the matter...Yes, I remember that, but, I do not mean any harm or offense or antagonism or criticism when doing so: only a pure, simple interest on something that I understand and I feel a strong need to express myself upon it .

Arrogance - No big deal, young tree . Besides, Lady Patience and I were almost at the end of our conversation : so , what's up ?

Young Tree - Well, as soon as you said "that"word, and it was"jealous", if I understood it correctly.......was it"jealous"....was it not ?

Arrogance - You heard it correctly, greenish wooden stick ! You heard it right, you did !

Young Tree - Well, now, if you all, that is you, Lady Arrogance, and you, Lady Patience and Lady Tolerance, will allow me to do good on my bursting into your conversation, I would reallylike it very much to comment on that word, "jealous", Lady Arrogance just had used .

Lady Tolerance - I do not see any reason why should any of us stop you from doing that . I feel certain that Lady Arrogance and Lady Patience will concur with me about it .

Arrogance - But, of course !

Lady Patience - Go ahead, dear child and we'll listen .

Young Tree - Oh! Thank you for your kindness and your understanding and what really I would like to say is the mentioning of what our Elders were teaching us, little growing seedlings, about vocabulary and idiomatic phrases and grammar and syntax and, what struck me, was that new word "jealous",used by Lady Arrogance as a grievance, I guess, against certain sources labeling her as the impersonation of presumptuousness and haughtiness and our Elders, at school or at meetings, never ever used that word : it just does not exist in the language of the forest .

Arrogance - What so strange about that word , boy ?

Young Tree - I had never heard that word before and, more, such word is not to be found in any forest dictionaries,or in school libraries or ever heard spoken in normal, average conversations among trees .

Arrogance - Come now ! I am sure that there would be some skimpy, skinny and slow growing trees in the forest who would look with envy and jealousy at other fully grown, majestic trees and wishing that they too could be like those majestic trees!

Young Tree - I don't know about that particular instance, Your Highness, since we, in this forest, are never confronted with such an eventuality. This term"jealous" is not in our vocabulary and we are unaware of its meaning and the purpose for using it . You see, our Elders, and some of them with a hundred years experience in life, never talked about such terms : just a while ago, I just purely guessed that "jealous" might have been a term of regret or disappointment at something, since you, Your Highness, had used it in reference to somethng unpleasant to your feelings

Arrogance - I hear you, little green stick of wood, but I still believe that something similar to"jealous" must be going on even in your forest among your trees. Even if in different forms, but, make no mistake, stick of wood, life is much the same everywehere and for everybody, regardless of shape, size or form .

Young Tree - I understand what you are saying, Your Highness, but, you see, and purely judging from your reactions, that word seems to indicate a sort of feeling of resentment against something or somebody, possibly secondary to rivalry, success or fortune and, among us trees, we have never had an occasion to feel that way, since a slender tree is not resentful........you, probably, would say "jealous"......of the size of a mighty big tree, on the contrary, it admires it and praises its glorious look and standing and feels very proud to be a part of its surroundings and be in its company .

Lady Tolerance - Well spoken, dear child .

Young Tree - Oh! I don't know ! That unusual word emboldened me in straying into your conversation and I hope that you all will forgive me for my audacity in acting so discourteously .

Arrogance - Never mind that, little stick of wood . What surprises me is your unexpected confrontation with a word unknown in your vocabulary, but, I assure you, it is in full existence in the vocabulary of other creatures as well as in their unforgiving mentality, creatures, those, who, unfortunately, do not resemble trees, which, if they did, it might help them .

Young tree - Oh ! That's something ! I had never heard of that either , that something or somebody could be made to look like us !....Even "think", like us....!!

Arrogance - In Fairy Tales stories, they do .

Young Tree - Ah ! I see ! Does that have any connection with Fairy Godmothers , Your Highness ?

Arrogance - It could .

Young tree - How could it be found out for certain , Your Highness ?

Arrogance - With some fertile imagination , I surmise .

Young Tree - Oh !

Arrogance - Anyway, don't let that worry you, unnecessarily : you are or, at least, you appear to be an honest, straight and clean growing tree with a wooden intellect that prevents you from absorbing unsavory, unethical and fruitless ideas, whichever way they may be coming from and prevents you from being adversely influenced or ensnared by distorted or dubious formulations .

Lady Tolerance - Our cousin is praising you, little green tree !!! Almost incredible ! May be, our "distinguished" cousin is still....."corrigible"....after all....!!!!!

Arrogance - Hardly !....And, most certainly, not a preferred turnaround, either !

Young Tree - Praising me ? Did you say that Lady Arrogance is praising me ?

LadyTolerance - It sounded that way .

Young Tree - I wonder why everything has to have a sound in order to be understood .

Arrogance - Nothing out of the ordinary, surprising or new, dear little green tree . It goes back to the old story about the mule which would follow commands if they were whispered into its ears but only after obtaining its attention by wacking him across his head with a large and hard stick .

Young Tree - Do creatures in the place where you are coming from carry these hard sticks with them so that they can get somebody's attention ?

Arrogance - No, little green tree, they don't, and there is the time when the "sound" comes in handy to get somebody's attention by a sometimes melodious, sometimes harsh, sonorous reminder, instead of hitting him or her across the head with a hard stick !

Young Tree - Strange customs !

Arrogance - The subtle improvements of progressive civilizations, always appear strange to the following civilizations, I surmise. But, let me finish what I was trying to point out to you : as you have the advantage of not being able to absorb anything said to you in a higher consistency of constructive expression or of more complex equations of thoughts, due to the ligneous consistency of your make-up, it follows that specialized information cannot be caught and assimilated by your wooden intellect . Sorry about it, but an undeniable reality .

Lady Tolerance - Yet, I am not so sure : wooden intellects are, as a rule, pretty solid even if not vivacious .

Arrogance - Well, I see what you mean, but we are talking about absorbability and not solidity, as the words, forming those more complex expressions and differing equations, have to go round and round following all those circles inside his trunk, as he describes them, and never be able to find a place where to"stick", stop and rest and be acknowledged .

Young Tree - Ah ! That's how it is : right ?

Arrogance - Right .
Young Tree - I didn't know that, but I am grateful to you, Your Highness, for letting me know about it and explaining it to me .

Arrogance - My pleasure .

Young Tree - Now, I shall pass on all that good information to my roots so that they might be able to inform my neighbours of it and, at the same time, thanks a million, Your Highness, for telling me all that !

Arrogance - My pleasure .

Lady Patience - Now, as it appears that you have completed and terminated a totally unnecessary conversation, I would like to have the privilege to complete mine, left hanging in the thin, aromatic fragrance of the forest air, some time ago, about Nature's masterful Wonders .

Arrogance - Don't you look at me, dear cousin, because not I, but your little protegee, your little green tree, came in, uninvited, into our conversation with some insipid remarks, so , if you have any influence on him, tell him, please, to keep to himself while we are talking and not to be unduly disturbed by literary variations in the common vocabulary . Now, please, dear cousin, kindly go right ahead and tell me all about Mother Nature's "various " motives for the infinite variety of creatures on this World, forests, mountains, seas and oceans, or something of that.......well....."nature" ?

Lady Patience - I do not really know if it is at all worth it to talk to you about the unknown motives of Nature : you are ....

Arrogance - But, my dear cousin, how can you talk, not only to me, but to anybody else, about motives of "anybody", and, least of all, of mighty Nature, if they are.........unknown..??!!

Lady Patience - It's just a way to express our owe about the entire mystery : what I mean is the mind-boggling kaleidoscopic appearance of an evolving parade of outstanding, incomparable marvels, well counterbalanced by similar mind-boggling catastrophic, rampaging, destructive forces, mercilessly bent on destroying what marvels they had just created .

Arrogance - Don't all sort of creatures, in this World of ours, practically follow the same pattern in their own lives, just as mighty Nature does with "her" life ?

Lady Patience - May be so it seems, at a glance, and natural events do affect us all, in one way or another .

Arrogance - I choose the"another" type .

Lady Patience - You are not seriously interested in this aspect of conversation, I see, and your basic interest remains in the world of greed, power, and supremacy, not on wordly events but on the least encomiable of all driving urges : offensive superiority .

Arrogance - But that, dear cousin, should not stop anyone from trying to do the same and use the power of their intellect to do their best with it .

Lady Patience - Likewise here : no one should be prevented from exercising the powers of intellect to explain things around us or around the World or in other Worlds,to the utmost of their power .

Arrogance - And I am the one constantly being accused of extolling the superiority of fine intellect to achieve the greatest possible range of success ..???!...I declare !!

Lady Patience - No one accuses you of that : your fault lies in abusing the right to intellect .

Arrogance - How can you stop a racing horse from winning when close to the winning line ?

Lady Patience - By riding with respect and fair talent : in that case, there is no need to stop it .

Arrogance - It looks to me that you must have never ridden a winning horse .

Lady Patience - But I have nursed to a glorious splendor many a famous trees !

Arrogance - So what ?! A tree is a piece of wood and does not even think of racing, can not even dream of racing : it really could not, even if he wanted to, so stuck as he is in the ground...!! Do you see what I mean ? Should we ask cousin Tolerance what she thinks about it , or just drop the subject ?

Lady Patience - Let's not "drop" anything : the "noise", caused by the inadvertent drop, could be interpreted as a controversial assumption in the matter and might wake up unnecessary and deviant thoughts about it , thoughts that always lurk at the foggy outer margins of dim intellects waiting for their undeserving chance of some limelight .

Arrogance - Noble words, dear cousin, for the defence of nobler thoughts from sneaky thoughts , indeed .

LadyTolerance - Whatever ,dear cousin! But Nature might have had different purposes when producing trees and when creating horses, defining their respective paths in different ways and in separate directions and the actual meaning of their intended functions not understood by any of us, and I doubt if it ever will be.

Arrogance - A noble and elegant assessment of arboreal destiny and equestrian carousel .

Lady Patience - As to their respective Destinies, they do not seem any different from ours, once their intended course reaches the end of the prescribed trajectory .

Arrogance - May be it is as you believe that it could be , Nature working and assigning different destinies to different entities and, it just dawned on me, while you were talking , that when Mother Nature was formalizing the destiny of trees, it must have been during a very cold Winter and it anticipated a good use of timber in a nice, warm and cozy glittering fireplace .

Lady Tolerance - Your retort, dear cousin, is not even worth laughing, rather crying, I would say, so much more appropriate to qualify its message . You take an unduly light regard for the surroundings in your sight instead of adopting a knowledgeable cognition of its intricacies , phenomena and mystery and live in awe in this privileged cradle of wonders, in an almost incomprehensible harmony that is so pervasive in all that has been created .

Arrogance - You must be a dreamer, dear cousin and, when you are not sleeping and dreaming, a visionary !!...Harmony, you say !...Where ?...I ask !!...In the way a volcano erupts ? Or, a hurricane wipes out entire communities ? Or an earthquake levels, nicely and neatly, an entire city ? Would that be a harmony in "C" minor or "D" major, or, more likely, a disaster in "F" flat ?

Lady Tolerance - In my limited opinion, it would be more likely a disaster in utter stupidity .

Arrogance - And not an unusual event in the exixtences of the two legged creatures !

Lady Patience - Which event, dear cousin ?

Arrogance - Their proverbial stupidity .

Lady Patience - Aren't you, perhaps, a little too hard in your appreciation of the two legged creatures ? After all they provide you with the necessary tools for your exploits, don't they now ?

Arrogance - What tools are you talking about ?

LadyPatience - But, dear cousin, I am surprised you asking !! The "tools" are represented by "they" "themselves": in other words, your pupils, your devotees !...Don't they play for you and your ego exceedingly sweet "harmonic" melodies ?

Arrogance - My dear Patience, Harmony is a noun coined precisely by those strange creatures with two legs, two arms, two feet, two hands and a long neck, at the end of which there is a pot-like form , some as large as a medium sized melon, some as a full melon and, some, again, smaller, like plump onions that make you cry as you start talking to them, anyway,.....

Young Tree - What's a melon ? What's an onion ?

Lady Tolerance - Never mind, little green tree !

Arrogance - Anyway, regardless of their respective sizes , all those pots at the end of their necks seem to have the tendency to be tethering on a precarious balance, pinned as they are on that stump.....their neck....that twists, jerks and goes back and forward, bending, at times, from one side to the other, depending from which side the wind blows : today my followers and devotees, tomorrow to be beguiled by something else . Harmony.....Bah !!

Lady Patience - Have you ever tried it ?
Arrogance – Tried what ?

Lady Patience - To be in harmony with yourself and your surroundings, in peace and tranquillity .

Arrogance - I haven't. Besides, why should "I" start "something" that was not even practiced when this World of ours was created ?

Lady Patience - You don't say !

Lady Tolerance - Our cousin is referring to the chronicle of the creation of the World .

Arogance - Precisely. And, apparently, it was not a tranquil and slow-paced affair as the awe-inspiring World and Universe were put together in seven days, the Creator did not seem to be choosing tranquillity in building it, or to be patient long enough, and hurried up everything, completed the task in seven days and then rested . I doubt that he had any incentive for harmony in mind, considering the cataclysmic relationships of all the parts that make up the whole thing ! It looks like that the Creator, in my mind, wanted to get the job done and in a hurry .

Lady Patience - You never fail, my dear Arrogance, or, at least, so it seems at a first impression, to show respect even for the Almighty by ignoring or sidelining His omnipotence in us, since, just in case you might have forgotten, you and all the rest there is, is part of the Almighty !

Young Tree - Are trees also part of the Almighty ?

Lady Tolerance - But of course they are .

Young Tree - Oh ! Thank you ! I feel so good about it !

Arrogance - I have known all that for a long time, dear cousin .

LadyPatience - Not long enough, so it seems .

Arrogance - And what all that has to do with "harmony", I wonder !

Lady Patience - For one, "harmony"is not entirely relegated to represent a sequence of pleasing sounds to the ear, but, also, an ordered, well adjusted, fluent mode of a creature's character, thinking and behaviour and, secondly, "harmony" may also identify itself in a balanced control of the innumerably available impulses so widespread in our daily existencies .

Arrogance - And who told you that ?

Lady Patience - No one . Just common knowledge with an extra "pinch" of common sense .

Lady Tolerance - Now, we are heading for deeper, darker waters, I 'm afraid !

Arrogance- I see no darker or deeper waters anywhere, except some impetuous silliness on the part of someone who plays the "know-all" type of fellow routine about the intricacies of some harmony and the creation of the Universe and everything else by the Almighty and, frankly, I really cannot make any sensible connection in all this !

Lady Patience - No one really can : no one has ever been able to make any connection but only to wonder in awe to even think of it all !

Arrogance - You are fantasizing, now, my dear, and flying high without any wings and that is not a good omen for the mental stability of a creature !

Lady Patience - I do not see any wings on you either, earth-bound cousin !

Arrogance - Do you think, may be, that with some....patience....!!....I might grow some wings , sometime...?!?..!!

Lady Patience - I believe that if "patience" is the issue in this particular case, then, I am certain that even you, yourself, might have noticed that this Almighty is highly PATIENT in tolerating for such long time, almost an unlimited amount of time.....his own Creation and the many false steps taken by some of the creatures he had created, like, for example......well....shall we say....an acquaintance of ours....let me think.....the name may be.........

Arrogance - If you, by any "casual" chance, are referring to me, I'd like to remind you of "something" that "your" little green tree had told me, that you had told him to tell me and that he, actually did tell me and that was that :"it is not good manners or a reflection of good up-bringing, to raise even veiled references of criticism about the characer and "virtues"(if any...) of other creatures "....Do you recollect that ?

Lady Patience - I am surprised at you, having the condescendence to so graciously recognize the real address to my ...query !

Arrogance - And, dear cousin, do you believe that the Great Almighty would have retained even a measly infinitesimal cognition of "my being" in the middle of that owe-inspiring UNIVERSAL, MIND-BOGGLING, INFINITE Construction??

Lady Patience - If the Almighty even had, at all, even a measly infinitesimal notion of you coming on in the midst of that universal soup, or even a double or even a triple infinitesimal cognition of you sneaking in...........

Arrogance - I resent that "insinuating" last remark........

Lady Patience - .....You would have been one,among some of the other creatures that "sneaked in", like the snakes, the wasps, the sharks and the black widows ." !

Arrogance - Apart from the fact that I , really, do not care to think about the possibility, or, to evaluate the possiblity whether the Almighy might have had or might not have had any cognition of my coming into being, but........

Lady Tolerance - Your insolence, despicable cousin, has no limits !

Lady Patience - May be, that, in itself, is, perhaps, the "tolerant key" safety valve of the Universe , I surmise .

Lady Tolerance - That is the part where I should come in, I guess !!

Arrogance - And this is the part where I come in and to be heard !

Lady Patience - Frankly, I do not think that there is anything left that much worth hearing , I guess !

Arrogance - That's up to you whether you want to hear it or not : it makes no difference to me .

Lady Patience - Same here !

Lady Tolerance - Likewise .

Young Tree - I don't understand !!!

Lady Tolerance - You are perfectly correct, Young little tree : there really is nothing to be understood .

Arrogance - That, of course, is entirely on a personal note : inability to understand has several variations, from hearing loss and all the way to brain loss and everything in-between....if you know what I mean...!

Lady Tolerance - We do not know what you mean, unless you are talking about yourself and worrying about your own....."hearing"..problems .

Arrogance - Ah ! Never mind ! What I wanted to say was that even if this Almighty had a glimpse of a thought about me, it must have been like a sudden spark and that is what I am : a glowing, glittering light of wisdom and wonders and, certainly, not a slow, lumbering form of a "patiently" growing silly little green tree.....(...."lumbering"...!...Strange that I thought of that noun.....!)

Young Tree - That's even stranger than the "lumbering" noun you thought about, but my Elders never told me that I was a "silly" tree : a green tree, a fragile seedling, yes, but that word, "silly", is "strange" to me . What does "lumbering" mean ?

Lady Tolerance - Do not pay any undue attention to what this facetious Herald of fortunes and misdemeanors blabs around to everybody who is so naive to listen to what he says !

Young Tree - Is that what"lumbering" means ?

Lady Tolerance - It expresses the degree of developed decency in a creature's mind, capable of variable speeds, these being painfully slow in some types of sparklets, that is some small forms of lesser sparks.....in the Universe, as I seem to have heard them mentioned by our eminent cousin.........

Young Tree - Oh! Our universal cousin...that what it means ?

Lady Tolrance - Not quite, but it comes close .....

Arrogance - Yes, indeed ! And it comes even closer to my clubbing all of you on your bald heads, since, as you all know, no hair grows on water melons .

Lady Tolerance - You see, just as I was saying : not quite but it comes close......

Arrogance - Indeed, close enough to a "patiently" growing tree with the unabating support of a "out of the blue!" Fairy GodMother, to help put together circles, one circle inside and one on the outside, destined to be stuck in circles, somewhere and finish up, by predetermined benevolent and all powerful omnipotent forces, as a nice piece of wood in a cozy fireplace or as an artistic object of furniture or a post in a fence !....Sorry, really sorry, but, definitely, that is not my way to interprete decency, but is certainly a very stupid way of proclaiming it , the way you described it...!!

Young Tree - Pardon my intrusion, dear Arrogance, Your Highness, but.............

Arrogance - Oh ! Never mind that : we have become quite accustomed to your intrusions, I assure you !!

Young Tree - Well, then, if my intrusion is acceptable to all of you, eminent listeners, I would like to throw some light unto the being of those circles.....

Arrogance - Fine, but, please, don't go around in circles, to describe them !

Young Tree - Oh ! No, dear Arrogance, nothing of the kind, because those circles have no scholarly intentions or pretensions, but simply describe wondrous events, so....

Arrogance - And I would hope that those"wondrous" events will show some "decency" and propriety of conformity to established standards of manners, so that our sweet cousin, Lady Tolerance, would be happy about them...!!!

Lady Tolerance - I am glad that you are catching on, dear cousin .

Arrogance - Just plain, tactical conformity, sweet cousin .

Young Tree - Oh ! Yes, Your Highness, full conformity, of course and more than that, I assure you, as there are no other known ways of expressing ourselves, us trees, I mean, but just straight up to the open sky !

Arrogance - Straight up is right, but, I hope, not as wide or we'll be here listening to you for the rest of time !

Lady Patience - You don't give this little young tree much of a chance ,don't you ?

Lady Tolerance - As I always feel about our cousin..: " Incorrigible !!" .

Young Tree - Please, dear Ladies, do not worry about me and my feelings and all that, since we are well adapted to adverse winds in this forest, but let me finish what I had meant to say at the beginning, and I'll try to be as quick as possible and down to the point so as to please your eminent cousin, Highness Arrogance : so, even poor and simple a young tree that I am.........

Lady Tolerance - There is your chance, cousin, to say something disparaging to the poor, simple and young tree, I dare you !

Arrogance - This way, is no longer fun .

Lady Tolerance - Nothing can vibrate in you as serious, I am afraid....Oh! Incorrigible !

Young Tree - Oh ! Dear Lady Arrogance, Your Highness, I do not mean any fun : on the contrary, mine is a simple explanation of the working of those circles....you see, these little circles that we talk about, are going inside and are going outside and, slowly but surely, build me up into a fully grown tree from a very modest beginning, a beginning so thin, that is void of circles, even void of any certain hope to remain alive !

Arrogance - What so "wondrous" about that ? That sort of uncertainty is common to everything there is around us, at the first light of birth .

Young Tree - Yes, that is true, but there is something else besides the circles and that is........

Arrogance - A Fairy GodMother, may be ??!!

Lady Tolerance - Cousin ! You are despicably and arrogantly incorrigible !

Arrogance - I just follow my nature, dear cousin, and, to think about it, Nature, herself, is pretty despotic and uncompromising, shall I say, may be, a little.....arrogant ?

Lady Tolerance - I am not even interested in continuing to chat with you: just listen to the little green tree !

Young Tree - Oh ! Yes, as I was saying, that "something else", besides the circles, is that magic-like power, an immense power, an undefinable power, just the same ancient and omni-present power, the very same power that built the millennia cedars of antiquity and the gigantic trees in many other forests, that very same power that builds me too into a fully grown tree from a tender and fragile shoot and, those circles, are all-encompassing, and that is to say that there is nothing more to say or to be said or whatever you may think to say, but only gasp at such a wonder !!.....

Arrogance - Really amazing ! Circular wonders !

Young Tree - You see, Your Highness, the circles seem to have a special meaning by their........

Arrogance - A famous ancient Greek mathematician might have argued with you on account of his famous triangles !!

Young tree - Oh ! Those circles do not mean any harm: they do not vie for supremacy, Your Highness, or to take away the luster from other forms or shapes, but they tell a story by recording my age and tell my years of existence better tha any triangle can tell.......besides, if I remember correctly what our teachers were telling us at school, someone, in ancient times, became a famous painter by being able to draw in one stroke a perfect circle ! These circles must have a meaning, don't you feel that way, Your Highness ?

Arrogance - Well, here we go with the old story that you are never too old or, I would add, never too late to learn something in this world of ours !

LadyTolerance - HALLELUJAH.....!!!

Young Tree - Did you mean : "....This forest of ours ", Your Highness ?

Arrogance - Whatever !.....What difference would it make, anyway: a world is a world and a forest is a forest, one and the other look the same to me !

Young Tree - Just asking, Your Highness . I did not know .

Arrogance - Very ,very good, little clever and green student ! And, tell me, what else you do not know ?

Young Tree - You mean, about the circles , Your Excellency ?

Arrogance - Damn those confounded circles, you ninny !..... I mean, anything else in general that you might not know...yet..or, do you know "it"all, little up-start..?

Young Tree - Sorry, Sir, but I do not follow you very well in what you are saying,Your Highness, but, anyway, in the very beginning of my existence, I did not know anything but, as I began to grow, I was told about many things by my elder Brothers .

Arrogance - Very attentive to your education, those elder Brothers, I see !

Young Tree - Well, they were very concerned about my well being, anyway,my seed began to germinate in the soil after I had fallen on it during a storm. Oh ! Dear Arrogance, that was a storm...!!....But, after the storm had passed and the ground was soggy and wet, just as I said, I began to germinate and, from a tiny green leaf I grew into a green stalk and this stalk, very slowly, began browning, from below and upwards and sprang green and tender branches in the coming of each Spring Season .

Arrogance - Astonishing .

Young Tree - I did not know it, then, but.........

Arrogance - ....but you still do not know it now, is that it ?

Young Tree - Oh ! Yes....well, NO !....I know it well now, Your Highness, and it was Patience, who told me all about my birth and accompanied me, tenderly and patiently, during the long journey from seedling to tree and I began to acquaint myself with all the intricacies of my developing existence, in this here forest of ours, with all the necessary patience that it required .

Lady Patience - You said it very well, my dear young little green tree !

Young Tree - Your teaching, dear Lady Patience...dear Patience, nothing but your teaching...!!

Arrogance - How touching, how touching, indeed, indeed !!So much kindness, so much devotion , so much nurtured sentimentality, all of them so well dispersed, with profusion,in a souped-up world of "make believe"! A little longer with this type of effusive conversation and we'll enter into an academic contest on forestation, vegetation, germination, orticulture, arboriculture, and, truly, I am a little tired of this long, too long, quite monotonous tirade of cheap rhetoric and sickly nostalgic lamentations mixed with a glorified representation of Fairy Tales GodMothers .

Lady Patience - You had said that already, just a while ago . As a matter of fact, you had said that several times over, in one way or another, on different occasions and, I guess, it's my turn now, to repeat what I , too, had said before in answer to what you had said and are saying, again, just now .

Arrogance - And what's that, dear cousin ?

Lady Tolerance - " THAT " is what she just said , or are you deaf, eminent cousin ?

Arrogance - "That" has nothing to do with what I said, did say or might have said. "That" is "What" I think, do think and think over and over and again and again and again.....!!

Lady Patience - That's good : at least you are explicit in your postulations .

Arrogance - Just tactical conformity , sweet cousin :.....just tactical conformity .

Lady Patience - But, dear sweeter cousin, you had that uncompromising chance to part from our company many a time before and foresake our talking, so injurious to your refined intellectual ears, but you didn't : what enticing aspect of that contested conversation prevented you from departing ?

Arrogance - Simply an overbearing sense of pride in fostering my inborn predilection for ostentatious civility towards a lesser equated reciprocal attitude from semi-mystical cretures and wooden stumps .

Lady Tolerance - And was the idea worth its conception ?

Young Tree - Oh ! Her Highness must have loved us !

Arrogance - Hardly .

Lady Patience - Please, continue, dear cousin : I'd really like to hear more about your decision to stay with us , regardless of the tenor of your explanation .

Arrogance - I just told you : pride of manners .

Lady Tolerance - That's fine, but "that" is just a polite opening into the real meaning of the issue which, when brought up with all candid reality, may not be so mannered, after all .

Arrogance - Sometimes, even strange as it may seem, but an inkling of "arrogance" in elucidating tangled situations or, in pointing out uncomfortable statements or, even criticizing certain debatable or controversial issues and stances, can be beneficial and not causing undue resentment by any opposing or supporting party for those debatable or cotroversial issues and stances .

Lady Patience - And even stranger it is listening to you talking so plainly and so conducibly on a situation of preferences and differing opinions !!....So, would I dare say that you, dear cousin, are, actually.......corrigible..!!??!

Lady Tolerance - "That", in my opinion, was definitely not the right key to hit in the harmonics of congenial understanding .

Arrogance - Not necessarily, dear cousin, but what I did not digest very well in our conversations was that persistent trend towrds that mixed up and glorified representation of sentimentalism, fairy tales stories and........

LadyPatience - Didn't anybody ever tell you fairy tales stories when you were just a "little" arrogance ?

Arrogance - With me it was different : I told "somebody" fairy tales stories, even when I was a"little arrogance ", about elves and hob-goblins and scaring the daylights out of my listeners!!......Well, anyway, all that fairy tales stories stuff and the introduction of some semi-spirituality of ill defined motives of coexistence with a young tree and some passers by or, as intimated, some permanent residents of this forest, namely my eminent cousins, Lady Patience and Lady Tolerance, (...and, perhaps, I'd better not say this too loud for fear that someone might hear me....!!)......well,.............

Lady Tolerance - ......Well, nothing wrong for anybody to hear a truth, if well meant ....

Arrogance - Well, yes, if within limits of sensible and appreciable consistency but, when the story seems to indicate that my eminent cousins, that is, Lady Patience and Lady Tolerance, have a permanent lodging in those trees and live in the trunk of those trees, guiding them, counseling them, encouraging them and instructing them on their long and slow growth, almost to the point of claiming to be their very soul, then, there, is where I draw the line and ask :"Who's now telling fairy tales stories " ??!

Lady Patience - No problem there, dear cousin, and no need to search wide and large, since we are the ones telling those stories, which may seem fairy tales stories to you but not to the trees because, to them, we are a reality .

Arrogance - Well, may be so, as you claim and, certainly, as you must believe too, but, regardless of who we are or think that we are, even if we do not know for certain of what we are talking about,there is a limit even for a facetious credibility of fanciful stuff for any brain to gleefully accept and enjoy it and I begin to think that now is a good time as ever to put a stop to this nonsense of "conversation-confrontation" type of jousting !!

Lady Tolerance - No one ever forced or even begged you to stay and joust with us, dear "facetious" cousin. So, why complaining ?

Arrogance - I am not complaining : I am saying "goodbye, Ladies, sweet cousins and tree stumps",and goodbye to all concerned, including spirits, trees, Fairies, God-Mothers, small trees, large trees, young trees, old trees and all the vegetation that can be found around here and good luck to the next "passer by" looking for a little rest under the shade of one of these trees...!!..........And I am very glad to get out of here..!!

Lady Tolerance - So, goodbye, old boy .

Lady Patience - Goodbye and come back , sometime, to see us .

Young Tree - I hope you will come back, sometime, Your Highness .

Arrogance - I doubt that I would ever come back to this forest : I was delayed already far too long and I cannot quite forgive myself for falling into the trap of all this nonsense, instead of continuing my journey after the refreshing rest under that silly young tree........and to think that I even allowed myself to be caught into a conversation, believe it or not, with a piece of wood and.........

Young Tree - I feel very glad, actually, more than that, and that is very proud, to have been able to be understood by such an eminent personality like you,Your Highness! You see, it isn't something that happens everyday, that a high ranking Creature takes time to talk to a tree and make sense out of it .

Lady Tolerance - And to make sense out of "anything" is, indeed, a remarkable achievement even for an.....arrogant creature, I surmise .

Arrogance - Oh ! You wouldn't get me into another argument, so , forget it, dear cousin ! And, besides the tree and on top of that, to be pinned down by a slow thinking, pedantic, cavillous creature, and I am not even quite certain whether that was a creature or something else and I haven't figured it out yet either,.......

Young Tree - Your Highness hasn't figured it out yet, after a whole day of conversation ? It seems incredible even for a little tree like me !

Arrogance - Figurative speech, little green tree:that's all !Anyway, that creature is a boring being who seems to be living inside the trees and goes under the name of Patience and another contemptuous creature, by the name of Tolerance, who contributes to the environmental protection of the forest and both of them calling me "cousin"....!!....Of all the audacity !!

Young Tree - Your Highness should not be upset by simple appellatives, sometimes, meaningless, and only used as a way to favour communication among creatures, inclusive trees . No harm is meant in that , I assure you !

Lady Patience - The little green tree speaks the truth.....cousin !

Lady Tolerance - How come you are still here.....cousin ?

Arrogance - I don't know ! It really beats me !!....I can see a little cottage, some distance away from the last standing trees at the end of the forest, resting between two pretty hills that I can spot very clearly from where I am standing. Oh ! I really better hurry because it's beginning to get dark in spite of the day still being young and I don't want to be caught in darkness in the middle of my journey! So , goodbye, again, to all and best wishes for a happy and illustrious growth to our....well...to YOUR little green tree , dear and sweet ....cousins......and let me get away from all this so "patiently endured" nonsense ! All the best and.....Ta!Ta! .

Lady Patience - «Au revoir »..and...« bien des choses chez vous »! It has been a real pleasure, dear Arrogance, to converse with you, Your Highness : "nous avons passé une soirée tres agréable" !

Arrogance - Cousin ...!?....Are you all right ?

Lady Patience - Fine, real fine, thank you .

Arrogance - I wonder if you realized that you addressed me in a foreign language !

Lady Patience - Did I ?

Arrogance - You mean to say that you did not know that it was a foreign language the one you used to address me ?....That's incredible !.. It was French !

Lady Patience - Was it, now ?

Arrogance - But you must have had some knowledge of the French language, even if only a foggy notion of it or of its most often used colloquialisms or something....!!

Lady Patience - Really, I didn't . I do not even know what that word that you used, "French", is or means .

Arrogance - But, then, you must have heard it spoken, somewhere, sometime, to be able to remember it : did you have some other friends who spoke foreign languages ?

Lady Patience - Oh ! No ! We do not get friends who speak a different language from the one spoken in this forest .

Arrogance - But, then, how did you know those sentences in French ? When did you hear them and where ? I am curious to know, really !

Young Tree - I think I know the answer to that, dear Arrogance, since it happened right here in the shadow of my branches, one fine day, in Summer time .

Arrogance - Quite interesting ! Even the young tree, now, becomes involved in Foreign affairs !!

Lady Patience - You shouldn't say anything about it, young little tree : it may be objectionable to our eminent cousin .

Young Tree - But, dear Lady Patience, how can something that's already happened be objectionable after it has happened, when it must have been objectionable even before it happened, so that the fact that it happened is...as they said....a" fait accompli' "...something like a gone and done affair, I guess, in our forest vernacular .

Arrogance - Did you say..: "As THEY said" ?.....THEY who ??

Young Tree - Well, it was a.........

Lady Patience - I'd rather wish that you would say no more, young little tree .

Arrogance - Why ? Do not stop him just now when it's becoming interesting and I am curious about the whole thing, stupid even as it might turn out to be !

Young Tree - It was a beautiful Summer night and the sweet, melodious song of the nightingale filled the air all around : ......the female nightingale flew, from far away, right to one of my branches, irresistibly attracted by the male nightingale exquisite and soothing song, while a young couple, close to me, on the ground, started an enduring embrace, bathed in the silver light of a full moon and............

Lady Patience - That's enough, young little tree

Arrogance - Well, he has not said anything extraordinary or improper ! What's so strange or objectionable about an embrace ? Why ! Creatures do that all the time all over the world without any second thoughts attached to it or is it because there are some Laws against its practice in this stretch of Land ...??!

Lady Patience - I do not like to talk about these things : they don't interest me. That's all .

Arrogance - I don't understand, dear cousin : the young tree didn't say anything about "things" or "anything"!...He had just praised the enticing song of the male nightingale in the moonlight of a beautiful Summer night and the joyful embrace of a resting couple.......what "THINGS" are you talking about ??

Lady Patience - I don't think that the young couple was resting .

Young tree - Our Lady Patience refers to the sequence of events that followed after the sweet song of the nightingale on one of my branches with his sweetheart that had flown to him from far away and the embrace of the young couple, close to me, on the ground, who had not flown in from anywhere but where just passers by, intending to take a rest but had changed their mind after hearing the sweet song of the nightingale .

Arrogance - That's all very well, exceedingly interesting and extremely fine but, in practical terms, this long redundant story does not answer my query of how could Lady Patience address her farewell to me in a foreign language, that happened to be the French language, when she does not have an inkling of that language and does not even know what French menas !!!

Young Tree - I see your point, and this is what happened : the young couple on the ground consisted of two passers-by, a girl and a boy, who were speaking in a foreign language so as not to reveal their true nationality, never calling each other by name but only moaning some unitelligible expressions except at the end of their embrace when they turned to each other and said those words that Lady Patience heard and repeated them to you, thinking that , if they had been said by the two "flightless" birds when parting, after the embrace had ended, they should be good to say goodbye to you too .

Arrogance - I see ! Well, but that still does not explain why would this mysterious couple choose to use French in an effort not to be recognized : chinese would have been far more intriguing and disguising !

Young Tree - Disguising , may be, but not exciting !.....You know..."cherchez la femme"..... ..."toujours l'amout"...."mon cheri"....."cocco cheri".......and so on and on under the light of the harvest moon ....!!

Arrogance - Ah ! Ah ! Our delightful cousin is annoyed about the whole thing because she only got some of the icing and none of the cake !.........".Une soirée tres agréable "....!! .....I bet !

Lady Patience - Happy now , Your Highness ?

Arrogance - Ah ! Shut up !! What are you up to, now, I wonder ?!....And why the sudden "buttering up" with that"Your Highness" stuff , when you always addressed me and, quite condiscendingly at that , just as simply as "cousin" ?......

Lady Patience - I haven't changed and I still call you cousin : I only echoed what the little young tree just told you, now , thinking, then, that it was an affectionate parting address and not a "sickly amorous adieu "! That was all .

Arrogance - Strange, really strange of you to come out with such insipid explanations of your doings, regardless of your justifications and adding sarcasm and ridicule with your impromptu "Your Highness" address, when you, were the very one, if you remember, at the beginning of our conversations, warning and instructing me on the inappropriatness and the incivility in acting that way, with your little green tree joining you gleefully in confirmimg your teaching and showing almost disdain to my lofty attitude, or so interpreted by you !!..... Really strange !

Lady Patience - My departing greetings to you were meant seriously and not as a joke or sarcasm and not in the least as ridicule . I do not make fun of anyone .There is always plenty of time at anyone's disposal for Mother Nature to make fun of all of us without we having to occupy ourselves in doing it . My"nature" tells me, instead, how much "real" patience is needed in this world of our existencies in this forest of ours , to make everybody happy and satisfied and to provide the necessary strength and courage to carry on .

Young Tree - I am very young, Lady Arrogance, Your Highness, but, please, look around, just a quick look to this immense forest before you leave us, and take notice of the patient growing of so much, of so many of us, from simple seeds and on and on into such an immense forest !

Arrogance - I really cannot figure out what this emotional outcry of yours, dear little green tree, has to do with parting greetings, however I am"almost" becoming used to the"almost" incomprehensible way things, thoughts and opinions are brought forward in this forest !......So , then, what did you have in mind or, should I rather convey my question as of what do you might have under your bark , to tell me with your"almost"poetical, semi-dramatic, emotionally laden remark ?

Young Tree - Oh ! Nothing much, really !All I wanted to point out was that without the persevering patience of our Fairy GodMother and her strictly applied diligence in observing it, this forest could not have been here, now . That is what I wanted to emphasize, before you left us .

Lady Tolerance - The little green tree tells the truth right from within his inner circles, dear Arrogance .

Arrogance - Quite interesting : and what's so important, anyway, that this forest be here at all ? Particularly so when "infested" with talking trees, with a soul inside them and a Fairy GodMother as their Instructor- Protector ??!!

Young Tree - Well, didn't you enjoy my shade and the refreshing rest under my spreading green branches ?

Arrogance - Of course I did, but a shade is not an uncommon commodity .

Young Tree - Granted: but it would be in a desert or in a plain without trees or buildings : right ?

Arrogance - It sounds like you are trying to run an advertising agency, portraying the desirable advantages and properties of trees and forests !

Young Tree - But trees do have advantages, I mean, they do offer advantages and opportunities that would be difficult to be found elsewhere unless Mother Nature had come up with innovative alternatives and, since She didn't, then ,forests and their trees are valuable essentials : don't you think ?!

Arrogance - My dear fellow, you, little green tree, should know that, for me, thinking is a waste of time : I am a creature of action, I aim at things to be done in earnest, well and completely. By just "thinking", a lot of opportunities are passing by, unobserved and unnoticed and lost for ever .

Lady Tolerance - Although I have no part in this conversation, yet, I cannot restrain myself from expressing my idea about "thinking ", so, what I.........

Arrogance - I guess that what you wanted to say was: " ....So, what ...I am thinking....", was it not ?

Lady Tolerance - < ...Was it yes...>....so to speak of, dear cousin, and I feel differently about thinking, perceiving it as a good "filter" to assess the actual value or no value of all those opportunities passing by :.......don't you think ??!!

Arrogance - What's so important about the "value" of an opportunity ? You grab what's coming, before someone else grabs it away from you and no questions asked .

Lady Patience - That's tantamount to gambling with life's essential virtues .

Arrogance - Isn't putting together a family and having children a fragile gamble, having no assurance of success whatsoever, except only a hope that success will follow and the children would be a blessing, this event not always a certain sequence, and even any "careful thinking", prior to the ensuing steps, may not help the uncertainty of the outcome .

Young Tree - But you, yourself, Your Highness, a while back in all these conversations, were thinking too, and I remember quite well you saying that trees were a good sourse of materials, particularly during the Winter months, when it is very cold, to keep creatures warm, offering them a good "opportunity" not to freeze to death...!!

Lady Tolerance - You see, that is a good opportunity for you to think things over : don't you think ?

Arrogance - Should I express what I am thinking, and would I think to express anything at all, I'd better not even say it or think of it for fear to set the stage for an "opportunity" by someone to accuse me of ......incivility !

Young Tree - And, Your Highness, in other instances, you had praised the usefulness of trees for the purpose of building furniture, to make life more comfortable, like the furniture used for resting, sitting, dining, sleeping and being protected from the inclement weather with protective walls, solid doors, strong roof and properly fitting windows, all of which is a lot more pleasurable than be sitting on a barren terrain with an open sky for a roof and wind, rain and dust for companions !

Arrogance - Interesting, yes, but not fully justifiable, yet . You see, even barring some new inventions or some spectacular pristine appearances of alternate materials by the benign hand of Mother Nature, whether this forest was or was not, another would grow in its place, somehow, somewhere .

Lady Tolerance - Tolerant as I am and delighted in preaching such an attitude towards our fellow creatures and their deeds, yet I am completely confounded at this last statement by our cousin, Lady Arrogance, that is, and her saying does not make any sense at all, it is out of place and it is disconnected and out of the entire contest being discussed ! I wonder, I just wonder, if she might have overdone herself !

Young Tree - Truly, Your Highness, your saying , I mean, what you just said is precisely the opposite of what you had said before and, frankly, it does not make any sense at all !!....Even more so when you had proclaimed the questionable need for "a forest" to be there...at all !!

Arrogance - I was suspecting it and I was expecting it .

Lady Tolerance - Suspecting an expectation is a senseless expression, in my opinion, since it is difficult to suspect something that you are already expecting .

Arrogance - Tralla-la-ra', hurrah ! Hurrah !!

LadyTolerance - Not even funny .

Arrogance - But effective : it stopped you cold in your rhetoric !

Lady Patience - «Tralla-la-ra' »! A nice tune to be remembered on the occasion of special events !

Lady Tolerance - Like , for example, the imminent departure of our cousin ?

Young Tree - Why do our conversations always finish up in confrontations ? Even with tempests, hurricanes and torturous winds, our branches hardly ever fight each other: they go down on the spot and do not "expect" others to go down with them !

Arrogance - Confrontation is a civil substitute for aggressive behaviour and if you ask me what all this has to do with the usefulness of trees, it beats me .

Lady Tolerance - That chapter has already been covered . Actually, it would have been better to have buried it, altogether .

Arrogance - Right !....Enough of all this .....yabbering, like they say in a far away land on this planet ! Enough of trees and forests ! The slow pace of your world, this world of trees and forests and Fairy God-Mothers, is really not "my cup of tea", as they say..........

Lady Patience - Did you say"yabbering"...??

Arrogance - I did . What's the problem ?

Lady Patience - Nothing, really : just unusual .

Arrogance - Anything can be "unusual" if not used .

Lady Tolerance - Smart Aleck .

Arrogance - How about "wise guy", for a change .

Lady Tolerance - Hardly worth the "change" !!

Young Tree - And here we go again..!! Confrontation, confrontation !! Can't some sense be made of all this....well....." far away land type of YABBERING " ???!....At least a measly ONE TIME ...????!!

Arrogance - Dear little young tree, has anything made sense "at all", ever since we started our conversations ??!...I doubt it !

Lady Tolerance - Now it's worth the "change"......WISE GUY !!

Arrogance - Thank you .

Lady Tolerance - Don't mention it .

Young Tree - Oh ! Oh !...Incorrigibles ! Hopelessly , incorrigibles ...!!!

Lady Patience - Apart from the "cup of tea" stuff, how would you prefer to identify yourself as a sign of personal recognition : the imposing fulgence of a lightning bolt, may be ??...

Arrogance - Thank you for your interest, but I do not need any special introduction : suffice myself .

Lady Patience - .That would be, of course, a catastrophic comparison with the slow growth of a tree, I understand that , and a significantly lower key representation of ready made accomplishments, according to the way you see and appreciate things, yet , a solid and strong growth, that of a tree, and not so destructive like the lightninmg bolt and its ostentatious image .

Arrogance - Frightening as a lightning bolt is in its horrendous power , yet, it impersonates a resplendent identity and I am fond of impressive appearances even if vane in their content, but, certainly, more impressive than a slow, monotonous growing of a tree .

Young Tree - I really do not understand you, dear Arrogance, although, believe you me, Your Highness, I am trying....I am really trying...!!

Arrogance - Try harder . After all, you are made of hard wood : it shouldn't be difficult !

Young Tree - There are creatures or other forms, our Elders told us, far harder than us trees and our Elders were not referring to rocks or mountains either .

Arrogance - Ah ! They must have been talking about those strange creatures with two legs, two arms and.............

Lady Tolerance - ....and two feet, two hands and a small tomato like fixture at the very top, precariously balancing itself on a skinny stick.....We have already heard this story, dear cousin .

Young Tree - Oh ! That's wonderful ! Wonderful ! Our Elders described them to us in a much similar way, only warned us of the indifference that these creatures have for trees and, generally, for almost anything that they choose to be indifferent about . Tell me, dear Arrogance, do these creatures have roots ?

Arrogance - Roots....??!?.....Listen, just listen, to this poor naive young little tree !! Roots, my dear, have only one purpose and that is to keep you stuck in one place without the possibility to move elsewhere in search of fortune and glory if the place where you were born would not offer you good enough opportunities .

Young Tree - This sounds strange and it it is even stranger to hear you say such things .You see, our Fairy GodMother had told us everything differently : that is that we, the trees, although standing solidly anchored to the soil where we were born with our penetrating roots, yet , we can reach many far away points, some even far, far away places, so to speak of, from where we stand and........

Arrogance - Amusing ! And would you or could you take those roots of yours along with you while running to those"far,far away"places?How I'd like to see this marathon !!

Young Tree - Oh ! Nothing like that, Your Highness ! Nothing like that, at all !!

Arrogance - I see : "hocus-pocus" with the magic of your Fairy GodMother".....and those "far, far away places" will be coming a running to you for a passing in review parade ! Will there be, also, a marching band to lead the triumphal parade ??!

Lady Tolerance - Oh ! You, incorrigible scoundrel, you...!!

Lady Patience - Dear little tree, why don't you tell to our cousin Arrogance what your Elders told you about those far away places !

Young Tree - Yes, I'll be glad to do it, but what the Elders told us is what you, dear Fairy GodMother, had told them, so , it is, really, what you had said that I shall tell to your eminent cousin : right ?

Lady Patience - You give me excessive merit in all these dispositions, dear little green tree: a lot of good comes also from you and your kindness in recognizing any enlightenment that you might have received from all of us . It is a rare gift for any creature, and I mean any "created" form, to show appreciation for received benefits without previous solicitation, and even a rarer virtue that of remembering it.

Arrogance - I can almost cry........!

Lady Tolerance - Oh ! Oh! Incorrigible !

Young Tree - Oh ! Yes, dear Lady Patience, thank you and , to the the best of my memory stored in my circles, our Elders had told us that it was not at all necessary for us to move from where we stand in order to reach far distant places and they never mentioned "marching Bands", whatever they are .

Arrogance - Quite interesting : arboreal soundless telepathy ! ....I declare !

Lady Patience - Nothing so aethereal, dear cousin, but a lot simpler mechanism , just as simple as it is efficient, with no aura of mystery or intervention of occult powers. Just listen to the young tree .

Young Tree - You are absolutely right, Fairy GodMother, you certainly are, because there is nothing mysterious in this mechanism which consists of a little "pinch" of Spring time and the.........

Arrogance - ....And, likely, a little "pinch" of salt, I guess, to give some taste to this insipid story.......

Lady Tolerance - It would not feel that insipid if you could "take it" with a little "grain of salt", distinguished cousin .

Arrogance - Grain of salt...!...Bah..!!...You would, probably, need a ton of salt just for listening to such stories and I thoroughly dislike anyone acting like that .

Lady Patience - Then, it is very simple : don't act that way .

Arrogance - Ah ! Forget it .

Young Tree - Whatever you say, whatever you said, whatever you may wishing to say that it is needed for us trees to reach far away places, what's needed is very simple, cheap, ready available, regularly recurring, abundant, reliable and effective,as I had mentioned, a little "pinch" of Spring weather, a few birds flying here and there, a little and gentle breeze to help Mother Nature to wake up from her Winter slumber and we can cover enormous distances, without any problems or encumbrances and without the need for path, road or compass .

Arrogance - You should start a travel agency, my boy : your commercial logo:"Fly with us, like a breeze, the cheaper, the better " .

Young Tree - Yes, dear Arrogance, Your Highness, it is so : just a little favourable wind and there we go far, far away to encourage other trees to grow, once our seeds carried by the propitious winds take hold on the soil of their new land and prosper from seed to sprout, to solid and sturdy big tall trees and generate a new majestic and powerful forest. Don't you think , Arrogance, that what I just told you is really very beautiful ? We do not have even to consider or worry about walking !!

Arrogance - Interesting, but I had not thought of that aspect in the long distance capabilities of trees .

Lady Tolerance - I can hardly believe my ears in hearing what I think I am hearing !! Heavens be witness of such a portent ! Our cousin Arrogance admitting ignorance of something ...!!!!!!!

Arrogance - Well, I am in good company in admitting some lack of knowledge about something. You, probably, might recall that amusing and historical episode about a famous French writer and philosopher who.........

Lady Tolerance - I know several who wrote about trees and forest and castles but I am not sure that I would know this particular one, about his lack of knowledge .

Arrogance - Nothing major, really, but interesting in the way this one that I am talking about, answered the subtle and unfriendly remarks of other royal Courtisans about the large salary given to him by the King on account of the great knowledge this famous writer possessed,: " If the King would pay me for what I do not know "...said Voltaire...,"the entire treasures of the empire would not be sufficient !"....So, I gladly share the company !

Lady Tolerance - Ah !....Voltaire...the hyper-sarcastic and caustic philosopher of immense talent, knowledge and vision....yes....Francois Marie Arouet.......Voltaire..!!

Young Tree - Oh ! Yes, I remember him too !

Arrogance - WHAT...!!!!...You...remember the great philosopher-writer Voltaire....????!! I can't believe what I am hearing and....from a tree !!

Young Tree - Oh ! Yes, I remember the man, taking some walks here in this forest with his peotegé Candide when out of the beautiful castle of Thunder-ten-tronckh for a breath of fresh air .

Arrogance - But, you young silly tree, you couldn't have seen that man because he lived some centuries back from your time !

Young Tree - Did he ?...That's interesting . He still comes through, though, from time to time, just for a walk .

Arrogance - You must be crazy, my boy . At a second thought, I believe that you ARE !

Lady Patience - You must understand, dear cousin, that our young tree just repeats what his Elders told him and what the Elders' Elders told the old Elders : it's a feeling of very sensitive perception for what cannot be seen but is thought of as a possibility of sight . You know, our young green tree cannot see .

Lady Tolerance - And that's a blessing in disguise.

Arrogance - And there you go again! All of you ! And again, and again.... you seem never to be able to stop on your careening trajectory of formulating veiled semi-philosphical, emotional, affective, seldom effective, hyperbolic loquaceous FANTASIES !!.....Well. if you see the old man come along ,again, for a walk in the woods with his precious Candide, say "hallo' to him for me !

Lady Patience Dreaming a little, fantasticating some, are, perhaps, signs of loneliness .

Arrogance - In a thick forest like this one, with thousands of trees all around ?!

Lady Patience - Multitudes do not perceive the inner needs of a single....tree, I guess and I was almost saying the spiritual needs of a single creature..so, old folks galore and fantasy come to the rescue and................

Arrogance - ......And "creatures" and "trees" see ghosts going around this forest for a stroll in the afternoons........

Lady Tolerance - You do not give anything or anybody a chance, do you ??!

Arrogance - You are right : I don't . I wasn't trained to indulge on the stupidity of lazy dreams and fancy imaginations : if you like them , fine, just fine and you can keep them, all of them, for yourself and enjoy them indefinitely, as for me, my dear, I do not give a hoot about your philosophical discussions over fantasies, Spring breezes, growing seeds in far, far away places, soil, wisdom and all the roots in the world ! So, it's goodbye and stay well, dear all !

Young Tree - Oh!Do not leave us in such a haste:we are not against you and it does not matter to us how you may be seen by others : you kept us company and, in some way, you refreshed and filled our day, so do not hurry away, now . The night is still some time away and you'll have still plenty of time to reach your cottage, there, between those two little hills, before darkness overtakes you .

Arrogance - Yes, that little cottage! I should have reached it already this mrning, but tiredness and the high heat of the day caused me to stop and lie down in your shade ! So, I really should hurry on, now !

Lady Patience - Dear cousin, you should kindly consider the spontaneous invitation of our little young tree for you to linger a while longer among us !

Arrogance - I do appreciate the kind invitation and I gave it my fullest and most sincere consideration, but I really must be on my way and not to be late for the quest of my disciples .

Lady Patience - The quest of your disciples...????!!

Arrogance - Yes, dear cousin : the moltitude of my faithful followers and students of my art, are not complacent at intervals of neglet of "action", never considering, not even in the least, a missing opportunity, possibly lost through self-indulgence towards the kindness of other creatures : that's why I must hurry now, too much time lost already !

Lady Patience - That's too bad .

Young Tree - I don't understand the logic behind all this complicated talking .

Arrogance - Better so, dear block of wood, better so !.....Opportunities, you must know, come one at a time and never repeat themselves, once they spun an opportunity .

Young Tree - I really cannot understand your way of representing things, Your Highness, and I do not understand why an opportunity cannot repeat itself . Why, in our forest, and, I guess, in many other forests, opportunities repeat themselves ad infinitum with the spreading of seeds all over there is a spot to stop and rest .

Arrogance - Your world, little green tree, is a well directed, pre-prescribed affair, where mine is directed by the shifty and unruly minds of the famous creatures with two legs, two arms and........

Lady Tolerance - ,,,,,two hands, two feet and a small head on top resembling a large tomato . We have heard that already, dear cousin. What the little green tree is telling you is a genuine invitation through his wooden soul and void of any artifice .

Lady Patience - Yes, dear cousin : that is exactly what the little green tree is telling you .

Arrogance - Contrary to my habit, to my character and to my personality, which do not accept nor appreciate advice of any kind or form and, least of all, exhortations, I have to admit that the little young tree has a way in his gentle address to starngers .

Lady Tolerance - The sun rising this morning from behind those sloping hills must have been in a radiant mood for allowing such a statement and recognition of other entities by the very Master of denial of other creatures' virtues and deeds !!!

Arrogance - Just folklore legend, dear cousin, about me . Those two legged creatures are constantly in need of a pinch of fabled content added to the insipid soup of their lives and I was a good "ingredient" for the folkloristic representation .

Lady Tolerance - And you are representing it....magnificently, dear cousin !

Arrogance - Perhaps you are overlooking an important fact or you are even unaware that you are using my way of expressions and response in the praising of an event, by using "adulation" in my favour !!

Lady Tolerance - As I just mentioned it to you, the sun must have risen this morning with radiant glory, causing us to come out with radiant expressions . Of course you do not need a risplendent sun to express yourself as your address works fine even under overcast skies .

Young Tree - But then, are you going to stay with us a little longer ? Your chatting with Lady Patience and Lady Tolerance has already detained you beyond the time that you would have wanted to be detained !!

Arrogance - Yes, just the last parting shots for good fortune and appropriate behaviour ! I, really, must go now and get back on my trail.....besides it is not my choice subject, really, any academic interpretation of soil, seeds and ceedlings in far, far away places, roots, forests and trees . No reference, of course, to anyone here present .

Young Tree - Of course ! Even I understand that .

Arrogance - So , my staying longer and the likely continuation of our discussions would, more likely than not, represent for me a loss of time rather than pleasure or interest . Well, then, goodbye, young little tree, and, by sober reflextion, it might not have been, in final analysis, a total waste of time our exchange of ideas, after all !!.......So long, to all of you !

Lady Tolerance - So long, then, if you MUST go, and so long from Lady Patience too . Bye !!

Young Tree - Oh Wait! Wait! Your Highness ! Don't leave right now : I want to tell you something !

Arrogance - Very well, then : what is it that you want to tell me ?

Young Tree - Well, Your Highness, in those last few fleeting instants of your presence among us, just as you were saying farewell and departing, you might have said something as an unrehearsed expression of formal departure, something wise but clear and straight enough, in its straightforwardness, that even a wooden stump of a tree, like I am, could understand !

Arrogance - You don't say !!

Young Tree - But I do, Your Highness and, when you made that remark : "after all, our exchange of ideas might not have been a total loss of time ", I felt very happy deep within my circles, I agreed with your thought , because, you see, I..........

Arrogance - Is this a subtle, insidious trick to try to keep me here longer, dear little tree ?

Young Tree - Not in a million forests,Your Highness, not in a million of a million forests, your Highness, I assure you ! It was that last parting remark that aroused my curiosity and it felt starngely close to my way of thinking because I firmly believe that any idea is not indestructible , but it can varie,undoing itself and, sometimes, even disappear altogether, like any one of us or anything else in this forest once our assigned time has expired, but.........

Arrogance - How true !

Young Tree - But, if nothing else, the thinking of ideas helps us creatures keep our spirits alive, and I did include myself in the "pot" with all the other creatures, not out of presumption, but only because I could not find another proper word to express that !

Arrogance - Even on the verge of my departure I am persecuted with philosophical quotations ! ....Oh ! Philosophy ! Philosophy ! Where art thou ...??! Why have you deserted this place and why are not coming among these trees and clear the fog around them !! It is hard to bear this onslaught of wisdom on such a hot day and, on top of that, just think of it, from a tree....!!!!!!

Lady Patience - Well, what's so strange about it ? A tree is also a sort of a creature, without presumption to be acting like one, of course, but, nonetheless, a created form, living, vegetating, producing fruits for squirrels and birds, and its real purpose in this world, apart from the obvious one of its well known immediate aspect and performance, is still totally unknown to us and its................

Young Tree - Please, Lady Patience, do not trouble yourself to such an extent just to protect my impulsive talking and defending my voiced feelings,often, coming in at the wrong time! I have a feeling, still, that Lady Arrogance did understand the meaning of my thought but, true to her character, would ridicule it instead !

Arrogance - I did not ridicule anything, but I am tired and overwhelmed by the ridiculously senseless logic of arboreal remarks .

LadyPatience - But this young tree's "philosophy", as you seem to define its simple straight talk and spontaneous expression, is nothing more than the natural projection of his roots above the ground : very simple, my dear Arrogance, and it is only your peculiar character that tends to enlarge upon everything , to exhault it to fulgid magnitude and that makes you, now, think that our little tree is a philosopher !! Dear cousin, he is just a good product of some good soil .

Young Tree - And, dear Arrogance, Your Highness, if I may, I'd like to......

Arrogance - You may, Oh! You certainly may, little green tree ! Are we not quite use to your intrusions ? That is or was, I am sure, what you were planning to do, was it not ?

Young Tree - I am impulsive, I know, may be the fierce winds of Winter and sudden early Spring squalls impressed upon me that kind of outbursts that come from within ! Yes, I wanted to butt in, as they say, and tell you that these here roots of mine, holding me firm and steady on this good soil, afford me the possibility to grow tall and taller ,every day, almost to reach the sky !

Arrogance - And get lost in the clouds for more peregrine and celestial "tall"philosophical remarks .

Young Tree - Your Highess,if I may be forgiven for saying what I am about to say, but I believe that it would be far more consonant with the character of my nature to.....

Arrogance - ......To quit talking, now, and have a rest .

Lady Tolerance - Oh ! Incorrigible !

Young Tree - You may be right,Your Highness, for me to quit talking as, I know, I am abusing my loquacity, encouraged by the constant rustling of my numerous and happy leaves , but I'd rather loosen up myself in the fringes of the sky, than to........

Arrogange - .....And, hopefully, remain there for good !

Lady Tolerance - Incorrigible ! Oh! Incorrigible !

Young Tree - Yes,Your Highness, even better to stay there, than to be lost in the un- healthy twirl of your kind of ideas and aims which only call,in the end, for the distrust and dislike of creatures who seek to grow tall enough to grasp the sky for pure pretentious show and self-conceit, but have no roots to prop them up and keep them steady in their frantic and anxious climb: I call that a worthless glory .

Arrogance - A worthless glory...???!!....Anf who seeks glory, green stick ??!...Only Idealists seek glory ! I , myself, seek only advantages and the lucky precedence to well stocked outlets of all meteriel of all materiel goodies available anywhere, anytime, all the time, in our existences .

Lady Patience - Dear cousin, what our little green tree, or, shall I correct that in order to pacify your exquisite sensitivity about that "our", and meaning just "my" little green tree......what, then, our ....oops....sorry....my little green tree refers to is the lack of esteem and consideration afforded those creatures who adopt and follow your type of "fortune foraging" that.......

Arrogance - What's wrong with any type of fortune making, let alone my particular type of foraging, any way ? Everybody in the forests of the world is trying to make a fortune, one way or another, except holy men who look, instead, in a different direction .

Lady Patience - It is not the actual desire to make a fortune that offends, sometimes, the more noble sensitivity of selected creatures, but it is the way that fortune is sought after, that gives it its sinister apparel, yours, for example, ususally saturated with pride, ostentation, haughtiness and presumption, at times, even with total disregard to civility, charity and compassion .

Arrogance - I begin to sense a strange feeling of insecurity to my very person as if threatened with an impending assault and doom !

Lady Patience - Do not worry! This is a peaceful, free and friendly forest and you must remain certain that what I am saying is not meant against you personally, but purely as a demonstartion of the general accepted way of defining that crowd of creatures that identify themselves as your followers, by their very deeds .

Arrogance - I sincerely appreciate your letting me out of that "Tribunal of Inquisition "! You must have given some serious and extended thought to the complexity of the issue, I imagine .

Lady Patience - The reason is that I have always believed that patience is necessary in our lives, so as to give time to all conflicting issues to present themselves more clearly and in a way that would offer a better reason for their proper identification .

Arrogance - But that's tantamount to losing precious time ! It is quite clear to me that, in our daily existences, no one is "patiently" waiting for some one else to ponder and linger on making up his, her or their minds !!

Lady Patience - Correct, and, generally, it is not an accepted practice in our world of forests for anyone to stand aside and say:"Sorry, but I think"YOU"were first in line"! So, to lose a few more moments may be better than years of regrets .

Arrogance - And, the way I can figure out the benevolent attitude of the world of created creatures as portrayed by you, patiently waiting for their chance at fortune, which may never materialize, is one of somnolent,slow moving, pious and depressed creatures just waiting, patiently again, of course, before jumping at each other's throat, contesting ideas, motives and plans and trying to grab what may be still grabbable as a consequence of that confrontation, under the aegis of " Patience Galore, Inc." !!

Lady Patience - That is "YOUR" construction of that situation : not mine and, most certainly, not that of "patient"and sober people,with neatly tuned intellective powers, reciprocal recognition of each others'thoughts and respect for each other and, respect for each other,means respect for each others' ideas, beliefs and the freedom of convincing, even if not be favoured by "either" side ...!!

Arrogance - Ah ! Yes, yes, I begin to understand, now, the meaning of all those nice and imposing appellatives that go under so many designations for various types of characters, as you describe them, from haughtiness to presumption, from pride to ostentation and so on and so on, the more the better, but you must have just, just missed one, my dear Lady Patience : did you not ?

Lady Patience - I don't think so : which one do you suspect I missed ?

Arrogance - Prejudice .

Lady Patience - Prejudice...??!....And why prejudice ?...And towards whom or what ? I really feel that it doesn't apply at all to the present issue .

Arrogance - But it does ! Prejudice towards me, my dear Patience, just towards me !

Lady Patience - Now, when did you feel that any inkling of prejudice was being formulated against you ?

Arrogance - Well embodied in all those distinctive appellatives that you have just mentioned, which, in my opinion, represent sheer envy for the glorious and magnificent achievements made possible by my way of living and by the practicing of my brand of virtues by the creatures who follow me !

Lady Patience - And you call this way to riches and fortune a way of pride, rather than the other interpretations I gave to it ?

Arrogance - You must be either blind....I know the little tree is, the poor thing.....or you must be "plumb dum", if you do not see it in its favourable aspect, so , since you are not blind, I am opting for the second possibility .

Lady Patience - Cousin, I am not thinking of anything bad about you : I only describe what the general thought is that prevails among simple creatures, simple, yes, yet very smart when it comes to differentiate between "good" and "not so good", and the majority of them do know what "good" is . So, they stay away from you, look upon your boasting followers with caution and try to avoid contact or confrontation with them . These simple ceatures'attitude, probably, is the reason why you feel that prejudice is practised against you .

Arrogance - Dear cousin, you and I know very well that prejudice is deeply ingrained in many aspects of our daily existences, in many places and in many forests, but it must not be blamed entirely on an adverse type of character of certain groups of creatures only, but it is a well balanced act where, many a time and, most of times, the so called "prejudiced" is not well disposed, sometimes even refractory and hostile to improvement and acceptance of wordly common and well established practices, adversely delaying, so , a smooth transition .

Young Tree - True ! Oh, how, how true ! So true that I almost cannot believe it !

Arrogance - Are you feeling well, little tree ?

Lady Tolerance - He is happy because you said somethng that pleased him enormously .

Arrogance - I am happy and sorpised about it, all at the same time : happy, because I pleased someone, and, surprised, because he understood it .

Young Tree - No surprise, Your Highness, and your description of certain character aspects of our common existences, reassured me and gave me hope of some improvement to comé, hopefully !

Arrogance - Like, for example, to be spared from the greediness of the two legged creatures, may be ?

Young Tree - Oh ! No , it's not the greedy two legged creatures that I am talking about, but those other terrible, and greedy too, creatures, the horrible fungi and the beetles who think tha I am just a gourmet meal for their own pleasure and, I believe, they are definitely prejudiced against me .

Arrogance - Yes ! For truth sake, it is, really, hight time for me to leave, after that talk !!

Young Tree - That is really a pity for you to leave now, when our ideas, thoughts and general conversation tended to a pleasant and common denominator, becoming pleasant, affable and peaceful . We will be sad without you !

Arrogance - Now, wouldn't you like to follow me and get out of this forest, get rid of goblins and ghosts promenading among the trees and bidding your Fairy GodMother an affectionate : "ADIEU"....??

Young Tree - You are also funny,dear Arrogance! You know that I cannot come,so stop teasing me !!....But I tell you what : one day, when some more time shall have passed and, according to my Destiny, I.........

Arrogance - Please! Please! ....Not again on that subject : Destiny would just upset me, I assure you, little tree !

Young Tree - Do not worry, Your Highness : no dissertation on it !!....All I intended to say was that when the purpose of my existence is fully completed, I shall make for you a very comfortable and artistic chair for you to sit on it, in your relaxing times and , so , perhaps, you might leisurely recall this time you spent with me in this forest and remember me : would you like that ?

Arrogance - Don't you even say that as a joke, little green tree !!....You'll live a thousand years, like the tall, old cedar trees that grew in that far away land called Lebanon !

Young Tree - But I am not a cedar, Your Highness !

Arrogance - Then, think of being one !

Lady Tolerance - For once, dear little green tree, you should capitalize on the good wishes of our cousin Arrogance: it is, indeed, an almost incredible event for Lady Arro-Arrogance, to soften to the point of feeling emotional about you, little tree !

Arrogance - But, now, little tree, I TELL YOU WHAT !!....If I will track by this path and by these woods again in the next hundred years or so, I will make sure that I would stop by and............

Young Tree - Oh ! Yes, yes, Your Highness, yes, please, do come again and stop by !...Oh! please, please, do come by again, Your Highness !

Arrogance - If I would come, I will talk to you about all the soil and the roots, the spirits and the ghosts, the goblins and the fairies and the Fairy GodMotheres that I might have encountered in other forests and add to it a "dissertation" on pride and prejudice, as it will have been written splendidly, by then, by a famous writer : is that a deal ?

Young Tree - I find it hard to believe that this is really real....!!!,,,YES ! Your Highness, it is a deal !!

Lady Patience - The little tree seems very happy with your proposition : you see, dear cousin, how gentle and how pleasant the attitude of that little tree is, in spite of all the contradictions and discussions and antagonistic thoughts ventilated during our heated conversations .

Arrogance - A fruit, perhaps, of his roots ?

Lady Patience - It is a possibility . His roots are good, his seeds were genuine, his ancestry of pure stock. It is a possibility .

Young Tree - Dear Lady Patience, is there ever anything that can be certain and not just possible ?

Lady Patience - If there was, no scholars would have invented the word of "possibility", I presume .

Arrogance - That is why I always aim straight at the obvious and the "solid" matter and the stuff at hand and let the world of dreamers argue about the inherent philosophy of the word"possibility".

Lady Tolerance - However, strange as it may seem, but it is a common knowledge in the writings, sayings, sermons and dissertations of wise men of all the past ages and scholars and learned men of all ages, that what is considered "possible" is an inexpliable feeling of something that may be vaguely perceived but not grasped .

Arrogance - Well, dear all, the way I perceive the philosophical meaning of the word "possibility", is the most certain of all the possibilities and that is that the philosopher is placed to rest in his burial place just as well as the grave digger who buried the philosopher and, each of them, happy or unhappy in their respective lives, are still nothing more than lonely mortals !

Lady Tolerance - Nothing really new in that, dear cousin : it's common knowledge that we are mortals, and that, since birth, we are careening down a sloping incline, to our final and most certain end...death I mean . Now, as to the "lonely" part of it, it is is a very subjective case and....well, shall I say....just a...possibility !

Arrogance - But I do not even like to talk or thnk about such depressive thoughts and I am annoyed at having been drawn into such an isuue: that constant gloomy reminder of the end of everybody and everything ! So what ??!....We all know that, every single creature knows that ! So , why to make a constant litany about the doomsday to come and cry long before the milk is spilled .

Lady Patience - But, my dear Arrogance, this beautiful sermon is just as good as a chip of philosophy, straight from the school of Atena ! I almost cannot believe that it is coming from you !

Arrogance - Well, dear cousin, it is not so : it just may sound that way to you because you do not know me that well yet, but, in my opinion,our times do not call for the help of philosophers even if a few of them, if real philosophers and not just "talkers", could do some good .

Lady Patience - For that short time spent with you,I was able to notice that,at least,you preserve your way of portraying things and opinion and, in itself, that might be a redeeming aspect of your character . Now, what else is there to be said before you leave us , dear cousin ?

Arrogance - Not much, I believe....seriously! Don't you think that we have"said " enough ? So , this chapter should conclude our discussions on I do not even remember what and why ! May be, the next time that we would encounter each other , we will have all the answers for ....I do not even remember what...!! Till then , my dear cousin, my warmest greetings and farewell !

Young Tree - Dear Arrogance, Your Highness, please, wait, do not leave yet, do not hurry away ! Please, look there, towards those hills, I.......

Arrogance - But how can you see anything towards those hills or anywhere, when you cannot see, period ?!!

Young Tree - I can see with what I can feel and, just a while ago, I began to feel some increased wind coming from that direction, since I am familiar with that side of the forest and, when that happens, the wind is usually accompanied by huge, large clouds, which the wind hepls in pushing them towards the forest and my Elders always tell me that, that type of wind, can be treacherous, violent and very destructive, with the appearance of heavy rain and, at times, also hail and lightning .

Arrogance - It might be just a little of wind, not an uncommon affair at this time of the year, hot days, moisture and you may get a squall or two.

Lady Patience - Don't you think that you should stay here a little longer before starting on your journey until, at least, we can see how the weather will turn out ?

Arrogance - As I said, a little wind at this time of the year does not really means a lot and, certainly, is not an anticipated guarantee of worst weather to come.

Lady Patience - But I believe that the young little tree feels that the wind is getting stronger than itwas, for example, last night : not a good sign . So, I urge you to reconsider and wait a little longer before starting off .

Arrogance - What for ? A little rain...?! We have seen it before !

Lady Patience - It seems to me, dear cousin, that even in the simple and common instances of every day life , like an aproaching rai or thunder storm, you never overlook to profess your derisive attitude about everything . The little young tree wanted to be kind and helpful to you and you compensated him rather poorly for his kindness and thoughfulness .

Arrogance - Control your language, cousin ! What's all the fuss about some rain, anyway?

Lady Tolerance - It isn't so much the rain to disturb our better senses but it is your insensitivity to kindness that disturbs us....!

Arrogance - Insensitivity towards an analphabet, silly little young tree, who tries to warn everybody of an approaching rain ?

Lady Patience - He does what he can with what he has got .

Arrogance - I see : some circles in and some circles out, frivolous fluttering leaves and a slow poke FauryGodMother nursing him : really remarkable ! How can you, cousin, at all dare accuse me of responding poorly to this little stump's concerns about some stupid rain approacing ?

Lady Patience - I see here, now, how true and even more convincing than ever was what an ancient philosopher used to say to one of his disciples :..." Of your own errors, justification is always readily at hand and defendedwith extraordinary tenacity and conviction of purpose..." !

Arrogance - That eminent philosopher of yours , my dear Patience, must have committed a great number of errors himself and was trying his best to cover them upin an easy way, speaking well, as they say, and acting foul !

Young Tree - Ah ! Look ! Look ! What did I tell you ?! I can even feel the first drops of rain falling on my leaves and the wind "growing" wild and stripping my branches of their leaves !!

Lady Patience - It looks like a bad shower : I hear a peeling of thunder and it seems to be coming from beyond those hills some distance from the end of the forest, just as our little young tree had forcast and those bad clouds seem to head just in our direction .

Young Tree - May be a severe downpour......even a hurricane !

Arrogance - Why not a "Universal Flood", like in the old times of ancient memories...??!!!

Young Tree - Oh ! No ! No !....Please, don't say those things, not even as a joke ! I want to live and continue to grow and I want to absorb this "life-giving"water even if it comes down in buckets together with cats and dogs, as they say, so that........

Arrogance - Why not adding some sentiment to such an enticing image of Mother Nature's ability to please and satisfy in many various ways her obedient subjects ? What about a little music ??!

Lady Tolerance - Oh ! Incorrigible !....Incorrigible !!

Young Tree - Nothing wrong,I believe,in praising something on account of "that" something that's providing "something" for me to be syphoned to the slender"stele"of the vascular system of my stem, that "something" consisting of a "complex pabulum" that will make me strong, tall and firm like the.........

Arrogance - ....Like the old cedars of Lebanon ??!

Young Tree - I am not a cedar , Your Highness : I am a tree .

Arrogance - That's a new one to me ! Aren't now cedars trees too ?

Lady Patience - The little young tree means something else, dear cousin . Of course, cedars are trees too but, for proper delineation of descent, cedars are coniferous plants of the Old World while our young little tree is a fagaceous tree of the genus "Quercus".

Arrogance - And are you going to tell me, now, perhaps, that this"subtle"differentiation of trees'class or category, is NOT a prejudicial slip against cedars ??!

Lady Patience - It is just a phylum, indirectly applied to the arboreal world .

Arrogance - A....WHAT..??!

Lady Patience - A phylum .

Arrogance - You mean an "affiliated" type of class or category, do you ?

Lady Tolerance - She told you, dear cousin :" A phylum ".

Arrogance - And I am telling you, dearest cousins : you are NUTS...!!

Young Tree - Ah ! That reminds me of something : we do make acorns, the cedars do not .

Arrogance - That's probably why the cedars of the Old World were smarter than the today's Oak trees : they were not making acorns but built the mighty, wonderful, sleek ships of the ancient Phoenicians on the shores of Lebanon .

Young Tree - But, Your Highness, our acorns are very good, have an artistic shape and provide excellent nourishment for the squirrels. I don't think that the squirrels, with their best of intentions, could eat ships, even if built by the ingenious Poenicians with Lebanon's cedars .

Arrogance - Obviously .

Lady Patience - And, just repeating "verbatim" what you had said to me, isn't your remark to the little young tree about the cedars of the Old World being smarter than the oak trees of the New World, plain "prejudice" ?

Arrogance - I don't think so, unless you choose to think so and never come up with an answer to that .

Young Tree - I feel more rain coming down on my leaves and branches, soaking the ground around me and increasing in intensity as well as the wind howling more fiercely through my branches : this is going to be a violent thunderstorm !

Arrogance - I detest dramatizations without the concept of an anticipation of a rewarding expectation, particularly so when uttered aloud by a stupid tree !

Young Tree - I heard you muttering some displeasure at my representation of the oncoming bad weather, Your Highness, but I would like to point out that there are no "stupid" trees .

Arrogance - All smart, right ?

Young Tree - Not even that, Your Highness . We are either small or big, soft wood or hard wood, some tall, very tall and, some, very short and, further up, I was told by my Elders that some of us, distant cousins to us and living in far away lands, are so precious that the forests that harbour them have special guards patrolling their enclaves to protect them .

Arrogance - The greedy two legged creatures, I guess !

Young Tree - I want to become a big tree, very, very big and even bigger, with many beautiful branches and so many green leaves to cover me up completely during the hot days of Summer and to able to feel the restful approval of the many creatures, young and old, of all types, shapes and sizes, who will enjoy my shade and cooling protection from the scorching summer sun or seek refuge in a sudden shower . Oh! I wish I could live long enough to do all that !

Arrogance - It is a widly spread notion among informed creatures that no one should seek shelter under a tree during a storm: are you aware of that recommendation ?.

Young Tree - I didn't say storm : I said"shower".

Arrogance - What's the difference ? The weather, in whichever form chooses to appear, is well known to carry, always, some unexpected and unpredictable changes, so , an unassuming shower could, suddenly, turn into a threatening storm. Experienced "Experts" have confirmed that hypothetical possibility .

Young Tree - "They" have to say something, always !! Well, just look around, Your Highness, and admire all those mighty trees and the magnificent oaks which, I am told by my Elders, have been here for longer years than anyone can count, and have lived through innumerable and fearsome thunderstorms and they are still here!

Lady Patience - Yes, these beautiful, old majestic trees, have learnt to live trough innumerable storms, some extremely severe, some, slightly less severe, just as any creature in this forest has and, I am sure, in many other forests, many other trees and other creatures have certainly lived through too . .

Arrogance - Indeed, our Destiny still remains hidden to us, but, as far as to the safety of standing under a tree during bad weather, regardless "whether the weather" is still just so bad or just not so bad, still commands caution and attention, because to take chances on known pitfalls is an act of irresponsibility .

Lady Patience - Strange for you to talk about responsibility and irresponsibility, when your general attitude is, to all practical expectations, a reckless one !......Certainly, not one type that could be recommended as a highly responsible "sensible ground level", when you try, always, to be above all and everything !!

Arrogance - I am always trying to be above , but with a shrewd judgement .

Young Tree - Your Highness, dear vague creature who wanders in our forest and whom I can hear but cannot see, please, pay no undue attention to what Lady Patience says to you, for she does not mean any harm or any antagonissm to you, as it is quite natural for anything or anybody to say things for pure instinct of a need for expression .

Arrogance - But did you consult with Lady Patience, before mentioning this intimate notion to me ??!

Lady Patience - No fear of contradiction or denial on my part and I believe that what the young green tree is telling you,is correct:I only point out what I see as a matter of cotradiction, but I do not raise a "case" for it .

Young Tree - Yes, Your Highness, even the rain behaves that way . You see, the rain, while falling, announces its presence in its penetrating liquid form, to bring life to our existences , a form of expression, in itself, I would say, just as equal to that of any other creature or form which tries to express itself in one way or another .

Arrogance - Listen, you green wooden philosopher, it starts raining stronger, now, and do I have to lend my ears to the sound of the falling rain and your stupid talking, both at the same time ..??!.....I might need a"double" umbrella !!

Young Tree - Of course, you do not have to, Your Highness ! Besides, apart from the fact that "double" unbrellas are not on sale anywhere in this forest, like they may be where you come from, the fact remains that, of course, no one has to listen to anything that they don't want to listen to, yet , no one can deny anyone his right to speak and express himself .

Arrogance - Noble thought .

Lady Tolerance - Yes, I think so too : a noble, sincere and enlightening thought, worth the strength of a forest of magnificent, proud, majestic trees .

Arrogance - You raised quite a quorum, little green tree, with your "power of expression" bit !!

Young Tree - I had no intention of causing such a favourable acceptance for what I said, and, honestly, I had not even thought of that, but, thinking about it or"thinking into the phenomenon", as that famous scientist said when asked how did he come up with his famous discovery, I too, in a far more modest and respectfully humble expectation, started thinking that how could........

Arrogance - Here we go again ! More......expectations ...??!

Young Tree - No, Your Highness, just pondering upon the right of anyone to express himself freely and for no one to deny that right to anyone and thinking of how could anyone, by any chance, tell the rain to stop falling, just because it may inconvenience somebody, or stop the peeling of thunder, just because the noise upsets somebody else, , or get the top of a mountain to come down to you, so that you could sit on it without having to climb up to it ?

Arrogance - What kind of nonsense are you talking about ! Your sense is as ligneous as that of a....wooden stick....!!!....And, guess what ?...YOU are one !!

Lady Patience - I don't think that was nice .

Arrogance - Can't anyone take a joke, down these lands ??

Lady Patience - Jokes, of course, yes, when they are jokes , smart jokes, I mean . We are less inclined to enjoy them when they foul .

Young Tree - Do not worry, Lady Patience, dear Fairy GodMother ! To me it makes no difference and it does not upset me to hear the opinions of different creatures, particularly when addressed to me . Every one is entitled to express opinions .

Lady Patience - Unfortunately .

Arrogance - That's prejudice, dear cousin !

Lady Patience - Ah ! Shut up !

Arrogance - !!!...COUSIN....!!!!!!

Young Tree - Yes, all I want is to grow big, with many branches and many green leaves on them and, perhaps, one day, someone will build a house in this vicinity and take me in within its enclosure, in their garden and take good care of me, and they will tell to their friends :"Look, just look at this oak how beautiful it is and how big, and it grows bigger every year...!", and their friends will say: "Yes, this oak tree is a splendid tree , the most beautiful tree in your garden!" and another visitor will say:"This oak is so beautiful, so beautifully proportio-ed,with majestic branches,thick with leaves and acorns!It deserves to be pain-ted on a beautiful, fine canvas by a renowned painter, a real artist !"....I will be, then, very happy and happy to be alive so desired and admired by all !.Oh! I wish I could be that big already now, and all of that dream promptly transferred into reality !

Arrogance - Listen,listen to the young tree who wants and longs to become big, very big and seems to suffer for not being at that stage yet, bound as he is, by Nature, to be "patient", before reaching for higher marks !!....What do you make out of your devoted disciple now, my dear Patience ?

Lady Patience - An impromptu of a wish to come true .

Arrogance - And it probably will .

Young Tree - Careful, careful, Lady Arrogance, Lady Patience and Lady Tolerance, take care : the rain is coming down thick and solid, now! The wind, also, has picked up a lot more strength !

Arrogance - Thank you for your concern, little tree: the rain is indeed very heavy now and the wind is fierce.

Young Tree - Oh! What a weather ! I can hear the thunder rumbling right abobe us ! And the rain, so heavy, so violent !!

Arrogance - I can see those black clouds pyiling up one against the other and so fast !!

Young Tree - I am afraid that this is no mere thunderstorm, o Arrogance, but a real hurrica-ne ! A real one !!...Hear, hear the thunder ever so much closer to us and so loud , and the intensityof the rain, coming down like a water fall ! This is a hurricane, dear Arrogance ! The Elders warned us of such a possibility, at this time of the year !.....I am glad you did not venture out on your journey while the weather apeared,then, so uncertain ! You might have been swept away by the violence of the wind !

Arrogance - Nothing sweeps me away : more likely I sweep anything else away ! So , I doubt that I would have been in danger and, by the time it took for the storm to build up, I could have reached that fine little cottage between those two hills a short distance from the end boundary of the forest and be fully repaired.

Lady Patience - It is always hard to tell what can happen:danger always lurks insidiously aro-und us , ready to strike whenever we least expect it !

Young Tree - And the wind is so strong, I can hardly keep my branches from snapping off me !

Arrogance - Indeed, were I not Arrogance, I, probably, would have had some difficulty in keeping my balance amidst the fury of this wind ! (then, to herself, just murmoring : "sometimes, when among strangers, is a good practice to play softly and low key...!) .

Young Tree - Oh ! Hear, hear that thunder, ever so closer and louder and loder than ever before ! This is a real tempest !

Arrogance - You might have been right, little green tree, suapecting a real hurricane !

Young Tree - Oh ! Oh ! A large branch broke off my trunk ! Be careful, Arrogance, that another one would not fall on your head !

Lady Patience - Hardly a possibility, little green tree ! Our cousin Arrogance head is always perched so high, I am wondering why it could not be out of danger altogether above the clouds . May be a good solid branch on her head would bring it back to where it ought to be, on her neck, that is, like anybody else, and she would, then, possibly, appreciate the virtues of patience and diligence with all the time that will be necessaryto heal her wounded head .

Arrogance - That was not nice, dear cousin . Have you, may be, lost your"patience" ?

Young Tree - Oh!Another terribly violent burst of wind....!...Oh! Another of my branches snapped off my trunk ! Be careful, Arrogance ! May be you better look for some better shelter , rather than counting on me : I feel so helpless ! If I only could see I could indicate to you some safer place where to take refuge !

Arrogance - I see a hanging rock just a short distance from here ; I shall run there and stay until the rain and the fury of the wind willsubside.....Oh! Another lightning bolt ! My goodness, and so close !

Young Tree - Run, quickly, Arrogance, to your shelter : it's getting worse !....My, another big lightning ! When will all this end ? ..Oh! Another lightning...and another one...my, my..this last one was pretty close but it fell in the open meadow.....this looks like the.....end !!

Arrogance - By Jupiter ! Another lightning bolt ! I had never seen one so frightful !!

Young Tree - Run, now, quickly to that hanging rock that will provide some better shelter.....run., run...quickly.....

...********** While Arrogance makes a quick dash towards the hanging rock, another terrific roar fills the forest and a frightful, powerful lightning strikes the little young tree ....

Arrogance - It was a frightning thing that last lightn.....Oh !..Oh!....What am I seeing??!!.... The little tree........the little green tree......is burning...!!!!!

****

Meanwhile, shortly after the lightning had struck the little green tree in a blinding flash of devastating fury, the violence of the wind lessens and the rain begins to taper off and the clouds, which had looked so menacing before, now are breaking up and dissipating, while a sun ray illuminates the scene of the smoldering little tree.

Consternation follows for Lady Patience and Lady Tolerance, leaving them in a paralyzing dismay, looking and hardly believing at what they were looking, at the sight of the smoldering little tree, and unable to utter a single word .

****

Lady Arrogance, now, emerges from underneath the protective hanging rock, in a somewhat annoyed attitude, and she didn't so much as look at the whole scene, throwing a casual look and, as the French would say, giving a"regard nonchalant", an indifferent look, at the tragic scene, then begins muttering to herself.................

****

Arrogance - Damn weather ! Damn, damn, damn !! Fortunately, I had just distanced myself from the little tree to seek shelter under that hanging rock which seemed to be able to provide a better protection from that pelting rain, when suddenly that lightning struck !!...Had I not moved away just seconds before it struck, I would be there, now, smoking too ! This damn weather, it always has to cause discomfort, when it does not cause more damage and destruction on its own accord and that tells me that it is high time for me to move on and leave this strange place !....After all, I really do not know how I allowed myself to be entertained....well...I would rather describe it better as "detained"......and kept here by some second rate and peculiar philosopher-like types of emotionally disturbed ghosts suffering from inanition and inanity as well, idolized by a stupid tree, duped into believing what wasn't there, and making a sucker out of me for listening and conversing with them, about sheer fantasies ....Oh!...well....anyone is allowed to be stupid once, but twice would be frowned upon !....So , goodbye and let me hurry towards that little cottage clasped between those two pretty hills and I'll hope I'll never see this forest again...!!!!

Arrogance departs and, Lady Patience, recovering after the earlier shock...

Lady Patience - Poor little tree ! So young and so well prepared with all your little rings inside and outside, now you are just a smoldering ruin ! What you took from Nature for the purpose of your life, you have now returned it as a "thank you" present to Nature herself . Chance, chose you, today . The unknown forces of that same Nature that created you, converged upon you and no one knows why or or for what reason, if there would have been one, or for what purpose, if destruction is, or would be, after all, a purpose . All of this, a mystery . No one, be it the rain, the wind, the thunder, the lightning and anyone of us included, can grasp its intended meaning, if a meaning can be either entertained for such events or one can be assigned to a restricted scale of repetitive probabi;ities . But, dear little tree, your roots are still there and they are alive, not quite reached by the intensity of the lightning and I am wondering whether the lightning was really meant to strike you or Arrogance ....I.wonder.... Anyway, a green sprout will rise from your roots . With renewed patience and my unabated care and assistance, you will be happy again in this magnificent forest ! So , adieu, for now, little tree : I have always loved you !

****

THE END

INDEX

The Dialogues & Stories Titles contained in the three Volumes

****

and where to find them in each Volume

****

****